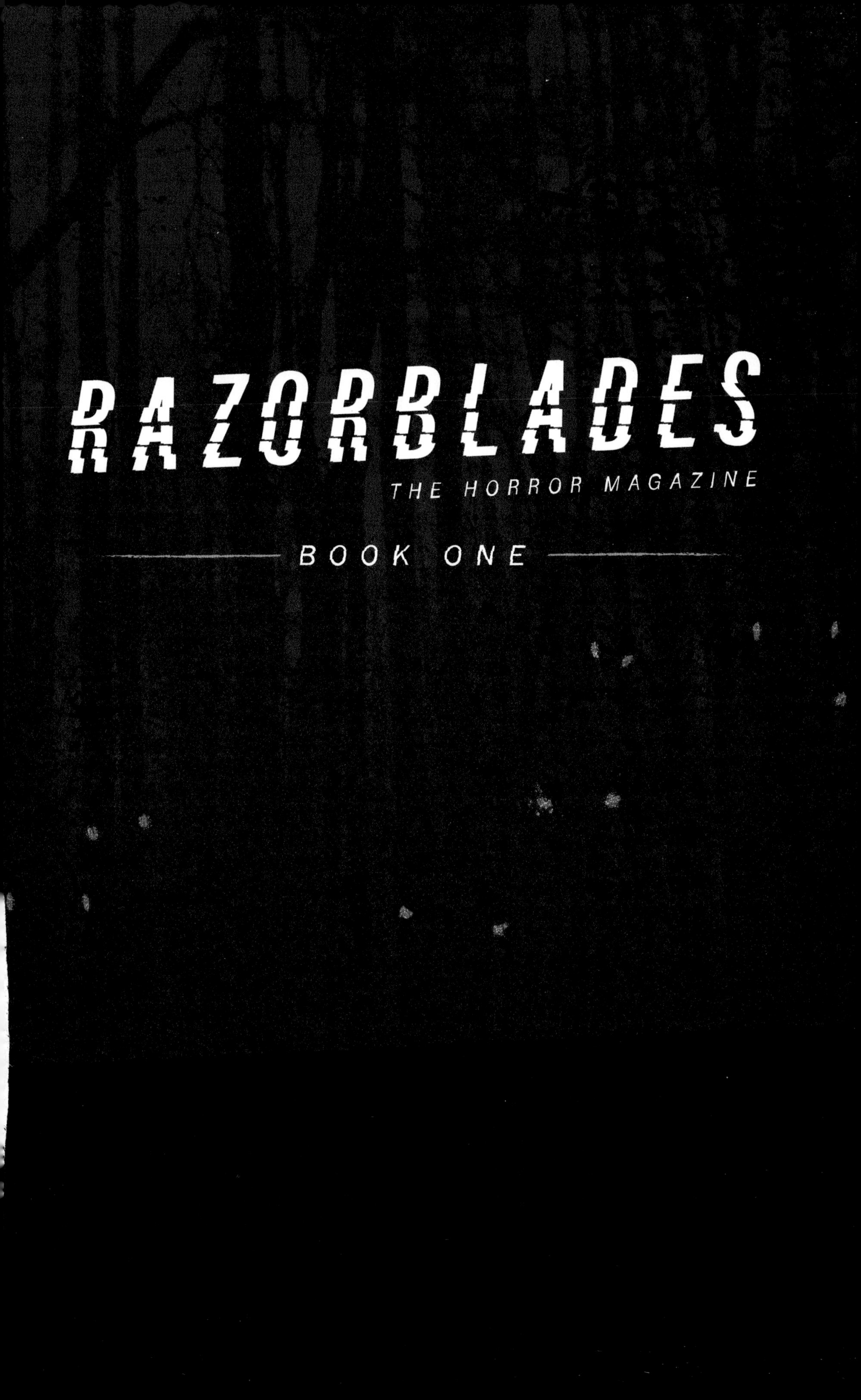
RAZORBLADES
THE HORROR MAGAZINE
BOOK ONE

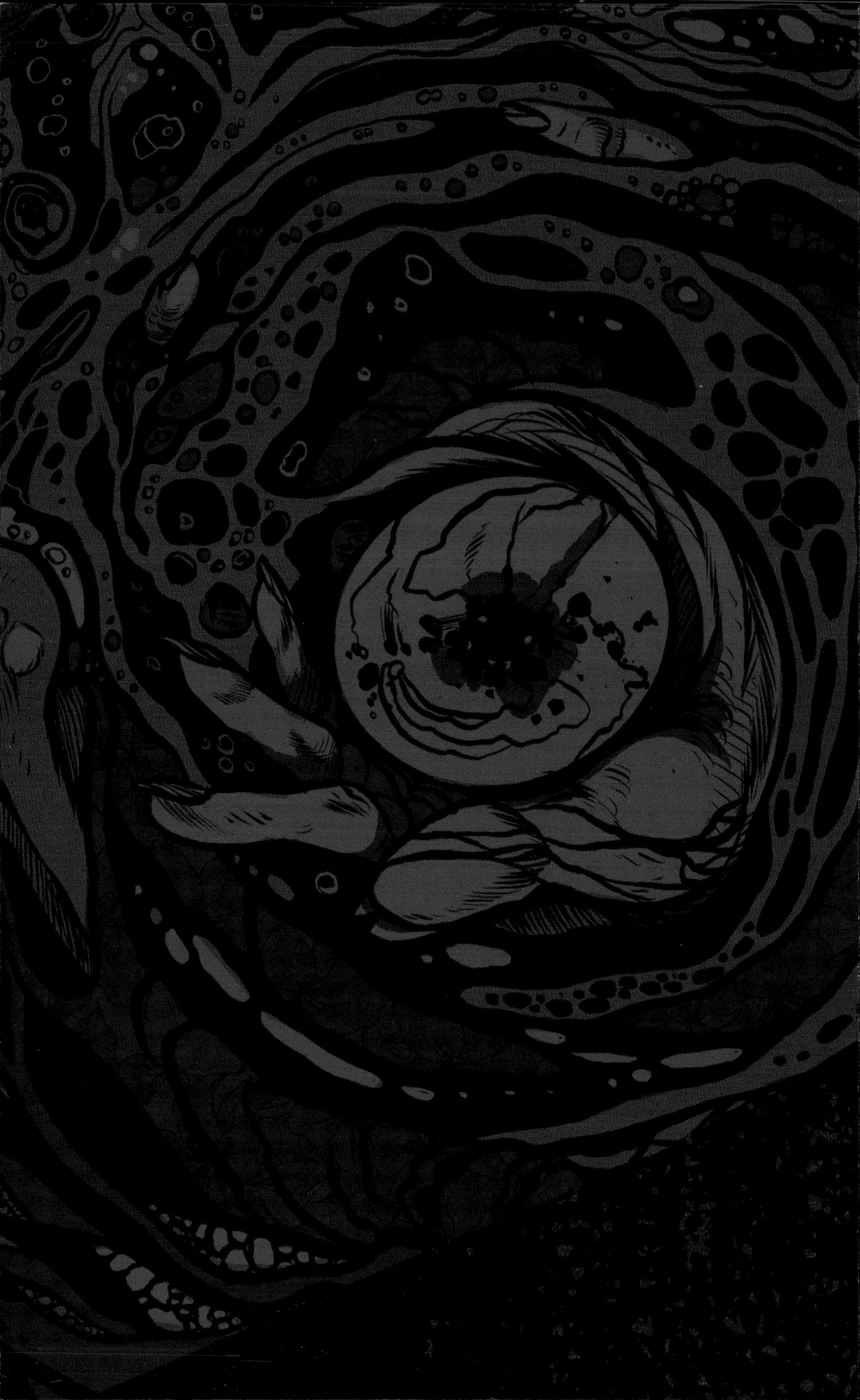

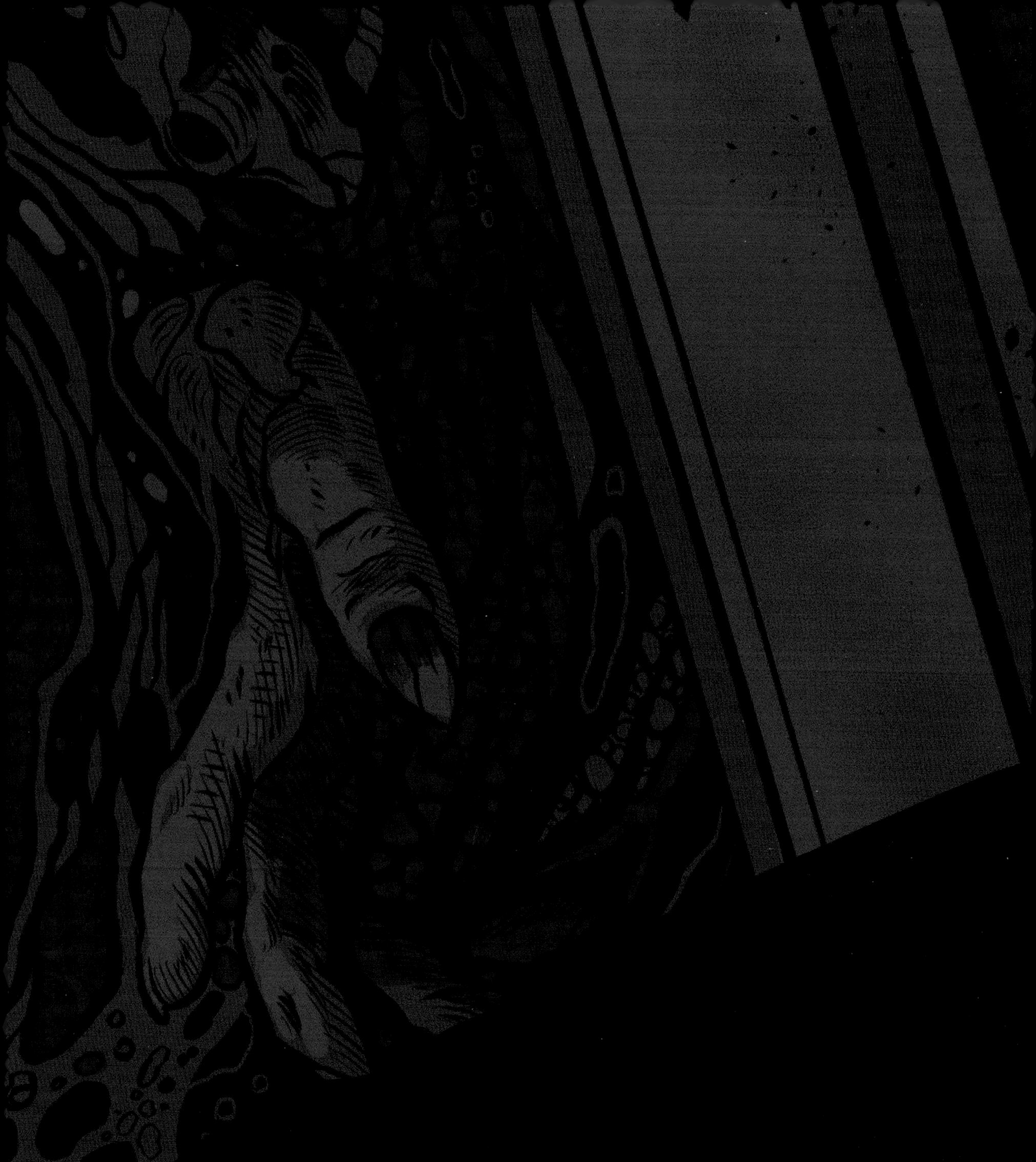

Co-Created & Published by JAMES TYNION IV

Co-Created & Edited by STEVE FOXE

Designed by DYLAN TODD

Collection Cover Art by DAVID ROMERO

Additional Production & Design by SECOND ROCKET COMICS

Special Thanks to
SAM JOHNS, JUNI SALGADO, *and* JJ'S COMICS & ART

TINY ONION

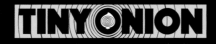

IMAGE COMICS, INC.

Robert Kirkman – *Chief Operating Officer*

Erik Larsen – *Chief Financial Officer*

Todd McFarlane – *President*

Marc Silvestri – *Chief Executive Officer*

Jim Valentino – *Vice President*

Eric Stephenson – *Publisher / Chief Creative Officer*

Nicole Lapalme – *Controller*

Leanna Caunter – *Accounting Analyst*

Sue Korpela – *Accounting & HR Manager*

Marla Eizik – *Talent Liaison*

Jeff Boison – *Director of Sales & Publishing Planning*

Lorelei Bunjes – *Director of Digital Services*

Dirk Wood – *Director of International Sales & Licensing*

Alex Cox – *Director of Direct Market Sales*

Chloe Ramos – *Book Market & Library Sales Manager*

Emilio Bautista – *Digital Sales Coordinator*

Jon Schlaffman – *Specialty Sales Coordinator*

Kat Salazar – *Director of PR & Marketing*

Monica Garcia – *Marketing Design Manager*

Drew Fitzgerald – *Marketing Content Associate*

Heather Doornink – *Production Director*

Drew Gill – *Art Director*

Hilary DiLoreto – *Print Manager*

Tricia Ramos – *Traffic Manager*

Melissa Gifford – *Content Manager*

Erika Schnatz – *Senior Production Artist*

Ryan Brewer – *Production Artist*

Deanna Phelps – *Production Artist*

IMAGECOMICS.COM

INTRODUCTION

Like many things in the last thirty years of the comic book business, RAZORBLADES wouldn't exist without Alan Moore.

Specifically, it wouldn't exist if I hadn't made the decision in college not to read FROM HELL.

I didn't have anything against the book. I had just finished reading his entire bibliography, and I wanted there to be one great Alan Moore comic I hadn't read on my shelf. Something I could call upon in a moment of need to bestow upon me great wisdom and inspiration. I almost relented a few times over the years, especially once I started working full-time in comics, but I had an almost supernatural aversion to sitting down and reading the book. It followed me on my shelf through four New York City apartments, and a house in Los Angeles. Waiting for the right moment.

The moment came in late April 2020. Nearly a month into the shutdown of the American Comic Book industry, and the country, due to Covid-19.

The funny thing is that this all happened because I was, for once in my career, ahead of schedule. I had kicked my ass in the first quarter of the year, getting on top of each of my deadlines, knowing that I had a gauntlet of conventions coming up this summer, and a new series with Image Comics in development. Suddenly I had an enormous amount of time, and shockingly little to do. Deadlines quickly became more of an existential quandary than hard, fast dates that needed to be hit. I was stressed all the time, doomscrolling through Twitter, with no place to go, other than occasional and frightening trips to the grocery store.

I started stacking comics on a pile on our dining room table. The rule I made for myself was that I wasn't going to go back and reread old favorites. I wanted to read a bunch of comics that I had never read before. Many of those comics were from the independent, alternative side of the comic industry, but after deliberation, I moved *From Hell* off my shelf to the top of that stack. I could feel it in my gut. It was time. The rainy day was here.

I wish I could bottle the manic episode I had reading that book over the course of a long weekend. It was like a second engine in the back of my brain, revving to life. There are so many obvious ways that that book is a work of absolute genius, but the simple fact that it existed was wondrous to me. That an acclaimed, but very mainstream writer, at that point best known for his DC work, paired up with a man best known for self-published black and white autobiographical comics, and created one of the best works of comic

book art ever put to the page. Read the first issue, and imagine any contemporary publisher putting it out. No, there would need to be a stronger hook, a more direct evocation of Jack the Ripper from the start. It would need to consider the page restrictions, or the number of issues. Unless they were just making it themselves, it wouldn't happen.

I was desperate to understand how a book like this had come to exist, and why there wasn't anything like it being made in our corner of the industry anymore. I would have been able to tell you, as a piece of comics trivia, that *From Hell* started as a serialized story in a horror anthology called *Taboo*, but I had never really considered what that meant. So, I ordered a full set of *Taboo* on eBay and I started researching.

In the late '80s, there was a whole generation of comic creator that had been raised on the classic horror anthologies. They had come of age, but the horror anthology hadn't. Most of the examples out there at the time were trying to capture the feel of old EC Comics. Few had the bite that something like Alan Moore, Steve Bissette, and John Totleben's *Swamp Thing* had. And so, Steve Bissette and John Totleben decided to create a platform that filled that void, with Steve taking point from the second issue until the last. They sought to create a home for vibrant, contemporary horror by the up-and-coming voices of the day. The people who did not want to recreate the trappings of the old generation of horror, but to embody the spirit of them. To push new boundaries and break the taboos of the day in an industry still by and large in the stranglehold of the Comics Code Authority.

Mind you, I say this with all the authority and conviction of someone who was just shy of his first birthday when the first issue of *Taboo* hit the stands, but oftentimes the myth of a moment is more important than the facts of it. And the way those myths can inspire fools like me, thirty years later. There's an incredible ambition to the book, in the way it asserts that all of these very different, smart comics belong in the same magazine together. Really, at the end of the day, the defining feature is the incredible curation by Steve Bissette, one of the true legends of the comic book industry. After burning through all nine issues and the special, I topped the experience off by ordering an almost full run of *Death Rattle* and *Gore Shriek* from the same era. Both feature some great horror work, but nothing matches the boundless ambition of *Taboo*.

And really, *Taboo* was only a platform. A brilliantly curated platform, that acted as midwife to some truly great works of comic book art. But it wasn't created to put a title like *From Hell* on the shelf. That wasn't a goal—merely a byproduct. *Taboo* was created to put together a bunch of the vibrant voices of the day and let them unleash their talents, without worrying about breaking taboos that would make other publishers nervous. And those principles created a platform on which great art could be created.

There are different taboos in the modern comics industry, and I'm not even talking the taboos of politics. In a world where the creator-owned side of the direct market has become dominated by IP generators, the potential for a long profit tail always wins against artists and writers just wanting to explore an idea or a feeling or a moment for the sheer art of it. And even the places that let you hold on to the rights are still curated with the tastes of a generation that's been around and making comics for a good long while. In some cases, as long as I've been alive. And they're still trying to make the kinds of comics they liked making ten, twenty, thirty years ago.

We live in a comics industry that is more disconnected than it has ever been before. The Young Adult Book Market feels like a foreign country to the Direct Market and neither of them seem to know what's happening in the exploding Webtoon/Webcomic space. The most popular superhero comic of the last decade is a Manga that most big two superhero editors have never heard of. The mainstays of indie alternative comics are putting out phenomenal work by young creators like Nick Drnaso, but most of his contemporaries in the superhero space don't know who the hell he is. There are hundreds upon hundreds of young illustrators dabbling in pseudo comics and pin-ups living off pins and artbooks they self-publish and distribute. There is a thriving, growing horror art community, and I keep following more and more of them every day.

There need to be more platforms that try and remind all of us that ALL these things are the same thing. And my generation, the rising Millennials entering our (no longer young) adult lives need to stop waiting for the older generations to present those platforms TO us. We need to make them ourselves. And to be fair, that's exactly what I keep on seeing. More and more of us aren't waiting for someone's permission to make comics. We're just making them ourselves. Folks in the Alternative space never STOPPED doing this. I'm sure they'd roll their eyes at me, the superhero kid, discovering the power of zines... But you know what? Fuck it. Zines are great. Self-published comics are great. I want more weird self-published shit by the big guns of the direct market comics industry. I would fucking love to see what weirdo comics some of my favorite writers and artists would make for themselves, with no interference.

But mostly I want to see what my peers create. The people who grew up with the same movies and influences as I did, who love the same comics as I do, who have the same frustrations I do about the industry as it exists today. I want to know what the young creators would make if they had total free rein to make exactly the kind of comic books they want to make, fueled by stupid enthusiasm and sheer creative joy. Those of us who like to write stories about people in costumes punching each other forget that *Teenage Mutant Ninja Turtles* started as a self-published black and white indie comic.

Creator-owned comics needs to reclaim its independent roots, and in doing so build some new platforms, new pathways, and new connections between all the disparate "cousin" industries that can all call themselves comics. I would love to have had a hand in creating the platform in which a Twitter horror artist connects with a great writer from the YA Book Market space and creates something beautiful and surprising and new that couldn't have happened with their worlds separated. I think horror is a great genre, and one that often pushes creative people to do their best work. To one-up each other's imagery, to find something perfectly unsettling in a way they've never seen before.

Also, horror is fucking great. I obviously love horror, and I plan on writing horror for my entire career. Of course, if I have some money that I want to throw at comic creators, I'm going to have them cook up something spooky.

That's where it all started. That and a kind of flashy, garish name. I remember texting my *Department of Truth* editor, friend, and fellow horror enthusiast Steve Foxe. At first, I was just trying to get him to tell me what a bad idea it was. But within hours, we were putting together a dream list of collaborators. We actually ended up getting most everybody on the list. It was Steve who would go on to give the flashy, garish name its meaning. This would be a collection of small, sharp things that can cut you. Which is all a lot of rambling to say that in creating *Razorblades*, Steve and I set out to create a cool venue for cool people to make cool scary shit. I think there need to be more platforms that allow for the intersection of disparate creators, that pits all of them against each other to try and come up with the most frightening stories they can imagine, in a bit of fun competition where we all win, because we all get some really fucking scary comic books.

I get that it's a privilege to be able to afford to do a project without a publisher, and it's a privilege I have, so I want to share that privilege the best I can and help some people who I think are capable of making some great comics, make some great comics. In doing that, I don't want to become what I'm saying we need to spend more time rejecting. To that end, *Razorblades* will always be a wholly creator-owned endeavor. The magazine reserves no rights to the work, save a right to reprint. All Steve and I own is the name and the logo. That's core to the ethos of the project.

And hey... Maybe this all crashes and burns in a couple of issues, and I spend the rest of my life warning others not to follow in my footsteps (much like Steve Bissette did many times in all these *Comics Journal* and Cartoonist Kayfabe interviews...). Maybe somebody smarter than me sees all the ways in which I'm doing it wrong and tries to one-up me with their own better self-published platform. Or maybe it works beyond all our wildest dreams, and we help lead to the creation of a whole bookshelf of seminal comic book classics...

But either way, I hope we create something that people find frightening, and enjoy reading as much as I've enjoyed putting it all together.

This is an experiment, and it's just getting started. I hope you'll come along for the ride with us.

James Tynion IV
Brooklyn, NY 7.30.20

Revised from the original post on jamestynioniv.substack.com

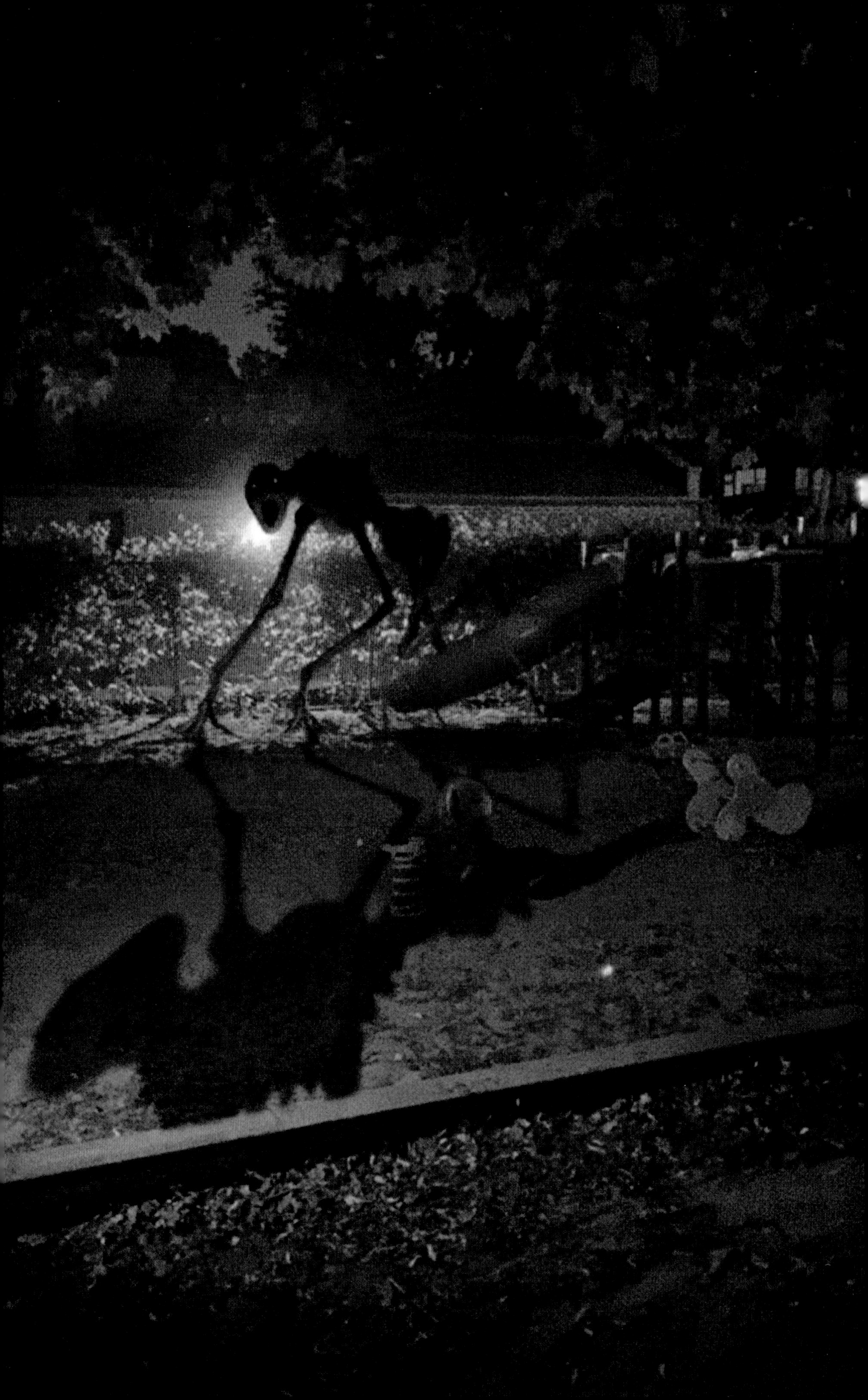

ISSUE #1

Cover Art By TREVOR HENDERSON

"THE WASHING MACHINE"
By JAMES TYNION IV & ANDY BELANGER | *Lettered By* SERGE LAPOINTE

"LOCAL HEROES"
By MARGUERITE BENNETT & WERTHER DELL'EDERA
Colored By EMILIO LECCE | *Lettered By* HASSAN OTSMANE-ELHAOU

Second Printing Cover Art By TREVOR HENDERSON

"MID-SEASON SLUMP"
Short Story By DANNY LORE | *Illustration By* AARON CAMPBELL

EXCERPT FROM "SLEEP STORIES"
By MICHAEL WALSH

"THE WEAVER"
By NICK ROBLES

"DEAD MEANS DEAD"
By STEVE FOXE & MICHAEL DIALYNAS | *Lettered By* HASSAN OTSMANE-ELHAOU

"SHE'S GOT IT"
By LONNIE NADLER & JENNA CHA | *Lettered By* HASSAN OTSMANE-ELHAOU

"KING OF FEVERS"
By FRANCINE B/WITNESSTHEABSURD

"KILLBOY"
By JAMES TYNION IV & RICARDO LOPEZ ORTIZ | *Lettered By* HASSAN OTSMANE-ELHAOU

THROUGH THE BLACK MIRROR:
JAMES TYNION IV *In Conversation With* SCOTT SNYDER | *Illustration By* JOCK

"ANATOMY OF THE RUT"
By SAM JOHNS & DANI

"BABY BLUE"
By TRUNG NGUYEN

"A DREAM OF TIME"
By RAM V & JOHN J. PEARSON | *Lettered By* ADITYA BIDIKAR

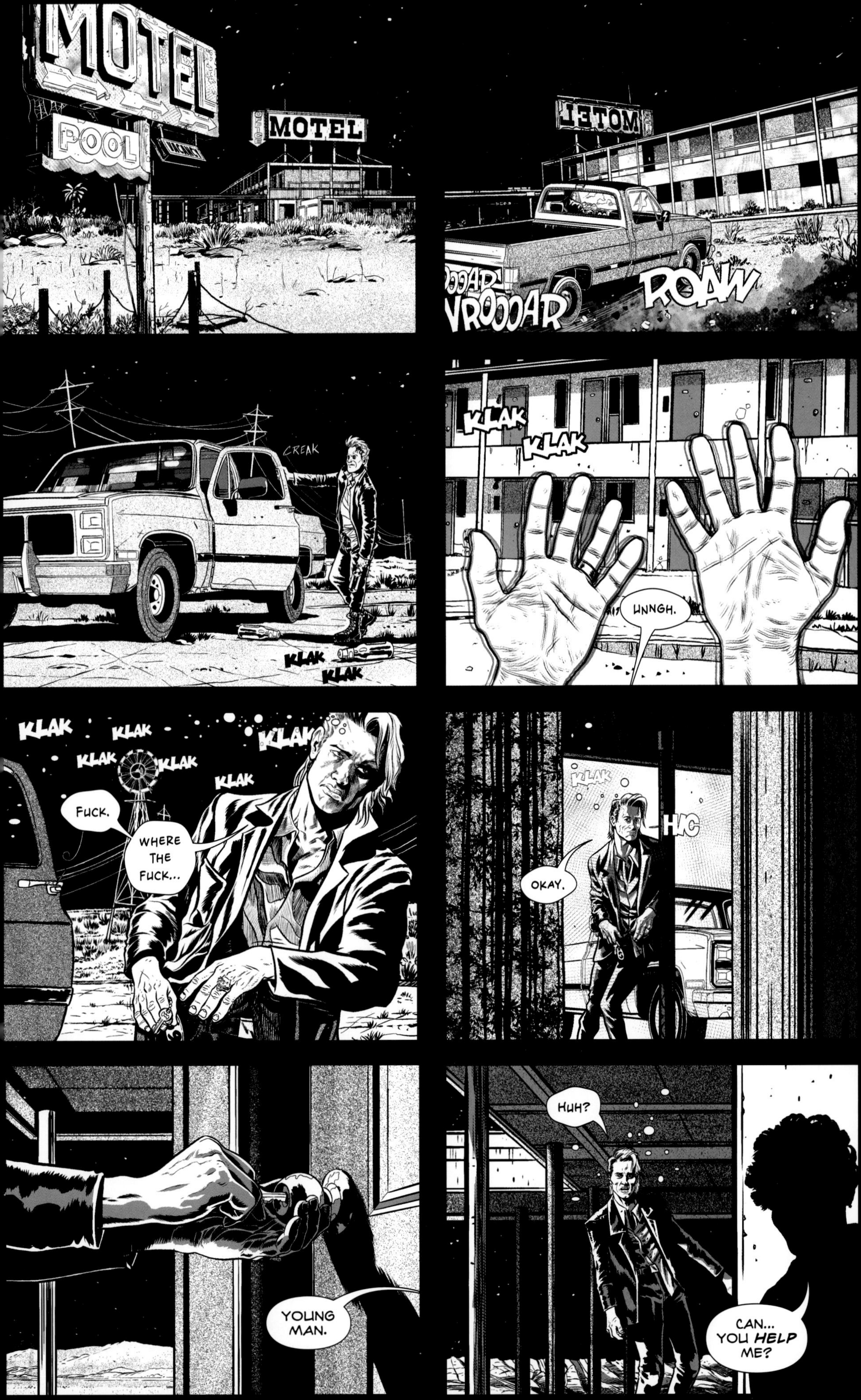
MOTEL
POOL
MOTEL
VROOOAR
ROAW
CREAK
KLAK
KLAK
KLAK
KLAK
UNNGH.
KLAK
KLAK
KLAK
KLAK
KLAK
KLAK
FUCK.
WHERE THE FUCK...
KLAK
HIC
OKAY.
YOUNG MAN.
HUH?
CAN... YOU *HELP* ME?

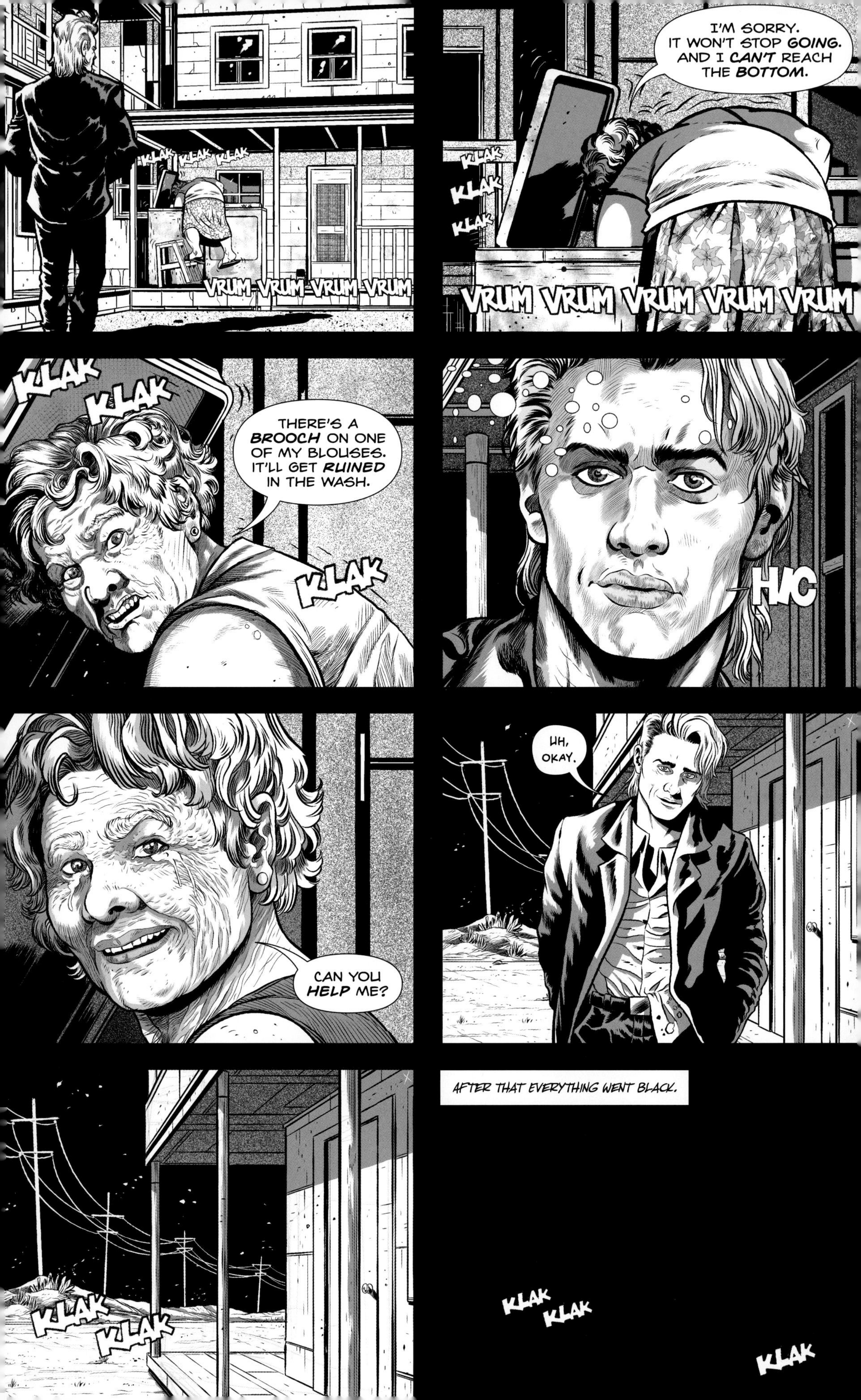
KLAK KLAK KLAK
VRUM VRUM VRUM VRUM
I'M SORRY. IT WON'T STOP GOING. AND I CAN'T REACH THE BOTTOM.
KLAK KLAK KLAK
VRUM VRUM VRUM VRUM VRUM
KLAK KLAK
THERE'S A BROOCH ON ONE OF MY BLOUSES. IT'LL GET RUINED IN THE WASH.
KLAK
HIC
CAN YOU HELP ME?
UH, OKAY.
KLAK KLAK
AFTER THAT EVERYTHING WENT BLACK.
KLAK KLAK
KLAK

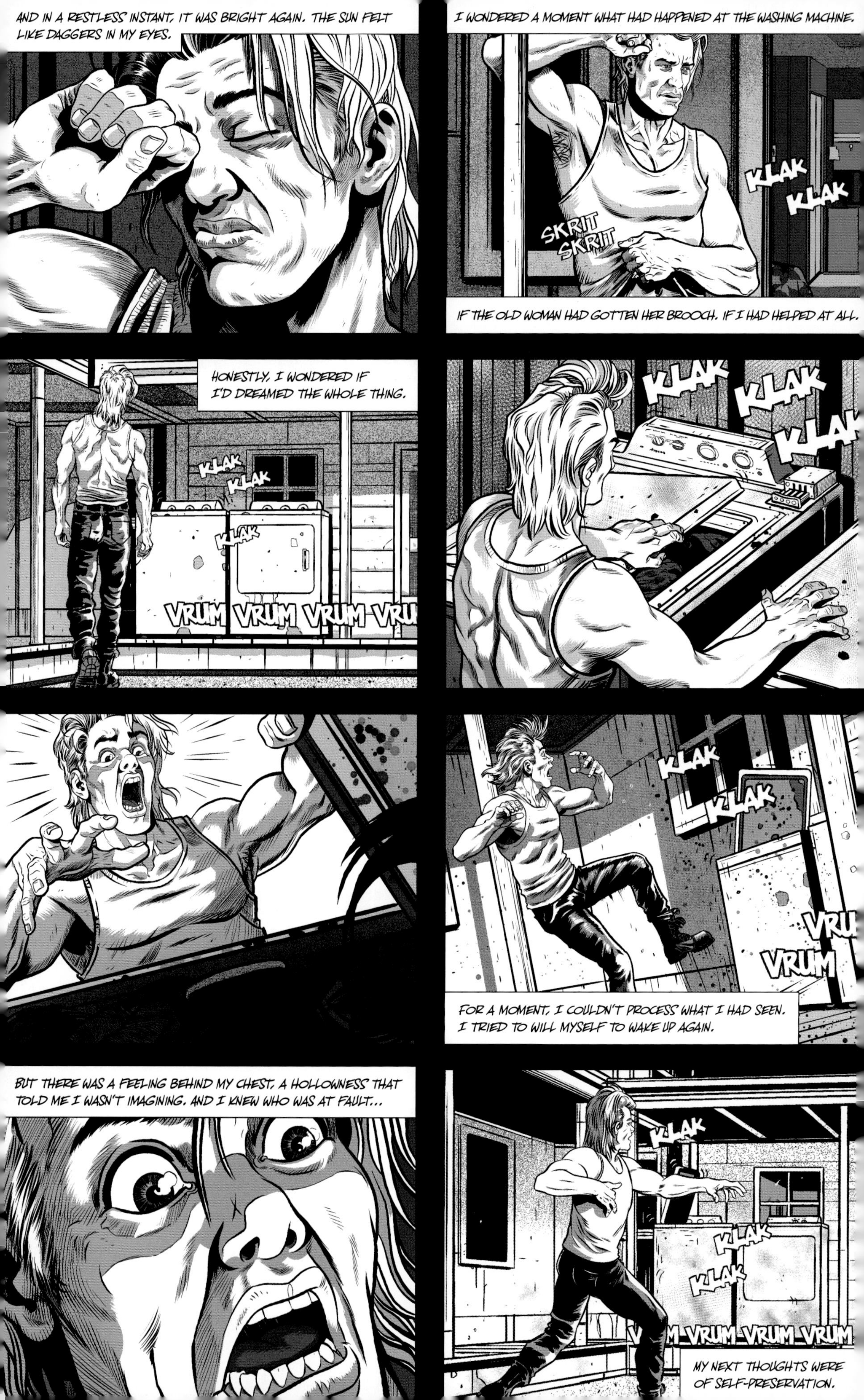

AND IN A RESTLESS INSTANT, IT WAS BRIGHT AGAIN. THE SUN FELT LIKE DAGGERS IN MY EYES.
I WONDERED A MOMENT WHAT HAD HAPPENED AT THE WASHING MACHINE.
KLAK
KLAK
SKRIT
SKRIT
IF THE OLD WOMAN HAD GOTTEN HER BROOCH. IF I HAD HELPED AT ALL.
HONESTLY, I WONDERED IF I'D DREAMED THE WHOLE THING.
KLAK
KLAK
KLAK
VRUM VRUM VRUM
KLAK
KLAK
KLAK
KLAK
KLAK
VRUM
FOR A MOMENT, I COULDN'T PROCESS WHAT I HAD SEEN. I TRIED TO WILL MYSELF TO WAKE UP AGAIN.
BUT THERE WAS A FEELING BEHIND MY CHEST, A HOLLOWNESS THAT TOLD ME I WASN'T IMAGINING. AND I KNEW WHO WAS AT FAULT...
KLAK
KLAK
KLAK
VRUM VRUM VRUM
MY NEXT THOUGHTS WERE OF SELF-PRESERVATION.

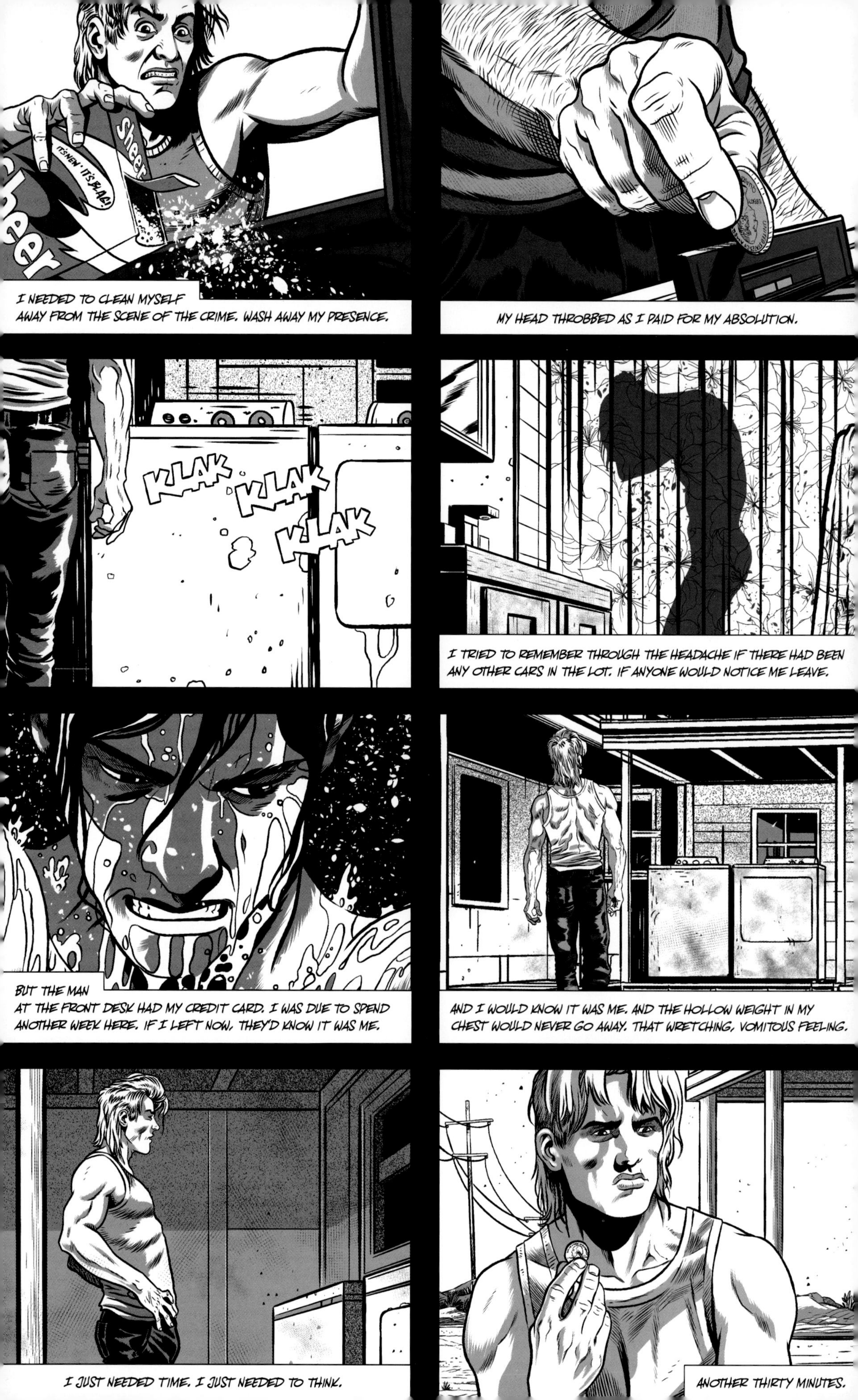
Sheer
IT'S NEW · IT'S BLACK!
Sheer
I NEEDED TO CLEAN MYSELF AWAY FROM THE SCENE OF THE CRIME. WASH AWAY MY PRESENCE.
MY HEAD THROBBED AS I PAID FOR MY ABSOLUTION.
KLAK KLAK KLAK
I TRIED TO REMEMBER THROUGH THE HEADACHE IF THERE HAD BEEN ANY OTHER CARS IN THE LOT. IF ANYONE WOULD NOTICE ME LEAVE.
BUT THE MAN AT THE FRONT DESK HAD MY CREDIT CARD. I WAS DUE TO SPEND ANOTHER WEEK HERE. IF I LEFT NOW, THEY'D KNOW IT WAS ME.
AND I WOULD KNOW IT WAS ME. AND THE HOLLOW WEIGHT IN MY CHEST WOULD NEVER GO AWAY. THAT WRETCHING, VOMITOUS FEELING.
I JUST NEEDED TIME. I JUST NEEDED TO THINK.
ANOTHER THIRTY MINUTES.

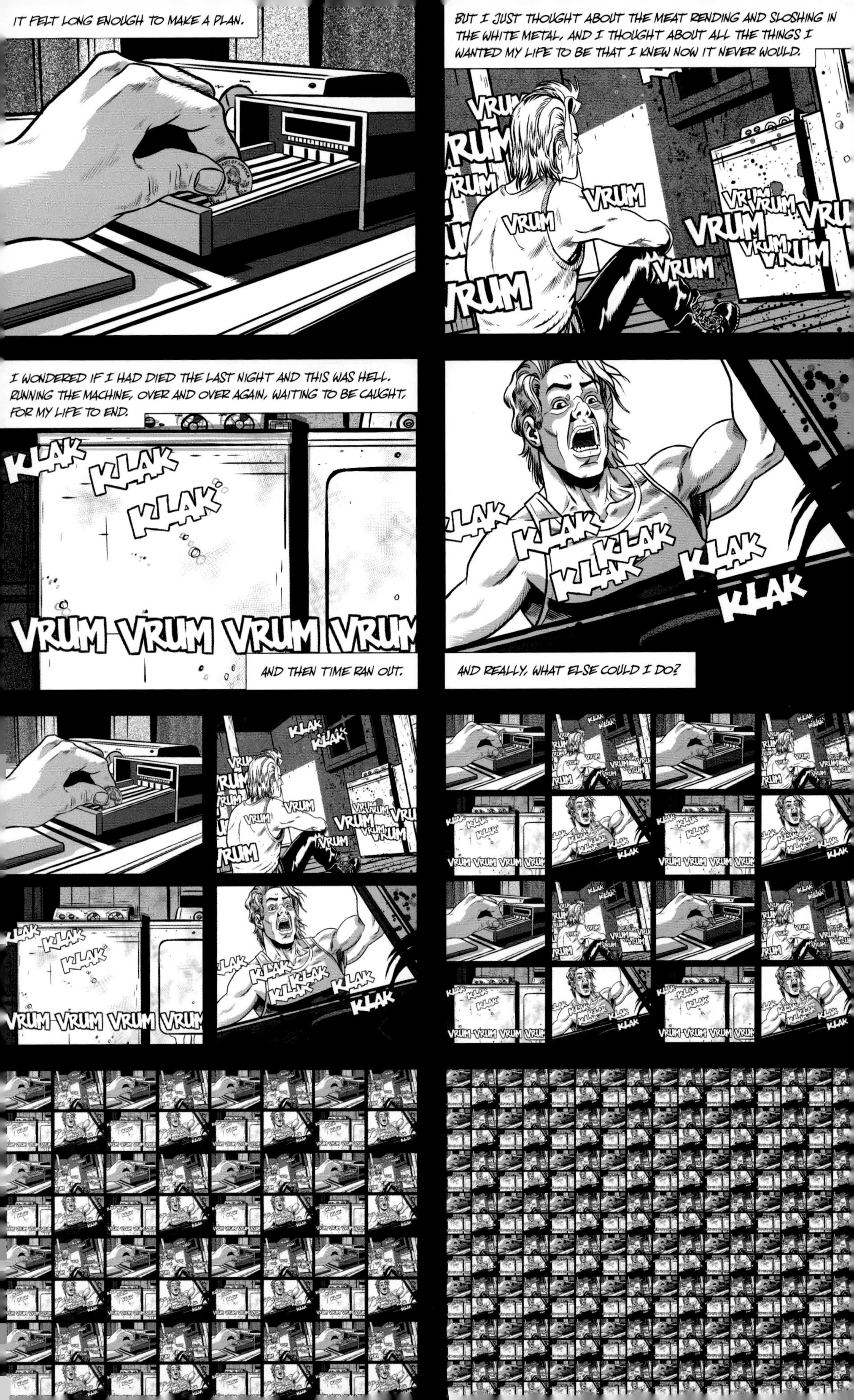

IT FELT LONG ENOUGH TO MAKE A PLAN.
BUT I JUST THOUGHT ABOUT THE MEAT RENDING AND SLOSHING IN THE WHITE METAL, AND I THOUGHT ABOUT ALL THE THINGS I WANTED MY LIFE TO BE THAT I KNEW NOW IT NEVER WOULD.
VRUM VRUM VRUM VRUM VRUM VRUM VRUM VRUM VRUM VRUM VRUM VRUM VRUM
I WONDERED IF I HAD DIED THE LAST NIGHT AND THIS WAS HELL. RUNNING THE MACHINE, OVER AND OVER AGAIN, WAITING TO BE CAUGHT, FOR MY LIFE TO END.
KLAK KLAK KLAK
VRUM VRUM VRUM VRUM
AND THEN TIME RAN OUT.
KLAK KLAK KLAK KLAK KLAK KLAK
AND REALLY, WHAT ELSE COULD I DO?
KLAK KLAK
VRUM VRUM VRUM VRUM VRUM VRUM VRUM VRUM VRUM VRUM VRUM
KLAK KLAK KLAK
VRUM VRUM VRUM VRUM
KLAK KLAK KLAK KLAK KLAK KLAK

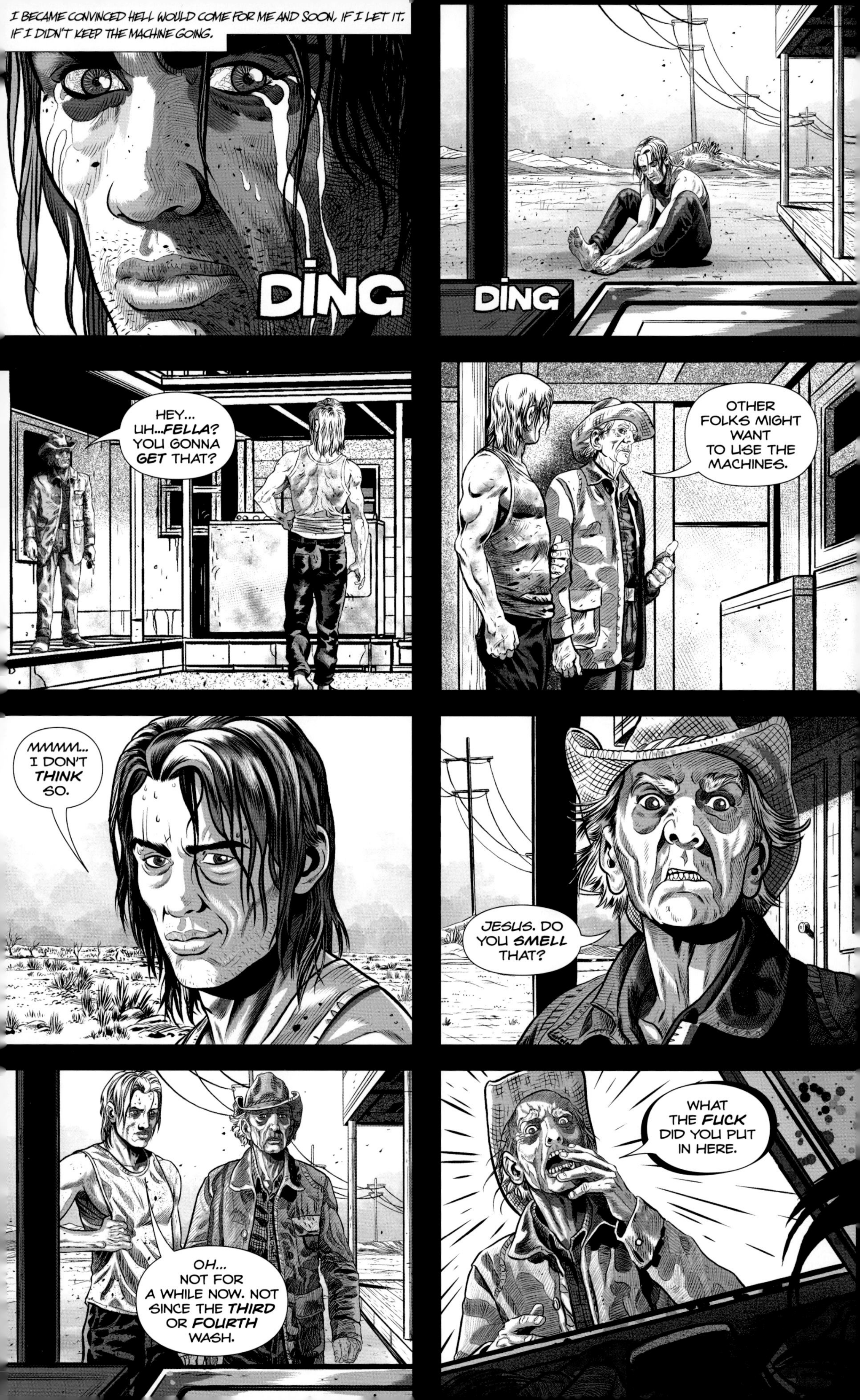
I BECAME CONVINCED HELL WOULD COME FOR ME AND SOON, IF I LET IT. IF I DIDN'T KEEP THE MACHINE GOING.
DING
DING
HEY... UH...FELLA? YOU GONNA GET THAT?
OTHER FOLKS MIGHT WANT TO USE THE MACHINES.
MMMM... I DON'T THINK SO.
JESUS. DO YOU SMELL THAT?
OH... NOT FOR A WHILE NOW. NOT SINCE THE THIRD OR FOURTH WASH.
WHAT THE FUCK DID YOU PUT IN HERE.

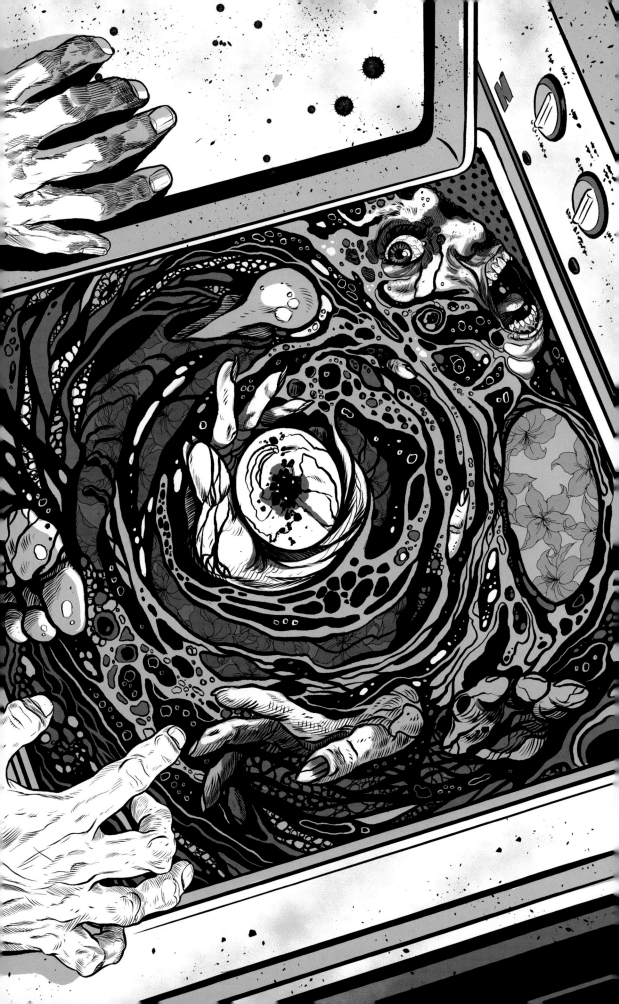

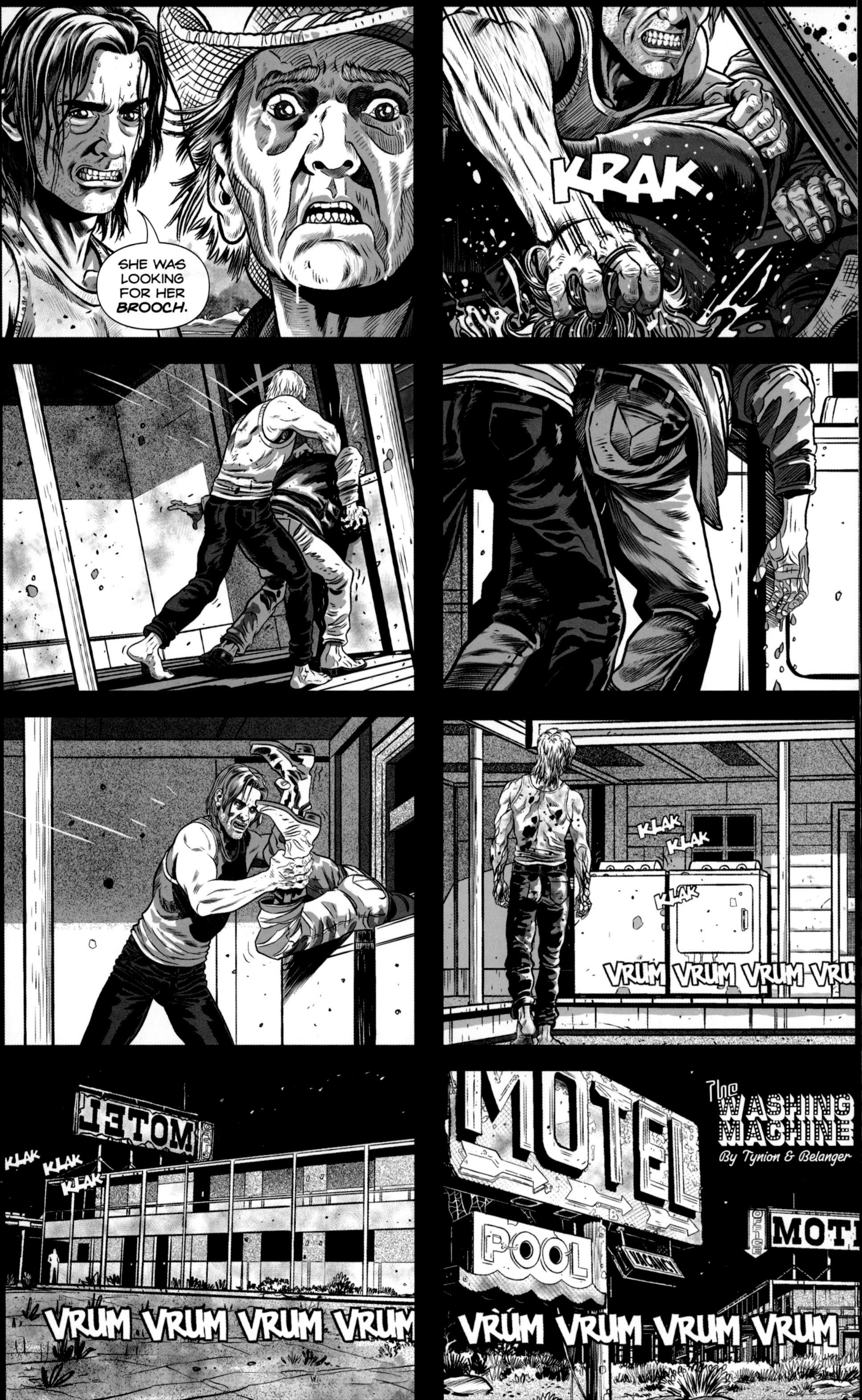
SHE WAS LOOKING FOR HER *BROOCH*.
KRAK
KLAK
KLAK
KLAK
VRUM VRUM VRUM VRU
KLAK
KLAK
KLAK
VRUM VRUM VRUM VRUM
MOTEL
The WASHING MACHINE
By Tynion & Belanger
POOL
OFFICE
MOT
VRUM VRUM VRUM VRUM

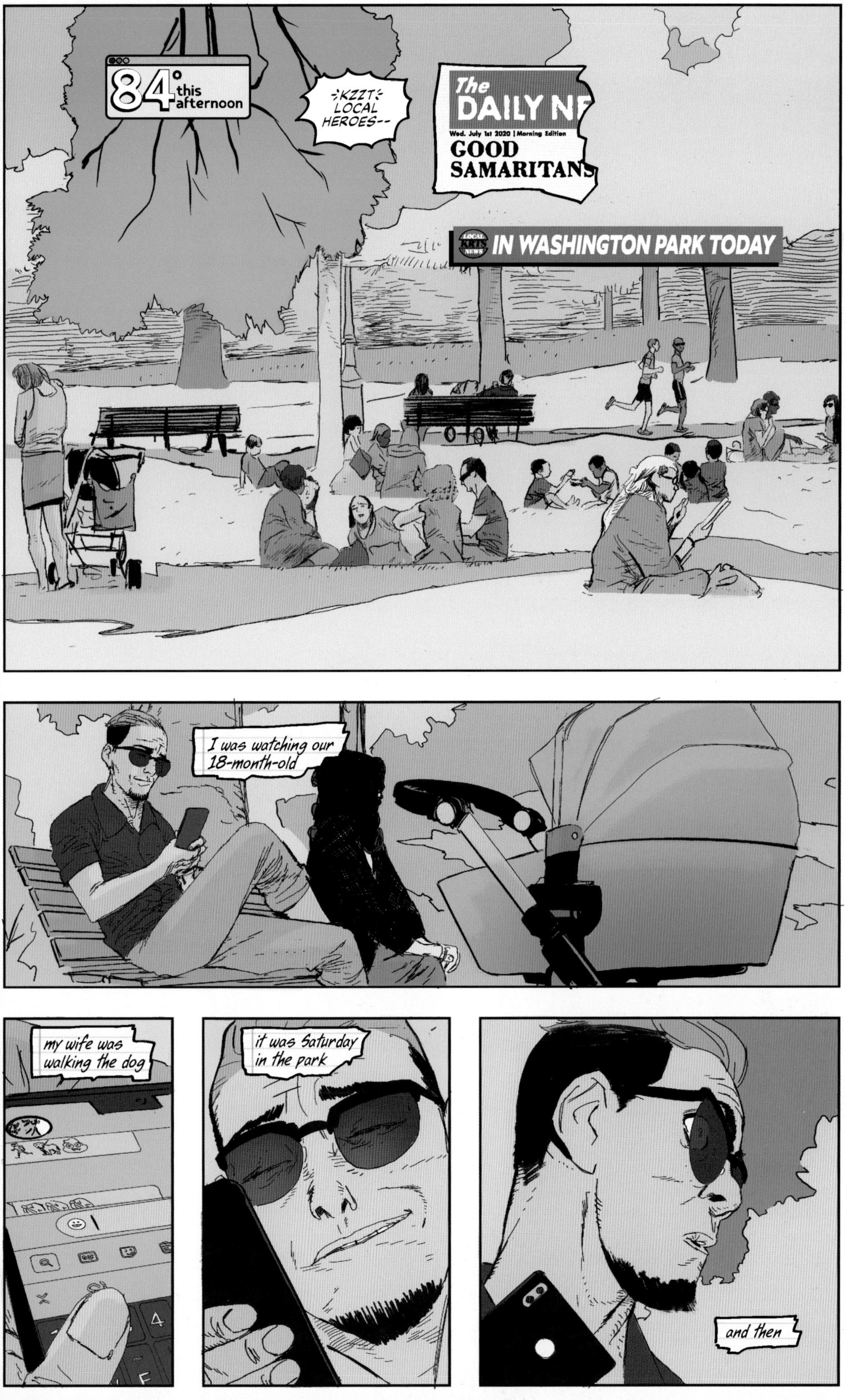
84° this afternoon
KZZT LOCAL HEROES--
The DAILY NE
Wed. July 1st 2020 | Morning Edition
GOOD SAMARITANS
LOCAL KRTS NEWS
IN WASHINGTON PARK TODAY
I was watching our 18-month-old
my wife was walking the dog
it was Saturday in the park
and then

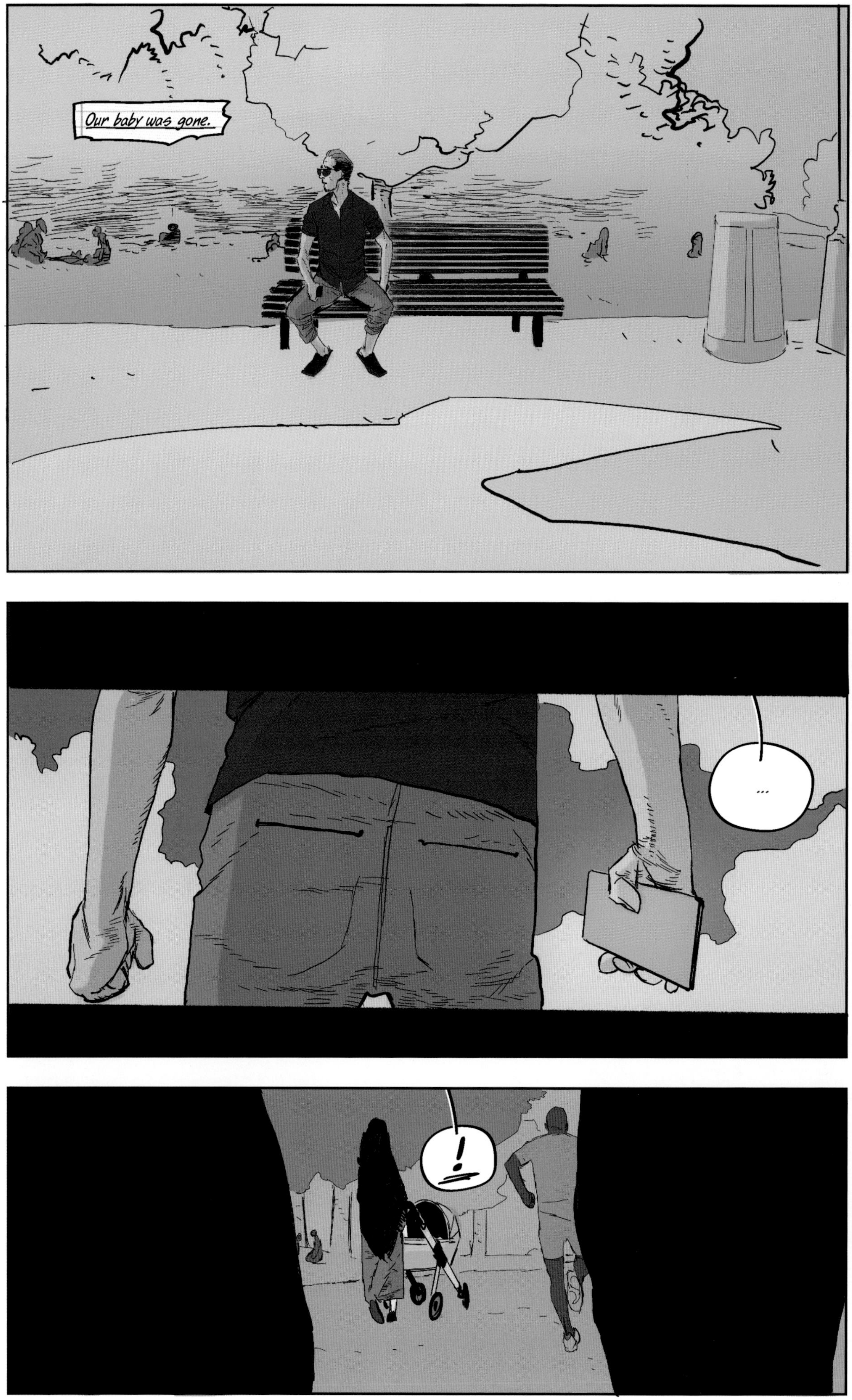
Our baby was gone.
...
!

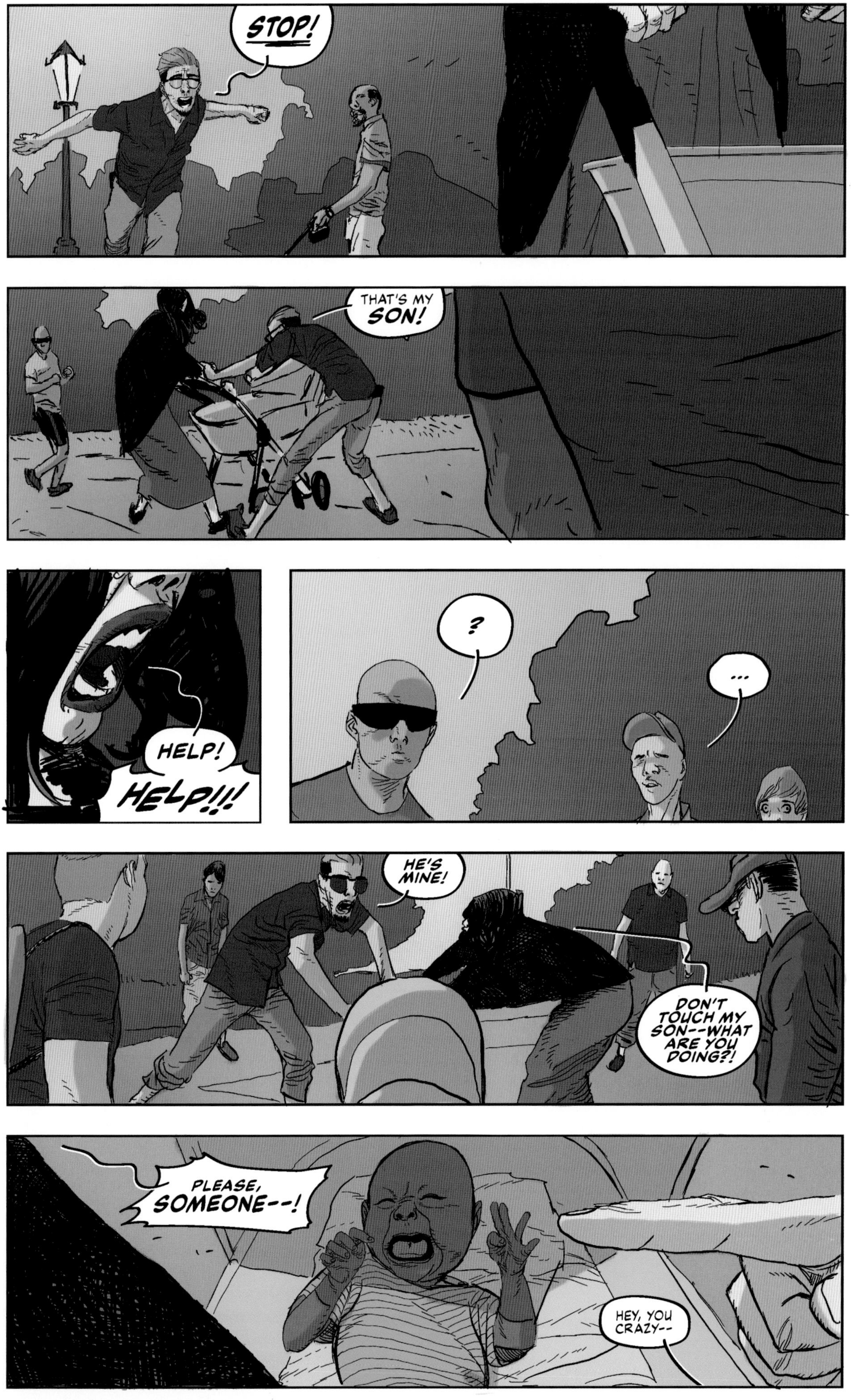
STOP!
THAT'S MY SON!
HELP! HELP!!!
?
...
HE'S MINE!
DON'T TOUCH MY SON--WHAT ARE YOU DOING?!
PLEASE, SOMEONE--!
HEY, YOU CRAZY--

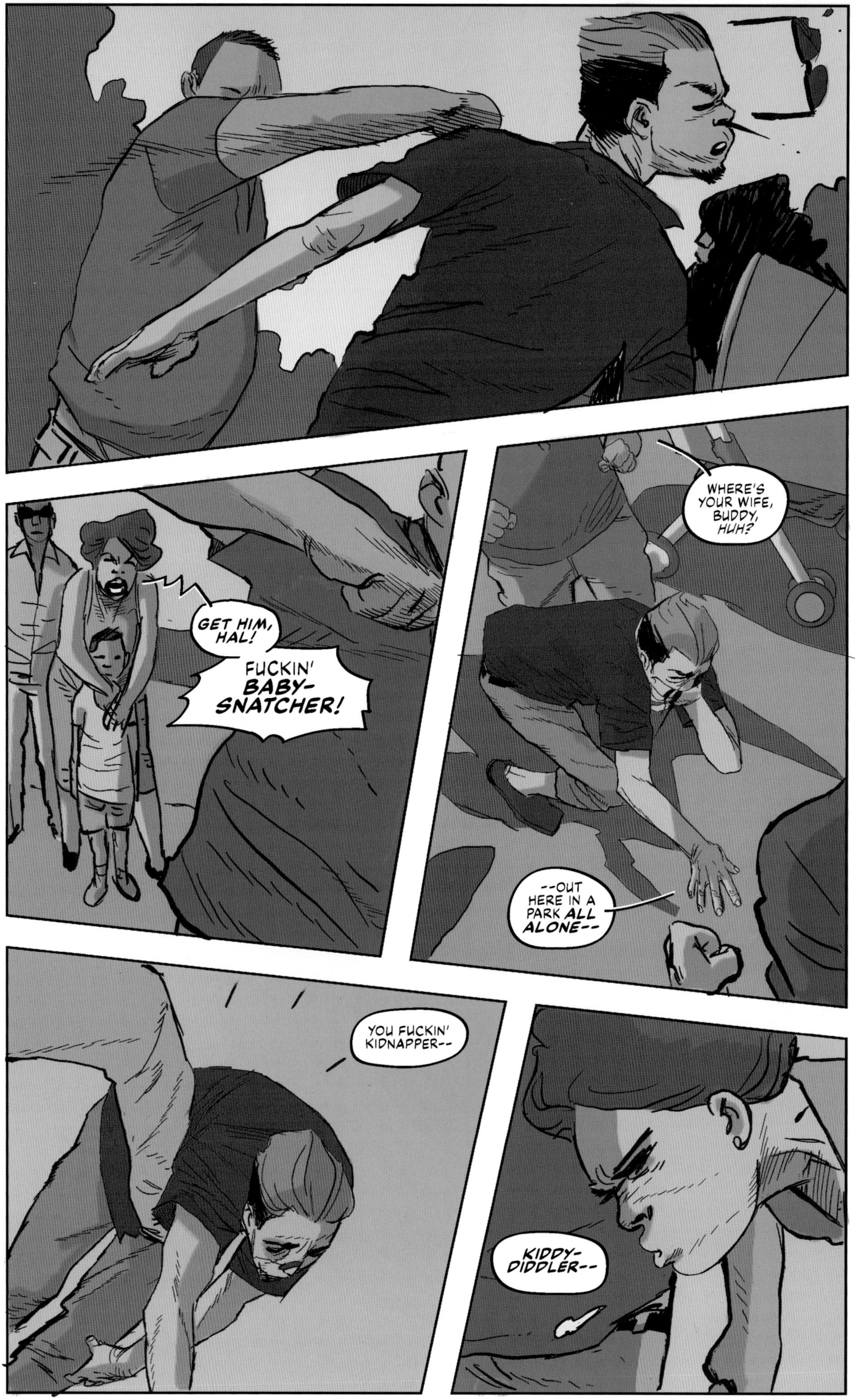
GET HIM, HAL!
FUCKIN' BABY-SNATCHER!
WHERE'S YOUR WIFE, BUDDY, HUH?
--OUT HERE IN A PARK ALL ALONE--
YOU FUCKIN' KIDNAPPER--
KIDDY-DIDDLER--

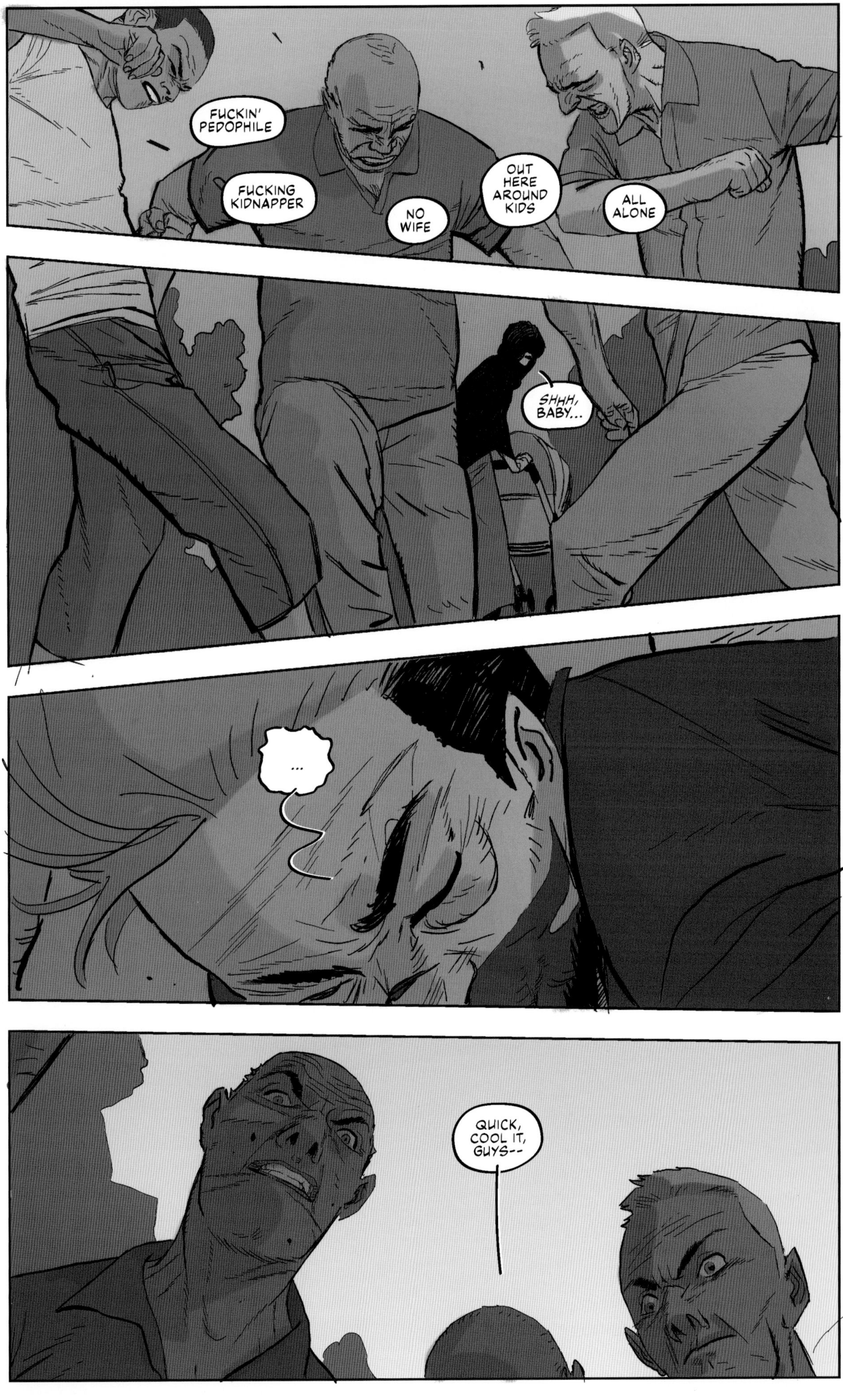
FUCKIN' PEDOPHILE
FUCKING KIDNAPPER
NO WIFE
OUT HERE AROUND KIDS
ALL ALONE
SHHH, BABY...
...
QUICK, COOL IT, GUYS--

--THE COPS ARE HERE.

...MY... SON...

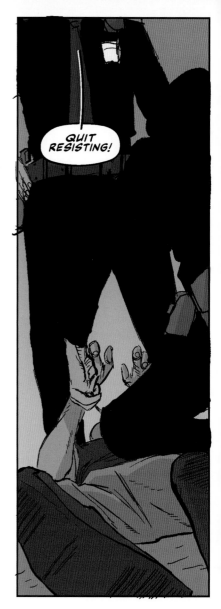

QUIT RESISTING!

STOP! WHAT ARE YOU DOING?!

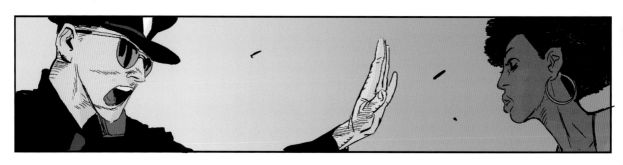

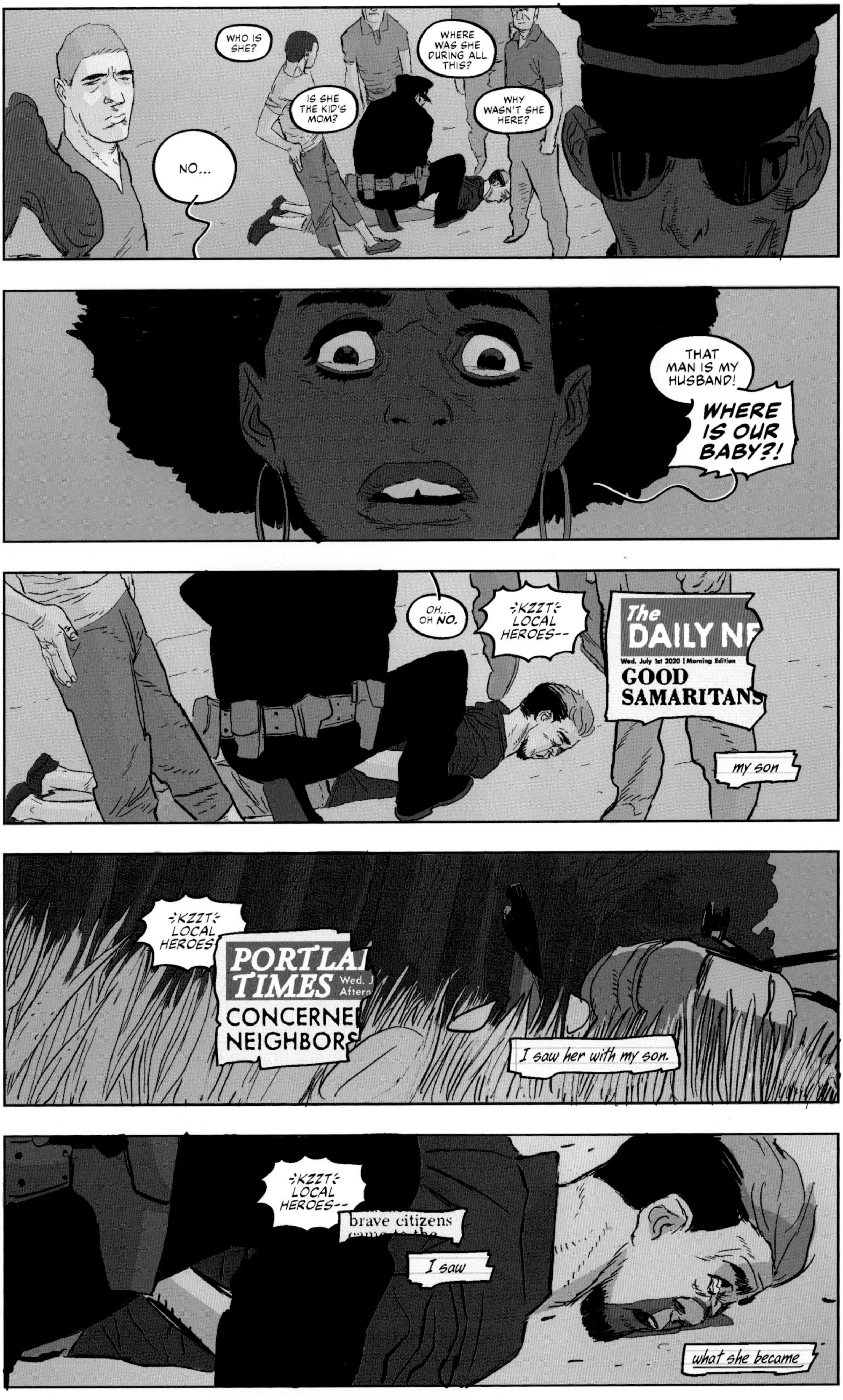
WHO IS SHE?
IS SHE THE KID'S MOM?
WHERE WAS SHE DURING ALL THIS?
WHY WASN'T SHE HERE?
NO...
THAT MAN IS MY HUSBAND!
WHERE IS OUR BABY?!
OH... OH NO.
-KZZT- LOCAL HEROES--
The DAILY NE
Wed. July 1st 2020 | Morning Edition
GOOD SAMARITANS
my son
-KZZT- LOCAL HEROES
PORTLA TIMES Wed. J Aftern
CONCERNE NEIGHBORS
I saw her with my son.
-KZZT- LOCAL HEROES--
brave citizens
I saw
what she became.

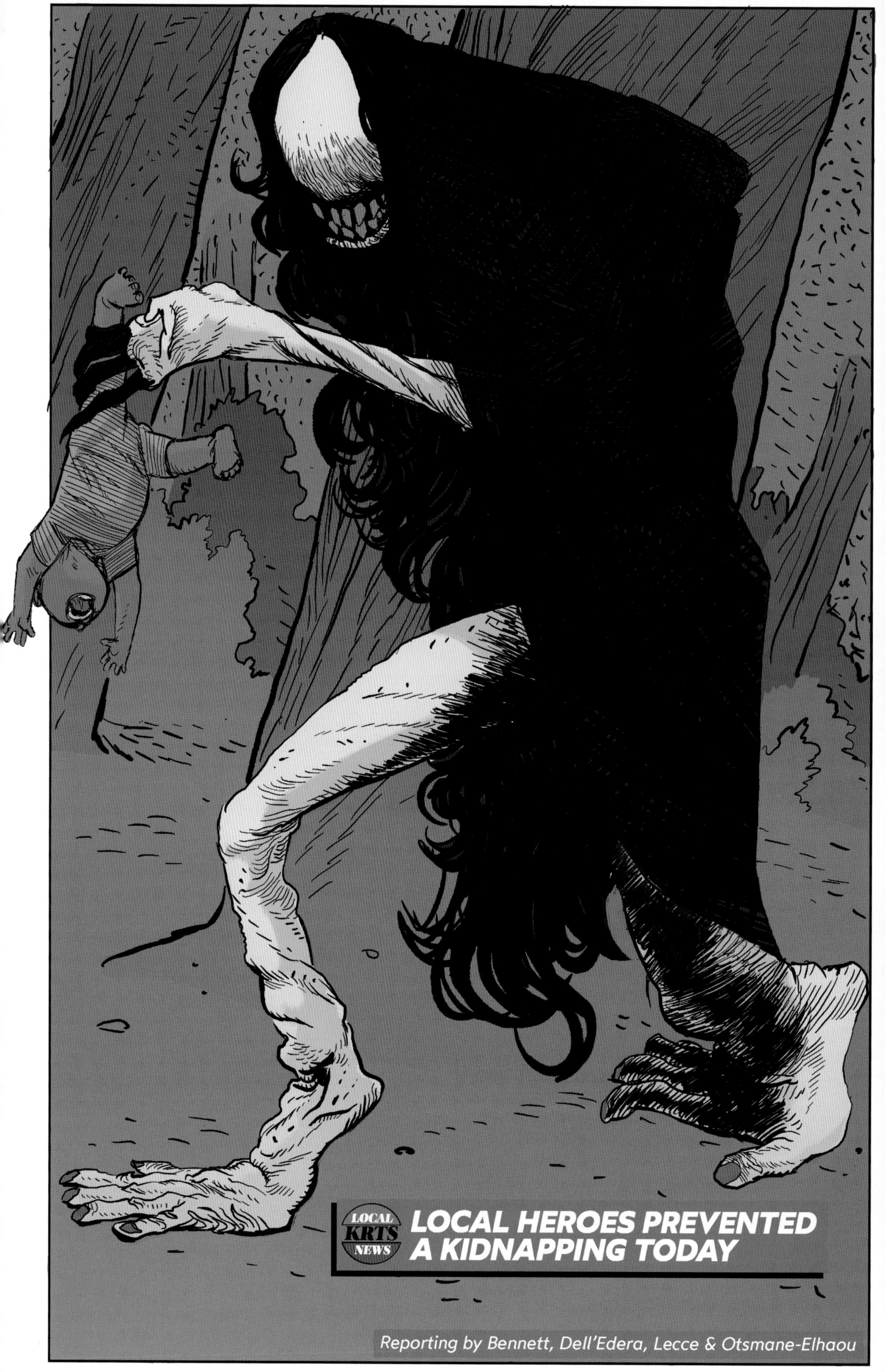
LOCAL KRTS NEWS
LOCAL HEROES PREVENTED A KIDNAPPING TODAY
Reporting by Bennett, Dell'Edera, Lecce & Otsmane-Elhaou

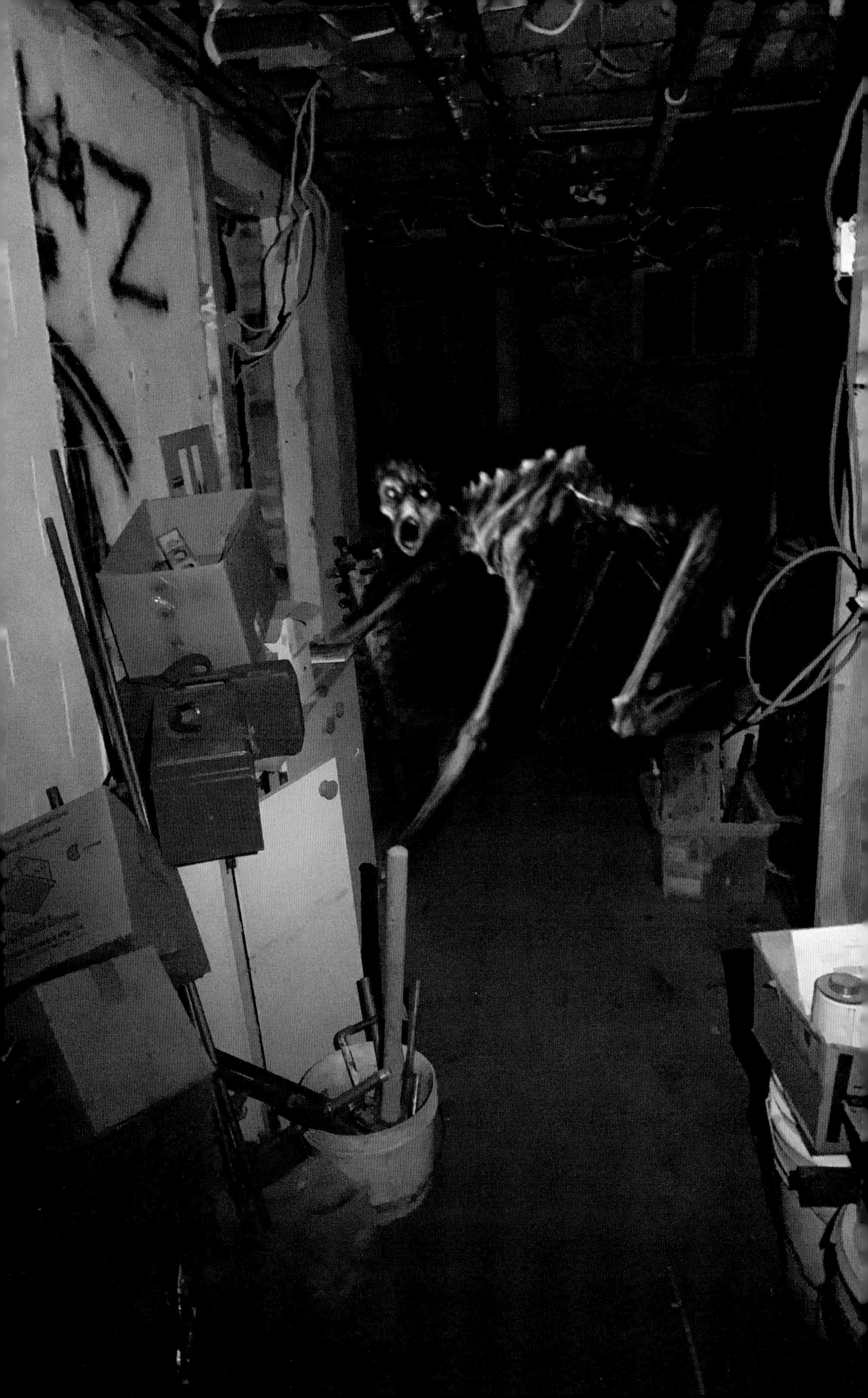

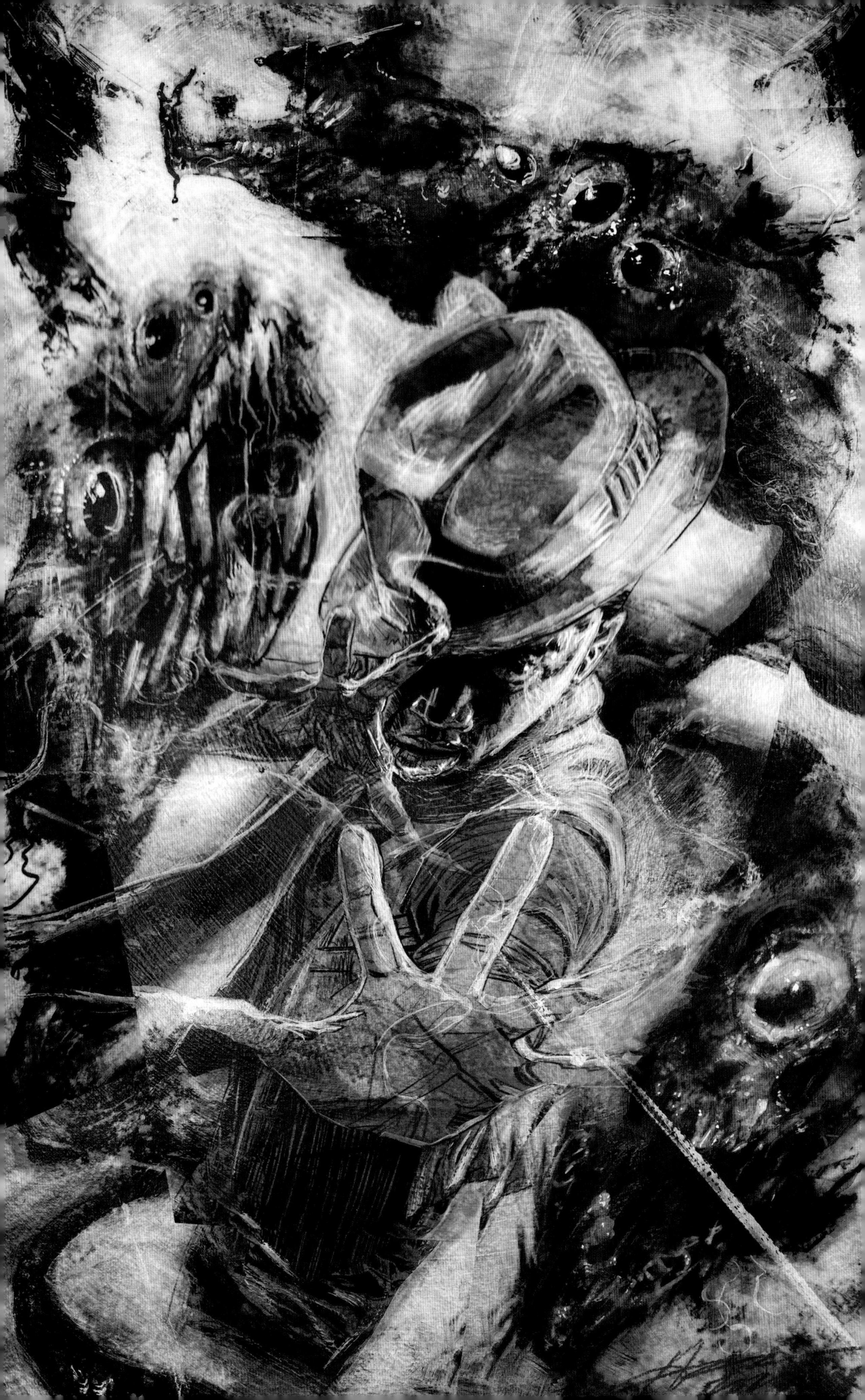

MID-SEASON SLUMP

WRITTEN BY DANNY LORE
ILLUSTRATION BY AARON CAMPBELL

The magic doctor is back! What ghoulish horrors will @jamaltrixs find in the all-new season of MAGICAL HOUSE CALLS? Check out the latest trailer below!

**

"Did you pop your *whole* load when you saw a picture of this place?"

Jamal's lip curled. He hated filming at Victorian-style houses for the same reason the show's producers loved it. Audiences assumed houses like that had a dark history: a murder, a séance, a past worth documenting. Jamal had yet to find even one of these houses that was any more magically influenced or haunted than the yellowing two-family place his grandmother had back in Queens.

And this house certainly was one of *those*, with its gray-purple fading bruise of a façade. The taller points of the roof reminded Jamal of skeletal hands with bloated, swelling joints. He looked at the heavily curtained windows and could already hear how every door would creak, how the groan of the wood would convince a man that the floor was about to sink beneath him.

The house was *obvious*. The only reason houses like this one held magic—if they even did—was because people gave them energy with their own beliefs and superstitions. It was the now giving the old home power. But that fear didn't need to be tied to terrors out of a Shirley Jackson story: it could be carried into co-ops and duplexes just as easily, if someone believed enough.

Enough was the reason that even this house felt dead to Jamal. Every one of these creep houses came with a twinge of amusement—tales of crazed owners not to be believed, and producers who saw storytelling rather than reality. Nowadays, the same quirks that made people think of haunted houses compelled skeptics to point out the ways in which the human mind played tricks on itself.

Ariaga smirked, pulling off his sunglasses, unconcerned with whether *anyone* believed in the power of Victorian architecture. Like the house, Ariaga was straight out of central casting—although, in Ariaga's case, Jamal suspected it was to make sure that the shiny bright-whites of Hollywood and television took him seriously. Pricey boot-cut jeans, a polo shirt, and a blazer over it, Ariaga's styling was a sharp contrast to Jamal's more "urban and authentic" gear. A fact that all the producers were sure to remind Jamal, of every time they tried to pry him out of his AF1s and oversized t-shirts.

"This is exactly the kind of thing that the audience digs. Makes the..." Ariaga tapped his now folded sunglasses against his palm. "...the illusion feel more real. Which you know already, Mr. Term-Searcher."

Jamal rolled his eyes. There wasn't much else to do in the car between filming locations at this point. He fantasized, momentarily, of spending the time between takes talking magic, talking *real shit*, with Ariaga. With anyone.

Then he remembered the stern talking-to he received the last time he'd tried. It was after the decision to pivot from debunking fakes into what the show was now. Jamal had kicked up a storm about how he didn't want to play along with the producers leading people on. That wasn't what he *did*. The point of the original show was protecting viewers from scams, not being one.

It was Ariaga who had taken him aside afterwards. They all put up with Jamal's eccentricities, because it was his Weird reputation, whispers on internet forums "confusing fact and fiction and rumor," that got the show its budget. But he couldn't start buying into his own myth, could he? The network wouldn't pay for the show of a madman.

Ariaga hooked his sunglasses onto

"Something about Miles or the house was staged, and Jamal wasn't sure which part."

the front of his shirt. He looked like a prick.

"Wait until you hear this guy's whole spiel. His audition tape?" Ariaga kissed the air. "This'll make for the perfect season finale."

They filmed out of order, so Jamal still had a supposed "séance gone wrong" to fix, a "possessed Pomeranian" to exorcise, and a "cursed plant" to cleanse.

This episode was supposed to look like a house cleansing. Most of the work would be done by the "reality" show's editing and SFX team. He just had to listen to a story, yell at the wannabe magic wielder, and pretend.

The real season's finale couldn't come fast enough.

**

Katiew3aves: Okay so I *get* why they call everyone a 'patient' (the whole house call/magic doctor thing)...but does no one else find that creepy? @jamaltrixs is no dr, & its got a whole predatory vibe... (1/?)

Katiew3aves:...like these are people who really believe they're seeing something, right? So they're probably really vulnerable. Idk. (2/2, shorter rant than I thought? Lol)

Garfthug69_: you know its all staged right? Bet you they're all actors who cant make it on real shows.

Katiew3aves: But not all.

Garfthug69: go back to your etsy store, bruh. You sound stupid.

Garfthug69: blocking me doesn't make you sound less stupid.

**

Every opening interview starts the same.

"So tell me something about the history of this house."

Miles was dressed up for the show: dark blue jeans and a light pink button up that complemented his skin, only a shade or two lighter than Jamal's. Jamal thought maybe Miles was self-conscious enough about his own crazy that he wanted to prove, through neat clothing, that he was sane.

Within a few moments, Jamal revised his evaluation. The man was obscenely... *normal*. Miles had a can of ginger ale tucked under his chair alongside a sandwich from catering. He chatted with the crew and seemed to have some level of understanding of things on the set, even if it was clearly informed by Google searches and bad television. He'd thrown Jamal a nod when they first crossed paths, a move that felt wickedly familiar to Jamal's easily irritable demeanor—too much camaraderie.

Miles's normalcy stood in stark contrast with Miles's house, which looked like someone took Halloween far too seriously. Too many leather-bound volumes (dust-coated, unread), too much wood stacked up for the fireplace (wiped down, clean but unused), and too many candles (half-melted onto surfaces as they burned). Something about Miles or the house was staged, and Jamal wasn't sure which part.

Still, when Miles answered Jamal's question, it was clear, unhesitating, sure. Not with belief—every patient thought they believed, although never enough to truly make the magic stick—but Miles wasn't nervous that Jamal *wouldn't* believe. Most patients had that shivering kind of discomfort, that pleading in their eyes that betrayed their doubt. They unintentionally begged the camera to believe in their hauntings and misfired hexes, because something still wasn't real about the situation to *them*.

Maybe that was why Jamal heard the inflection in Miles's voice more than he heard the story, and found it discomfited him. As soon as the filming of this segment stopped, Jamal stood up, wiping his hands on the sides of his pants.

Miles stood up after him, almost jumping up to follow.

"Yo, man, much appreciated," Miles said. Jamal was pulling out his phone, looking at hundreds of notifications. "I've spent a lot of time in here, trying to figure out what to do about..." Miles gestured around him, referencing the story they'd just repeated. "None of the local guys in the paper could help." Jamal snorted; of that he was sure. "They're not the real shit, you know? Not like us."

At that, Jamal's head shot up from his phone. Miles didn't flinch at the full weight of Jamal's stare; he was, instead, waiting expectantly. It took a moment for Jamal to glance down and realize why. Miles's fist was outstretched, waiting for a dap.

Jamal could feel a couple of crewmembers holding their breath, nervous at the familiarity of the gesture.

"Like us?" Jamal echoed, each word a blade against a sharpening stone.

Miles withdrew his hand. He glanced around the room, sucking his teeth as he remembered there was an audience to his shunning.

"Yeah. Us. You know what I mean."

Jamal tucked his phone, and the thread he was reading about him being a fraud, into his pocket.

"There ain't no 'like us.'" There was none of the carefully put-on seriousness of Jamal's interviewing voice. This was piercingly tinted with sincerity, and it didn't sound "nice" or "good."

He took a step forward, and Miles didn't step back. Maybe he shrank in Jamal's shadow, but not enough.

"You're on a show, my dude. This is all staged. But at least when we're playing pretend, throwing in some props and spooky music, people know. Your ass signed a release to be on this show." Jamal glanced around the room, past all the cables and lights brought in for recording. "But at least we're better than the game you're pulling here."

"Excuse me?" Miles didn't stutter.

"There ain't a damn thing about this place that's haunted, is there?" Miles opened his mouth wide, but Jamal barreled on. "I know what you told the producers, but we do our homework. You've lived here your whole life? You bought this in a foreclosure auction five years ago. That grandpa whose entire line studied 'dark arts' to avenge their legacy? He's still alive in...Ariaga, it was Miami, wasn't it?"

There was no answer, and fuck it, Ariaga might have stepped out. What there was, though, was that tension, coalescing, spooling. It felt like something buried deep in Jamal's memory, back in the day before release forms and teams of researchers, something that felt wrong in front of cameras.

"There's no Ouija board your older cousin used to tie a demon to this house before being murdered, because that cousin doesn't exist. So don't get it twisted: there's nothing real about either of us. No magical energy, no portals. I feel *nothing*."

The corner of Jamal's eyesight burned with spots of orange. A candle flame growing and subsiding? A lens flare exploding and going dim? He refused to notice it.

Miles clear his throat, looking down for a minute before speaking. "Do you feel nothing," he started, this time a little more careful, a little more deliberately, "Because magic isn't real, or because you know what magic feels like, and it's not here?"

Jamal was startled by the question, by the way Miles' eyes narrowed. As if the man was seeing Jamal, but...the Jamal from before four successful seasons of this show.

Jamal considered telling Miles to fuck off, that he could pick either answer and shove it up his ass. That Jamal was just going to finish required filming over the next couple of days and then they would never talk about what Jamal felt ever again.

**

Of course I'm going to watch the new season, but I can't be the only one feeling like its getting boring? I wish we'd just get a special episode that was just about Trixs. I know, wishful thinking.

**

"What do you fucking mean, you don't know where Ariaga is?"

Amanda, the newest of Ariaga's on-set interns, quaked under Jamal's bafflement. She shrugged, hands up, nothing to offer.

"We haven't seen him since he went to check out a few ideas for B-roll shots. I called him, like you and Reggie asked, but..." Another shrug, with a look that said she was calculating how much she was going to get blamed for Ariaga's actions and her inability to fix them.

Jamal shook his head with irritation. He'd gotten a text message from Ariaga not ten minutes ago, something about being upstairs, that they should workshop an apology to Miles...but no one seemed to *find* him when they went upstairs.

"Fuck this, he's being a little shit," Jamal grumbled, turning from Amanda and starting towards the stairs. The steps groaned and creaked, exactly how Jamal predicted. "Surprised Ariaga isn't recording you for later eps," he told them. The stairs didn't answer.

**

While most of the Q&A was entertaining, with light-hearted tales of behind-the-scenes antics from the ghost-hunting shows, the comic-con panel wasn't without awkward moments. During audience questions, one "fan" of Magical House Call *got up and asked how Jamal Trixs dealt with accusations of the show losing its edge. Jamal's response was mostly bleeped out in the livestreams, and critics pointed out that the answer verged on bullying, embarrassing the fan for the sake of Trixs's "image."*

And it still didn't hit at the heart of the question: What happens to a magic doctor when he's clearly getting bored by his own patients?

**

There was a door cracked open to the left of the stairs. Jamal pushed it, letting its joints whine at him. There was a thickness, a pressure as he opened the door. He imagined that it was— no, he *knew* the pressure was just ill-oiled hinges not wanting to comply. It wasn't the feeling of a weak ward attempting to withstand a final assault.

The goosebumps rising on his arms weren't because of the door, but what lay on the other side. Jamal felt as if he'd walked into a museum exhibit of his own career. No, not the exhibit, but the back room messily storing the exhibit pieces until they were all filed away. Walls of pictures, screen captures, reviews of episodes with parts annotated and highlighted. A rumor rag that had inset photos of a blurred Jamal next to a larger sketch of a demon or a fae: STRING OF POSSESSIONS IN DETROIT, AND THE *MAGIC DOCTOR* IS ON THE CASE, read the headline.

It was the first time anyone had used that name for him, three, four years before the start of the show. But not the first time one of those supermarket magazines managed to stumble upon his link to eerie happenings.

And there were *notebooks*, spiral and composition, well worn, some taped to stay together, piled on various surfaces. Candles, currently unlit, slumped and melted into the wood.

Jamal's ears popped like he was on an airplane, and suddenly he was aware of Ariaga in front of him, the producer's back towards him. Ariaga, staring at the walls with the same tension that Jamal had in his own body, a horrific kind of shock...except.

"Ariaga, man, what the fuck is going on?" Jamal asked. His voice was harsher than he intended, "You knew about this shit before we started filming?"

"I..." Araiga didn't turn, although his hand was reaching up at one of the articles, slowly, jerkily skimming the lines. "...didn't..."

He sounded *off*, somehow simultaneously stretched and staccato.

Jamal sucked his teeth and reached out, grabbing Ariaga's shoulder to jerk him around.

Buffering, Jamal realized in horror as Ariaga turned. Ariaga sounded like he was stuck *buffering*, and his face...it flickered, warping and twisting in unnatural, blocky contortions, as if it was attempting to deform but couldn't quite get enough of a signal to do so. An eye bulged and then swam in his face, and then all of Ariaga's features blurred and squared and widened and narrowed, a picture forming as the flesh-video loaded.

"...know..." Ariaga's words were separate from his mouth, staggered against the way his face moved. "...t-t-this..." Jamal felt nauseous as he realized he couldn't tell the difference between Ariaga's eyes widening in horror and the distortion of whatever *this* was, because they were both happening now, right in front of him.

Not *whatever this was*, Jamal thought.

"Magic," Jamal spoke out loud. That didn't make sense, Jamal didn't *feel* anything, there wasn't anything here except a subtle pop, and there was nothing subtle about what was happening to Ariaga.

And it was still happening, moving out like a digital spiderweb from Ariaga's face to the rest of him. A shuddering, blistering metamorphosis slowly catching on—spreading, installing, still fucking *buffering*—made the edges of Ariaga and the air around him blur. He threatened to become indistinguishable from the wall and floor and the headlines that framed him.

And then reality stuttered. Reality *burst* before smoothing out, and Jamal felt sticky warmth, and his nostrils were filled with a smell he didn't want to name, but which made him want to vomit.

As reality smoothed out, ignoring the wretched splatter of human that hung from the macabre gallery of Jamal's greatest hits, it didn't load Ariaga. Jamal's nausea hit a roiling pitch.

"*Miles.*"

**

Have you read that blog post, CONFESSIONS OF A TRIXSTER? I think it really illustrates what's happening in the fandom right now. We're seeing a shift of sorts: We used to exist on conspiracy theory reddits and forums, but after the expose about that show's use of CG, and the statements made by 'patients' from the first season, we just had to accept the show for what it was: entertainment.

**

"I wanted to feed them each to the house before you got up here."

Miles was mostly clean, but pressed his fingertips against the front of his shirt, wiping off producer bits onto the pale pink of his shirt. It left a smear, comical in its solitude. He grimaced.

"Thought it would be the intern next. Figured you'd send her up here, acting all lazy and shit." Jamal didn't speak, but not for lack of trying; he was gagging on the slaughter, on the blurring of reality.

Miles shrugged, looking at Jamal as if he was inconvenienced, but not concerned, by the change of script.

"I wanted to feed them each to the house before you got up here," he explained. "Panic and fear, when they realized the house was real, that magic was real. It would have been useful for what happens next." He snorted, shaking his head. "But you know that already. This is your wheelhouse, right Trixs?"

Jamal stumbled backwards before he bolted. He wasn't thinking when he ran towards the door, when the thick pressure that he'd attributed to hinges *was still there* as he passed through the open exit.

"Oh, this is going to be easier than I thought."

Miles's voice boomed in the hallway, not coming from the room that Jamal had just left. Nothing came from the room that Jamal just left. The doorway opened to a gray, aborted nothing. (It didn't *load*, his brain told him; it was rebooting, resettling into reality.) Jamal wasn't fool enough to lean back into it, to see what happened if he crossed that threshold one more time.

The hallway wasn't much safer, though, Jamal soon realized. It stuttered and flickered like Ariaga had, pulsing its way into a stretched, skewed distortion. Where it had been mere footsteps between and the stairs before, now there was...it was both miles away and seconds away, the way a damaged digital file merged pixels from two moments in time. Jamal shook his head as if it would right the world.

"Heard you never ran from *any* magic."

Miles's voice loomed. Jamal was reminded of a browser tab blaring sound in the background, the frantic search to find and close it. He kept moving toward the steps.

"This the first time, *Trixs*?"

Jamal didn't want to answer, but his pride did the work for him.

"Don't...fucking...flatter yourself." Oh, words were hard, but not *buffering*-hard, he told himself. "How'd you pull this off?"

"Which part?"

Before working in television, Jamal heard dozens, hundreds of screams. He'd heard human and inhuman screams. Screams of pains, earsplitting choruses of demons, the soundless shrieks of ghosts, and the way the fae still sounded beautiful during a cacophony of terror. What he heard from

downstairs qualified as screams, but it was almost digitized—audio destroyed by bad reception. Muffled and booming, with sharp seconds of silence intercut as if breaking up on the other line.

He heard Amanda's audio overlay Reggie's—Reggie, who had come onto the show in season two—which then crackled into Naomi's from hair and makeup. The sounds weren't supposed to be *simultaneous*, part of Jamal's brain told him, even as his logic told him they shouldn't exist at all.

"The house was obvious." Miles's voice was the clearest, too clear, as it echoed Jamal's thoughts. Too clean. Too real, as reality crashed around them. "Any house would have done, but it doesn't take a genius to know what you'd pick. So make a house look like a horror, weave some stories...make your team *believe* it's the perfect house for an episode."

Jamal got to the top of the stairs, and the bottom was a technicolor, digital soup. Sometimes, briefly, the pulsating reality swelled together into something recognizable— part of a camera with Amanda's arm coming out of the lens, Ariaga's sunglasses as large as a reflector, his screaming mouth emblazoned upon it— before glitching away into the sea of noise.

"That's what I learned from you, about magic. That no matter the style or tradition you adapt, it's belief. If I could make the team believe what I *knew*, that was enough."

Jamal could hear his younger self in those words, could almost feel those words rising up out of the static below. He hesitated to touch the stair railing, ready to imagine it falling away into errors at his grip. Caught his own imagination before it fell in line with the image in front of him. Reminded himself of the rules of magic. He couldn't lend Miles power like that, right? That was how this was supposed to work?

So he grabbed the bannister, hard, told himself that he was sure it would remain firm under the heat of his hand. The wood was unsure of which reality held sway over it. It squished and chunked and pixelated slightly but didn't collapse.

Jamal took a step down. Took a breath.

"If you learned from me, you know what I can do," he bluffed. "You know who I am."

"I know who you were," Miles retorted smoothly. Jamal's steps were slow, as he tried to remember how to exert his will over Miles's. "I fucking *idolized* you, man. I had some talent already, but I read everything about you. Watched that first season, where you'd talk about what magic was and wasn't while revealing all these fakers."

Jamal closed his eyes and tried not to be as nauseous from that revelation as he was from the bits of human still clinging to his shirt. He took another step.

"I don't like much of the other seasons," Miles admitted. For a second, the bannister was warm like Jamal, the wood darkened to only a few shades lighter than Jamal's skin. The gold design painted on its surface tinted rose-gold before falling away, a few steps down, into the noise. But every time Jamal took a step, the ground was solid under him. Solid enough. The noise pushed back a bit more. "But I could see you...die." Jamal didn't snort in amusement or agreement, but felt the sweat on his temples drip. "That's why I sent in an audition tape. Sorry about lying but...I thought I could save you."

"Save...me?" Jamal's voice was choked, and as the shock hit him, squared chunks of reality blurred, fell, and reassembled. "From what?"

"Becoming one of them." Now Miles's voice came from below, from the noise. A lump of the noise lifted, raised, the shape of it reminding Jamal of the dome of a whale. Still, there were flashes of recognizable images: was there a logo in there, collapsing into the credits of *Magical House Call*? Or was it bits of Reggie, and the shingles of the house? "The boring, the skeptics. I didn't want you to lose your power. Trade it for fame."

Is that how Miles saw it? Jamal Trixs, signing a devil's deal for media appearances in exchange for the magic that got him this far? Wasn't that how *Jamal* saw it? Wasn't that what Jamal *believed* he'd done?

Belief was everything; knowing was God.

"So is this you scaring me into believing?"

"No, you believe in magic," Miles countered, and the tumor of digitization grew larger still, started to craft itself into a shape. "I realized that when you went off on me, Trixs. You never stopped believing."

Then why was this so hard, Jamal didn't dare ask. Why couldn't he swoop in and crush Miles's magic, tear apart what was illusion and what magic made real? That was what he did, that was why he was the magic doctor, that's why he was Jamal Trixs—

The noise was an oval shape now, leaning up towards Jamal on the steps. Big enough that when the bottom part opened, yawning wide, it could have consumed Jamal. Big enough that Jamal had to realize he'd *stopped moving*. Stopped walking. The bannister was softer.

"You thought you couldn't feel the magic because there wasn't any." The sound was coming from the yawn, as the noise formed a face, formed Miles's face, his broad nose and searching eyes writ humongous in discordant pixels. "But that wasn't why. You couldn't feel it because of the cameras, the producers, and the audition tapes. The squabbles online that you keep seeking out, reading and rereading to confirm what you already know. You believe in magic..."

Powerless, Jamal felt his mouth finish his greatest fear.

"...but I know *I've* become a lie."

It wasn't the bannister that was softer as the large mouth opened. It was Jamal's own hand, his limbs, as the edges blurred. He was choppier, blockier, as he remembered the message boards, as he thought of his own words, echoed back to him in audio that needed desperately to get cleaned up in post.

So don't get it twisted: I feel nothing.

End

THERE WAS A TICKLE IN MY THROAT.
I COUGHED, GASPING FOR AIR.

WET HAIR BRUSHED MY LIPS.

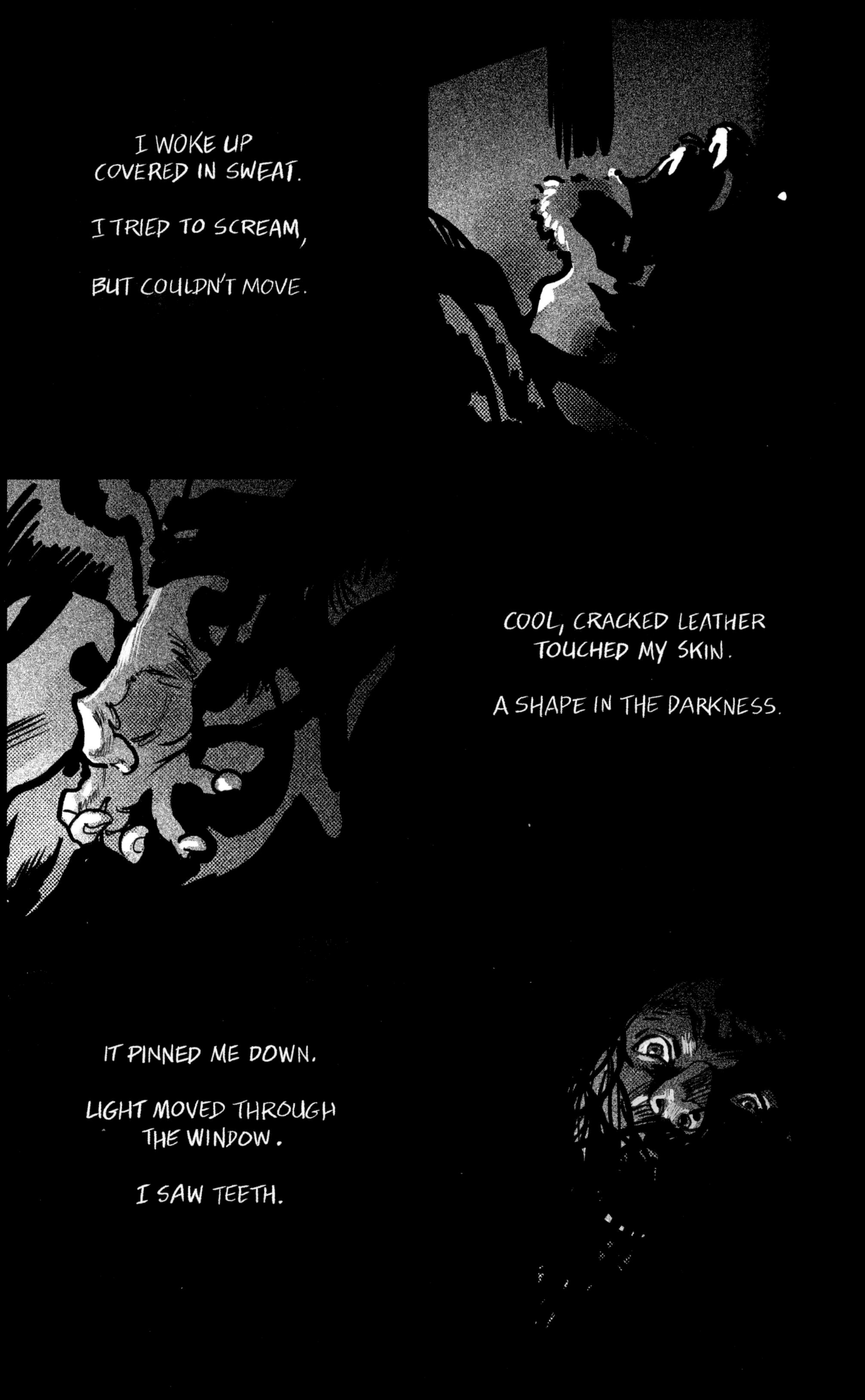
I WOKE UP COVERED IN SWEAT.
I TRIED TO SCREAM,
BUT COULDN'T MOVE.
COOL, CRACKED LEATHER TOUCHED MY SKIN.
A SHAPE IN THE DARKNESS.
IT PINNED ME DOWN.
LIGHT MOVED THROUGH THE WINDOW.
I SAW TEETH.

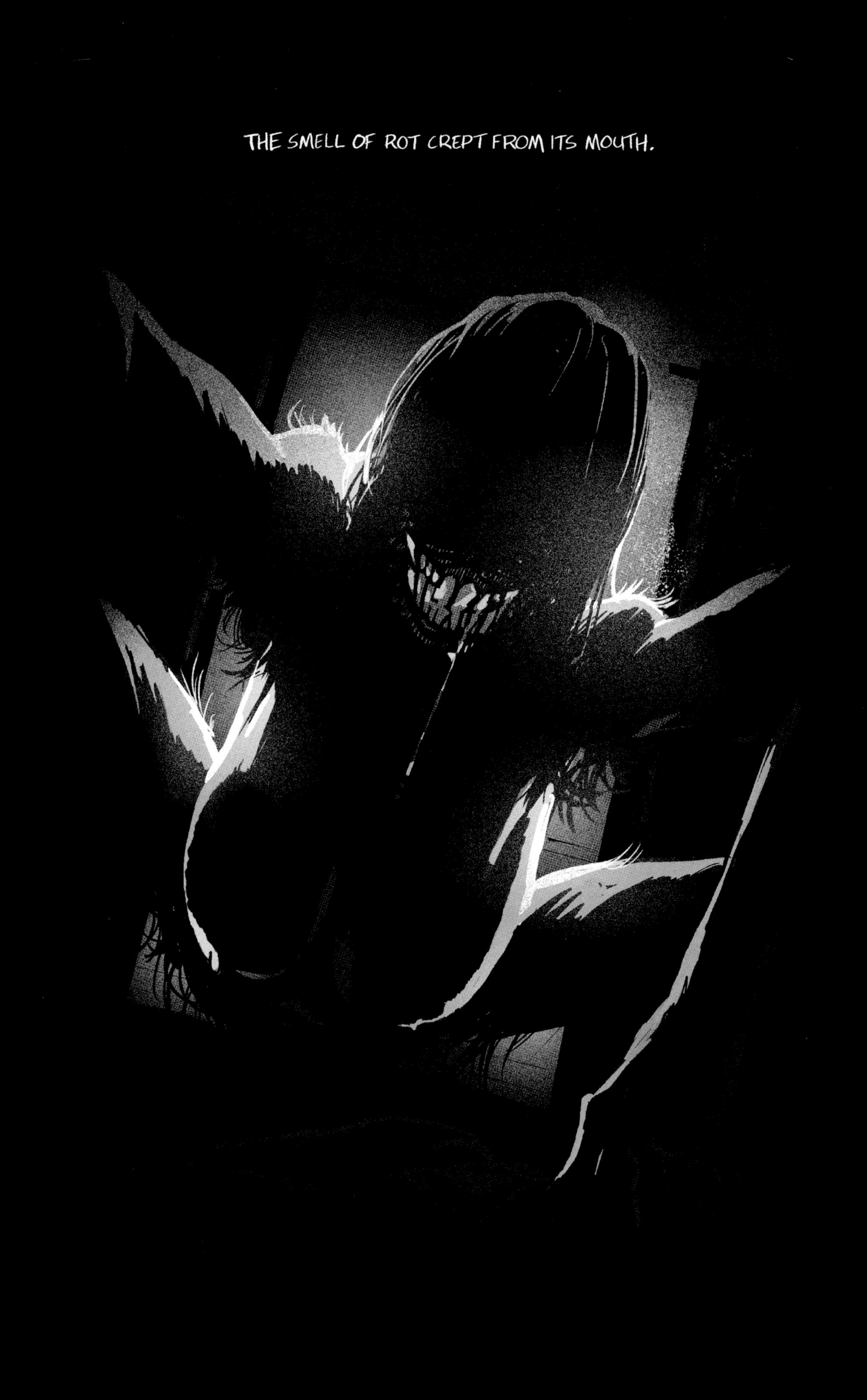
THE SMELL OF ROT CREPT FROM ITS MOUTH.

I OPENED MY EYES TO THE SOUND OF SPLATTERING GREASE.

YOU WERE MAKING SOME REALLY STRANGE NOISES.

DID YOU WANT SOME BACON AND EGGS?

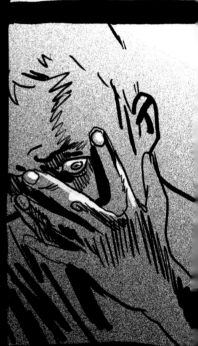

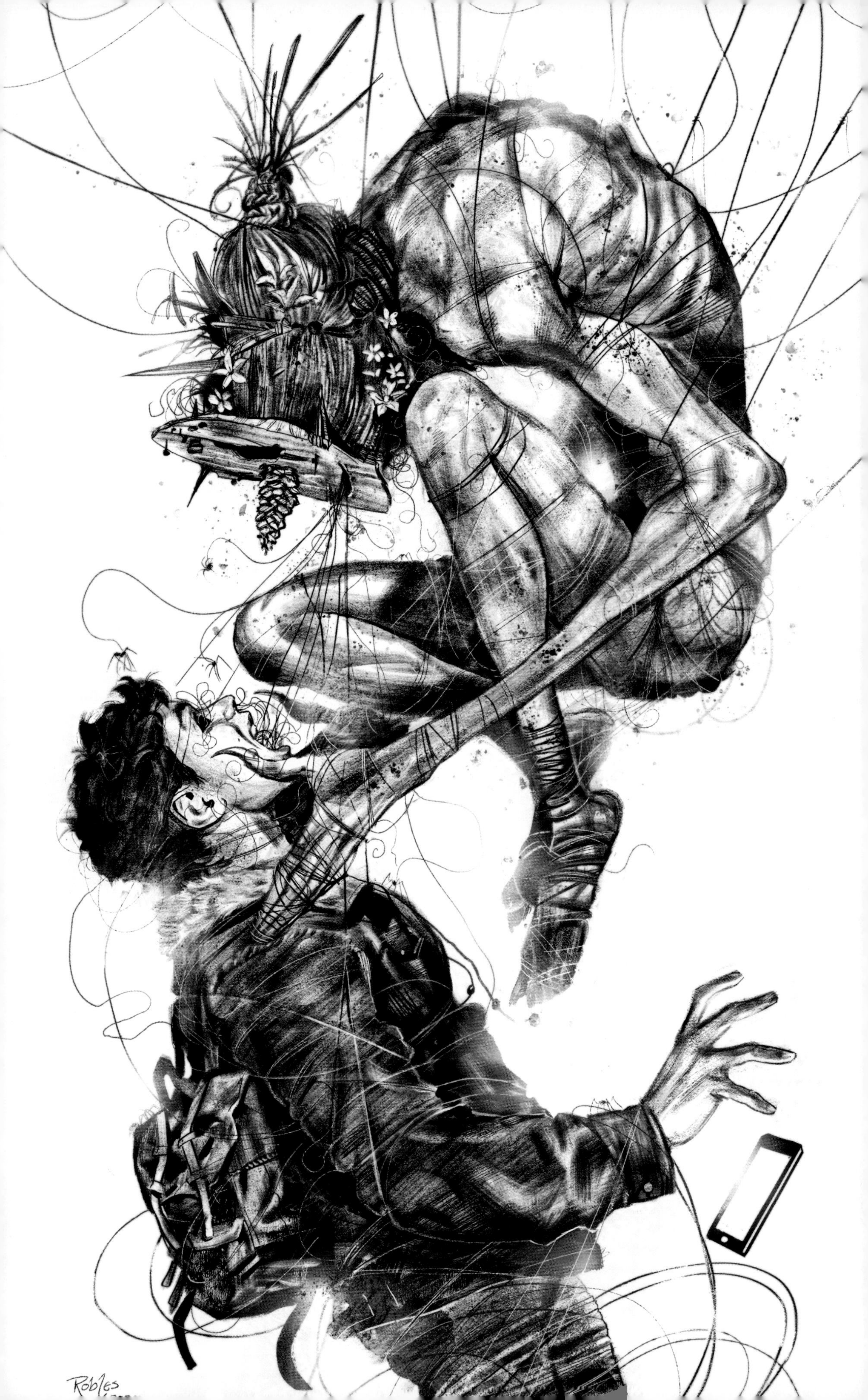
Robles

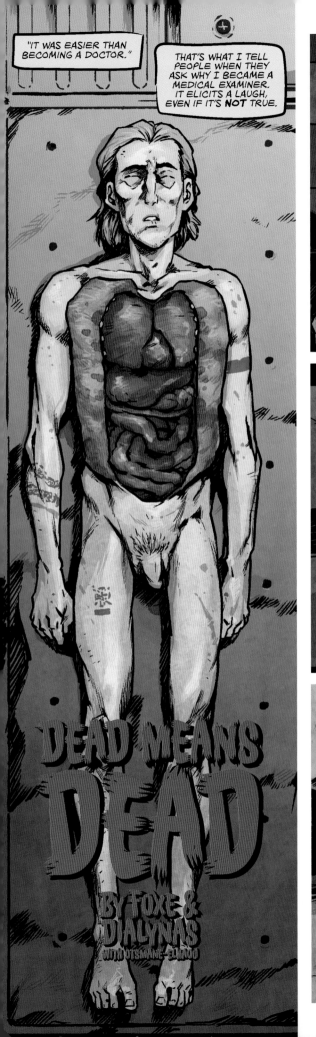

"IT WAS EASIER THAN BECOMING A DOCTOR."

THAT'S WHAT I TELL PEOPLE WHEN THEY ASK WHY I BECAME A MEDICAL EXAMINER. IT ELICITS A LAUGH, EVEN IF IT'S **NOT** TRUE.

DEAD MEANS DEAD

BY FOXE & DIALYNAS
WITH OTSMANE-ELHAOU

IT TOOK ME **YEARS** TO LEARN THE INS AND OUTS OF THE HUMAN BODY. I NEVER AIMED TO BE A DOCTOR.

BUT NO ONE WANTS THE **REAL** ANSWER.

MY DAD PASSED AWAY WHEN I WAS NINE. I HANDLED THE GRIEF OKAY FOR MY AGE.

BUT A FEW MONTHS AFTER HIS FUNERAL, I WOKE UP WITH A TERRIBLE THOUGHT:

WHAT IF HE WASN'T REALLY DEAD WHEN WE BURIED HIM?

BEING BURIED ALIVE BECAME AN ALL-CONSUMING FEAR OF MINE. I EVEN REFUSED TO TAKE ELEVATORS OR SLEEP UNDER HEAVY COMFORTERS.

BUT MY DAD, WHO HAD BEEN IN AND OUT OF HOSPITALS MY ENTIRE LIFE, **ALWAYS** URGED ME TO FACE MY FEARS HEAD-ON.

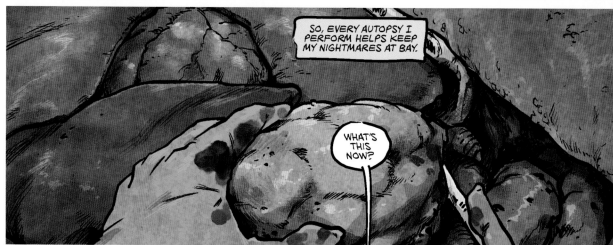

SO, EVERY AUTOPSY I PERFORM HELPS KEEP MY NIGHTMARES AT BAY.

WHAT'S THIS NOW?

THIS JOHN DOE WAS AN APPARENT **OVERDOSE** IN AN AIRPORT BATHROOM.

MOST PEOPLE I EXAMINE HAVE **MESSY** ENDS.

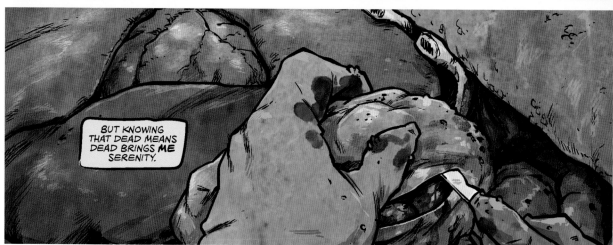

BUT KNOWING THAT DEAD MEANS DEAD BRINGS **ME** SERENITY.

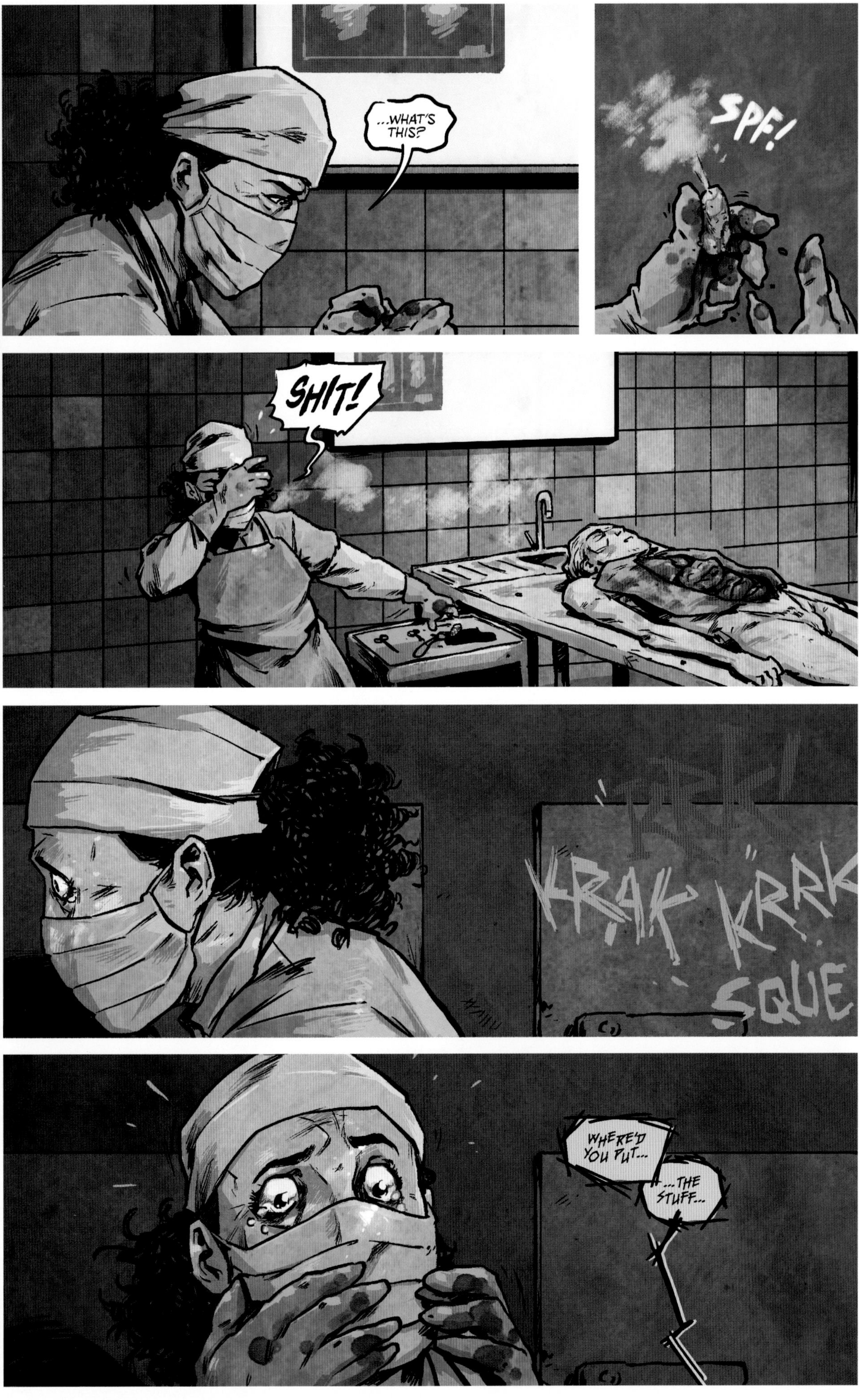
...WHAT'S THIS?
SPF!
SHIT!
KRAK KRRK
SQUE
WHERE'D YOU PUT...
...THE STUFF...

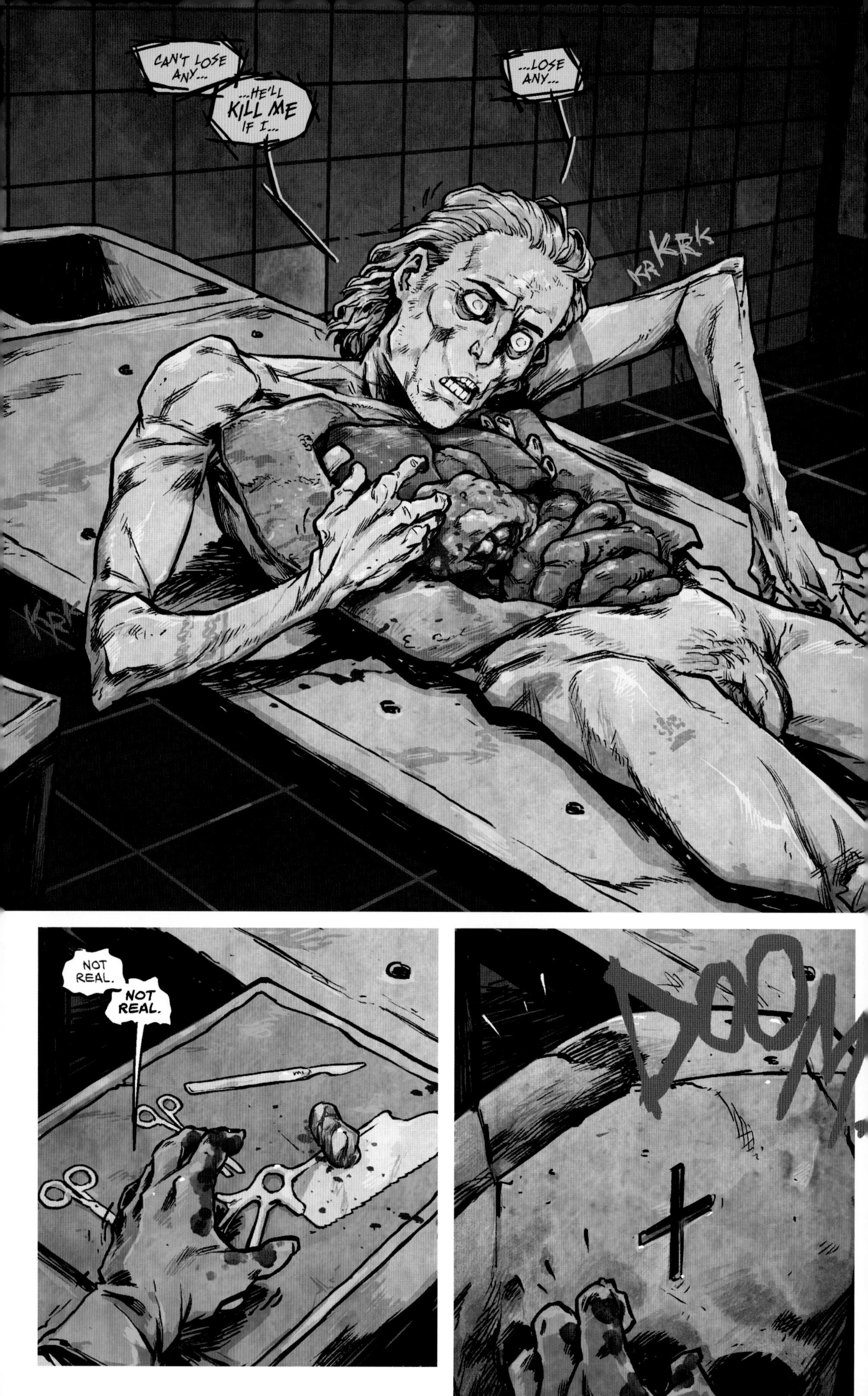
CAN'T LOSE ANY...
...HE'LL KILL ME IF I...
...LOSE ANY...
KRKRK
KRK
NOT REAL.
NOT REAL.
DOO

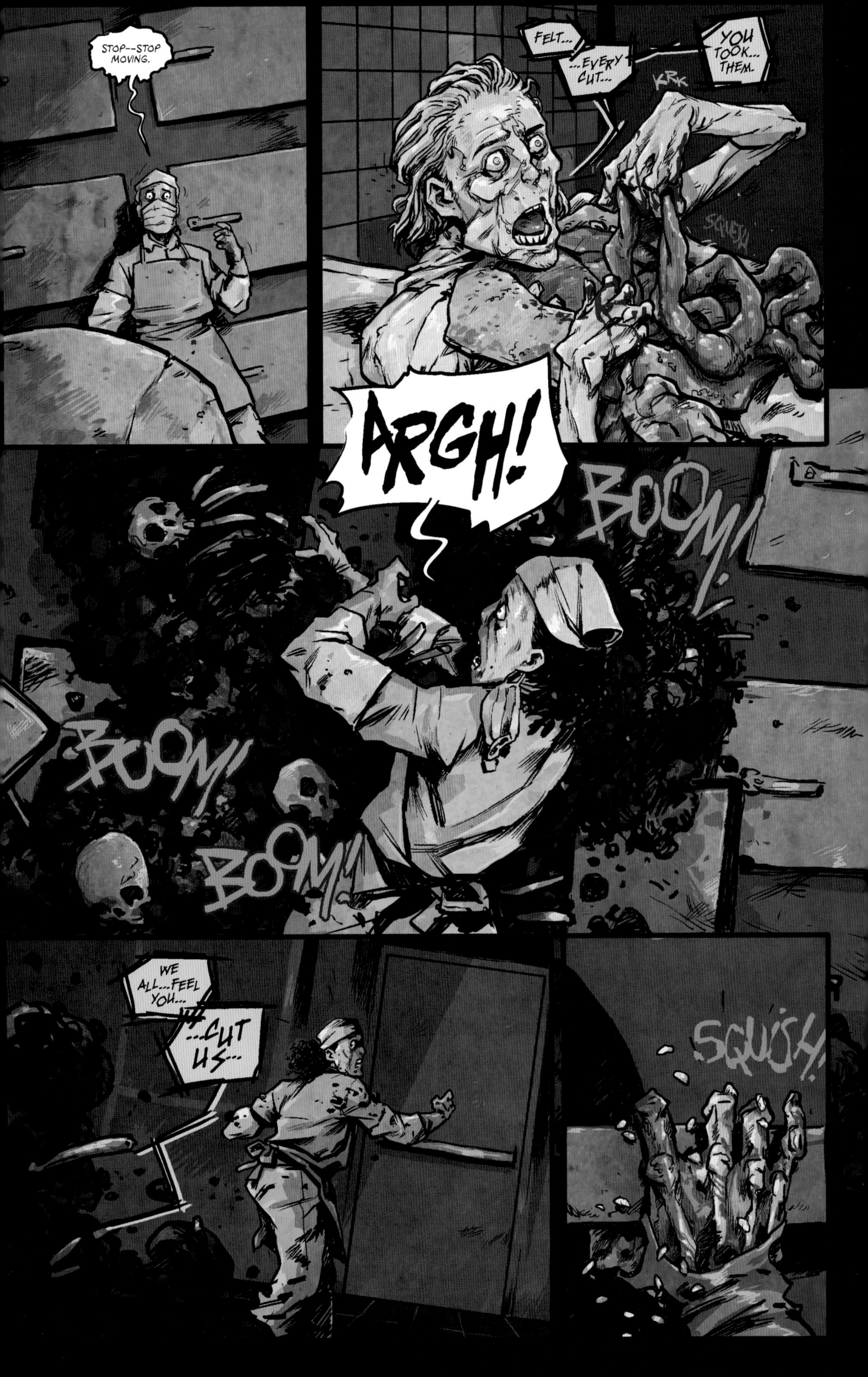
STOP--STOP MOVING.
FELT...
...EVERY CUT...
YOU TOOK... THEM.
KRK
SQUISH
ARGH!
BOOM!
BOOM!
BOOM!
WE ALL...FEEL YOU...
...CUT US--
SQUISH!

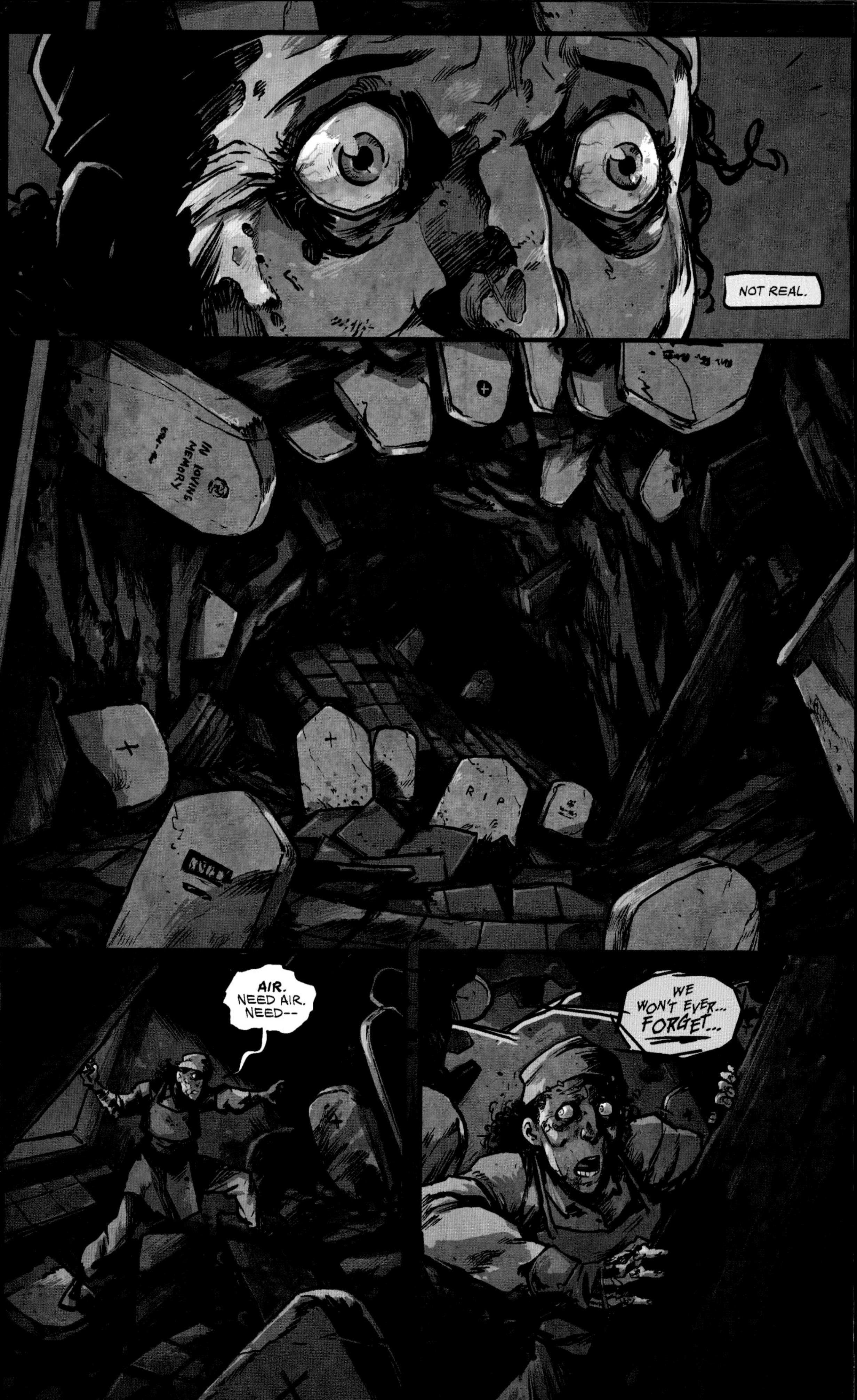
NOT REAL.
IN LOVING MEMORY
RIP
AIR. NEED AIR. NEED--
WE WON'T EVER... FORGET...

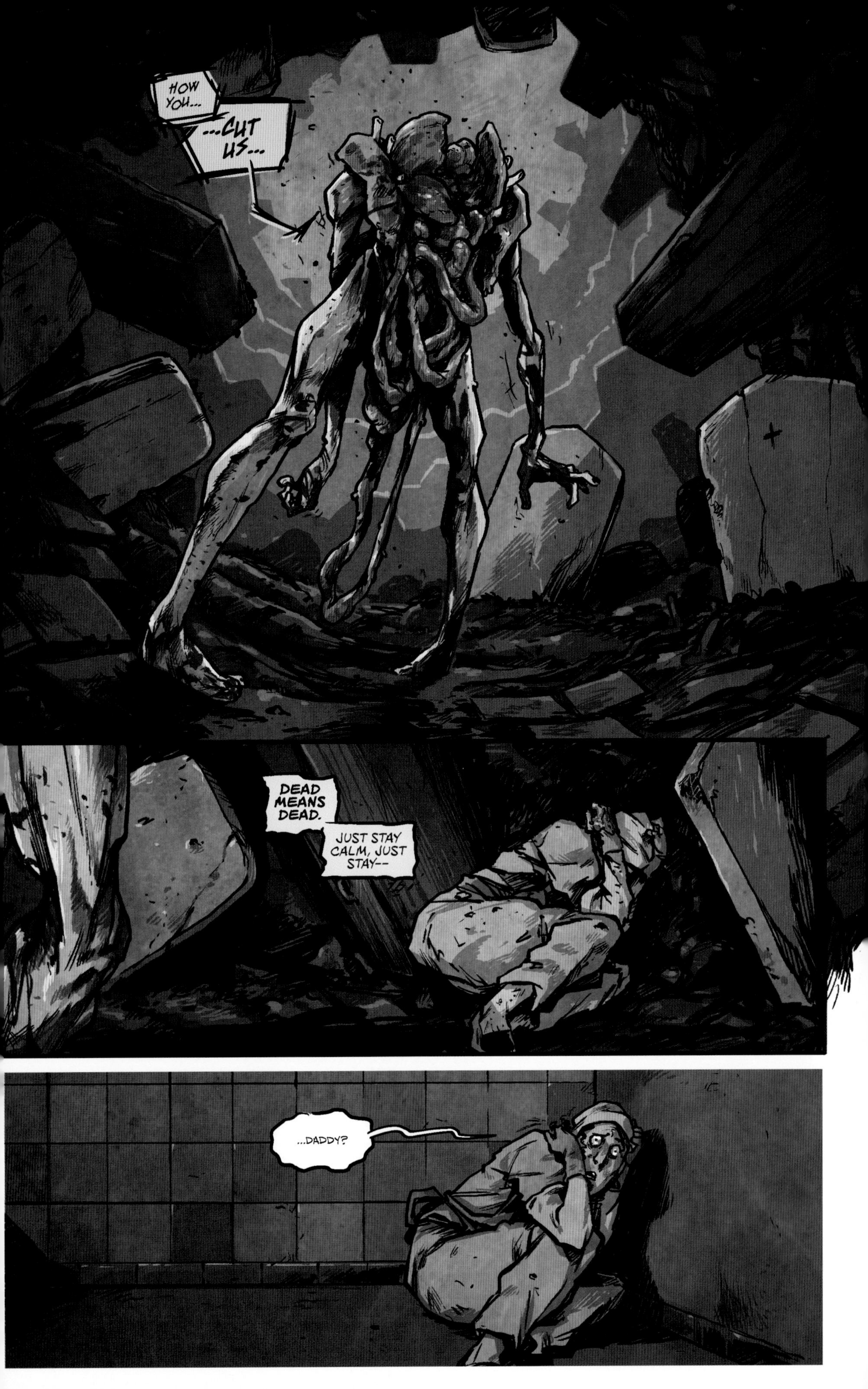
HOW YOU...
...CUT US...
DEAD MEANS DEAD.
JUST STAY CALM, JUST STAY--
...DADDY?

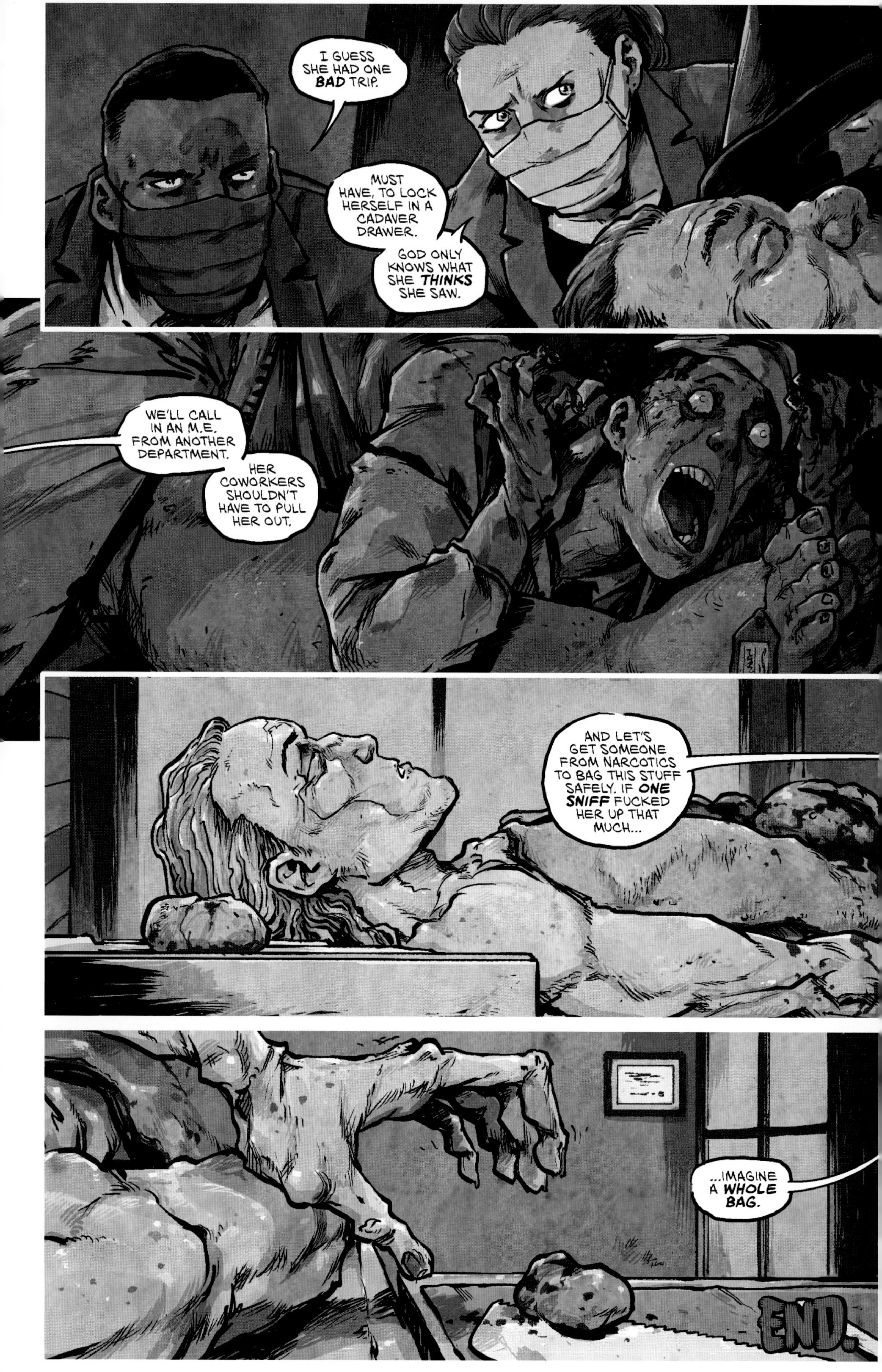
I GUESS SHE HAD ONE BAD TRIP.
MUST HAVE, TO LOCK HERSELF IN A CADAVER DRAWER.
GOD ONLY KNOWS WHAT SHE THINKS SHE SAW.
WE'LL CALL IN AN M.E. FROM ANOTHER DEPARTMENT.
HER COWORKERS SHOULDN'T HAVE TO PULL HER OUT.
AND LET'S GET SOMEONE FROM NARCOTICS TO BAG THIS STUFF SAFELY. IF ONE SNIFF FUCKED HER UP THAT MUCH...
...IMAGINE A WHOLE BAG.
END.

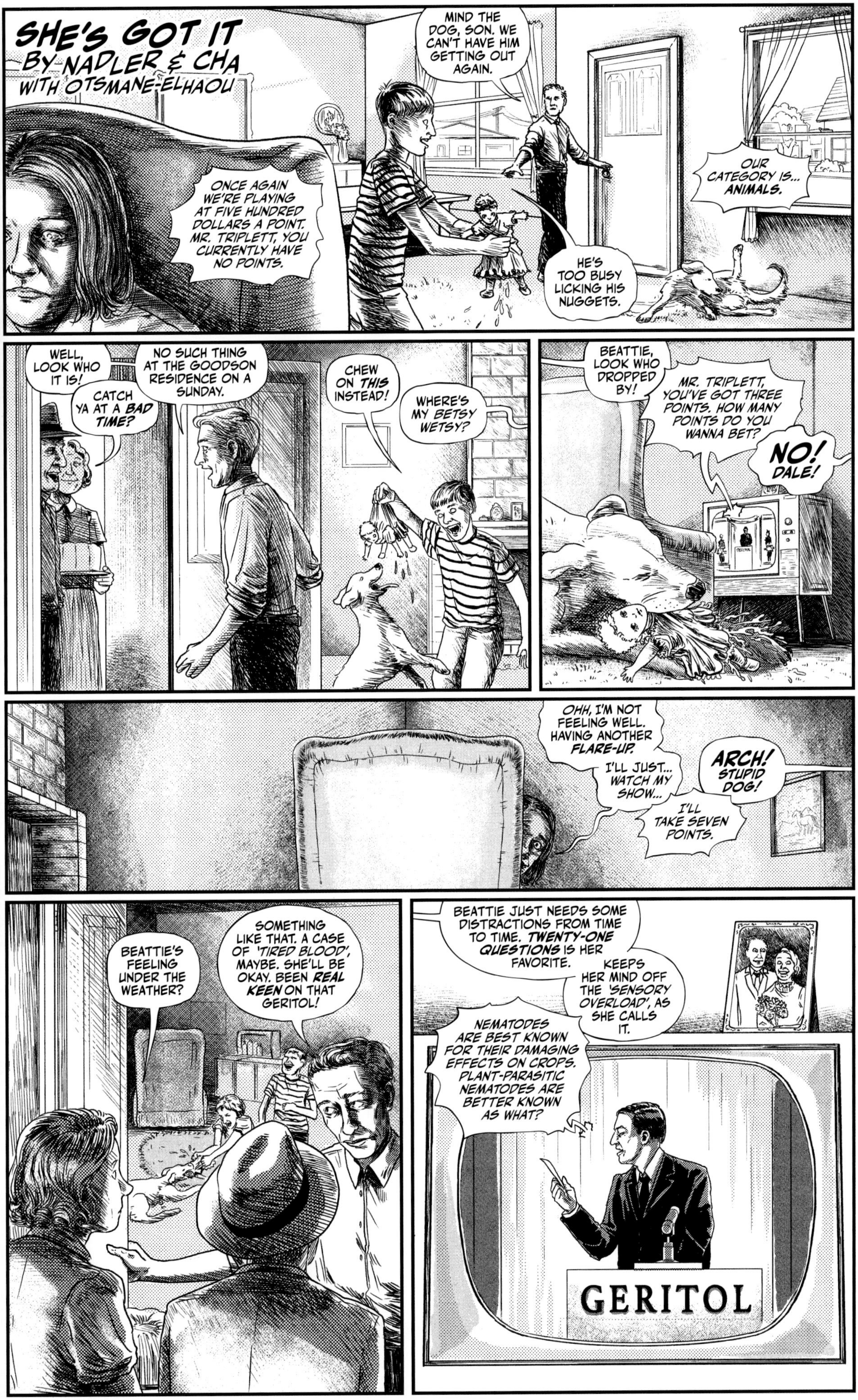
SHE'S GOT IT
BY NADLER & CHA
WITH OTSMANE-ELHAOU
ONCE AGAIN WE'RE PLAYING AT FIVE HUNDRED DOLLARS A POINT. MR. TRIPLETT, YOU CURRENTLY HAVE NO POINTS.
MIND THE DOG, SON. WE CAN'T HAVE HIM GETTING OUT AGAIN.
HE'S TOO BUSY LICKING HIS NUGGETS.
OUR CATEGORY IS... ANIMALS.
WELL, LOOK WHO IT IS!
CATCH YA AT A BAD TIME?
NO SUCH THING AT THE GOODSON RESIDENCE ON A SUNDAY.
CHEW ON THIS INSTEAD!
WHERE'S MY BETSY WETSY?
BEATTIE, LOOK WHO DROPPED BY!
MR. TRIPLETT, YOU'VE GOT THREE POINTS. HOW MANY POINTS DO YOU WANNA BET?
NO! DALE!
OHH, I'M NOT FEELING WELL. HAVING ANOTHER FLARE-UP.
I'LL JUST... WATCH MY SHOW...
ARCH! STUPID DOG!
I'LL TAKE SEVEN POINTS.
BEATTIE'S FEELING UNDER THE WEATHER?
SOMETHING LIKE THAT. A CASE OF 'TIRED BLOOD', MAYBE. SHE'LL BE OKAY. BEEN REAL KEEN ON THAT GERITOL!
BEATTIE JUST NEEDS SOME DISTRACTIONS FROM TIME TO TIME. TWENTY-ONE QUESTIONS IS HER FAVORITE.
KEEPS HER MIND OFF THE 'SENSORY OVERLOAD', AS SHE CALLS IT.
NEMATODES ARE BEST KNOWN FOR THEIR DAMAGING EFFECTS ON CROPS. PLANT-PARASITIC NEMATODES ARE BETTER KNOWN AS WHAT?
GERITOL

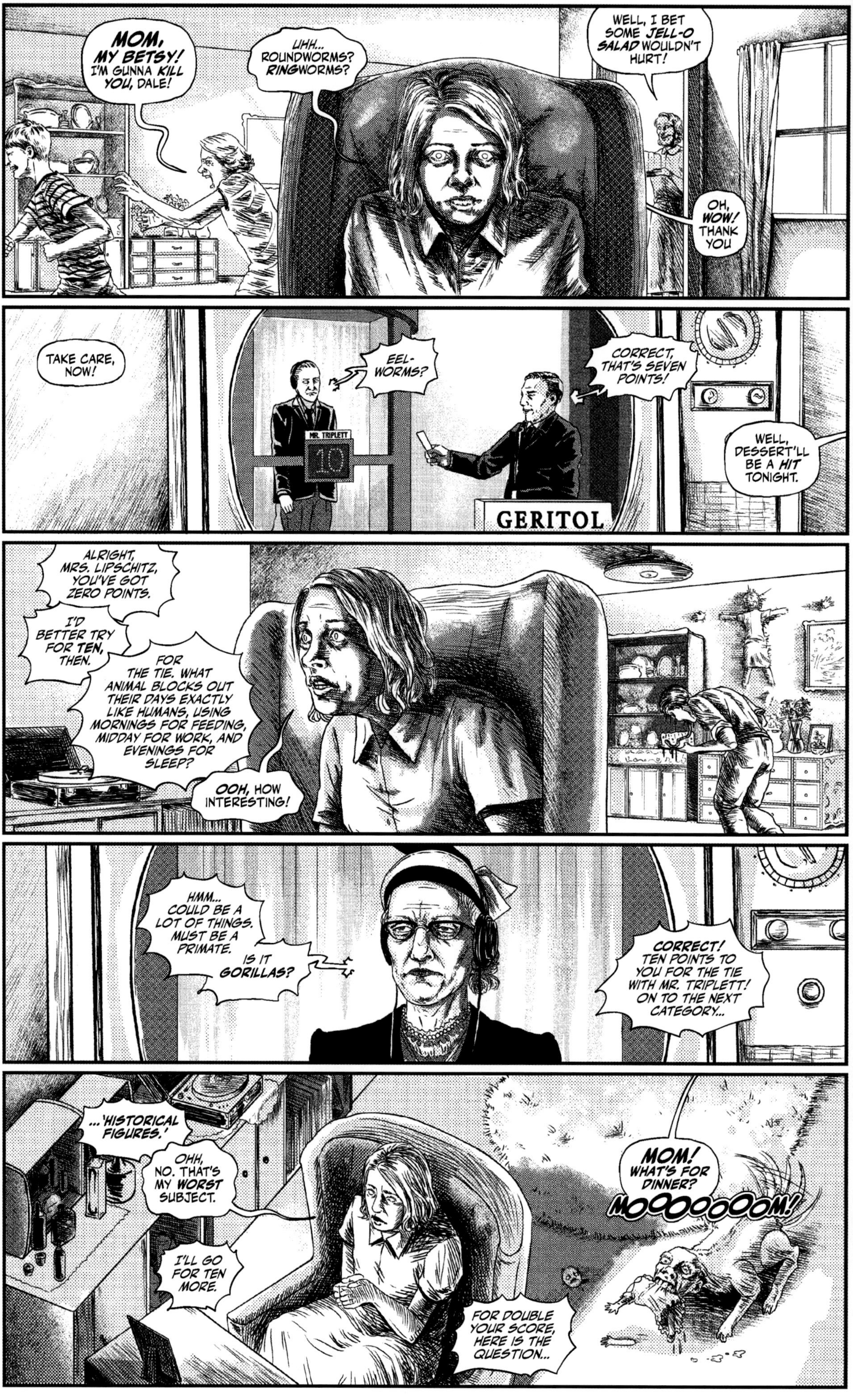
MOM, MY BETSY! I'M GUNNA KILL YOU, DALE!
UHH... ROUNDWORMS? RINGWORMS?
WELL, I BET SOME JELL-O SALAD WOULDN'T HURT!
OH, WOW! THANK YOU
TAKE CARE, NOW!
MR. TRIPLETT
10
EEL-WORMS?
CORRECT, THAT'S SEVEN POINTS!
GERITOL
WELL, DESSERT'LL BE A HIT TONIGHT.
ALRIGHT, MRS. LIPSCHITZ, YOU'VE GOT ZERO POINTS.
I'D BETTER TRY FOR TEN, THEN.
FOR THE TIE. WHAT ANIMAL BLOCKS OUT THEIR DAYS EXACTLY LIKE HUMANS, USING MORNINGS FOR FEEDING, MIDDAY FOR WORK, AND EVENINGS FOR SLEEP?
OOH, HOW INTERESTING!
HMM... COULD BE A LOT OF THINGS. MUST BE A PRIMATE.
IS IT GORILLAS?
CORRECT! TEN POINTS TO YOU FOR THE TIE WITH MR. TRIPLETT! ON TO THE NEXT CATEGORY...
...'HISTORICAL FIGURES.'
OHH, NO. THAT'S MY WORST SUBJECT.
I'LL GO FOR TEN MORE.
FOR DOUBLE YOUR SCORE, HERE IS THE QUESTION...
MOM! WHAT'S FOR DINNER?
MOOOOOOOM!

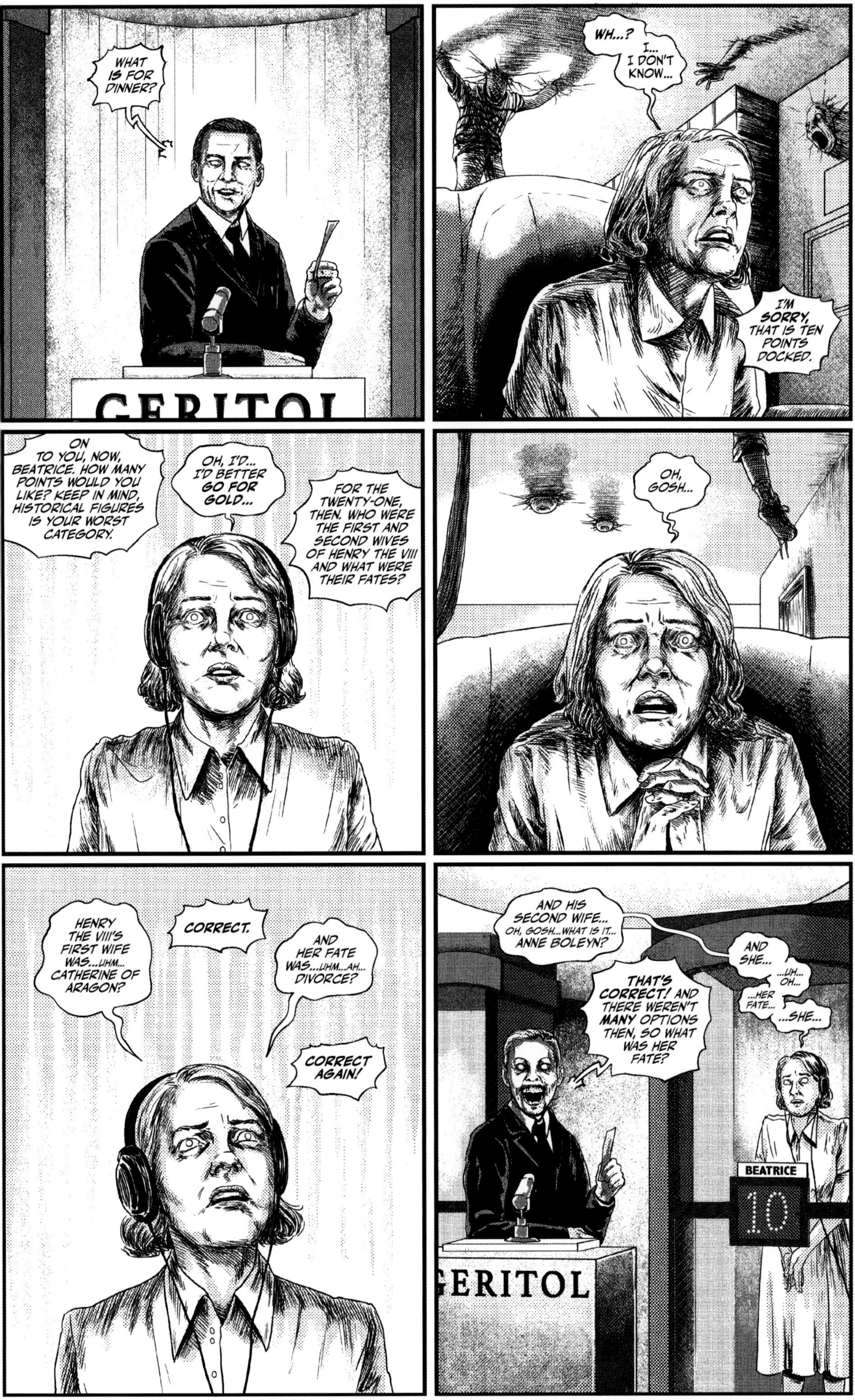
WHAT IS FOR DINNER?
GERITOL
WH...? I... I DON'T KNOW...
I'M SORRY, THAT IS TEN POINTS DOCKED.
ON TO YOU, NOW, BEATRICE. HOW MANY POINTS WOULD YOU LIKE? KEEP IN MIND, HISTORICAL FIGURES IS YOUR WORST CATEGORY.
OH, I'D... I'D BETTER GO FOR GOLD...
FOR THE TWENTY-ONE, THEN. WHO WERE THE FIRST AND SECOND WIVES OF HENRY THE VIII AND WHAT WERE THEIR FATES?
OH, GOSH...
HENRY THE VIII'S FIRST WIFE WAS...UHM... CATHERINE OF ARAGON?
CORRECT.
AND HER FATE WAS...UHM...AH... DIVORCE?
CORRECT AGAIN!
AND HIS SECOND WIFE... OH, GOSH...WHAT IS IT... ANNE BOLEYN?
AND SHE... ...UH... OH... ...HER FATE... ...SHE...
THAT'S CORRECT! AND THERE WEREN'T MANY OPTIONS THEN, SO WHAT WAS HER FATE?
BEATRICE
10
GERITOL

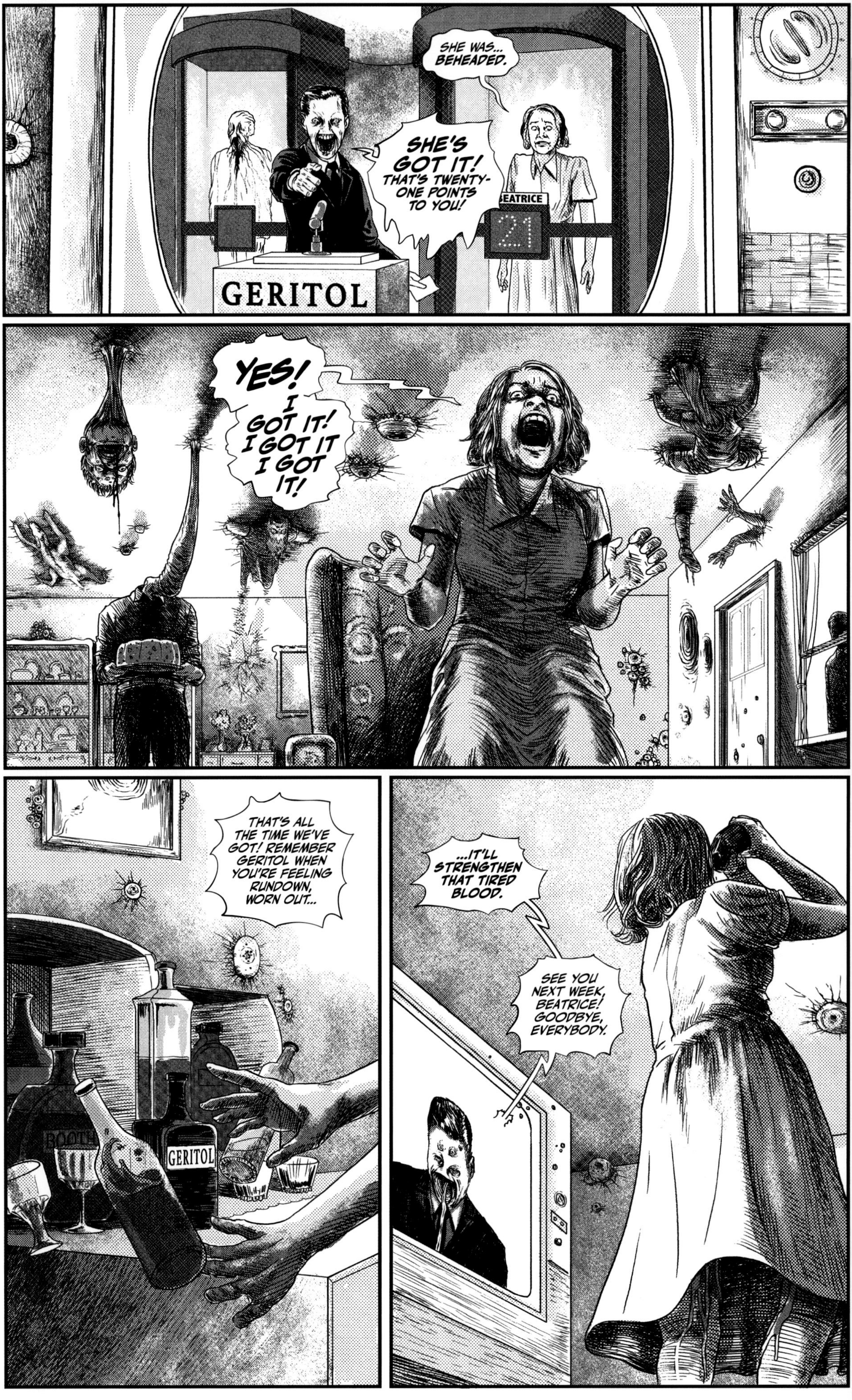
SHE WAS... BEHEADED.
SHE'S GOT IT! THAT'S TWENTY-ONE POINTS TO YOU!
GERITOL
BEATRICE
21
YES! I GOT IT! I GOT IT I GOT IT!
THAT'S ALL THE TIME WE'VE GOT! REMEMBER GERITOL WHEN YOU'RE FEELING RUNDOWN, WORN OUT...
BOOTH
GERITOL
...IT'LL STRENGTHEN THAT TIRED BLOOD.
SEE YOU NEXT WEEK, BEATRICE! GOODBYE, EVERYBODY.

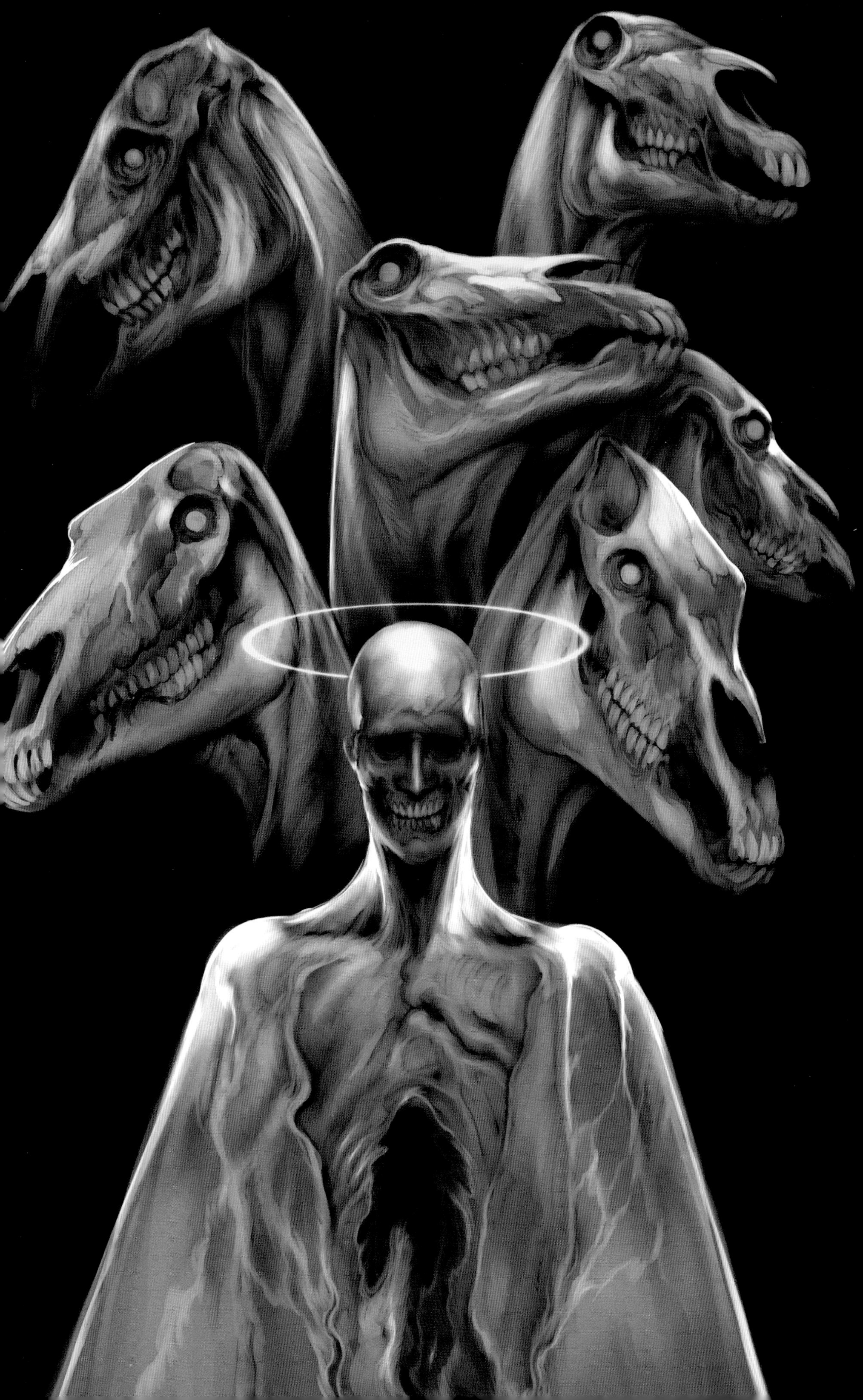

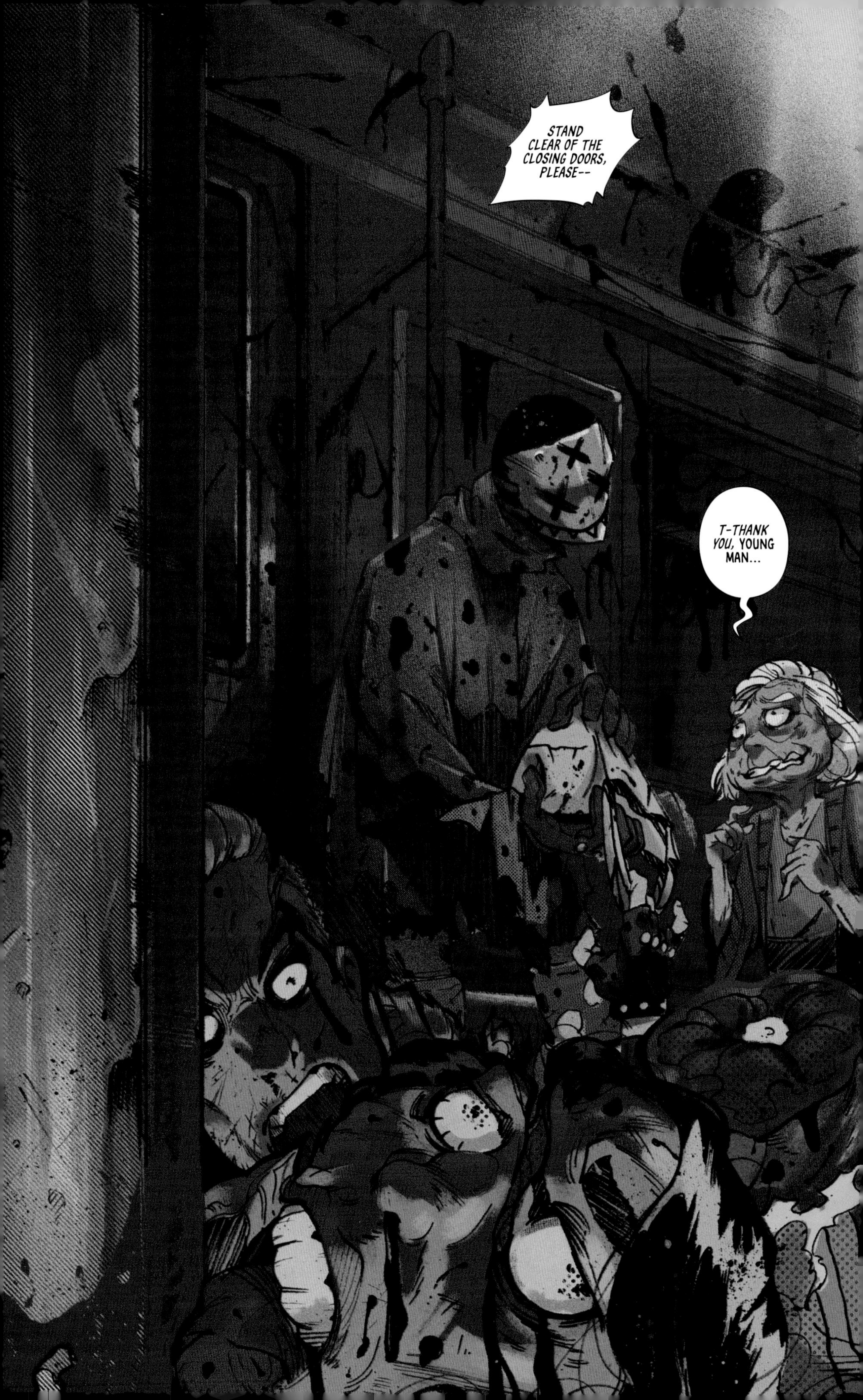
STAND CLEAR OF THE CLOSING DOORS, PLEASE--
T-THANK YOU, YOUNG MAN...

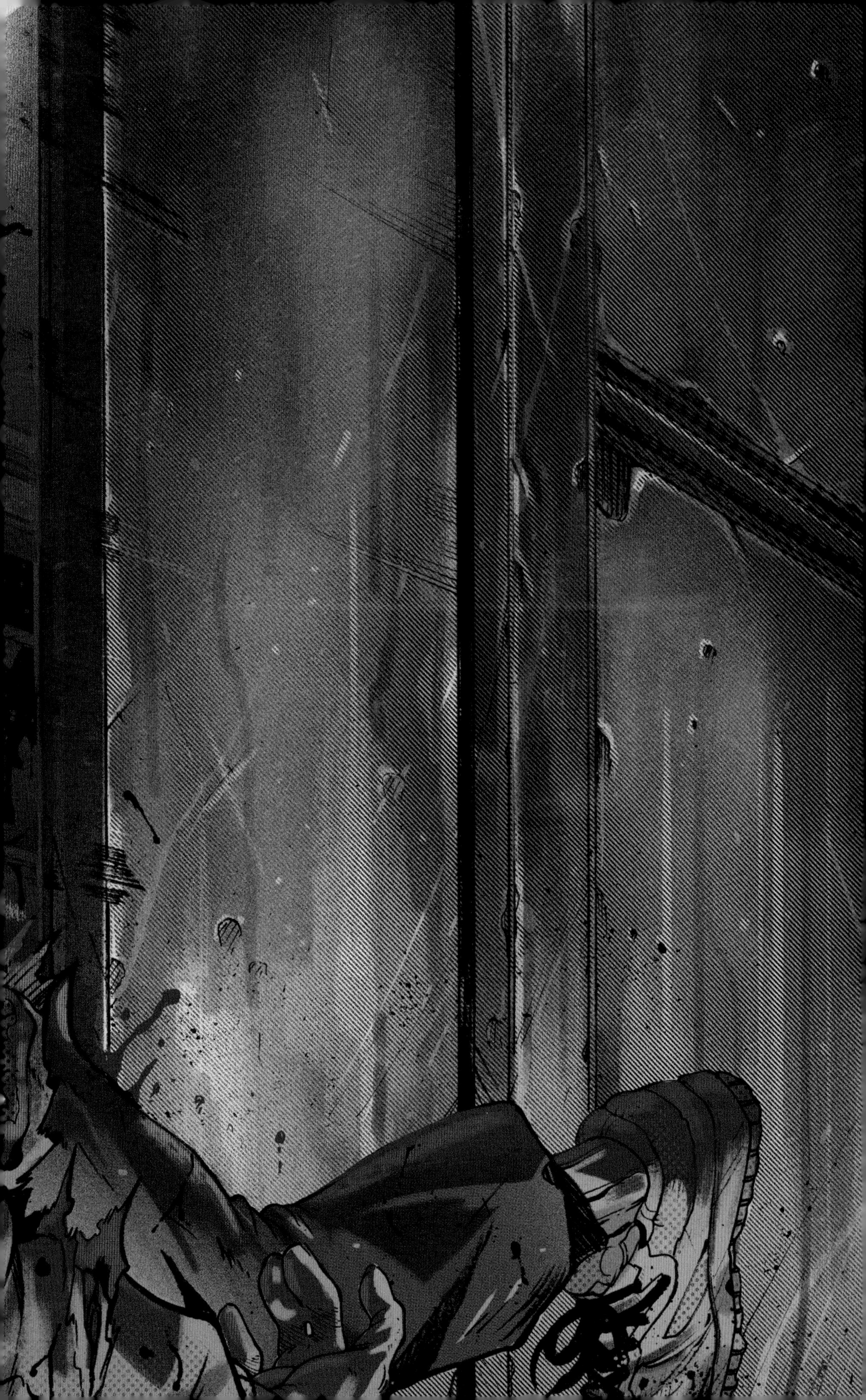

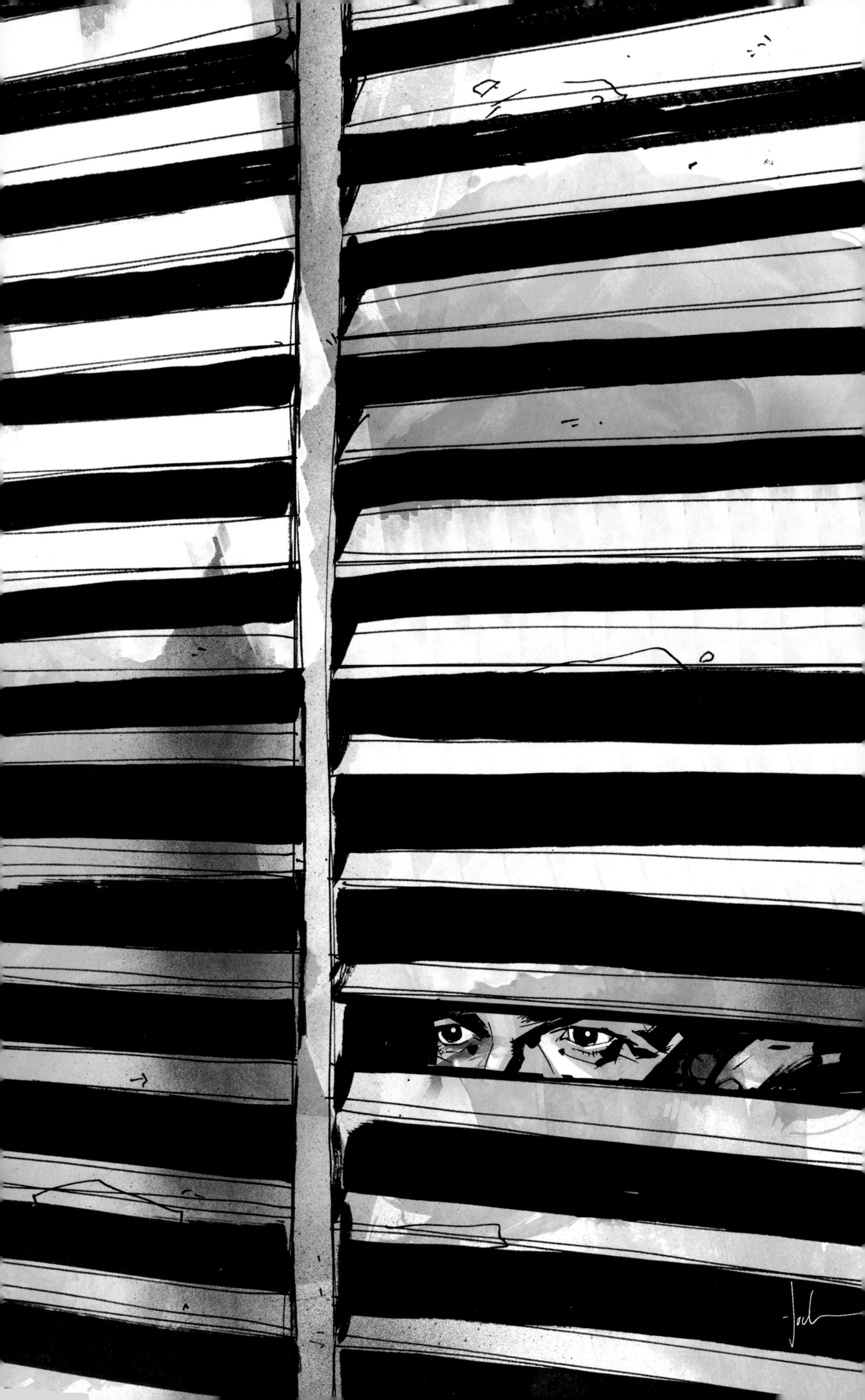

THROUGH THE BLACK MIRROR

JAMES TYNION IV INTERVIEWS SCOTT SNYDER

Whether it's murderous clowns stalking the dark alleys of Gotham City, vampires slaughtering their way through the Wild West, ancient witches eating children in the forests of New England, or merpeople killing their way through the Arctic, Scott Snyder has spent his storied career in comics writing about monsters of all shapes and sizes. But the darkest veins in his work come from its stark and often bleak humanity. Razorblades Publisher James Tynion IV sat down with the co-creator of Wytches, American Vampire, *and* The Wake *to discuss the craft of horror.*

JAMES TYNION IV: From your most intimate work, to your most bombastic superhero projects, your comics have always had a strong through line of horror. How much of that is by choice, and how much of that just comes naturally? Do you consider yourself to be a horror writer?

SCOTT SNYDER: I do consider myself to be a horror writer, honestly. I think I tried to resist the label for a long time, and then in the last few years, decided to embrace it entirely. I think it's because, after looking back at work that's inspired me over the years, I realized that horror is really at the center of my DNA as a writer. The things that I gravitated towards as a kid were all versions of horror, from '80s slasher films to Stephen King to works like *Frankenstein*, which is my favorite book. And so in the last few years, I tried to figure out why and figure out what is so magnetic to me about horror, and what has always been so magnetic to me about it. And I think really what it is, is [that] I was always a very anxious kid. I've always felt afraid of the other shoe dropping. I wasn't a kid that was happy-go-lucky or carefree. I always was worried about losing my parents or something going wrong. I just had a lot of anxiety. And I think horror, for me, gave me a way of confronting my own fears in a very aggressive and pure way, and at the same time in a safe way. I guess my first real experience with it, [the] touchstone by which I sort of figured this out, was watching *Night of the Living Dead* when I was about 10 years old.

When I was a kid, I grew up in New York City on the Lower East Side, and there was a video store called The Video Stop on 26th Street and Third Avenue. And they wouldn't rent R-rated movies to kids, but they would deliver them to your house if you called. So, it was this neighborhood secret. And, you know, at that time it was the height of '80s cheeseball horror, slasher films, all the *Friday the 13th* movies and everything. I got *Night of the Living Dead* because I had heard it was scary, but then it came and it was black and white. I remember at first being incredibly disappointed and thinking it was going to be super corny, and then watching it and walking away from it unsettled and then having nightmares just night after night, and really being terrified of that movie and kind of hating it for a while and not really understanding at that age, you know, 10, 11, something like that, why it had done such a number on me. And then years later, coming back to it, watching it again and realizing that the reason was because it forced me to confront things that I was afraid of in a really honest and truthful and terrifying way.

When horror is done right, I feel like the monsters aren't scary creature-feature beings, but extensions of the characters' fears and the creators' fears about the world, about themselves, about human nature. That film was so merciless in that respect, where everybody you think is going to make it out alive—because they have in every other sort of horror movie up to that point—don't. The young couple in love; Ben, the hero; the daughter of the couple housed in the basement who's been bitten; everybody. There's a reason for every character to survive. And one by one, they all go down and it's not just because the zombies are so terrifying (which they are), it's because of a failure of the characters' abilities to get along.

And that kind of cruelty and brutality, emotional brutality and emotional horror, just did a whole number on me, and [that's] why it's my favorite film now. And similarly, when I read *Frankenstein* for the first time it really unsettled me, and later I went back and realized that it touched on all these fears about mortality and about creating a monster out of your own anxieties. And so for me, I think what I've come to really embrace is this idea that horror gives me an opportunity to experience the fears that I'm really uncomfortable with in their most frightening and pure form, so that I can work through them in a way that's safe, and yet also very honest. I love horror as a pure form of conflict. And I do try to really embrace or espouse that same kind of approach when I'm doing drama or I'm doing superhero action. I try to put the main character up against the thing I think they're most afraid of in a distilled or crystallized way, so it might not have the semantics or the aesthetics of horror, but it always has that same priority that horror is all about.

JT: Going back to when you were my teacher at Sarah Lawrence College a million years ago, you've always been a huge proponent of writing from the heart. The idea that a story needs a very intimate fear or emotion that it's trying to tap into. You've always treated it as broadly true, but I think there's something almost baked into that idea that makes it particularly suited to horror. You give a character a powerful fear or emotion, and then you attack that fear from the darkest angles. Do you think the way you structure stories pushes them toward horror?

SS: Yeah, I do. I had teachers and influences in writing that really all lean in that direction where the emotional conflict always trumps the plot conflict. That's the thing that I think was one of the biggest lessons that I learned when I was in my teens and twenties studying writing, was that you can come up with any plot that's magnificently surprising and twisted and all of that, but if it doesn't have an element—it sounds hokey, but it's true—if it doesn't have an element of the personal and something that's really emotionally wrenching in it, it'll feel hollow. I think we can all think of movies or books or comics that we liked because they're propulsive and they're engaging and they're scary and they have cool ideas, but you walk away from them and they're not your favorites necessarily because they didn't hit a nerve.

So if you invert the kind of priorities that I think you would assume come with horror, or you would assume come with superhero comics—big bombastic stuff, or terrifying stuff—and [those] that you only associate with drama. Like if you invert the idea that plot trumps emotion, then it kind of pushes you towards the priorities of good horror, in my opinion. And it's true of all genres, when you look at it closely. It's true of all writing, but I think it's harder to see through the kind of scaffolding of action and horror and adventure, but it's always true. I think horror, when done right, really is an intensified form of that motto. You can have an action movie and make it personal and have it be a personal journey, but the only way a monster is going to be scary is if it plays on your fears. So it demands that deeply intimate exploration.

JT: One of my favorite high concepts in all of your work is the idea of the Black Mirror from your *Detective Comics* run. Not just because it informs your entire DC library of work up to and including The Batman Who Laughs and the Dark Multiverse, but because it's this great horror thesis about the relationship between Batman and Gotham. The idea that the city itself gathers up your worst fears and confronts you with them. Why do you think Batman and horror mix so well together?

SS: Because Batman is a character who is born in a moment of horror. What happens to him in the alley is noir and it's crime, but at its core, it's a kid's worst fear. Losing your parents in front of you in a random act of violence that almost has no logic. It shatters all preconceptions about the world, all the kinds of bedtime stories and all the things that we as parents—I have kids that age—promise them won't happen. You know, when you send them to school or you walk them to the ice cream shop and say, "Oh, of course everything's okay." It just destroys all of the sense of safety in every way.

So, he's born in terror, you know, Batman as a character. And what he does is, by going out night after night to prevent what happened to him from happening to other kids, he's confronting that very fear over and over and over again. Obviously he tries to stop all kinds of crime, but at the core, what he's trying to stop is that same murder. He wants to stop kids from suffering what he suffered. And if he fails, he's confronted all over again with being responsible for the horror he experienced growing up. So I think at the core, baked into the DNA of Batman is horror, is terror, is all of that.

But I think that's why he's such a relatable character, too. Because ultimately he's human, he doesn't have powers, and the car is awesome, and all those kinds of things that attracted us to him. But I think the motto that "Batman always wins" has a deeper truth to it, which is people want to see people overcome their deepest fears. They want someone to go out there and say, "Everything is terrifying. Don't be afraid. We're going to get through this together. We have to confront the things we're most afraid of." And Batman is built on that. The very thing that scared him the most is his sigil, the bat, is his symbol. He is about taking your worst fear and transforming it into your greatest triumph.

JT: I gave an interview the other day, where I described the Joker, as you wrote him, as the devil at the crossroads. Not the beautiful tragic, fallen Lucifer, but a grittier, darker Satan.

A solitary, allegorical evil. Can you talk a bit about what you find scary about The Joker, and how that has informed your work with him?

SS: Everybody has their own version of him. I love what you're doing with him now in *Batman: Joker War*. And I love when you read a version of him that's different than your own. I think mine is really black in terms of his heart. What I tried to do with him was have him be almost like—and I didn't think of this comparison until more recently—the joker card itself. The idea that the joker card in a deck of cards can take on any value that is needed to win that hand. And so Joker is this malleable and completely adaptable character who tries to bring your worst fears, or primarily Batman's, to life in order to say, "You have to face these fears. And I'm going to make them so deadly, so horrible, that it's going to make you feel that all your worst nightmares and terrors about yourself, about the world, about all of it, are true. And I'm going to laugh at you when you deny that they are. And you're going to go down in flames fighting."

Deep down, there's almost a kind of nobility to what he's doing, where he sees himself as someone whose job it is to be the Lord of Nightmares, to be the Devil, because if you can beat him or overcome him, then you come out stronger. So that's how I've always played him. Someone who's willing to do anything to make you believe that all the things you don't want to admit you're afraid of, or don't want to admit are true, are true.

He's not openly supernatural in any way, but he borders on that idea. He's just on the line of someone that lives under your bed and knows all of your worst secrets and comes out and says, "I know exactly what you're most afraid of and it's absolutely true. Let me show you how, and as you try to argue with me or fight that, I'm going to laugh at you while you go down swinging." He's pure horror for me.

I love him because he's a conflict generator. He's like an engine of bringing everybody's worst fears to life, including my own.

He voiced my worst fears many times, like in *Batman: Death of the Family*. You know this because we've been friends for a long time, but we were pregnant with my son, Emmett, when I came up with the concept for the story. And my big fear at that time, as my career was starting to take off, was that I was not really fit to be a father a second time, or maybe I didn't want to be a father a second time. And those are very hard things to admit. And that story is all about Batman feeling some of the same things about the Bat Family, because it gives him vulnerability. Joker is the only one that sees that and says, "I know what your big fear is. It's that you shouldn't have ever been a father. So, let me do what you really want and kill your whole family then we can go back to just being the two of us." And then in *Batman: Endgame*, he voiced a lot of my fears of when I'm at my worst. When I'm most depressed or anxious. He's saying the things that I've said to myself, to my wife, or to my doctor about feeling like, what is the point? What is the point of trying to really accomplish anything when the world is totally random? Joker always gives voice to the voices in your head [that] you don't want to admit are there. So, I love working with him. It takes a lot out of me, but I love working with him.

JT: I think part of where your horror shines is in the dialogue. You've always been incredibly good about finding the exact place to stick the knife in. Most recently, I can remember talking to you about a line of dialogue from The Robin King in Death Metal, but it goes back to every Joker story you've written. More than that, I know there's a kind of glee to writing bad people saying absolutely horrible things. Can you talk a little about finding that horrible voice that says the worst possible thing?

SS: That's a great, great question. And it's so true. I feel bad because I'm really not a mean guy. I never say those things to people, but I get tremendous pleasure in coming up with the most villainous things you can possibly say when they're appropriately coming out of the mouths of the darkest characters. I think what it really is, is that, when you're depressed or you really are in a bad spot, for me at least, it's almost like everything you look at in the world is a twisted funhouse mirror that reflects the worst of you back at yourself. Anything you try and do to get out of that state, or any hope you have, or anything that you are positive about in your mind, gets thrown back at you negatively.

So, it's a kind of like, "You know what, today I'm going to try and go for a run or try and write something." *You're going to write something? Well that's going to be shit. Whatever you write's going to be horrible.* Those moments when you really feel at your lowest, it is words. It is a voice or a comment that goes through your own mind when you're being your own most brutal and vicious critic. And you can't stop that attack, and I feel like the scariest thing is when you're locked in your own head and you're attacking yourself. There's no escape from that incredibly astute, laser-like critical eye that just comes at you and sees everything you don't want it to see. [It] just says that all the things you are worried are true about yourself are true.

And so there is a kind of satisfaction, or like you said, almost a glee in finding lines like that for villainous characters who really are worthy of those lines, because I feel like the heroes confronting those things are overcoming them. And them fighting back gives me hope, as somebody who definitely is the target of those kinds of comments from the worst facets of my own psychology.

JT: Your work has always played with the history, mythology, and symbols of America, and the horror that rests under it. *American Vampire*, obviously, embodies that more than any other title, but you can see it in all of your work. What's so scary to you about America's past? Why do you find that such fertile ground for horror stories?

SS: I try to have a deep belief in the cumulative, if not consistent, progress of not just America, but of human nature. I'm a hopeless romantic about the idea that we stumble and we fall backwards and all of it, but ultimately we will evolve to a better state. The sins of the past and the things that we try to move away from have such a grip over us, because when we look not only at great national horrors, from the most obvious like slavery, but even small things… You go to a small town, or you look into a family history, and you'll find things that people want to forget. I feel as though mining history, or going back and looking at it, is a way of coming to terms with the worst of ourselves. Not just because I believe that we get better as we go, but [because] that constant recognition of who we were is an important part of being able to move forward. Letting it go or burying it or covering it up is something that winds up only having it come back in a more haunted, frightening way.

On the other hand, I think the fun of it for me too, is [that] history allows for a kind of imaginative leap just because we live in a world right now that's so intensely examined: in a literal way, where there's very few places to escape off the grid; to a more figurative way, where we understand so much scientifically in all these different ways that there are few kind of magical or mystical areas left, except the bottom of the ocean. So, I think, and again, I mean more figuratively, I think there's not the same sense of wonder and terror at natural phenomena and undiscovered places. And so, going back in history allows for almost a revisiting of a time when there weren't so many mechanisms to dig into things or explore or know places. And so there's a more potent sense of possibility for horror, for supernatural, for all of that. Although, I think when you look at it, there's really nothing about the present that makes it less fertile than the past for wonder and terror.

When I was growing up, my grandparents took care of me a lot. My mom was in school to be an optometrist and my dad was in the military and then in school to be a doctor. And my grandmother was fascinated by antiques and she would take me to antique fairs. Sometimes we'd go at like five in the morning to these crazy antique fairs in Westchester. And part of the rule was, if you got something, you had to make up a story about where it had been. I loved this, by the way. But from a very early age, I think I was always fascinated by the idea of the secret history of things and where they came from. Now it's in my house, but how many houses was it in before? What did it witness? What was it a part of? And also growing up in New York City, the area that I loved exploring with my friends, down by the South Street Seaport, was one of the oldest parts of the city. There was always a sense of wonder at how many generations had been there. I think there's a built-in kind of terror to the idea of how small you are in the face of history. And that there's a kind of horror element that just comes in naturally with exploring that. Whenever you go back in history, it makes you understand how tiny you are in the scope of things.

JT: One thing I've always found really fascinating, because it's a huge difference between us, is that you prefer science to superstition. You almost always ground the supernatural in at least one scientific element, like the bloodlines of *American Vampire*, or the way *Wytches* are an evolutionary branch off of humanity. Why do you think you do that? Do you find magic inherently less frightening?

SS: You know what it is? I'm from a family of scientists. I mean, I'm the black sheep. My parents are both doctors. My sister is in medicine. My grandparents were doctors. I mean, my wife is a doctor. So, I always joke with my father that she's the son that he never had. But for me, I think what it really is, is that I spent a lot of time convincing my parents of the validity of what I wanted to do. And I always loved the idea of history and science, the things that my parents, and my father in particular, were fascinated by. He's a big history buff in addition to being a kind of a science nerd. So I think my horror, and the things that I like to build out of, were those types of stories. If I could figure out a way to just use something scary that was happening in science or history, and work my way into the territory of horror or the supernatural in such a way that you wouldn't see where it jumped the rails, that's what I love. And those were my favorites growing up as well. I mean, I like fantasy and I love when it's done well, but I really gravitate towards things where it's almost like one suspension of disbelief that's built on something that's almost real. So you can't quite tell where the science or the history ends and the supernatural begins. And then you're down the rabbit hole. I think that's really what it is. It probably just comes from trying to convince my parents that horror and comic books and all of it weren't that different than what they were doing or what they like.

JT: Have you ever crossed a line, where you think you've written something too frightening? And when that's happened, is that because you think it'd be too much for the audience, or too much for yourself?

SS: Too much for myself. I mean, I think especially as a parent, now, I worry about that sometimes. You know what I mean? Because with something like *Wytches*, for example, and *Batman: Death of the Family* as well, there was a lot on display there on how uncomfortable I was with parenthood at first. And there are days that I worry about my kids reading those books when they're older and wondering whether their father was hesitant to be a dad. And I'm uncomfortable with that, to be honest. But Jock and Greg Capullo, my partners on those books, were very encouraging, as were you, about really trying to write to the truth of those fears. So, I'm very proud of those. Those are some of the things I'm most proud of in my library of stuff. What I tried to point to for myself, when I think about that, is [that] my favorite Stephen King book is *Pet Sematary*. I think *The Stand* is the most enveloping for me—it's

the one that, you know, carried me away. But *Pet Sematary* is the one that really terrified me, really scared me. And I remember reading about it in an interview with him and then talking to him about it when I got to know him in real life. It was the one book that he actually put away and didn't think he was going to finish because it was written, again, about the fears of parenthood. And the boy, Gage, is the age that his son was when he wrote it, Owen King. And that notion of writing your most powerful stuff, that and *The Shining*—the fear of being a parent. About things that are embarrassing and ugly about yourself. You know, it's a very weird balance, when you have kids, because I think part of it is [that] you are afraid that they're going to see it and be angry or be ashamed of you, but at the same time, you have to be truthful about those things. And what I hope is that my kids will read those when they are parents, or when they're going to be parents, and be like, *Oh, everybody feels like this sometimes.* But it's an uncomfortable balance. It really is.

JT: What, to you, is the essence of a horror scene? If you're sitting down staring at a script, and you know a moment isn't scary enough, what's the math problem going through your head? What are you trying to solve for?

SS: Well, if it's not scary enough, that usually means to me that it's not getting at the stuff that is going to expose the vulnerable, embarrassing, ugly things about the main character in such a way that you are going to put them in the spotlight in a way that's uncomfortable.

When I'm writing a horror scene and it feels not scary enough, it usually means I'm not digging enough emotionally. I'm not going to that place with Bruce Wayne or with one of my own characters, Sailor or Pearl Jones. It's really getting at their fears. And a lot of the time, that means making them less heroic, making them admit that they're not as good as they pretend to be.

Sometimes it's as simple as a comment and sometimes it's a whole architecture of how to choreograph a scene that slowly leads you down into the big scare, but the scare really has to be emotional. It has to be something that rips your heart out of your chest and shows it to you and says, *Look at this thing, isn't this horrible, isn't this ugly?* I think I can think of scenes in particular—for example, when we were doing *Death of the Family* and Joker reveals that he's taken the faces off all of the Bat Family, that's inherently a horrible moment, a scary moment. But I remember when you and I were talking about it, there were times when I felt like there was a way in which it was just going to feel sensational.

If there wasn't a real cumulative build and a logic to the idea that he says to Batman, "I cut off their faces because I'm trying to prove to you that beneath their faces and their masks, they're just soft flesh and tissue and sinew and bone. But you, if I cut your face off, it would be a bat. And me, when I cut my face off, it doesn't hurt me because I'm just more clown, more jester." And if you can get that in there, then that moment's scary because you realize, as Batman, it's your fault. If you don't, it just becomes scary because it's horrible and gory. So it's getting to the emotional core of why that scene, even if you showed nothing that was scary, if it was like a black page, and there was just words—why would it be scary?

JT: I find that nowadays, I get more excited when I read or watch horror than I get scared, just because I love the genre and I love its possibilities. Do you still get scared by horror stories? What's the last bit of horror you can think of that really got under your skin, and why did it?

SS: I do still get scared, but not for the same reasons I did when I was younger. I mean, again, going back to *Night of the Living Dead*, what scared me then was the brutality of how truthful and how ugly Romero was willing to go when it came to the human characters at that moment in the '60s, and show, culturally and psycho-logically, how disgusting we were. There are books and movies now that I feel like, when I read something that really convinces me that it can't be as bad as it seems, and then it goes there and it is that bad, those things really still scare me because they speak to a truth that I think all of us feel right now. Things are so uncertain. Whatever side you're on politically, there's no sense of linearity. There's no sense of any kind of coalition. Everything is becoming more fractious and more volatile and more contentious.

In the seventies, you watch the films, everything from *The Exorcist, The Omen, Texas Chain Saw Massacre*, all those films spoke to a moment of tremendous cultural anxiety about who are we and what do we want to be? What was our past? How ugly is it coming back to get us? And I think we're in one of those moments in a way right now. When you watch some of the films coming out now, like *Midsommar*, the A24 films, films like *The Babadook*. Films that are pushing emotional boundaries that go back to almost that late '60s, early '70s, kind of horror that was built on building cumulative dread and emotional anxiety. I feel like there's a real resurgence of that. And that, to me, speaks to this moment as being a time that's incredibly ripe for horror. I mean, I really feel like right now, it's needed because we have so many things that are being exposed about us, as a country, a race, as a human race, that are so frightening that we need these kinds of stories to confront them and to make us look at them in a way that is really uncomfortable and really unsettling—but also ultimately allows us to move past the horror and try and reconcile some of our uglier parts.

***

Scott Snyder is one of comics' bestselling authors. His works include Batman, American Vampire, The Wake, Undiscovered Country, Severed, *and* Wytches *among others. He has also been published in* Zoetrope, Tin House, One-Story, Epoch, Small Spiral Notebook, *and other journals, and has a short story collection,* Voodoo Heart, *which was published by Dial Press in 2006. He has taught at Columbia University, Sarah Lawrence University and NYU and lives in New York with his wife, Jeanie, and his three sons.*

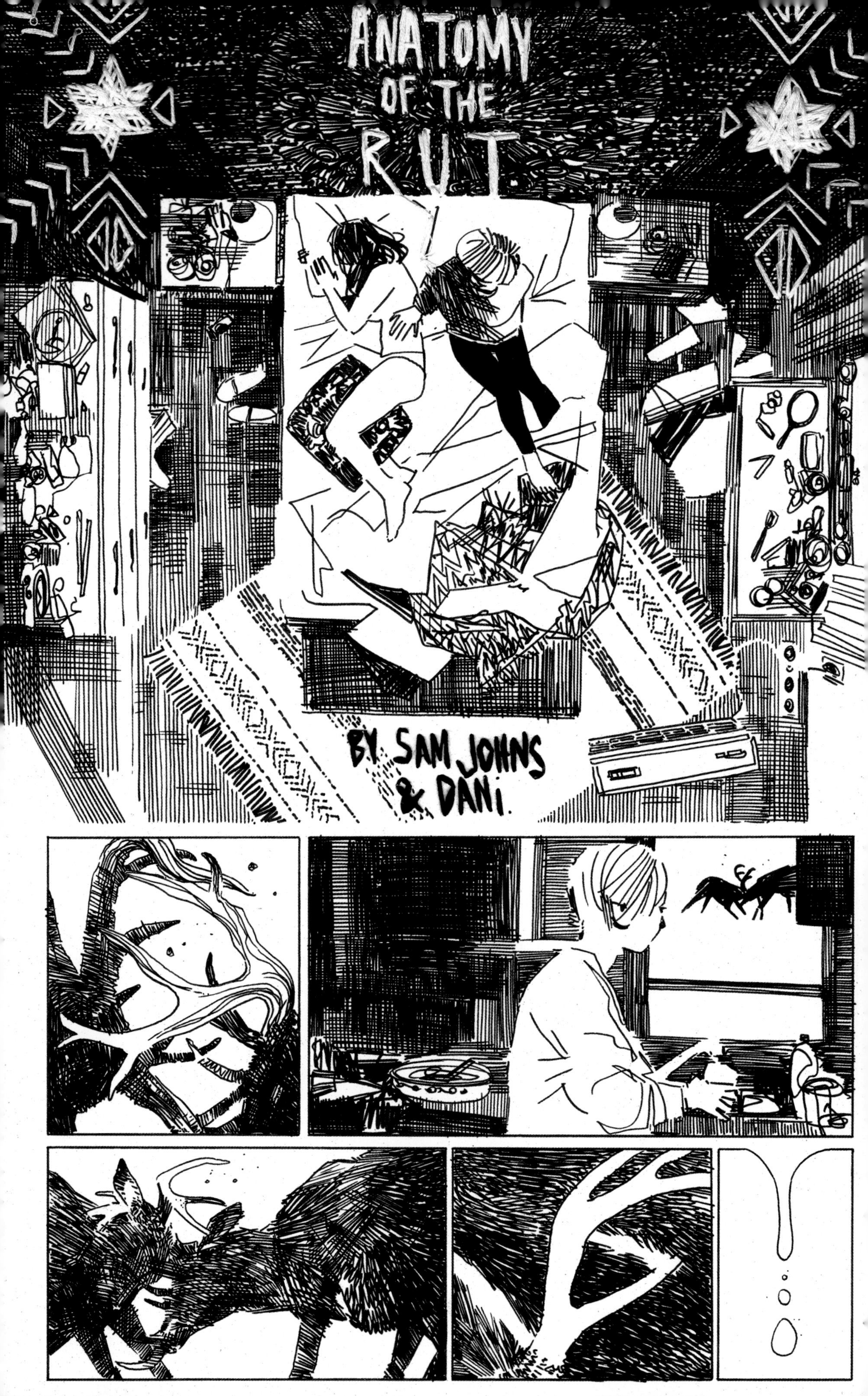
ANATOMY OF THE RUT
BY. SAM JOHNS & DANI.

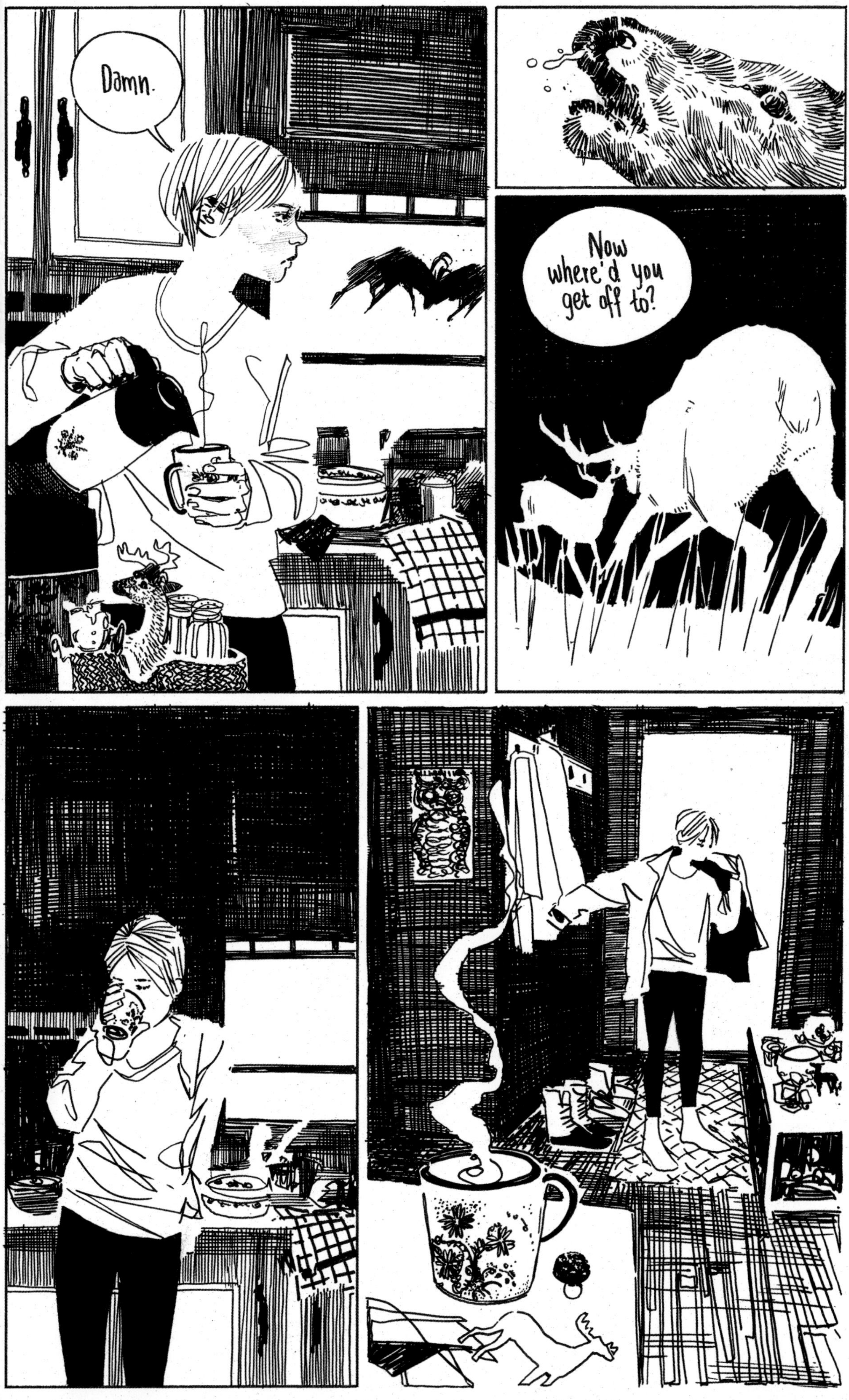
Damn.
Now where'd you get off to?

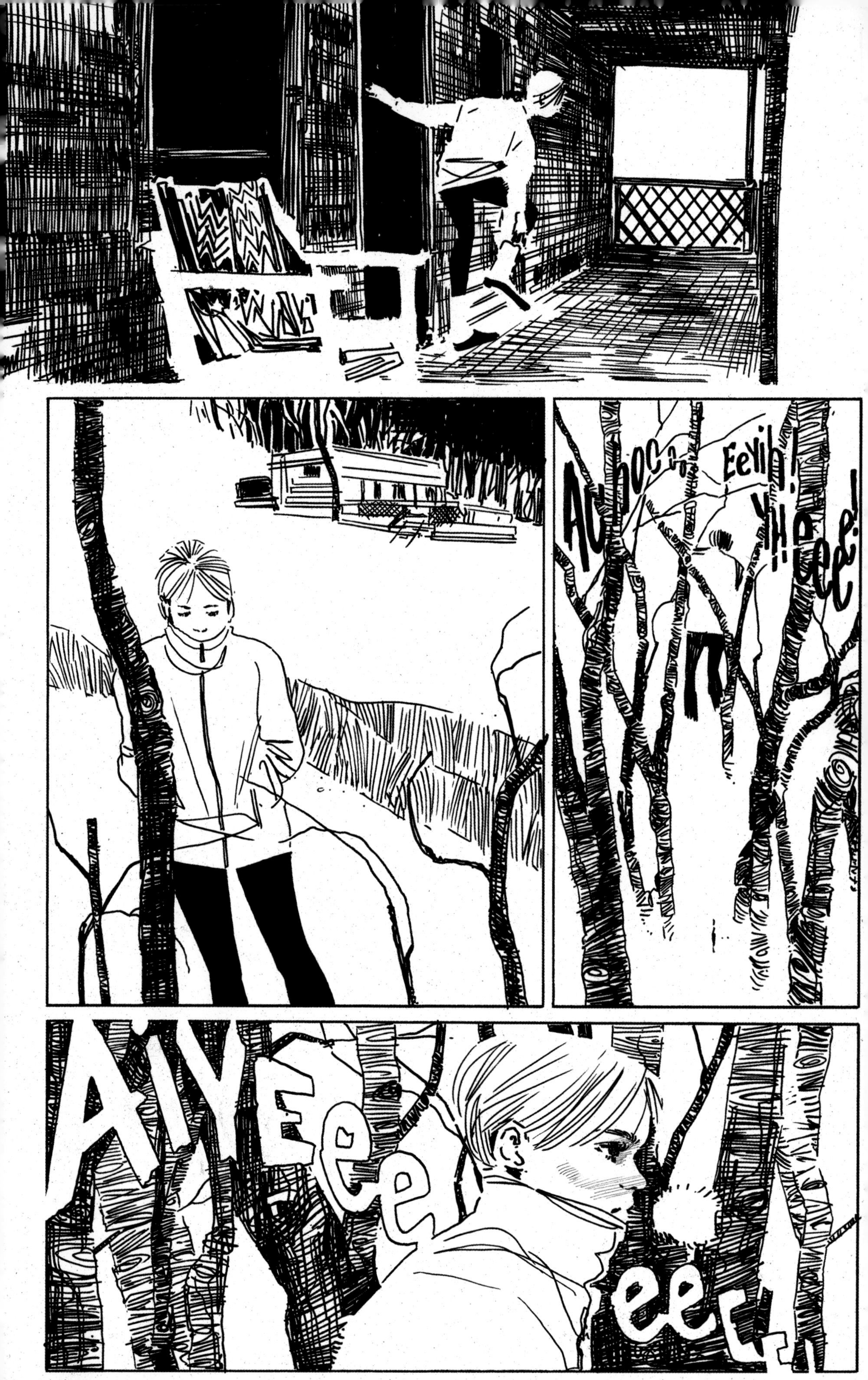
Aahoooo
Eeyih!
YHeeee!!
AIYEeeeeet.

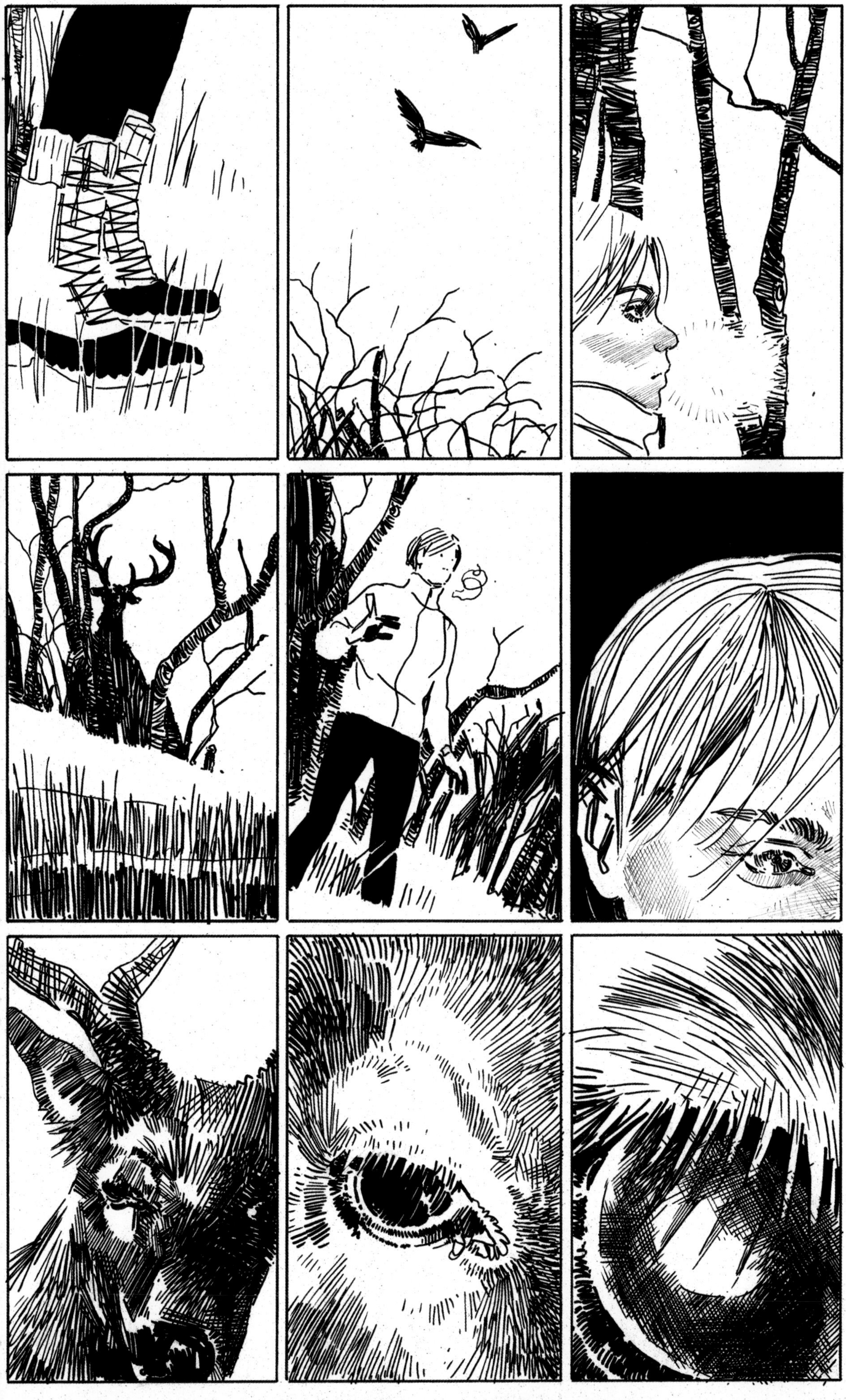

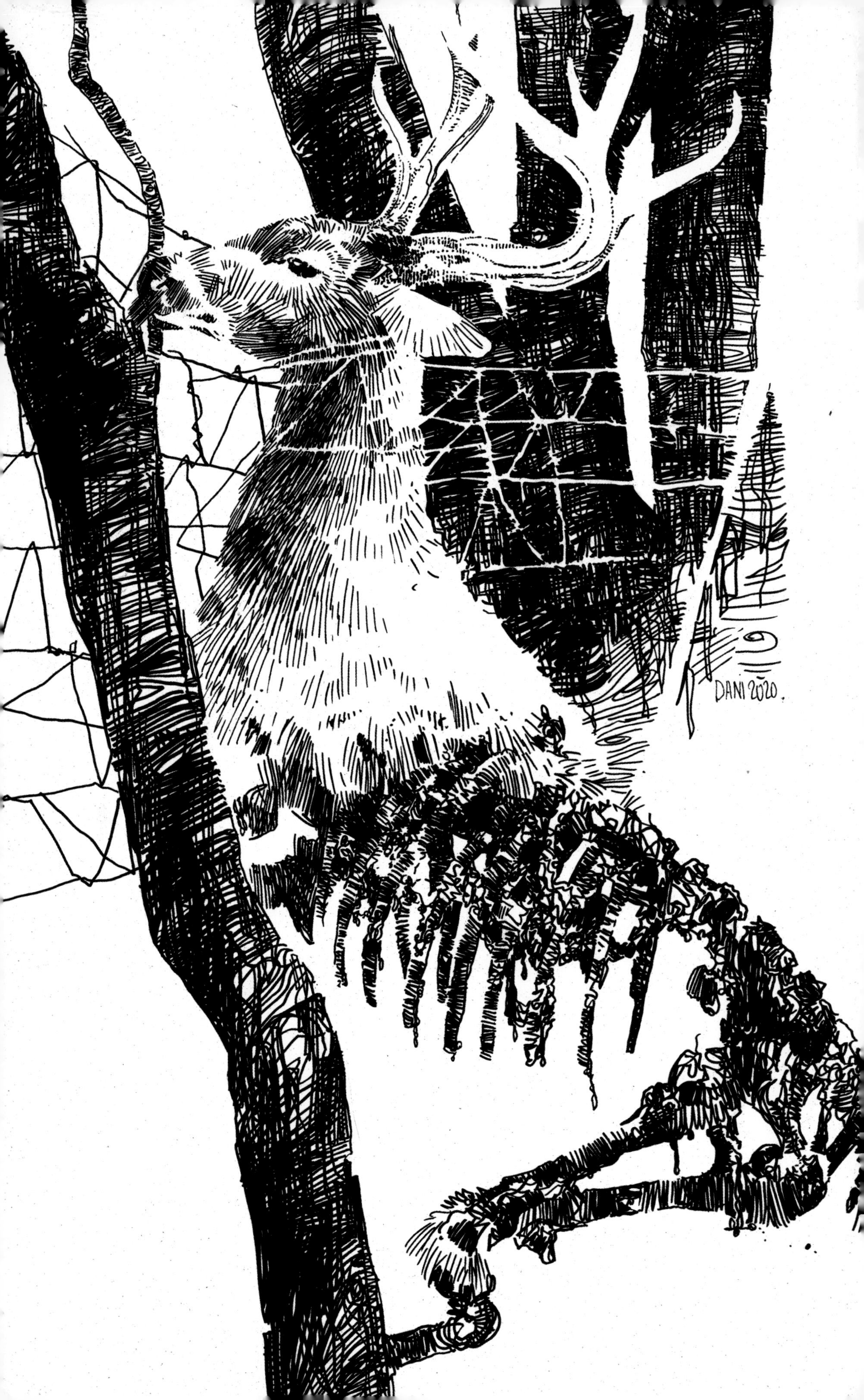
DANI 2020.

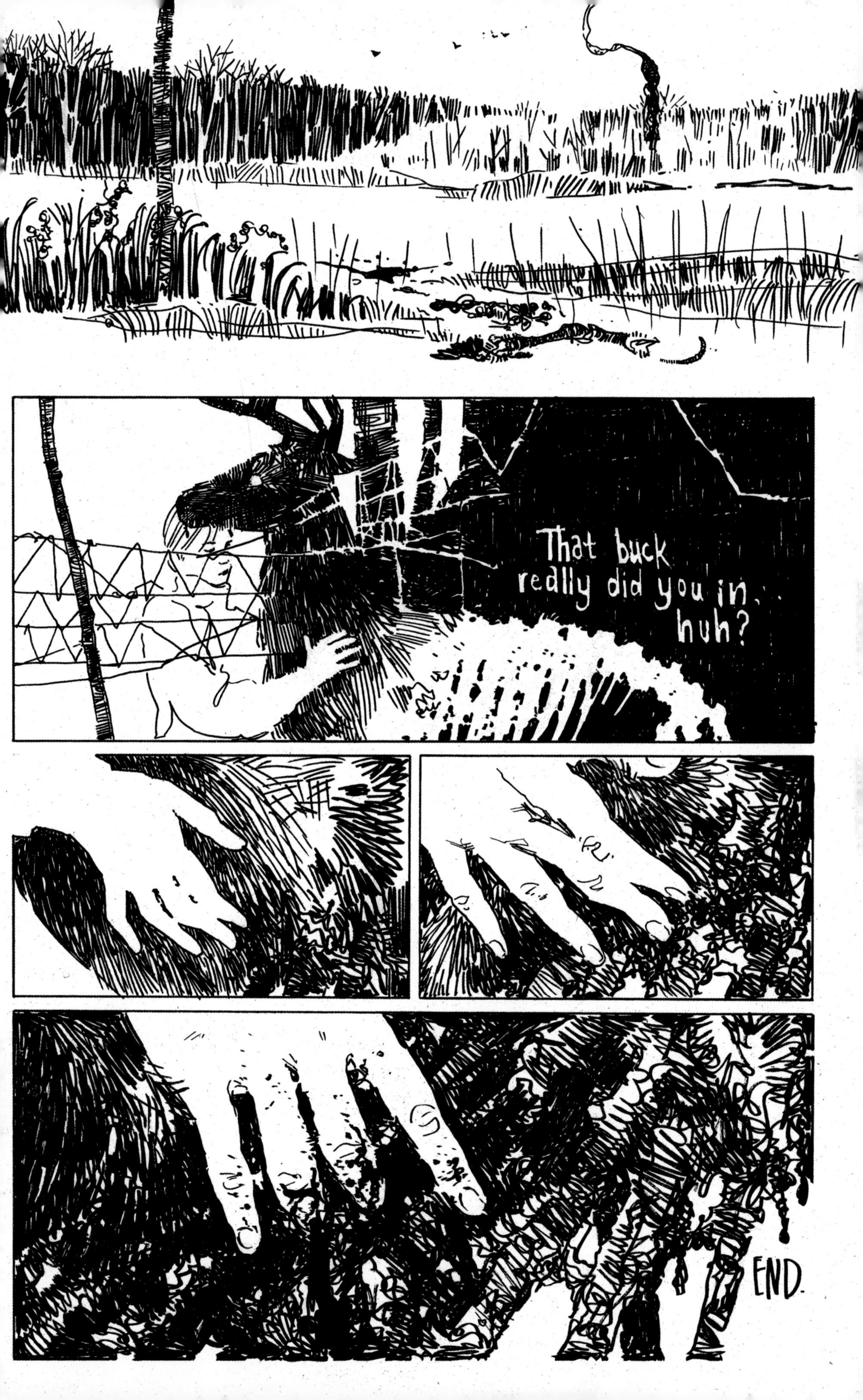
That buck really did you in, huh?
END.

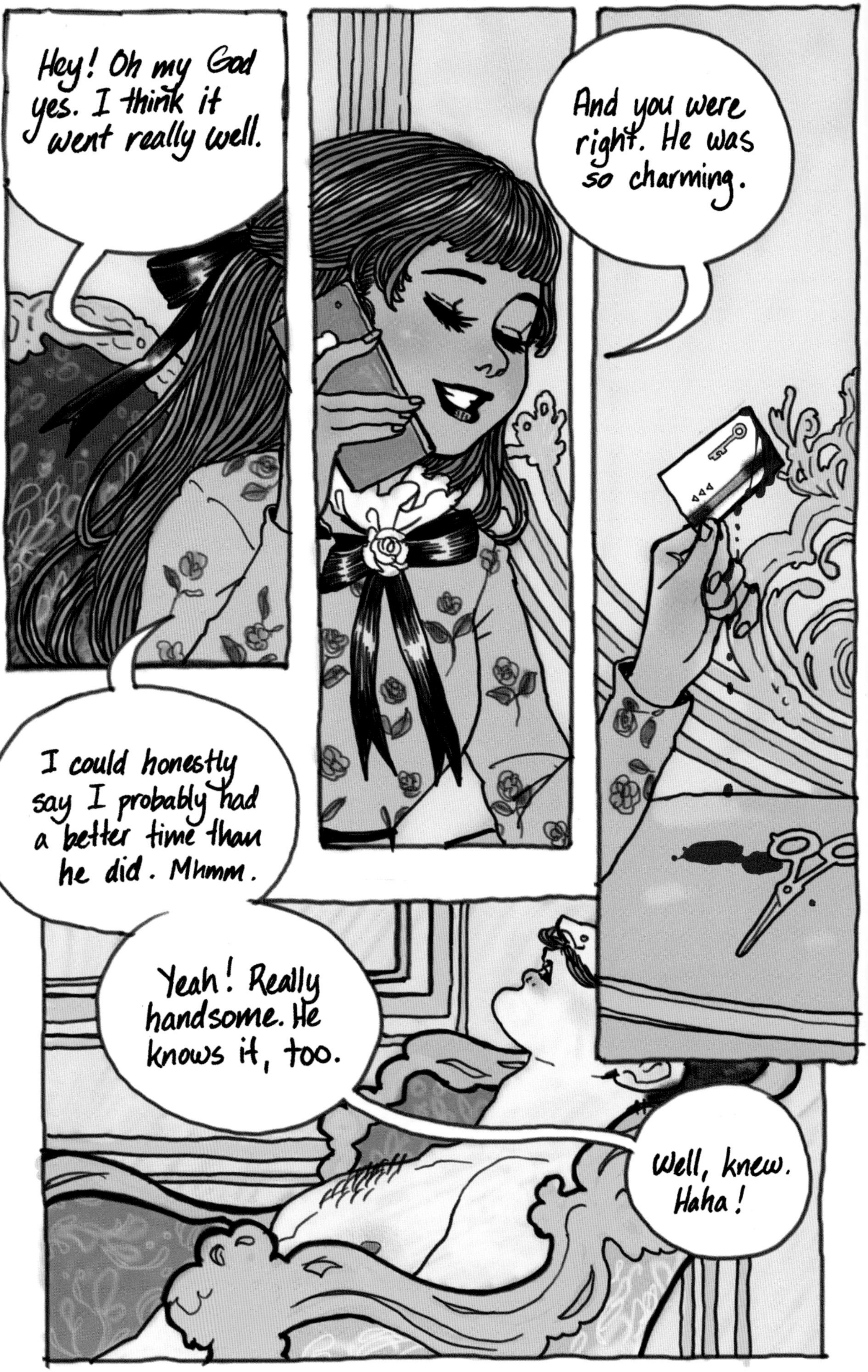
Hey! Oh my God yes. I think it went really well.
And you were right. He was so charming.
I could honestly say I probably had a better time than he did. Mhmm.
Yeah! Really handsome. He knows it, too.
Well, knew. Haha!

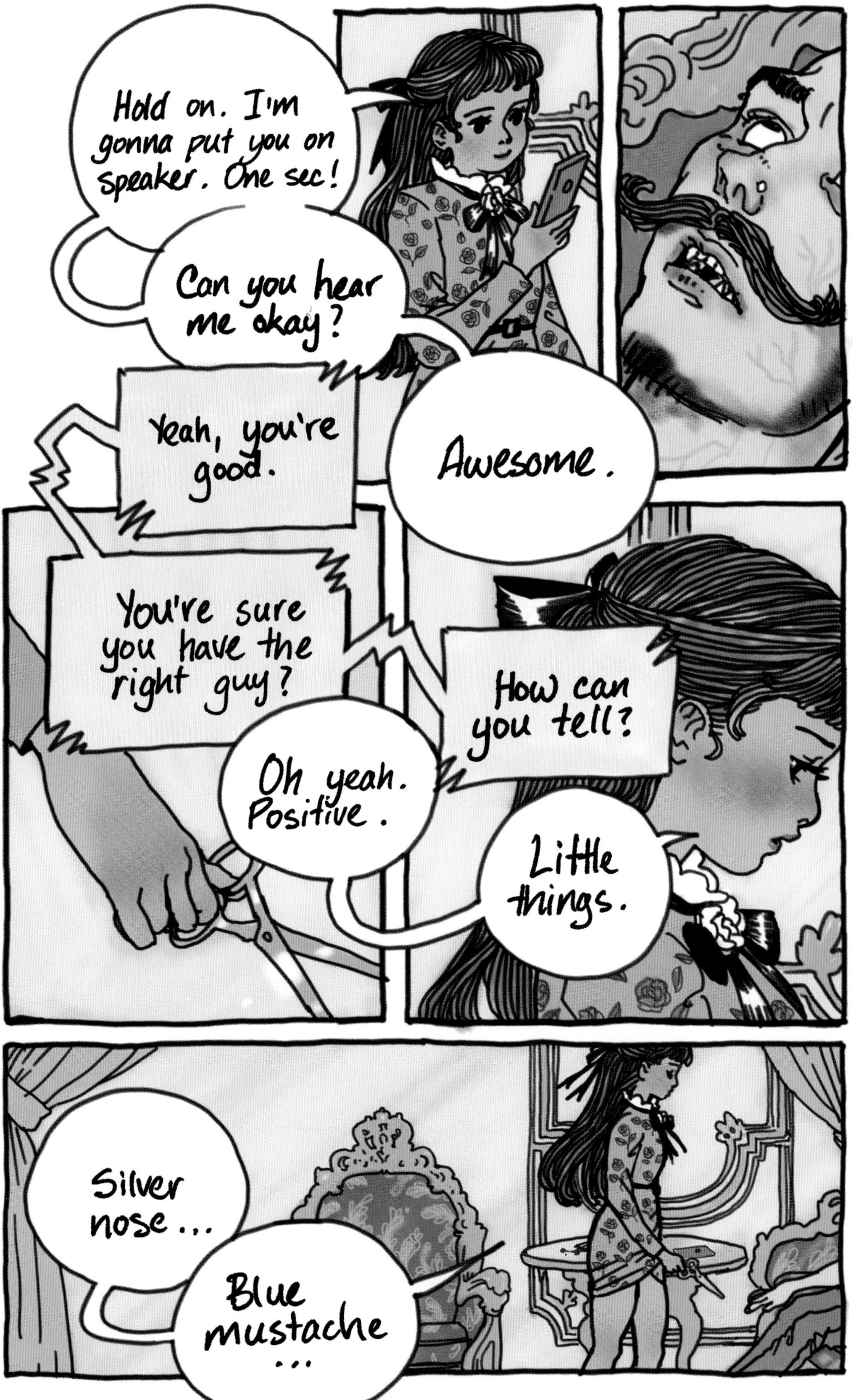
Hold on. I'm gonna put you on speaker. One sec!
Can you hear me okay?
Yeah, you're good.
Awesome.
You're sure you have the right guy?
How can you tell?
Oh yeah. Positive.
Little things.
Silver nose...
Blue mustache...

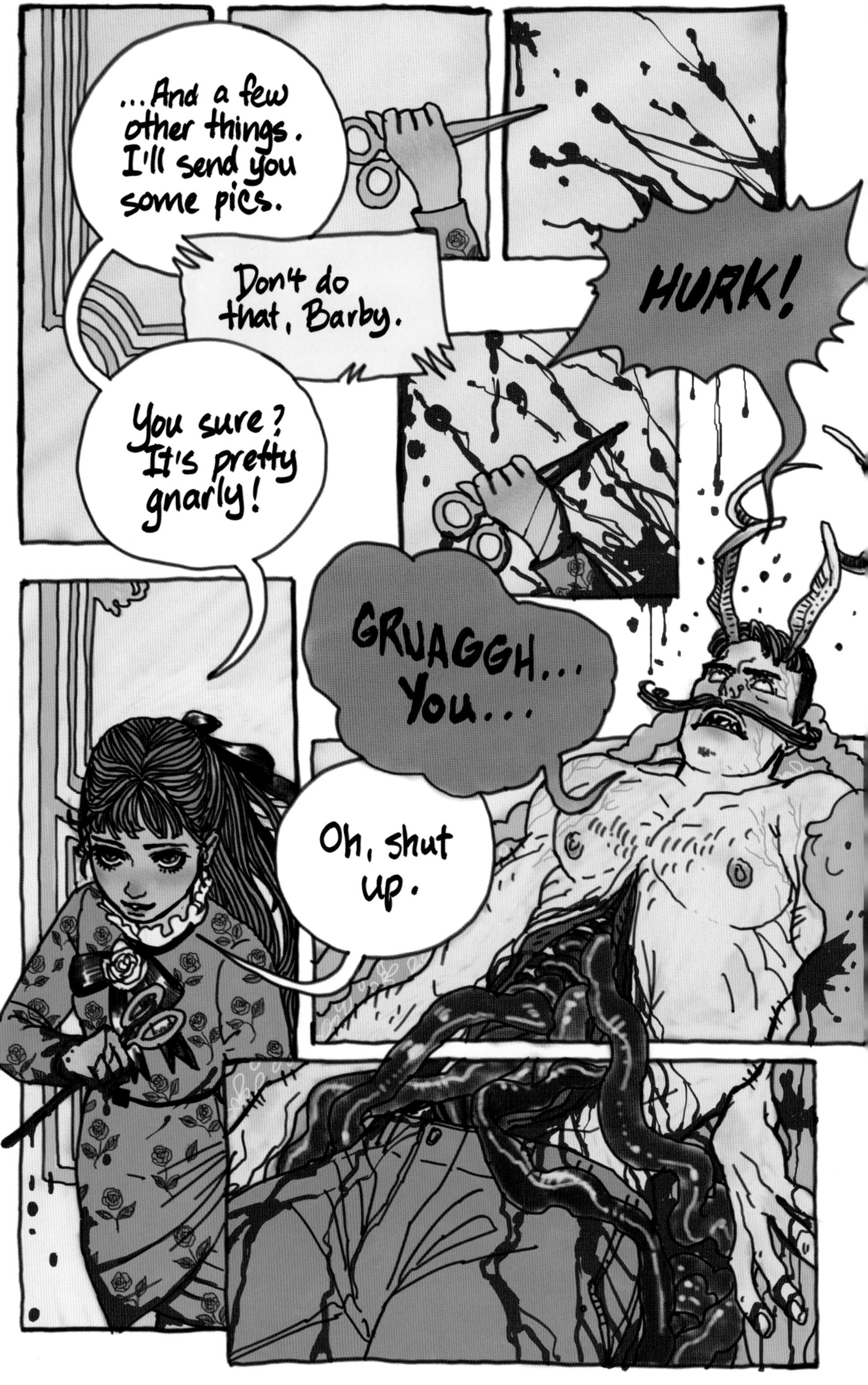
...And a few other things. I'll send you some pics.
Don't do that, Barby.
HURK!
You sure? It's pretty gnarly!
GRUAGGH... You...
Oh, shut up.

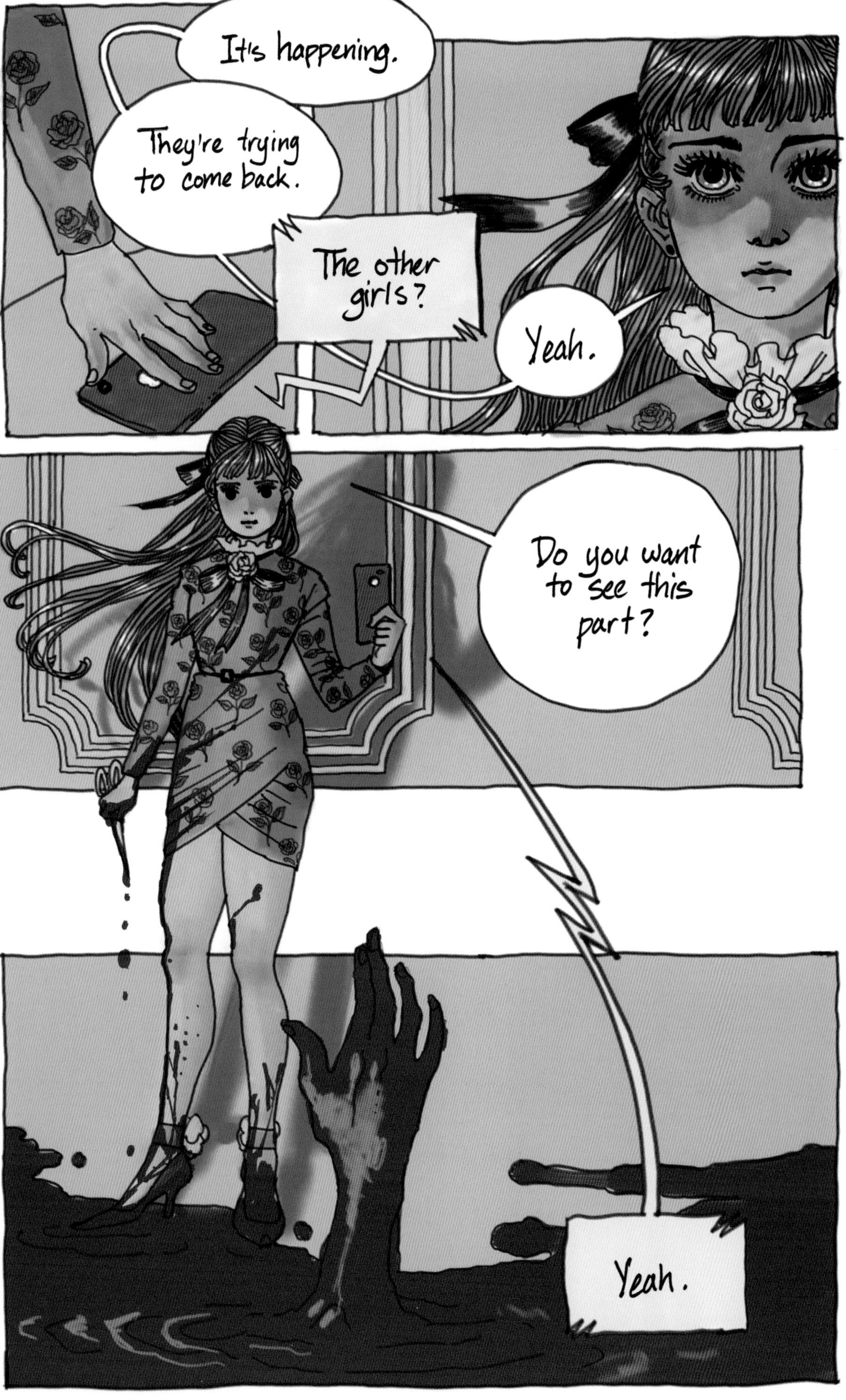
It's happening.
They're trying to come back.
The other girls?
Yeah.
Do you want to see this part?
Yeah.

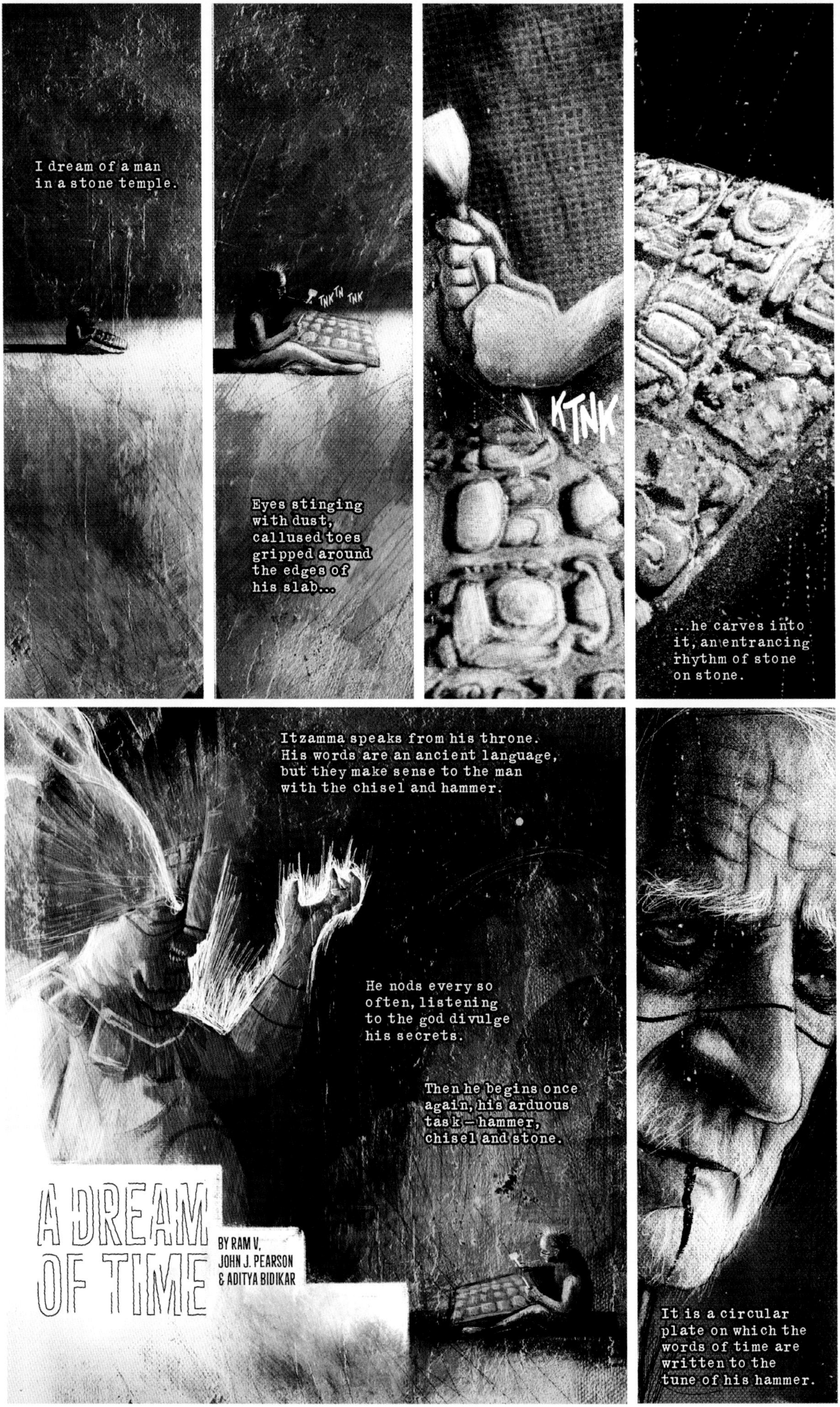

I dream of a man in a stone temple.
TNK TN TNK
Eyes stinging with dust, callused toes gripped around the edges of his slab...
KTNK
...he carves into it, an entrancing rhythm of stone on stone.
Itzamma speaks from his throne. His words are an ancient language, but they make sense to the man with the chisel and hammer.
He nods every so often, listening to the god divulge his secrets.
Then he begins once again, his arduous task — hammer, chisel and stone.
A DREAM OF TIME
BY RAM V, JOHN J. PEARSON & ADITYA BIDIKAR
It is a circular plate on which the words of time are written to the tune of his hammer.

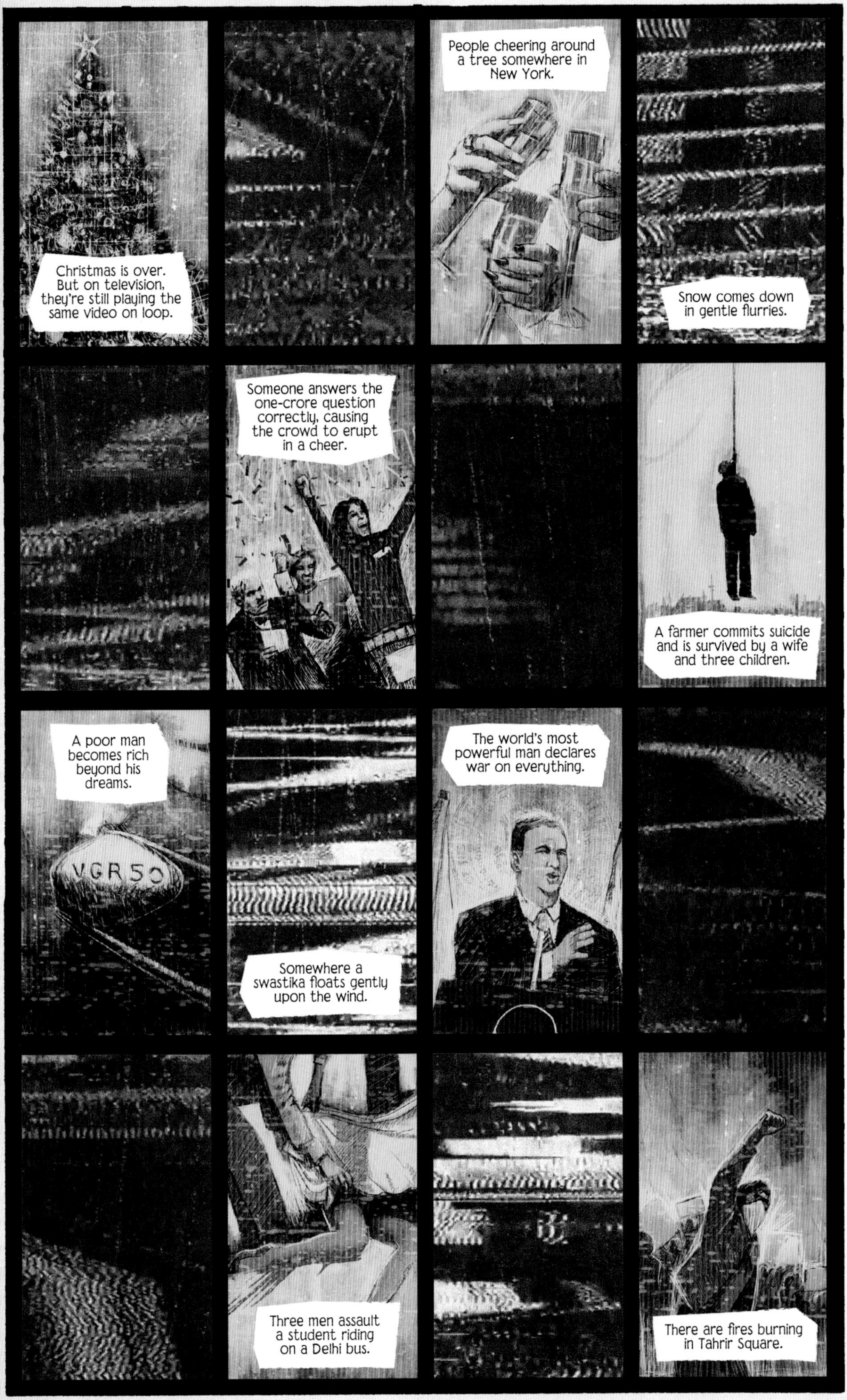
Christmas is over. But on television, they're still playing the same video on loop.
People cheering around a tree somewhere in New York.
Snow comes down in gentle flurries.
Someone answers the one-crore question correctly, causing the crowd to erupt in a cheer.
A farmer commits suicide and is survived by a wife and three children.
A poor man becomes rich beyond his dreams.
VGR50
Somewhere a swastika floats gently upon the wind.
The world's most powerful man declares war on everything.
Three men assault a student riding on a Delhi bus.
There are fires burning in Tahrir Square.

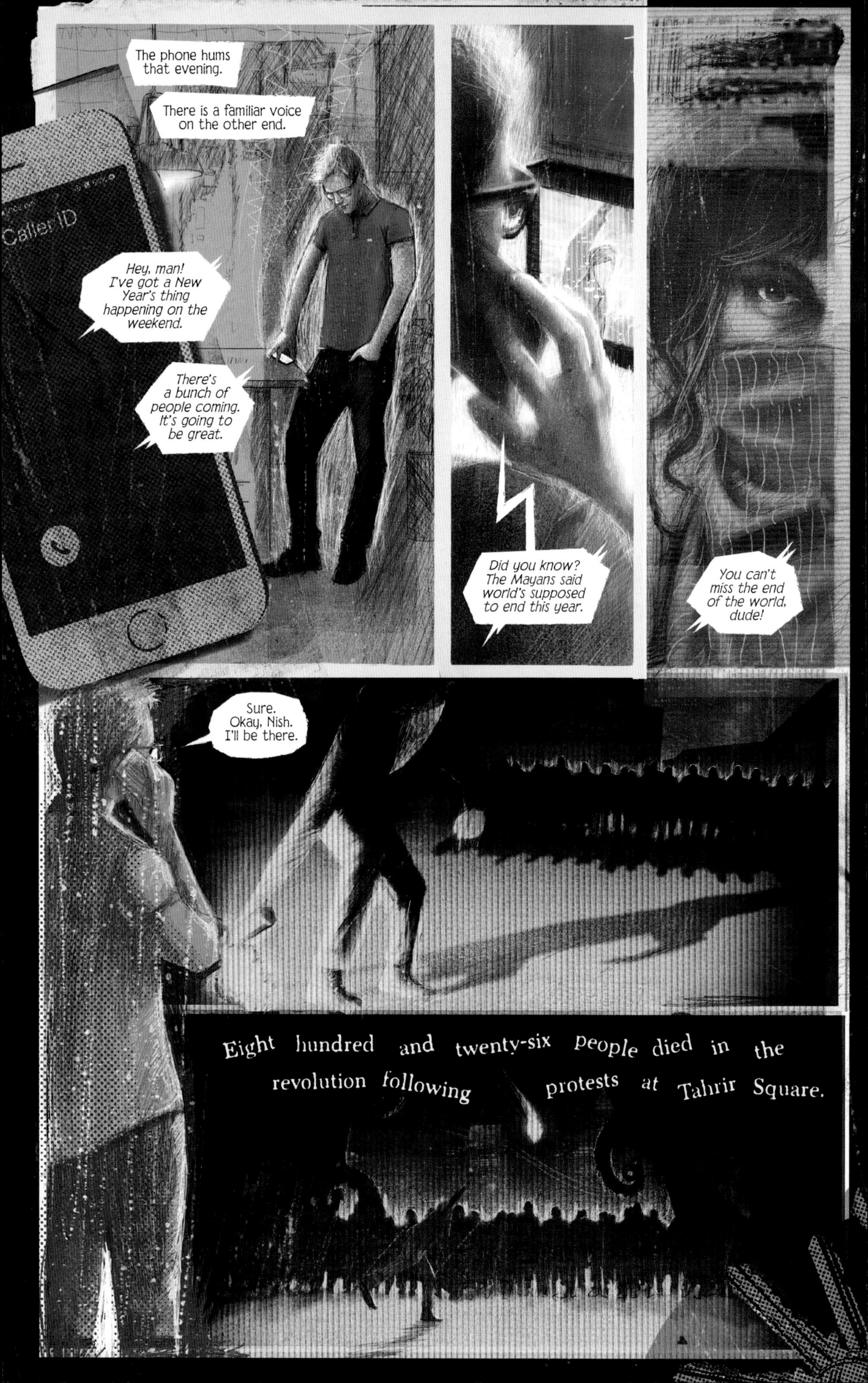

The phone hums that evening.
There is a familiar voice on the other end.
Caller ID
Hey, man! I've got a New Year's thing happening on the weekend.
There's a bunch of people coming. It's going to be great.
Did you know? The Mayans said world's supposed to end this year.
You can't miss the end of the world, dude!
Sure. Okay, Nish. I'll be there.
Eight hundred and twenty-six people died in the revolution following protests at Tahrir Square.

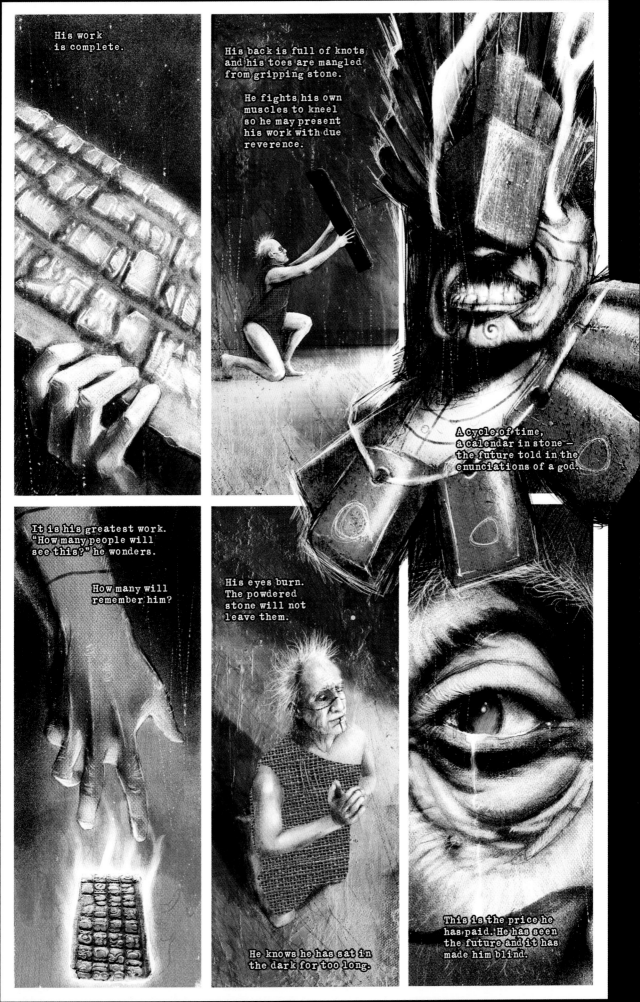

His work
is complete.

His back is full of knots
and his toes are mangled
from gripping stone.

He fights his own
muscles to kneel
so he may present
his work with due
reverence.

A cycle of time,
a calendar in stone —
the future told in the
enunciations of a god.

It is his greatest work.
"How many people will
see this?" he wonders.

How many will
remember him?

His eyes burn.
The powdered
stone will not
leave them.

He knows he has sat in
the dark for too long.

This is the price he
has paid. He has seen
the future and it has
made him blind.

The evening spirals into a dancing throng, flickering toward New Year's Eve.

Glimpses of people shining for the briefest moments.

I find a quiet balcony where strangers come by to smoke.

There, I meet a girl who's running away from home. She thinks Tokyo will solve her problems.

We fall into a conversation about euthanasia. She tells me she's against it.

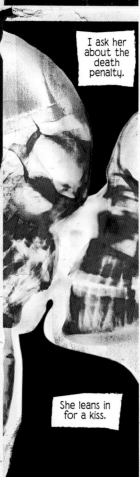

I ask her about the death penalty.

She leans in for a kiss.

I don't understand how you can be for the death penalty and against euthanasia.

"Life is suffering," she says.

Woman assaulted in New Delhi dies in hospital eight weeks later.

I watch her disappear.

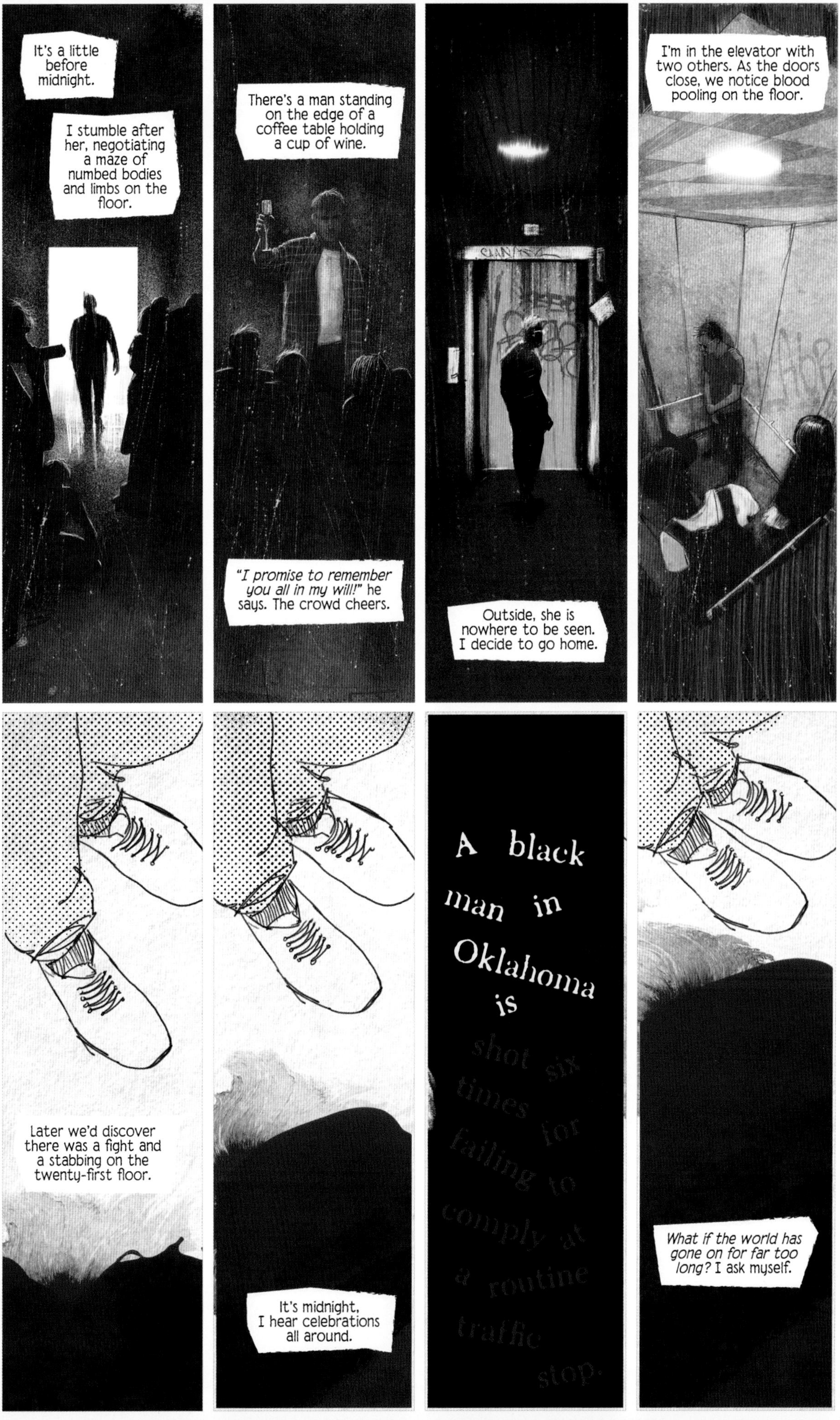
It's a little before midnight.
I stumble after her, negotiating a maze of numbed bodies and limbs on the floor.
There's a man standing on the edge of a coffee table holding a cup of wine.
"I promise to remember you all in my will!" he says. The crowd cheers.
Outside, she is nowhere to be seen. I decide to go home.
I'm in the elevator with two others. As the doors close, we notice blood pooling on the floor.
Later we'd discover there was a fight and a stabbing on the twenty-first floor.
It's midnight, I hear celebrations all around.
A black man in Oklahoma is shot six times for failing to comply at a routine traffic stop.
What if the world has gone on for far too long? I ask myself.

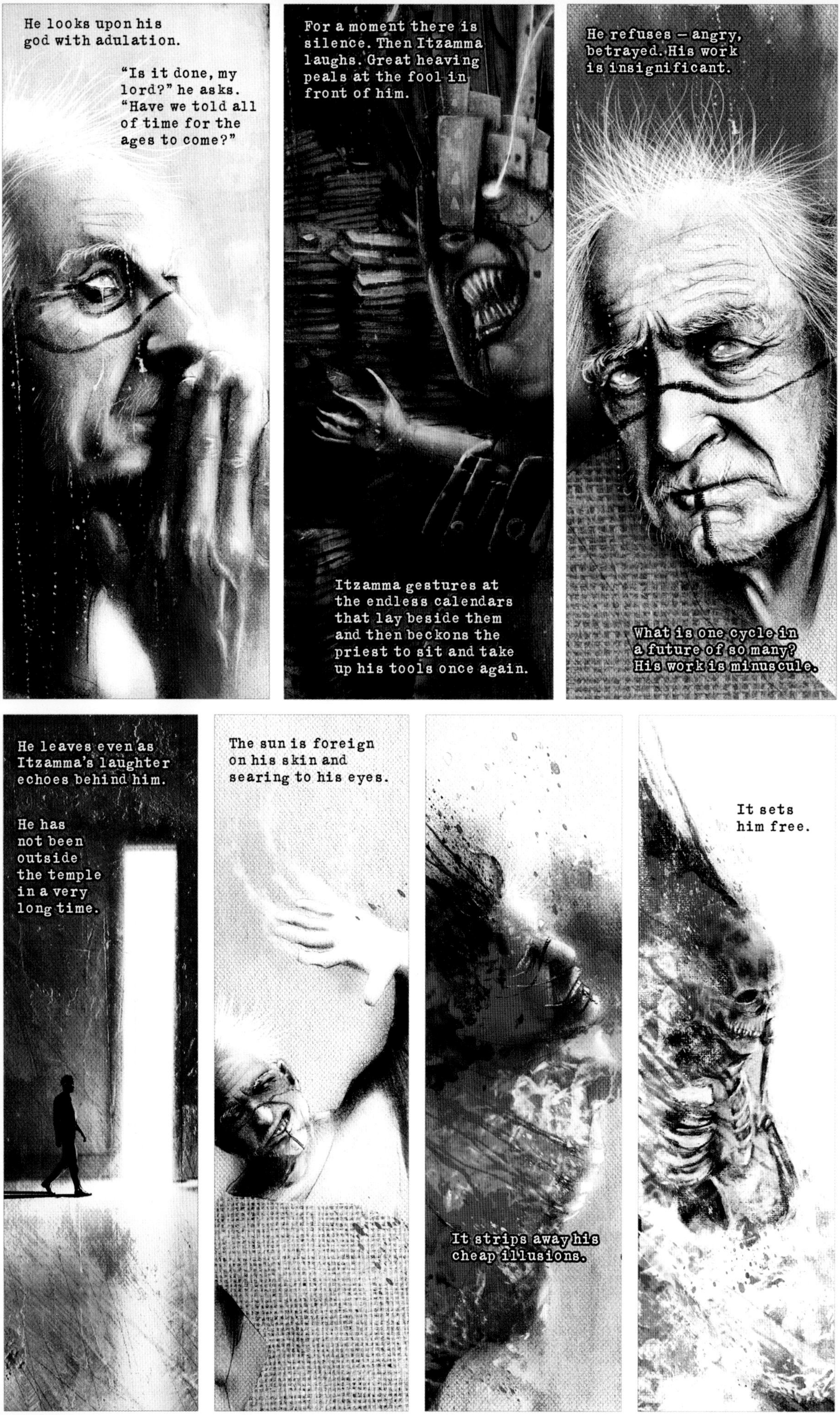
He looks upon his god with adulation.
"Is it done, my lord?" he asks. "Have we told all of time for the ages to come?"
For a moment there is silence. Then Itzamma laughs. Great heaving peals at the fool in front of him.
Itzamma gestures at the endless calendars that lay beside them and then beckons the priest to sit and take up his tools once again.
He refuses — angry, betrayed. His work is insignificant.
What is one cycle in a future of so many? His work is minuscule.
He leaves even as Itzamma's laughter echoes behind him.
He has not been outside the temple in a very long time.
The sun is foreign on his skin and searing to his eyes.
It strips away his cheap illusions.
It sets him free.

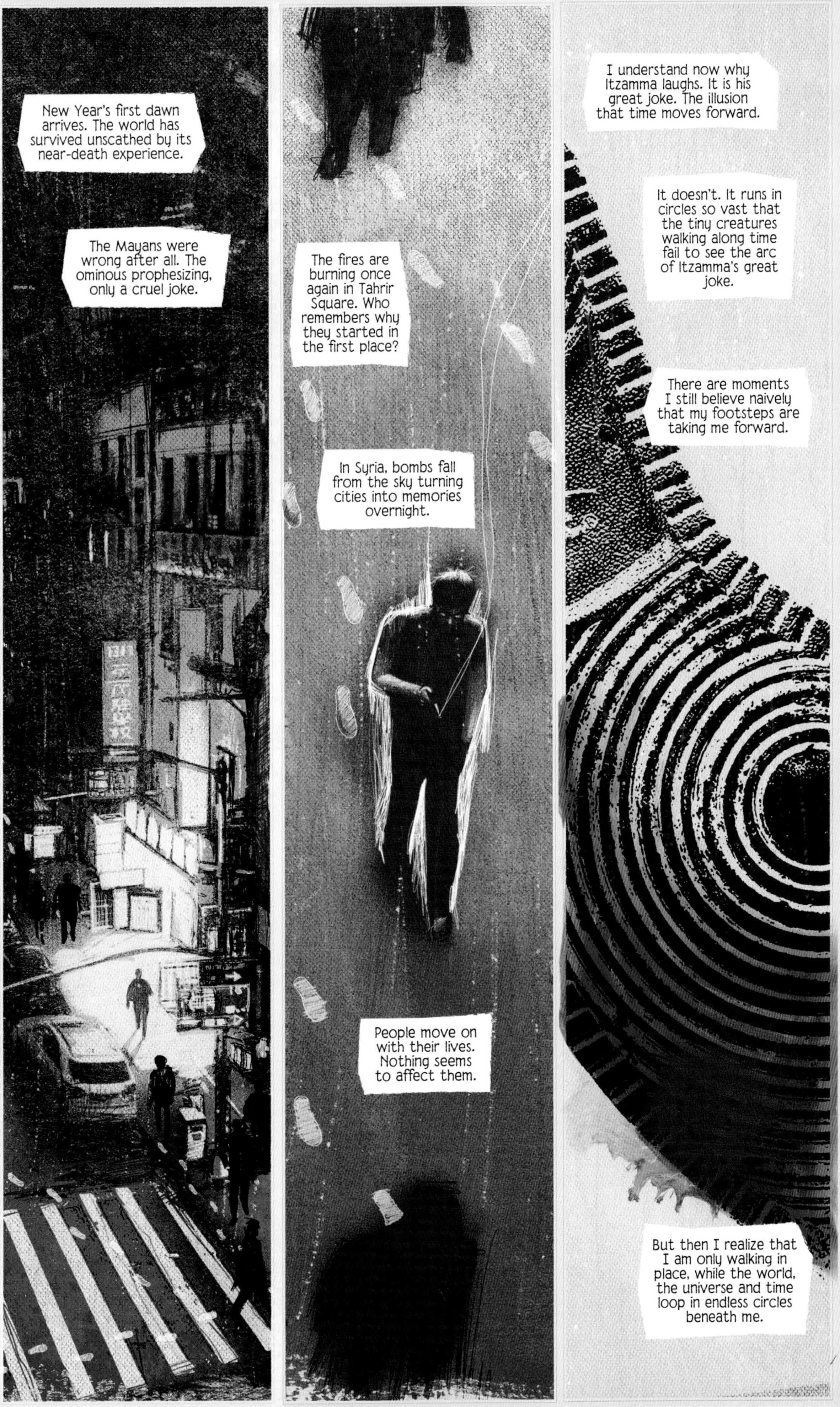
New Year's first dawn arrives. The world has survived unscathed by its near-death experience.
The Mayans were wrong after all. The ominous prophesizing, only a cruel joke.
The fires are burning once again in Tahrir Square. Who remembers why they started in the first place?
In Syria, bombs fall from the sky turning cities into memories overnight.
People move on with their lives. Nothing seems to affect them.
I understand now why Itzamma laughs. It is his great joke. The illusion that time moves forward.
It doesn't. It runs in circles so vast that the tiny creatures walking along time fail to see the arc of Itzamma's great joke.
There are moments I still believe naively that my footsteps are taking me forward.
But then I realize that I am only walking in place, while the world, the universe and time loop in endless circles beneath me.

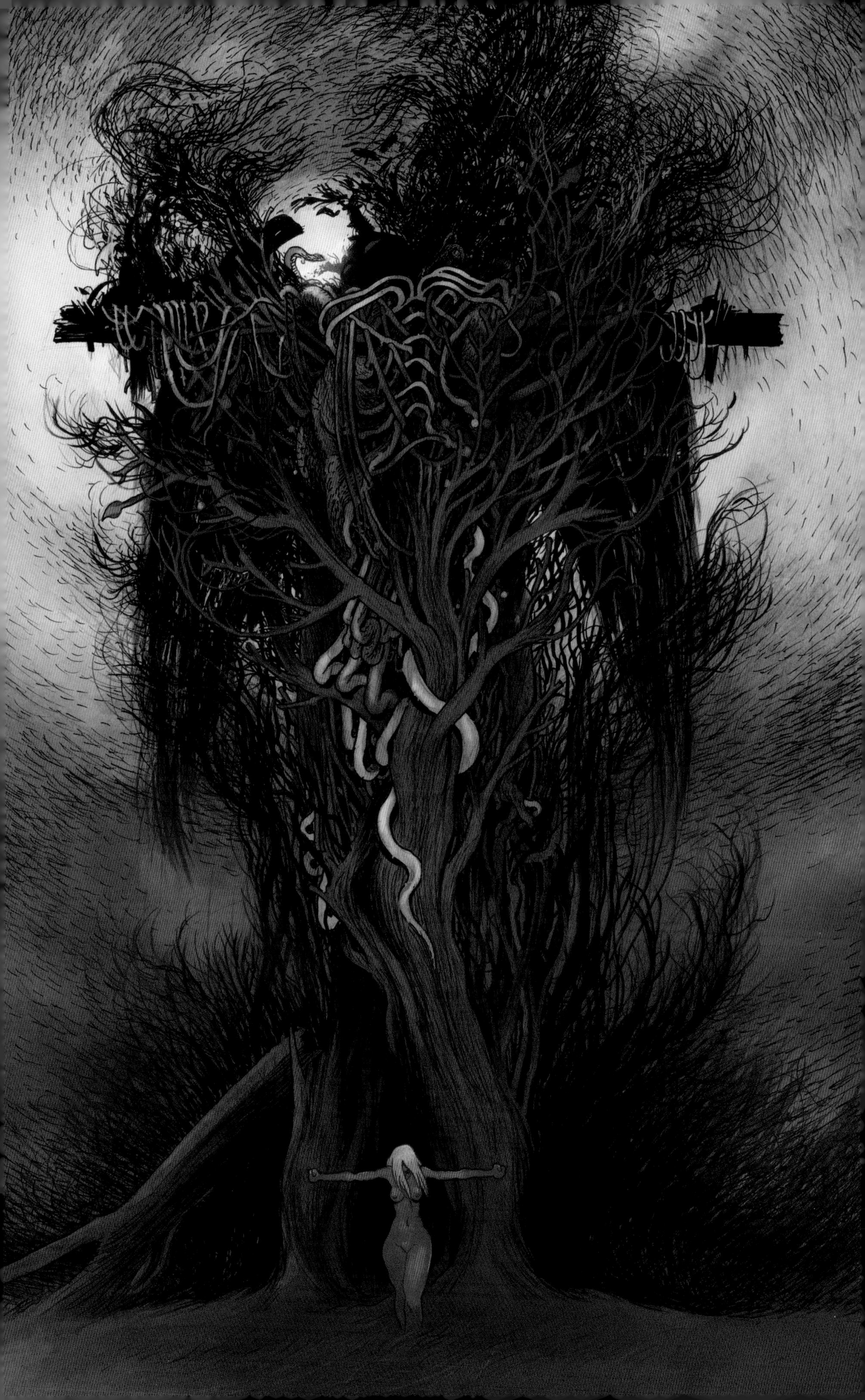

ISSUE #2

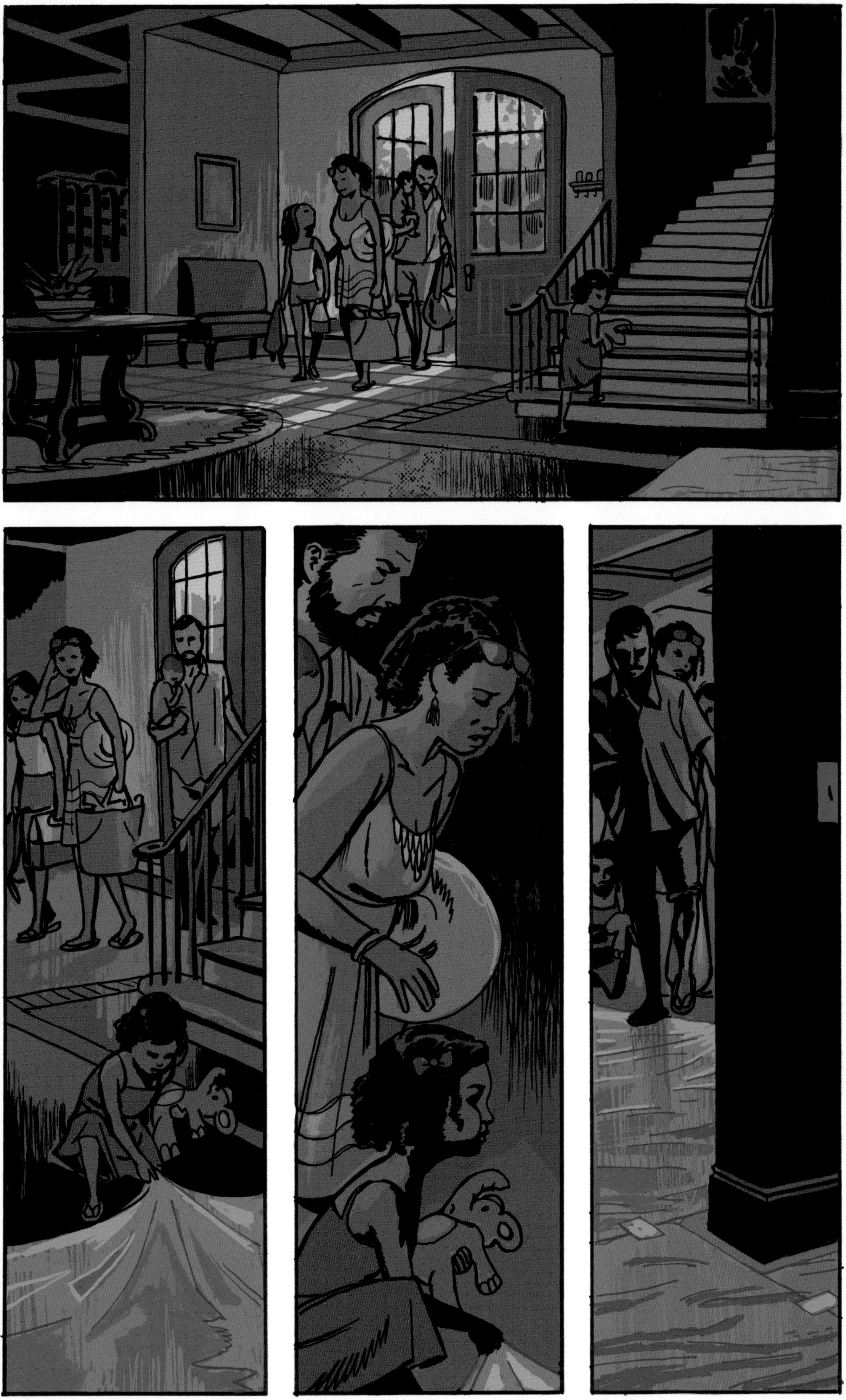

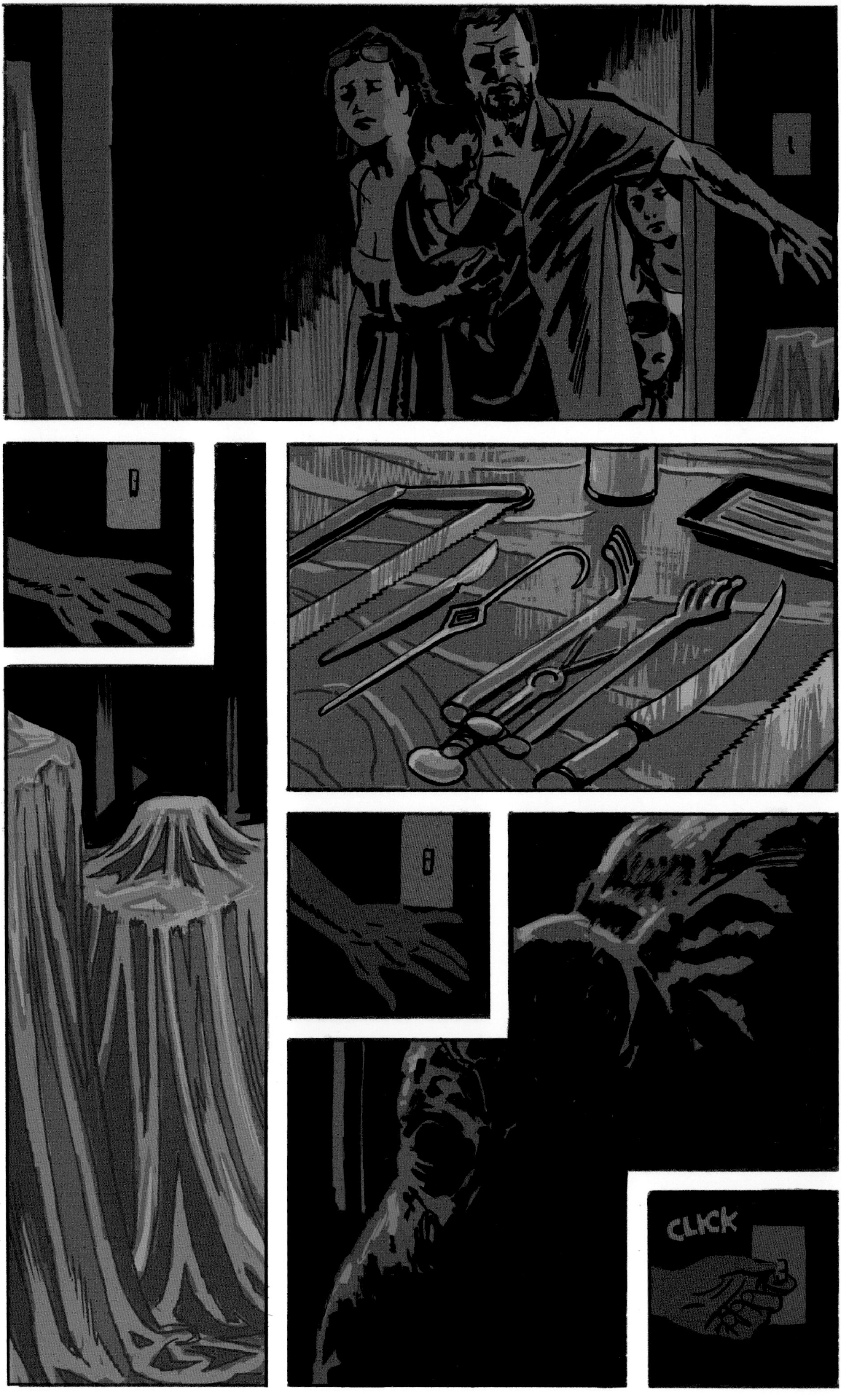
CLICK

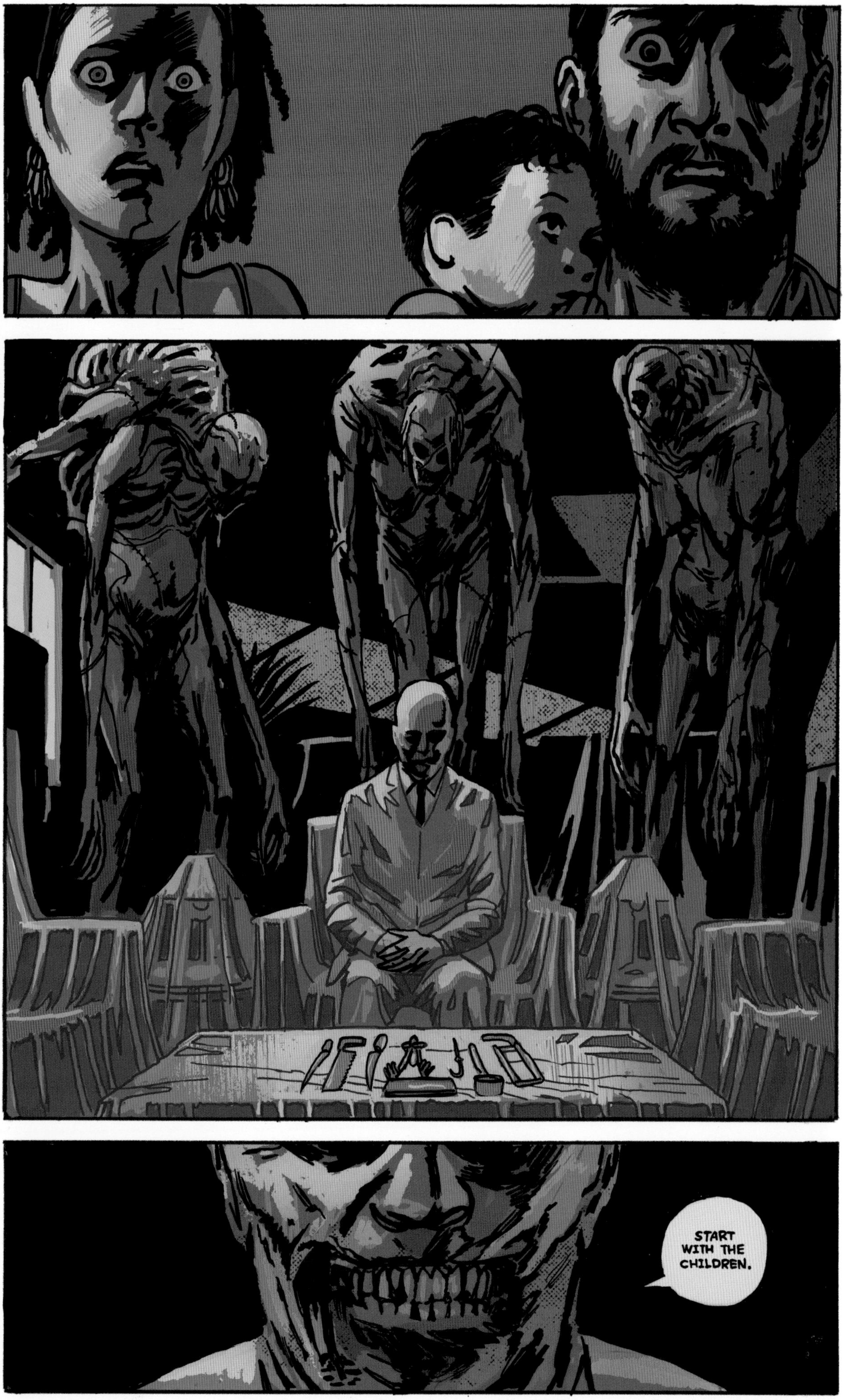
START WITH THE CHILDREN.

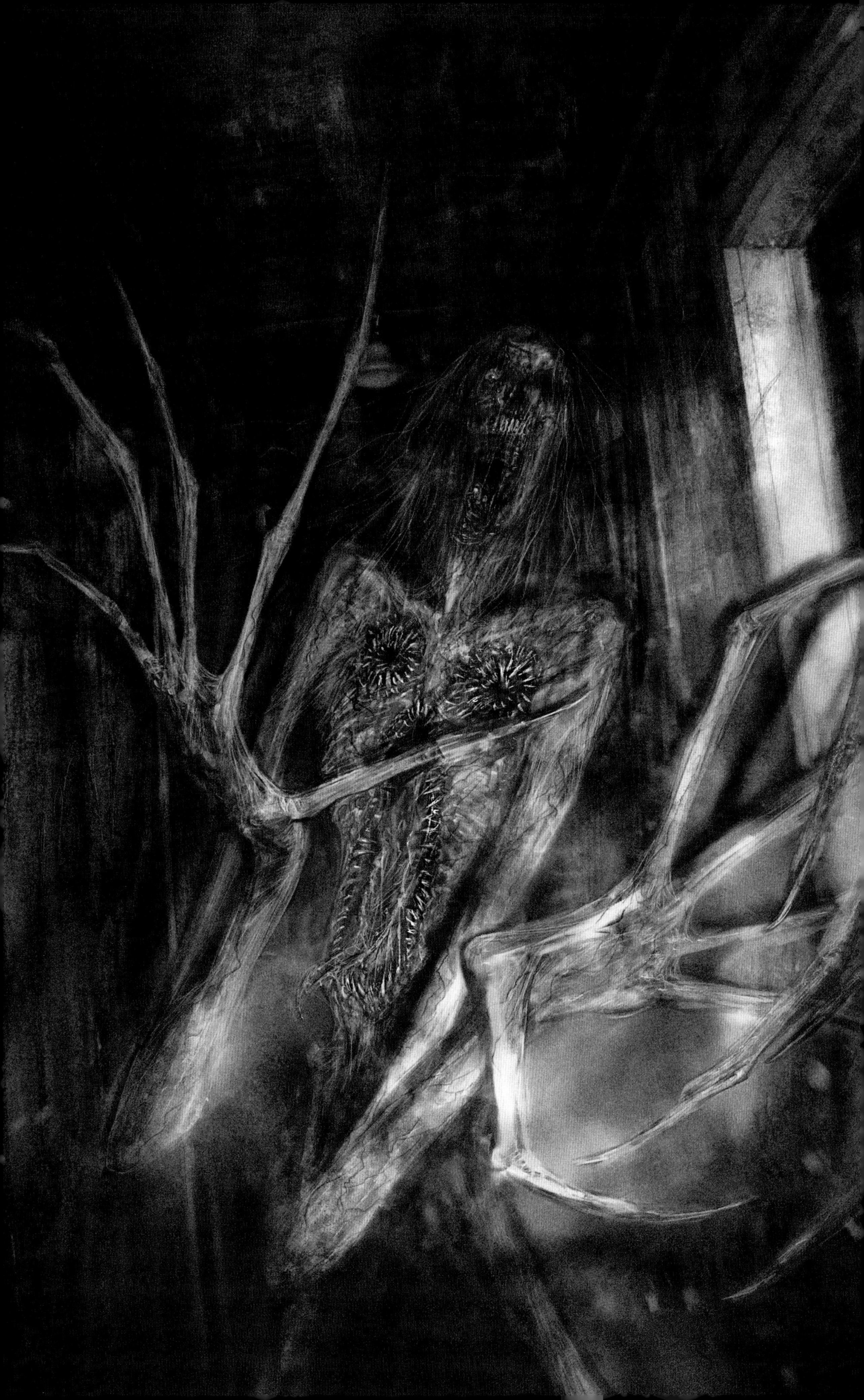

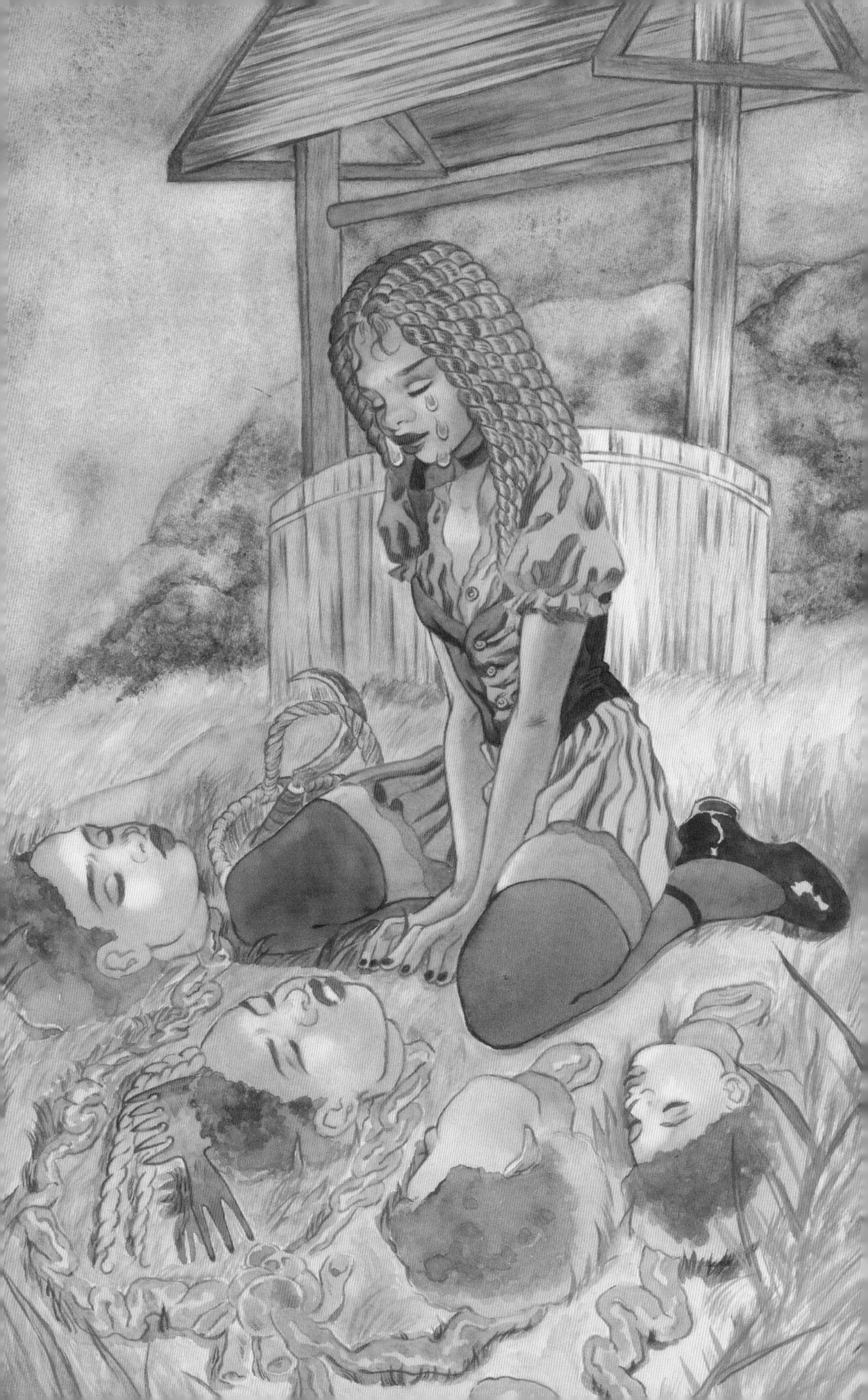

You don't remember, but we were fucking here, years ago.
You were ranting, your thoughts racing, mine were slow.
You didn't seem to worry, or if you did, it didn't show.
You finally shut out those stains polluting the world, like we didn't know.
We've forgotten you can't see the horizon from the Green.
Forgotten we're trapped here, forced to live in between.
You've evolved, I've evolved,
But somehow we're finally free.
Whoever you've changed into, whoever I've become, whoever we want to be.
Now, here we are, doing what you did one day on a spree.
Touched me, licked me, enveloped me

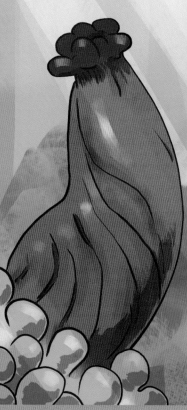

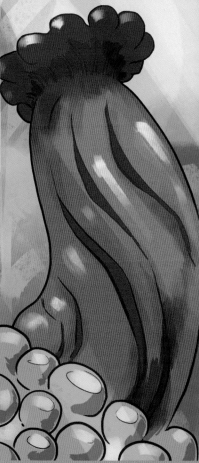

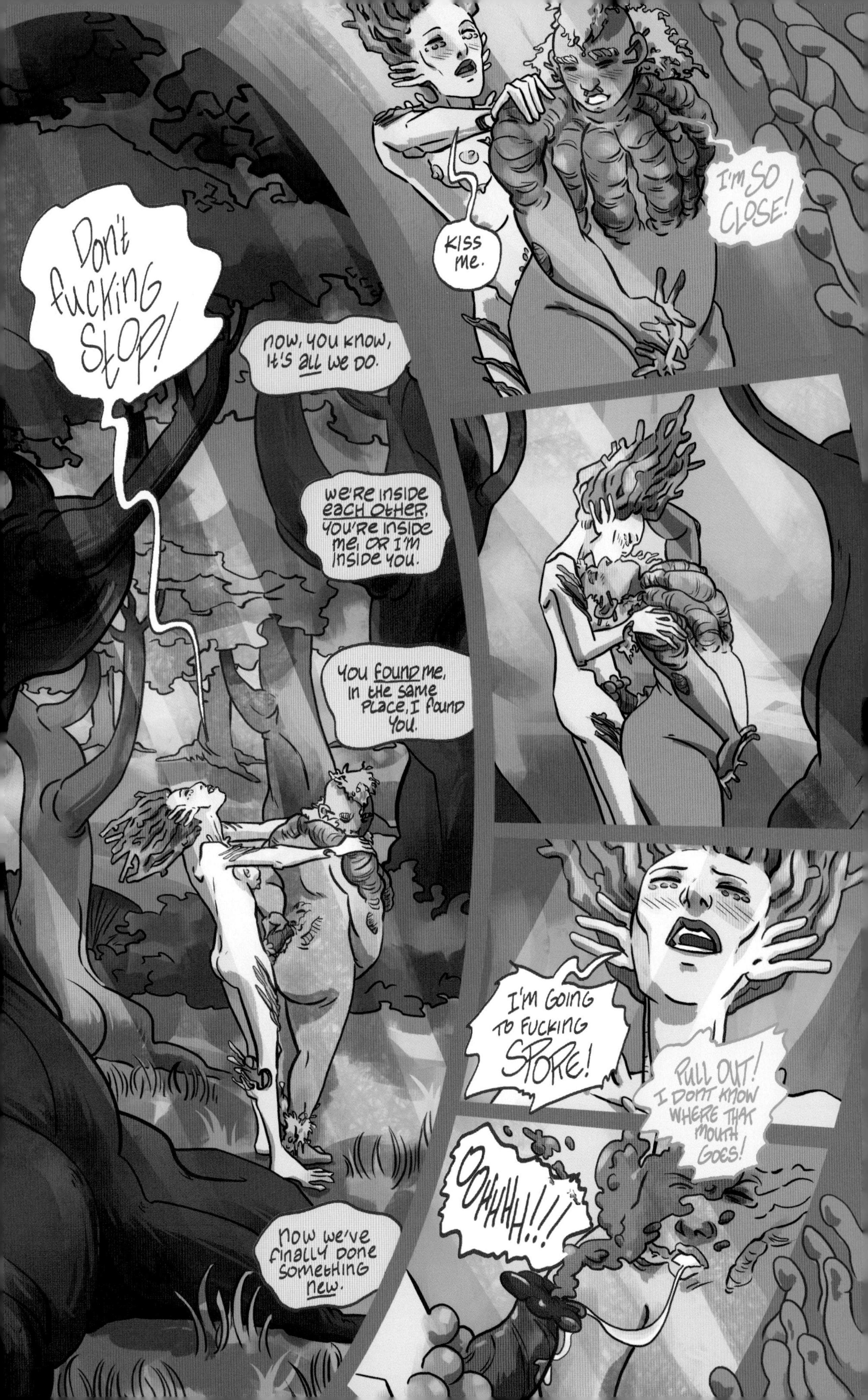
Don't fucking Stop!
now, you know, it's all we do.
we're inside each other, you're inside me, or I'm inside you.
You found me, in the same place, I found you.
now we've finally done something new.
Kiss me.
I'm SO CLOSE!
I'm Going to fucking SPORE!
PULL OUT! I DONT KNOW WHERE THAT MOUTH GOES!
OOHHHH!!!

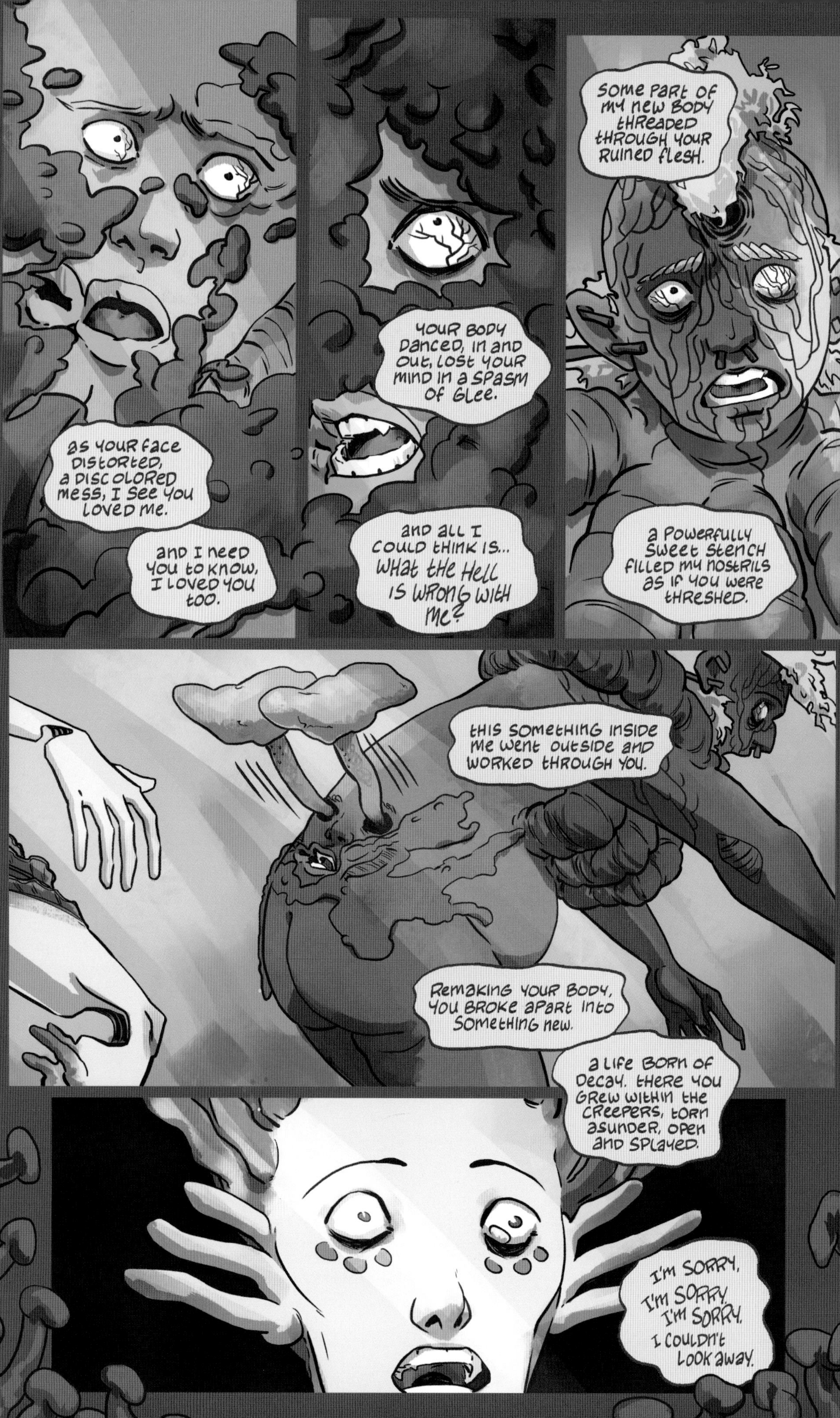
as your face distorted, a discolored mess, I see you loved me.
and I need you to know, I loved you too.
your body danced, in and out, lost your mind in a spasm of glee.
and all I could think is... what the hell is wrong with me?
some part of my new body threaded through your ruined flesh.
a powerfully sweet stench filled my nostrils as if you were threshed.
this something inside me went outside and worked through you.
remaking your body, you broke apart into something new.
a life born of decay. there you grew within the creepers, torn asunder, open and splayed.
I'm sorry, I'm sorry, I'm sorry. I couldn't look away.

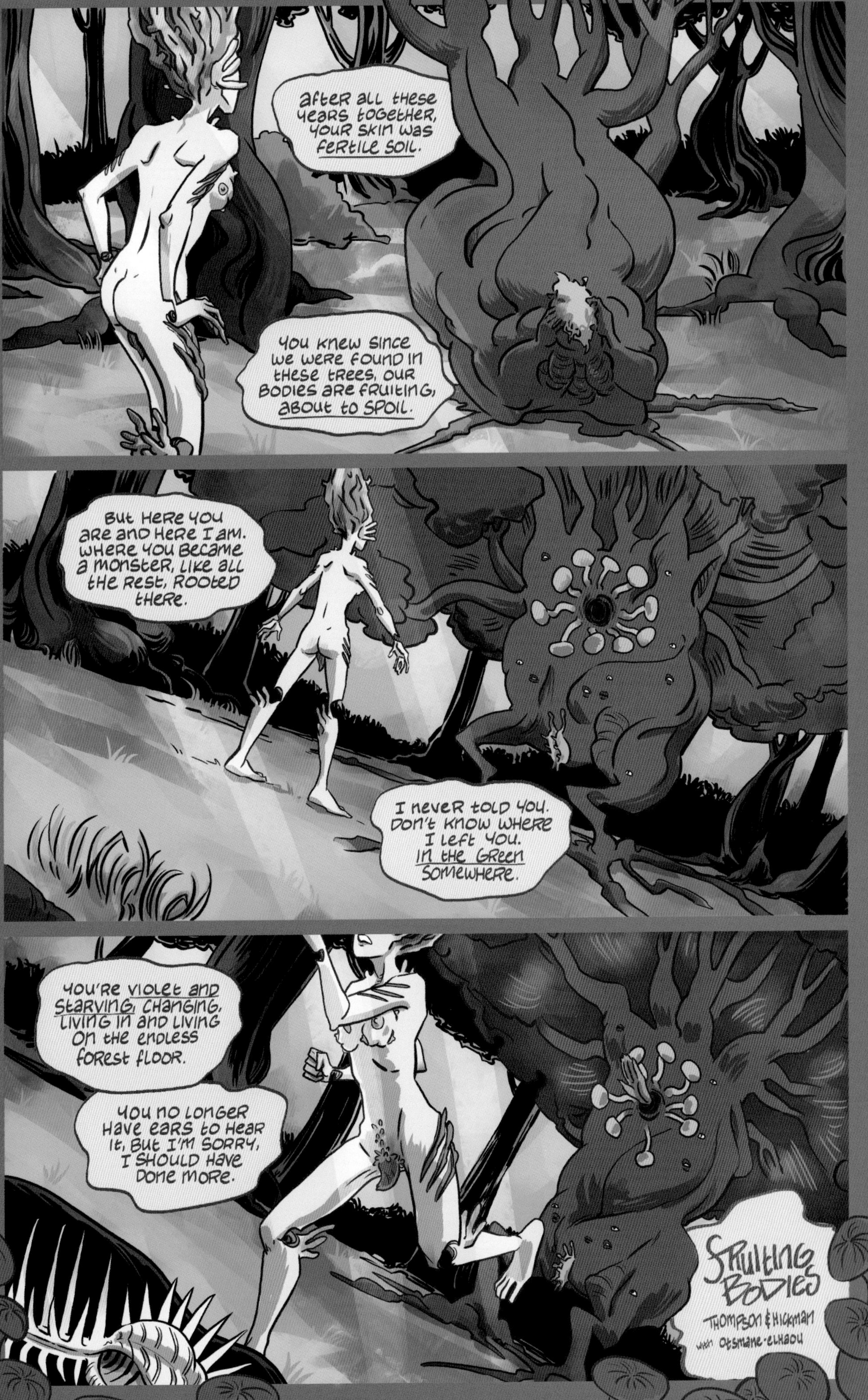
after all these years together, your skin was fertile soil.
You knew since we were found in these trees, our bodies are fruiting, about to spoil.
But here you are and here I am. Where you became a monster, like all the rest, rooted there.
I never told you. Don't know where I left you. In the Green somewhere.
You're violet and starving, changing, living in and living on the endless forest floor.
You no longer have ears to hear it, but I'm sorry, I should have done more.
Fruiting Bodies
Thompson & Hickman
with Otsmane-Elhaou

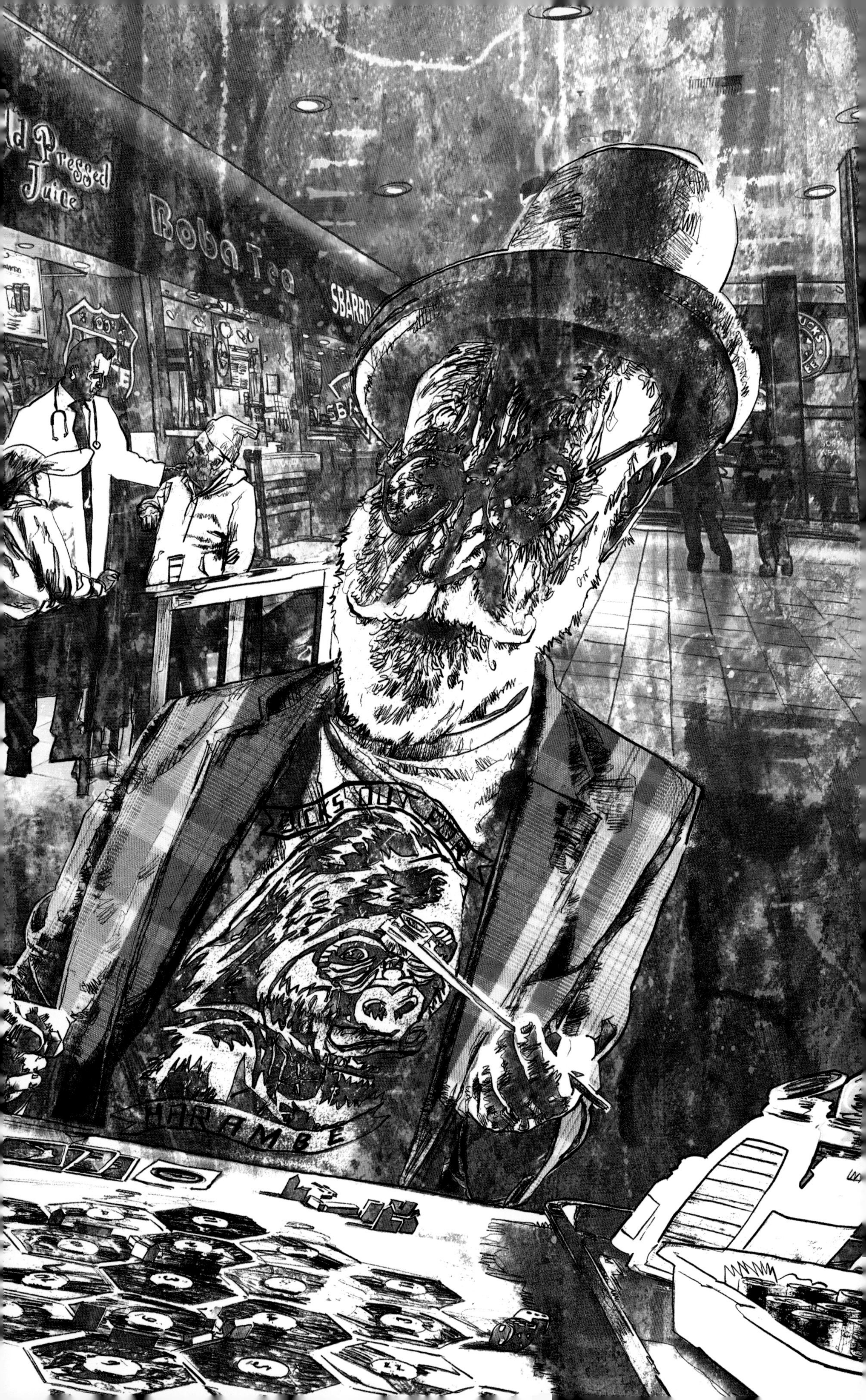
Pressed Juice
Boba Tea
SBARRO
HARAMBE

THE OLD FOLK

WRITTEN BY TINI HOWARD
ILLUSTRATION BY AARON CAMPBELL

"How sick *is* she?"

This was one of the primary problems I'd been having with my girlfriend. Stuff like this. I don't know if Deanni thinks it's funny, or edgy, or if she'd just been reading too many of the archives from back when social media was still a thing, but I never liked it. It was like she wanted to shock me into being her adversary.

"She's not *sick*." I was trying to sound measured. I was "driving," out of some weird sense of misplaced comfort. Not that the car needed my help, but it's what my grandmother would have done. She insisted on driving until the day they put her in the home.

Grandma said that when *she* was young, taking your car keys away was how they told you that you were too old to drive. Back then, cars were actually dangerous, like unchecked weapons, sliding around the road, piloted by *individuals*. I told her that didn't make any sense—there were *plenty* of stupid, rude, or just otherwise *distracted* people who wouldn't be safe behind the wheel these days.

Grandma said she knew, and that it was the same then. That's why she resented it. Taking the keys away was just another way to make you feel old. Truthfully, I didn't know if I could do it, if I had to—drive a car like she did, actually having to steer the thing around. But there were plenty of

things Grandma Krista couldn't figure out these days, so we got along.

I wondered if it was normal to get along with your grandmother better than you did your girlfriend. Then I felt Deanni staring at me like I owed her an argument. So I responded.

"She's just *old*. Old enough that—"

"I just asked!"

TICK TICK TICK TICK

Deanni had installed an app on the car that played old-fashioned noises, like wipers swishing, or blinkers ticking. She thought stuff from the '10s and '20s was *so cute*. Her grandparents were all dead already.

I was tense in the seat, my hands on the wheel, pretend-driving, like I could have gotten us there faster.

"I'm sorry. I'm stressed out. I really don't like this. I don't like that she has to live in a home, or that I'm supposed to go visit her there. It seems wrong. She was *fine* at her house."

"Siobhan, come *on*. Remember before? You didn't think it was safe for her to be alone in there, her lungs the way they were. She couldn't go outside without oxygen. Her immune system was a mess."

Deanni's hand was warm on my thigh, her tiny wrist encircled in my grandmother's vintage timepiece, *Betsey Johnson* in pink scrawl on the face. Everything about her light, fun, feminine. A human balloon, bouncing across the fingertips of everyone on the dance floor. She wasn't bogged down by the sins of the past, or survivor's guilt, or any of the shit that chewed at me.

She was cute.

"You were being *obnoxious* about it."

And she liked to ruin things when she was ahead.

"Okay." I folded my arms. I didn't even want to pretend to drive the car anymore. "We're almost there."

Deanni twisted fully in her seat as we approached the nursing home.

"There's no way. Are you serious? There's *no way.*"

I jiggled my leg against what would have been the gas pedal, a habit that just rubbed in how ill suited I'd be to actually drive one of these things. Utterly too anxious.

"It's an experimental treatment, Deanni. I didn't want to tell you because I didn't want you to get *weird.*"

"You should have let me prepare." She turned around, her eyes saucer-wide, made bigger by black eyeliner that she called her *wings.* "I have so many questions. I needed to do *research.* I didn't bring the right photo lens in my implant—this is the first time I've ever *seen* one of these in reality!" She was downright giddy. As if she'd entirely forgotten the reason for our visit. As if she'd completely forgotten—

"Why is your *grandmother* living at a fucking *shopping mall?*"

****

"FUCK!"

"That is a Critical Failure."

The table erupted into a roar.

"Bullshit. Mulligan. Do-over! Can I do-over?"

The table grew quiet. As a Dungeon Master, Richie had rules. In exchange for a fully immersive tabletop role-play experience, he expected a few reasonable things. *One,* no distractions at the table. No chitchat, no music in your ears, and no phones. No endless scrolling through archives with one hand. "Those things are a fucking *pacifier,*" Richie would say derisively, and he wasn't wrong.

(You could eat at the gaming table. They were, after all, in a food court, and brain food was a concept they all believed in.)

Two, long conversations between only two people were to be reserved for between sessions. And *three,* you *had to know how to use your abilities.* He found it impartial for him to tell his players how to play their character. It wasn't *asking for a Mulligan* that was the problem, it was Krista *not knowing whether or not she could.*

She felt the pressure, tapping at the character sheet projected on the table before her. "I'm sorry, I don't—I wish we could just use fucking *paper,* man, I can't read it like this. Where are my spells, my—yes. Okay. I have the Sorcery points, I can reroll."

"Then go ahead."

"Mrs. Delano." A polite demand, from the table's central speaker.

"Shit. One second! Okay, gimme the D20, I'll do it now—"

Richie's face was impassive. For all its wrinkles and soft, sagging skin, his face was without expression, his jaw like a bulldog's, artificially widened by his old-fashioned dentures.

"I'd prefer if we did this without distractions, Krista." He tapped the table and the projection sheets disappeared. "We'll pause until next session."

"Mrs. Delano. I hope you can hear me. I'd hate to have to subject you to a forceful *ear-cleaning*."

Krista looked around at the rest of the table. Traitors. Not a single one of them pushed him to wait for her. She sniffed and got to her feet, not breaking eye contact with Richie.

"Coming, nurse."

Krista leaned on her walker as she got to her feet. A required stumble, the slide-clack of moving along with the wheels and the little rubber feet, a second to get her bearings. A moment later, she pressed a foot to the metal slat at the bottom of her walker and *pushed*. The silent battery motor kicked on and she rested her other foot atop it, letting the tiny-wheeled walker-scooter take her through the mall to the nurses' station.

"I'd hate to have to subject you to a forceful ear-cleaning."

Krista's eyes weren't great anymore, but the walker knew where to go, and the smells themselves were a map. The food court stopped at the pizza smell, and then she turned left past the open-air candy store. They were all artificial, of course. Not one of them had an immune system that would have endured the germy depths of a shared candy bowl.

The scented candle store—that was real. But Krista suspected that the scent they put in the candy-scented candles was the same fake candy scent that they blew into the air outside of the candy store. But the candle shop was real. You could go in there and purchase scented candles, and take them back to your room. It meant that the very same scent was "fake" in one context but "real" in another.

Krista wrinkled her nose. Young people didn't think old people thought about stuff like that anymore, but they did. She herself was still full of curiosities unfulfilled, and planned with no irony to die that way. Her generation had been cursed with it. The need to know everything, compulsively—to scroll the old archives for new anxieties, like a thumb-sucker. Anyway, her mind was still sharp. Too sharp.

Popcorn-kiosk smell. Leather-boot-and-foot-stink roller-rink smell. Arcade lights—those didn't have a smell, but they glowed brightly enough to cut through the eyestrain and cataract haze. Through the grates of the department store she could see beds, dozens of them, in chevron-V displays. All dressed in different lovely five-piece brocade satin bed sets. Wide, wide beds, but short, with ample room to walk between the aisles.

The gate was down now, of course. No access to your bed during the day. That made you depressed.

Left past the department store, her scooter whirred, heralded by rubber plants and skylights. Above, the carefully measured memory of sunlight glimmered through the glass in tessellating triangles, buttressed by large frames. A hyper-modern mall cathedral. The real light of the sky outside—Krista couldn't see that.

The hallway opened up into the secondary lunch spot. There was no small amount of discourse as to whether or not this area should also be considered a food court. It was a communal area with food smells, food tables, and the *aesthetic* of a food court. No food was served there, but if there was anything the old folk around here loved, it was endless bickering over genre and catalogue.

Before they took down the inter-mall network and replaced it with archives, the old folk would spend *hours* just arguing about *nothing*.

There was that comforting smell: buttered pretzels. She backed off of the walker's step as she came into sight of the nurses in their blue-and-white-striped paper aprons, returning to what she considered her staggering hobble act. She singsonged her greeting to the nurses.

"I'm *heeere*."

"*Careful*, Mrs. Delano," a young Californian nurse laughed. "Don't get too excited now."

Krista pursed her lips. The white-hot rage at the sound of their airy giggles made her feel like a child. "Don't you *fucking* laugh at me," she spat. "I'm here because of your stupid announcement. You fucked up my fucking game. What do you want?"

"You old folk *loooove* that word," the nurse smiled, tapping a few pills into a white biomatter condiment cup. The sound was all wrong. It was supposed to be paper. It *wasn't* paper. "*Fuckin'* this and *fuckin'* that. You think it sounds so scary!" The cup, the pills. The small globule of gel added on top to make them easier to swallow. "Here you are, ma'am. Hot-n-fresh," the nurse grinned, setting the cup down.

The cup, the pills, the weird stickiness of the globule. Krista coughed.

"That sucked. Can I please have a slushee now?"

"You know we don't have any treats for you, Mrs. Delano. Just good smells, good vibes. Doesn't it make you happy? Didn't you used to eat pretzels at the mall back in the day like the rest of your friends?"

Krista frowned.

"No fucking point in wearing aprons and hats if you don't even have real pretzels."

"It's cute," said the nurse. "Don't you old folk like cute?"

Krista stepped onto the walker and zipped off quietly. The nurse called after in a fake-candy voice: "Don't you wanna take a *selfie* with me?!"

****

Deanni was running back and forth, zigging and zagging from one side of the big, shiny hallway to the other like a marble on a hill. A shop that advertised nothing over five dollars sent her into fits. An earring shop, utter bric-a-brac, tin trash on wires, and she swooned.

"This is incredible. This place should be a museum! I would pay to host parties here. I would *die* to host parties here." Deanni returned to my side, her little nails like a vice on the soft flesh of my upper arm. "Is there a food court? Can we eat there? I'm sorry I keep blinking so much, I've taken so many pictures. The smells are *insane*. Do they have an arcade here?"

I gave her an answering look. It said *nothing* regarding arcades.

"What? I'm much more interested in visiting your grandmother now, if that helps." Her perfect teeth in a row. "Now that she lives in a real, actual, old-as-shit refurbished *shopping mall* with the *carpet* and *kiosks* and *everything*."

"It's not—"

"I want an overpriced band t-shirt."

"Deanni—"

"I want a bath bomb."

"Honey—"

"And an Orange Caesar smoothie. A huge one. I mean, whatever, you know what I mean."

"Come *on*, Deanni, *please*!" The shiny tile made a chorus of my voice. Deanni raised her eyebrows.

"Wow. Forgive me for being excited. Ready to have a lot to talk about with Grandma."

"I want to be clear before we talk to her. She doesn't *live in a shopping mall*. She's part of an experimental treatment to help people like her. They need as little stress as possible so that their bodies can continue to function. This space is...*comforting* to her."

"Do you think it's true that old folks like them are just like...too *soft*?"

I felt my lips twist.

"No, Deanni. How can you simultaneously be so fascinated with her generation and so derisive of it in the same breath?"

"I like history, Siobhan." She put a piece of gum grasped off a newsstand kiosk into her mouth. "The ugly parts too. I respect it all."

The rows of shops were like a time capsule, a dollhouse. Every storefront packed with items. Rows of obsolete CDs and DVDs lined the shops, old junk that Grandma Krista and her friends hoarded and traded like kids on the playground.

But where I'd found comfort before in Wild West villages and Renaissance Fairs, something about this place didn't feel comforting. I didn't want a pretzel or a slushie. I wanted to see my grandmother. The thought of this place being open for the masses made me *sad*. Dozens of people just buying things for fun? From other people, who worked tirelessly to sell items they didn't own, making money to pay for more things?

"You're muttering, Siobhan, and it sounds pretentious."

"I don't think I'm pretentious.

I think it's okay to learn from history."

We checked in at the reception area, an Information Desk complete with large colorful maps and a place to rent hermetically sealed strollers for visiting grandkids. Deanni cycled through being overly friendly to the nurse, to asking too many questions about the antiques, to getting irate when she was told to spit out her gum. "I got it *here*. What kind of mall doesn't let you chew bubble gum?"

"It isn't a *mall*." God, I hated repeating myself. I didn't want to admit to being stunned. But I was, every time. It was almost a *joke*, the kind of terrible low-fruit sort of thing you'd see on a greeting graphic. A food court straight out of a movie, rubbery (or perhaps, actual rubber) pizzas under glass, rotating slowly. We walked past a woman who passed out nutritional supplements with small sticks in them, gently encouraging each patron with a lilting "Free sample?"

"Do you think it's true that old folks like them are just like...too soft?"

And the patrons: stooped and bent, crotchety and weathered, as expected. They'd certainly weathered a storm or two. But they were all so *frail*. Septuagenarians, most of them, and they were as bent and slim as the sort of ancient, ageless people you heard about on mountaintops.

I recognized Grandma Krista's friend—"fucking Richie"—at the head of the table in his little porkpie hat. He had a bunch of printed biomatter tiles on the table before him, running yet another game for his little clique. But she wasn't there.

I knew right where to find my grandmother. If she wasn't in the food court playing *D&D*, she was at the arcade.

****

"Mrs. Delano?"

"Hold *on*." That was sharper than she meant it to be, really. But she was still pissed at Richie and his rules, and needed a distraction. The archives barely interested her anymore, but she still found herself staring at the screen in her hand more than she meant to, cycling through and through the 30-year-old interactions left behind. Nothing more than a journal, a photo album now. That kind of Wild-West personal sharing had gone way out of fashion, not to return until long after it had been forgotten.

Long after Krista Delano was long gone. A real dead woman instead of just a half-dead woman. Another '80s Baby haunting a half-empty mall.

"Mrs. Delano. This is the second time today you have been *unresponsive*."

Krista looked up. The arcade beeped around her. Her hip was screaming at her to sit properly, as her arthritis demanded, not perched as she was inside a *Cruis'n World* cabinet. The games were free to play, but she wasn't playing them. Not this time. The sound, the darkness, the screens, it all soothed her, made her feel young again. Back when the world was shit, but it was *hers*.

"She's fine, nurse, thank you."

Krista tensed and relaxed immediately, recognizing her granddaughter's strong, measured voice calling out to the nurses' speakers, and a young woman holding her hand beside her.

"Siobhan." She was tall and slim, and *healthy*, damn healthy.

Healthy in a way people had never been before, robust, and happy, blooming with all of it. Better people from a better future. Krista stood, sure that the sudden burst of joy would catch up with her body. It didn't, but Siobhan did, tall and lovely, her dark hair and soft skin like steel underneath as her granddaughter caught her. And bless her, Siobhan didn't *hold* Krista, but brought her to her feet, stood her there. Less like a hug than a cover. Siobhan would never let her look a fool.

Krista pressed her feet against the arcade's carpet, steadying her footing. With her glasses on, she could properly see the other girl. Deanni, Siobhan had prepared her. Deanni was fascinated with the games, putting herself in front of several.

"This must be Deanni. Nice to meet you. So what brings you here, my girl?"

"Wanted to see you. I'm worried about how you're doing in here. The doctors said this was the best thing for you by a long shot, but..." They sat across from one another, in shiny plastic chairs that seemed an affront to ergonomics. "Deanni is—I'm sorry about her. She got excited because she likes these sorts of old-fashioned places."

Krista leaned back in her booth and shouted in Deanni's direction. "This one sucks now," she said, nudging her slippered feet against the table and pushing the chair back on two feet. "I mean, I never came to *this* one when I was alive—I didn't live here—but this one *does* suck now. You can't actually get any of the mall food."

Deanni strode over as Siobhan gently grasped her grandmother's hands, encouraging her to return all four chair feet to the floor.

"That's stuff's no good for

anyone, Grandma. It was just cheap trash from people who didn't care what they were served. We have better stuff now."

Deanni sat down next to Grandma Krista. "I'd try the real thing. Take the risk. A hot dog. That fake red dye."

Grandma cracked a smile. "You'd be smart to. Plenty of things did this to me. My parents ate that shit too, and it didn't kill 'em. That shit didn't kill me. Not like *they* killed me!" She started laughing, then coughing, then stopped. "It was good, though. Nothing's really that good, anymore. I mean, for you guys it is. Better'n ever. That's good. Fuck yeah to that."

Deanni folded her legs in the chair. "Fuck yeah," She repeated. Siobhan watched, braced for the next thing out of Deanni's mouth. She was already dangerously comfortable.

"Siobhan says you were *hot*."

"Yeah, I was." Grandma Krista whipped out the palm-sized screen, eagerly tapping into years of old archives. Siobhan had seen the archived photos of her grandmother before, digitally enhanced curves shining in a tiny bikini, her lips pursed at the camera. Grandma Krista carried herself with the same recklessness even now, but her bones were all angles. Her skin sagged and draped in powdery folds, the tattoos along her arms faded and sheer, but still bright against the paper-white wilt of her skin. This body's the only thing I ever had around long enough to invest in, she used to say.

Siobhan came around and folded her grandmother into her arms. She was small, weightless like a child, and sullen like one too. The sort of belligerence oft ascribed to dementia patients hung over all of them here. The last of their kind, the last of the Old Folk. A whole generation

dead—from stress, disease, a toxic planet—and now those who were left were bubbled into a time before their stresses, into the comforts of their childhood.

"You don't like it here, Grandma?"

Krista breathed, a sigh that was surely meant to sound petulant, but didn't. It was a rasp, a rattle. "It's fine."

"Good." Siobhan resisted the urge to squeeze the tiny woman like a child might a comfort toy. The Old Folk had missed the threshold by so little, it seemed. She knew 50-year-olds, like her parents—and they were as fit as she herself was, and expected to stay that way, well into their early 110s. To Grandma Krista and everyone like her, it was mostly good news: their children will live a long, long time, because we can fundamentally change the planet to help both it and the human race thrive.

The bad news for Krista's generation: they are ravaged fossils of a toxic world. This brave new world is not meant for them. The even *worse* news—the answer to the unprecedented amount of stress and uncertainty faced by your generation—is forever confining them to the past.

"I wish I had some paper, though," Krista said. "I keep fucking up at *D&D* without it."

Deanni grinned. "Oh! I have some here in my bag, no problem."

Grandma Krista waved her hand. "Not the same thing. Those are all biomatter pages, it's not *real* paper. Used to feel different."

Siobhan let out a groan that seemed fit to crack her through the middle. "You do like the games and stuff, yeah? And your friends?"

"The games are fine. My friends are assholes." Grandma Krista gently extricated herself from

Siobhan's arms. "Don't be sad. I'm glad things are so good for you girls. It was bound to happen sometime, honey. Humanity was gonna take that great leap forward. And a whole lot of people were gonna have to die for it to happen. A whole generation of us.

"Maybe shoulda been the one before mine. Or the one before them. But it wasn't."

Deanni sniffed. "Wow. You're still real sharp, Grandma Krista."

"Yeah," she said flatly. "Always had to be."

Krista looked at Siobhan, the angles of their face the same underneath, even where the lines diverged, or had not yet bloomed on the younger woman.

"That's wisdom," Krista said. "Knowing when you're the sin-eater. Knowing when you need to go away to die for everyone's sake. And if the sin-eaters before you won't go, then someone else gets the job. They don't go away. The sins of the past just pile up. Someone's gotta eat. They died rich, and we inherited their sins.

"Humanity was gonna take that great leap forward. And a whole lot of people were gonna have to die for it to happen."

"My grandparents didn't know it, honey. My parents didn't know it. And it cost me and my whole generation our lives. I'm here because we didn't let it cost you *yours*."

****

It was time to go. I gave her a hug. We took some pictures on her phone and she showed me, again,
how she would have uploaded them to the sites that were now all archives. I couldn't believe it, the way she missed it.

"Giving all of those secrets about your life away for free?" I chided her gently into her thin, wiry hair.

"It didn't feel like giving it away, then," she muttered. She pulled back from the hug, squinted. "Your girlfriend's pretty. I think."

"You're a fucking *baddie*," Deanni fried. It was a pretty good impression of the way girls talked in Grandma's day. I smiled. So did Grandma.

"I wanna go outside," said Grandma Krista.

"No!" my reaction was immediate, prescriptive. "Absolutely not."

"What's gonna happen?" She had a point. "It's not like you're air-locking me into space. This place has an entire hospital where the Belk's used to be. If I stop breathing, they'll come help me back up. Just take me to the door and open it?"

She could tell she had to bargain. Grandma was shrewd like that. "I won't even step outside," she tried.

"C'mon, Grandma!" Deanni stood up, slapping her palms on the table. "Let's do this! But we have to stop to steal some earrings on the way."

We followed right behind her as she zipped ahead on her walker-scooter, trailing like parents at the park.

"Don't be worried."

"I'm not letting her out. First of all, the sun alone—"

"It's just her getting to see a door open! It'll make her feel like a badass."

"I'm going to have the nurse on standby."

"No, they'll stop you. Besides, it's a nursing home. *Nursing mall.* Whatever. Just yell if you need a *nurse.* One'll show up."

Grandma Krista leaned toward the door, a little closer than I would have liked. But there were two doors between her and the outside. Both had once been glass, but were now replaced with more modern materials manufactured under up-to-date protocols. None of these doors would open for any patient. But they would open for Deanni and me.

Grandma slid a pair of plastic knockoff RayBans onto her face and threw her arms back like a skydiver.

"I'm ready."

I opened the doors, and for a moment everything seemed perfect. Grandma stepped over the threshold and her old roguish smile came back into her face, like the cat that had caught the canary. The air rushed in and out. From my side of the door I saw the walker topple and for a scant second, thought she'd thrown it into the street, a superhero casting off her glasses to reveal her true form. The light that hit her hair *bloomed*, from gray into the old-fashioned teal-blue and pinks she washed into it. The pink became orange, and then red, and then white, and I thought perhaps that something *magical* was happening, something her body was resisting, and then I felt Deanni's little nails on my arm again.

"*Oh no.*"

Grandma Krista was burning.

Not up in flames, but simmering, expanding burns, like old pieces of film. She grew white hot and came apart. Where the air outside hit her skin, it turned bruise-black and blistered, swelling and bubbling up with a sickening sound. Grandma Krista made a sound like "*up!*" and simply raised a hand in shock as her knees turned to liquid and her feet buckled out below her.

The doors whooshed with the blood in my ears as I sprinted through to her. I heard screaming. It wasn't Grandma's. Her throat was mostly liquid.

The air, the light, the heat, the germs, it was all too much. All she'd wanted was my help, and I was willing to give her anything—but this was all wrong. She had accepted sickness, like all of the Old Folk had, but not this. Not a pure rejection from the only planet she'd ever known. Nothing could undo what had been done to her body and mind. Nothing could erase the burden of the sins the Old Folk had eaten. And now Grandma Krista was dead.

She hadn't meant to die like this. Another betrayal. That was clear from her panicked, bodiless look in her final moments. A woman who'd never been given anything, who worked herself into nothing, had to spend her dying days in a monument to things no one needed. And she died in the parking lot, trying to breathe the air.

A nurse touched me. She threw a sheet over the remains of Grandma Krista. The sheet became wet, and soaked her up. I could see two small, hard orbs I distantly realized had to be her eyes, somehow preserved into marbles when everything else became jelly.

"Stress, viruses, their whole life spent in war? The toxicity of the environment they were raised in?" The nurse said, matter-of-factly. "Their bodies can't handle it, sweetheart. That's why we have rules.

"You didn't mean to kill your grandma. This world just wasn't meant for them."

End

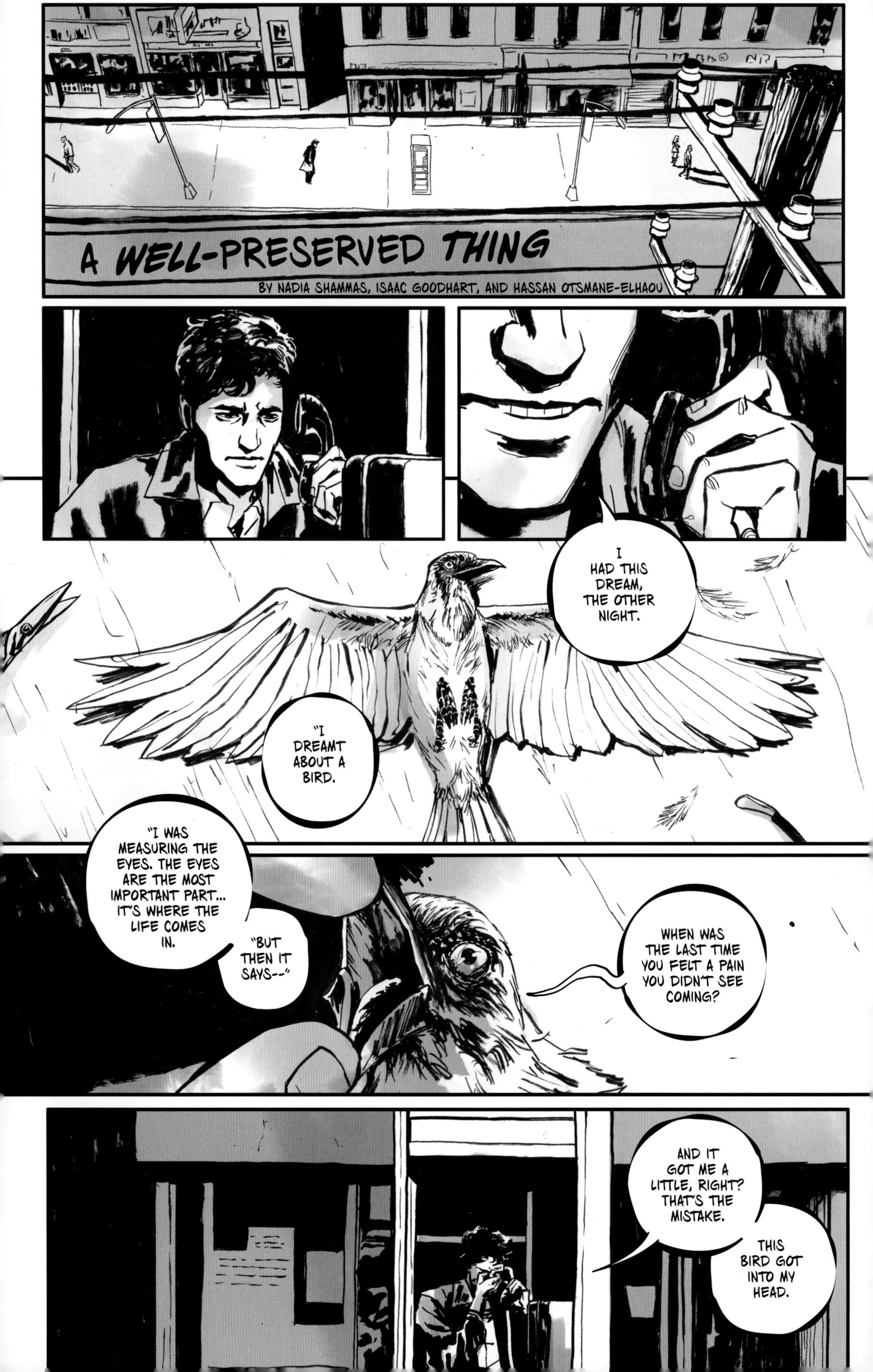
A WELL-PRESERVED THING
BY NADIA SHAMMAS, ISAAC GOODHART, AND HASSAN OTSMANE-ELHAOU
I HAD THIS DREAM, THE OTHER NIGHT.
"I DREAMT ABOUT A BIRD.
"I WAS MEASURING THE EYES. THE EYES ARE THE MOST IMPORTANT PART... IT'S WHERE THE LIFE COMES IN.
"BUT THEN IT SAYS--"
WHEN WAS THE LAST TIME YOU FELT A PAIN YOU DIDN'T SEE COMING?
AND IT GOT ME A LITTLE, RIGHT? THAT'S THE MISTAKE.
THIS BIRD GOT INTO MY HEAD.

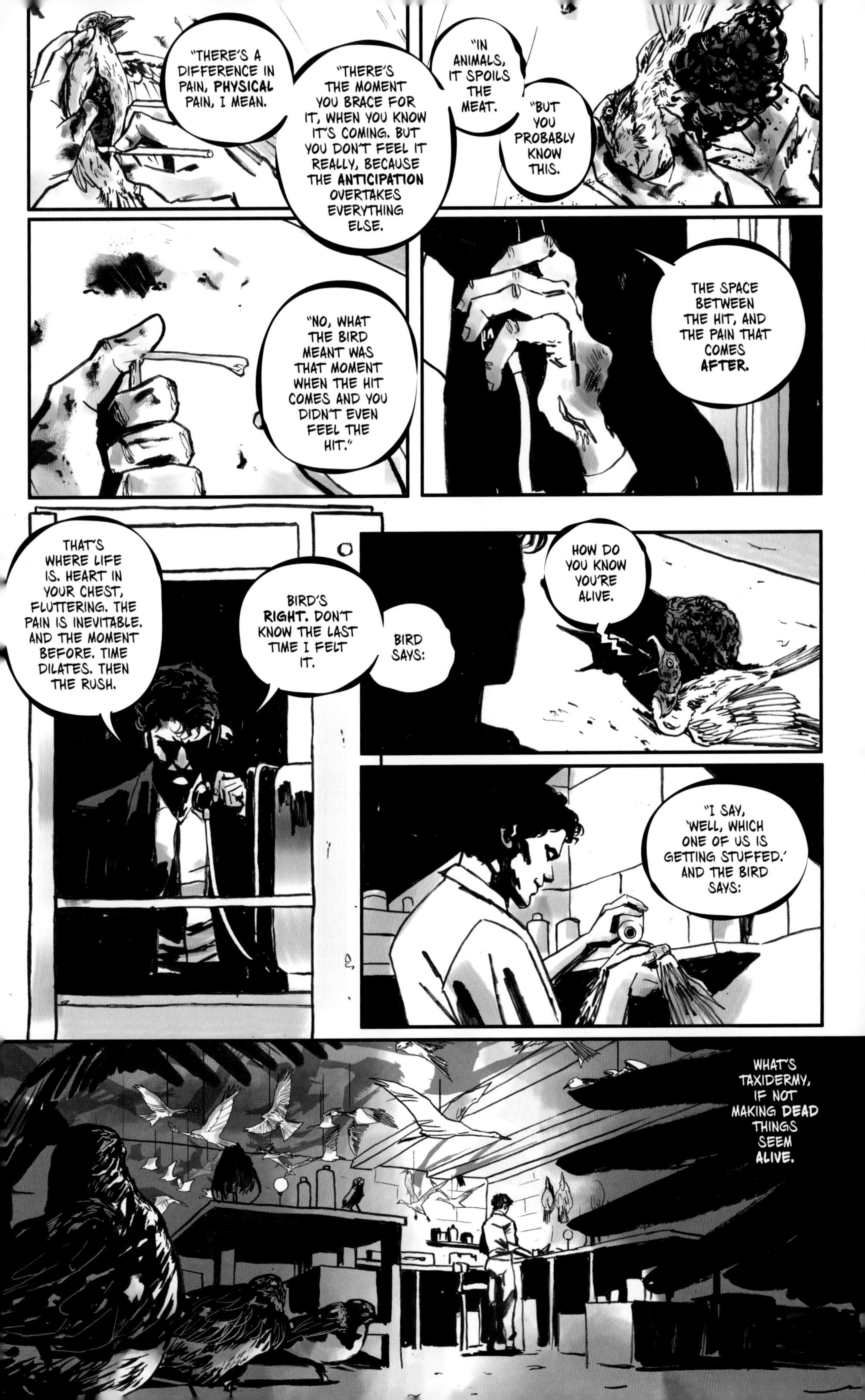
"THERE'S A DIFFERENCE IN PAIN, PHYSICAL PAIN, I MEAN.
"THERE'S THE MOMENT YOU BRACE FOR IT, WHEN YOU KNOW IT'S COMING. BUT YOU DON'T FEEL IT REALLY, BECAUSE THE ANTICIPATION OVERTAKES EVERYTHING ELSE.
"IN ANIMALS, IT SPOILS THE MEAT.
"BUT YOU PROBABLY KNOW THIS.
"NO, WHAT THE BIRD MEANT WAS THAT MOMENT WHEN THE HIT COMES AND YOU DIDN'T EVEN FEEL THE HIT."
THE SPACE BETWEEN THE HIT, AND THE PAIN THAT COMES AFTER.
THAT'S WHERE LIFE IS. HEART IN YOUR CHEST, FLUTTERING. THE PAIN IS INEVITABLE. AND THE MOMENT BEFORE. TIME DILATES. THEN THE RUSH.
BIRD'S RIGHT. DON'T KNOW THE LAST TIME I FELT IT.
BIRD SAYS:
HOW DO YOU KNOW YOU'RE ALIVE.
"I SAY, 'WELL, WHICH ONE OF US IS GETTING STUFFED.' AND THE BIRD SAYS:
WHAT'S TAXIDERMY, IF NOT MAKING DEAD THINGS SEEM ALIVE.

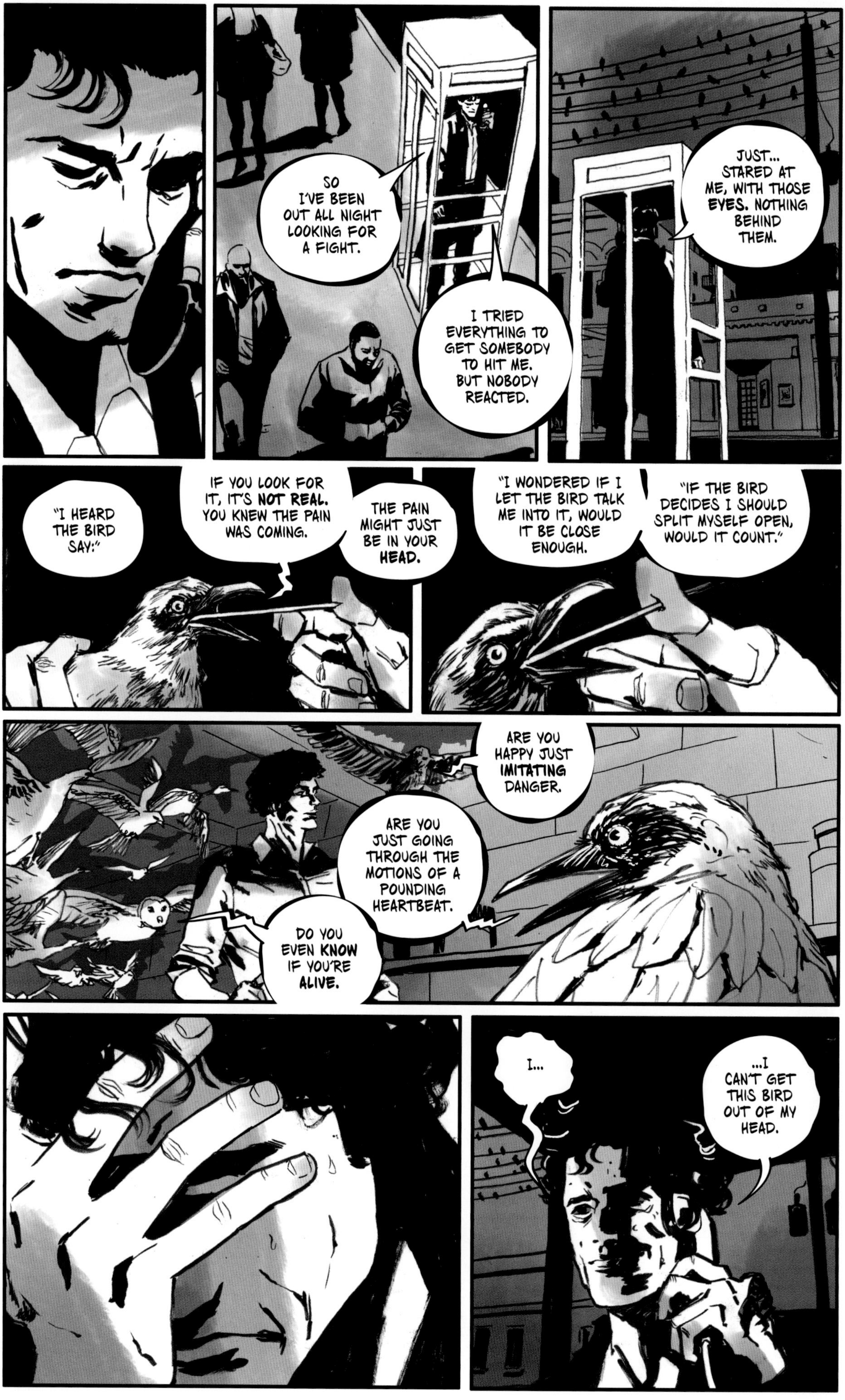
SO I'VE BEEN OUT ALL NIGHT LOOKING FOR A FIGHT.
I TRIED EVERYTHING TO GET SOMEBODY TO HIT ME. BUT NOBODY REACTED.
JUST... STARED AT ME, WITH THOSE EYES. NOTHING BEHIND THEM.
"I HEARD THE BIRD SAY:"
IF YOU LOOK FOR IT, IT'S NOT REAL. YOU KNEW THE PAIN WAS COMING.
THE PAIN MIGHT JUST BE IN YOUR HEAD.
"I WONDERED IF I LET THE BIRD TALK ME INTO IT, WOULD IT BE CLOSE ENOUGH.
"IF THE BIRD DECIDES I SHOULD SPLIT MYSELF OPEN, WOULD IT COUNT."
ARE YOU HAPPY JUST IMITATING DANGER.
ARE YOU JUST GOING THROUGH THE MOTIONS OF A POUNDING HEARTBEAT.
DO YOU EVEN KNOW IF YOU'RE ALIVE.
I...
...I CAN'T GET THIS BIRD OUT OF MY HEAD.

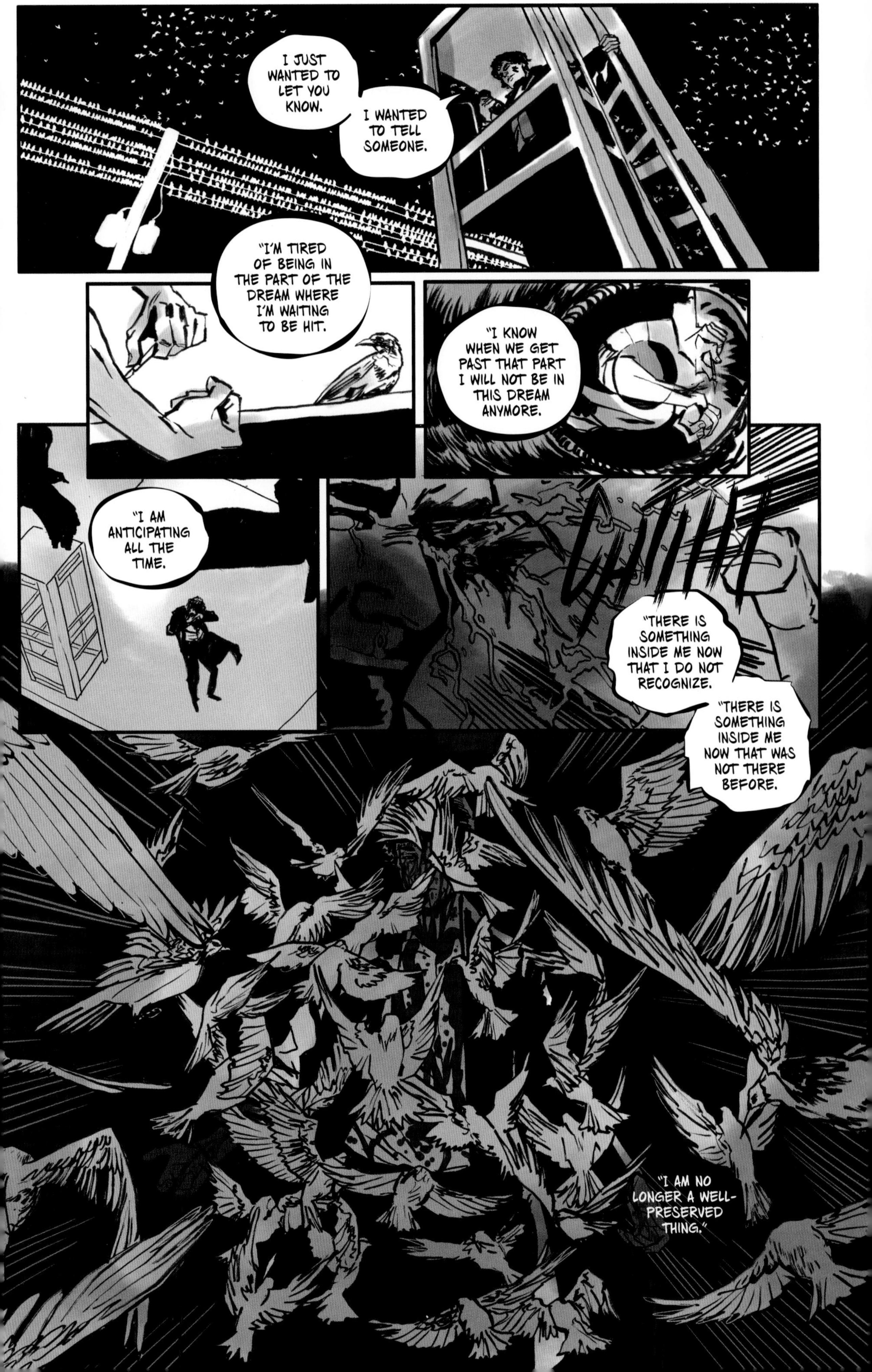
I JUST WANTED TO LET YOU KNOW.
I WANTED TO TELL SOMEONE.
"I'M TIRED OF BEING IN THE PART OF THE DREAM WHERE I'M WAITING TO BE HIT.
"I KNOW WHEN WE GET PAST THAT PART I WILL NOT BE IN THIS DREAM ANYMORE.
"I AM ANTICIPATING ALL THE TIME.
"THERE IS SOMETHING INSIDE ME NOW THAT I DO NOT RECOGNIZE.
"THERE IS SOMETHING INSIDE ME NOW THAT WAS NOT THERE BEFORE.
"I AM NO LONGER A WELL-PRESERVED THING."

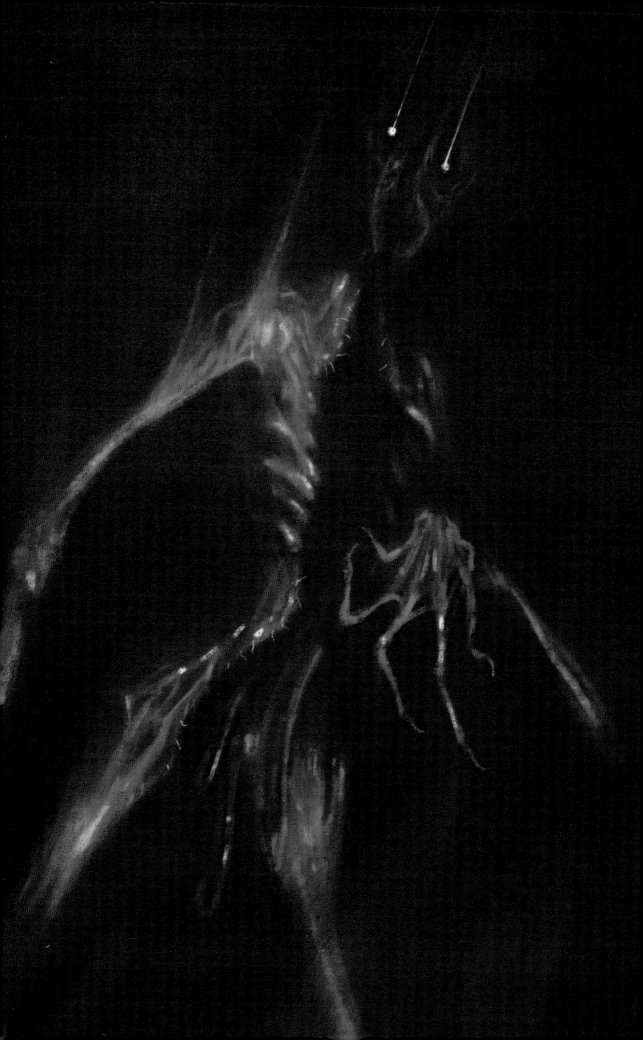

"The Empty Man"

In regards to the new one that's been giving us so much grief lately:

An emaciated figure, with a gaping wound through its midsection devoid of any internal organs. At least semi-tangible, it seems to be able to interact with the physical world at will, with disastrously violent effect.

This entity has been seen on multiple occasions, all within a two-block radius of the presumed resting place. Time of day does not seem to matter, we've seen it in the daylight just as often as night encounters. As it differs wildly with the exhumed [redacted] currently in agency custody, it's presumed that the appearance of the [redacted] serves a specific purpose that we are not aware of as of yet. It is possible that it is actively trying to scare us.

Unlike other [redacted] this one seems to be particularly vicious, with quite the tally of presumed victims and missing persons cases attributed to it. It is unclear what exactly it is doing to the people it takes, as it never leaves any corpses behind when it "leaves." If it hadn't wandered into a previous operation in-progress, it's possible we never would have known it was here.

When it's "hunting," it seems as though only its intended victim can see it. Whether this is a tactic designed to disorient and weaken its prey, or whether unveiling its true form holds a ritualistic factor in its ability to influence the natural world, remains to be seen. The open chest cavity and split face seem to factor into how it feeds, opening wide to engulf its victims (See night vision footage of the Connelly house feeding, 10/04/99)

Operation is ongoing, please report to [redacted] with any additional questions.

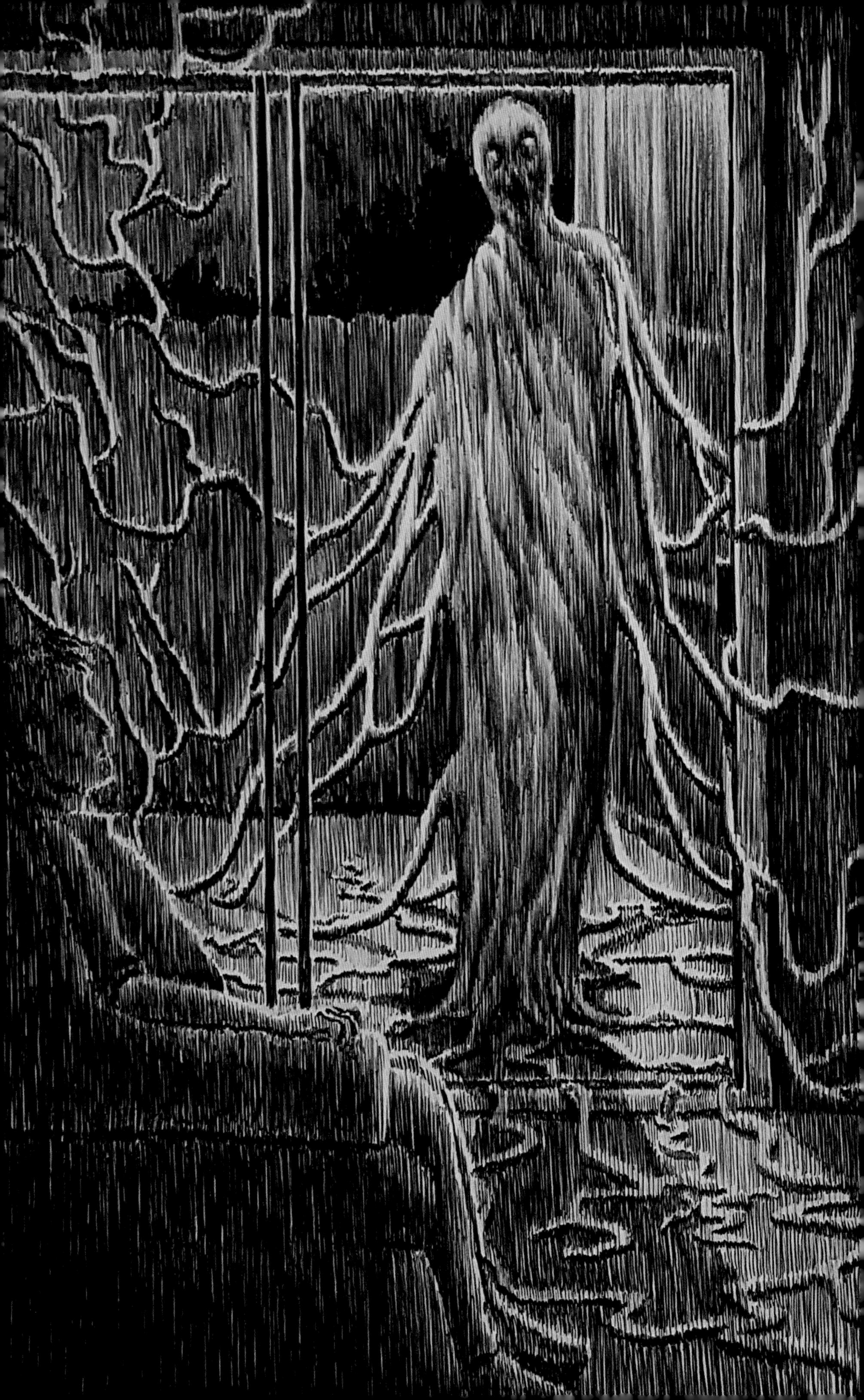

PART OF LEMP COLLAPSED LAST NIGHT.

IT'S WEIRD THAT NO ONE'S FUCKED WITH IT...

RIGHT?

CITY DIDN'T COME PUT UP TAPE. HELL MAN, NO TWEAKERS EVEN CAME TO RIP OUT THE WIRING OR STEAL THE FUCKIN' CEILING TILES!

AND THAT'S WEIRD.

RIGHT?

AIN'T *NOTHIN'* IN THAT PILE OF TRASH WORTH TOUCHIN' – EVEN THE TWEAKERS KNOW THAT.

LOTTA PEOPLE DIED IN THERE.

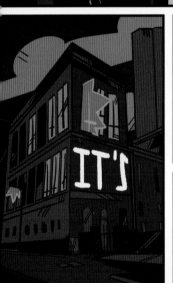

IT'S

HAUNTED

AS FUCK.

THAT PLACE...

(YOU DON'T KNOW 'CAUSE YOU AIN'T BEEN HERE THAT LONG.)

BAD SHIT HAPPENED IN THAT PLACE,

THIS AIN'T THE FIRST TIME IT'S COLLAPSED.

(DAMN NEAR EVERYTHING TOUCHES THAT P.O.S. BUILDING COLLAPSES.)

AND I KNOW WE DON'T KNOW EACH OTHER REAL WELL...

(...WHAT WITH YOU NOT REALLY BEIN' FROM HERE AND ALL...)

...BUT YOU LOOK LIKE YOU GOT ENOUGH GHOSTS HAUNTIN' YOUR HOUSE ALREADY.

MAYBE YOU LEAVE THIS ONE...

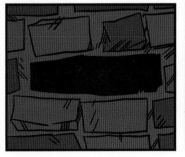

ALONE.

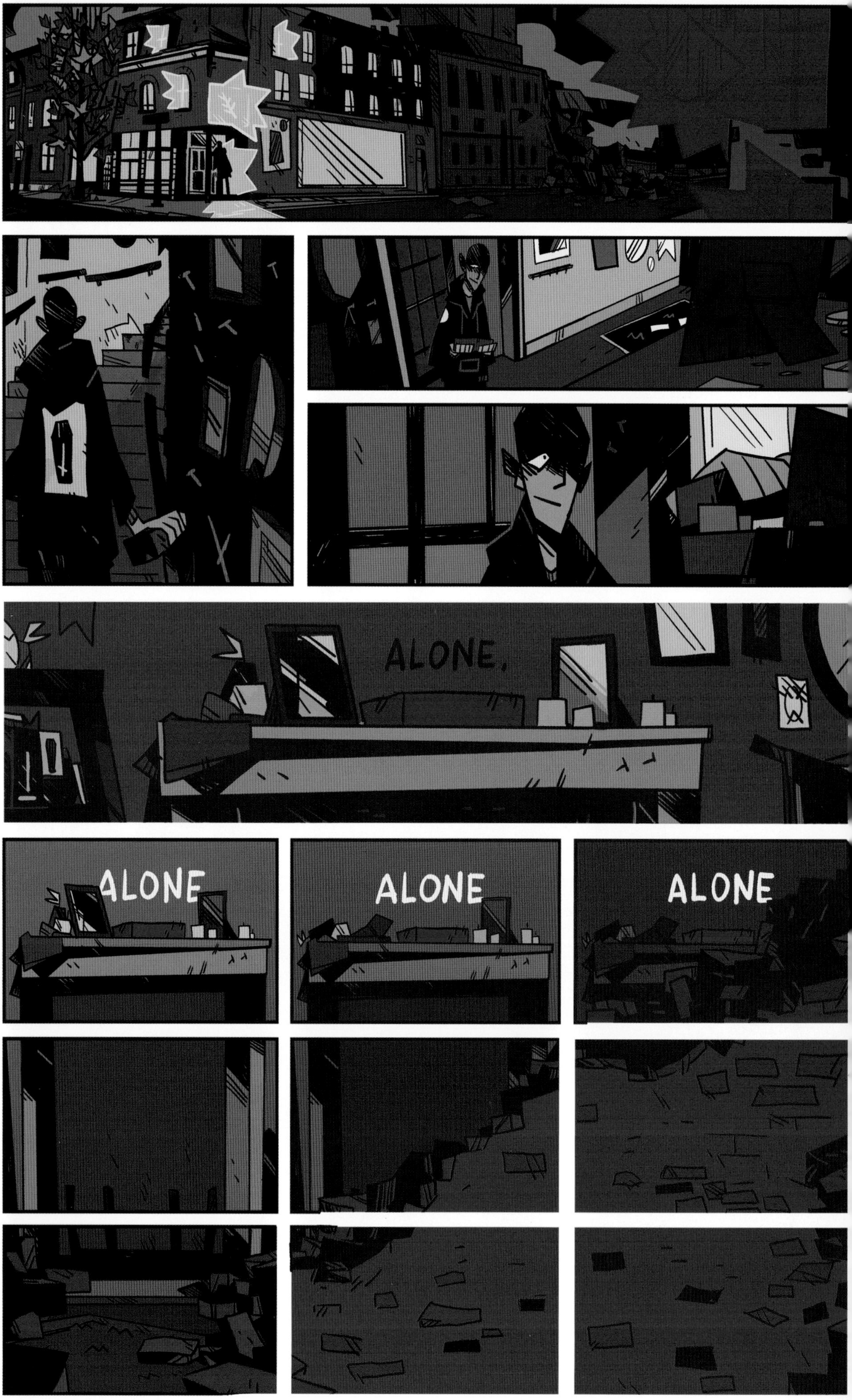
ALONE.
ALONE
ALONE
ALONE

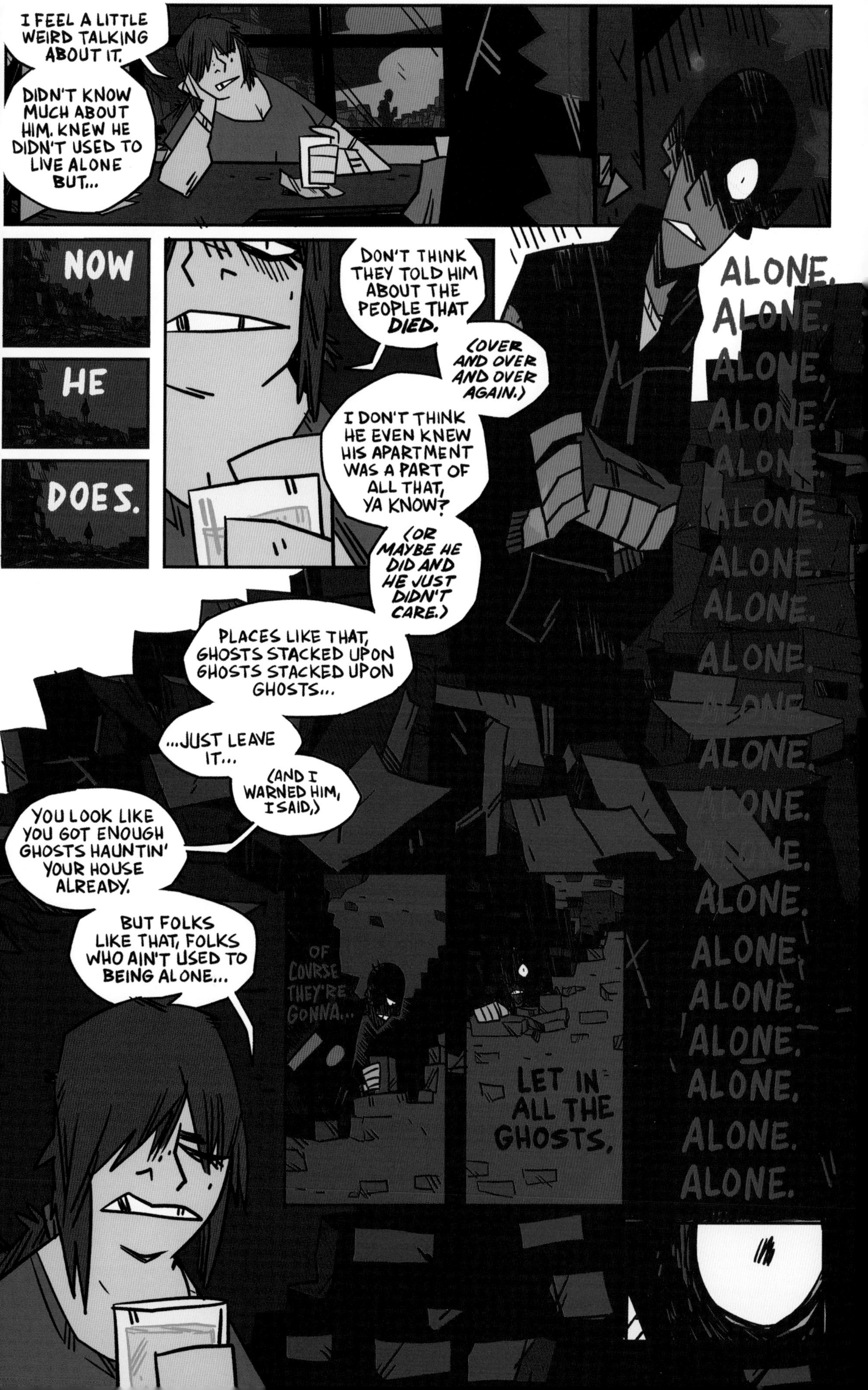
I FEEL A LITTLE WEIRD TALKING ABOUT IT.
DIDN'T KNOW MUCH ABOUT HIM. KNEW HE DIDN'T USED TO LIVE ALONE BUT...
NOW
HE
DOES.
DON'T THINK THEY TOLD HIM ABOUT THE PEOPLE THAT DIED.
(OVER AND OVER AND OVER AGAIN.)
I DON'T THINK HE EVEN KNEW HIS APARTMENT WAS A PART OF ALL THAT, YA KNOW?
(OR MAYBE HE DID AND HE JUST DIDN'T CARE.)
PLACES LIKE THAT, GHOSTS STACKED UPON GHOSTS STACKED UPON GHOSTS...
...JUST LEAVE IT...
(AND I WARNED HIM, I SAID,)
YOU LOOK LIKE YOU GOT ENOUGH GHOSTS HAUNTIN' YOUR HOUSE ALREADY.
BUT FOLKS LIKE THAT, FOLKS WHO AIN'T USED TO BEING ALONE...
OF COURSE THEY'RE GONNA...
LET IN ALL THE GHOSTS.
ALONE. ALONE. ALONE. ALONE. ALONE. ALONE. ALONE. ALONE. ALONE. ALONE. ALONE. ALONE. ALONE. ALONE. ALONE. ALONE. ALONE. ALONE.

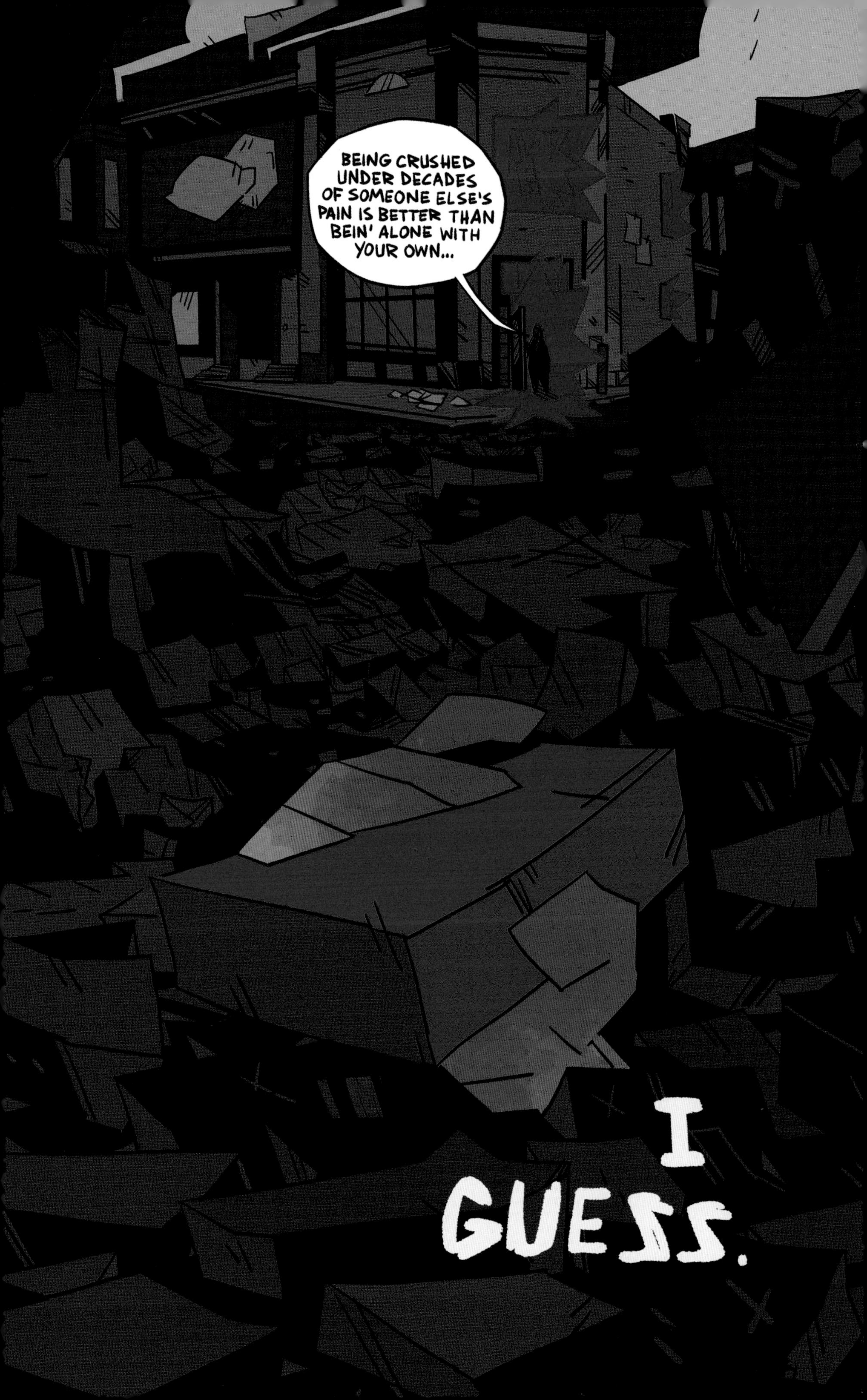
BEING CRUSHED UNDER DECADES OF SOMEONE ELSE'S PAIN IS BETTER THAN BEIN' ALONE WITH YOUR OWN...
I GUESS.

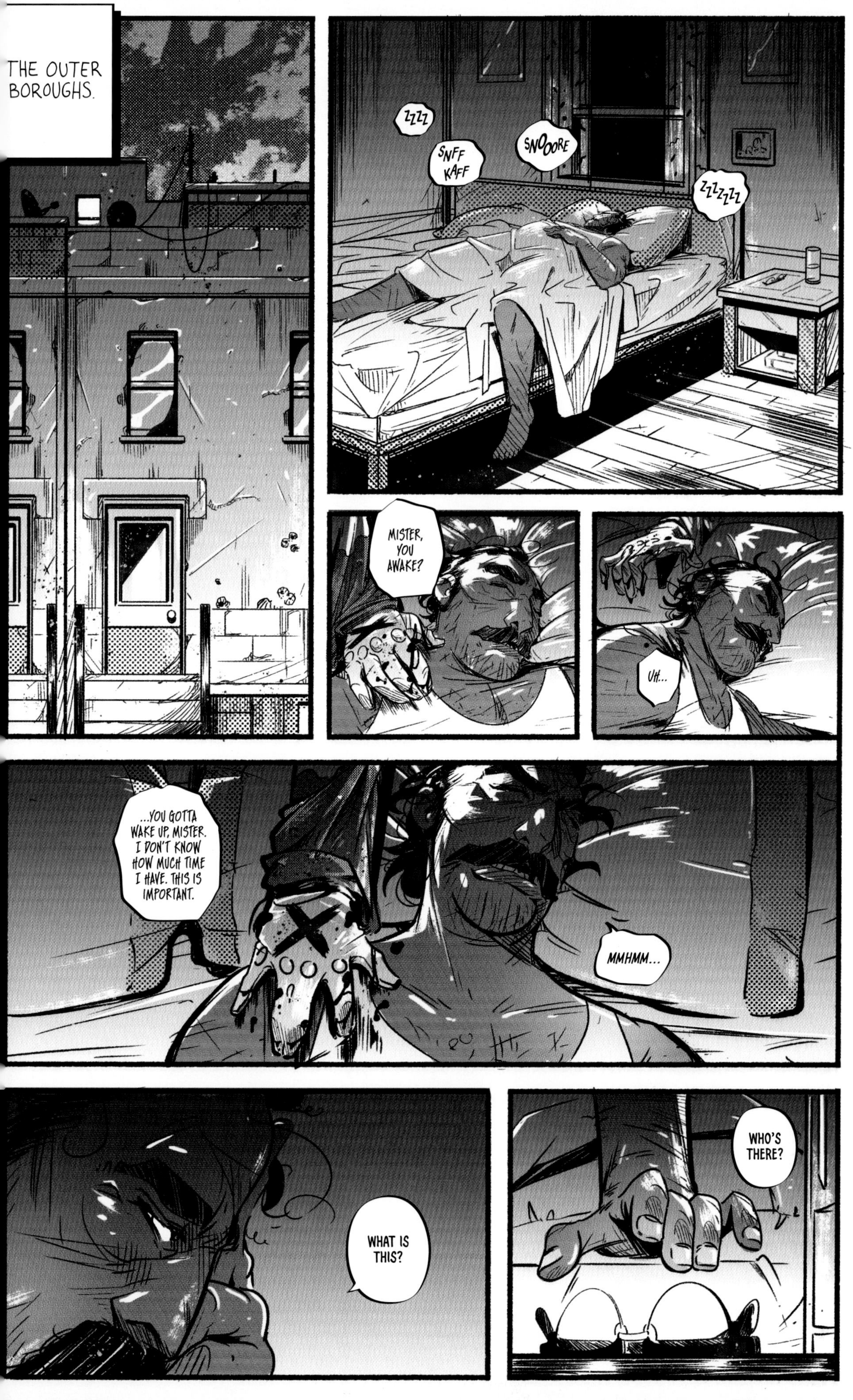
THE OUTER BOROUGHS.
ZZZZ
SNFF KAFF
SNOOORE
ZZZZZZ
MISTER, YOU AWAKE?
UH...
...YOU GOTTA WAKE UP, MISTER. I DON'T KNOW HOW MUCH TIME I HAVE. THIS IS IMPORTANT.
MMHMM...
WHAT IS THIS?
WHO'S THERE?

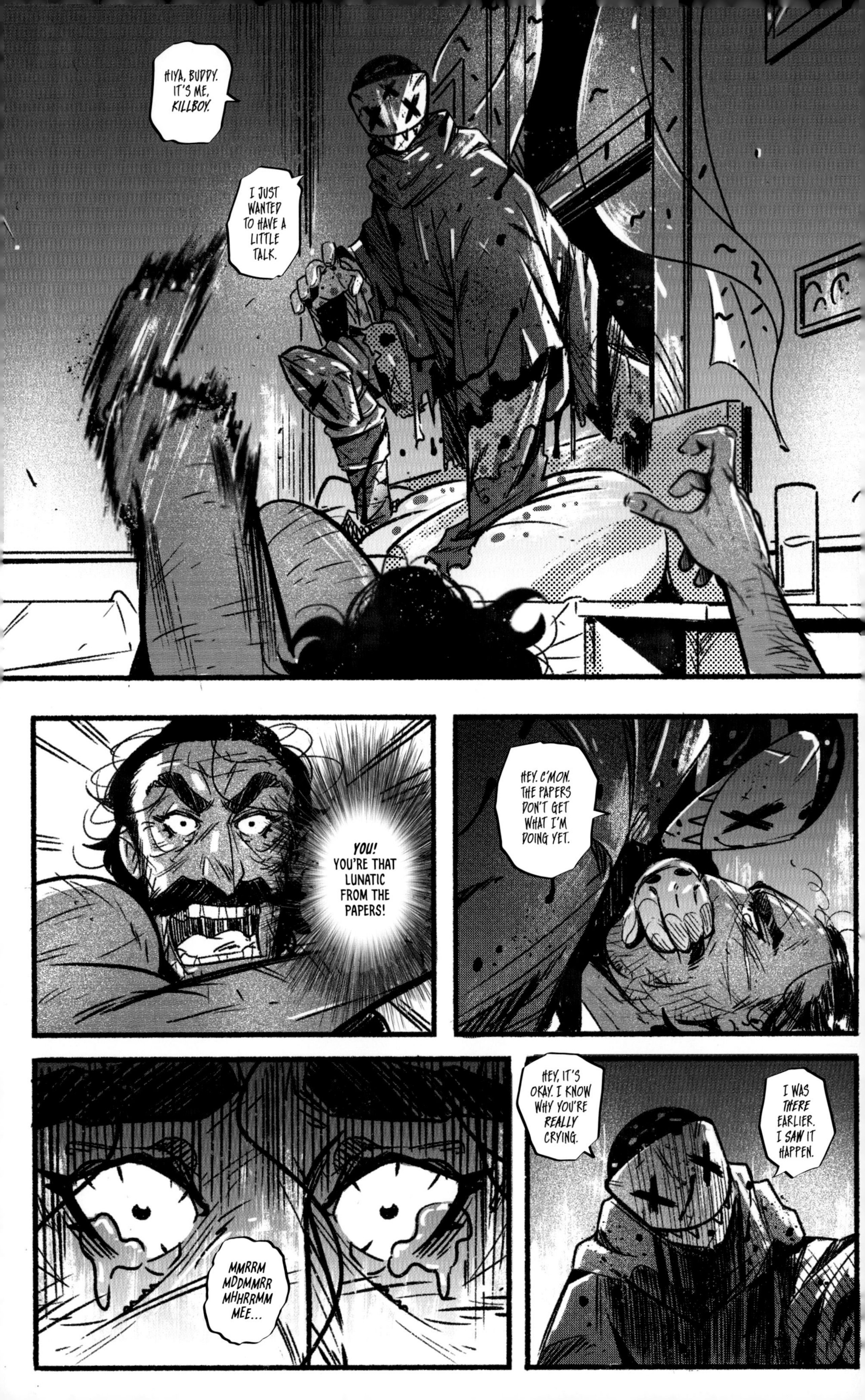
HIYA, BUDDY. IT'S ME, KILLBOY.
I JUST WANTED TO HAVE A LITTLE TALK.
YOU! YOU'RE THAT LUNATIC FROM THE PAPERS!
HEY. C'MON. THE PAPERS DON'T GET WHAT I'M DOING YET.
MMRRM MDDMMRR MHHRRMM MEE...
HEY, IT'S OKAY. I KNOW WHY YOU'RE REALLY CRYING.
I WAS THERE EARLIER. I SAW IT HAPPEN.

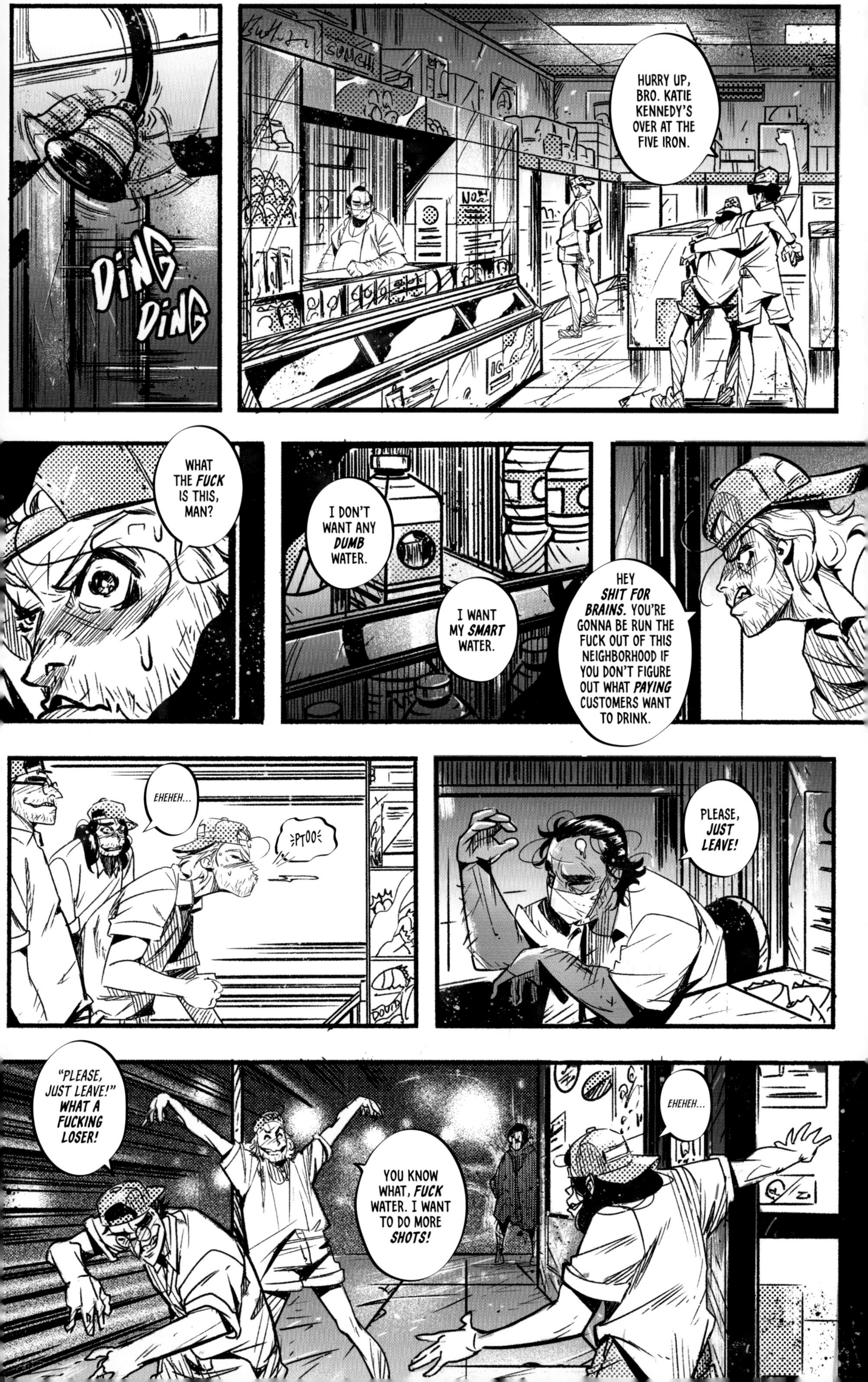
DING
DING
HURRY UP, BRO. KATIE KENNEDY'S OVER AT THE FIVE IRON.
WHAT THE FUCK IS THIS, MAN?
I DON'T WANT ANY DUMB WATER.
I WANT MY SMART WATER.
HEY SHIT FOR BRAINS. YOU'RE GONNA BE RUN THE FUCK OUT OF THIS NEIGHBORHOOD IF YOU DON'T FIGURE OUT WHAT PAYING CUSTOMERS WANT TO DRINK.
EHEHEH...
PTOO
PLEASE, JUST LEAVE!
"PLEASE, JUST LEAVE!" WHAT A FUCKING LOSER!
YOU KNOW WHAT, FUCK WATER. I WANT TO DO MORE SHOTS!
EHEHEH...

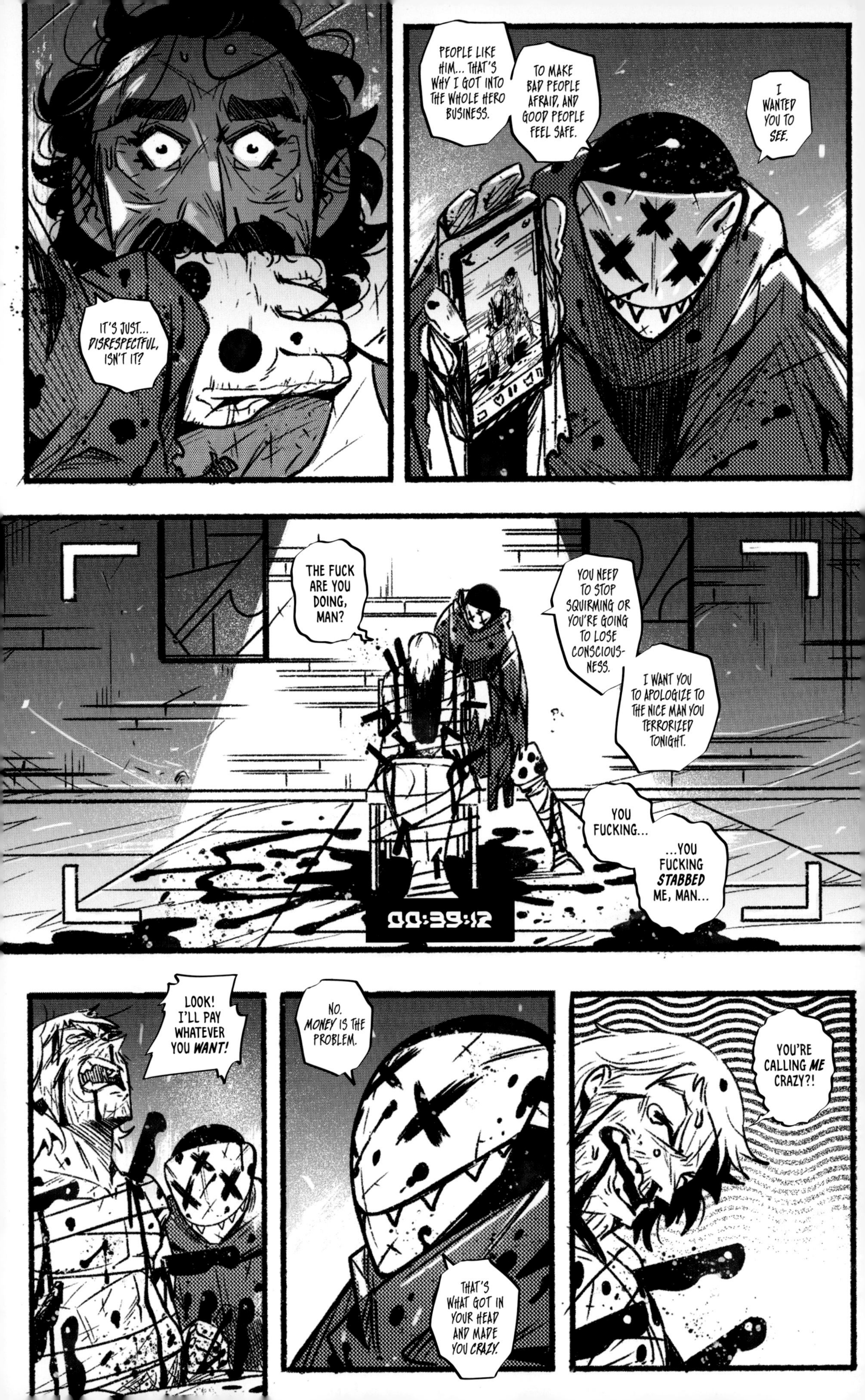
IT'S JUST... DISRESPECTFUL, ISN'T IT?
PEOPLE LIKE HIM... THAT'S WHY I GOT INTO THE WHOLE HERO BUSINESS.
TO MAKE BAD PEOPLE AFRAID, AND GOOD PEOPLE FEEL SAFE.
I WANTED YOU TO SEE.
THE FUCK ARE YOU DOING, MAN?
YOU NEED TO STOP SQUIRMING OR YOU'RE GOING TO LOSE CONSCIOUS-NESS.
I WANT YOU TO APOLOGIZE TO THE NICE MAN YOU TERRORIZED TONIGHT.
YOU FUCKING...
...YOU FUCKING STABBED ME, MAN...
00:39:12
LOOK! I'LL PAY WHATEVER YOU WANT!
NO. MONEY IS THE PROBLEM.
THAT'S WHAT GOT IN YOUR HEAD AND MADE YOU CRAZY.
YOU'RE CALLING ME CRAZY?!

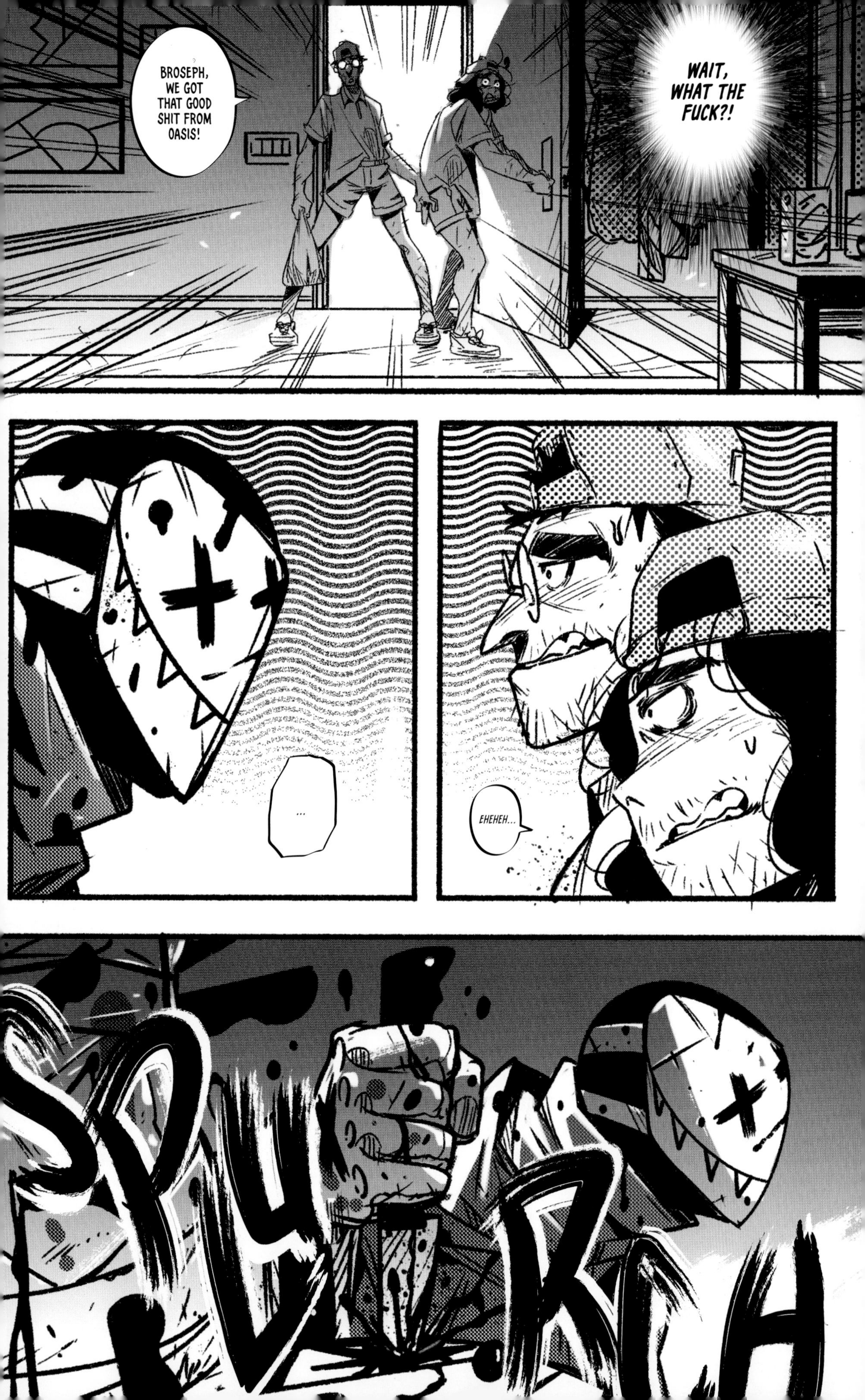
BROSEPH, WE GOT THAT GOOD SHIT FROM OASIS!
WAIT, WHAT THE FUCK?!
...
EHEHEH...
SPLURCH

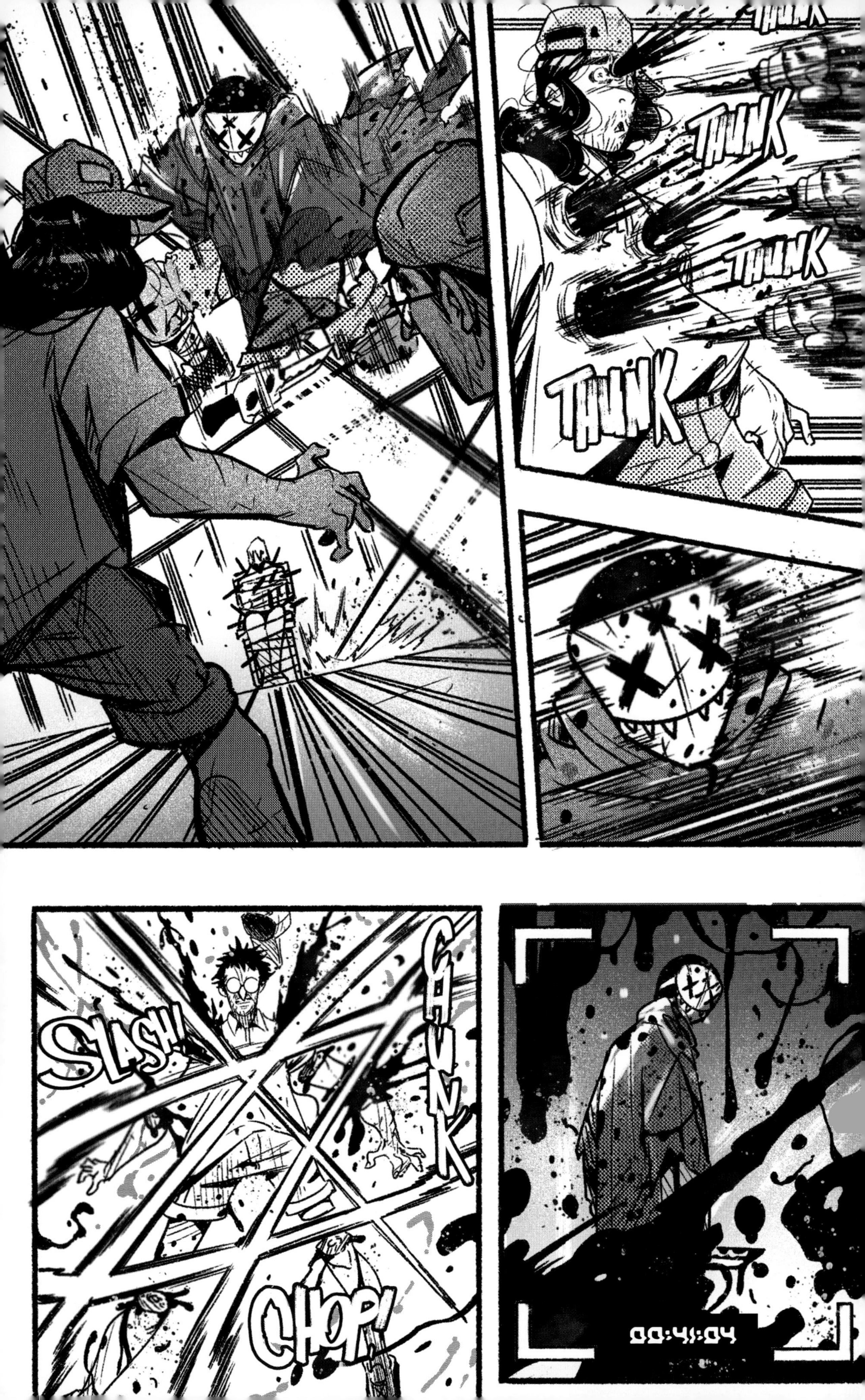
THUNK
THUNK
THUNK
THUNK
SLASH!
CHUNK
CHOP!
00:41:04

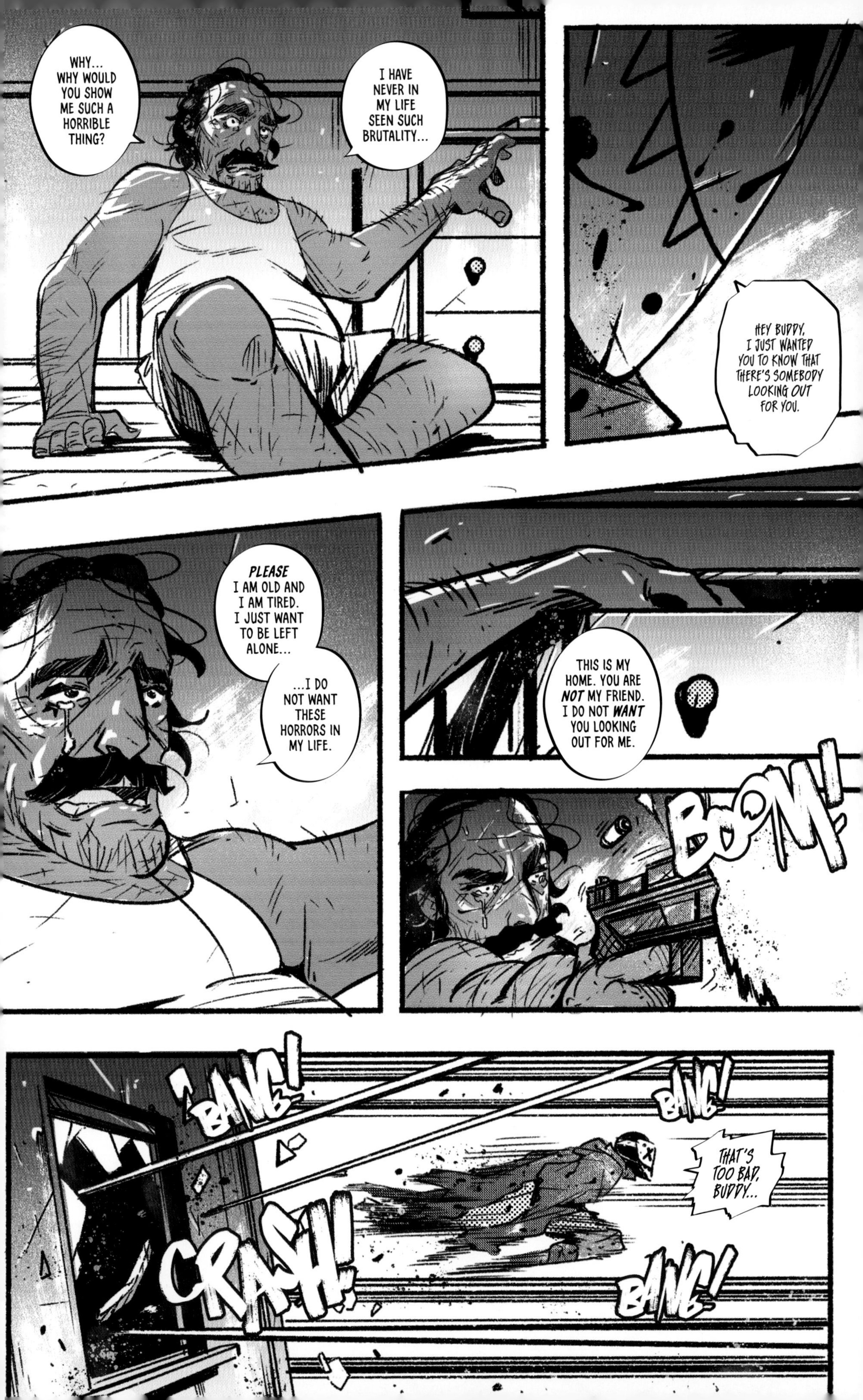
WHY... WHY WOULD YOU SHOW ME SUCH A HORRIBLE THING?
I HAVE NEVER IN MY LIFE SEEN SUCH BRUTALITY...
HEY BUDDY, I JUST WANTED YOU TO KNOW THAT THERE'S SOMEBODY LOOKING OUT FOR YOU.
PLEASE I AM OLD AND I AM TIRED. I JUST WANT TO BE LEFT ALONE...
...I DO NOT WANT THESE HORRORS IN MY LIFE.
THIS IS MY HOME. YOU ARE NOT MY FRIEND. I DO NOT WANT YOU LOOKING OUT FOR ME.
BOOM!
BANG!
BANG!
THAT'S TOO BAD, BUDDY...
CRASH!
BANG!

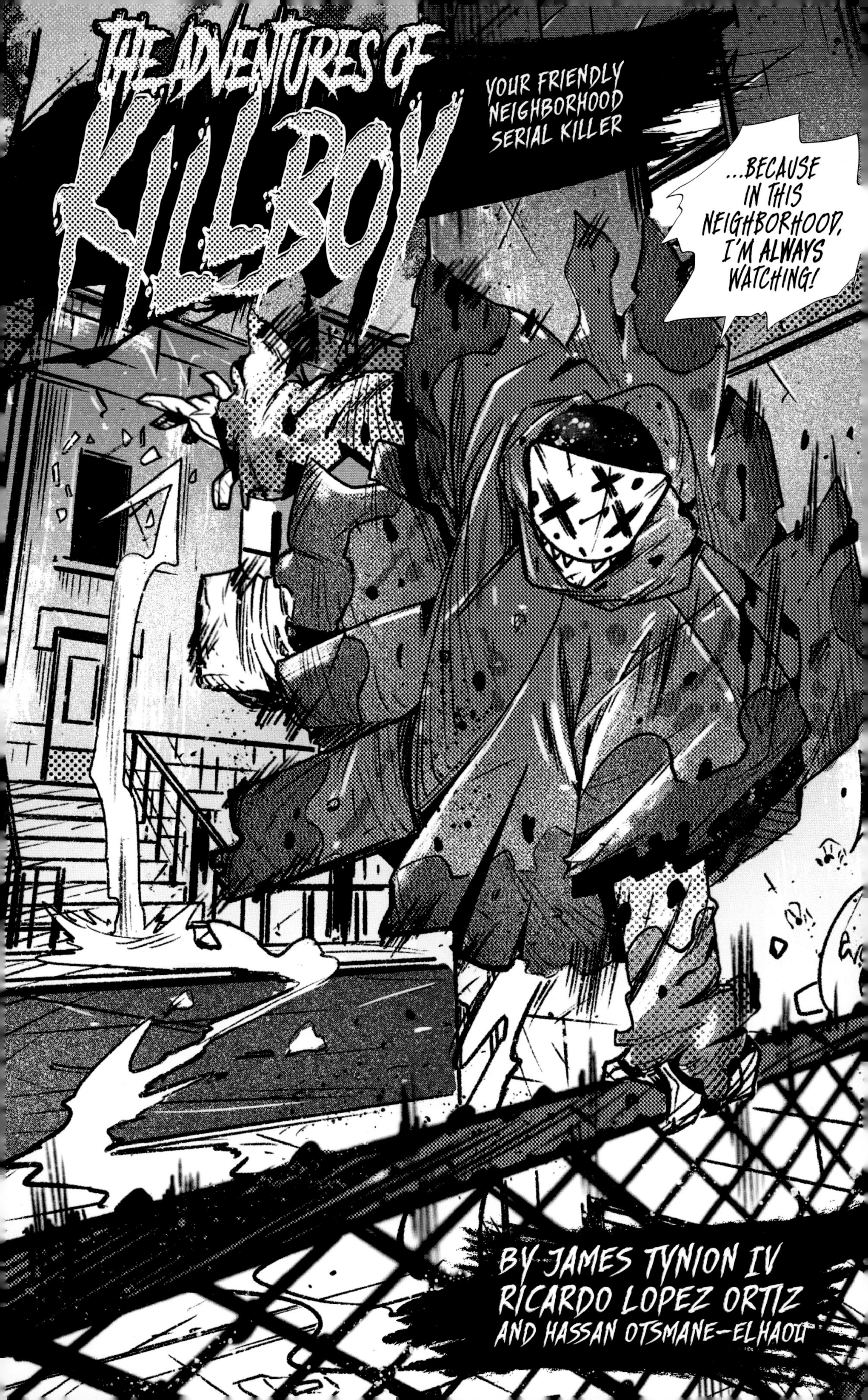
THE ADVENTURES OF KILLBOY
YOUR FRIENDLY NEIGHBORHOOD SERIAL KILLER
...BECAUSE IN THIS NEIGHBORHOOD, I'M ALWAYS WATCHING!
BY JAMES TYNION IV
RICARDO LOPEZ ORTIZ
AND HASSAN OTSMANE-ELHAOU

KINDRED SPIRITS

ZACK DAVISSON INTERVIEWS GOU TANABE

The first time I heard of Gou Tanabe was on a panel at Rose City Comic Con. I was onstage with Carl Horn, who was announcing upcoming manga licenses for Dark Horse. In the list was an adaptation of HP Lovecraft's *The Hound and Other Stories*. I immediately started scheming on how I could be given the job to translate it. It wasn't that I was a fan of the artist; to be honest I really didn't give much thought to who made the comic. But I loved Lovecraft. I was (and am) a lifelong Lovecraft fan, since my mother bought me a copy of *Bloodcurdling Tales of Horror and the Macabre: The Best of H. P. Lovecraft* when I was about eight years old. Warts and all—and yes, Lovecraft has MANY warts, which we will get into later—he remains one of my favorite authors. Long story short, I begged and pleaded my way into the job. I didn't have many expectations beyond getting to work on something Lovecraft. And then I got the book...

From the first page, I knew that Gou Tanabe was something special. His artwork was amazing, of course. But other amazing artists have tackled Lovecraft with less success. No, Tanabe brought something special. Something other artists hadn't managed to achieve.

Part of it was that Tanabe was tackling Lovecraft's, well, worse stories. He wasn't playing the hits, or even the B-sides. Or the C-sides. Tanabe was all the way down into the Z catalog. The first story in the book was "The Temple," a minor short story I had forgotten Lovecraft had even written. The other stories were equally obscure. "The Hound." "The Nameless City." Not exactly blockbusters. This ended up in Tanabe's favor. While there are numerous adaptations of "The Call of Cthulhu," "The Colour Out of Space," and *The Shadow Over Innsmouth*, by digging into Lovecraft's back catalog, Tanabe was able to essentially tread new ground. There was no one to compare him to. We could take in these stories as if we had never seen them before; because likely, we hadn't. No one had bothered.

The other thing was Tanabe's approach. So many artists attempted to manifest the craziness of Lovecraft, the madness. But Tanabe was the opposite. His work was coldly clinical. It was precise. Almost scientific. And he let Lovecraft be Lovecraft. Tanabe made no attempts to stylize the work, or to transform or redeem it. Instead, Tanabe took what was on the page and rendered it in intricately detailed line. And by doing so created what I believe to be the greatest adaptations of Lovecraft's stories made in any medium.

And there is one more thing about Gou Tanabe that is unique, although this one is personal. Tanabe is personable. This may not sound like much, but in the world of Japanese comic artists it is almost unheard of. Most artists cloak themselves behind pseudonyms and carefully hide their image. One artist, Paru Itagaki, famously only makes public appearances wearing a chicken mask in order to protect her identity. I have signed multiple contracts where it is expressly written that I am forbidden contact with the artist. By contrast, when *The Hound and Other Stories* was announced and with me as the translator, much to my surprise Gou Tanabe hit me up on Twitter and jumped into my DMs saying, "Hey!" We've stayed in touch ever since.

Razorblades offered me the chance to chat with Gou Tanabe and learn more about him.

We were both thrilled.

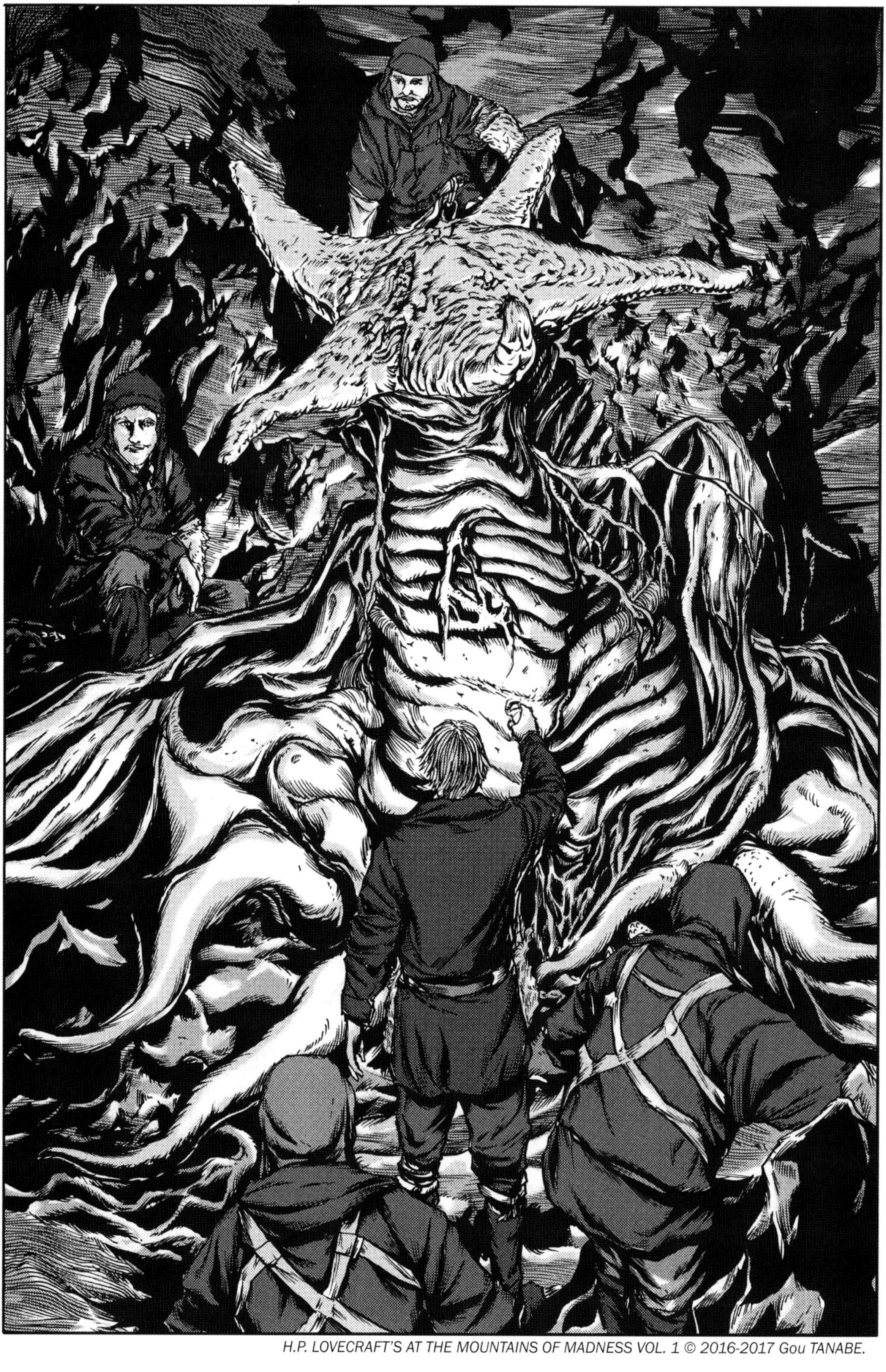

Like many artists, Gou Tanabe combined a lifelong love of art with a dream of breaking into a professional art career. He worked as a delivery man while honing his skills and sending off samples. Finally, he got his break.

"I started drawing comics when I was about 25 years old, I think." said Tanabe. "I started out as an assistant for Kentaro Ueno."

In Japan, it's common for upcoming artists to apprentice with established artists in order to build up their skills and learn the ropes. As assistants they may draw backgrounds, or do inks, or any other number of odd jobs for their boss. Each assistant is hoping for their debut, for an editor to see enough promise in their work that they are given a short solo project. How long you are an assistant can depend on many things, including talent, drive, and potential. Some can stay working as assistants for years.

"I was an assistant for about a week."

Tanabe got his first shot in 2003, creating a comic called *Sunakichi* for *Monthly Comic Beam*, the same magazine where he was working as Ueno's assistant. It told the story of a young boy trapped underground and building a bomb to escape. The story went on to win the Four Seasons and *Comic Beam* New Faces awards for that year.

"I was ecstatic. I remember running home shouting and forcing my grandmother to cheer for me."

He used the prize money to buy drawing tools and supplies, and got ready to produce his next work. But Tanabe had a problem. He was interested in drawing monsters and the macabre but was having a difficult time generating story ideas. An editor he was working with suggested that Tanabe read masterpieces of literature from both inside and outside of Japan. Tanabe read books by Chekhov and Gorky, and Ueda Akinari's *Tales of Moon Light and Rain*. And H.P. Lovecraft.

"I wasn't familiar with Lovecraft at all. I hadn't read any comic adaptation of his work. In Japan, I think most people might know the game *Call of Cthulhu* more than anything else. The role-playing game is popular, as are video games. I'd say the games and the Cthulhu mythology [are] far more popular than Lovecraft himself."

Indeed, Lovecraft is best known in Japan from games, where *Call of Cthulhu* is as synonymous with role-playing games as *Dungeons & Dragons* is in the U.S. Lovecraft's works have been published in Japanese since the 1950s, though they remained obscure. Influential artist Shigeru Mizuki adapted "The Dunwich Horror" in 1962 as *Footsteps from the Depths of the Earth*, although he restaged the story in Japan and many readers may not have even been aware it was an adaptation.

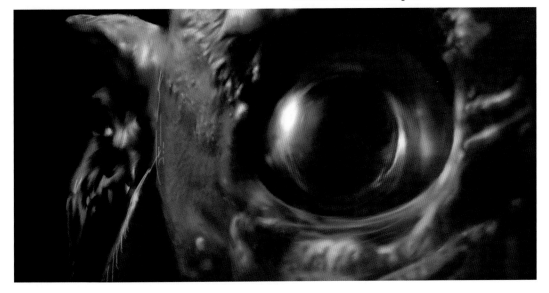

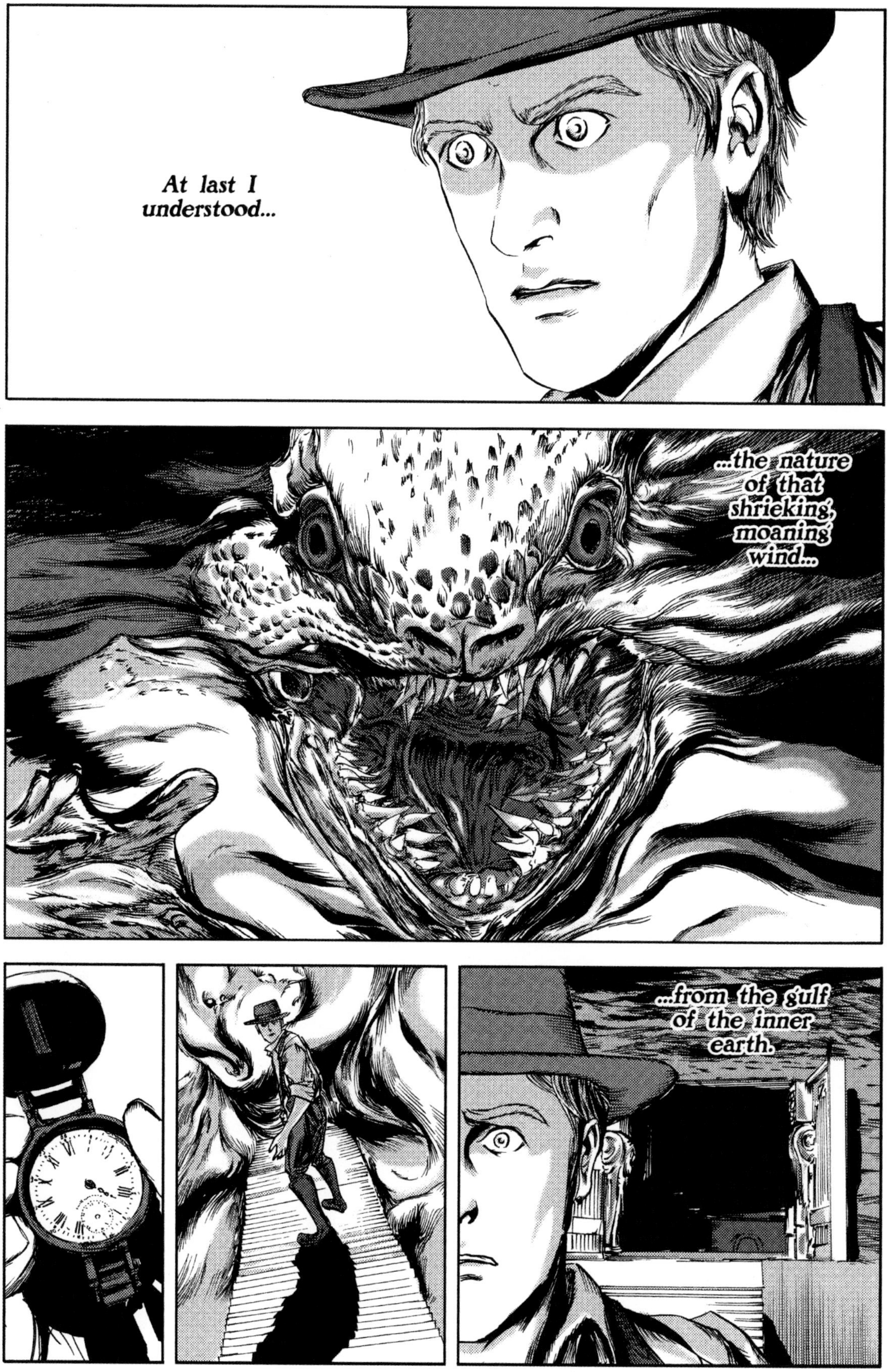
At last I understood...
...the nature of that shrieking, moaning wind...
...from the gulf of the inner earth.

Tanabe was inspired by many of the authors recommended to him by his editor but found what he was looking for in the works of H.P. Lovecraft. Tanabe empathized with the loneliness of Lovecraft's characters. As a self-professed outsider himself, Tanabe identified with Lovecraft's world of isolated artists. He sensed a kindred spirit of sorts and felt that he could make something of this.

In 2004, that same editor asked him to produce another comic. Tanabe did an adaption of Lovecraft's "The Outsider."

"I was still very new and had no real experience as a cartoonist. The editor wanted a 24-page story, so I had to find something to fit that. I think the editor was more enthusiastic about Lovecraft than I was. He could read English and knew the original stories. He was watching my adaptation closely, making sure I didn't stray too far."

Tanabe also said "The Outsider" fit his own feelings at the time. He didn't feel comfortable around other people. He was pessimistic and lonely. There was also a symmetry that "The Outsider" was the first Lovecraft story to be published in book form, in *The Outsider and Others* in 1939.

The editor was very pleased with Tanabe's work and encouraged him to do more Lovecraft. Tanabe followed with adaptations of "Dagon," "The Hound," and "The Nameless City." He found it challenging and fascinating.

"Visualizing that world was challenging, trying to make it a real world where people could live. That was key to me; the hero had to live in the story. And that meant using my own experiences, my own emotions, and the world around me.

"Facial expressions were also important and something I struggled with. I often doubted myself, but my editor was highly skilled and able to guide me through my own fears.

"And then there are monsters. How do you draw something that the writer felt could not be described? I looked at the monsters of some other creators. I love the work of Harryhausen, Mad George, and Takayuki

Takeya. I found many people could do great monsters, but they lacked atmosphere. They lacked mystery. I needed the monsters to work in the mood of the story.

"Physically it is challenging as well. To get my hands to do what I can see in my head."

When talking about Lovecraft, Tanabe rarely mentions words like "horror" or "fear."

"In pop culture, I think the image of Lovecraft has changed completely. No one is scared of Cthulhu anymore. In fact, I wouldn't call what I do horror at all. I would call my work dark, perhaps, but not horror."

Tanabe has done only one comic that he thinks is horror, and adaptation of a classic Japanese ghost story, *Kasane* by Sanyutei Encho.

"I did *Kasane* in 2007 but frankly it was too scary for me. I don't think I'll ever do anything like that again. I realized I hate being scared."

In creating fantastic worlds, Tanabe feels realism is key.

"I'd say my art style is realistic. Artistically, my influences are artists like Daijiro Morohoshi, Hiroshi Hirata, Shigeru Mizuki, and Kazuo Umezu.

"I work in a mix of digital and physical. Digitally, I used software to compose scenes with perspectives, including referencing photographs and using 3D modeling software. From that I break out the ink and pens. I do all the drawing by hand, then scan it and use software called Comic Studio to add tone and color.

"Manga production software has made the whole process easier. Even though I got my break as an assistant, I don't use any myself. It's all me!"

It's impossible to discuss Lovecraft without talking about his racism. Recently the World Fantasy Award has removed the image of Lovecraft from their award. And Tanabe grapples with this as well.

"I'm Japanese, which means I have a difficult time understanding the history, emotions, and feelings of racism in the United States. I only know what I see on the news, and it seems like a difficult problem.

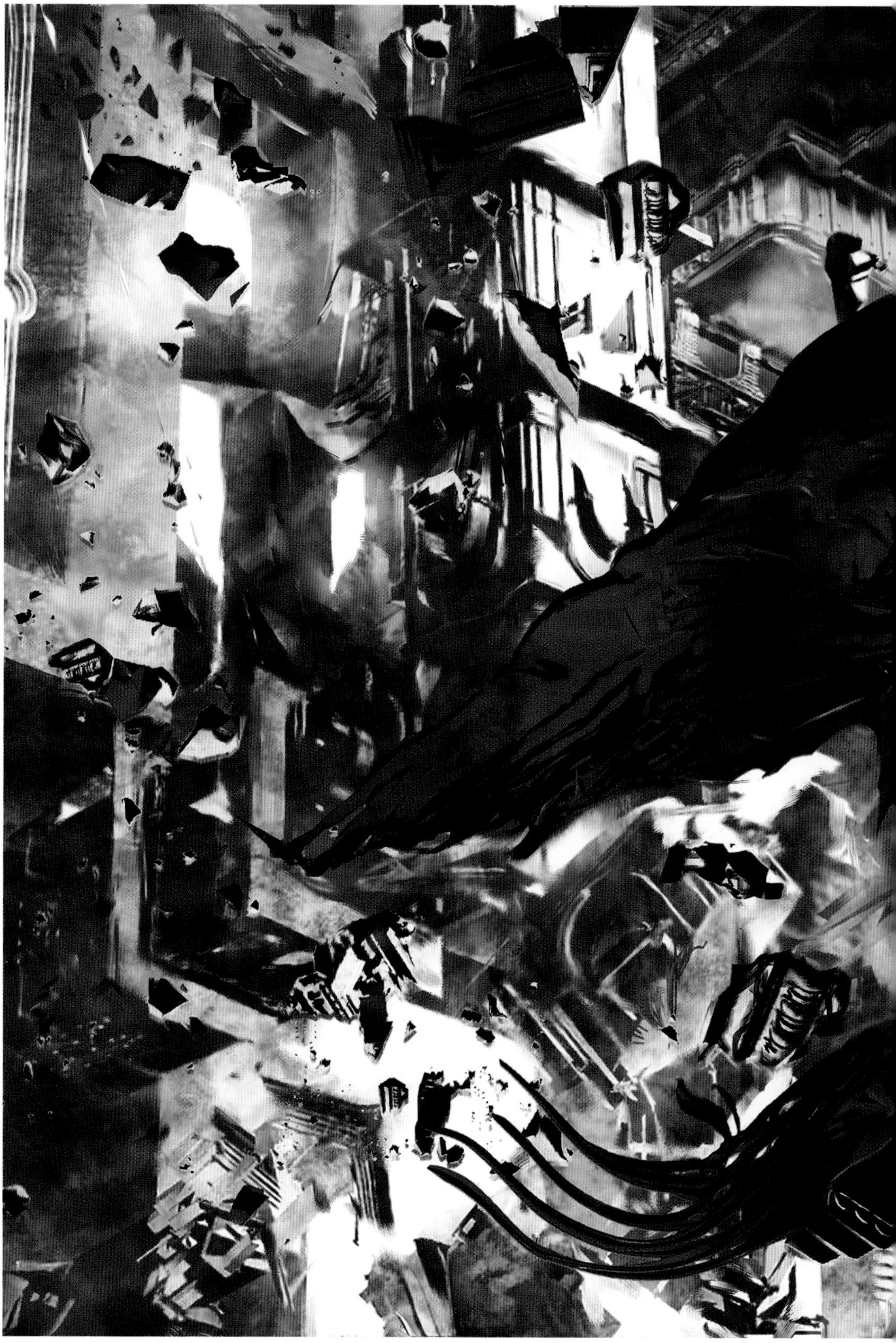

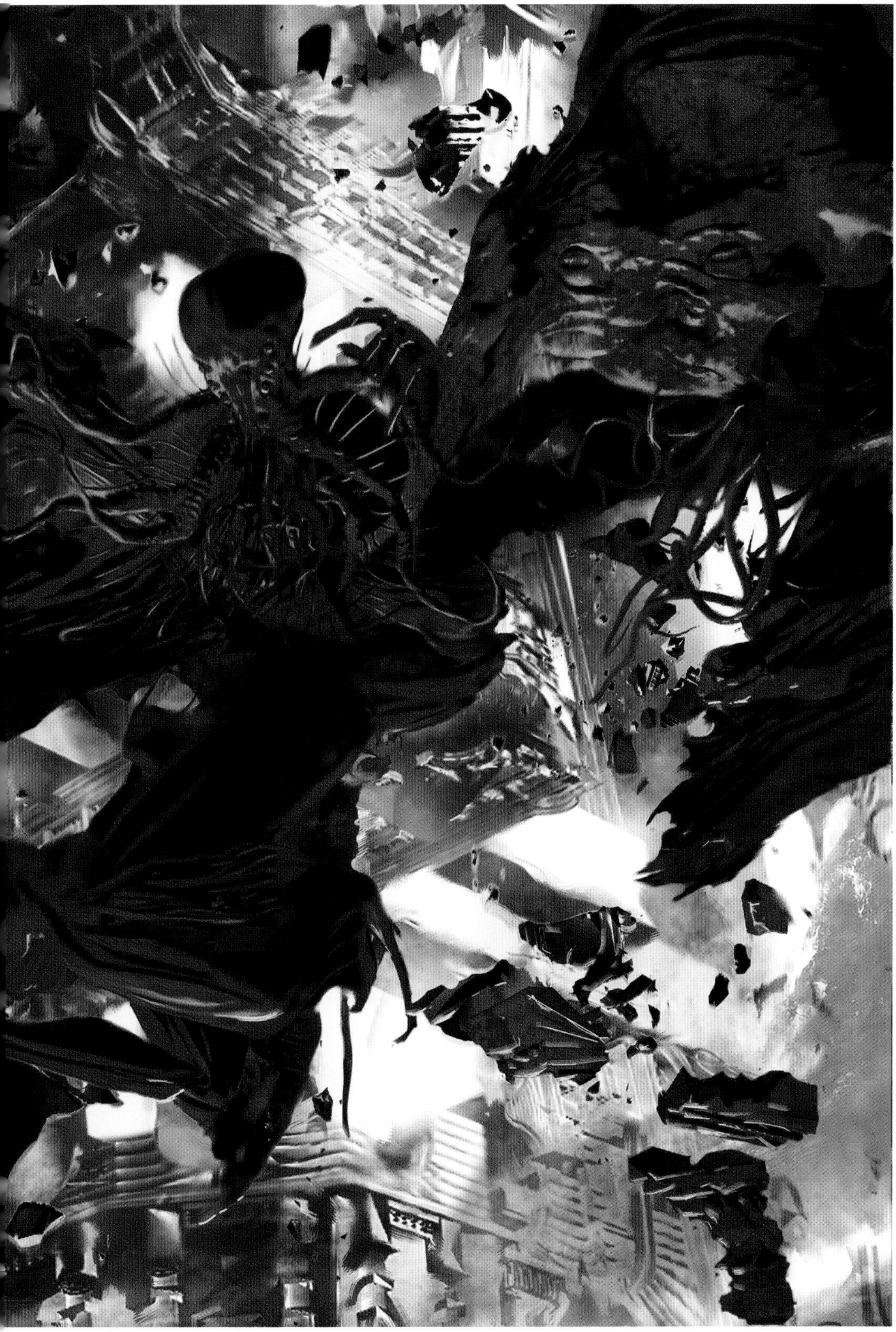

"Of course, Japan also struggles internally with racism. I hate it. I hate anyone who sees a human being as anything other than a fellow human.

"With Lovecraft, I think to myself, well, he was born over a hundred years ago, in a different time and a different society. Racism was perhaps more common then, although no less horrible. But I don't know."

Tanabe thinks maybe it is easier to not think about Lovecraft the human, Lovecraft the racist.

"Instead I think of him as some sort of...higher being...some distant god who created the Cthulhu mythos, who breathed life into this fantastic world.

"But again, I don't know. I feel helpless."

With *At the Mountains of Madness*, there was a notable shift in Tanabe's approach to Lovecraft. While previous adaptations had held closely to the original text, in this larger work Tanabe started moving around scenes, manipulating the pacing. The balance of Tanabe and Lovecraft began shifting.

"The editor in charge changed. I was more on my own. Trying to find myself as an artist in the world of Lovecraft was immensely challenging. When reading the novels, there are parts I don't understand, parts that are unclear.

"When working on *Call of Cthulhu*, I did even more. The original work has large gaps, and I found it less interesting among Lovecraft's works. Much of the details of the novel are lacking, and so I tried to fill that in. It was one of the more challenging adaptations I have done. Now, it is my best-selling work in Japan, so it seems to be okay."

Outside of Japan, Tanabe has received a lot of recognition. He won the Angouleme International Manga Festival Award and has been nominated for the Eisner Award several times.

"I'm thrilled, of course, and many fans are overjoyed. But it's difficult to see what sort of effect this will have on my career in the future. To be honest, in general, Japanese comic fans have very little interest in what happens overseas. But we will see!"

Speaking of his plans for the future, Tanabe plans to continue adapting Lovecraft.

"I tried branching out into a few areas, doing detective comics like *Genius Loki* and *Mr. Nobody*. I like detective comics too, but unfortunately, they didn't sell very well and were cancelled.

"For now, I will continue to work on the Lovecraft Masterpiece Collection. I'm currently working on *The Shadow Over Innsmouth*."

And finally, when asked if Tanabe had a favorite amongst the various Lovecraft adaptations done over the years.

"Mine, of course!"

Thank you, Tanabe-sensei. Me too. And I think I speak for everyone when I say we are looking forward to more.

***

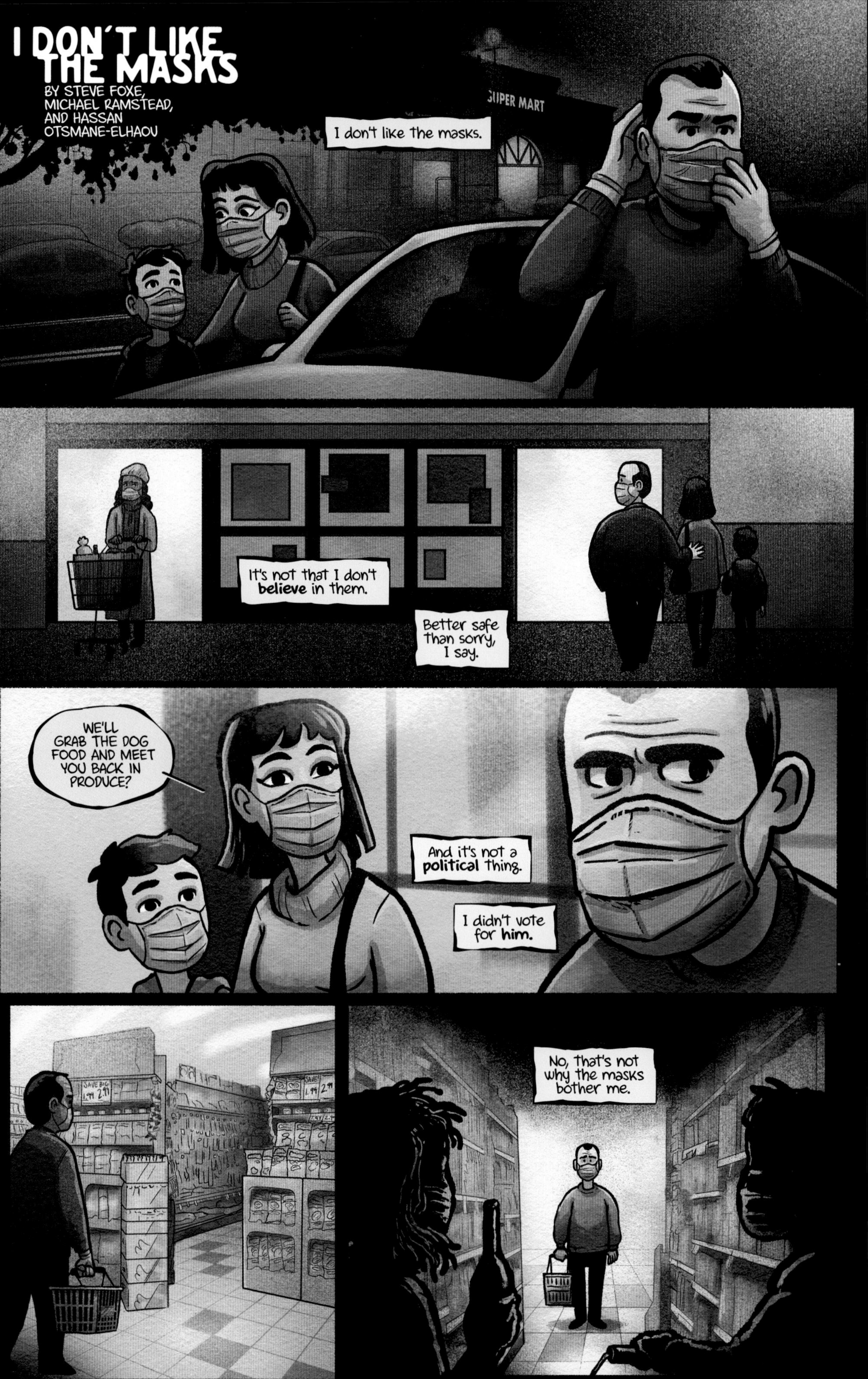
I DON'T LIKE THE MASKS
BY STEVE FOXE, MICHAEL RAMSTEAD, AND HASSAN OTSMANE-ELHAOU
SUPER MART
I don't like the masks.
It's not that I don't believe in them.
Better safe than sorry, I say.
WE'LL GRAB THE DOG FOOD AND MEET YOU BACK IN PRODUCE?
And it's not a political thing.
I didn't vote for him.
SAVE BIG 1.99 2.99
SAVE! 1.99 2.99
No, that's not why the masks bother me.

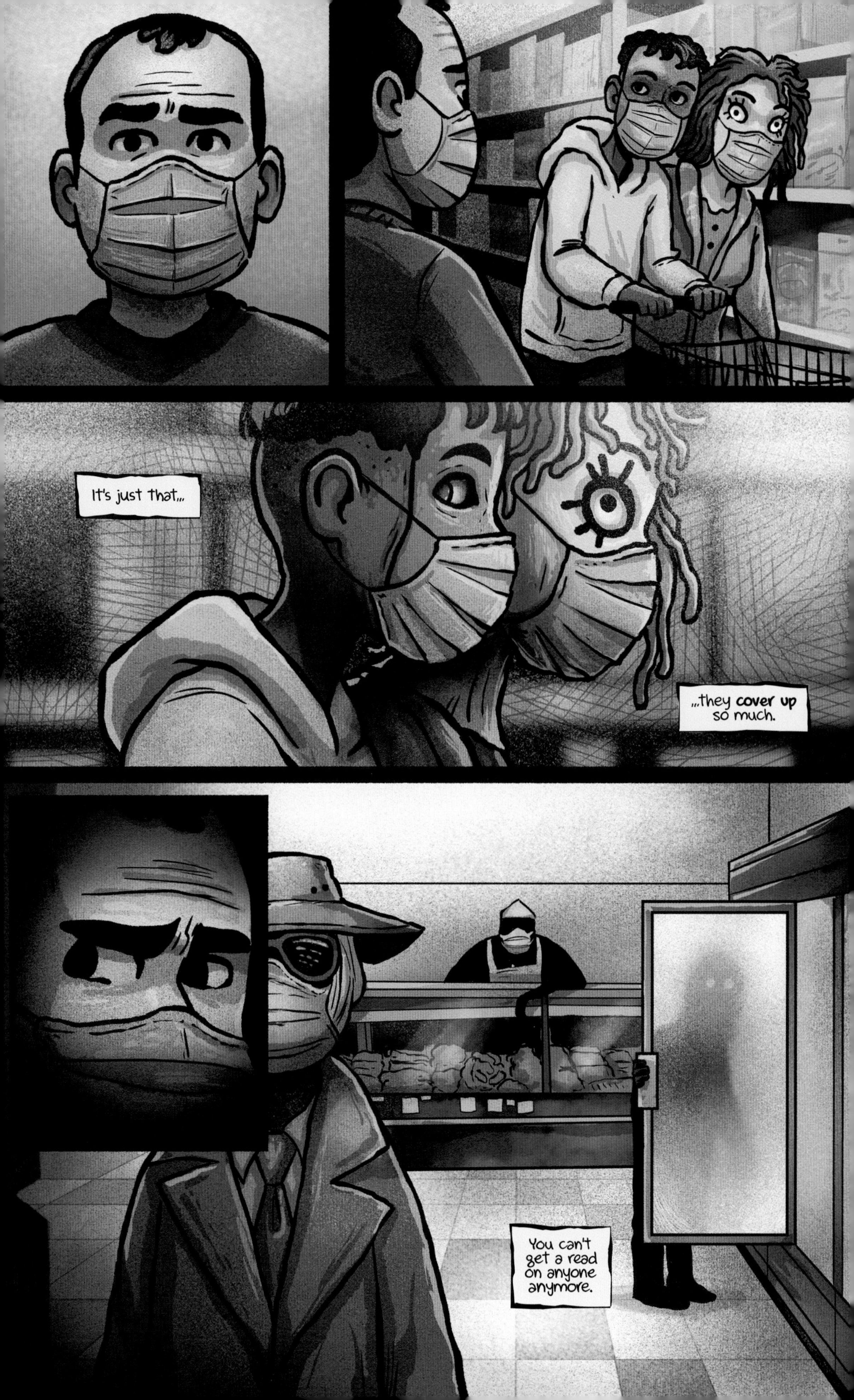
It's just that...
...they cover up so much.
You can't get a read on anyone anymore.

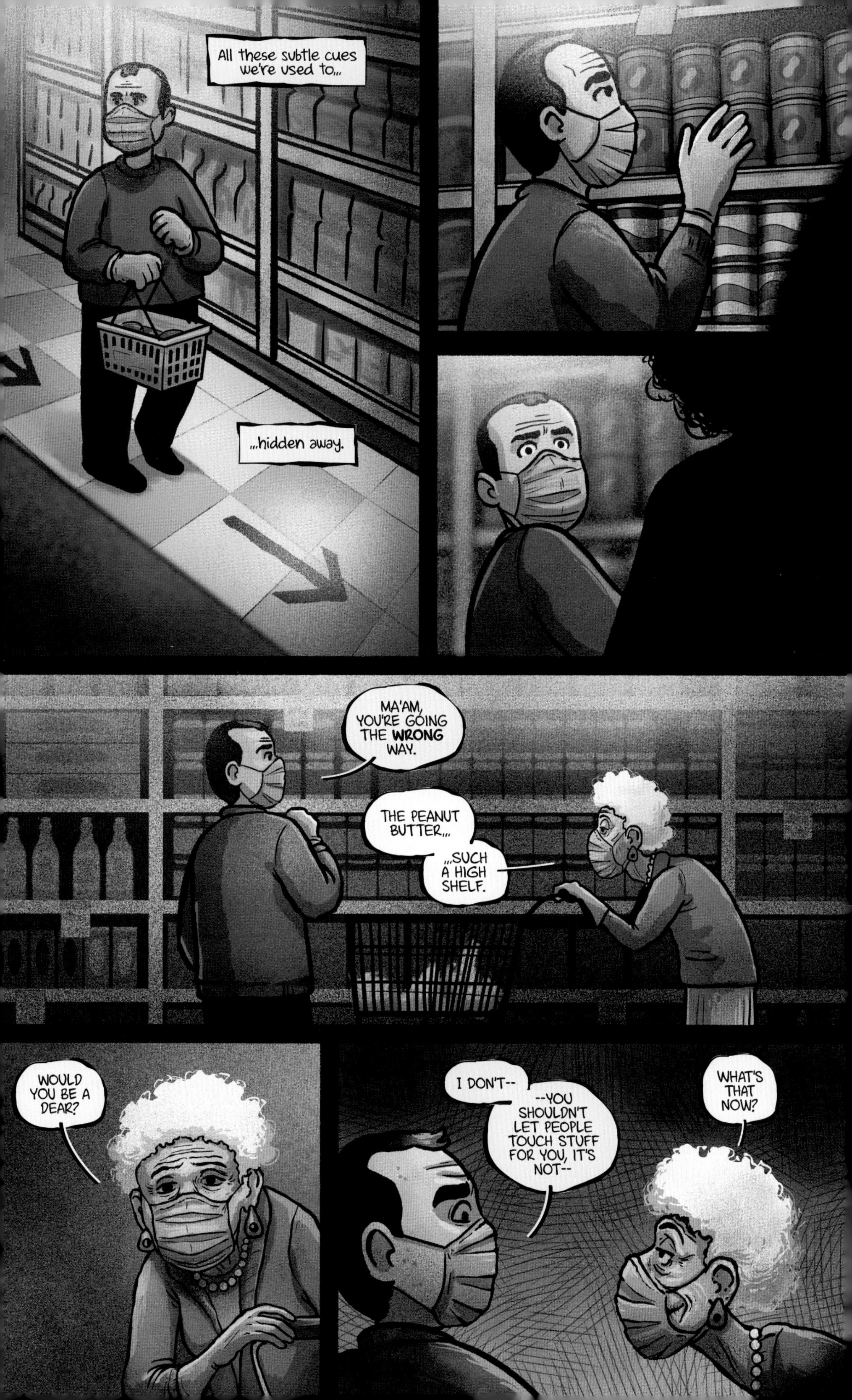
All these subtle cues we're used to...
...hidden away.
MA'AM, YOU'RE GOING THE **WRONG** WAY.
THE PEANUT BUTTER...
...SUCH A HIGH SHELF.
WOULD YOU BE A DEAR?
I DON'T--
--YOU SHOULDN'T LET PEOPLE TOUCH STUFF FOR YOU, IT'S NOT--
WHAT'S THAT NOW?

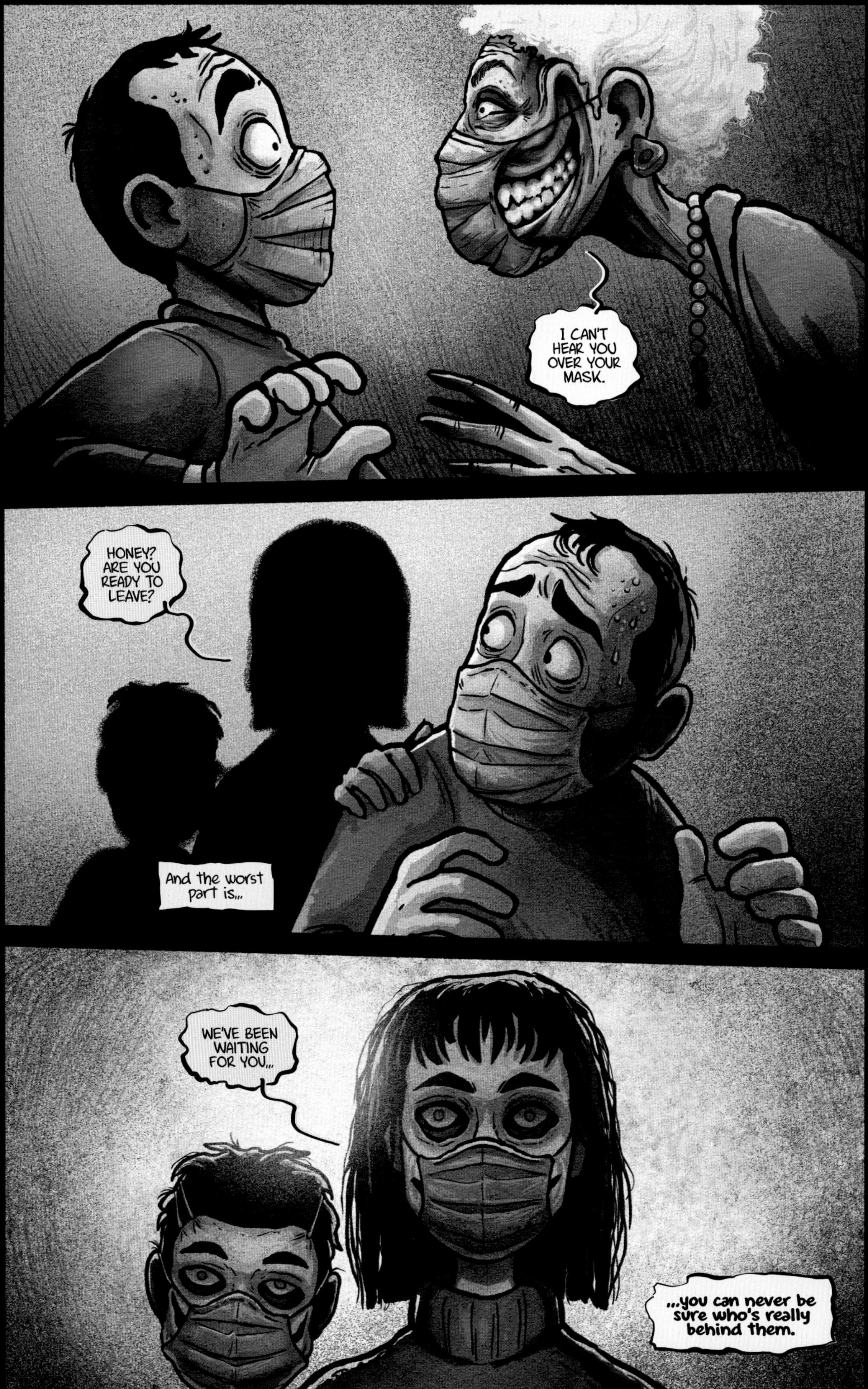
I CAN'T HEAR YOU OVER YOUR MASK.
HONEY? ARE YOU READY TO LEAVE?
And the worst part is...
WE'VE BEEN WAITING FOR YOU...
...you can never be sure who's really behind them.

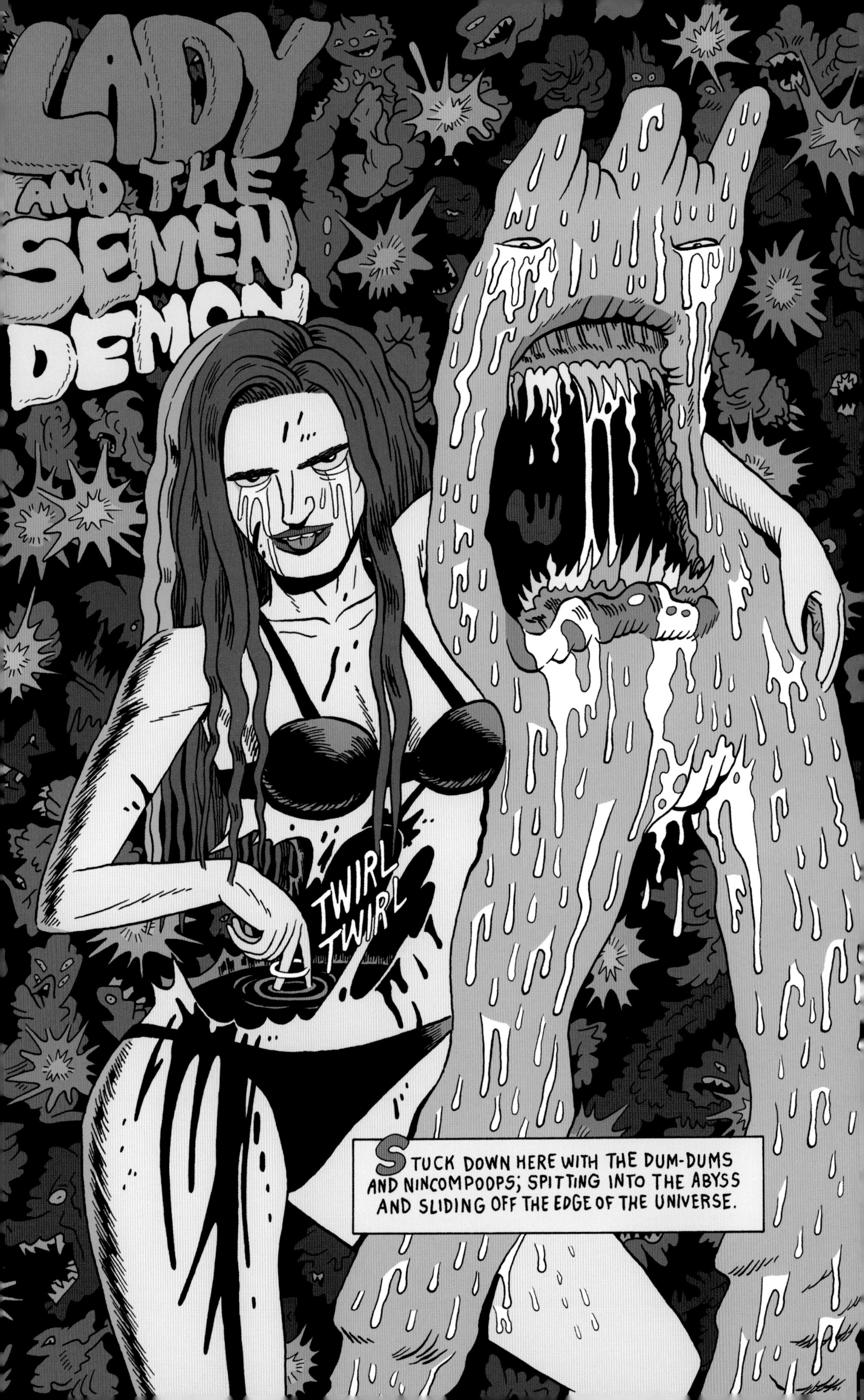
LADY AND THE SEMEN DEMON
TWIRL TWIRL
STUCK DOWN HERE WITH THE DUM-DUMS AND NINCOMPOOPS; SPITTING INTO THE ABYSS AND SLIDING OFF THE EDGE OF THE UNIVERSE.

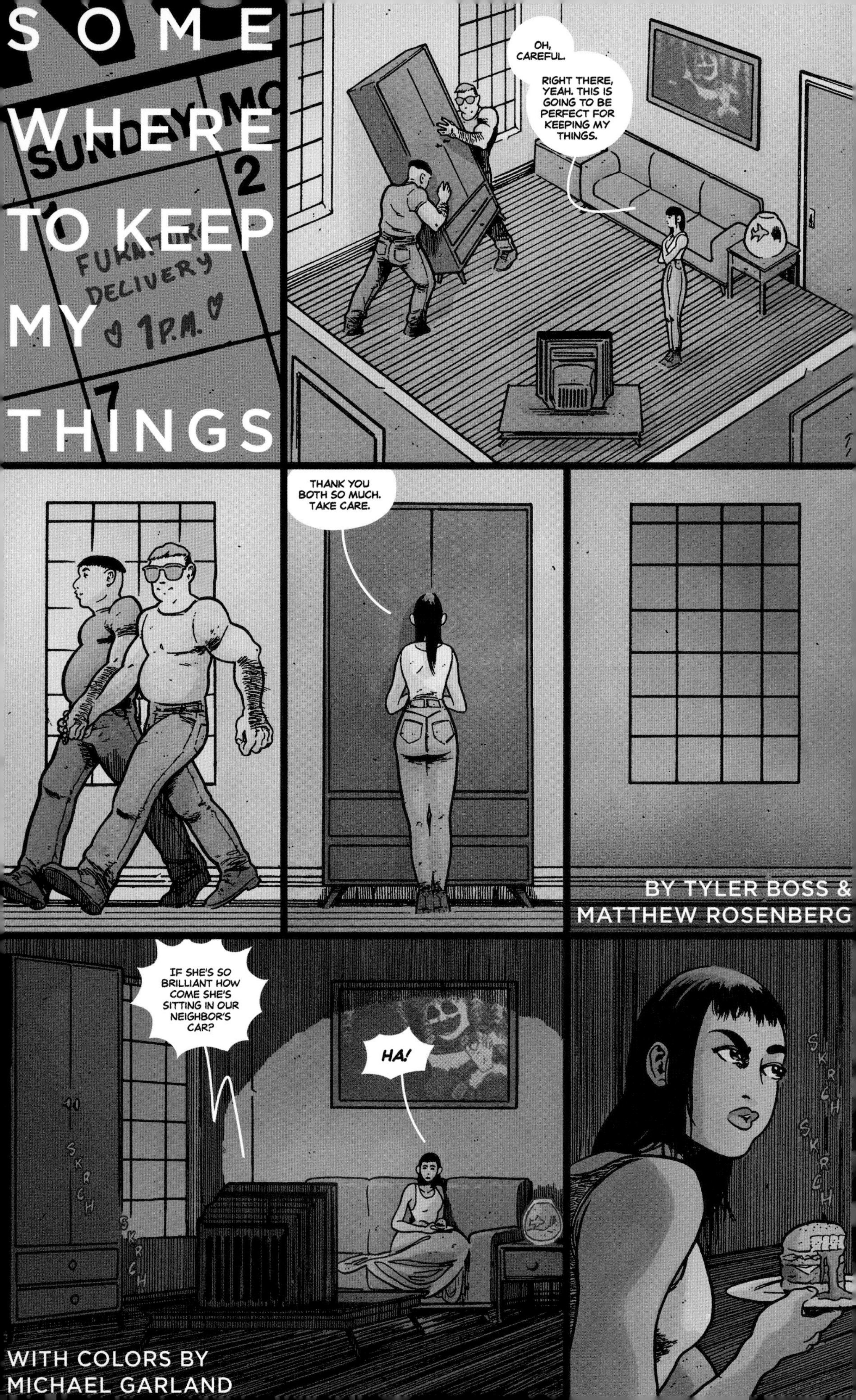
SOME WHERE TO KEEP MY THINGS
SUNDAY
MO
1
2
DELIVERY
1P.M.
7
OH, CAREFUL.
RIGHT THERE, YEAH. THIS IS GOING TO BE PERFECT FOR KEEPING MY THINGS.
THANK YOU BOTH SO MUCH. TAKE CARE.
BY TYLER BOSS & MATTHEW ROSENBERG
IF SHE'S SO BRILLIANT HOW COME SHE'S SITTING IN OUR NEIGHBOR'S CAR?
SKRCH
SKRCH
HA!
WITH COLORS BY MICHAEL GARLAND
SKRCH
SKRCH

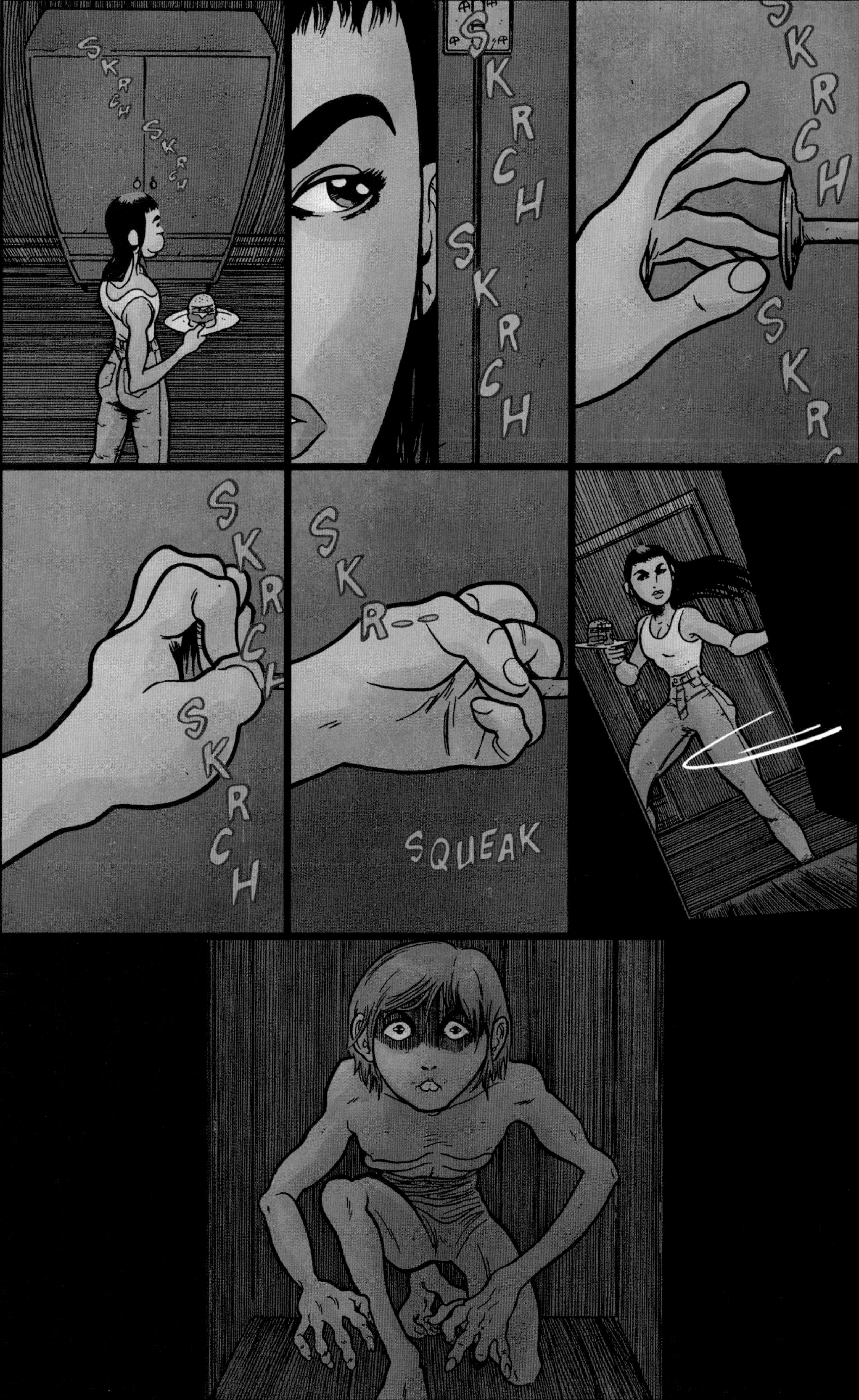
SKRCH
SKRCH
SKRCH
SKRCH
SKRCH
SKRC
SKRCH
SKRCH
SKR--
SQUEAK

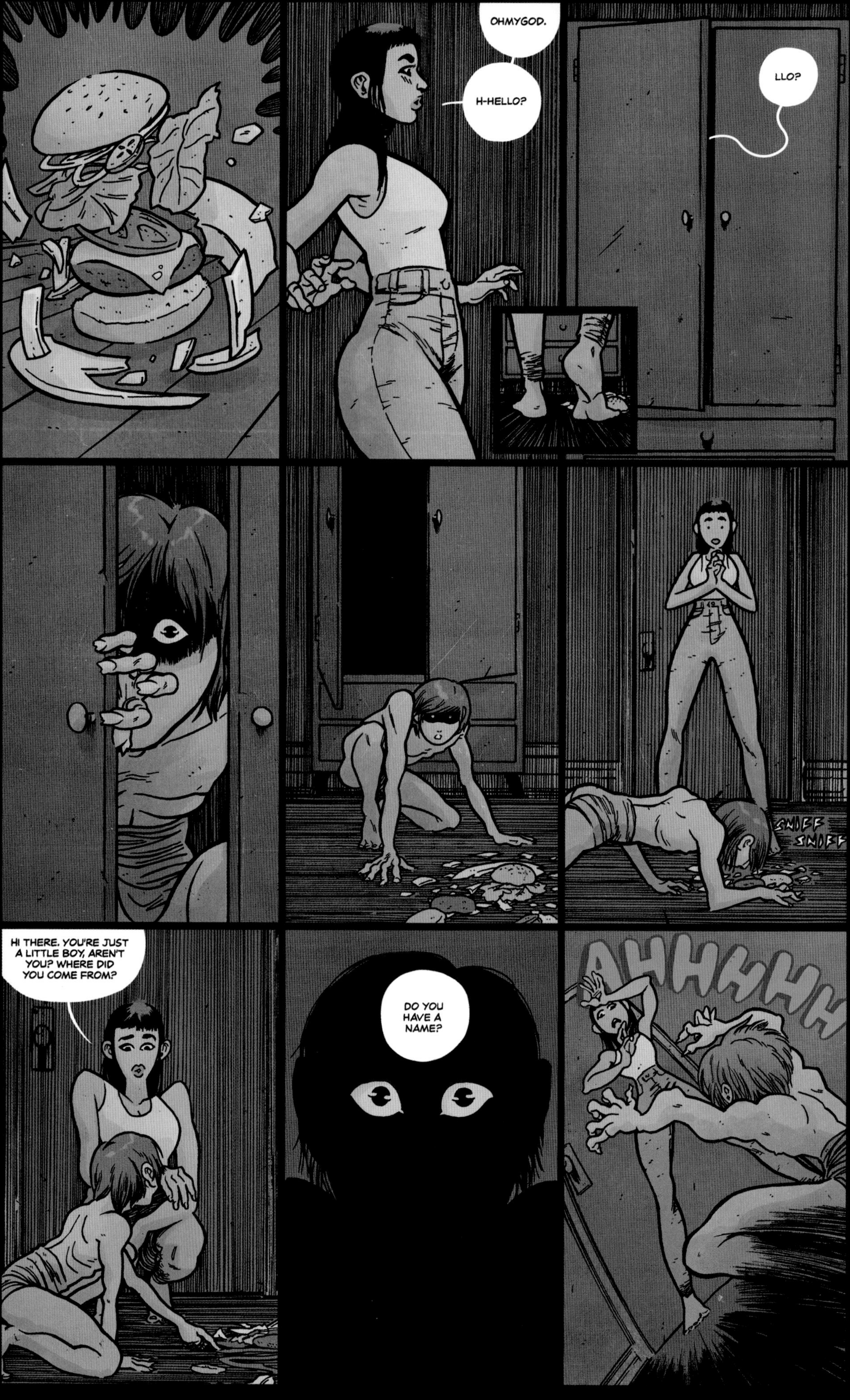
OHMYGOD.
H-HELLO?
LLO?
SNIFF
SNIFF
HI THERE. YOU'RE JUST A LITTLE BOY, AREN'T YOU? WHERE DID YOU COME FROM?
DO YOU HAVE A NAME?
AHHHHHH

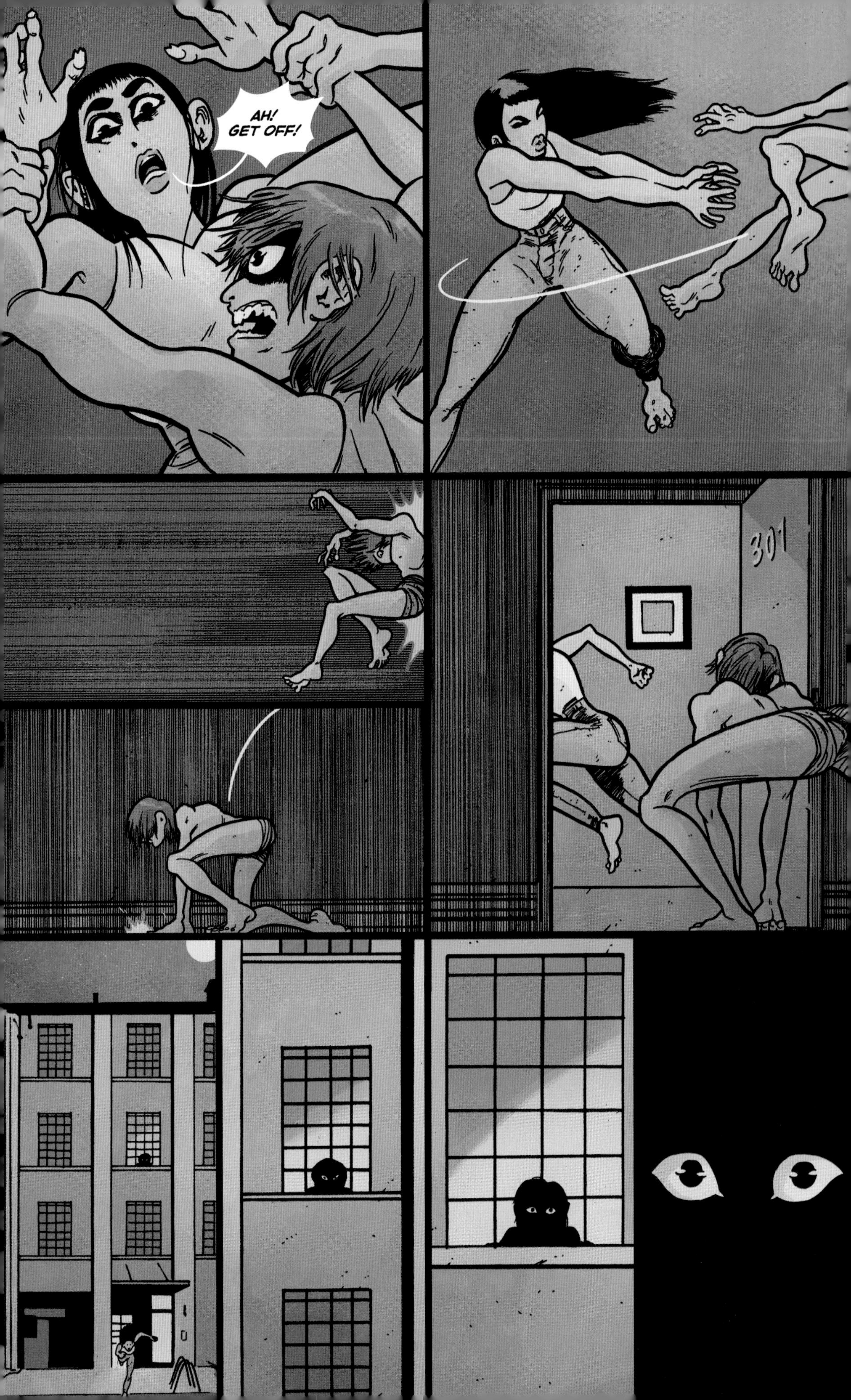
AH! GET OFF!
301

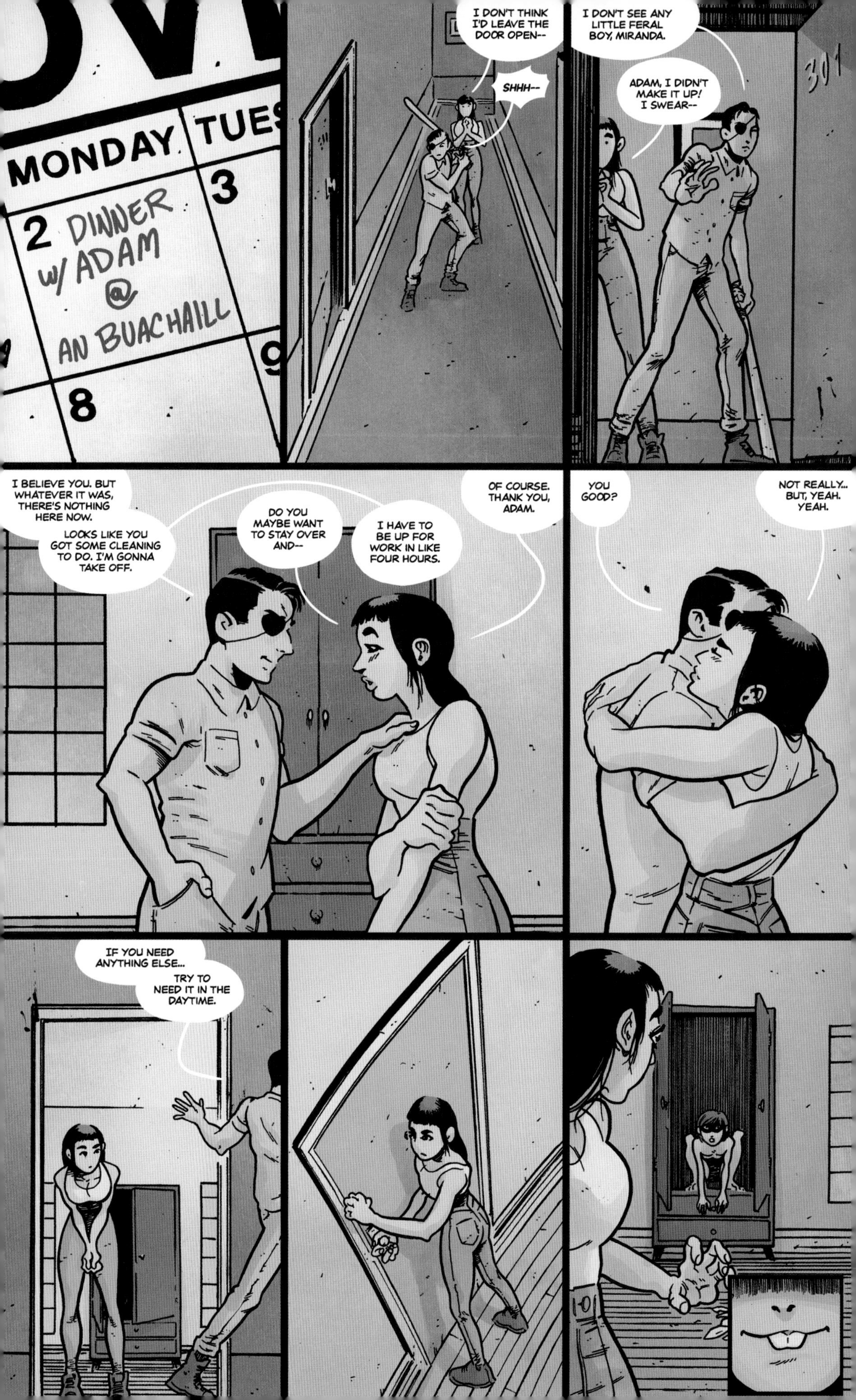
MONDAY
TUES
2 DINNER w/ ADAM @ AN BUACHAILL
3
8
9
I DON'T THINK I'D LEAVE THE DOOR OPEN--
SHHH--
I DON'T SEE ANY LITTLE FERAL BOY, MIRANDA.
ADAM, I DIDN'T MAKE IT UP! I SWEAR--
301
I BELIEVE YOU. BUT WHATEVER IT WAS, THERE'S NOTHING HERE NOW.
LOOKS LIKE YOU GOT SOME CLEANING TO DO. I'M GONNA TAKE OFF.
DO YOU MAYBE WANT TO STAY OVER AND--
I HAVE TO BE UP FOR WORK IN LIKE FOUR HOURS.
OF COURSE. THANK YOU, ADAM.
YOU GOOD?
NOT REALLY... BUT, YEAH. YEAH.
IF YOU NEED ANYTHING ELSE...
TRY TO NEED IT IN THE DAYTIME.

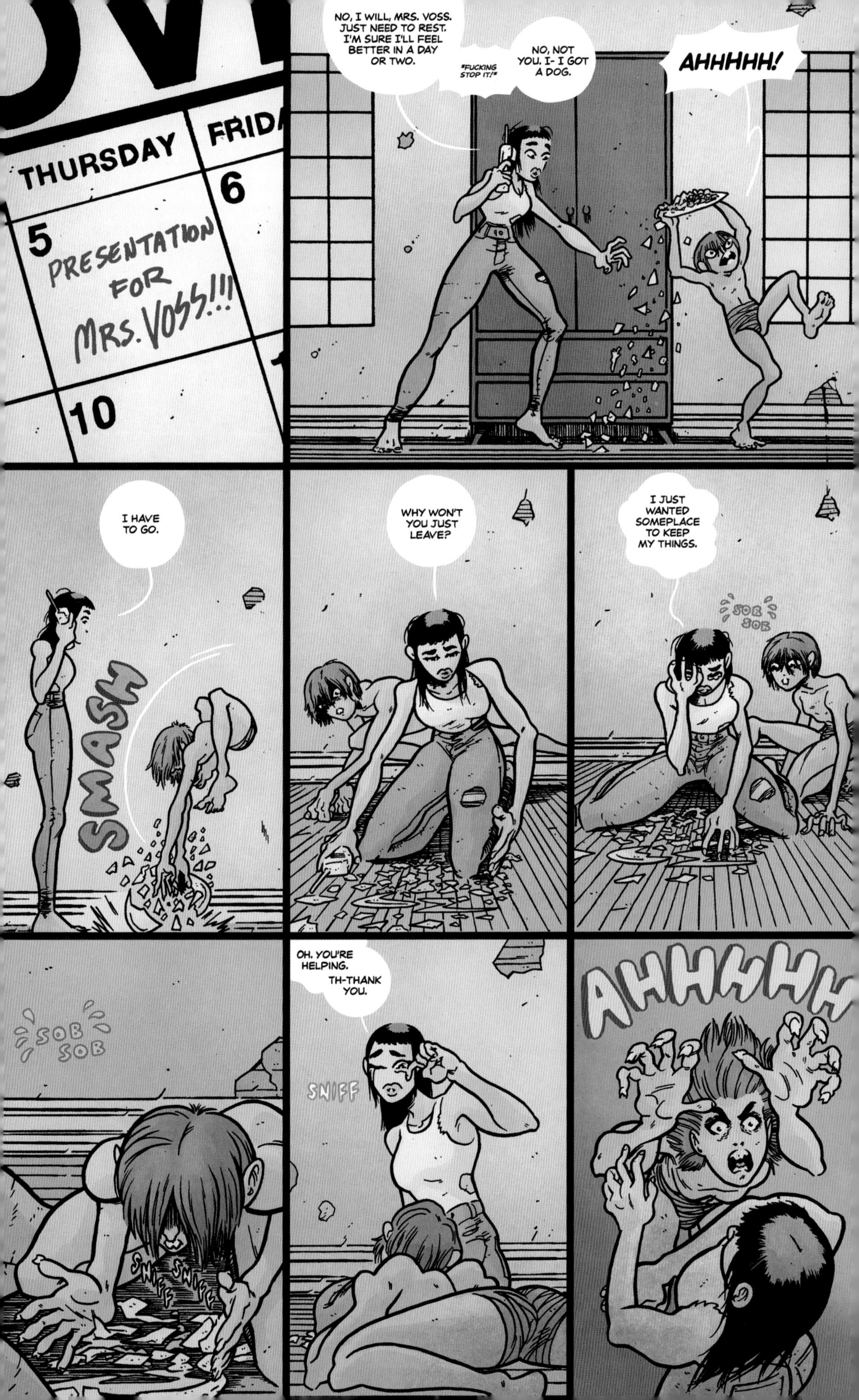
THURSDAY
FRIDA
5
PRESENTATION FOR MRS. VOSS!!!
6
10
NO, I WILL, MRS. VOSS. JUST NEED TO REST. I'M SURE I'LL FEEL BETTER IN A DAY OR TWO.
FUCKING STOP IT!
NO, NOT YOU. I- I GOT A DOG.
AHHHHH!
I HAVE TO GO.
SMASH
WHY WON'T YOU JUST LEAVE?
I JUST WANTED SOMEPLACE TO KEEP MY THINGS.
SOB SOB
SOB SOB
SNIFF SNIFF
OH. YOU'RE HELPING.
TH-THANK YOU.
SNIFF
AHHHHHH

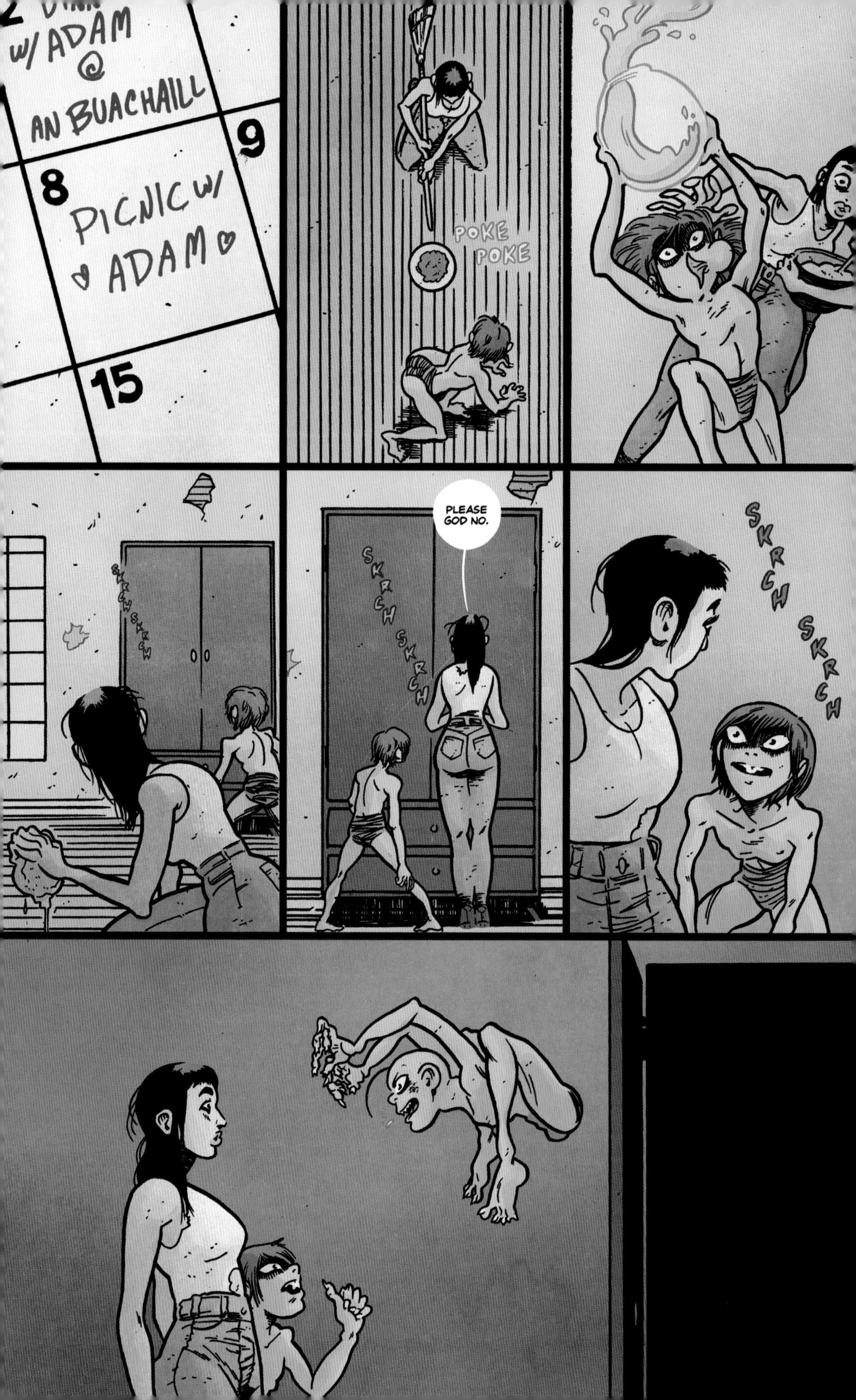

W/ ADAM @ AN BUACHAILL
9
8
PICNIC W/ ADAM
15
POKE POKE
SKRCH SKRCH
SKRCH SKRCH
PLEASE GOD NO.
SKRCH SKRCH

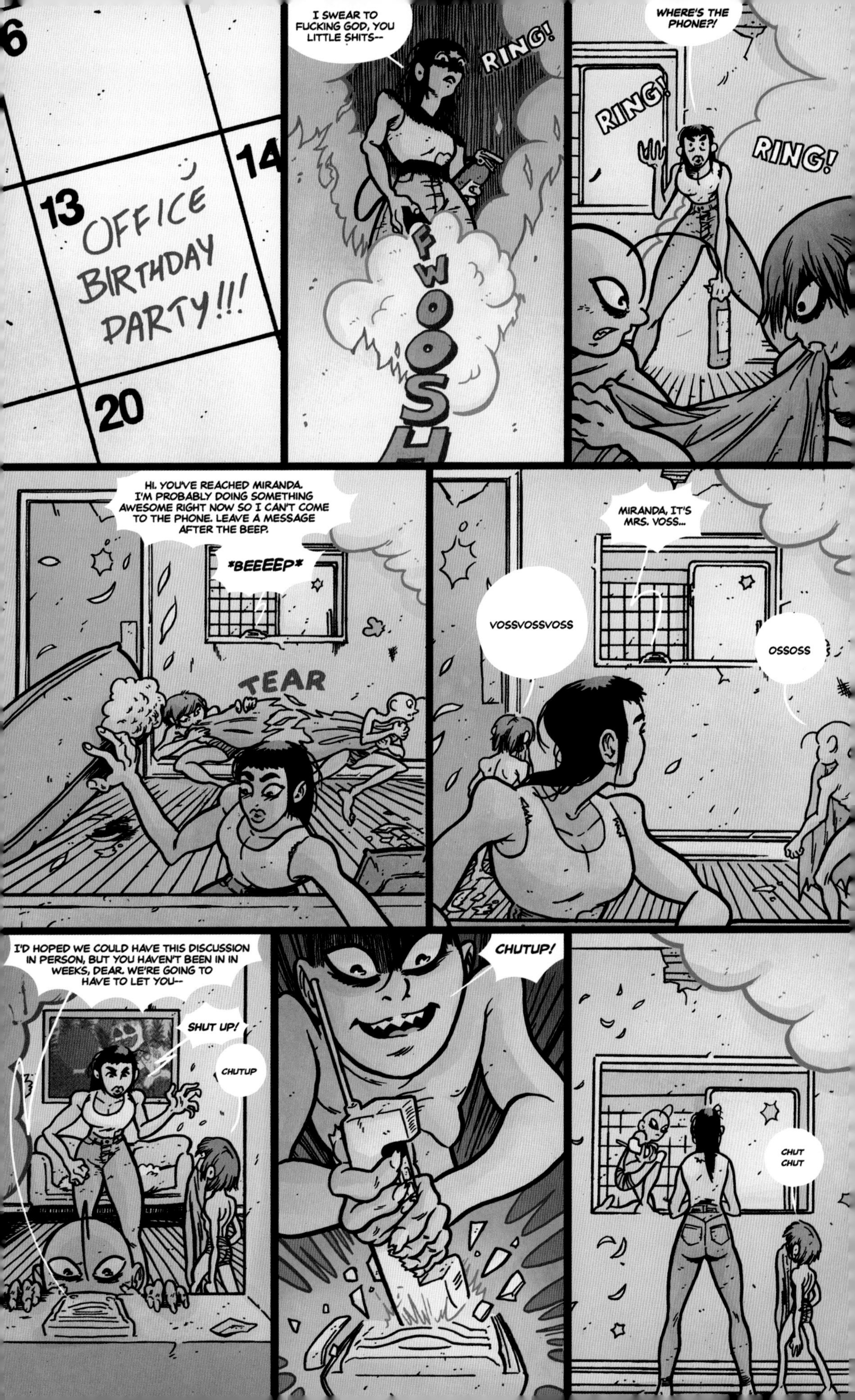
6
13
OFFICE BIRTHDAY PARTY!!!
14
20
I SWEAR TO FUCKING GOD, YOU LITTLE SHITS--
RING!
FWOOSH
WHERE'S THE PHONE?!
RING!
RING!
HI. YOU'VE REACHED MIRANDA. I'M PROBABLY DOING SOMETHING AWESOME RIGHT NOW SO I CAN'T COME TO THE PHONE. LEAVE A MESSAGE AFTER THE BEEP.
BEEEEP
TEAR
MIRANDA, IT'S MRS. VOSS...
VOSSVOSSVOSS
OSSOSS
I'D HOPED WE COULD HAVE THIS DISCUSSION IN PERSON, BUT YOU HAVEN'T BEEN IN IN WEEKS, DEAR. WE'RE GOING TO HAVE TO LET YOU--
SHUT UP!
CHUTUP
CHUTUP!
CHUT CHUT

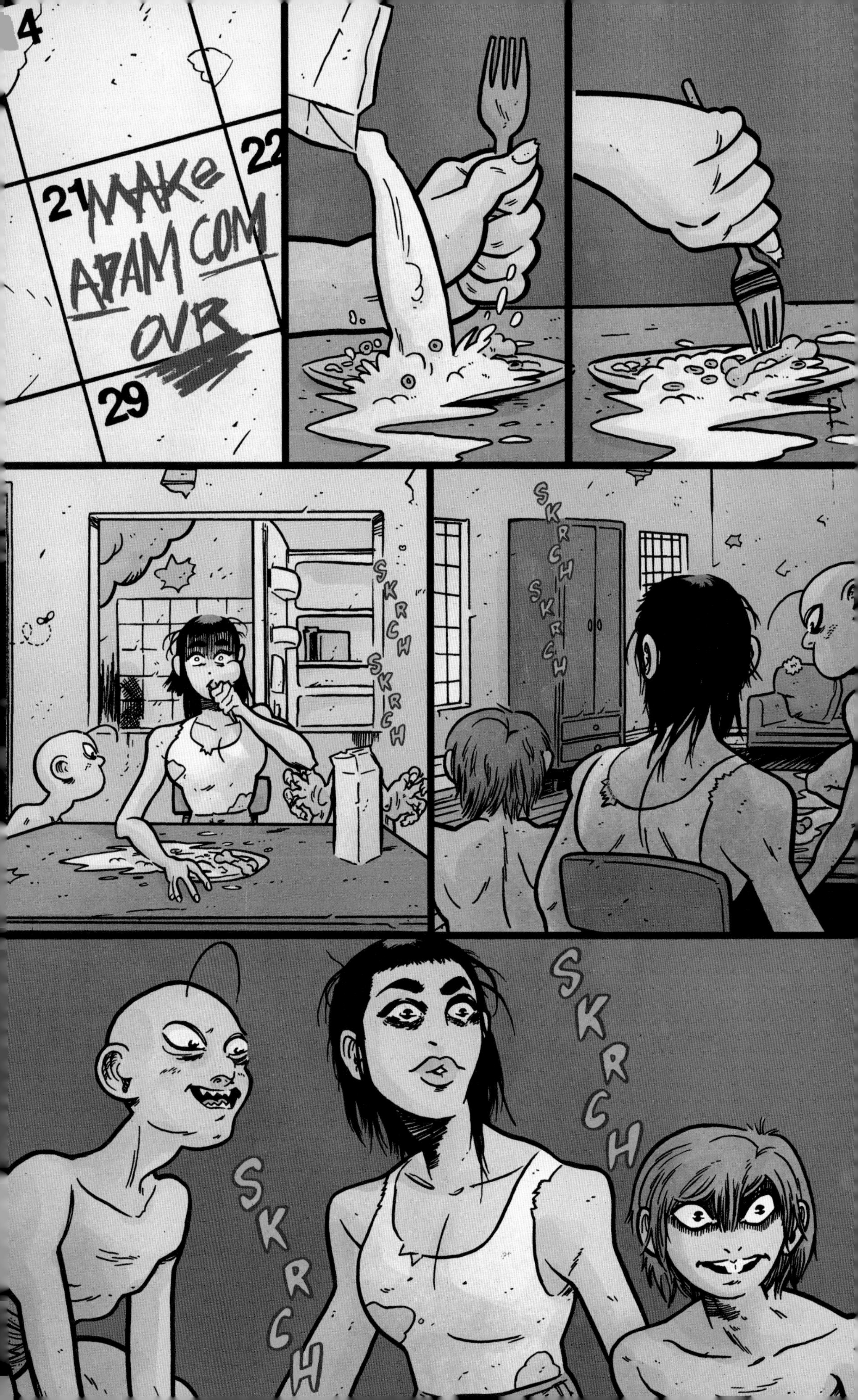

14
21
22
MAKE ADAM COM OVR
29
SKRCH SKRCH
SKRCH SKRCH
SKRCH
SKRCH

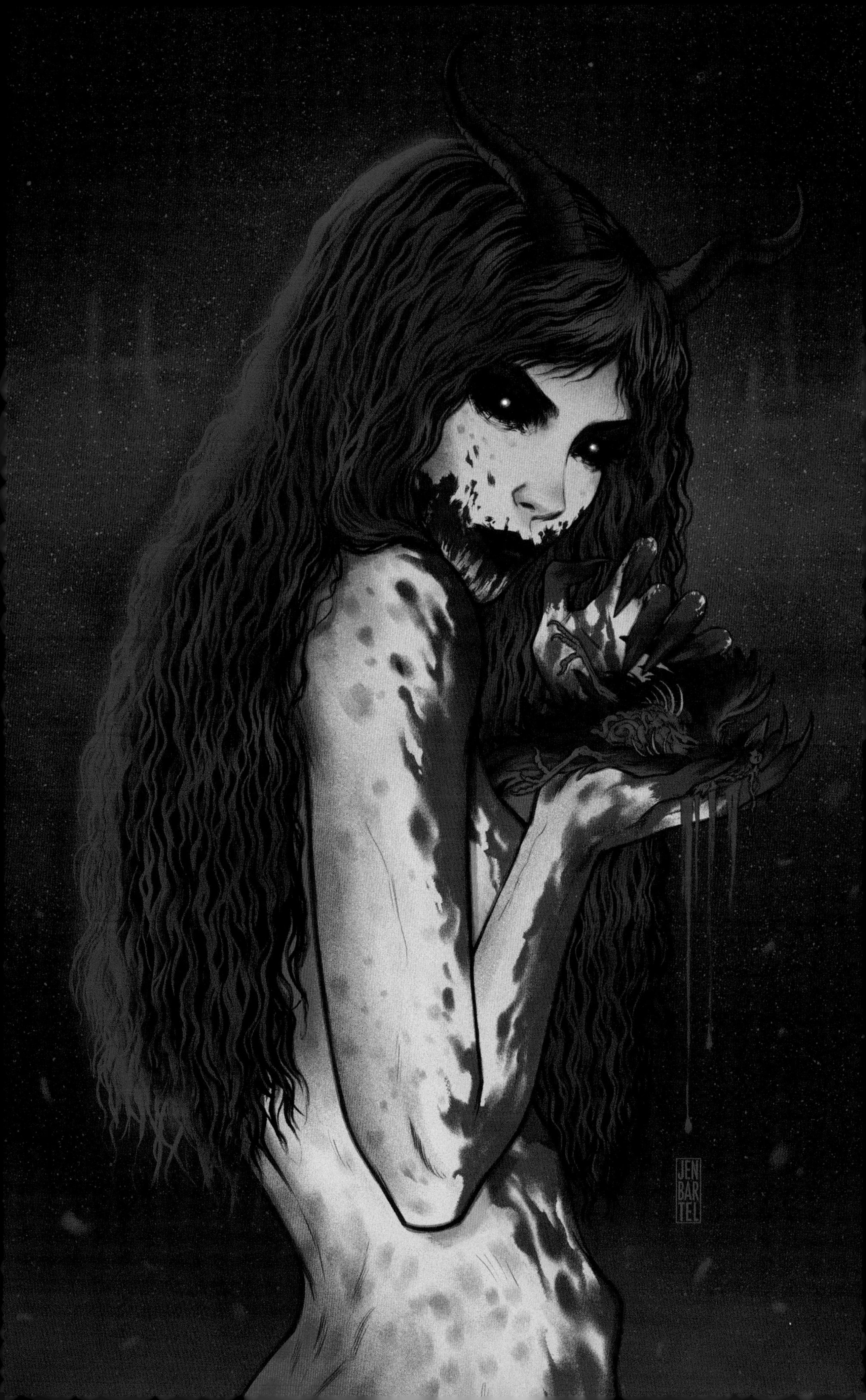
JEN BAR TEL

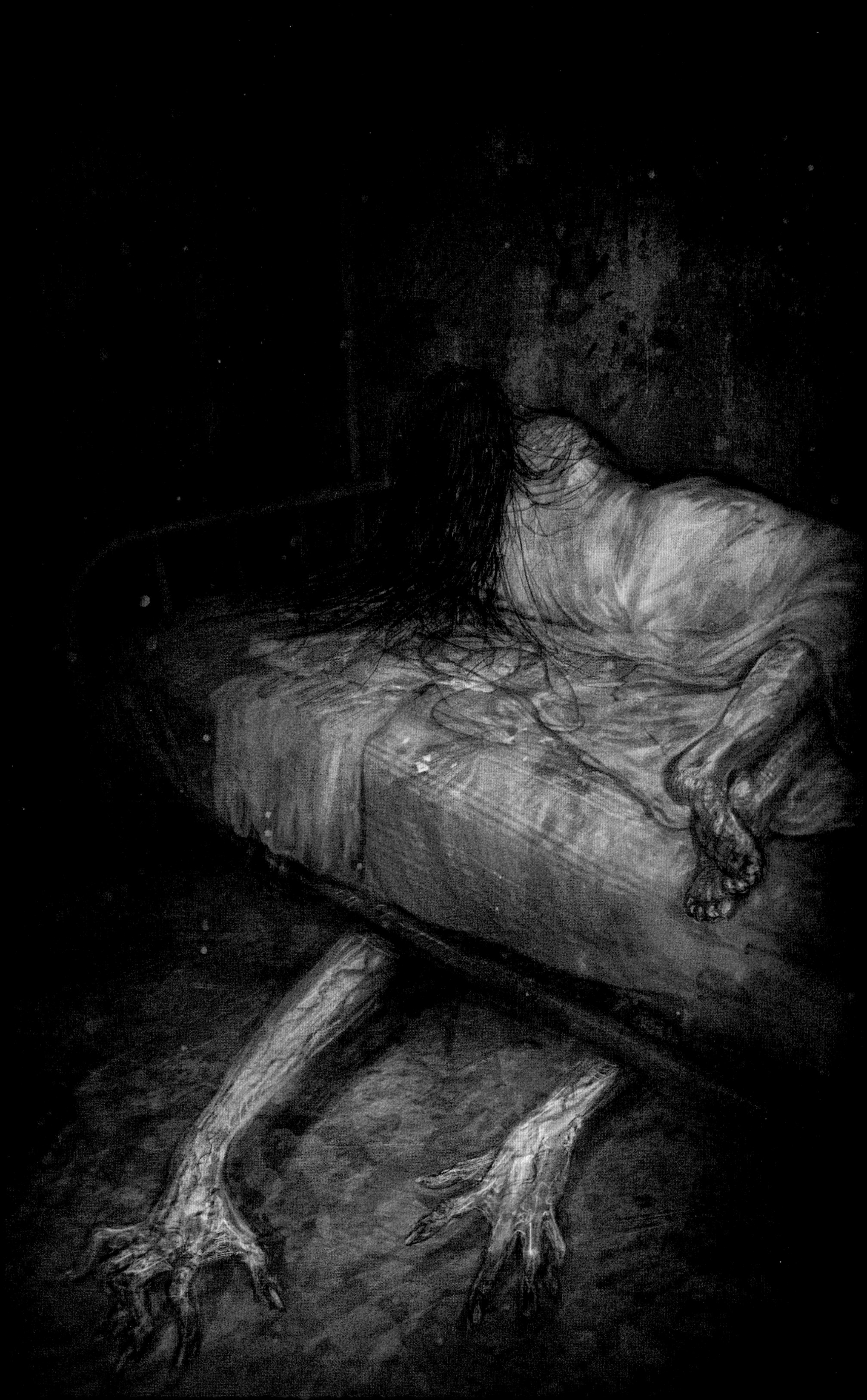

ISSUE #3

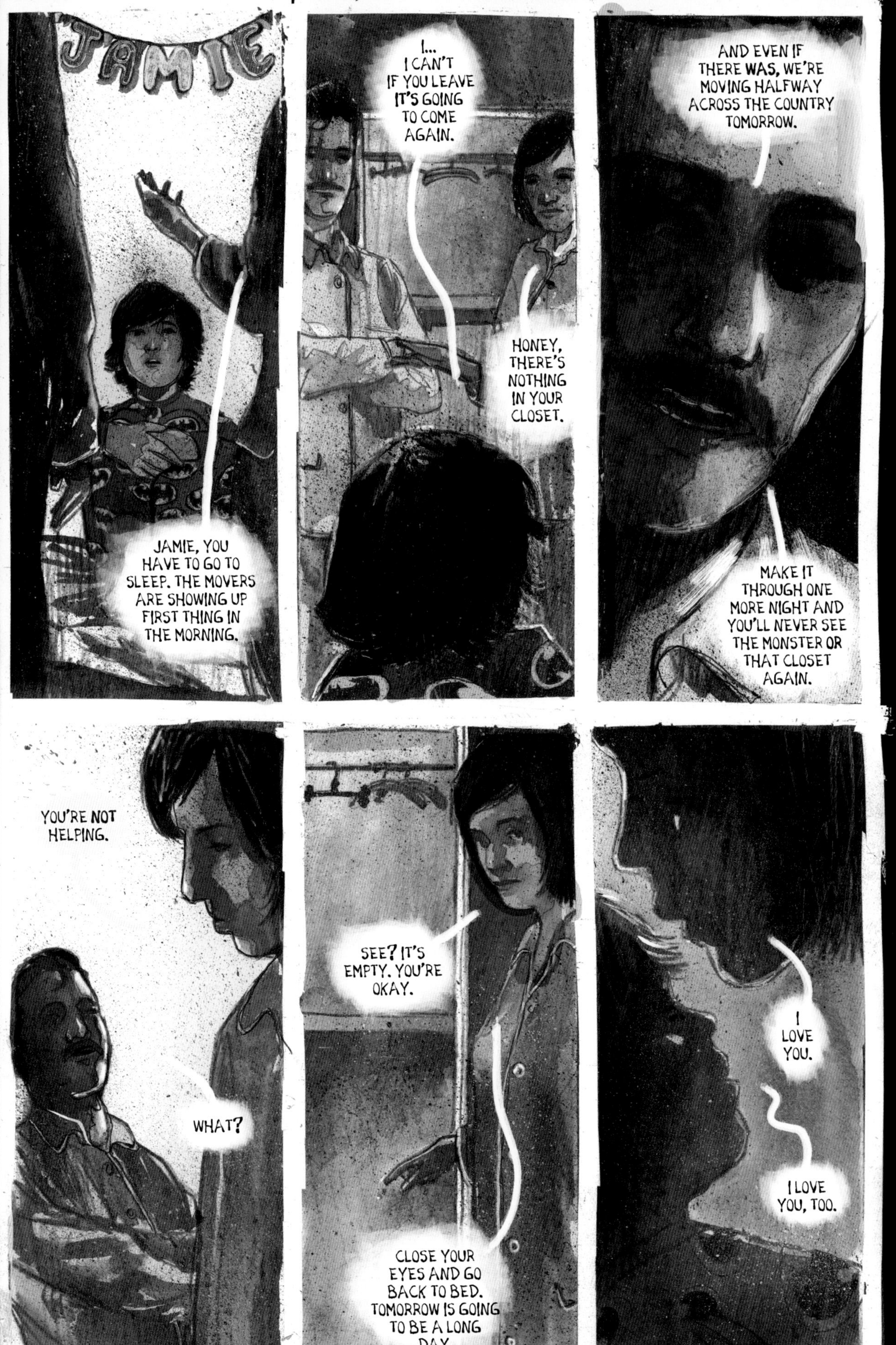
JAMIE
JAMIE, YOU HAVE TO GO TO SLEEP. THE MOVERS ARE SHOWING UP FIRST THING IN THE MORNING.
I... I CAN'T IF YOU LEAVE IT'S GOING TO COME AGAIN.
HONEY, THERE'S NOTHING IN YOUR CLOSET.
AND EVEN IF THERE WAS, WE'RE MOVING HALFWAY ACROSS THE COUNTRY TOMORROW.
MAKE IT THROUGH ONE MORE NIGHT AND YOU'LL NEVER SEE THE MONSTER OR THAT CLOSET AGAIN.
YOU'RE NOT HELPING.
WHAT?
SEE? IT'S EMPTY. YOU'RE OKAY.
CLOSE YOUR EYES AND GO BACK TO BED. TOMORROW IS GOING TO BE A LONG DAY.
I LOVE YOU.
I LOVE YOU, TOO.

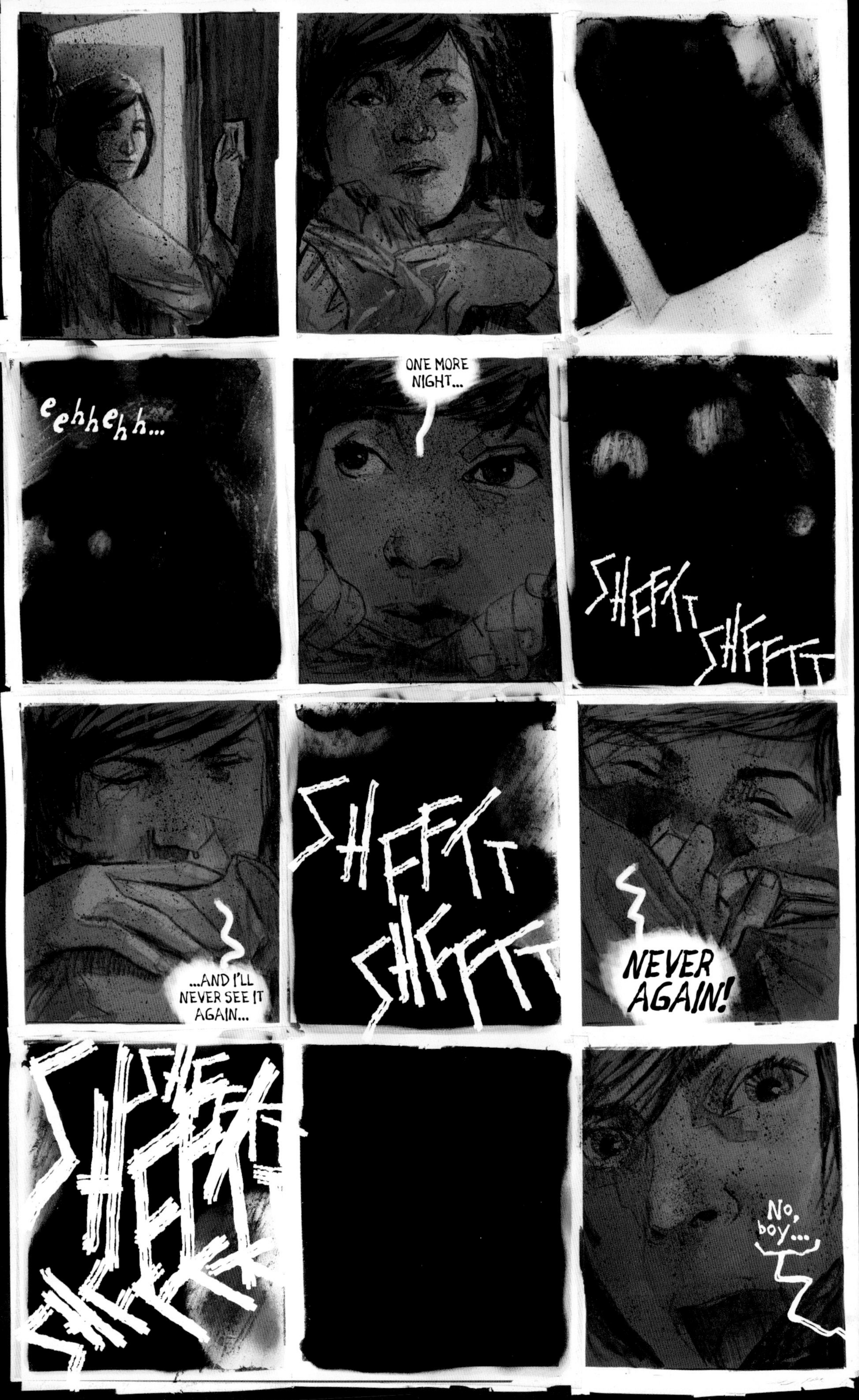
ehhehh...
ONE MORE NIGHT...
SHFFKT SHFFTT
...AND I'LL NEVER SEE IT AGAIN...
SHFFKT SHFFTT
NEVER AGAIN!
No, boy...

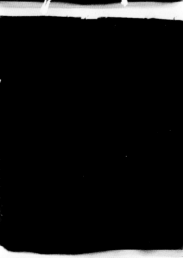

I'm coming with you.
ONE MORE NIGHT
by Tynion IV, Simmonds, & Otsmane-Elhaou

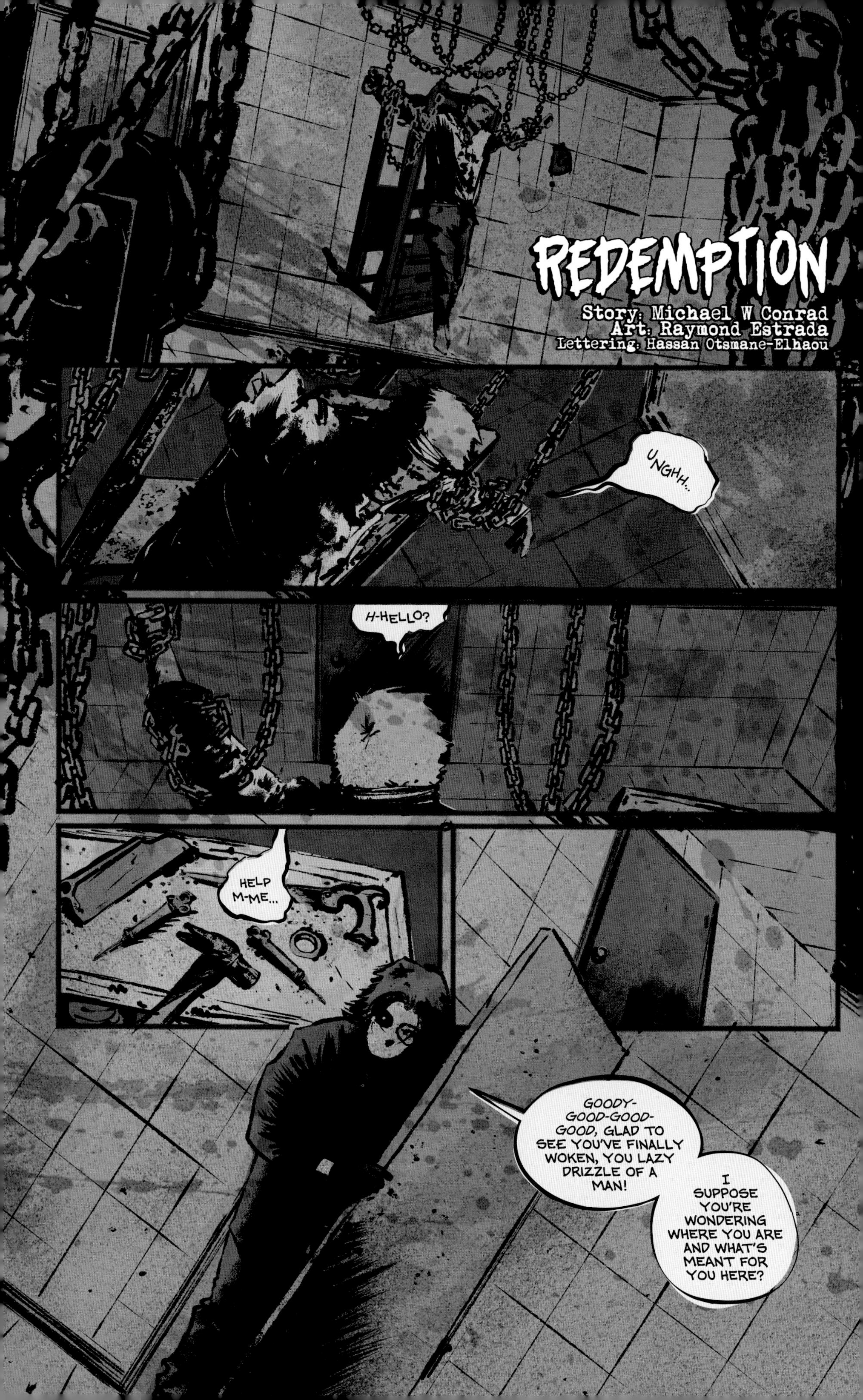
REDEMPTION
Story: Michael W Conrad
Art: Raymond Estrada
Lettering: Hassan Otsmane-Elhaou
UNGHH..
H-HELLO?
HELP M-ME...
GOODY-GOOD-GOOD-GOOD, GLAD TO SEE YOU'VE FINALLY WOKEN, YOU LAZY DRIZZLE OF A MAN!
I SUPPOSE YOU'RE WONDERING WHERE YOU ARE AND WHAT'S MEANT FOR YOU HERE?

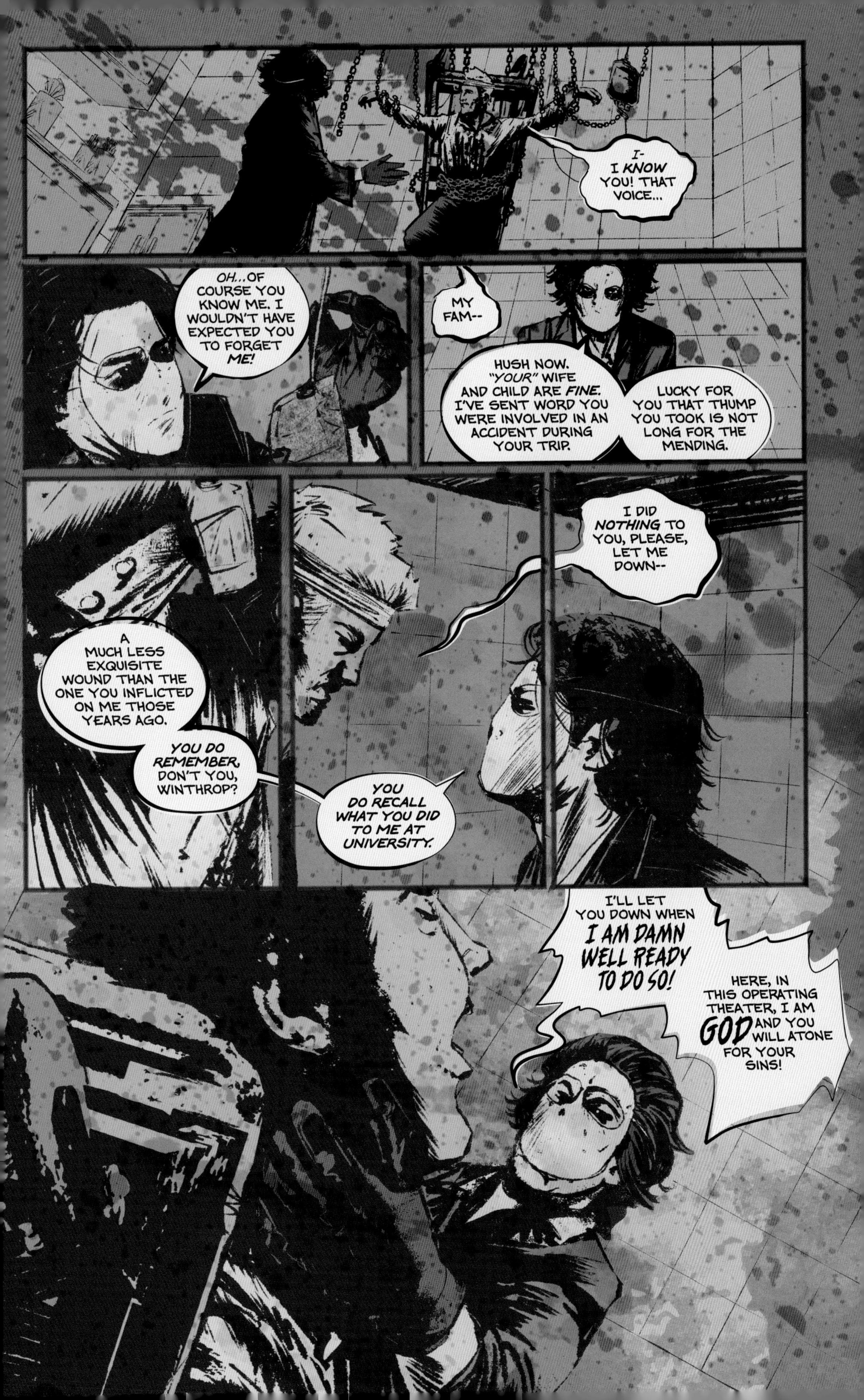
I- I KNOW YOU! THAT VOICE...
OH... OF COURSE YOU KNOW ME. I WOULDN'T HAVE EXPECTED YOU TO FORGET ME!
MY FAM--
HUSH NOW. "YOUR" WIFE AND CHILD ARE FINE. I'VE SENT WORD YOU WERE INVOLVED IN AN ACCIDENT DURING YOUR TRIP.
LUCKY FOR YOU THAT THUMP YOU TOOK IS NOT LONG FOR THE MENDING.
A MUCH LESS EXQUISITE WOUND THAN THE ONE YOU INFLICTED ON ME THOSE YEARS AGO.
YOU DO REMEMBER, DON'T YOU, WINTHROP?
YOU DO RECALL WHAT YOU DID TO ME AT UNIVERSITY.
I DID NOTHING TO YOU, PLEASE, LET ME DOWN--
I'LL LET YOU DOWN WHEN I AM DAMN WELL READY TO DO SO!
HERE, IN THIS OPERATING THEATER, I AM GOD AND YOU WILL ATONE FOR YOUR SINS!

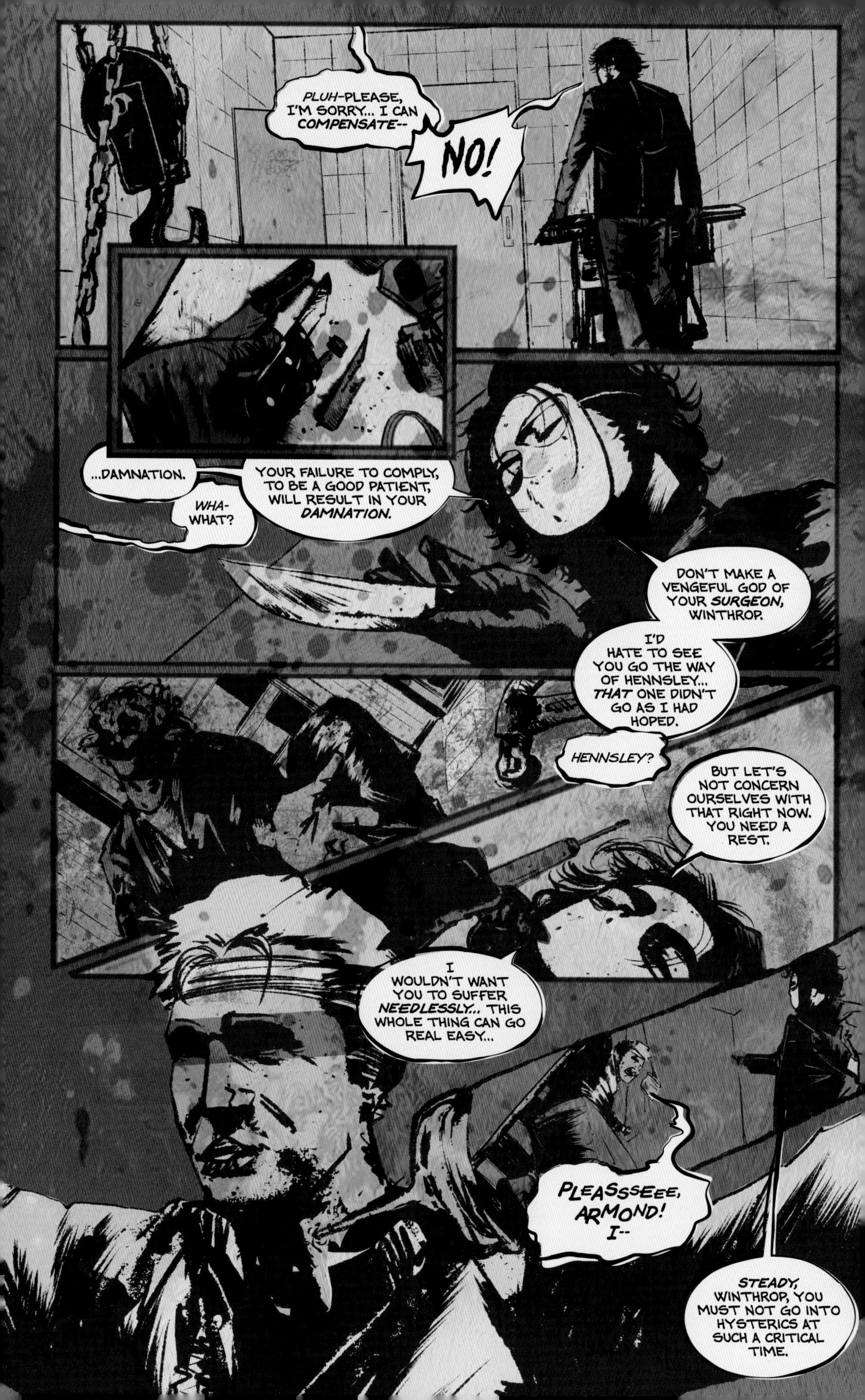
PLUH-PLEASE, I'M SORRY... I CAN COMPENSATE--
NO!
...DAMNATION.
WHA-WHAT?
YOUR FAILURE TO COMPLY, TO BE A GOOD PATIENT, WILL RESULT IN YOUR DAMNATION.
DON'T MAKE A VENGEFUL GOD OF YOUR SURGEON, WINTHROP.
I'D HATE TO SEE YOU GO THE WAY OF HENNSLEY... THAT ONE DIDN'T GO AS I HAD HOPED.
HENNSLEY?
BUT LET'S NOT CONCERN OURSELVES WITH THAT RIGHT NOW. YOU NEED A REST.
I WOULDN'T WANT YOU TO SUFFER NEEDLESSLY... THIS WHOLE THING CAN GO REAL EASY...
PLEASSSEEE, ARMOND! I--
STEADY, WINTHROP, YOU MUST NOT GO INTO HYSTERICS AT SUCH A CRITICAL TIME.

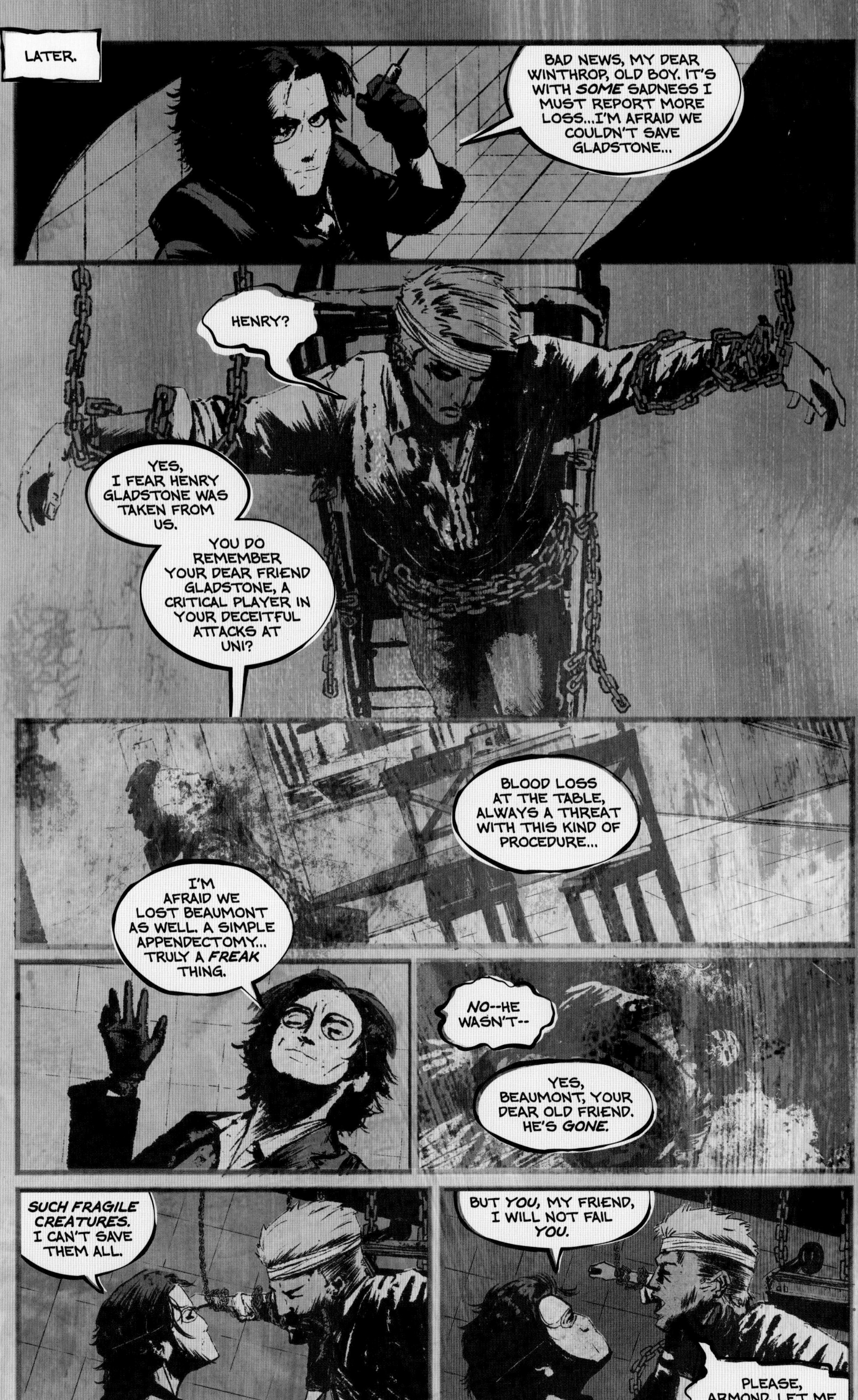
LATER.
BAD NEWS, MY DEAR WINTHROP, OLD BOY. IT'S WITH *SOME* SADNESS I MUST REPORT MORE LOSS...I'M AFRAID WE COULDN'T SAVE GLADSTONE...
HENRY?
YES, I FEAR HENRY GLADSTONE WAS TAKEN FROM US.
YOU DO REMEMBER YOUR DEAR FRIEND GLADSTONE, A CRITICAL PLAYER IN YOUR DECEITFUL ATTACKS AT UNI?
BLOOD LOSS AT THE TABLE, ALWAYS A THREAT WITH THIS KIND OF PROCEDURE...
I'M AFRAID WE LOST BEAUMONT AS WELL. A SIMPLE APPENDECTOMY... TRULY A *FREAK* THING.
NO--HE WASN'T--
YES, BEAUMONT, YOUR DEAR OLD FRIEND. HE'S *GONE.*
SUCH FRAGILE CREATURES. I CAN'T SAVE THEM ALL.
BUT *YOU*, MY FRIEND, I WILL NOT FAIL *YOU*.
PLEASE, ARMOND, LET ME MAKE IT RIGHT!

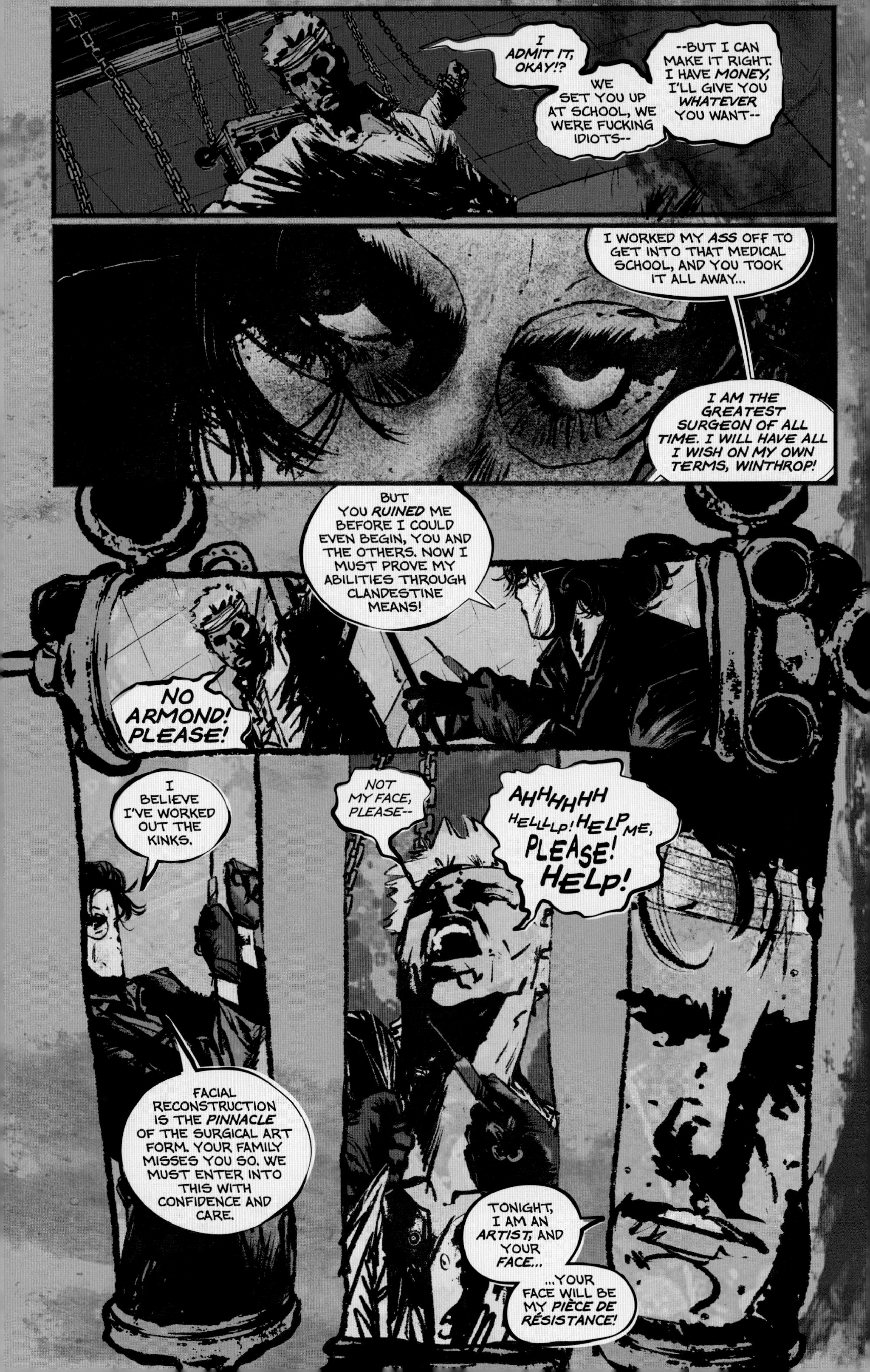
I ADMIT IT, OKAY!?
WE SET YOU UP AT SCHOOL, WE WERE FUCKING IDIOTS--
--BUT I CAN MAKE IT RIGHT. I HAVE MONEY, I'LL GIVE YOU WHATEVER YOU WANT--
I WORKED MY ASS OFF TO GET INTO THAT MEDICAL SCHOOL, AND YOU TOOK IT ALL AWAY...
I AM THE GREATEST SURGEON OF ALL TIME. I WILL HAVE ALL I WISH ON MY OWN TERMS, WINTHROP!
BUT YOU RUINED ME BEFORE I COULD EVEN BEGIN, YOU AND THE OTHERS. NOW I MUST PROVE MY ABILITIES THROUGH CLANDESTINE MEANS!
NO ARMOND! PLEASE!
I BELIEVE I'VE WORKED OUT THE KINKS.
FACIAL RECONSTRUCTION IS THE PINNACLE OF THE SURGICAL ART FORM. YOUR FAMILY MISSES YOU SO. WE MUST ENTER INTO THIS WITH CONFIDENCE AND CARE.
NOT MY FACE, PLEASE--
AHHHHHH HELLLLP! HELP ME, PLEASE! HELP!
TONIGHT, I AM AN ARTIST, AND YOUR FACE...
...YOUR FACE WILL BE MY PIÈCE DE RÉSISTANCE!

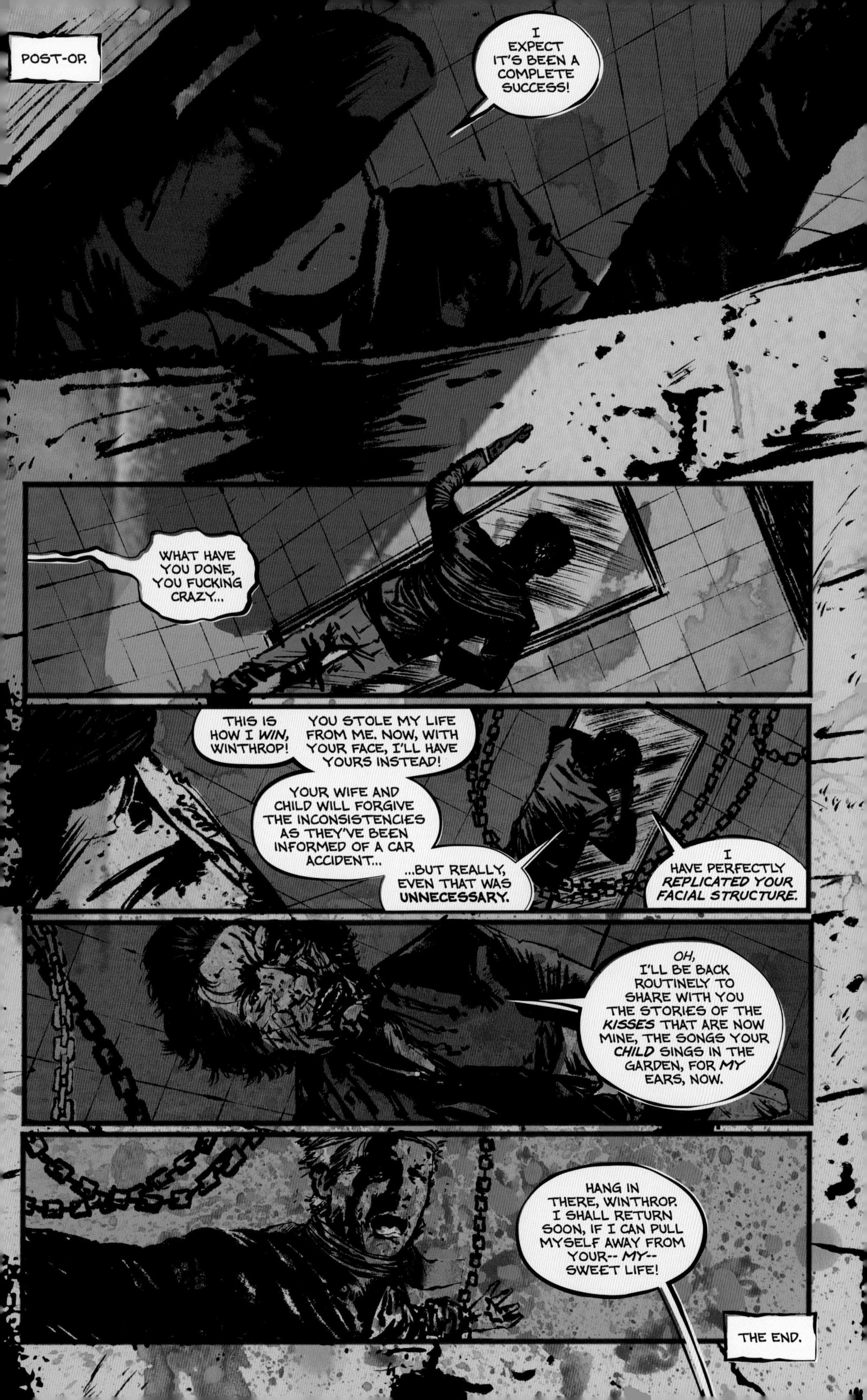
POST-OP.
I EXPECT IT'S BEEN A COMPLETE SUCCESS!
WHAT HAVE YOU DONE, YOU FUCKING CRAZY...
THIS IS HOW I *WIN*, WINTHROP!
YOU STOLE MY LIFE FROM ME. NOW, WITH YOUR FACE, I'LL HAVE YOURS INSTEAD!
YOUR WIFE AND CHILD WILL FORGIVE THE INCONSISTENCIES AS THEY'VE BEEN INFORMED OF A CAR ACCIDENT...
...BUT REALLY, EVEN THAT WAS **UNNECESSARY.**
I HAVE PERFECTLY *REPLICATED YOUR FACIAL STRUCTURE.*
OH, I'LL BE BACK ROUTINELY TO SHARE WITH YOU THE STORIES OF THE *KISSES* THAT ARE NOW MINE, THE SONGS YOUR *CHILD* SINGS IN THE GARDEN, FOR *MY* EARS, NOW.
HANG IN THERE, WINTHROP. I SHALL RETURN SOON, IF I CAN PULL MYSELF AWAY FROM YOUR-- *MY*-- SWEET LIFE!
THE END.

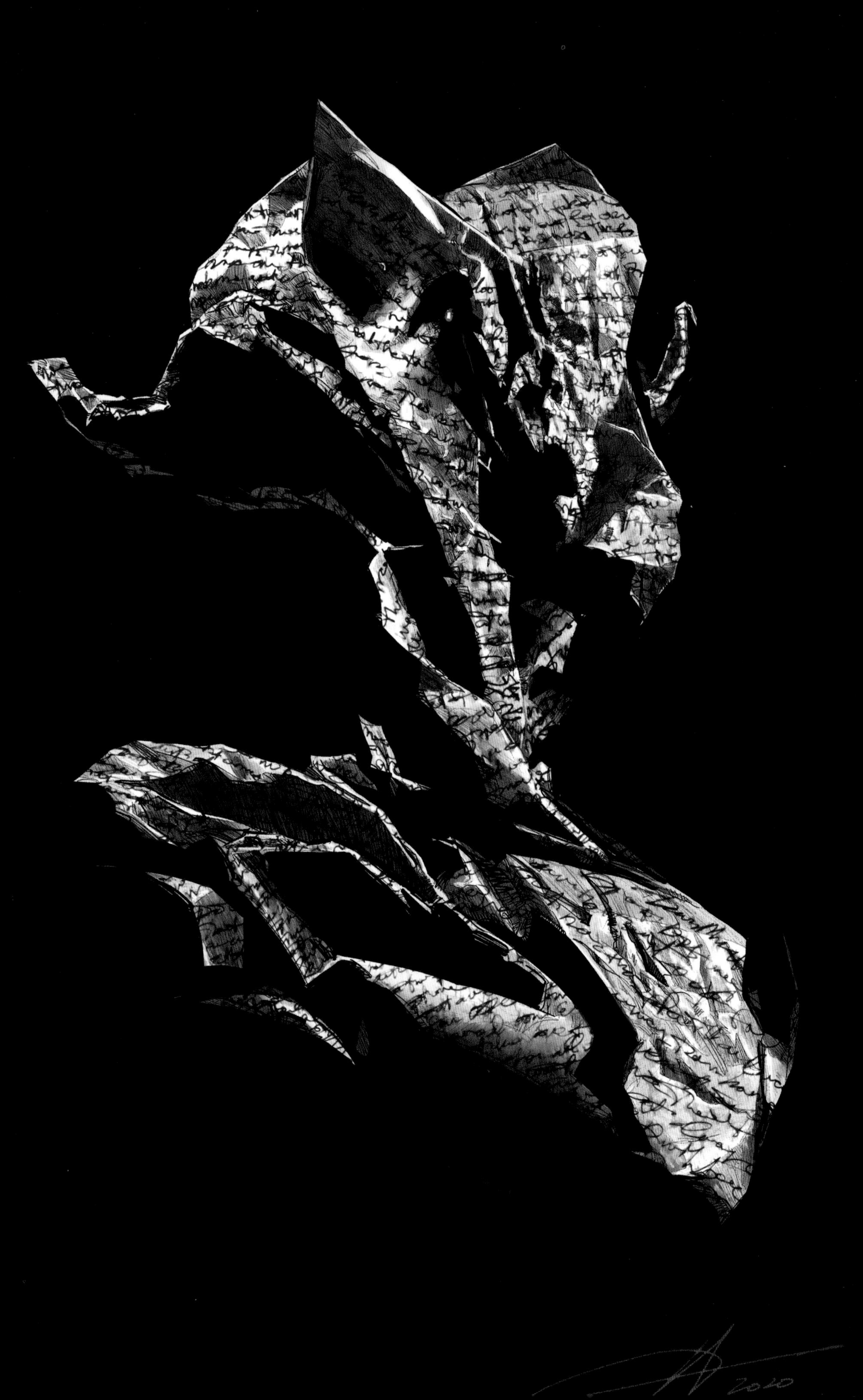

INSIDE

WRITTEN BY MICHAEL MORECI
ILLUSTRATION BY AARON CAMPBELL

The last of the casserole dishes arrived unceremoniously, exactly as the ones that'd preceded them. Natalie heard the faint knocking on her front door, the familiar sound of receding footfalls hurrying down her front steps, then a car shifting into gear and driving away. Once the car's engine was lost in the sycamore trees that surrounded Natalie's home, silence, steady and warm, returned. Her home, now, was mostly that: silence. The Sickness had claimed her husband, Gerald, and no one came near. Furtive casseroles and the occasional bouquet of flowers—requisite expressions of mourning—were the only things friends and families dared to offer.

It had only been a week since Gerald passed, alone in an overcrowded hospital, and Natalie had spent much of that time in her husband's home office. She was surprised, in fact, by how much of the house's varied noises—from people knocking on the door to water pushing through pipes to squirrels scurrying across the roof—she was able to hear in this secluded corner. Gerald was an academic, almost to the point of parody: his tweed blazers were worn out and carried his scent; his absentmindedness had been a running joke since the day he and Natalie met. Natalie always imagined this room to be a kind of cocoon of quiet solitude. This is where Gerald came to think and analyze historical accounts and grade his grad students' thesis papers. The outside world didn't intrude on this space—

But the more time she spent in this confined, musty room, the more Natalie realized how inaccurate her perception of it was.

Natalie sat back in Gerald's weathered desk chair, thinking. Spread out before her on Gerald's desk was a series of letters that, until just days ago, Natalie never knew existed. Seventeen years of marriage, over twenty devoted to one another. While Natalie wouldn't consider their relationship to be one of the world's greatest romances, she was comfortable in the life they shared. They folded into one another, proud of their strengths, forgiving of their weaknesses, understanding of their desires. They were generous enough in spirit to give themselves to each other while still retaining enough confidence to allow one another to be individuals.

And yet—and *yet*.

These letters.

Natalie stood up and pressed her palms down on the desk. She'd only read the first two of the letters she'd found, caught somewhere between not wanting to intrude on her late husband's privacy and wondering why he'd kept this relationship from her. Natalie knew she'd never gain any kind of clarity as to the reasons Gerald had never told her about any of this, and it wasn't like it mattered— the letters were nothing. It was unlike Gerald to hide things from Natalie, and unlike him to even do something like this. But they were nothing.

Natalie took a deep breath and left her husband's office, leaving the remaining letters unread.

Nothing, she reminded herself.

Downstairs, on the house's main level, Natalie scrubbed, cleaned, and disinfected until the day's gray gloom faded into night.

Ten days ago, Gerald was rushed from their home in an ambulance. He'd been showing signs of being what the TV experts called "Unwell"—a very generous term for those afflicted by the Sickness,

Natalie had come to discover—for a few days. Gerald said he was simply tired. Fatigued from his classwork. At worst, he had a common cold. But it wasn't that. Soon, Natalie was calling 911, and shortly after, men in hazmat suits came to take Gerald away. She never saw him outside of a grainy computer monitor again.

Subtracting those ten days—Natalie's last day of exposure—left her with ten more in quarantine. Not that it mattered much. While Gerald was still active in the world outside their home since the start of the Sickness, Natalie had stayed confined. There was part of her that simply didn't want to take the risk; she didn't want to chance her own health, and she didn't want to pass that risk on to others. But there was something else, too. In the months between when the Sickness began and when Gerald died, Natalie would find herself gazing out her living room window and seeing something out there—seeing but not seeing.

It was like an intrusion. Something got inside of you if you went out there; it got inside of you, then you brought it into your home, and it got inside there, too. Then it was everywhere. Down on her hands and knees, scrubbing the living room's hardwood floor, Natalie felt that intrusion all around her. Gerald, of course, was the point of incursion. Whether through a department meeting, one of his lectures, or somewhere else, the Sickness got inside of him. And he carried it right into their home.

The experts said the Sickness didn't last long—within hours, it was undetectable on nearly any surface. Gerald had been gone for over a week; Natalie had already washed all his clothes, she'd disinfected their house from top to bottom; she'd already scrubbed the very floor she was scrubbing now. Twice. But she could never feel at ease, not for long. The border separating herself, within these walls, and whatever was outside had been breached, and that couldn't be undone.

Something was inside. Natalie was certain of it.

So, she scrubbed. And she washed down the walls, she sprayed disinfectant on doorknobs and light switches, she removed curtains and stuffed them into the laundry machine. She went online and purchased more cleansing products. The night's darkness became absolute, and Natalie didn't even realize she'd forgotten to eat dinner. She couldn't believe it was already past midnight.

Her hands were raw, her knees were stiff, and her back ached. Natalie climbed the steps leading upstairs and paused at the landing. Those letters were still resting there, just over her shoulder, on Gerald's desk, alone in the dark. They begged to be read, nagging at Natalie's thoughts no matter how thorough her conviction over their nothingness. The sight of them just lying there, the words exposed for anyone to see, flashed across her mind until—

Natalie was standing before them. She didn't remember making the turn toward Gerald's office—right, when her bedroom was left—and she wasn't even certain how long she'd been standing there. But she was there. And so were the letters.

There was nothing to consider. Outside, the wind had begun to pick up and was howling through the trees. Natalie hardly noticed. She sank into Gerald's leather chair and picked up the third letter in the correspondence.

Like the other two Natalie had already read, this one seemed to be equally as innocuous. The letter was handwritten by a young boy—his valediction simply "Your Friend"—who was either lacking a proper education, wasn't comfortable with English as his preferred language, or both. He wrote about how he'd recently played soccer with his friends and how his school had recently purchased new books for his classroom—due, in part, to Gerald's generosity. From what Natalie could tell, Gerald had sponsored this young child, and the letters were simply an expression of gratitude and a means to show Gerald's generosity in action. But at the heart of her husband's kindness was a question that Natalie couldn't ignore: Why keep this a secret? Had he just forgotten to tell her? Or maybe there was a different reason? He didn't think Natalie would discourage him from being charitable—did he?

Natalie leaned back in the chair, its old, dried-out base sighing as she did. She turned the letter facedown, onto her lap. Every marriage has secrets, and Natalie's was no different. But you hid your sins and things you were ashamed of—not your goodness. Outside, the wind continued to throttle the trees. Natalie could hear their branches groaning as they were pushed and pulled; the air currents' howls sounded almost like laughter, as if they were mocking the trees' protestations. Natalie again picked up the letter, determined to let this entire thing be. She wouldn't torture herself over questions she'd never be able to answer.

But as she returned the letter to the desk, she noticed a line at the bottom. Right before Your Friend signed off—

I'm sorry your wife is so sad but it is good you are not.

Natalie's heart sank. She understood—in a detached, distant way—that she was in mourning. Most of these past ten days, she felt numb, the numbness interrupted by bouts of uncontrollable, and unpredictable, sobbing. Her feelings of loss, and the realization that she'd never see her husband again, were some of the most intense she'd ever experienced in her life. But the idea that she was *sad*, even now, felt so wrong to her. She may not have radiated ebullience, but Natalie felt content, if not happy. More importantly, she and Gerald were happy together.

And yet. *And yet*, Gerald was so convinced of her sadness, and maybe even so troubled by it, that he unburdened himself with a complete stranger—a child, no less. What did Natalie's husband see

when he looked at her? That question, loaded with anxiety and dread, weighed heavily on her.

What did Gerald see within her that she didn't?

A crashing sound erupted from downstairs, severing Natalie's thoughts. She raced to the living room and found glass shattered all over the floor she'd just scrubbed. A branch, torn from a nearby tree, had plunged through the picture window—penetrating her carefully maintained boundary. The curtains billowed as wind blew whatever was outside into her home.

Natalie grabbed her slippers from the couch, kicked the broken glass out of her way, and shoved the tree branch back outside. She stood for a moment, studying the gaping hole that now existed in her house. She felt the wind racing in; she saw the rainwater starting to pool in front of the baseboards. Who knew how far the wind, carrying whatever it carried, would reach within her house. Who knew how much water would collect. Who knew how much of the Sickness had gotten inside. But Natalie could feel it—in her lungs, coating her skin. She didn't need to see it, didn't need to heed what experts said about the unlikelihood of the Sickness existing long in the air without a human host. Natalie could feel it, and that was all that mattered.

Supplies. Natalie needed supplies, and quickly. Plywood, hammer, nails. She could clean the glass and soak up the water later. Right now, the breach needed to be sealed.

Natalie raced to the basement, to Gerald's workroom. Everything she needed was there, and she could get the window patched up in no time.

And then—the real cleanup would begin.

The cleaning, washing, and disinfecting carried Natalie all the way to late morning. She felt her weariness in her bones. But more than that, her throat was raw; every swallow was hot, every breath just a little bit constricted. It was the chemicals, she told herself. All those chemicals that she'd been using to eliminate whatever had gotten into her house during the night—she'd huffed so much of it in, and hadn't been drinking any water. That's why her throat was this way. And it was why her head was feeling light, and why her thoughts were so unfocused.

It was just chemicals and exhaustion.

Natalie forced her body up from the couch. She looked around. There was still so much to do, and Natalie couldn't help but wonder if she'd ever get it done. But, right now, she needed to rest. She needed a shower—scrubbing the past few hours off of her body was imperative—and a long nap.

Upstairs, she got as far as the bathroom—her hand hovering over the faucet—before her mind, free from concentrating on the task of eliminating any trace of the Sickness in her home, wandered to Gerald's letters. The idea that there was this sadness within her that even she didn't recognize frightened her. Those letters were the only clue Natalie had—her only way of understanding what this sadness was. It was imperative that she discover more.

She returned to Gerald's office. Natalie started with the letters she'd already read, combing through the niceties and trying to find any clue or hint that could help her understand. But there was nothing. Just that single, aching line:

I'm sorry your wife is so sad.

She forged ahead. More pleasant updates from Your Friend, more gratitude for Gerald's generosity. She went through one letter, then another; she was about to chalk it up as a misunderstanding and forget this entire episode. But then another line clawed its way up from the surface of Your Friend's parchment:

Why do you think your wife doesn't understand you?

Cold burned inside of Natalie. How desperate had Gerald been, to unburden himself to a child? It was like loading missives into a bottle and launching it into the depths of the ocean. And what had he seen in her? What did Gerald not *understand*? Was it her supposed sadness he couldn't grasp, or was it something else, something more intrinsic to Natalie as a person, that, somewhere along the way, began to elude him?

The crumpled paper felt satisfying in Natalie's grasp. She flung it across the room and shoved Your Friend's letters from the desk. They floated down to the floor, softly, and Natalie sneered at them before bringing both her fists down on Gerald's desk, hard. She pounded the desktop again, and again, then collapsed onto it, burying her head in her arms as she began to sob.

Her eyes were still wet with tears when she fell asleep.

It was night when Natalie awoke. She peeled open her eyes then pulled away the crust before turning on the desk's lamp. Her throat was rawer than it had been that morning, and her head was throbbing. Natalie reminded herself that she hadn't drank or eaten anything all day—but then she noticed her arm.

There were bruises along her right forearm. Four slender, dark bruises. Like someone had grabbed her.

She raced to the kitchen and gulped down water straight from the tap. The cold water helped awaken her mind, but she was nowhere close to achieving clarity. Natalie felt like she was looking at life through a sheet of smoky glass. She reminded herself that she was tired. And dehydrated. But—was bruising a sign of being Unwell? Her breathing became labored. Her throat still ached. More signs?

The Sickness now felt pervasive. Oppressive, even. She shouldn't have taken a break to shower. She definitely shouldn't have allowed herself to be distracted by Your Friend's letters. Natalie chastised herself—there was still so much of the house that needed to be fully disinfected, and she'd let it go unattended for hours. It could have spread while she was asleep. It could be anywhere by now. Everywhere. She'd have to start all over again.

Natalie forced herself to take a couple bites from an apple; it tasted like nothing, but revolted her anyway. The Sickness was crawling on *everything*.

Wasting no time, Natalie got back to work. She turned on every light, creating an artificial boundary between her home and the darkness outside that seemed determined to get in.

Over the past ten days, cleaning had been therapeutic. It was white noise that helped drown out Natalie's sorrow. But now, those same sounds—the scrubbing, the sloshing water—were abrasive. Her mind wouldn't drift into blissful distraction, nor would it allow Natalie to focus on a single thought. So many were competing for her attention—the Sickness, Gerald's absence, the bruises on her arm—that by the time she started considering one, another rose to the fore. Natalie scrubbed the floor harder. Her breathing was heavy, her throat felt like it was lined with gravel. She scrubbed even harder. There was no way she'd finish this entire house tonight, not in the condition she was in. Not with those letters crawling inside her head, driving her toward a compulsion to know more. They kept calling out to her, and Natalie tried to quiet their voice, and the sparring got her angrier, and angrier. She punched her sponge into the bucket but misjudged her aim—and the bucket toppled to its side.

A screamed ballooned inside of her, but Natalie knew how painful it'd be to release it. Stifled, she got to her feet and stomped up the stairs and back to Gerald's office.

Her phone. She needed to re-search symptoms of being Unwell—symptoms she could, just days ago, recite like the Pledge of Allegiance. But now they escaped her. Natalie walked over the letters she'd shoved onto the floor and grabbed her phone from the desk—

Dead. She pounded her thumb into the home screen, then the power button. Nothing. Natalie smashed her phone down on the desk, shattering the screen. And then, the scream came, though it wasn't much of a scream. Raspy and broken, her voice pushed up through her throat like shards of glass rejected by her lungs. Natalie collapsed onto the floor, burying her head into her knees, wondering what, if anything, she could do to stop all of this from happening.

Out of the corner of her eye, she spotted another letter. They were all out of order now, and there was no way of knowing at what point this particular correspondence between Gerald and Your Friend had occurred. But what mattered, only, was the line she drew from it:

Maybe you're right. Maybe there is something inside of you.

Natalie jumped to her feet and tumbled back against the desk.

Something inside of you. Not something inside of *her*.

The logical and most obvious conclusion was that Your Friend was speaking to Gerald. But Natalie knew that wasn't the case. Your Friend was—beyond reason, beyond any plausible means she could imagine—addressing her.

Slowly and carefully, unsure whether she actually wanted to touch the missive or not, Natalie bent down toward the letter. She reached out her hand, and the tips of her fingers were about to make contact with the parchment, parchment that didn't seem nearly as simple as it once had, but just before they did—

There was a knocking on the front door.

Natalie's head—eyes wide, mouth trembling—whiplashed to the side. She wondered who could possibly be at her door at this time of night. But she realized, then, she had no idea what time of night it was. It could have been eight, it could have been three in the morning.

With her phone broken and the only clock in the living room, there was no way for her to know.

She raced to the office's narrow window. The vantage didn't give her a clear glimpse of the front door; the light adjacent to the door cast no shadow, and there was no car in the driveway. It could have been one of the neighbors, checking on her—but Natalie dismissed this idea just as quickly as it formed in her mind. The same neighbors who were too frightened to bring their tokens of condolences into her home would now pay her an unexpected visit? It couldn't be.

The knocking came again, louder this time. Four thumps that Natalie felt in her bones.

"Go away!" she screamed, her throat shredding from the exertion.

More knocking. Three this time, and slower. Thoom. Thoom. Thoom.

Natalie pressed her hands to her ears, as if denying sound would help push everything out—the knocking, the pain in her throat, the letters that were inexplicably speaking directly to her.

The letters. Suddenly, Natalie was driven by an urge to get rid of them. All of them. They were the cause of everything that was happening—Your Friend may have gotten inside Gerald's head the way he was trying to penetrate Natalie's. She raced around the office, picking up the loose sheets of paper, intending on bringing them downstairs, straight to the fireplace, where she'd reduce them to ash. But as she picked up each correspondence, she couldn't help but see the words that were leaping off the page at her. One by one, in each letter, a word stabbed into her mind.

There
Is
Something
Inside

Natalie tore the letters that were in her grasp in half, and she was going to rip them again, when—

ThoomThoomThoomThoom

Natalie bared her teeth. Her breath came out in ragged, uneven pants; her eyes were unblinking. She threw the scraps of Your Friend's letters into the air and thundered to the stairs. She'd tell whoever was trying to intrude on her sanctuary, she'd tell them—

But Natalie's foot caught at the top of the stairs. Her ankle twisted, bending at an unnatural angle, and before she could reach out and grab the banister, her body was tumbling uncontrollably forward.

She hit the steps hard, rolling and careening, the world going end over end again and again and again.

Natalie dropped to the hardwood floor, her shoulder crunching upon impact. Everything felt like it was still spinning, like her mind had been thrown off its own axis. She blinked, hard, trying to regain her perspective—and she saw, through her bleary, fading vision that her front door was ajar. She had to close it—that thought overwhelmed all others. It was all coming *in*, everything outside, everything beyond, was coming in, and it had to be stopped. Through the pain—in her shoulder, in her ankle, in her entire body—Natalie crawled forward, willing herself toward the door. Darkness flooded the edge of her vision, but still she reached out with her one good arm and pulled the rest of her ahead. Her need, desperate and essential, to not be too late, flickered like a flame inside of her—and she was nearly to the door, it was just out of her grasp, when that flame was extinguished.

A voice called from behind her—

"It's okay," the voice said. Distant—maybe even childish. "I came to help—I'm Your Friend."

It was the last thing Natalie heard before her world turned to black.

End

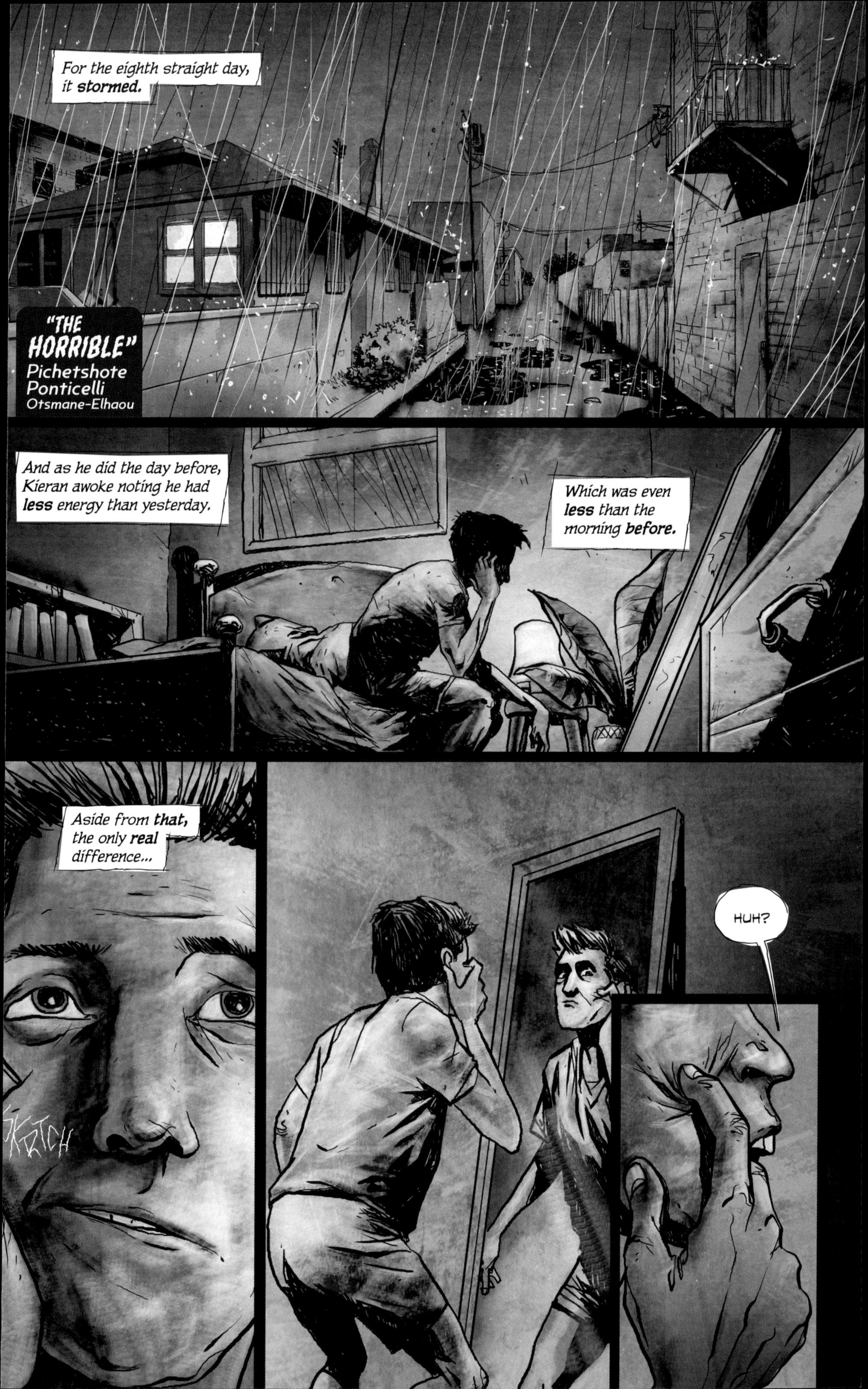

For the eighth straight day, it **stormed.**
"THE HORRIBLE"
Pichetshote
Ponticelli
Otsmane-Elhaou
And as he did the day before, Kieran awoke noting he had **less** energy than yesterday.
Which was even **less** than the morning **before.**
Aside from **that,** the only **real** difference...
HUH?

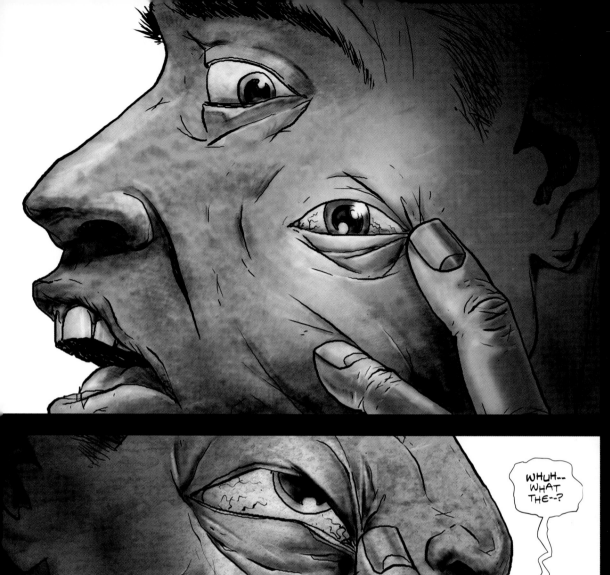

WHUH-- WHAT THE--?

SLRPP

AAAAH!

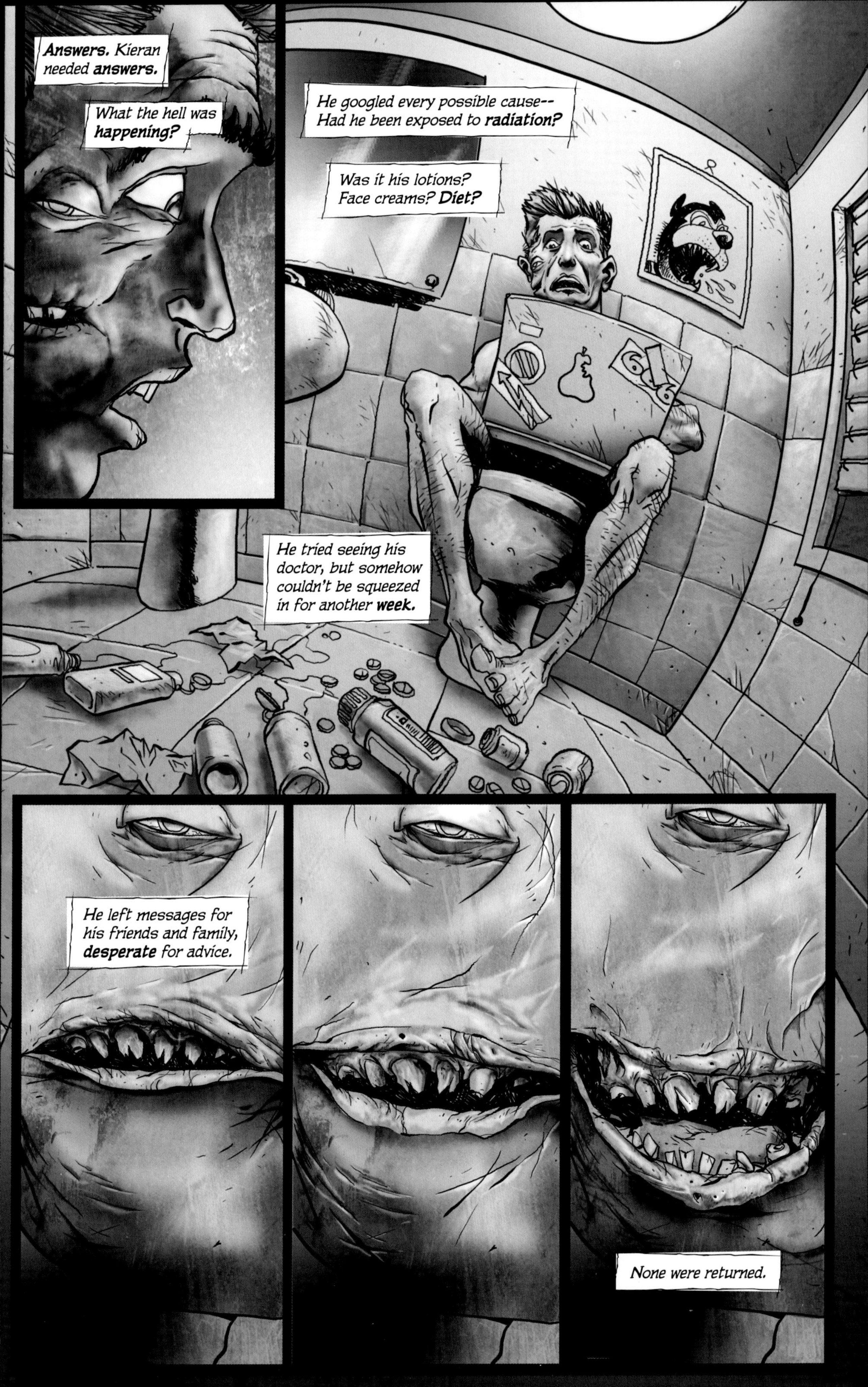
Answers. Kieran needed answers.
What the hell was happening?
He googled every possible cause-- Had he been exposed to radiation?
Was it his lotions? Face creams? Diet?
He tried seeing his doctor, but somehow couldn't be squeezed in for another week.
He left messages for his friends and family, desperate for advice.
None were returned.

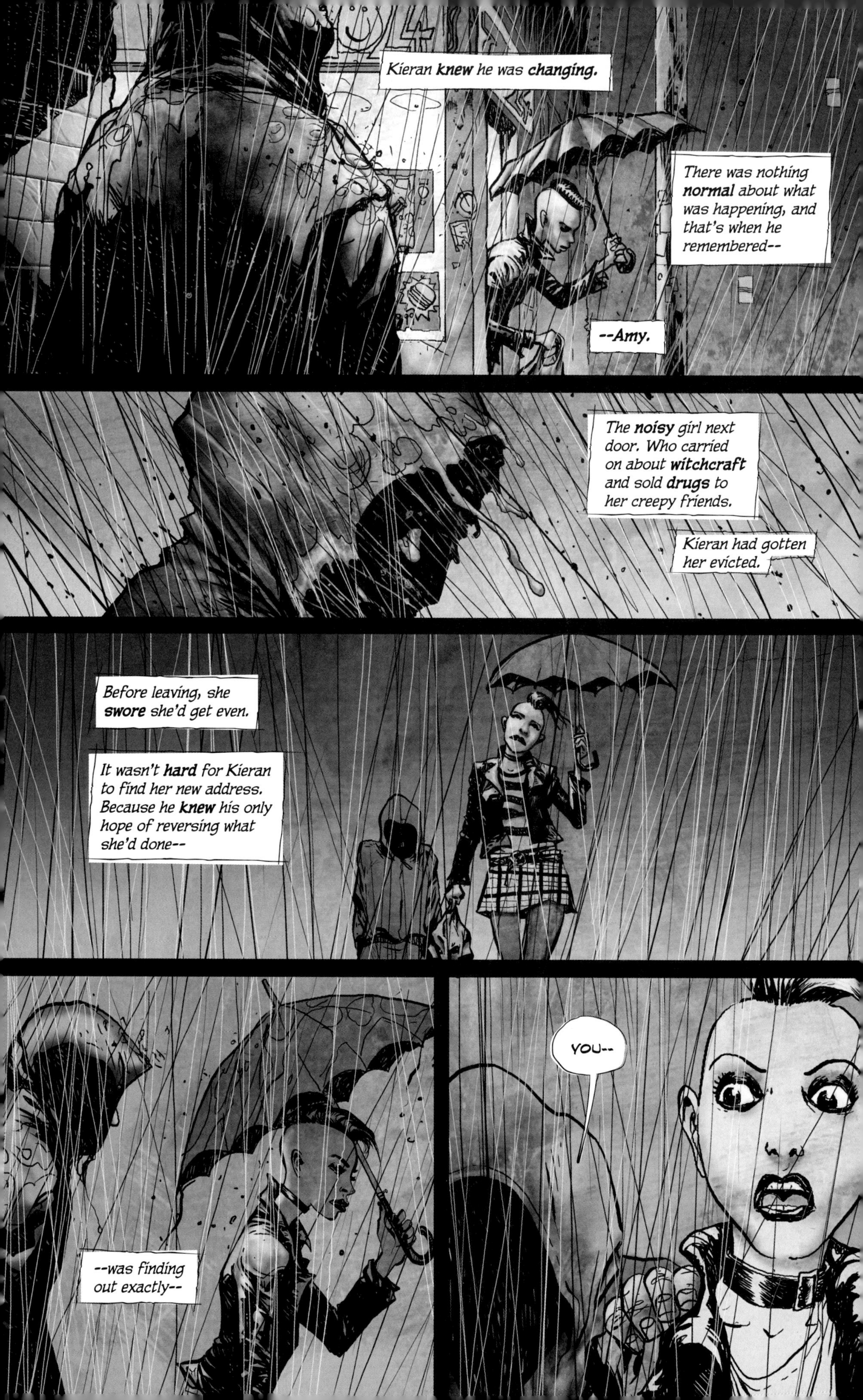
Kieran **knew** he was **changing.**
There was nothing **normal** about what was happening, and that's when he remembered--
--**Amy.**
The **noisy** girl next door. Who carried on about **witchcraft** and sold **drugs** to her creepy friends.
Kieran had gotten her evicted.
Before leaving, she **swore** she'd get even.
It wasn't **hard** for Kieran to find her new address. Because he **knew** his only hope of reversing what she'd done--
--was finding out exactly--
YOU--

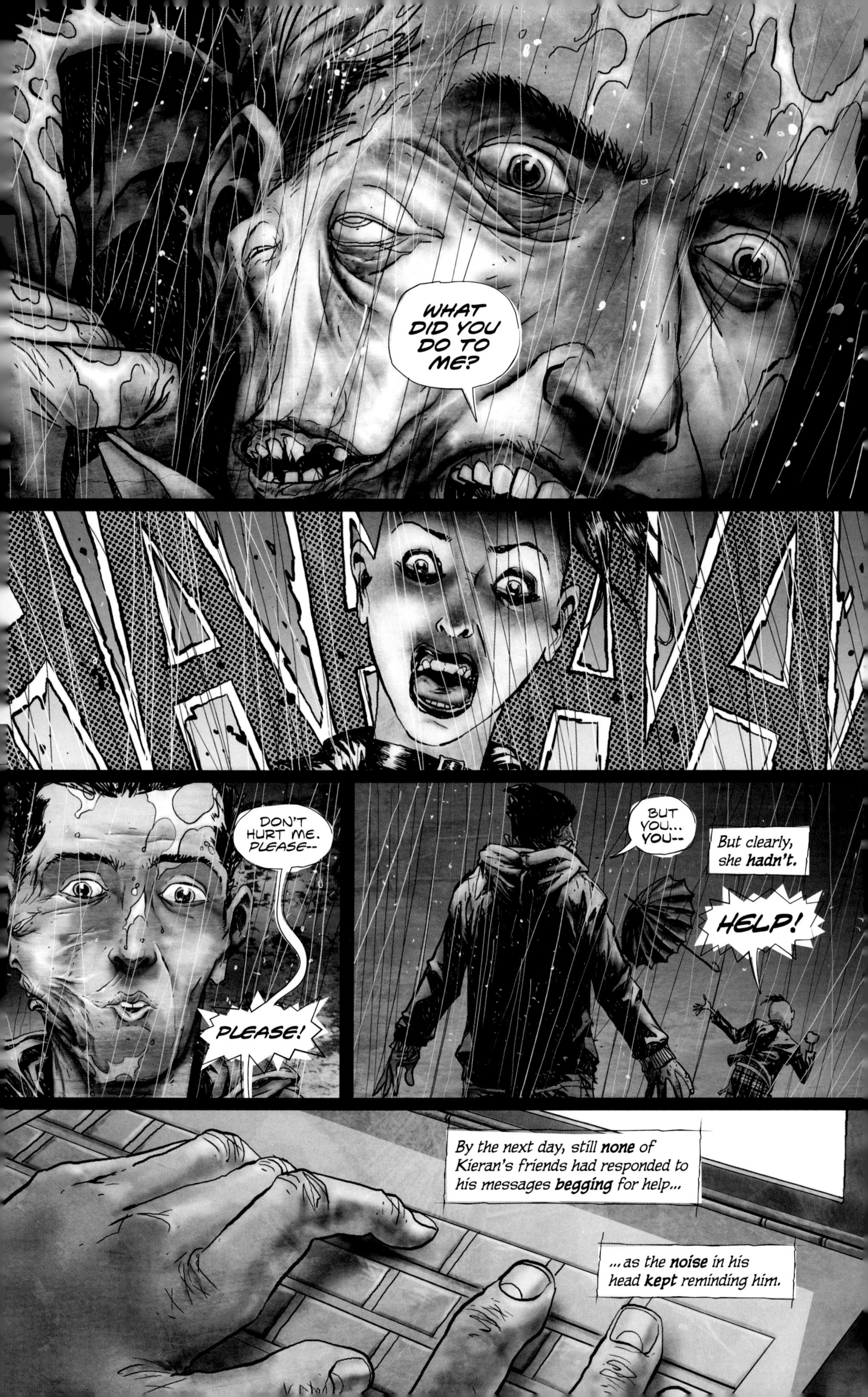
WHAT DID YOU DO TO ME?
DON'T HURT ME. PLEASE--
PLEASE!
BUT YOU... YOU--
But clearly, she **hadn't.**
HELP!
By the next day, still **none** of Kieran's friends had responded to his messages **begging** for help...
...as the **noise** in his head **kept** reminding him.

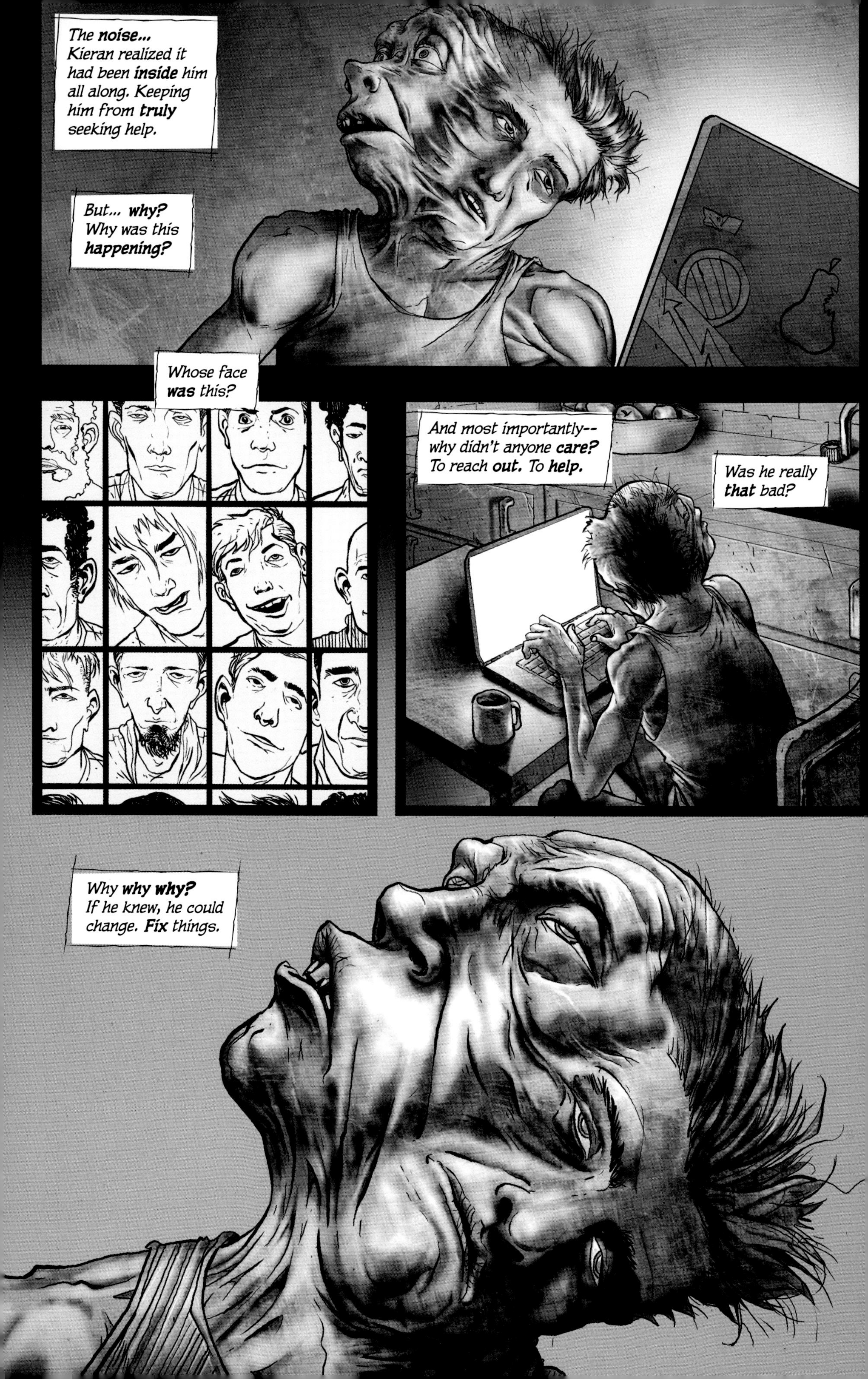
The **noise...** Kieran realized it had been **inside** him all along. Keeping him from **truly** seeking help.
But... **why?** Why was this **happening?**
Whose face **was** this?
And most importantly-- why didn't anyone **care?** To reach **out.** To **help.**
Was he really **that** bad?
Why **why why?** If he knew, he could change. **Fix** things.

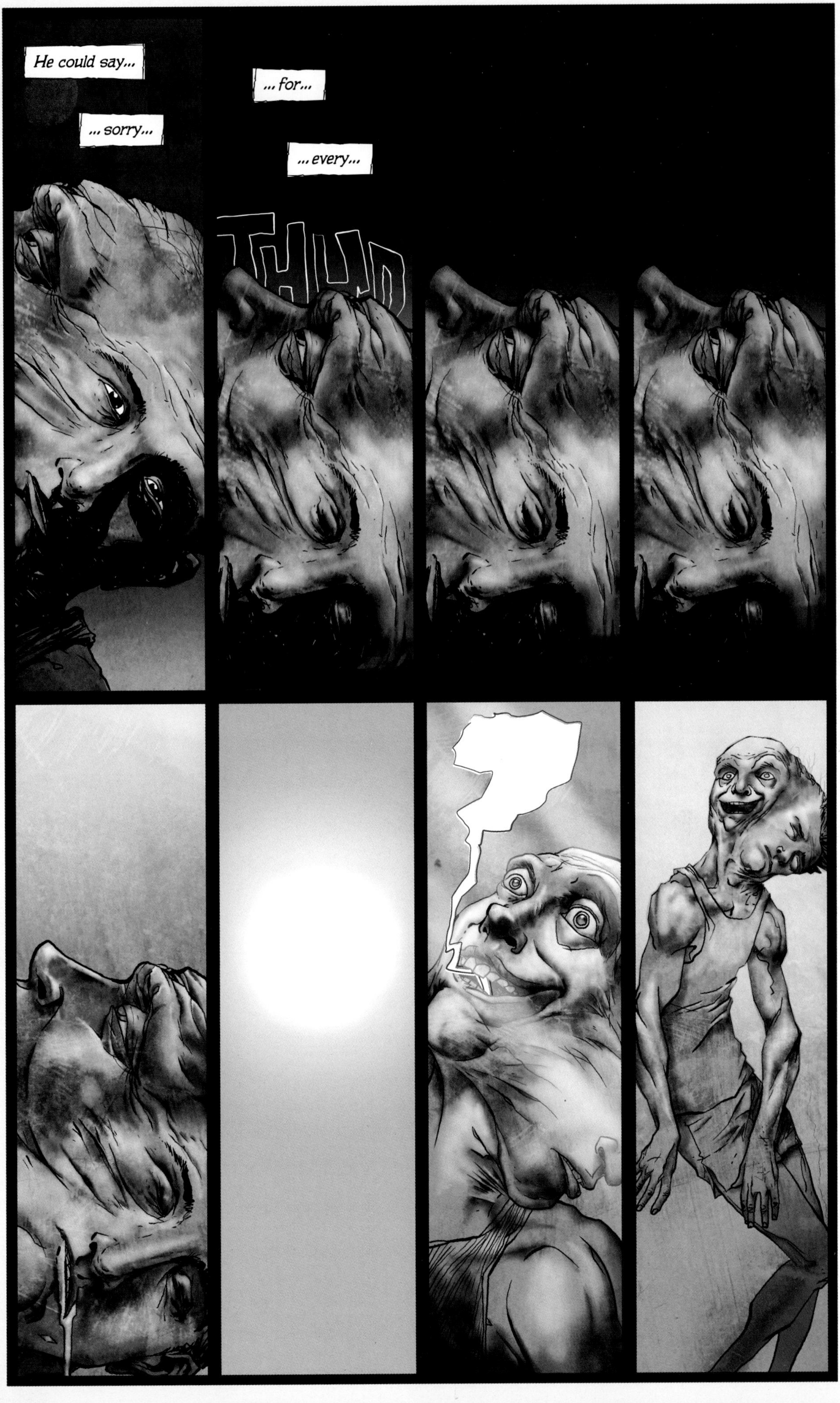
He could say...
...sorry...
...for...
...every...
THUD
?

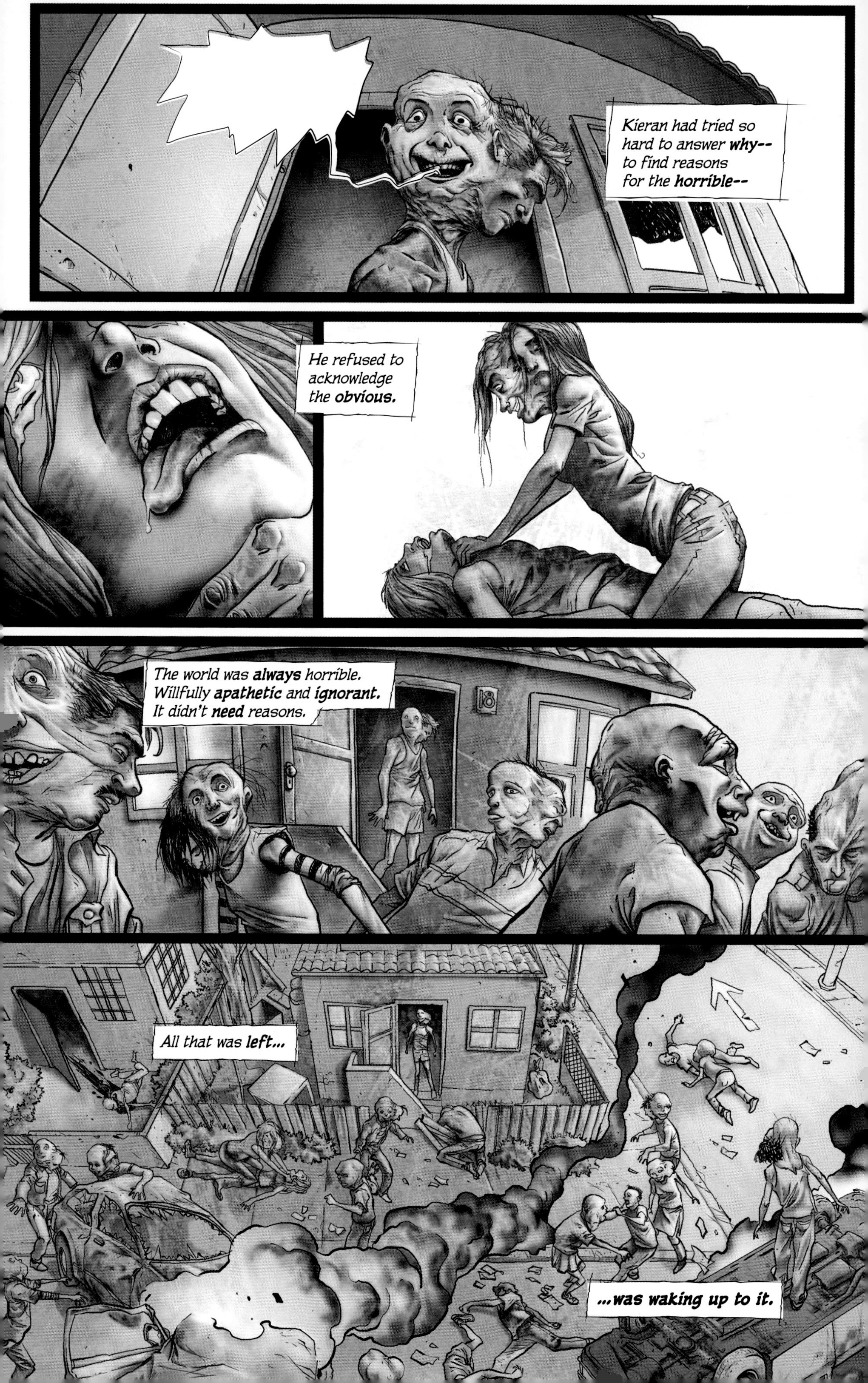
Kieran had tried so hard to answer **why--** to find reasons for the **horrible--**
He refused to acknowledge the **obvious.**
The world was **always** horrible. Willfully **apathetic** and **ignorant.** It didn't **need** reasons.
18
All that was **left...**
...was waking up to it.

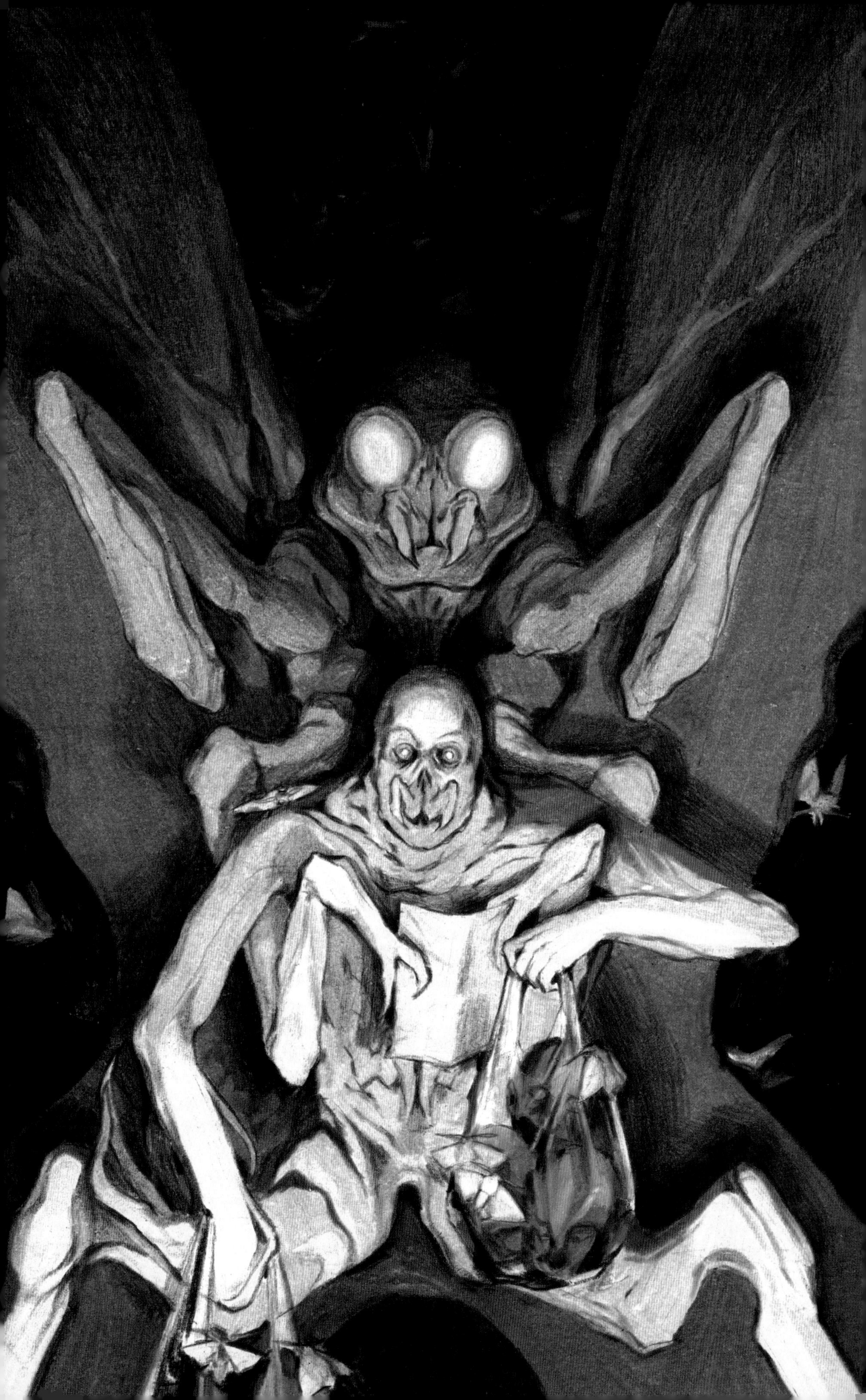

by Jess Unkel &
Jenn St-Onge

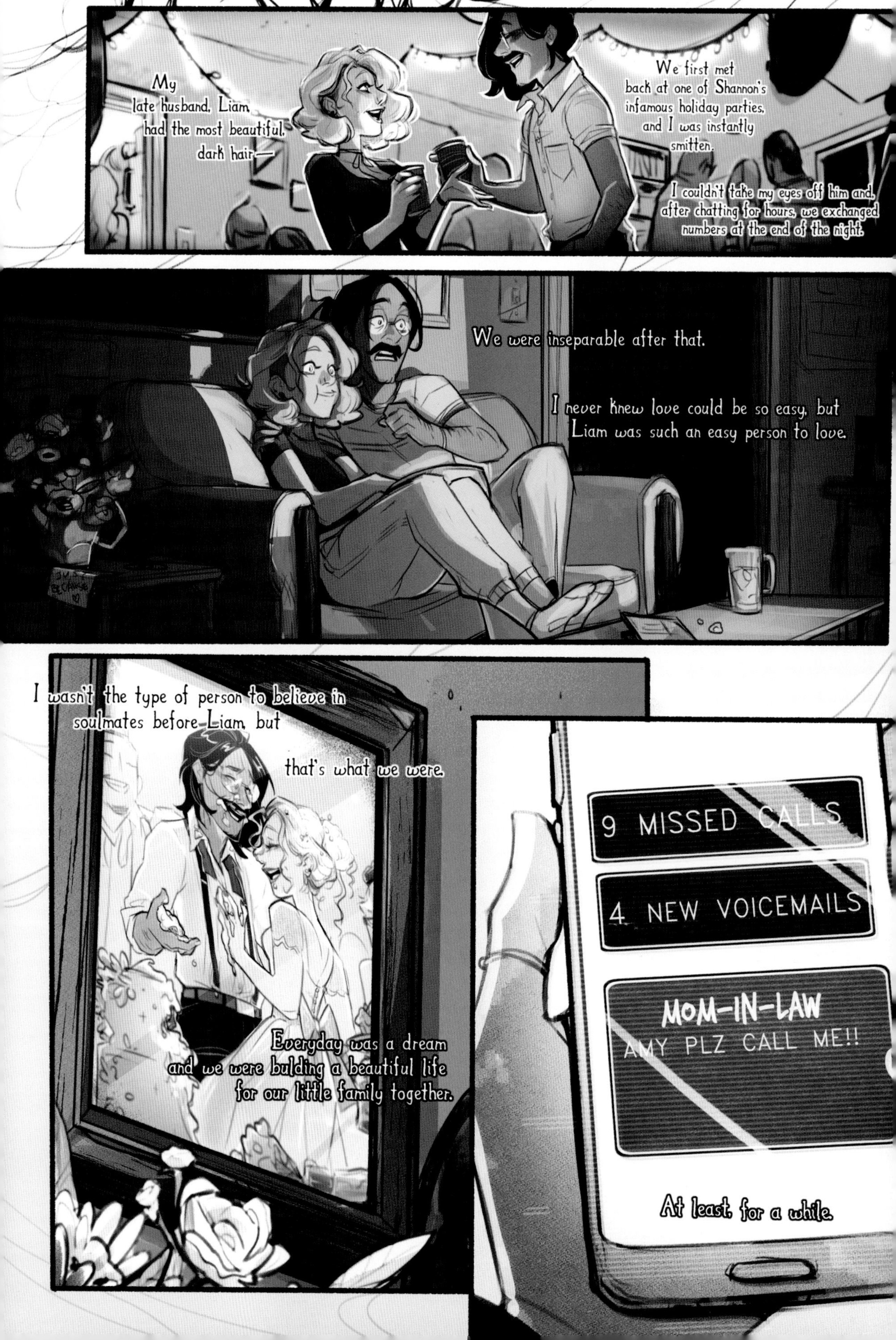
My late husband, Liam, had the most beautiful, dark hair—
We first met back at one of Shannon's infamous holiday parties, and I was instantly smitten.
I couldn't take my eyes off him and, after chatting for hours, we exchanged numbers at the end of the night.
We were inseparable after that.
I never knew love could be so easy, but Liam was such an easy person to love.
I wasn't the type of person to believe in soulmates before Liam, but
that's what we were.
Everyday was a dream and we were bulding a beautiful life for our little family together.
9 MISSED CALLS
4 NEW VOICEMAILS
MOM-IN-LAW
AMY PLZ CALL ME!!
At least, for a while.

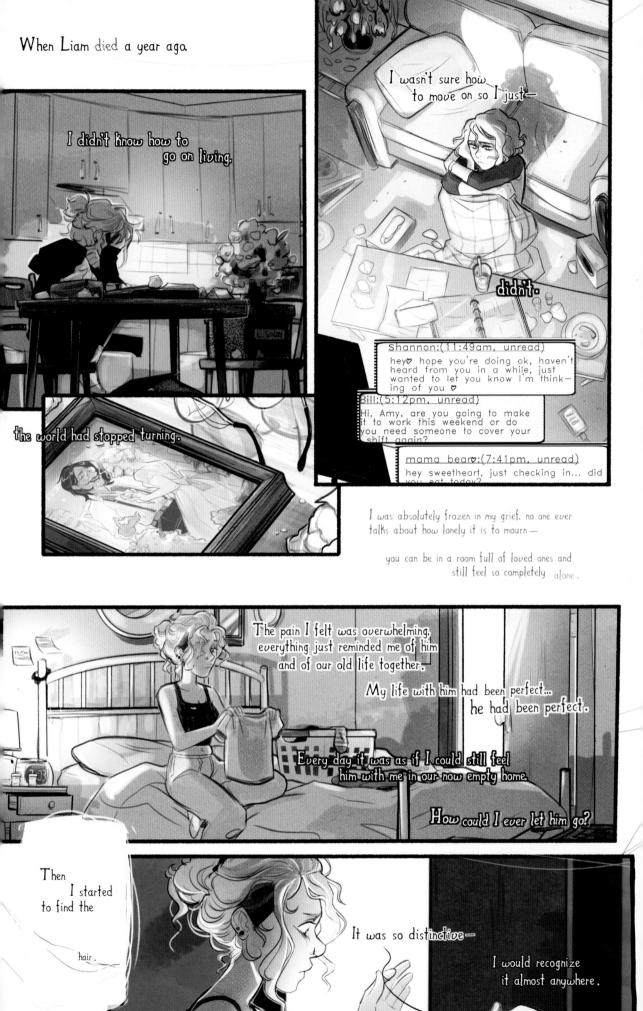

When Liam died a year ago,

I didn't know how to go on living.

I wasn't sure how to move on so I just—

didn't.

the world had stopped turning.

Shannon:(11:49am, unread)
hey♡ hope you're doing ok, haven't heard from you in a while, just wanted to let you know I'm think-ing of you ♡

Bill:(5:12pm, unread)
Hi, Amy, are you going to make it to work this weekend or do you need someone to cover your shift again?

mama bear♡:(7:41pm, unread)
hey sweetheart, just checking in... did you eat today?

I was absolutely frozen in my grief, no one ever talks about how lonely it is to mourn —

you can be in a room full of loved ones and still feel so completely alone.

The pain I felt was overwhelming, everything just reminded me of him and of our old life together.

My life with him had been perfect... he had been perfect.

Every day it was as if I could still feel him with me in our now empty home.

How could I ever let him go?

Then I started to find the

hair.

It was so distinctive—

I would recognize it almost anywhere.

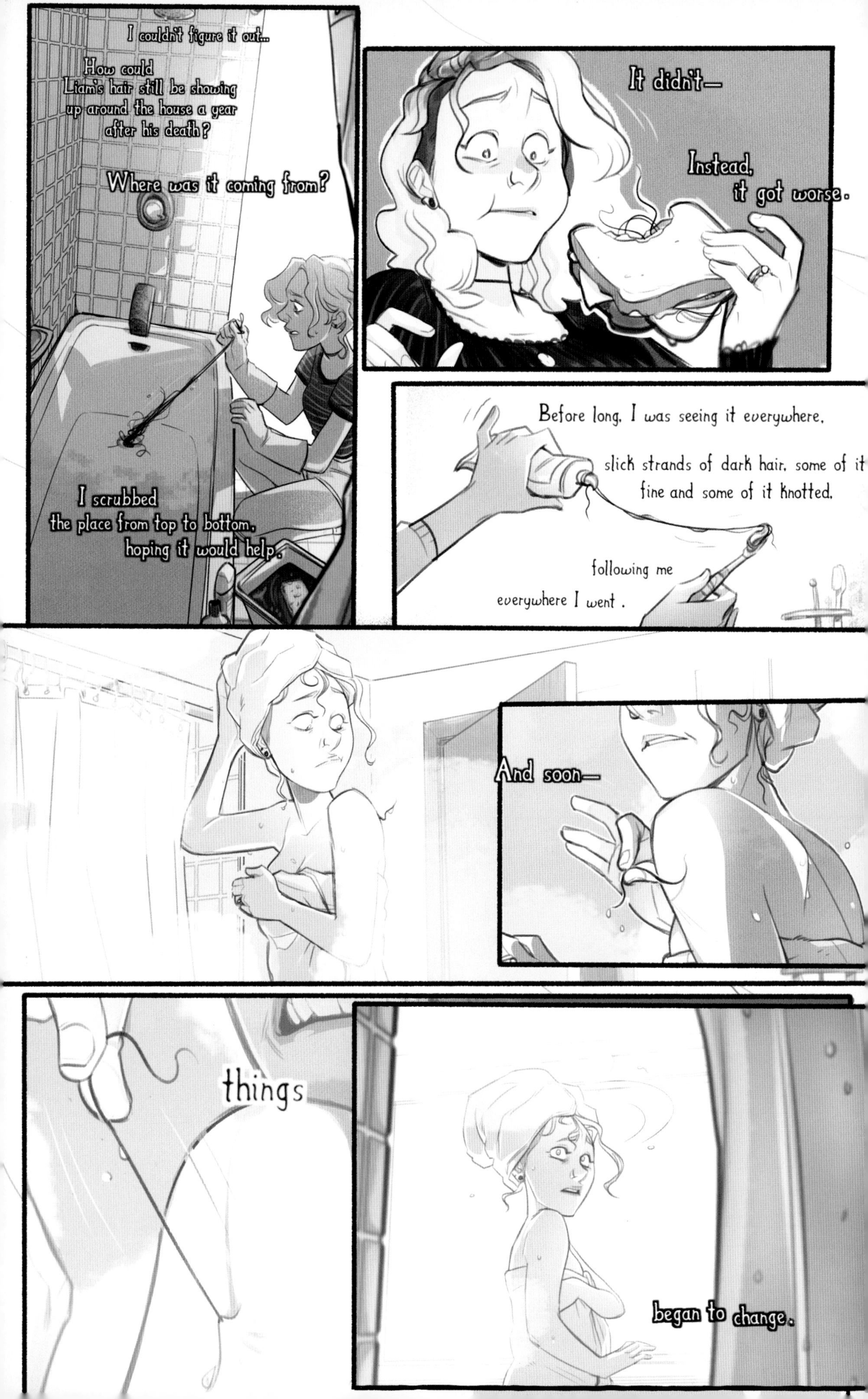
I couldn't figure it out...
How could Liam's hair still be showing up around the house a year after his death?
Where was it coming from?
I scrubbed the place from top to bottom, hoping it would help.
It didn't—
Instead, it got worse.
Before long, I was seeing it everywhere,
slick strands of dark hair, some of it fine and some of it knotted,
following me
everywhere I went.
And soon—
things
began to change.

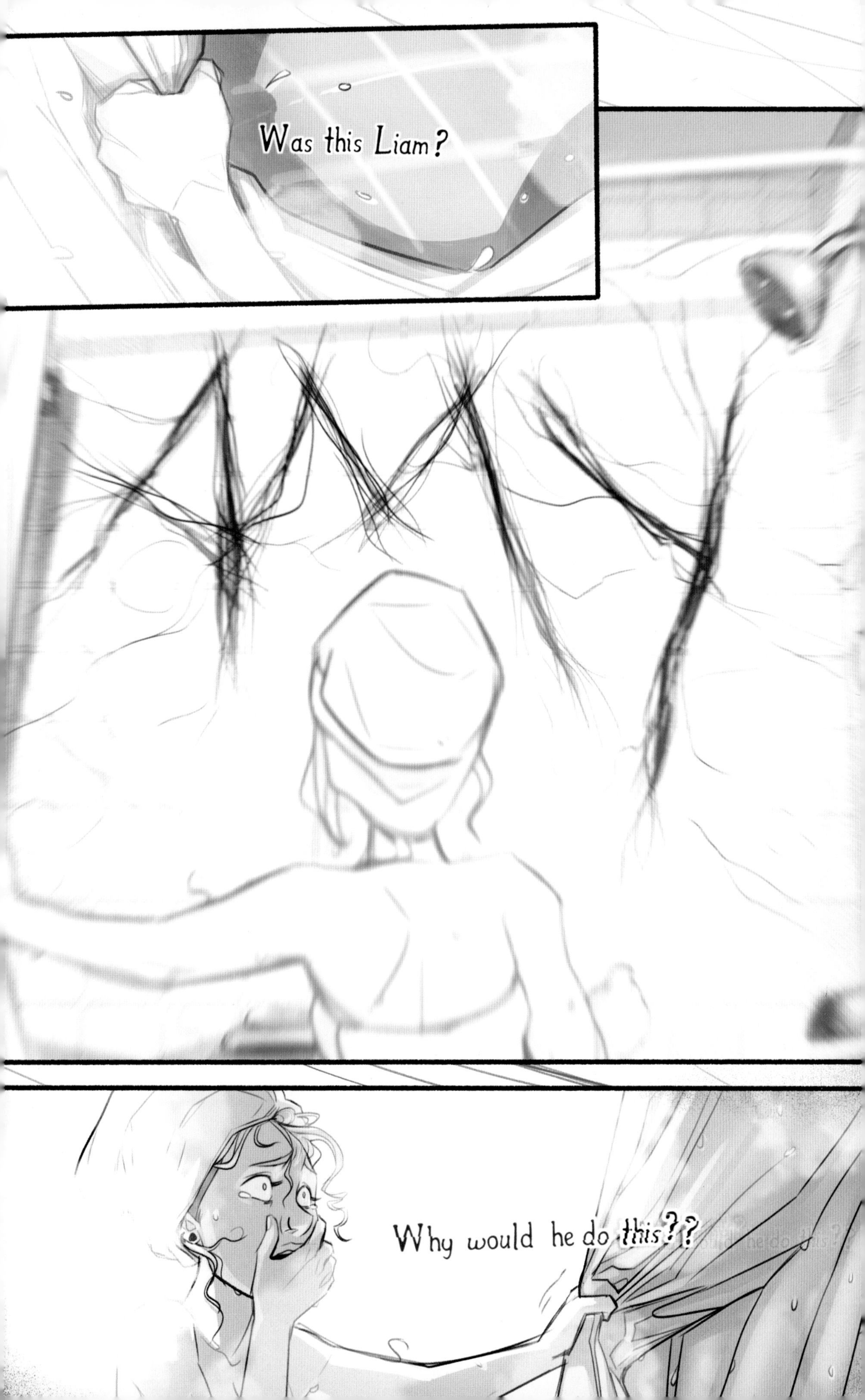
Was this Liam?
Why would he do this??

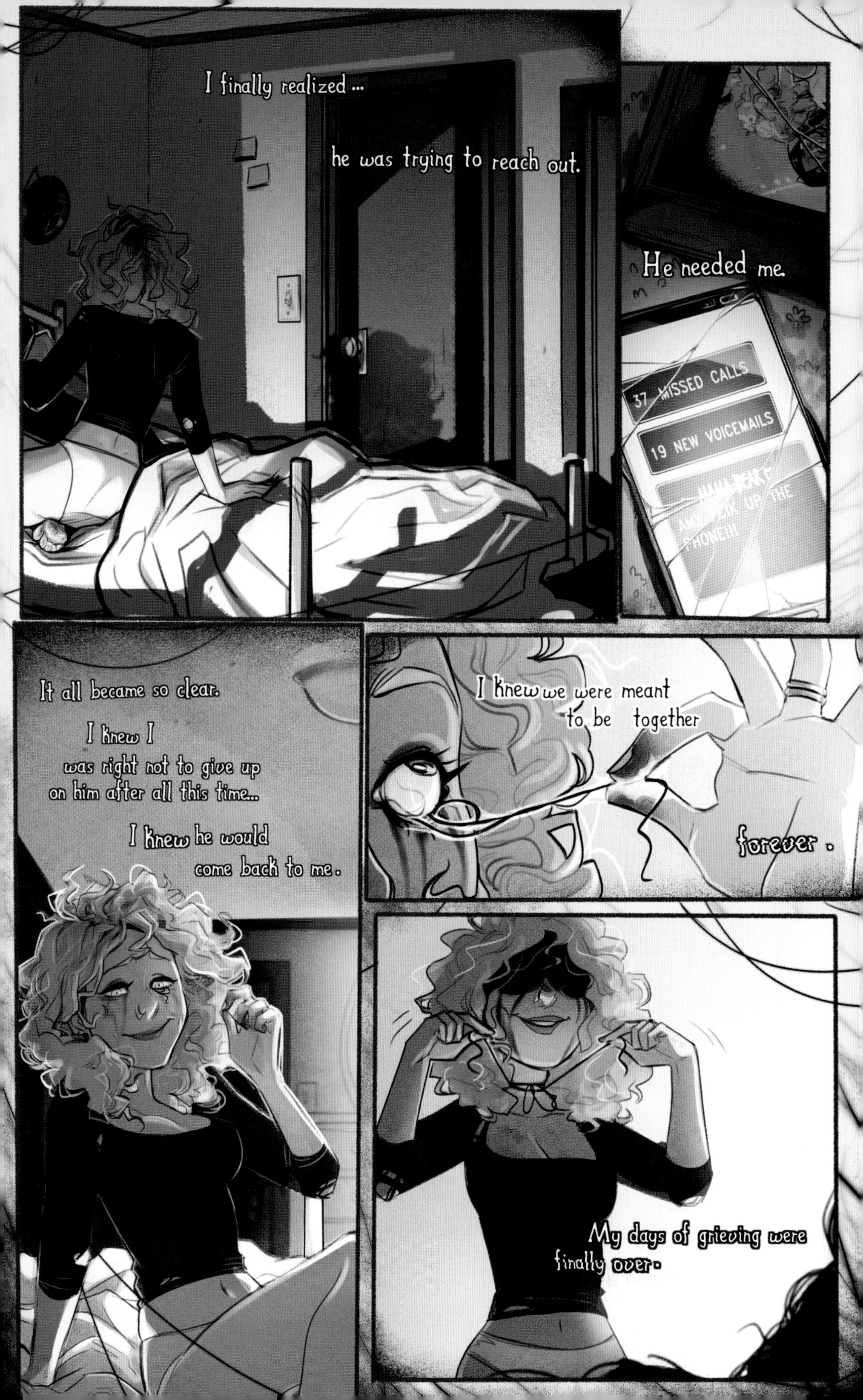
I finally realized ...
he was trying to reach out.
He needed me.
37 MISSED CALLS
19 NEW VOICEMAILS
UP THE
PHONE!!!
It all became so clear.
I knew I
was right not to give up
on him after all this time...
I knew he would
come back to me.
I knew we were meant
to be together
forever.
My days of grieving were
finally over.

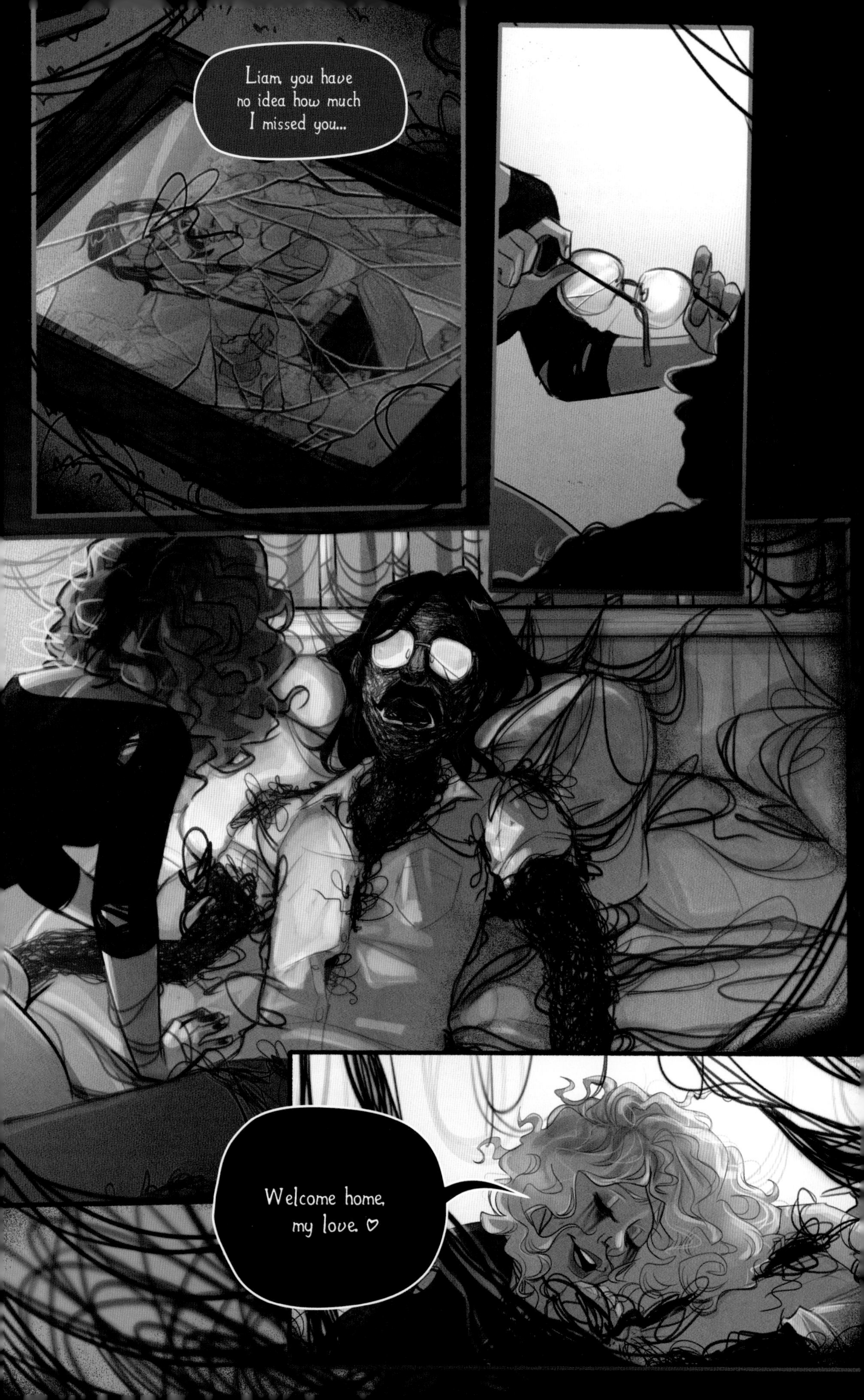
Liam you have no idea how much I missed you...
Welcome home, my love. ♡

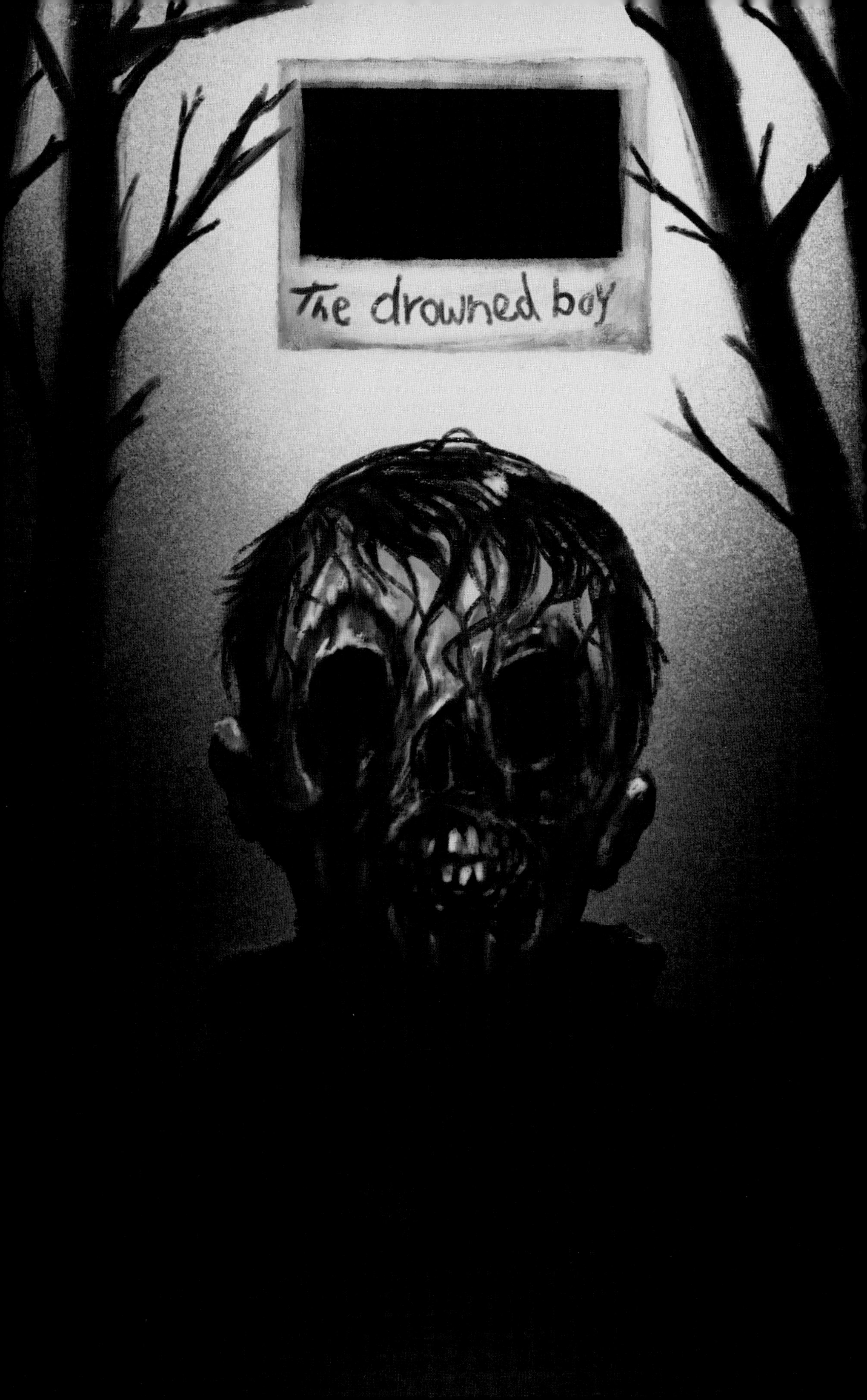
The drowned boy

Patrick is missing.

Last Saturday, we ~~#~~ went up to the lake together,
and that's the last anyone has seen of him.
I'm getting really worried.

He heard about The Drowned Boy over summer break,
at one of Kelly's parties, and ever since, he's been
obsessed.

He wanted to see him, summon him. And last
Saturday, he brought me along while he tried.

To summon The Drowned Boy, you have to go to the
spot where he died. You bring a candle to see your
way, and a camera, the kind that spits out the
photos so you can tack them up on your wall.

The key is to use the last photo looking out over
the water, and if it comes out black then it's
because the boy is peering into the lense with an
empty, watery eye socket. That's what they say, ~~###~~
~~###############~~ And that's exactly what happened.

Patrick laughed it off, and I just thought it was
his shitty old camera, so we hung out for a while
and drank his piss beers. But no one has spoken to
him since then. His parents are really worried.

I haven't told anyone, but I've been having these nightmares
like I'm floating in a black void. No one can hear me
calling out. I'm screaming and I can see the skin
peeling off my fingers and floating away.

Last night I found bare wet footprints soaked into
the carpet next to my bed. I think Patrick is gone.

I think we woke up The Drowned Boy. I think I'm next.

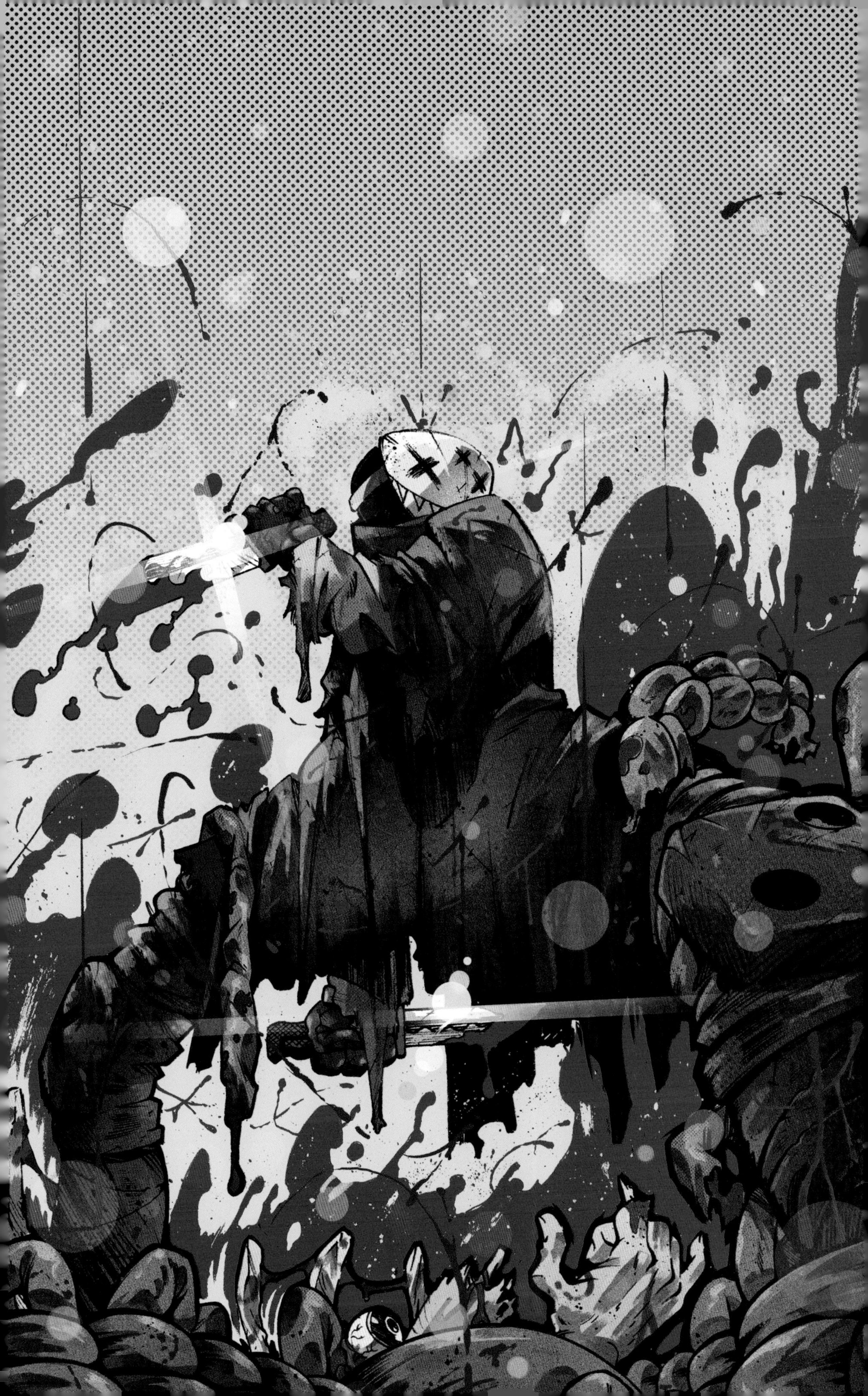

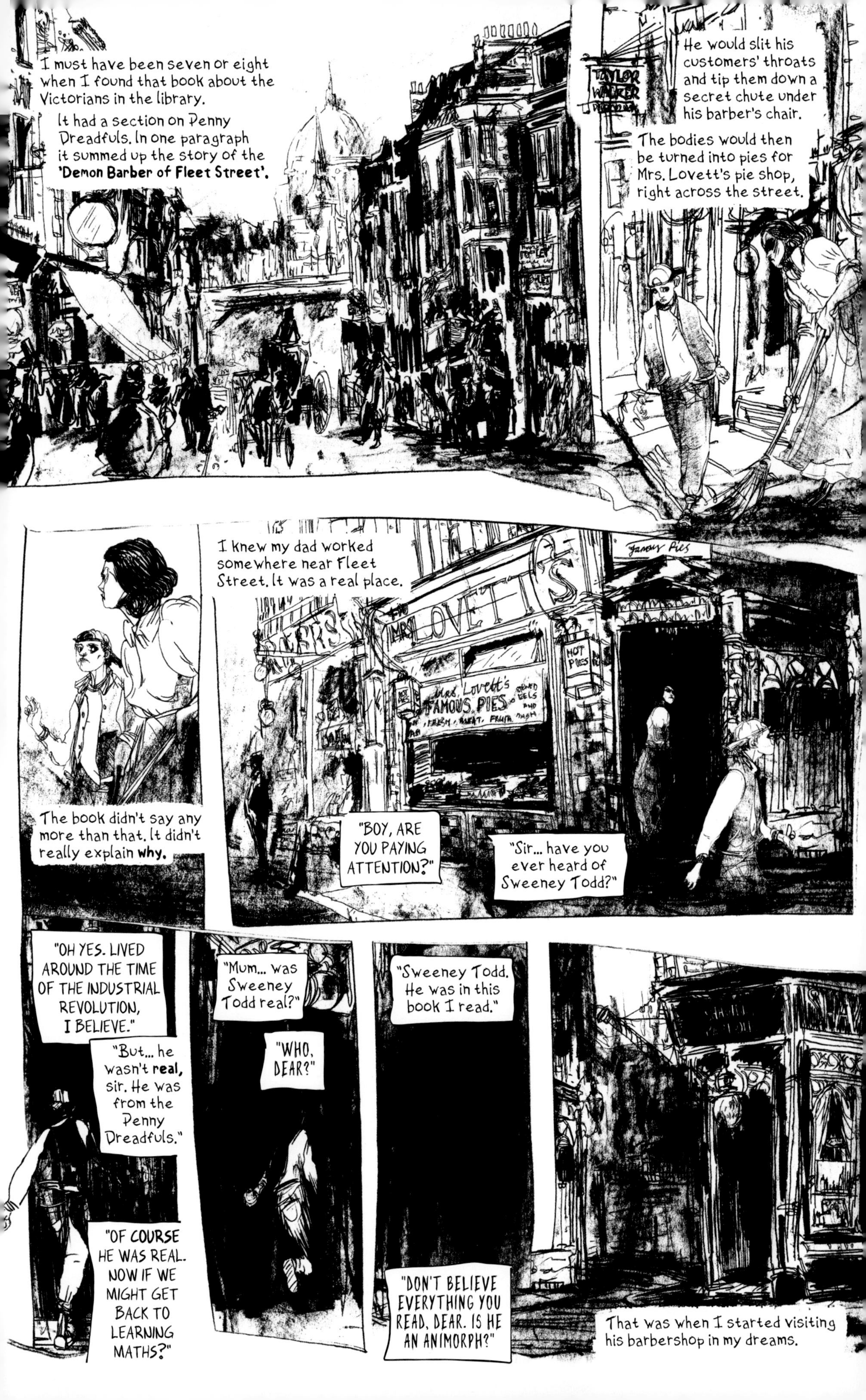
I must have been seven or eight when I found that book about the Victorians in the library.
It had a section on Penny Dreadfuls. In one paragraph it summed up the story of the **'Demon Barber of Fleet Street'.**
TAYLOR WALKER
He would slit his customers' throats and tip them down a secret chute under his barber's chair.
The bodies would then be turned into pies for Mrs. Lovett's pie shop, right across the street.
The book didn't say any more than that. It didn't really explain **why.**
I knew my dad worked somewhere near Fleet Street. It was a real place.
MRS LOVETT'S
Mrs. Lovett's FAMOUS PIES
HOT PIES
"BOY, ARE YOU PAYING ATTENTION?"
"Sir... have you ever heard of Sweeney Todd?"
"OH YES. LIVED AROUND THE TIME OF THE INDUSTRIAL REVOLUTION, I BELIEVE."
"But... he wasn't **real,** sir. He was from the Penny Dreadfuls."
"OF COURSE HE WAS REAL. NOW IF WE MIGHT GET BACK TO LEARNING MATHS?"
"Mum... was Sweeney Todd real?"
"WHO, DEAR?"
"Sweeney Todd. He was in this book I read."
"DON'T BELIEVE EVERYTHING YOU READ, DEAR. IS HE AN ANIMORPH?"
That was when I started visiting his barbershop in my dreams.

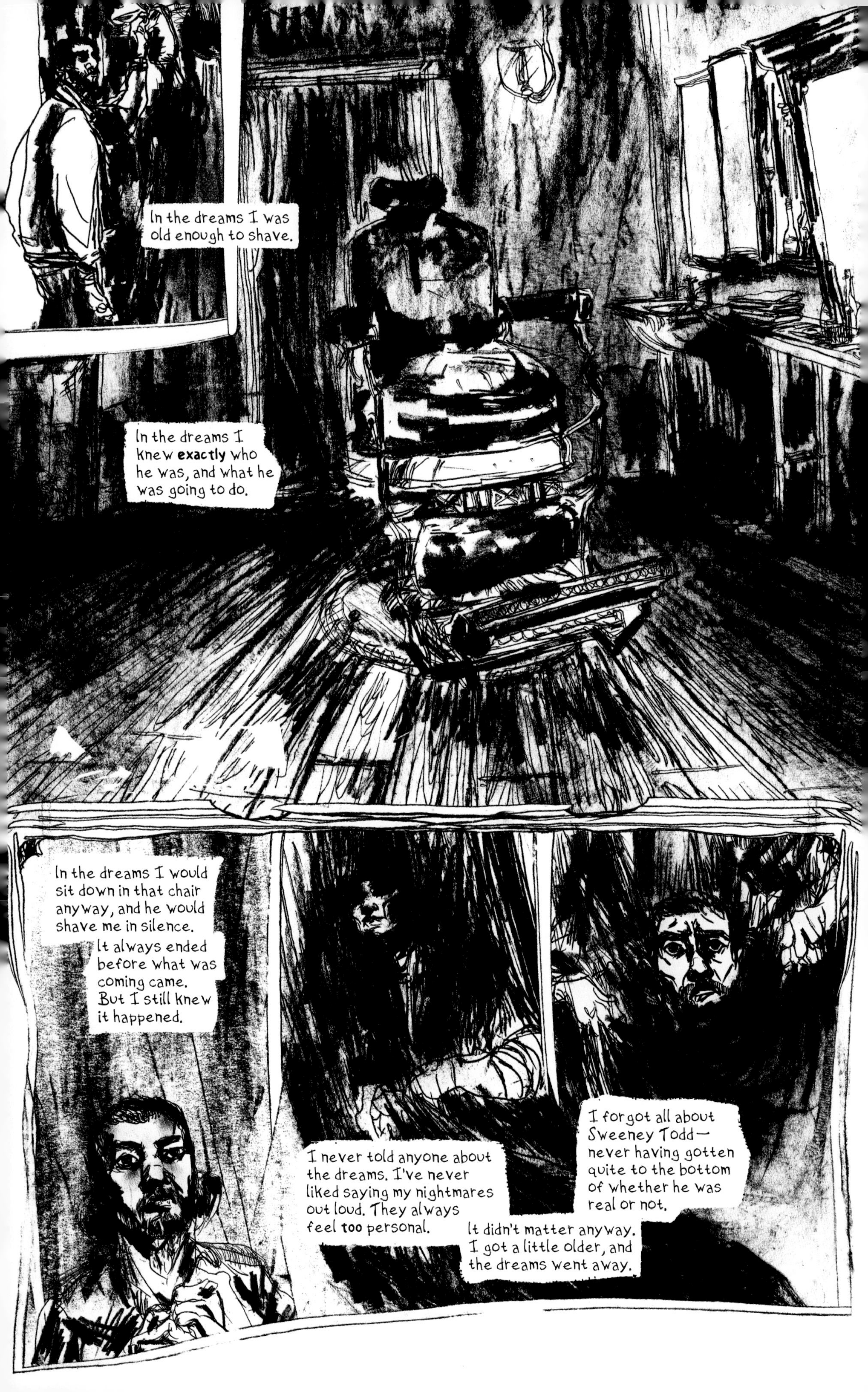

In the dreams I was old enough to shave.
In the dreams I knew **exactly** who he was, and what he was going to do.
In the dreams I would sit down in that chair anyway, and he would shave me in silence.
It always ended before what was coming came. But I still knew it happened.
I never told anyone about the dreams. I've never liked saying my nightmares out loud. They always feel **too** personal.
I forgot all about Sweeney Todd— never having gotten quite to the bottom of whether he was real or not.
It didn't matter anyway. I got a little older, and the dreams went away.

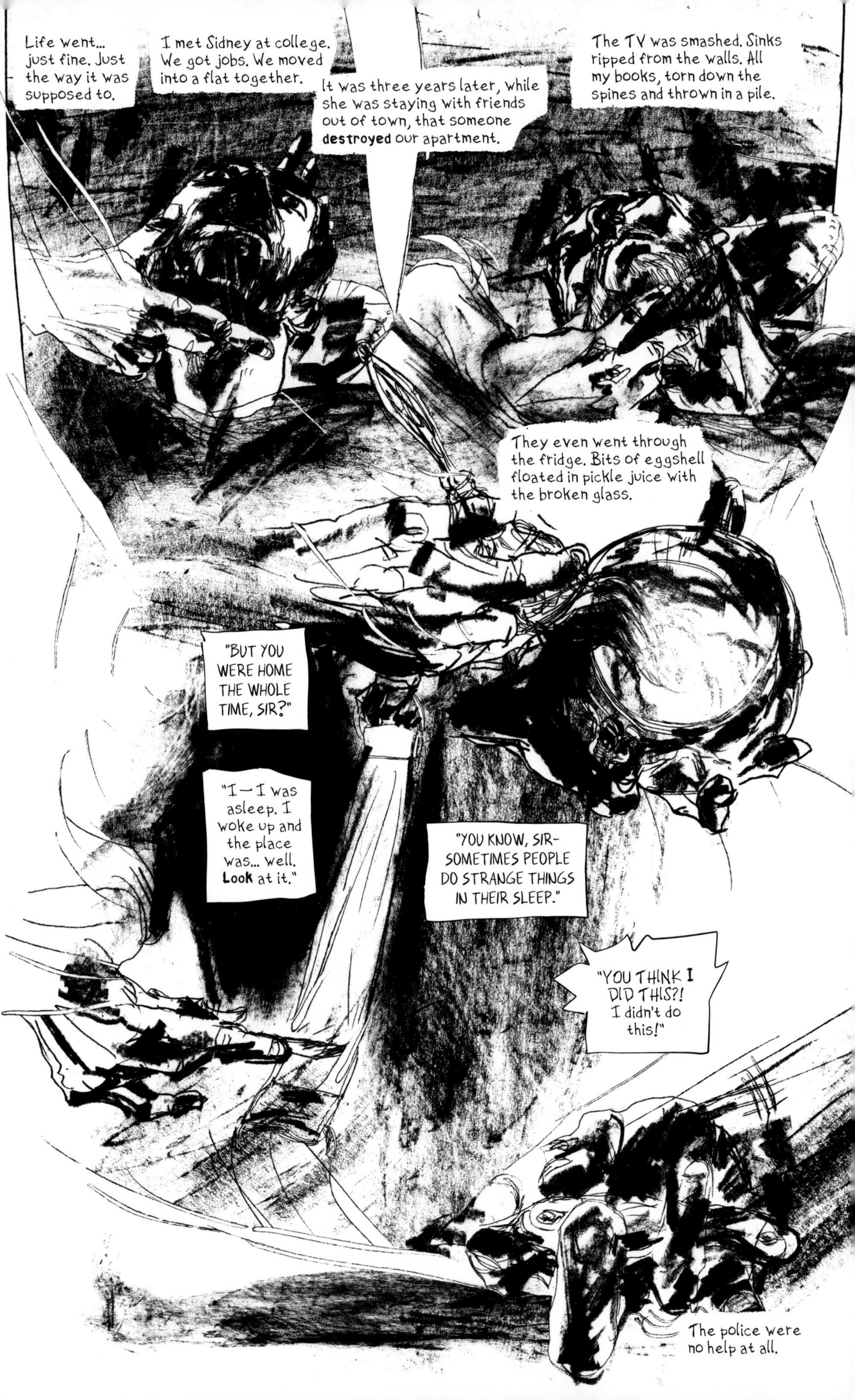
Life went... just fine. Just the way it was supposed to.
I met Sidney at college. We got jobs. We moved into a flat together.
It was three years later, while she was staying with friends out of town, that someone **destroyed** our apartment.
The TV was smashed. Sinks ripped from the walls. All my books, torn down the spines and thrown in a pile.
They even went through the fridge. Bits of eggshell floated in pickle juice with the broken glass.
"BUT YOU WERE HOME THE WHOLE TIME, SIR?"
"I — I was asleep. I woke up and the place was... well. **Look** at it."
"YOU KNOW, SIR- SOMETIMES PEOPLE DO STRANGE THINGS IN THEIR SLEEP."
"YOU THINK **I** DID THIS?! I didn't do this!"
The police were no help at all.

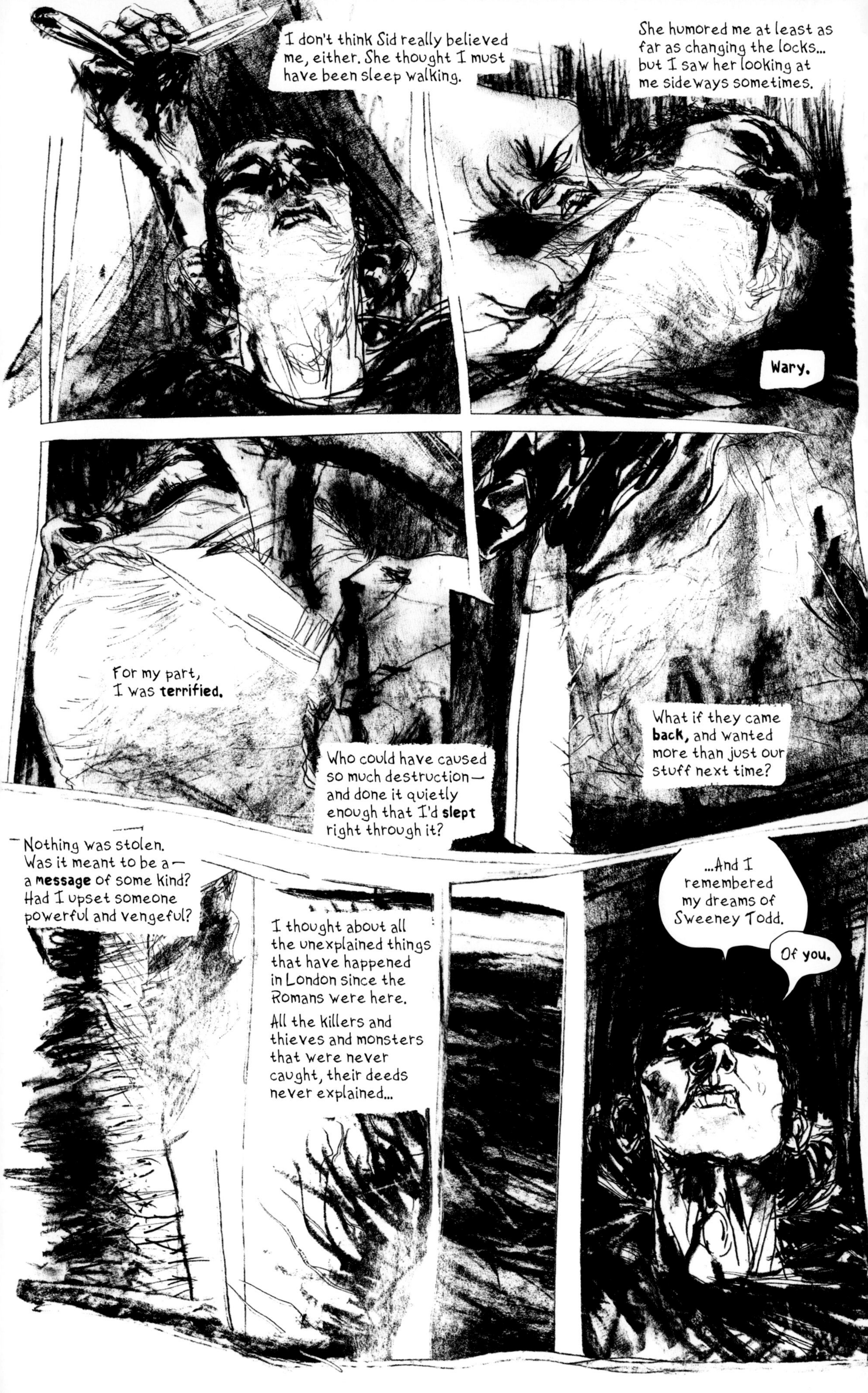
I don't think Sid really believed me, either. She thought I must have been sleep walking.
She humored me at least as far as changing the locks... but I saw her looking at me sideways sometimes.
Wary.
For my part, I was terrified.
Who could have caused so much destruction— and done it quietly enough that I'd slept right through it?
What if they came back, and wanted more than just our stuff next time?
Nothing was stolen. Was it meant to be a— a message of some kind? Had I upset someone powerful and vengeful?
I thought about all the unexplained things that have happened in London since the Romans were here.
All the killers and thieves and monsters that were never caught, their deeds never explained...
...And I remembered my dreams of Sweeney Todd.
Of you.

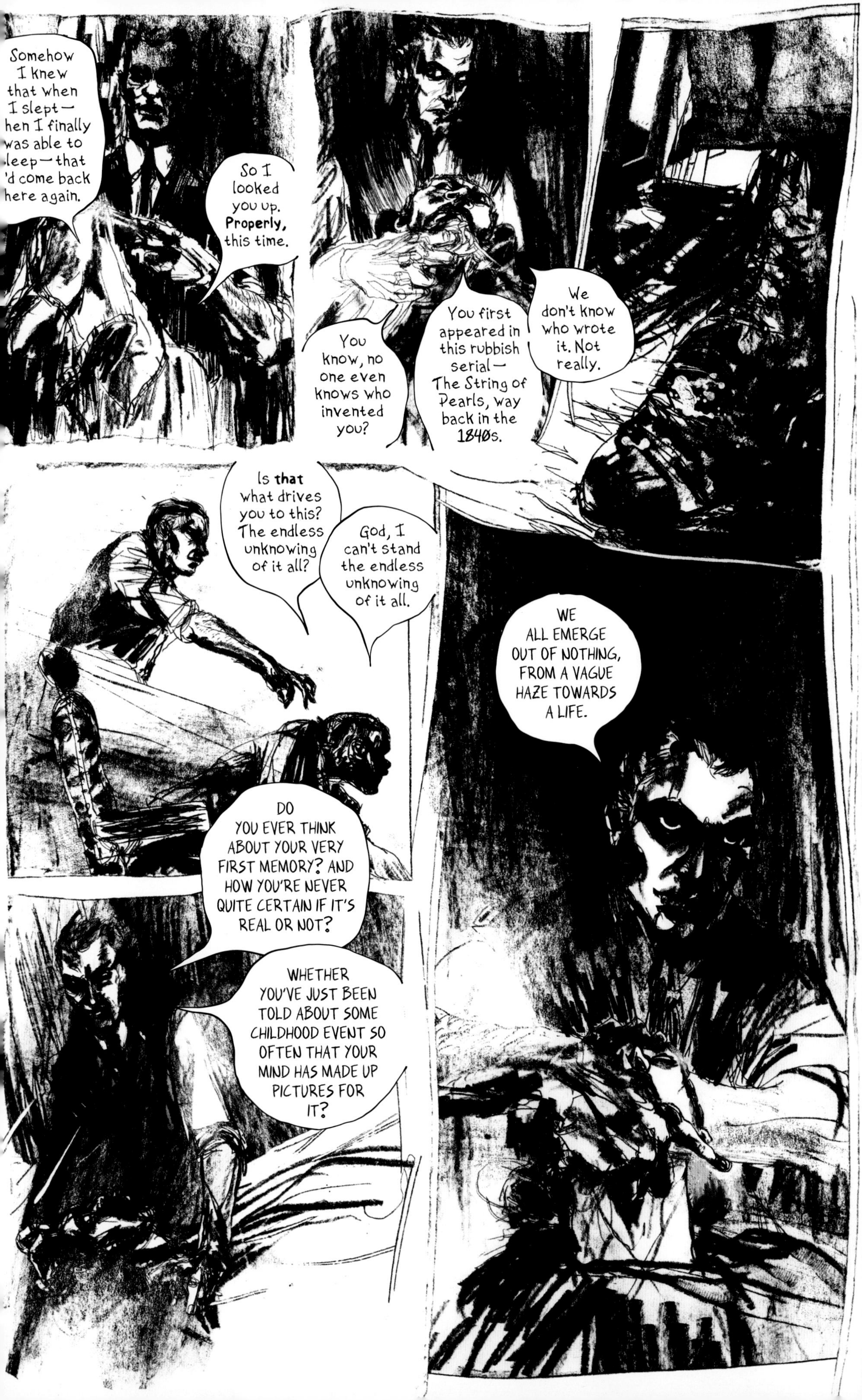
Somehow I knew that when I slept— hen I finally was able to leep—that 'd come back here again.
So I looked you up. **Properly,** this time.
You know, no one even knows who invented you?
You first appeared in this rubbish serial— The String of Pearls, way back in the 1840s.
We don't know who wrote it. Not really.
Is **that** what drives you to this? The endless unknowing of it all?
God, I can't stand the endless unknowing of it all.
DO YOU EVER THINK ABOUT YOUR VERY FIRST MEMORY? AND HOW YOU'RE NEVER QUITE CERTAIN IF IT'S REAL OR NOT?
WHETHER YOU'VE JUST BEEN TOLD ABOUT SOME CHILDHOOD EVENT SO OFTEN THAT YOUR MIND HAS MADE UP PICTURES FOR IT?
WE ALL EMERGE OUT OF NOTHING, FROM A VAGUE HAZE TOWARDS A LIFE.

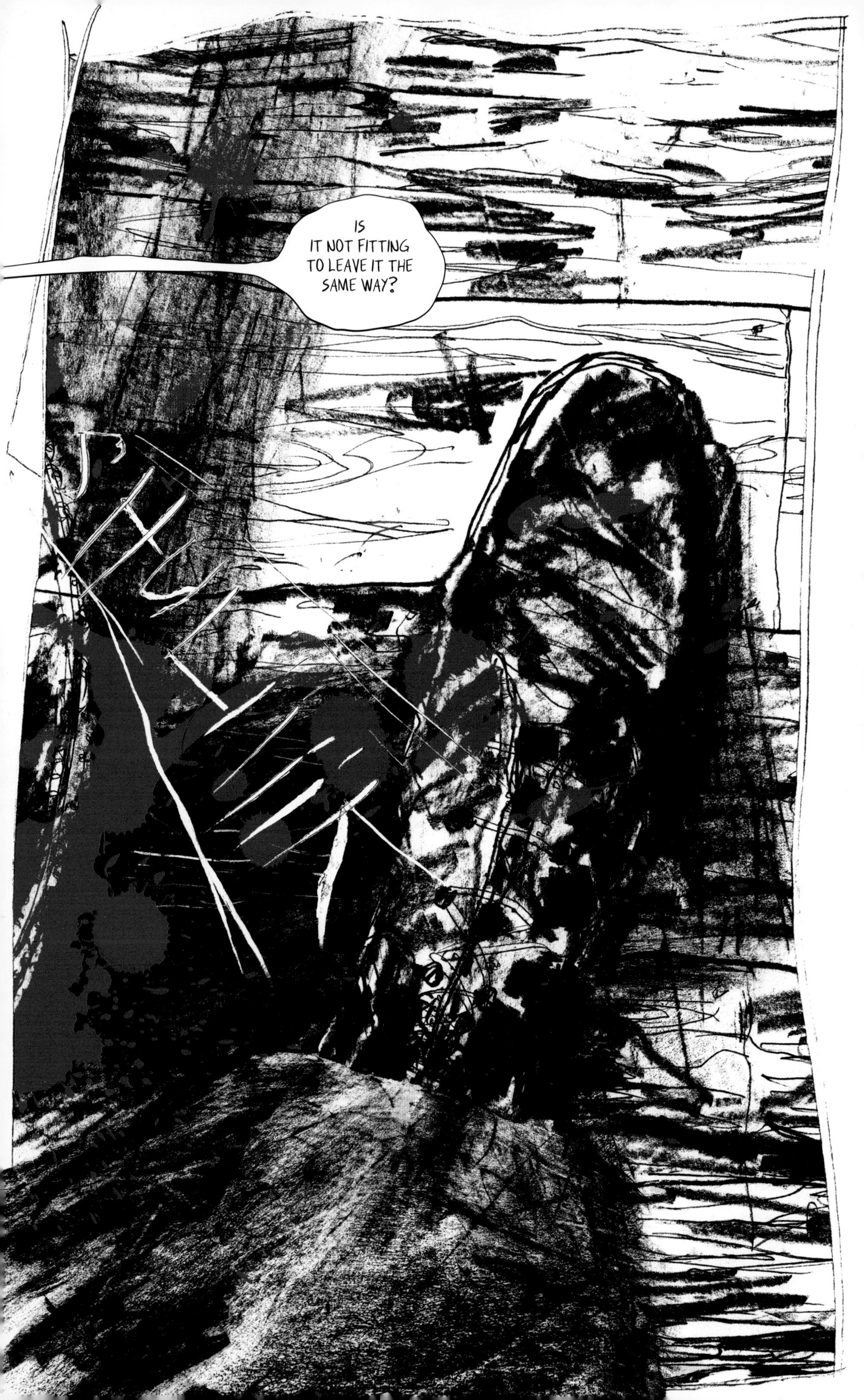
IS IT NOT FITTING TO LEAVE IT THE SAME WAY?

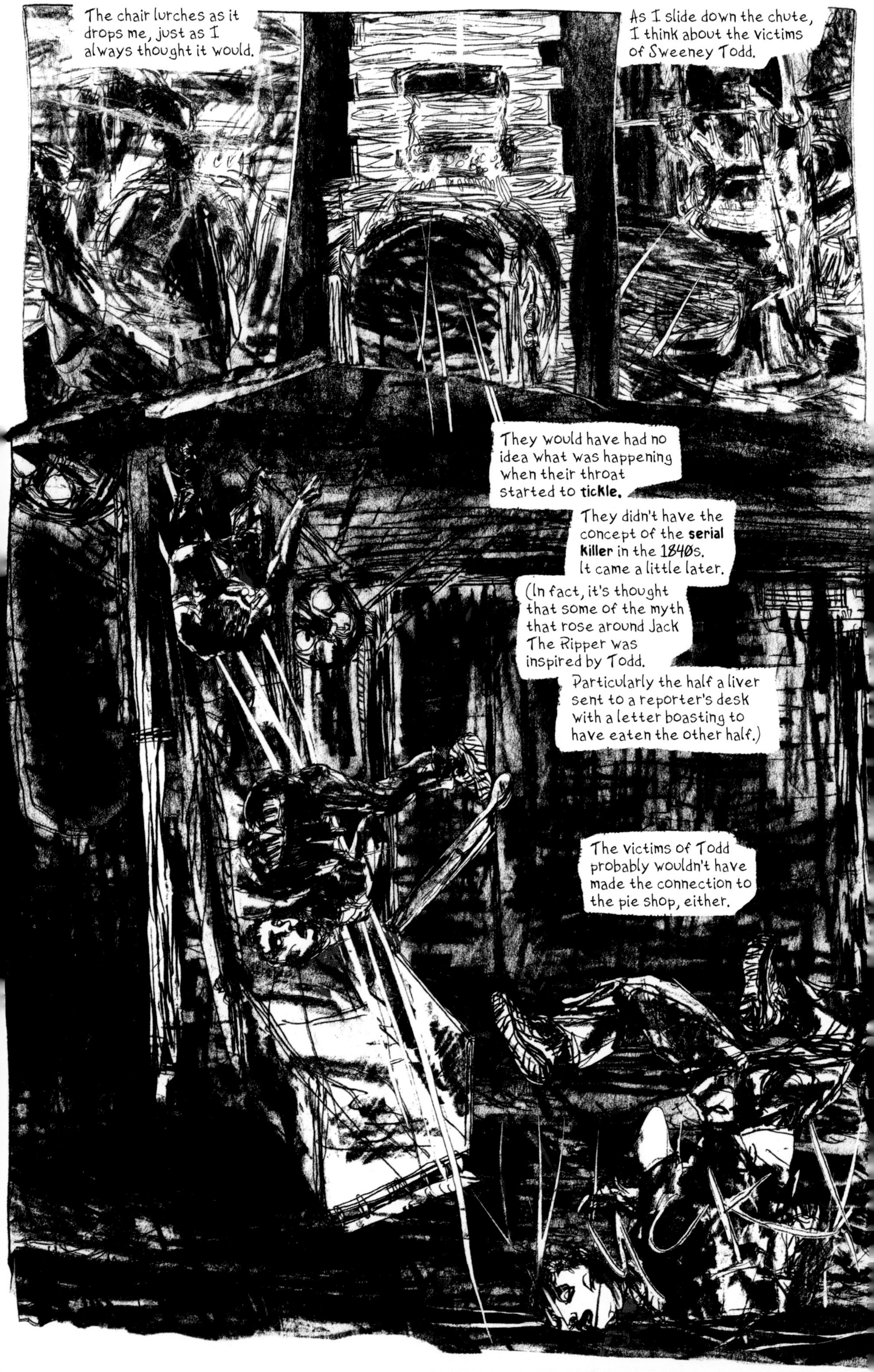
The chair lurches as it drops me, just as I always thought it would.
As I slide down the chute, I think about the victims of Sweeney Todd.
They would have had no idea what was happening when their throat started to **tickle.**
They didn't have the concept of the **serial killer** in the 1840s. It came a little later.
(In fact, it's thought that some of the myth that rose around Jack The Ripper was inspired by Todd.
Particularly the half a liver sent to a reporter's desk with a letter boasting to have eaten the other half.)
The victims of Todd probably wouldn't have made the connection to the pie shop, either.

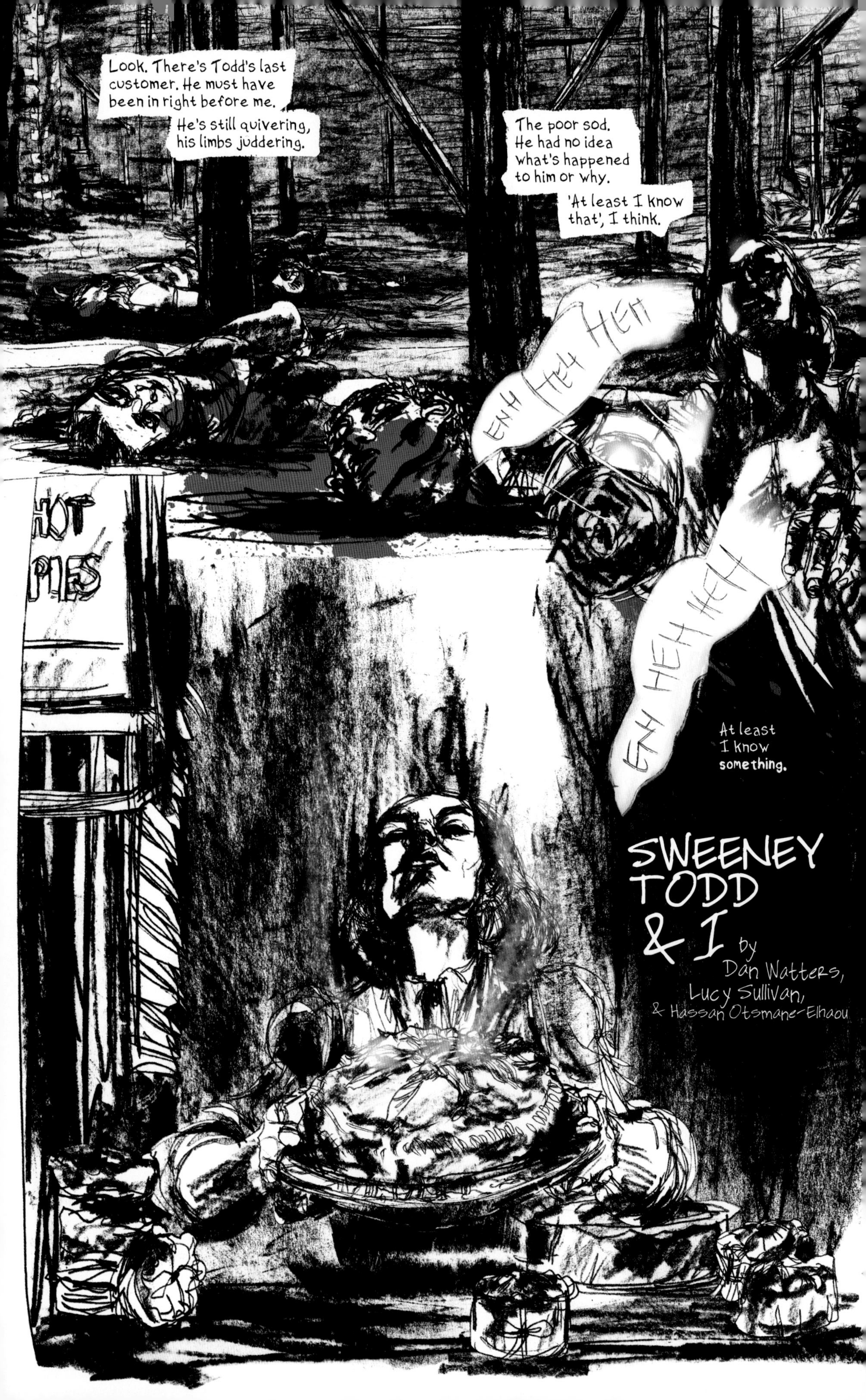
Look. There's Todd's last customer. He must have been in right before me.
He's still quivering, his limbs juddering.
The poor sod. He had no idea what's happened to him or why.
'At least I know that', I think.
ENH HEH HEH
HOT PIES
ENH HEH HEH HEH
At least I know **something.**
SWEENEY TODD & I
by Dan Watters, Lucy Sullivan, & Hassan Otsmane-Elhaou

YOU CAN'T GET PAST THE STAKES

STEVE FOXE INTERVIEWS KILLADELPHIA'S RODNEY BARNES

STEVE FOXE: One of the few guidelines we give *Razorblades* contributors is that we're typically not very interested in classic monsters and horror tropes unless you have a really new take on them. How do you approach vampires in 2020 without falling prey to the been-there, done-that feeling?

RODNEY BARNES: I wanted to actually go in the opposite direction and look at vampires more from a place of—not so much a monster, but as another entity, an evolution in existence. We've all seen vampire movies where, you know, they're in the coffin, they come out of the coffin. They sleep, they get up, they chase people around for blood. And if you think about it, if you're gonna be immortal, that's a pretty crummy way to have to live the rest of your life—to have to go about just seeking blood like humans seek food. So my thing was, if I could approach the idea that trauma-based issues in life, especially early

in life, that don't leave us, they form habits. And how could I get that idea into the idea of a vampire?

They couldn't shake the part of them that was human. They couldn't shake their mistakes that they had made in life. And so when they're in the coffin, supposedly asleep, really they're just ruminating on the lives that they led. And I wanted to [show] that part of their existence because oftentimes in the horror tropes, vampires can be in a coffin for hundreds of years. So if you were trapped with nothing but your thoughts and the mistakes that you had made in life, that would be pretty traumatic. And so I wanted to give that idea some existence, some relevance, and just try to evolve the idea of what a vampire was. Especially for today's times, where we're trying to figure out what life is, and what the meaning of life is, I wanted to get into that from the mindset of a vampire—from an immortal, more so than a vampire.

SF: It's funny that you talked about the coffin part because I'm very claustrophobic. And when I realized that's where you were going with James Sr., that he was willingly going back under the dirt—that was one of the scariest parts of the series so far for me. But then you have this really lovely sequence where he's able to reunite with his wife, so he's chosen to go back under the ground with a goal.

Along those lines, you introduce a fairly significant amount of the supernatural to your vampire lore. You have magic, you have the crossing of that border between life and death, and I always find magic tricky in horror because it's another step away from the real world. Can you speak a bit about balancing the more fantastical elements with those truer-to-life scares?

RB: I think it's keeping it to a minimum more so than anything else, because once it becomes so magical, you're right—you sort of lose all touch with any reality. And it's hard from that point to really connect yourself to, if that's not your thing. It's not really my thing *en masse*. What I wanted to do was take the limitations away. If I'm immortal and I have information at my hands—this book that the folks that turned them into vampires gave the big guys—it would have all the answers of the wonders of the universe: time, space, magic, all of that stuff. And I just wanted to be able to open a door to the possibilities of doing more than, like I said before, just sucking blood and just walking around saying really cool stuff. I think the thing with Sangster Sr. wanting to go back to the grave—again, it's the idea that the limitation isn't the coffin. The limitation isn't your body. There's a soul there. Whereas as human beings, the soul sort of fires us and moves us through life, in the vampires' cases, it's a prison, and you can move about in a spirit form, almost like a ghost, through realms, through the netherworld, through wherever it is that you're trying to go, whatever your goal is. But you always have to come back if you want to exist in the mortal world as a vampire.

So again, it's more or less trying to expand the boundaries of what we've seen vampires to be, and also to be able to give me as a storyteller other places to go than just wandering around Philadelphia seeking blood. I think that would wear out pretty quickly, and I would get bored with it. So trying to add the human element to it, saying that, because you're a vampire, that you're not limited to the idea of what a vampire is, that you can go in a myriad of directions, I think helps the reader not get bored as well. And from month to month, you don't know what's gonna happen. You don't know, because sometimes *I* don't know. I try to work off of themes more than anything else, more than just pure plot. And being able to open up all of those different doors helps.

SF: And talking about opening up different doors, I think it would have been easy to frame the whole series through the perspective of James Jr., or James Jr. and his father, but *Killadelphia* ends up pulling back the curtain on just as many of its antagonists as it does its quote-unquote heroes. There are plenty of horror stories where we root for the monster, but it's not as often that we hear their internal monologue and we learn about their sympathetic motivations. Can you talk a bit about the decision to have characters like Jupiter and Abigail tell their own stories rather than to see those through the perspective of the Sangsters?

RB: I think the thing for me has always been: everybody's flawed. My therapist told me once that everybody's flawed. There are two types of people, though—I actually use this line in the book. One sort of stands on their flaws and defines themselves by it. The other walks with their flaws and they try to work on it and make it better. To me, that's the line in this book between the protagonists and the antagonists. [The antagonists] have given way to the things in life that angered them or hurt them, and they've sort of defined themselves by it. But the protagonists, if you want to say the Sangsters, you know, they're working on their relationship. Their relationship has its ups and downs, and it gets better. But the bad guys are looking to, for lack of a better word, hurt other people in the name of their own hurt.

As a history buff—don't quiz me on anything—I always heard people say that the past really doesn't have that much effect on the future, when you talk about some of the societal stuff that we're going through right now. And I don't believe that to be true; I think it's all connected. So I wanted to create a narrative that was flexible enough that you could go back to the past and see how the past influenced the way that these people felt and [how] those feelings manifest today. They may be doing something different than they were; Toppy was in Deadwood, and that's when his trauma hit. And he's still angry today, hundreds of years later. That anger may not be about the same thing, subject-wise, but it manifests itself as anger that he's able to put forth out into the world today.

And I think a lot of our societal issues sort of stem from that place. We were born—America was born—in violence, and a lot of that violence, I think it's still in the DNA of what America is. So I wanted to be able to tell a story without necessarily just pointing to it and saying it. It's in the DNA of what *Killadelphia* is, but without necessarily making it feel like medicine, like *Ha ha! Here's the point!* I'm putting these two together. I want the reader to be able to make that jump.

SF: Speaking to the American history of violence and also the difference between intent and execution, *Killadelphia* is part of a long tradition of horror stories that are interwoven with police and detective drama. But it wastes no time in complicating the book's police force when it comes to things like racist violence and neglecting marginalized communities. Has it been challenging or intimidating to play with the detective drama format throughout such a sea change in how America discusses law enforcement and its systemic shortcomings?

RB: Not really. I mean, I try to be objective with that thing because—as I'm sure you know—we live in a polarized society, and both sides believes that their side is right. And I'm sure that being a police officer is a really difficult job, and so, from the outside, you look at them, you say, *Oh, they're the bad guys.* But they have a really difficult job. And on the other side, you look at all the societal stuff in the history of policing in America, and that side has its opinion as well. And that's sort of how I wanted to tell the story. That's how I wanted to tell the story with the politics of it. As soon as you take a side, you immediately alienate the *other* side. And that's not what I wanted to do.

Oftentimes when you're dealing with race in genre, it's hard to lose yourself in the story because you have to service this other thing. And I didn't want that to happen in *Killadelphia*. I wanted to have behavior rule the day, and then the reader can take away from it what they take away from it. I didn't wanna make any judgments about cops. I didn't wanna make any judgments about society at large. I wanted to just show behavior and tell the story of human/vampire behavior and allow the reader to take away from it what they take away from it. As soon as I say one side is bad, then I sort of got to stay in that place, and I gotta make them one dimensional. Whereas I think, more often than not, it comes down to behavior. It comes down to belief systems. It comes down to those unconscious biases that I think everybody has. And judgment limits your ability to have a conversation, to tell a story. I just didn't want to limit myself with the story in that way.

SF: There is an impulse in horror to try to figure out what stories are "really about." You have *The Babadook* which is about a scary boogeyman, but also about a mother's grief and guilt. *It Follows* is about a shape-shifting monster, but also the nature of mortality. *Killadelphia* directly addresses everything from slavery to prison abolition to living in the closet. How do you balance the social and real-world commentary you want to address with the more

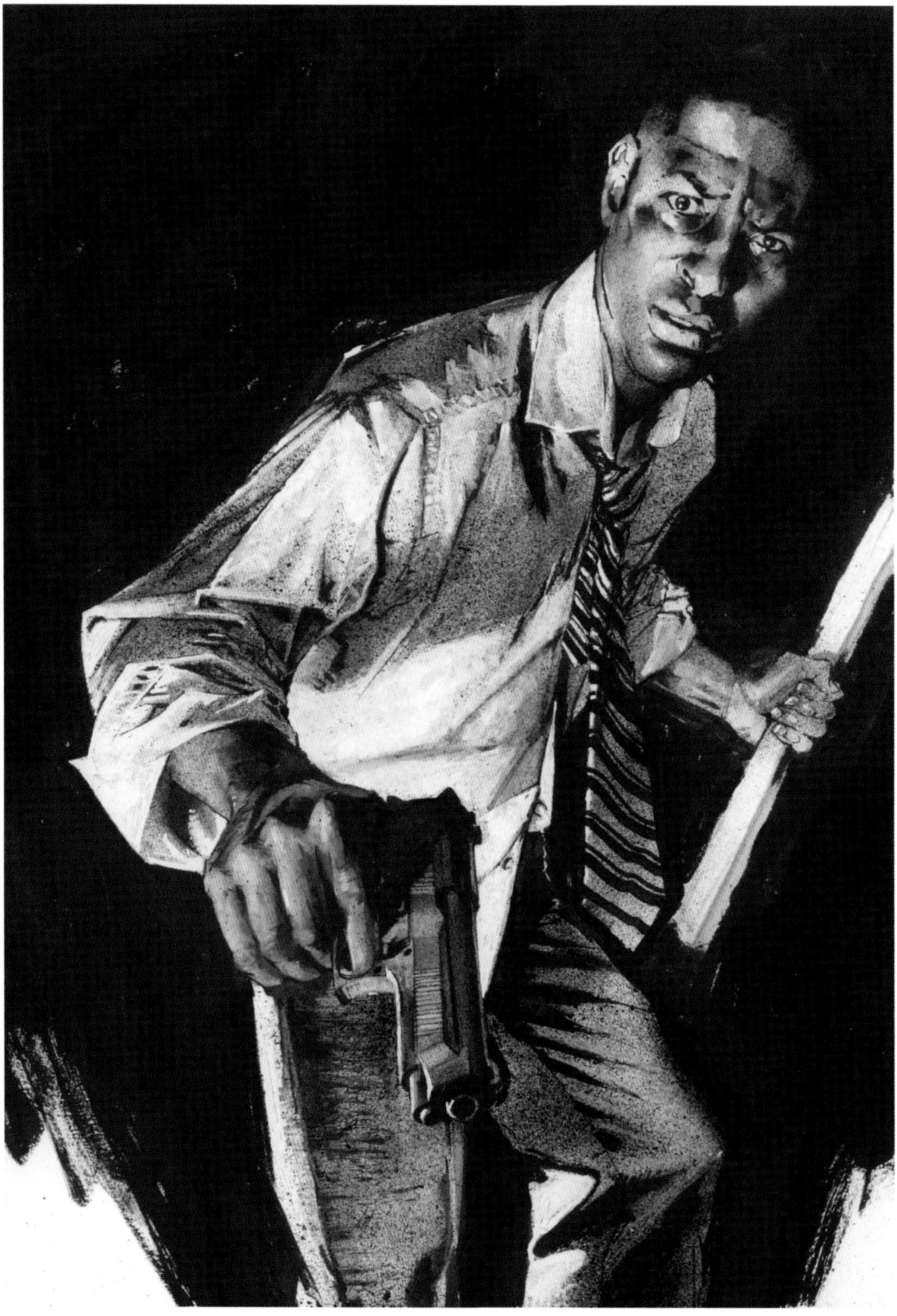

propulsive horror/action plot? You spoke a bit already about how you go about handling those themes themselves, but in the recipe of what *Killadelphia* is, how do you keep that from overwhelming the ongoing, more action-heavy plot that you have going on?

RB: I do try to keep it to just behavior. I don't want it to be, *this is the racial violence issue*, and this is the, you know, whatever subject matter it's gonna be about. Of course there're some exceptions, but to folks that deal with racism, it's not like an everyday component that's in your face in that way. Whether it's the George Floyd stuff or any of that, it's almost like a roller coaster. It's omnipresent, but it's not an everyday aspect. The heightened part of it isn't in your face every day, and so I didn't want the characters to be burdened, because they're characters of color, to have to talk about it all the time. That's why the Sangsters are really dealing with their interpersonal relationship as much as they're dealing with anything else, but there're moments where you're reminded, whether you reminded in an in-your-face type of way, or you're reminded from the periphery, that these things still exist and that they're still factors in your life.

It's so easy when you're dealing with subject matter like this to become medicine, and it's not fun anymore. And a lot of other books or a lot of other stories, you can just go to and enjoy the book or enjoy the story. You don't have to think about any of this stuff. And so I think sometimes when you're a reader, you look at the book and you say, *Uh oh, Black vampires—I know what they're gonna be talking about.* And you immediately dismiss it, because you believe that this is the book where you're supposed to come and learn something, or it's gonna be something where it's just not gonna be fun. And I never wanted the social commentary, for lack of a better term, to overwhelm the story. I still wanted it to be about themes that matter: the love, the hate, the anger, fear, vanity, all of that stuff. To me, that's the star of *Killadelphia* more so than anything else. And I always want it to be that way.

Now that doesn't mean, as you pointed out, that those other things won't be a part of the story, but just not so much a part of the story that that's what [the series is] about. You know, Toppy was part of the institution of slavery in his own unique way, and he suffered the horrors and was part of the horrors of slavery. But it's not about slavery, per se. It's not like we're stuck in that period of time, because he's gonna jump out. He's gonna have a very human thing happen to him, And so, typically, that's the place that I'm going to go. It's more of a garnish, being able to talk about all of that stuff, than it is leaning into it to where, this month in *Killadelphia*, this is what we're gonna be talking about. *You're gonna come out a better person because you read this book!* It's never that. It's always like, I'm going back to my love of Hammer films and that stuff and saying, okay, Christopher Lee and Peter Cushing did a thing that I loved as a kid. And I want that feeling. I want that feeling here. But in order to set it in today's world, instead of wolves running by a carriage, you're probably gonna have cops down a main street in Philadelphia say, *Hey, where are you going?* I want it to feel natural to the world that it's in, not so much this thing that I'm throwing in because I have a point to make. And hopefully, so far, it seems like it's working.

SF: I don't want to suggest it's a one-to-one comparison, but what you said about the presence of racism in your life—as a gay creator, any single day, I can tell you sort of the macro things affecting the LGBTQ+ community. But I might go weeks without thinking *so directly* about it. And I don't, as a creator, necessarily want the pressure of, *Okay, well, this is a gay writer. There's a gay character. This book is gonna be about gay stuff.* Because we also just do other stuff. So that's very relatable.

RB: Yeah, there's a human tie that connects all of us, regardless of what group we happen to be in that's not part of the dominant idea of America. And, yeah, we're in that group, but that doesn't make us less human. We still have the same pros and cons that come with life.

And that's the connecting stuff. Regardless of how any of us live our lives, we're still people, we still love, we still hate, we still have problems that fall into the realm of being a human being. And I'd rather talk about that stuff, and more from a cultural place, how specifically that impacts someone that happens to walk through life in a different cultural idea. I'd rather talk to that as it relates to being a human being than talk about race or the tropes and all of that other stuff that we've seen, you know, for the past 50 years or so, if not longer.

SF: I still have to ask—I don't want to impose the label onto *Killadelphia* or suggest the Black creators haven't *always* participated in the genre, but it feels like there's undeniably more eyes than ever on Black-focused horror after *Get Out*, *Lovecraft Country*, *Horror Noire*, etc. Do you feel actively involved with that push, or are you just keeping your nose down and letting other people worry about the labels or categories?

RB: Labels and categories, yeah, I kinda don't focus on that as much. I'm cognizant of the fact that there *is* a moment right now, and there seems to be moments over time where you get this stuff. And to me, the best thing that I can do to be a part of it is try to be a craftsman. It'll survive regardless of what it's about if it's good and well-crafted.

I'm honored and blessed to be working with Jason Shawn Alexander on the book, and his art, I think, is as big of an idea of why the book works as my storytelling. His ability to tell the story sets a tone and an atmosphere that makes it feel like what I always wanted it to feel like. And so, you know, therein lay what this moment is: I think you see more good stuff.

I'm old enough to remember the Blaxploitation movement. And *Blackula* was the first horror movie I saw as a kid. My mom took me to it. I'm actually doing a *Blackula* remake, the book. Hopefully sometime in 2021. And I remember how much fun the movie was.

And then, as I got older, how problematic it became, because I wasn't a kid anymore. You know, why, when his fangs got longer, did his afro grow? His bellbottoms got bigger! It's like, *what power?* You know, we can go with the afro and the sideburns, but how did his lapels get bigger? Where did that come from? And there was some guy in the back, you know, probably figuring that, afros were a big deal in the '70s, and bellbottoms were the style, and hey, we're gonna throw it all in there.

Being able to tell those stories like *Get Out* and *Lovecraft Country* and a few others, from a human place, I think, is a big jump, and being able to bring the degree of sophistication in without the problematic areas, or at least not as many of them, into today's world—it's sort of what I think any of us are trying to do.

Not trying to speak for anyone else, but when I see books like *Excellence* or *Bitter Root* or some of the others, I think we're all trying to just raise the bar because, for so long, these stories sort of languished in the idea that, if there were Black leads in the story, those Black leads had to be doing "Black things," whatever that is. Someone came up with an idea that this is how Black people behave, and if we're gonna put them in the story, that story has to either become a comedy or it's got to be so deeply rooted into some social issue or something that it's not gonna be fun anymore. You know, they're gonna be vampires, but they're gonna be vampires with a *purpose*. And they're basically gonna be the Black Panthers or whatever they're gonna be. I think now what you see is, as you were talking about earlier, you see the human element in it, because you see people of color behind the camera, and pen to pad, telling these stories and telling the stories from intrinsic places within themselves, not just places that are dependent upon the color of their skin or whatever place they come from or whatever cultural idea they come from. You see it coming from an honest place, and I think that's part of this movement right now. It's not so much just about color as much as it is about culture. And it is about being honest in your storytelling.

SF: I'm glad you brought up both Jason and the craft side of producing comics because I wanted to ask you about both. As someone with experience in film and television, how do you approach horror on the printed page where you don't have the same control over pacing or things like audio cues and jump scares?

RB: It's a funny struggle. My first book was *Falcon*, and I struggled for a while to figure out the relationship between words and art. I thought it would be a lot easier. And so, in my arrogance, I deserved the tongue-lashing I got from Twitter, which is a *wonderful* place.

You learn over time how to tell a story, the bridge between prose and graphic storytelling. How to make a splash page work, in regards to a certain pacing. And Jason was very helpful in that as well. He would read the script and he would guide me to a place where, you know, *this would work better if you did this*, to magnify the horror when that was needed or to even elevate the idea of an emotional moment that we were trying to hit. And once you start doing it, after a while, like anything, it gets easier, it gets better. It becomes a natural part of who you are, if you do it enough.

I've been fortunate enough that every artist I've had on every book that I've worked on so far has been a friend as well. And they taught me along the way, because I came from TV and film, as you say, and TV and film do a lot of the work for you. You have an actor interpreting the thing in his way, so you hear it in the actor's voice. The reader hears it in their voice when they're reading it, even if they see an image. And I wasn't as aware of that when I first started on *Falcon*. So I think for me, that process of continuously needing a script—when I turn in a script, that's just the first draft. It'll probably go through ten more revisions before we actually get to Jason illustrating it or me feeling comfortable with it and the pacing. And in the early issues of *Killadelphia*, we would get galleys done so that we could have a printed thing in hand and be able to look at it and see what works and what doesn't.

It's funny because I've been a comic book fan, collector, reader my entire life. I believe the first book I ever read was a comic book when I was four or five years old, and it's an honor to be able to do it. I don't think anybody does this to get rich. So it's one of those things that's just like, for the love of it more than anything else that I've ever done.

Not to say that I don't love TV and film, but no matter where you are in the business, those are still sort of group dynamics. You know, it's not like I write a script and it becomes a TV show. There're a lot of producers and studio heads and networks that play a role in what the final product is. In comic books, it was frightening because no one told me anything. They just gave me a job and I turned in a script and I was terrified because I was so used to, okay, I turned in a script and people tell me what they think and I changed things and I move things around. And here it was like, no, just have it in by Thursday, and maybe there would be a couple of things and whatever, and really, that's it. And you learn your mistakes.

Like I said, Twitter became my critic, and that's a *horrible* place to have a critique, because there's no filter. If somebody feels something, they're gonna say what they feel, and it could be good or, you know... And *Killadelphia*, it's been pretty good. But you learn quickly, if there's a consensus, it's probably best that you take a look. You take a step back and look at that thing, because everybody's saying this thing. That level of awareness actually helped me.

There was this one guy, on *Falcon*, he would screen-capture whatever dialogue he hated, and he would put it on Twitter. I remember I was in a movie, *The Post* with Tom Hanks and Meryl Streep, and I was holding my cell phone and it kept beeping, and it was Twitter. It was this guy, and all weekend, he was killing me about, I think, issue three of *Falcon*. And I was dying inside because I felt like, *I'm never gonna be able to do a book again, this guy, this guy.*

And once I was able to separate my feelings from what he was saying and how it never feels good to have someone not like your work—as soon as I was able to do that, and to look at what was under what he was saying, I could see some semblance of truth in it. Because I *was* writing dialogue for TV. I was doing my other job in this job, and I stopped doing that, and I started to write to the character. And I started to come to the stories from an intrinsic place, more so from the extrinsic, *I'm writing a comic book* place. I started to apply some of the same principles that work for me in TV and film, which seems obvious, but at the time it wasn't. I was so much into my fanboy, *oh my God, I get an opportunity to work with my favorite characters ever, this is great.* And I really don't do that with TV and film, even though I've had some relatively cool gigs, I just approach the work from a certain place. And I returned to that place in comics, and I think it served me well. At least that's what Twitter's told me.

SF: I want to make sure we talk a little bit more about Jason because, like you said, he's such an intrinsic part of this book. And he has a long history with the genre, including writing *Empty Zone*, which was a sci-fi/horror story. Is it fair to say you have a more collaborative relationship on this series than you've had on other books, and has his experience changed how you structure the story as it's gone along?

RB: Jason is my husband, for lack of a better work. We fight, we argue, we wrestle—I win the wrestling matches because I'm much bigger. But Jason lives a mile away from me, or I live a mile away from him, and we spend a lot of time together.

A guy reached out to me to interview Jason for an art magazine, for his horror art. And once we realized we were so close to each other, we just started going to dinner every couple of weeks, and we would pitch each other ideas. He hated my ideas, and I hated his ideas. And one night, he had been drinking, and I pitched him *Killadelphia*, and he liked it. And I didn't know whether he really liked it or if it was the liquor. And the next day, he said, "That vampire thing that you were talking about, have you written it down?" I said, no, not yet. It's just something I've been rolling around in my head for a while. And he said, "You should write it down, I think that one works." And I said, well, what was the difference between this and all the other pitches? And he said it was the way I pitched it, because I said that it was *Hamilton* meets *Dracula* meets *Sanford and Son.*

As we got closer, I would come over to his place and look at his art, and Jason is an incredible fine artist as well, not just comic art, and there was always this sadness that was there, and melancholy. And I was thinking, if the tone of *Killadelphia*—I actually knew the tone before I knew the story, how I wanted it to feel—there was this sadness that was there and Jason's ability to capture that in his art. If I could write to that, I think we would have something that would really work. And again, if you look at his facial expressions, not even just the stuff that's horrifying, like the ripping off arms and biting necks and all of that, the subtle stuff to me works as much as the horrifying stuff. It really nails the emotion.

I call him a director more so than anything else, because in television and film, a director takes a script, and they interpret how it makes them feel, that's an aspect of it. I look at Jason as doing the same thing, and I'm sure every artist does that to an extent. But in a book like *Killadelphia*, which is character-driven more so than just plot-driven, you need to be able to bring those characters to life. When I write a script, I see the images in my head in a particular way, but when I get it back from him and he reinterprets it, it's the same thing, but it's *different*. It's exactly what it was on paper, but he sees it differently and oftentimes he sees it better than I do. The emotion is heightened in such a way. And for everything that we do, I'd love to be able to stick with him or guys who think like him for the rest of my career.

I'm starting my own imprint for horror and fantasy and sci-fi. I wanna keep doing stories

like this that sort of, not just genre-bend, but also play to the idea of the emotional connection, because that's where I made it. Horror spoke to that, the stakes of horror, life and death. You can add the supernatural elements in and all of that other stuff, but you can't get past the stakes. It's not about somebody robbing somebody or stealing or, you know—when you're dealing with superhero comics, people, they don't die.

SF: Not for long.

RB: Exactly. They're coming back eventually. In horror, though, there are real stakes involved. I remember, I worked on the movie *The Green Mile*. I was Michael Clarke Duncan's stand-in, and there's a long story that goes with that, because we look nothing alike. But no one figured that out. And the only reason I wanted to be there is because I wanted to meet Stephen King, because I love Stephen King. Stephen King and Richard Matheson were my two favorite writers of all time, and still are to this day, but there's a whole lot of other folks who have joined the club. But I

remember meeting Mr. King and having the opportunity to talk to him for a while. And he was talking to me about kind of his formula and the way that it worked. Being able to get you to care about the protagonist and making it feel like it was a real person.

And that's what I think Jason does with the Sangsters, more so than anyone else, even Abigail and John and all of them. But he makes you care about their relationship. It matters that one is a vampire and the other one isn't, but what really, *really* matters is the tie that binds them emotionally and the frustration, the anger, the love, and all the stuff that goes into that. Without a guy like Jason to make that feel real month to month to month, it just becomes like, okay, they're not getting along. Okay, now they're getting along. But being able to add that element that makes it feel real, that's invaluable.

SF: *Elysium Fields*, the back-up feature—six issues into *Killadelphia*, you and Jason decide, oh, let's reinvent another standard horror creature.

How did that come about? Why do it the way you're doing it? And is it correct to say that you're intentionally trying to be a little more pulpy on this one and kind of homage a different style of horror?

RB: We both love Bernie Wrightson, who also worked on *The Green Mile* and gave me a *Frankenstein* portfolio. [Jason and I] wanted to do something like that *Frankenstein* because we both loved it, and we kept referencing it. And Jason was like, let's do something that's black and white. We already worked in this world of vampires, and we both love werewolves, specifically the movie *The Howling*, [though] I go back to Lon Chaney Jr. and the Universal stuff.

A lot of our conversations start with, *Wouldn't it be cool if...* I'm a big fan of the '60s and '70s. I was working on a Fred Hampton movie set in the time of the Black Panthers. I'd done all of this research and then another movie was made. My movie died. So I'm sitting here with all of this stuff in my head, like, what do I do with it? And so, after many conversations, we were like, hey, let's do something like a revolutionary story that dealt with the idea of a curse and how that curse influenced the perspective of time in the same way as *Killadelphia*, but with a different spin. Instead of being on the bottom like slavery, let's have it to where these characters were on top in a period of time when they weren't just free, but they were conquering lands. They were coming from a place of power, not so much from a place of lack. And then they're compromised by one of their victories, and that leads them on a journey through time. How do you manifest having come from the opposite place from *Killadelphia*, where you're not coming from slavery to today, but you're coming from a place of, hey, wait a minute—these people have been influenced, the world has been influenced, by slavery. And how do we make an adjustment and fit in today's world coming from a place where we don't know anything like that?

It's sort of like Wakanda in the *Black Panther* movie, where that place had never been touched in the same way that other places have been touched by slavery in history. This was more of a mindset that had never been influenced in that way to where the self-esteem issues, that sense of hopelessness or anger or any of that, none of that was present in the quartet that makes up this group. And so they have to fit into a modern America where they also have this curse, when the moon is full and they become werewolves. But they, too, much like the vampires of *Killadelphia*, are seeking purpose in the world. As I think all of us are, to a lesser or greater degree, but they're coming from another place where they have to temper themselves to the mindset of the people around them, more so than try to figure out a way to find a sense of hope within themselves, like the world of *Killadelphia*.

So you're right in the sense that we wanted to do something with the traditional idea of what werewolves were, but we just wanted to do it in a way that didn't feel like it was weighed down by anything else. And that it was different than *Killadelphia*, but still attached to the same math of what it means to be a human being with human psychology.

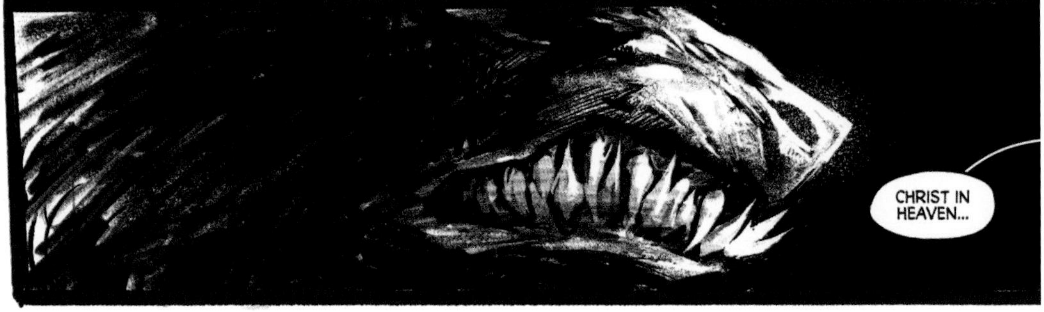
CHRIST IN HEAVEN...

SF: I want to end on a broader question. Without getting too invasive, what scares you?

RB: When you get to an age where you're certain you're going to die—I'm at that age, and, you know, as a younger person, it's not that I thought I was immortal, but you sort of think that death is something that's gonna happen way down the road, you don't have to think about it right now. Fortunately or unfortunately, I've lived long enough and have gone through enough where you start to realize that you've got more days behind you than you do in front of you.

I spent a lot of time on this journey confused, afraid, riddled with insecurities and, you know, just fear, for a lot of different reasons, childhood trauma, my own insecurities and fears. And [eventually] you get to a place where you realize, A. everybody has that stuff, it's not just you, and B. again, if you work on that stuff, it can get better.

What I hope is, by the time I make it out of this life, I've done something to make things a little bit better for other people, so that I've been a positive force and not a negative one. And so the fear would be not being able to live up to that idea. As much as I talked about the hard part of Twitter, there's been some really great people in the little *Killadelphia* world that have been really supportive, really inspiring, and I feel connected to all of them. And there's something beautiful under all of this that I love being a part of, wanting to just really do good work.

Even when we're talking about Bernie Wrightson right now, Bernie was so fantastic. You know, Bernie Wrightson and Neal Adams, those where my guys as a kid growing up. Those early *Swamp Thing* books and Bernie's other horror stuff, they gave me purpose. I actually ran up to my corner store and I couldn't wait until the new books came because I loved those *House of Mystery* or *House of Secrets* or whichever ones they were. And I just want to be a part of life in that way, that I'm making things that make people feel better and make

this difficult time that we're all living in a little bit more enjoyable. And hopefully just adding something to the world. Not being able to do that would be my fear. That's what scares me.

SF: That's a very beautiful answer. I was expecting you to say vampires.

RB: No, no, no. Part of being a vampire is kind of cool! If you're the Bela Lugosi or Frank Langella, the sexy kind, the guys who come in kind of like pimps but they're vampires? I wouldn't want to be the kind I'm doing, the *Killadelphia* kind, they're crawling and groveling. Not them, but the sexy ones, that wouldn't be the worst thing.

***

Rodney Barnes is the award-winning writer/ producer of HBO's Showtime, *Hulu's* Wu-Tang: An American Saga, *Marvel's* Runaways, *Starz's* American Gods, *and a host of other television programs and films. He is also the author of Lion Forge's* Quincredible, Star Wars—Lando: Double or Nothing, *and* Falcon *from Marvel Comics. He is now writing* Killadelphia *for Image Comics. Rodney resides in Los Angeles.*

All process art courtesy of Jason Shawn Alexander.

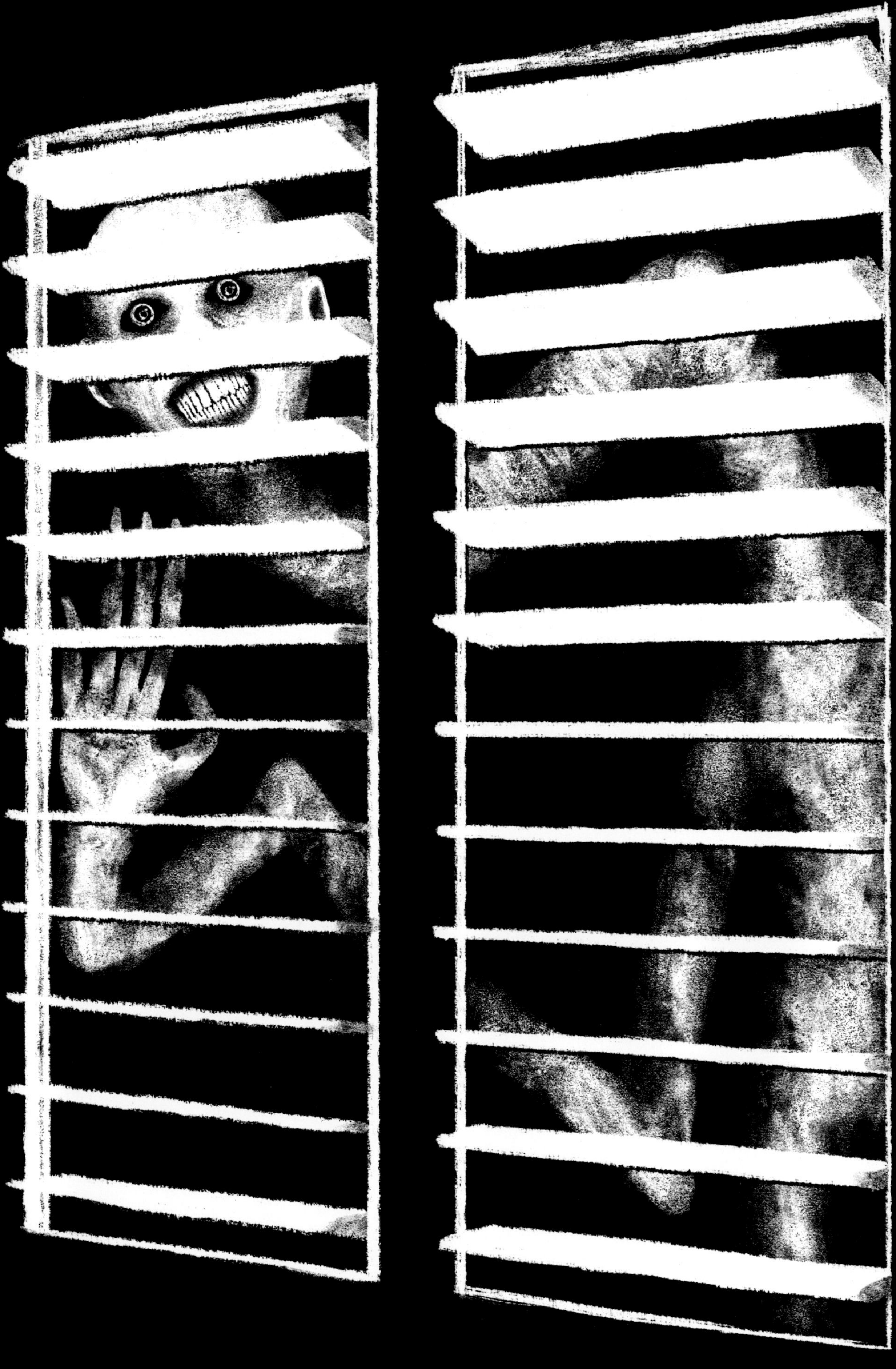

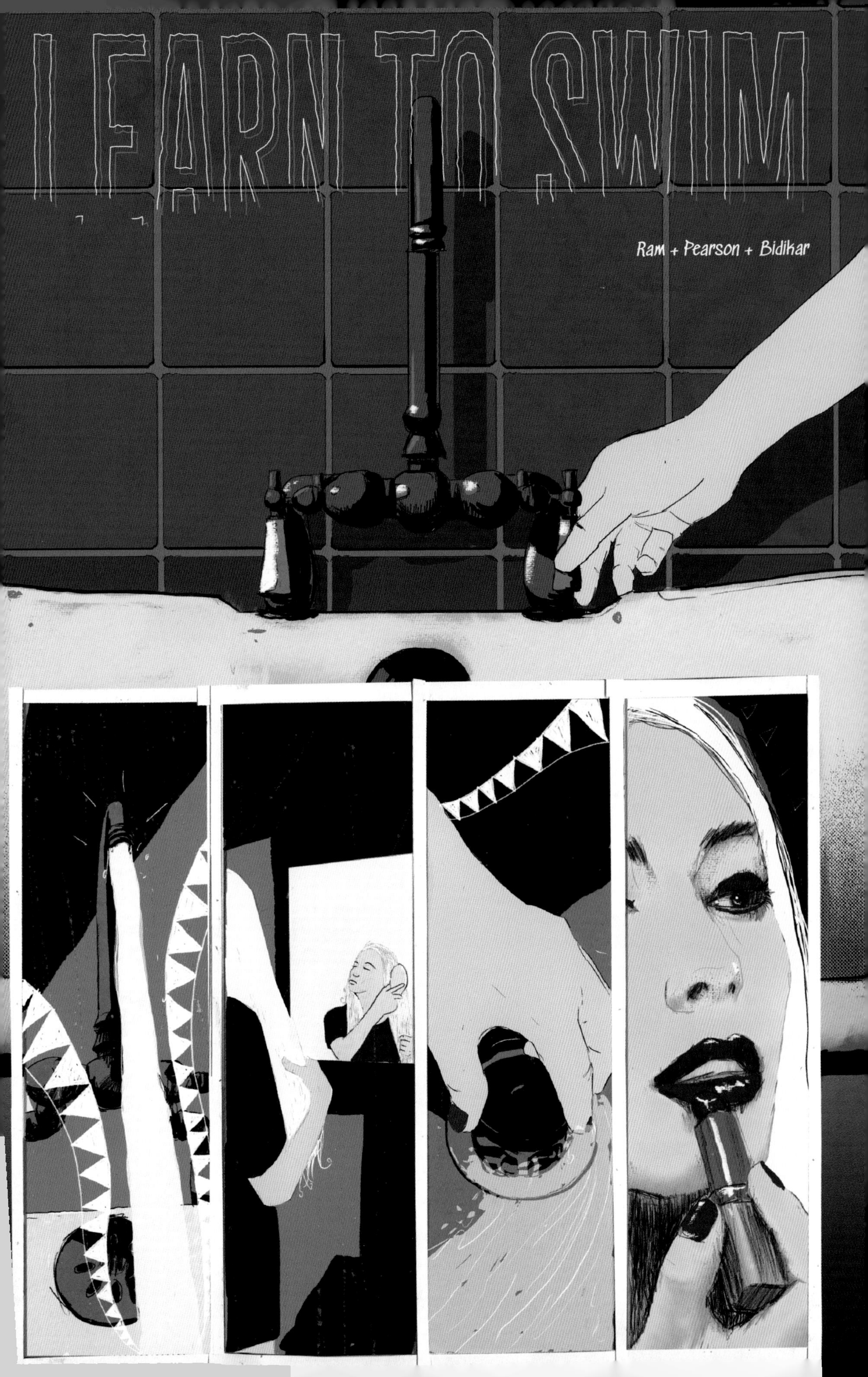
LEARN TO SWIM
Ram + Pearson + Bidikar

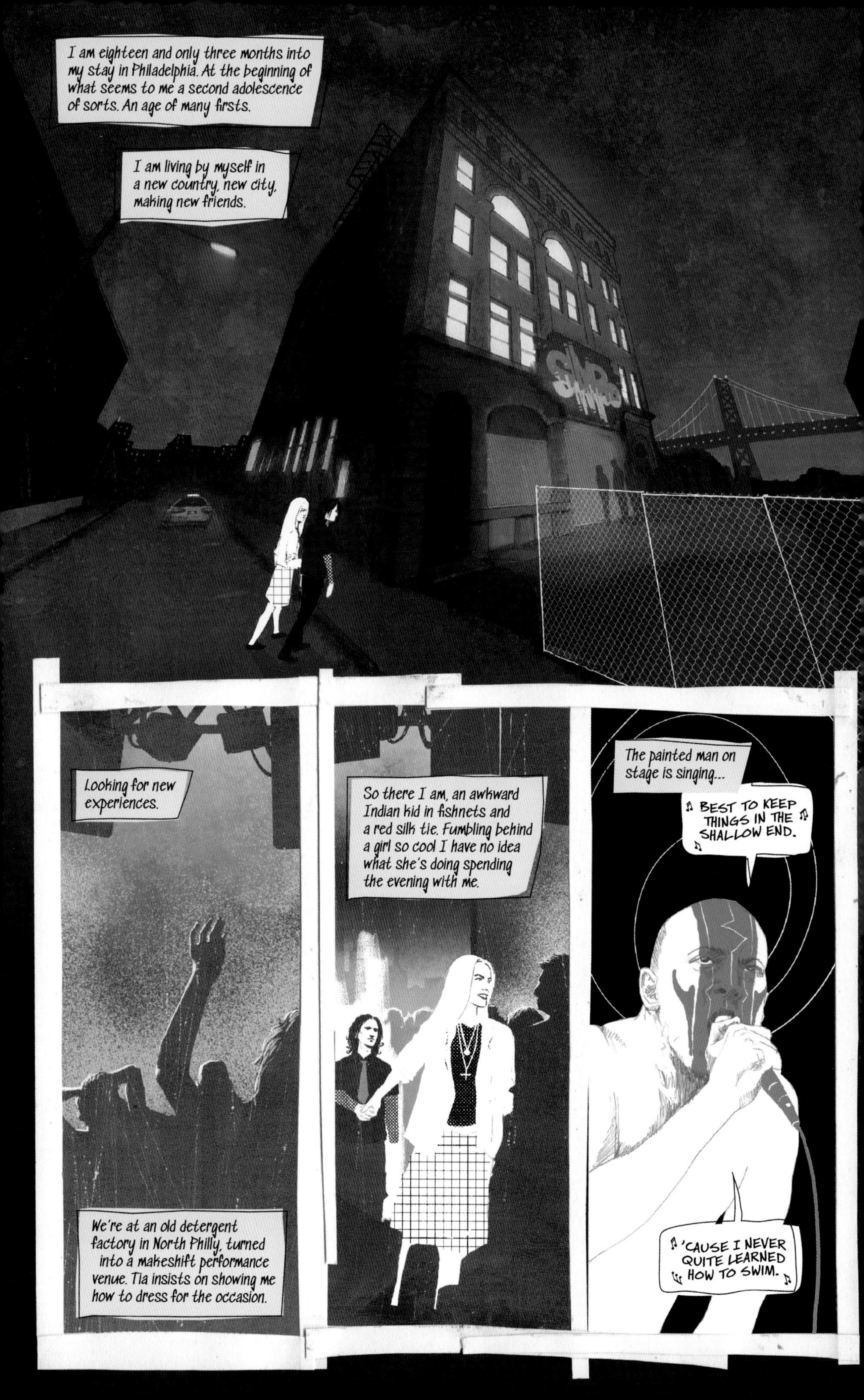
I am eighteen and only three months into my stay in Philadelphia. At the beginning of what seems to me a second adolescence of sorts. An age of many firsts.
I am living by myself in a new country, new city, making new friends.
Looking for new experiences.
We're at an old detergent factory in North Philly, turned into a makeshift performance venue. Tia insists on showing me how to dress for the occasion.
So there I am, an awkward Indian kid in fishnets and a red silk tie. Fumbling behind a girl so cool I have no idea what she's doing spending the evening with me.
The painted man on stage is singing...
BEST TO KEEP THINGS IN THE SHALLOW END.
'CAUSE I NEVER QUITE LEARNED HOW TO SWIM.

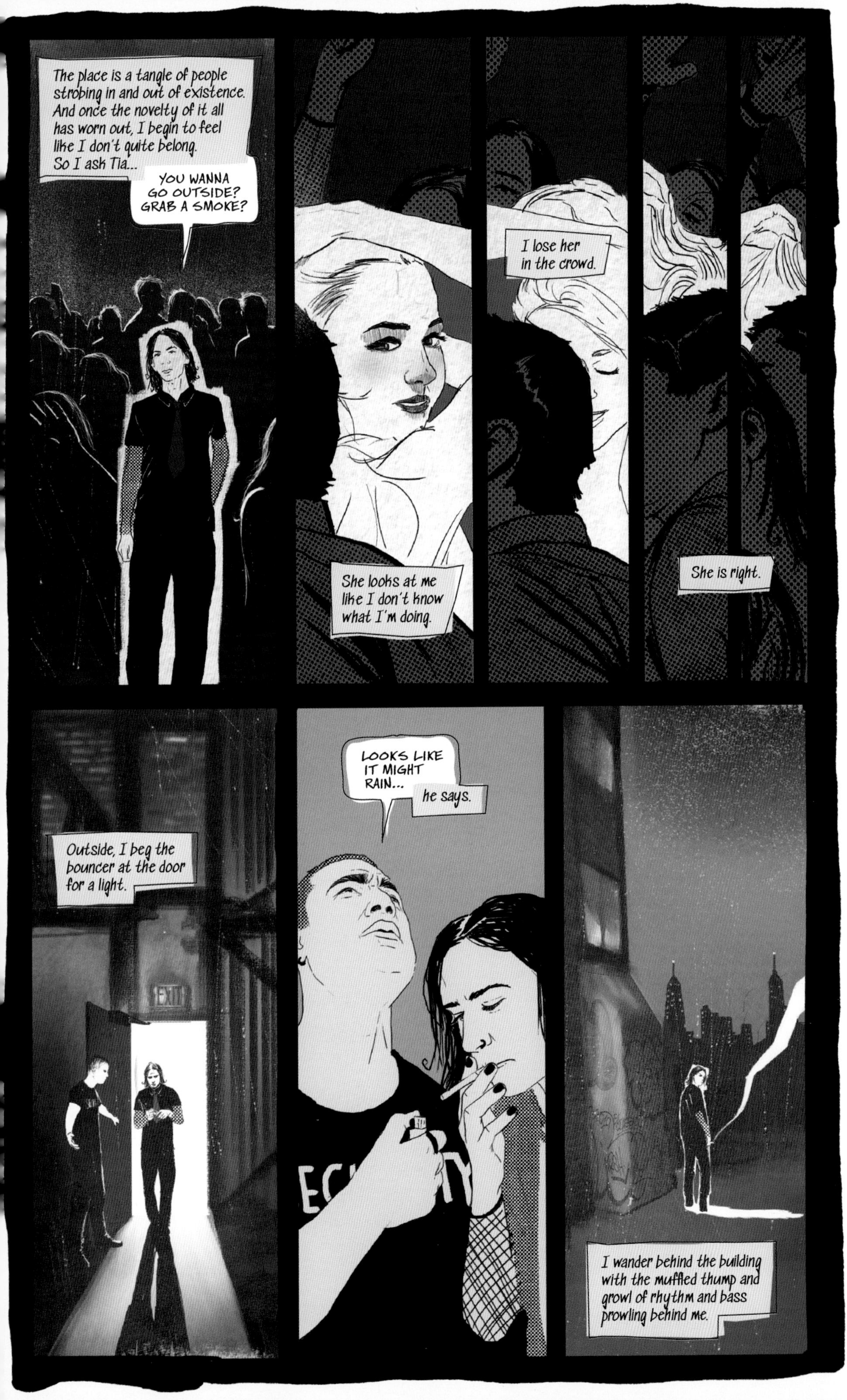
The place is a tangle of people strobing in and out of existence. And once the novelty of it all has worn out, I begin to feel like I don't quite belong. So I ask Tia...
YOU WANNA GO OUTSIDE? GRAB A SMOKE?
She looks at me like I don't know what I'm doing.
I lose her in the crowd.
She is right.
Outside, I beg the bouncer at the door for a light.
EXIT
LOOKS LIKE IT MIGHT RAIN...
he says.
I wander behind the building with the muffled thump and growl of rhythm and bass prowling behind me.

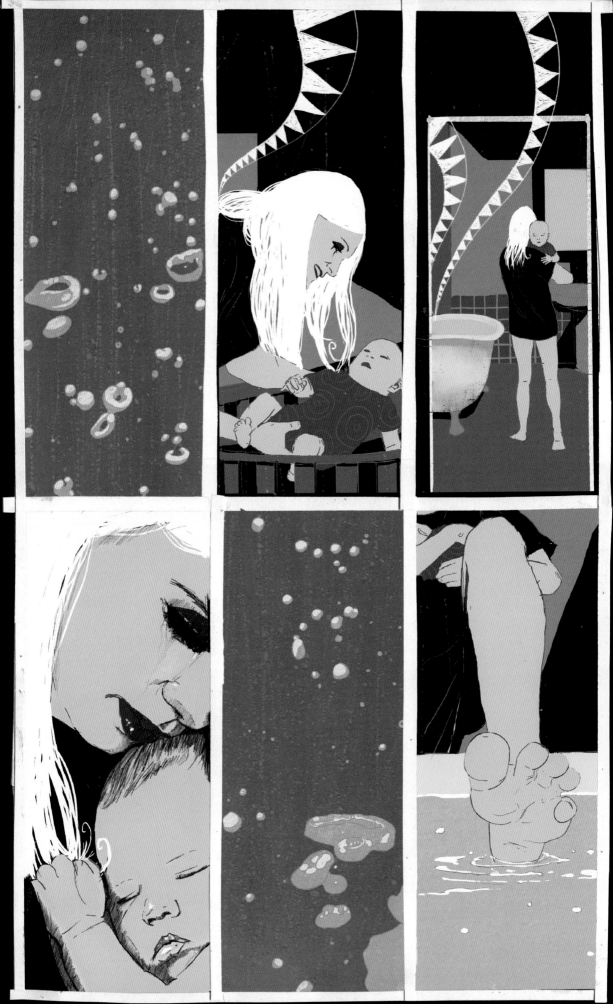

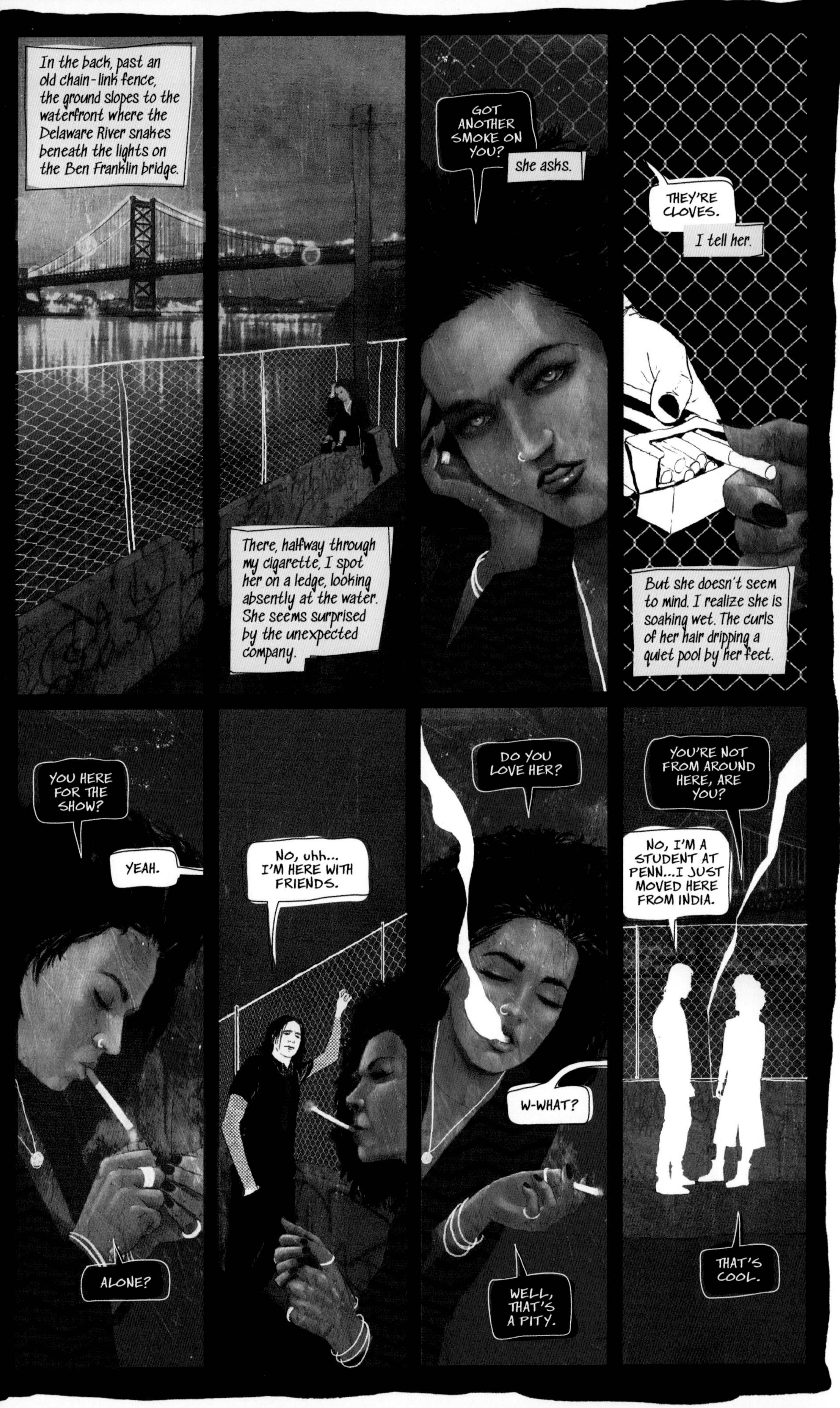
In the back, past an old chain-link fence, the ground slopes to the waterfront where the Delaware River snakes beneath the lights on the Ben Franklin bridge.
There, halfway through my cigarette, I spot her on a ledge, looking absently at the water. She seems surprised by the unexpected company.
GOT ANOTHER SMOKE ON YOU?
she asks.
THEY'RE CLOVES.
I tell her.
But she doesn't seem to mind. I realize she is soaking wet. The curls of her hair dripping a quiet pool by her feet.
YOU HERE FOR THE SHOW?
YEAH.
ALONE?
NO, uhh... I'M HERE WITH FRIENDS.
DO YOU LOVE HER?
W-WHAT?
WELL, THAT'S A PITY.
YOU'RE NOT FROM AROUND HERE, ARE YOU?
NO, I'M A STUDENT AT PENN...I JUST MOVED HERE FROM INDIA.
THAT'S COOL.

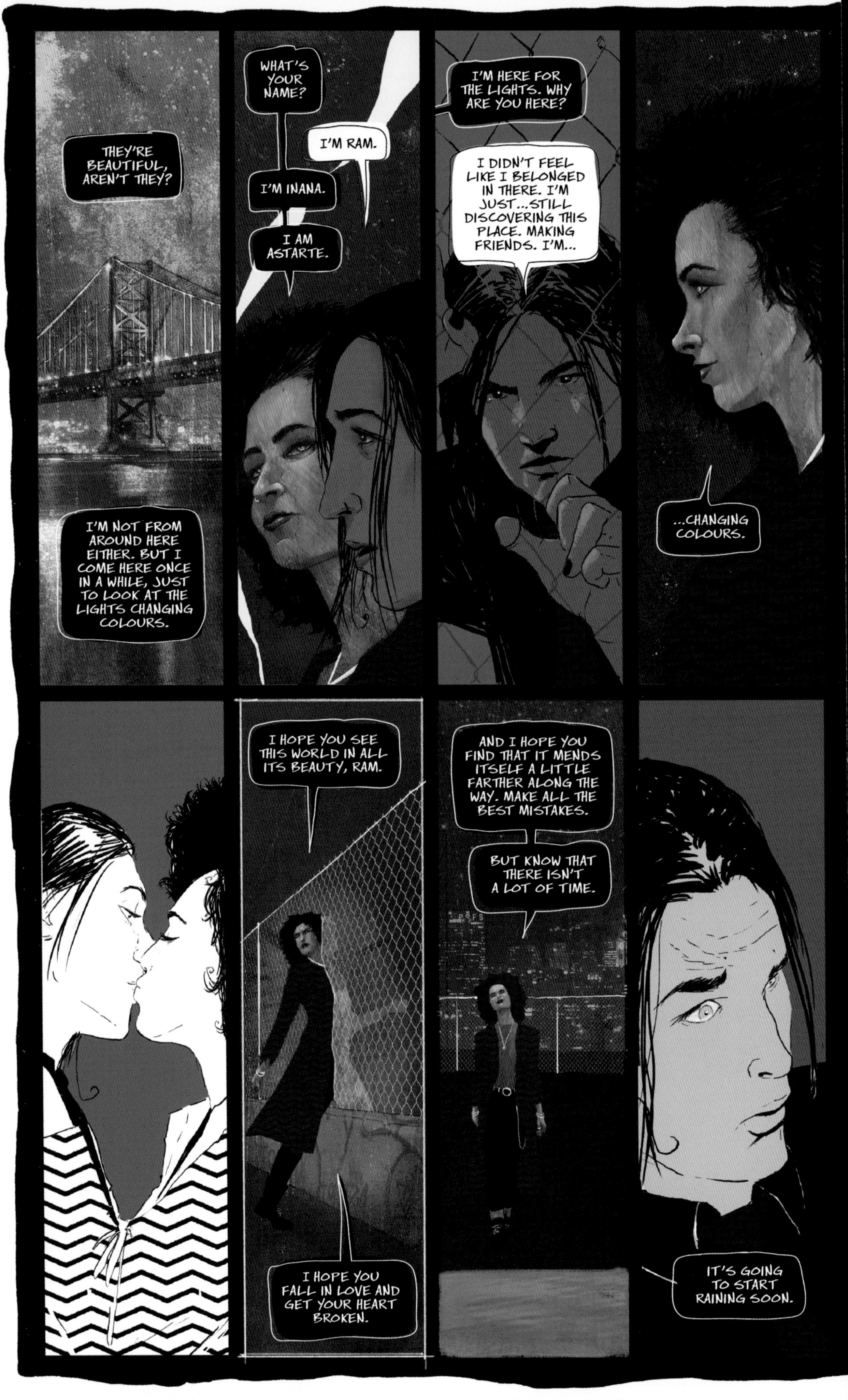
THEY'RE BEAUTIFUL, AREN'T THEY?
I'M NOT FROM AROUND HERE EITHER. BUT I COME HERE ONCE IN A WHILE, JUST TO LOOK AT THE LIGHTS CHANGING COLOURS.
WHAT'S YOUR NAME?
I'M RAM.
I'M INANA.
I AM ASTARTE.
I'M HERE FOR THE LIGHTS. WHY ARE YOU HERE?
I DIDN'T FEEL LIKE I BELONGED IN THERE. I'M JUST...STILL DISCOVERING THIS PLACE. MAKING FRIENDS. I'M...
...CHANGING COLOURS.
I HOPE YOU SEE THIS WORLD IN ALL ITS BEAUTY, RAM.
I HOPE YOU FALL IN LOVE AND GET YOUR HEART BROKEN.
AND I HOPE YOU FIND THAT IT MENDS ITSELF A LITTLE FARTHER ALONG THE WAY. MAKE ALL THE BEST MISTAKES.
BUT KNOW THAT THERE ISN'T A LOT OF TIME.
IT'S GOING TO START RAINING SOON.

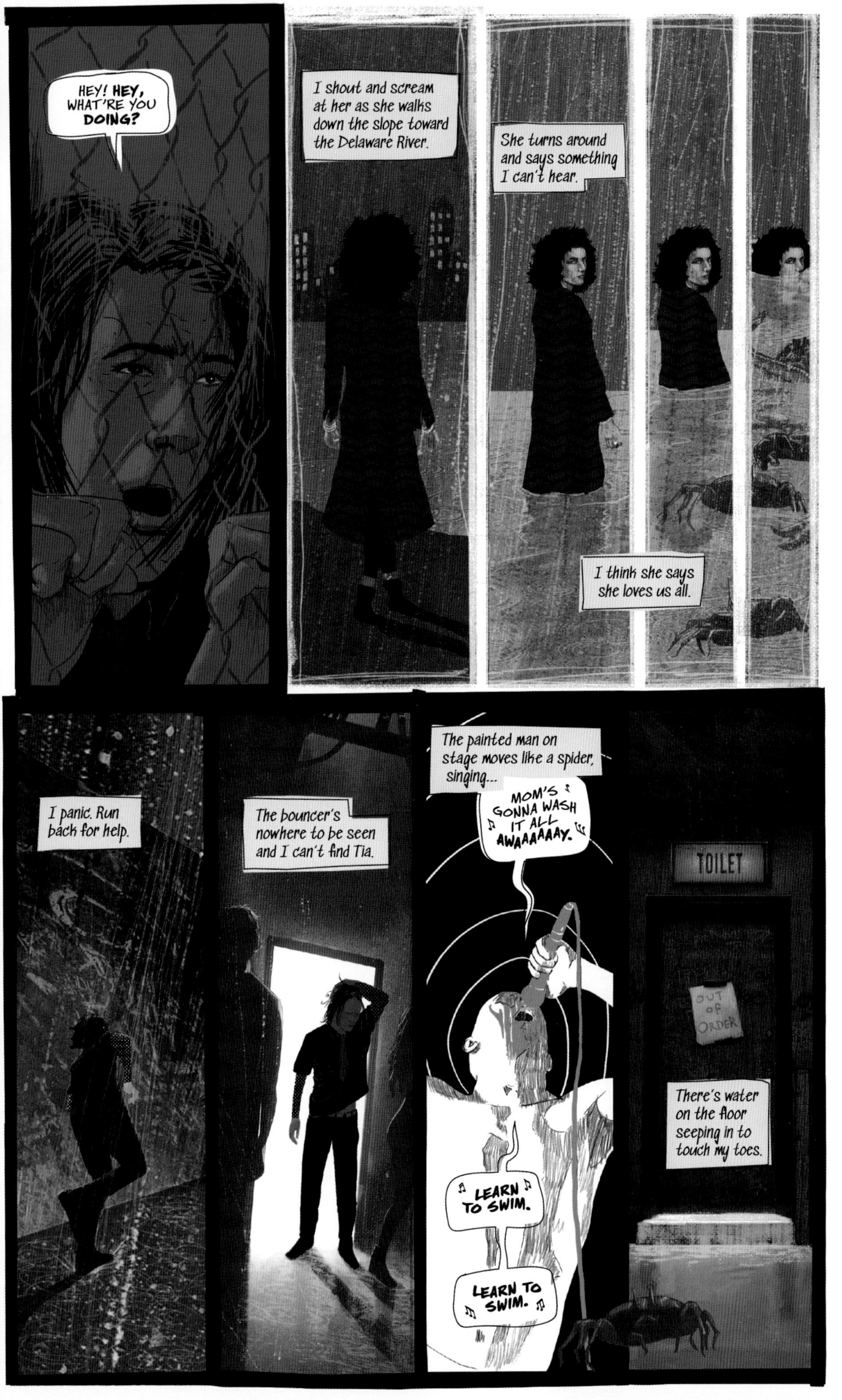
HEY! HEY, WHAT'RE YOU DOING?
I shout and scream at her as she walks down the slope toward the Delaware River.
She turns around and says something I can't hear.
I think she says she loves us all.
I panic. Run back for help.
The bouncer's nowhere to be seen and I can't find Tia.
The painted man on stage moves like a spider, singing...
MOM'S GONNA WASH IT ALL AWAAAAAAY.
LEARN TO SWIM.
LEARN TO SWIM.
TOILET
OUT OF ORDER
There's water on the floor seeping in to touch my toes.

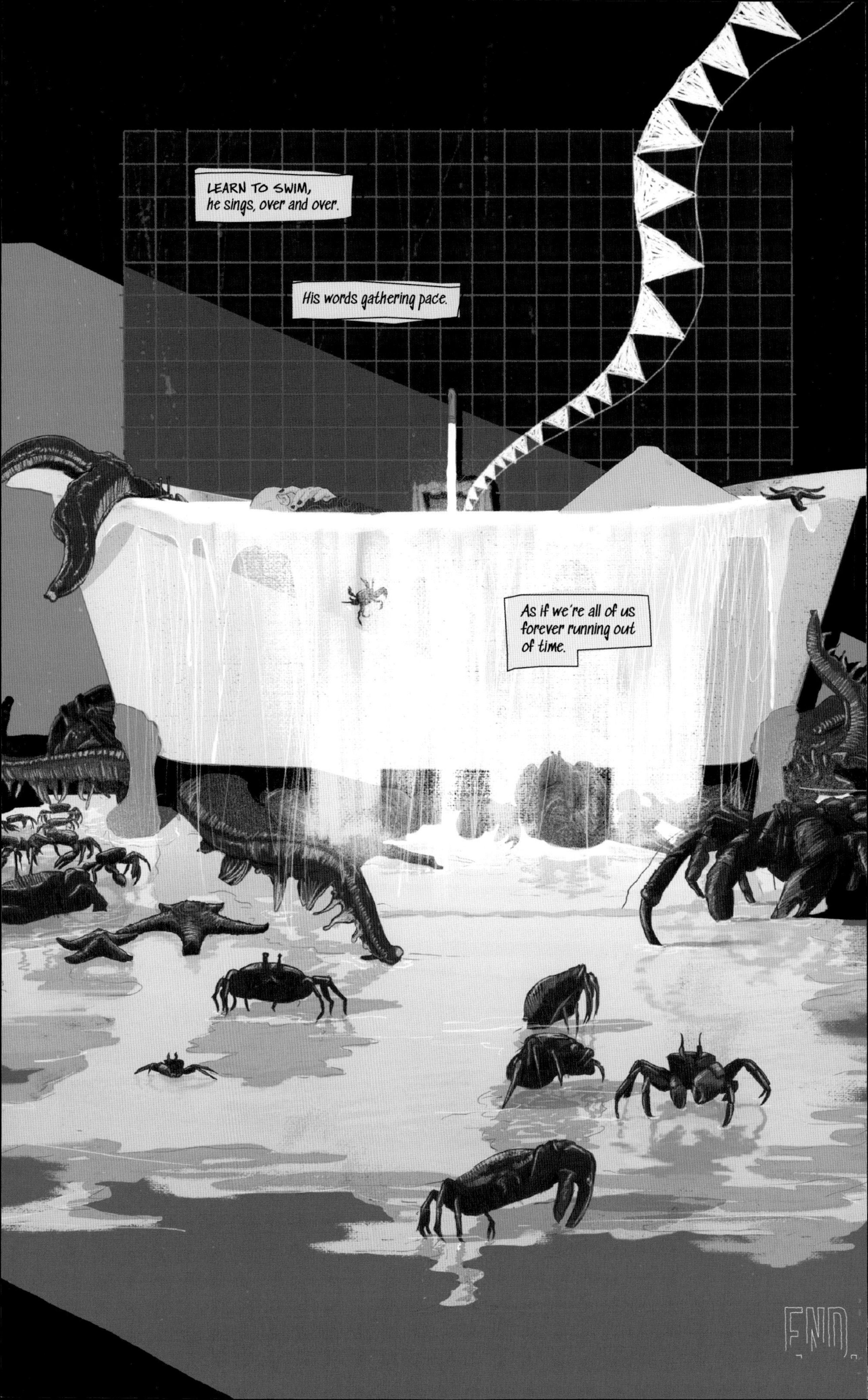
LEARN TO SWIM,
he sings, over and over.
His words gathering pace.
As if we're all of us forever running out of time.
END.

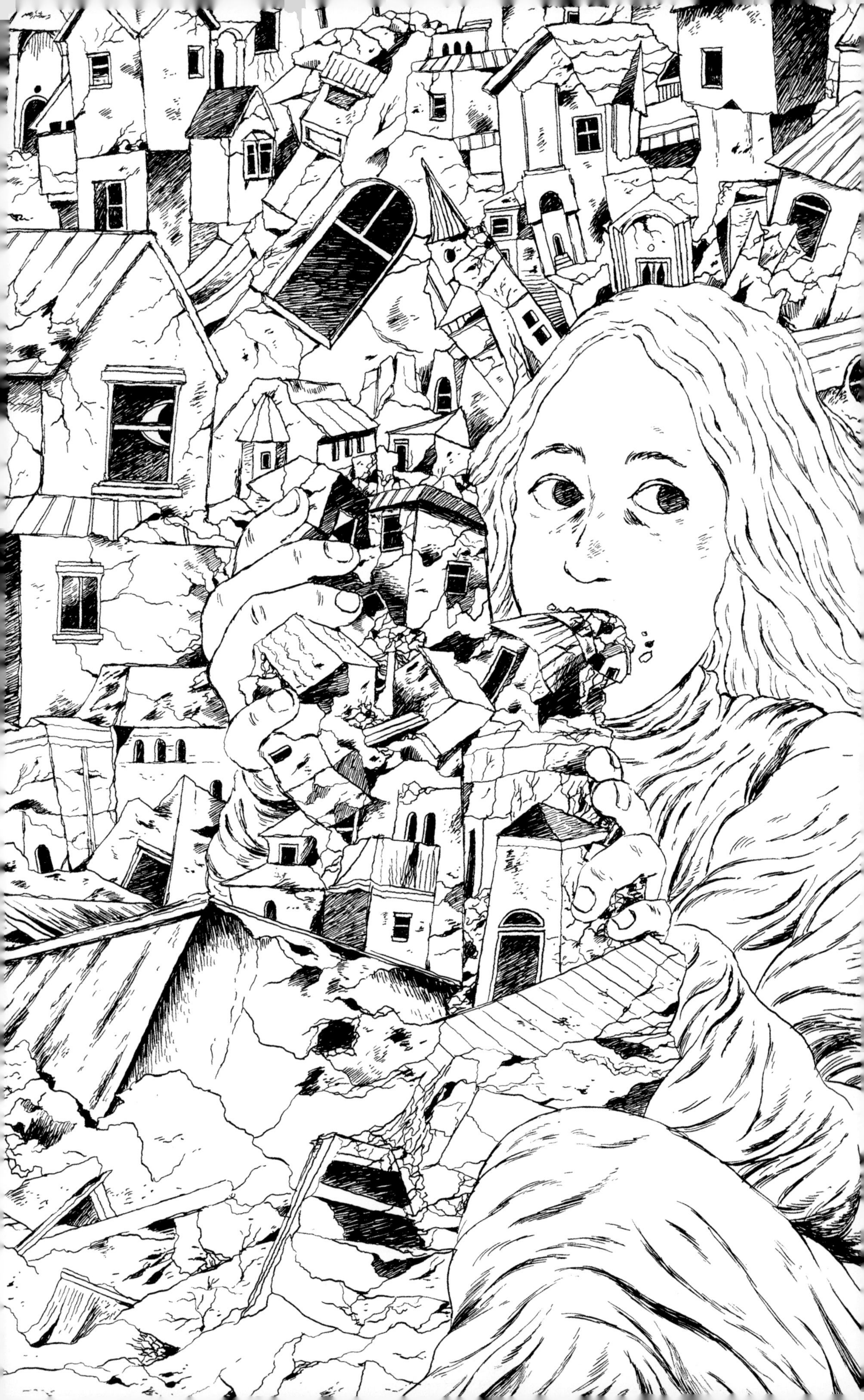

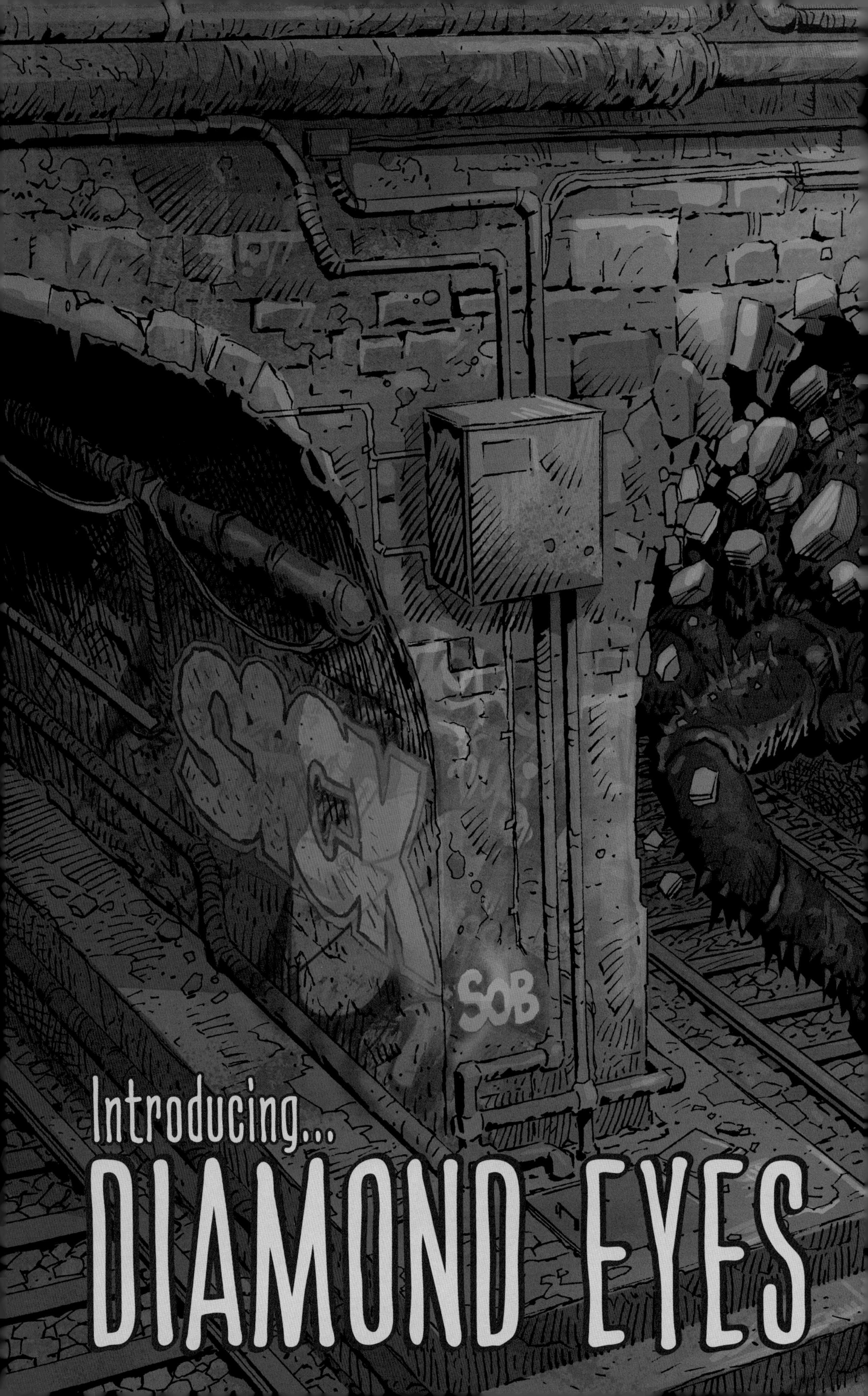
SOB
Introducing...
DIAMOND EYES

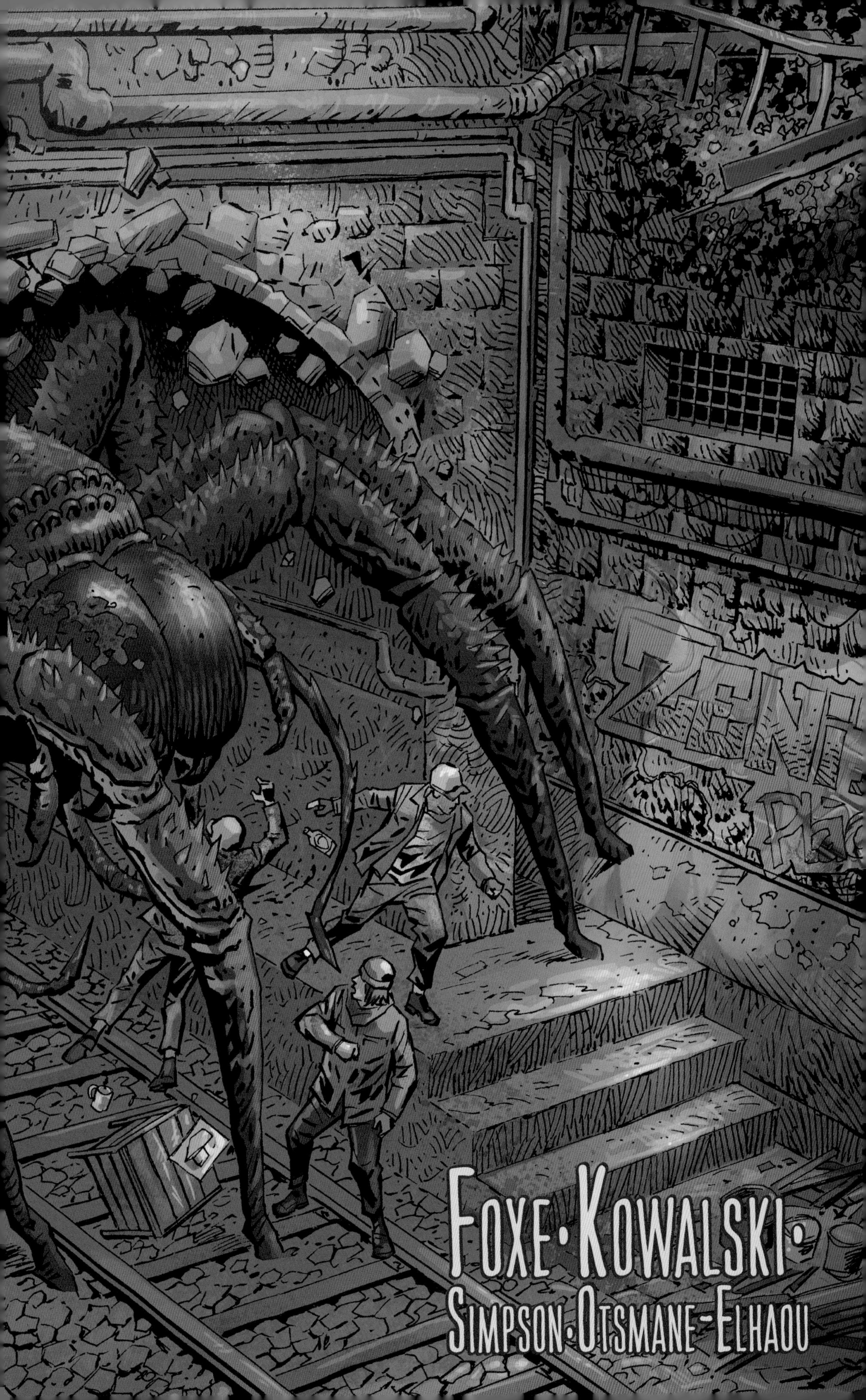
FOXE·KOWALSKI·
SIMPSON·OTSMANE-ELHAOU

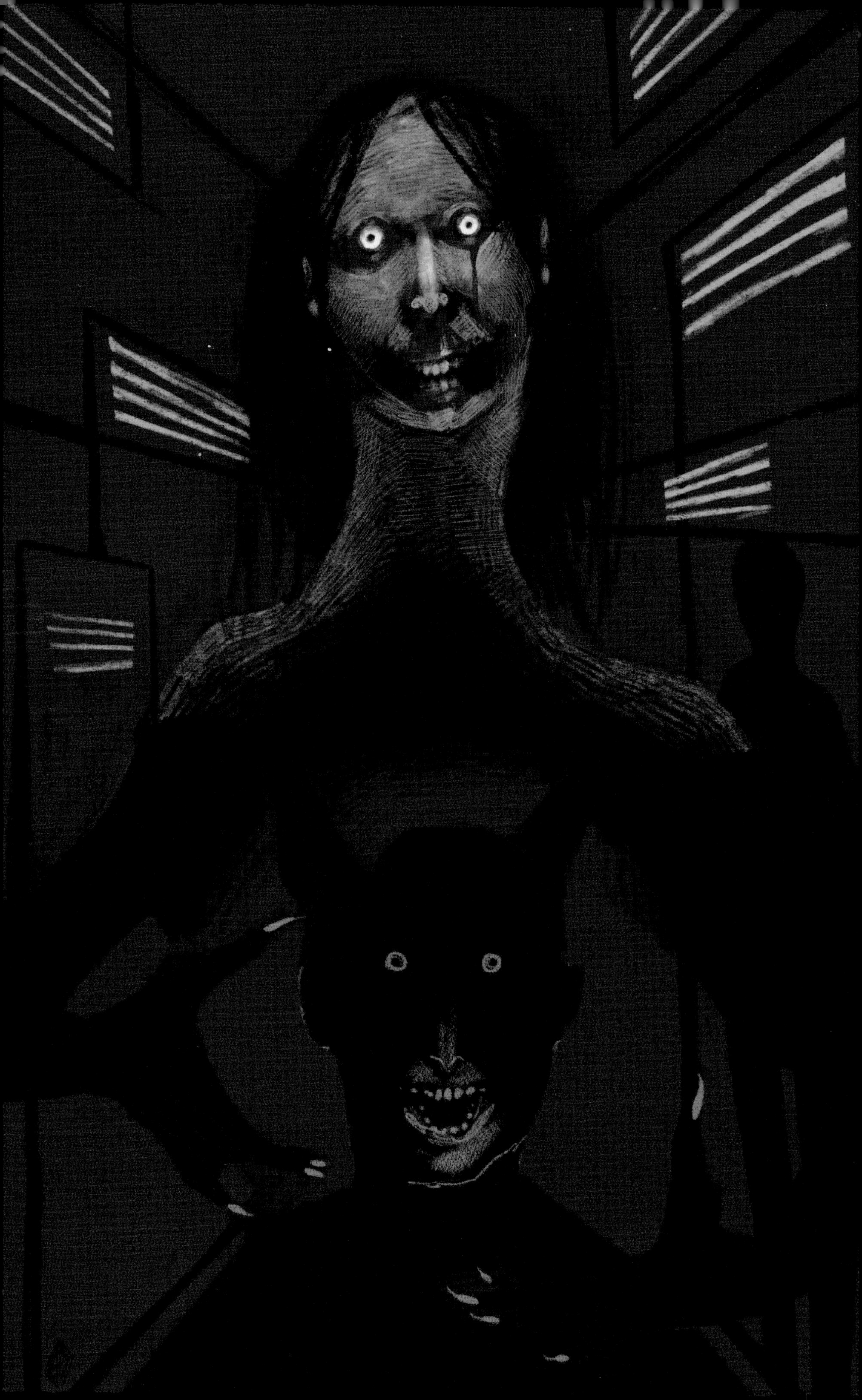

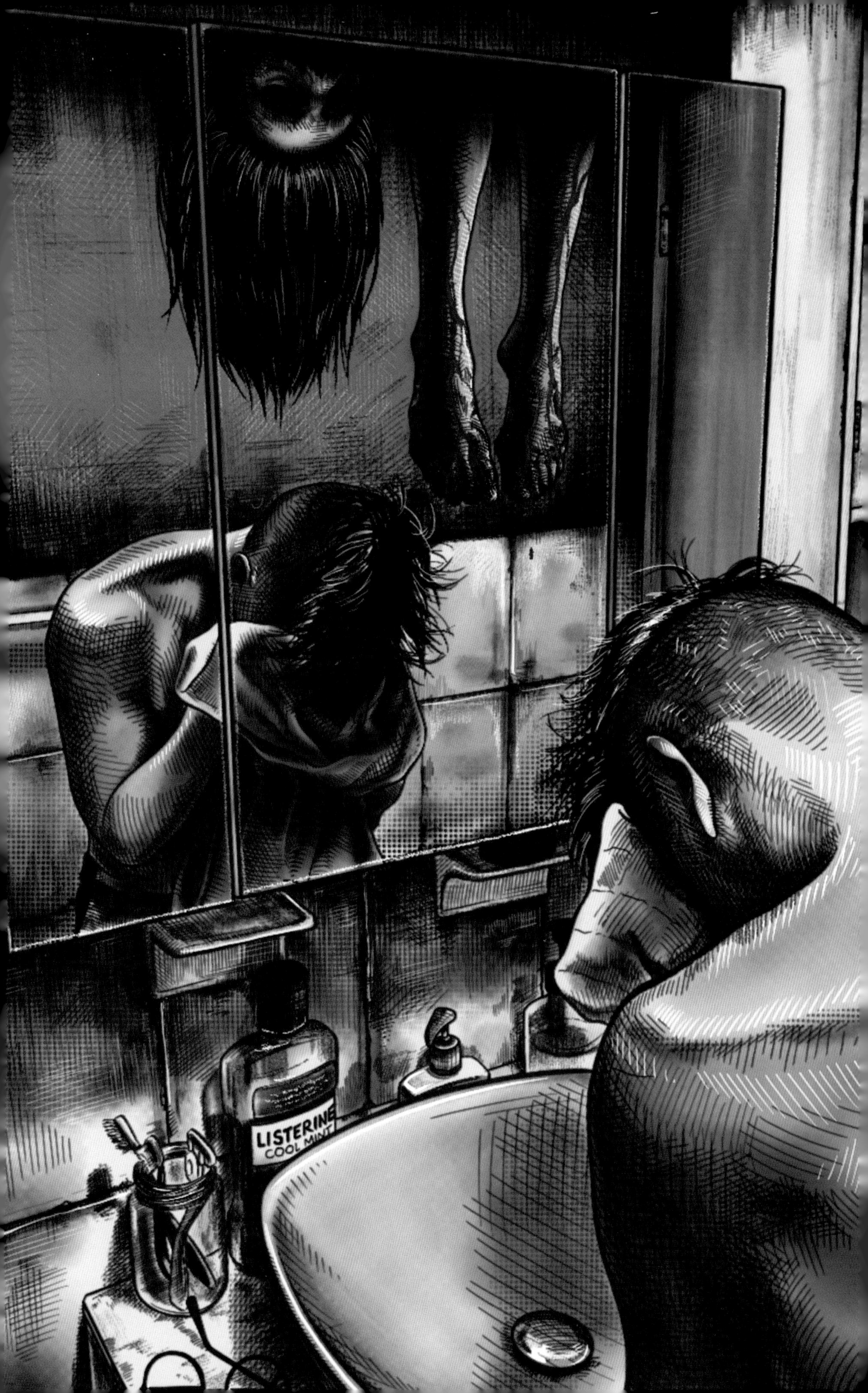
LISTERINE
COOL MINT

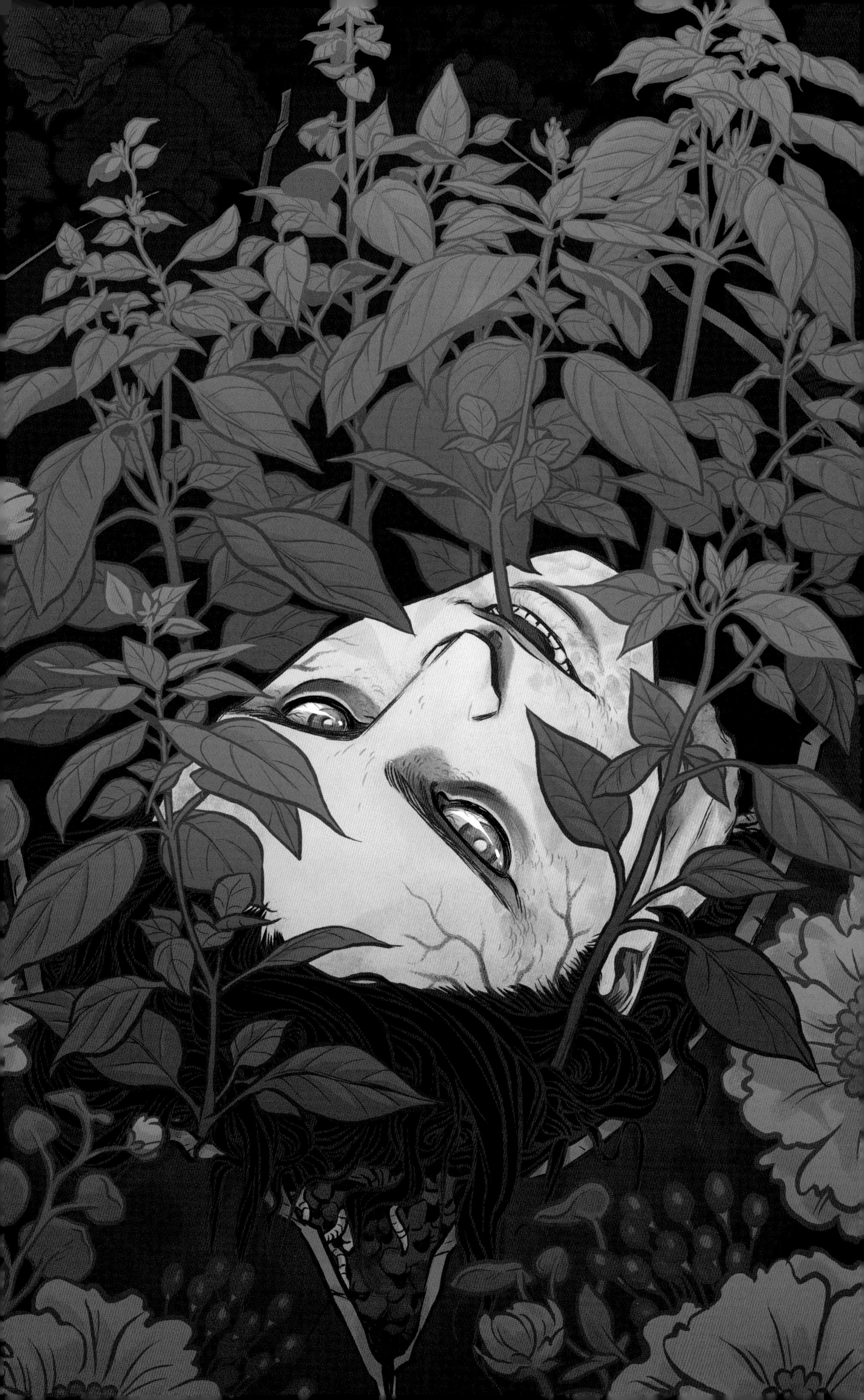

ISSUE #4

Cover Art By BECKY CLOONAN

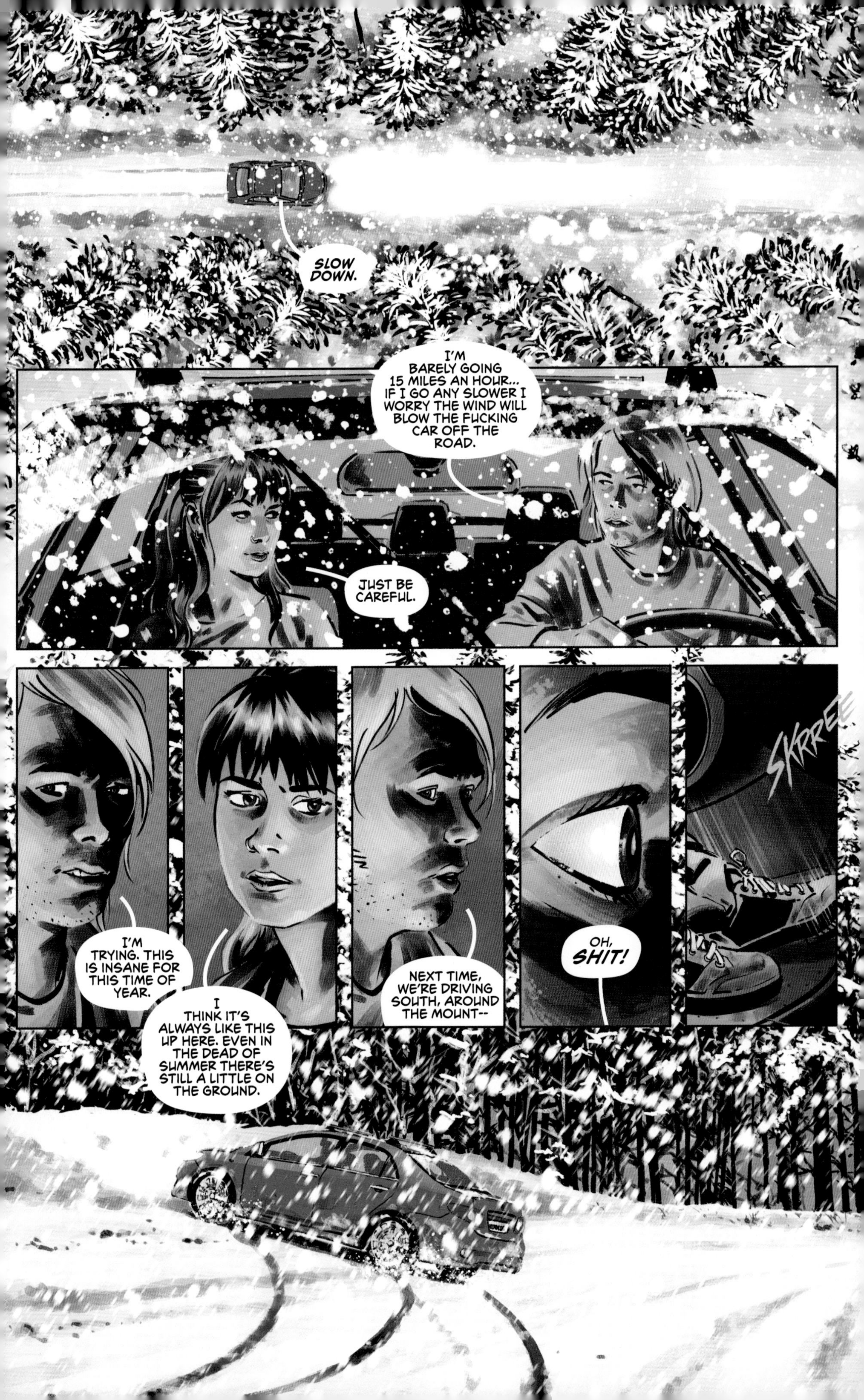
SLOW DOWN.
JUST BE CAREFUL.
I'M BARELY GOING 15 MILES AN HOUR... IF I GO ANY SLOWER I WORRY THE WIND WILL BLOW THE FUCKING CAR OFF THE ROAD.
I'M TRYING. THIS IS INSANE FOR THIS TIME OF YEAR.
I THINK IT'S ALWAYS LIKE THIS UP HERE. EVEN IN THE DEAD OF SUMMER THERE'S STILL A LITTLE ON THE GROUND.
NEXT TIME, WE'RE DRIVING SOUTH, AROUND THE MOUNT--
OH, SHIT!
SKRREE

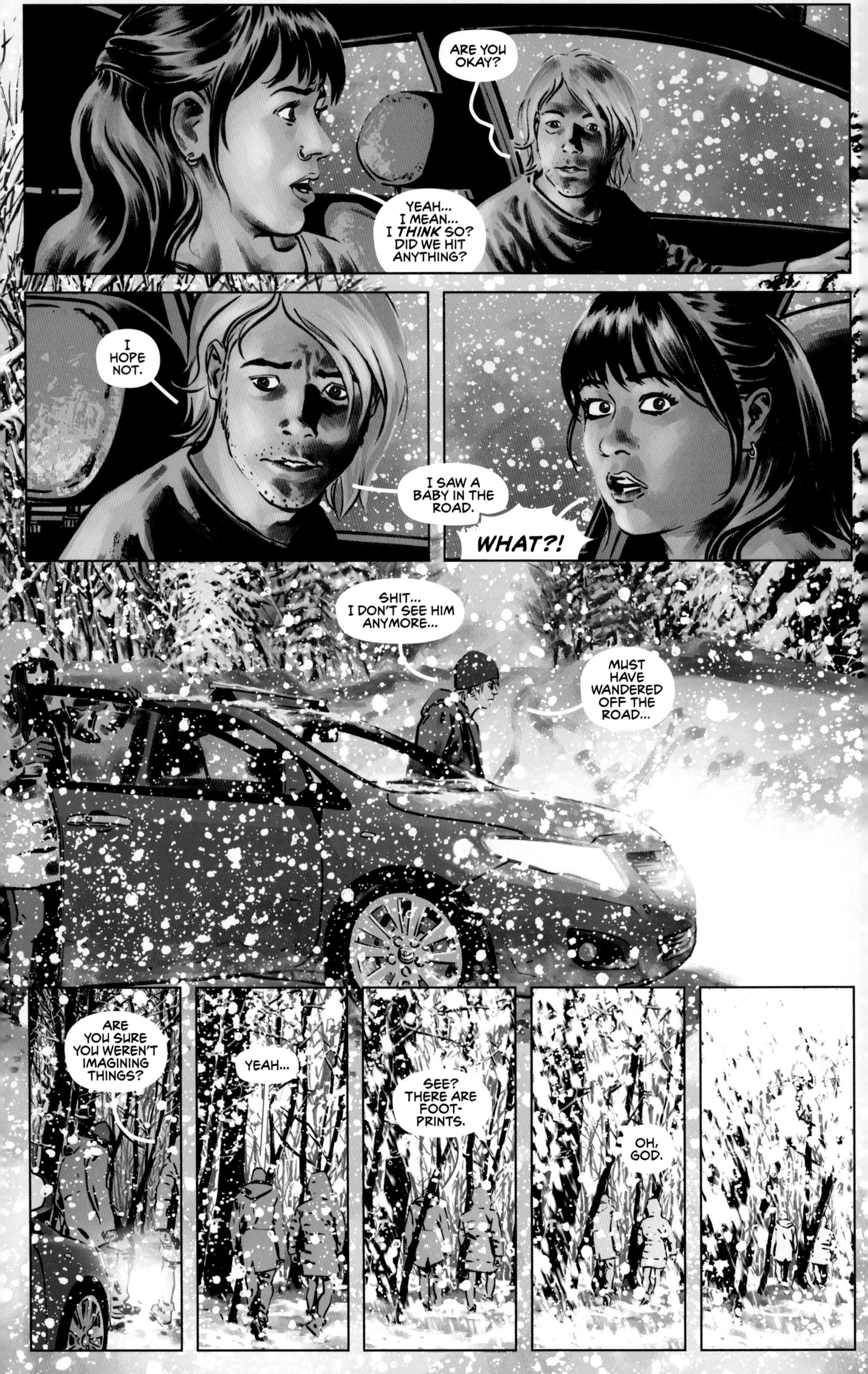
ARE YOU OKAY?
YEAH... I MEAN... I *THINK* SO? DID WE HIT ANYTHING?
I HOPE NOT.
I SAW A BABY IN THE ROAD.
WHAT?!
SHIT... I DON'T SEE HIM ANYMORE...
MUST HAVE WANDERED OFF THE ROAD...
ARE YOU SURE YOU WEREN'T IMAGINING THINGS?
YEAH...
SEE? THERE ARE FOOT-PRINTS.
OH, GOD.

WHO WOULD JUST LEAVE HIM OUT HERE... HE MUST BE FREEZING TO DEATH.

HEY! WE'VE GOT A KID HERE!

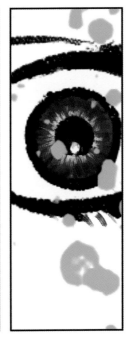

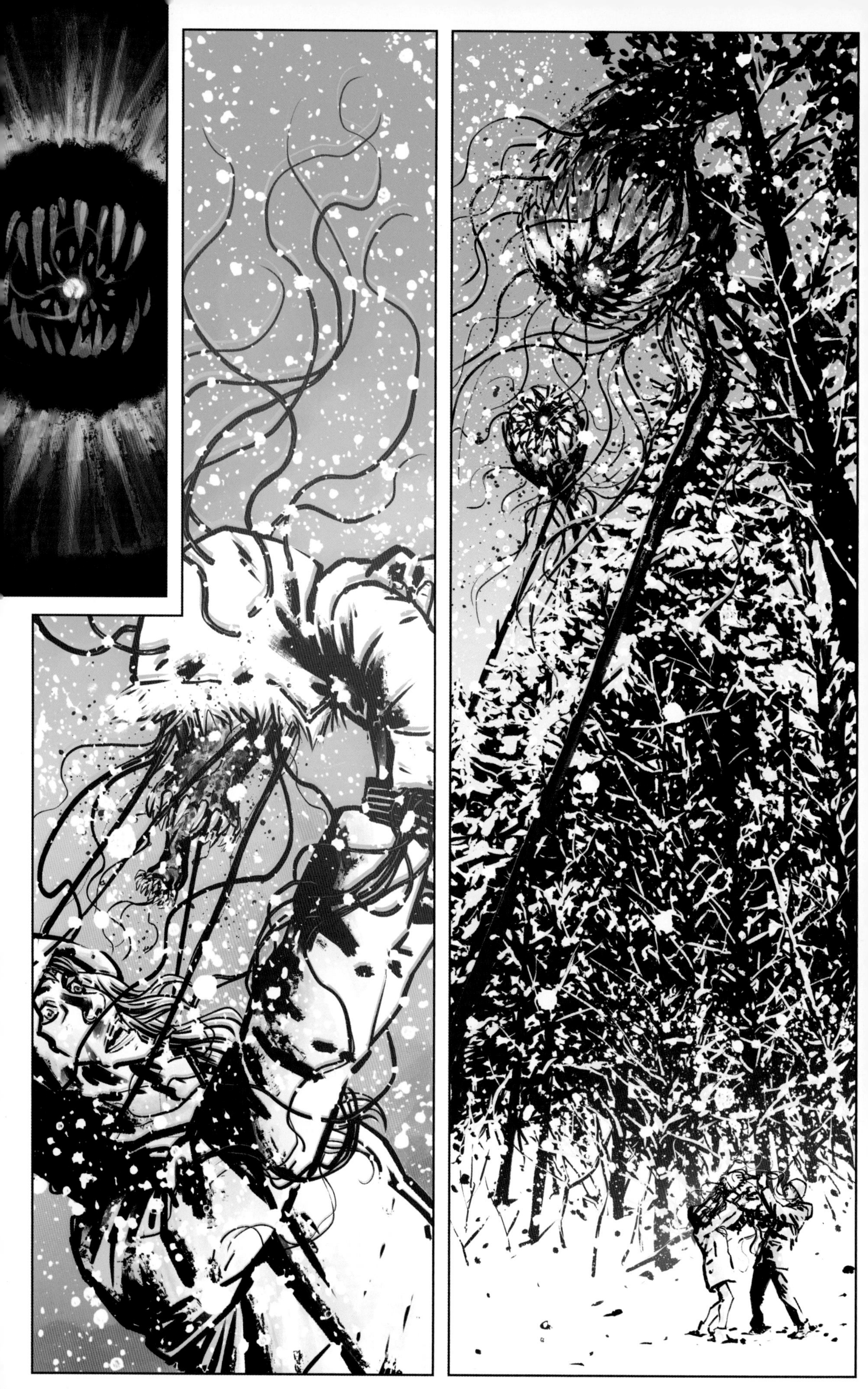

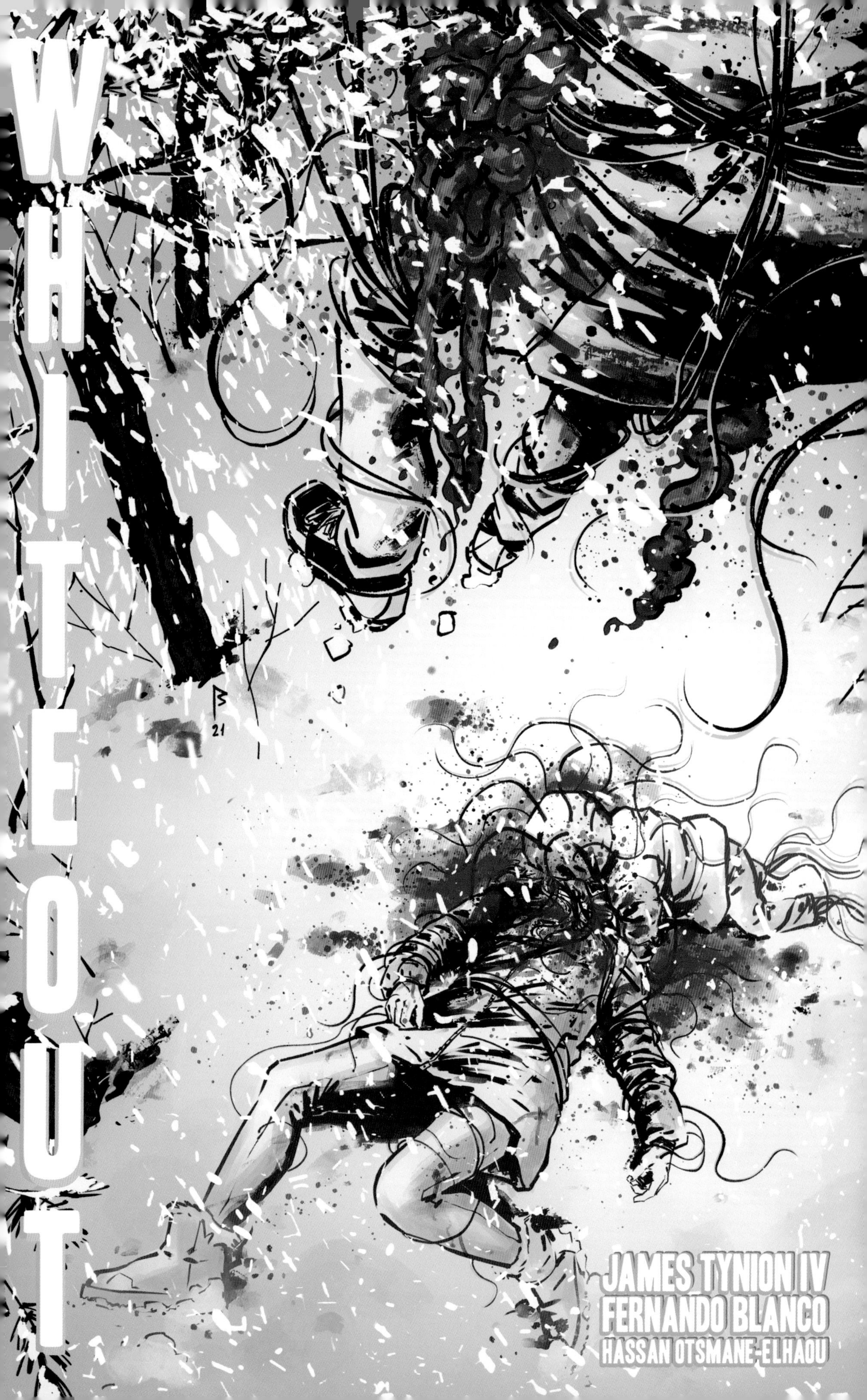
WHITEOUT
JAMES TYNION IV
FERNANDO BLANCO
HASSAN OTSMANE-ELHAOU

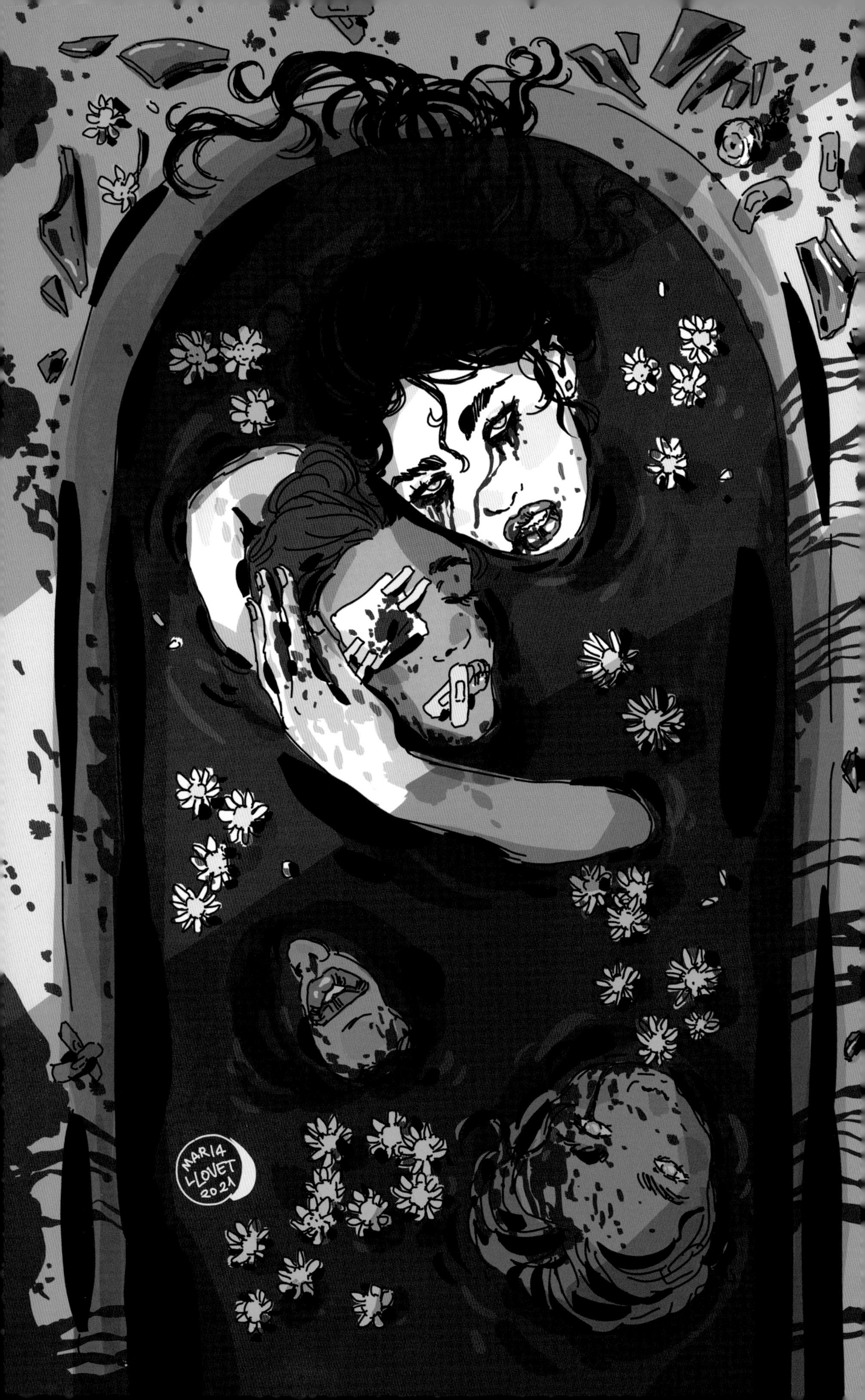
MARIA LLOVET 2021

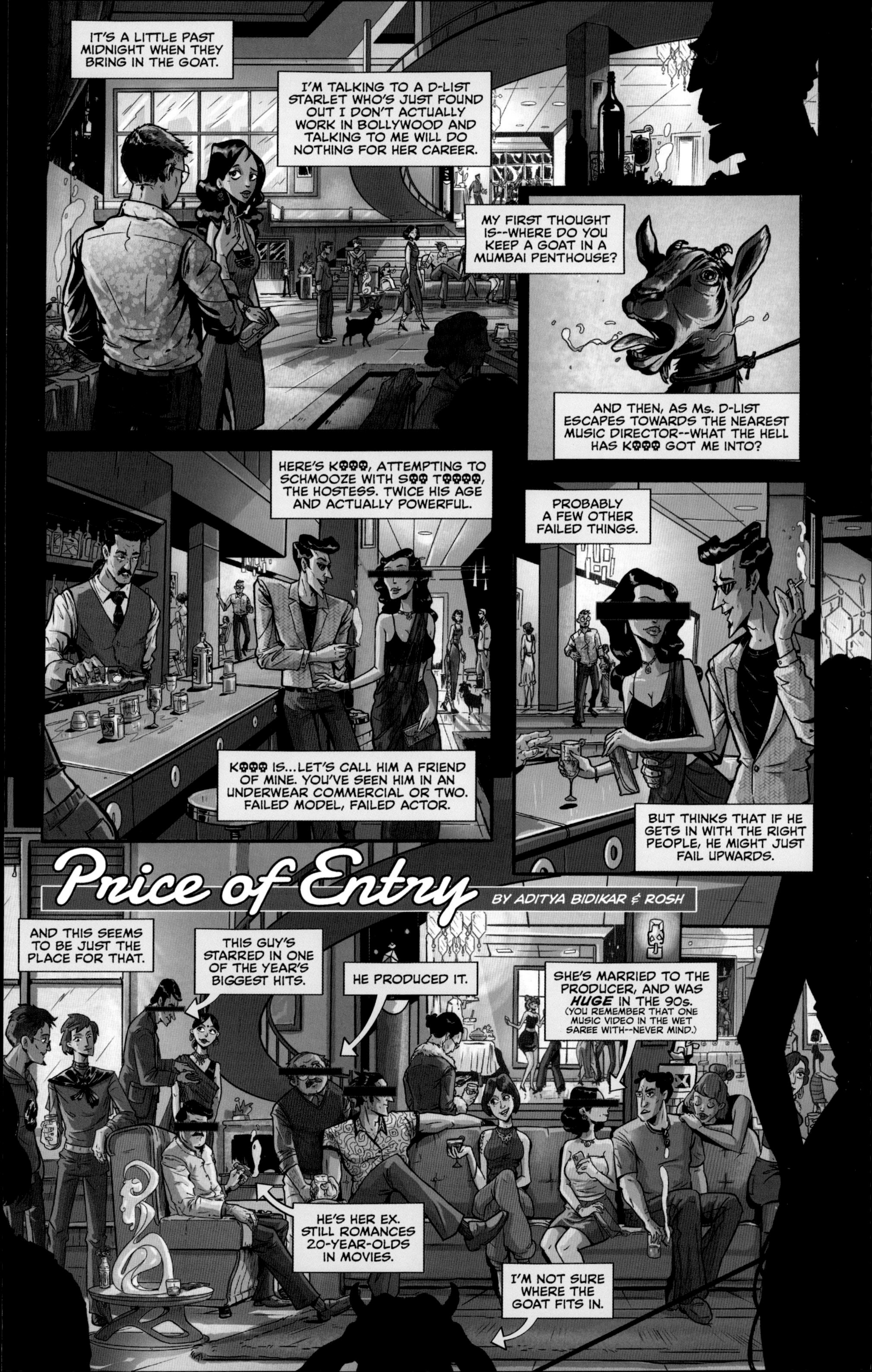
IT'S A LITTLE PAST MIDNIGHT WHEN THEY BRING IN THE GOAT.
I'M TALKING TO A D-LIST STARLET WHO'S JUST FOUND OUT I DON'T ACTUALLY WORK IN BOLLYWOOD AND TALKING TO ME WILL DO NOTHING FOR HER CAREER.
MY FIRST THOUGHT IS--WHERE DO YOU KEEP A GOAT IN A MUMBAI PENTHOUSE?
AND THEN, AS Ms. D-LIST ESCAPES TOWARDS THE NEAREST MUSIC DIRECTOR--WHAT THE HELL HAS K☠☠☠ GOT ME INTO?
HERE'S K☠☠☠, ATTEMPTING TO SCHMOOZE WITH S☠☠ T☠☠☠☠, THE HOSTESS. TWICE HIS AGE AND ACTUALLY POWERFUL.
K☠☠☠ IS...LET'S CALL HIM A FRIEND OF MINE. YOU'VE SEEN HIM IN AN UNDERWEAR COMMERCIAL OR TWO. FAILED MODEL, FAILED ACTOR.
PROBABLY A FEW OTHER FAILED THINGS.
BUT THINKS THAT IF HE GETS IN WITH THE RIGHT PEOPLE, HE MIGHT JUST FAIL UPWARDS.
Price of Entry
BY ADITYA BIDIKAR & ROSH
AND THIS SEEMS TO BE JUST THE PLACE FOR THAT.
THIS GUY'S STARRED IN ONE OF THE YEAR'S BIGGEST HITS.
HE PRODUCED IT.
SHE'S MARRIED TO THE PRODUCER, AND WAS *HUGE* IN THE 90s. (YOU REMEMBER THAT ONE MUSIC VIDEO IN THE WET SAREE WITH--NEVER MIND.)
HE'S HER EX. STILL ROMANCES 20-YEAR-OLDS IN MOVIES.
I'M NOT SURE WHERE THE GOAT FITS IN.

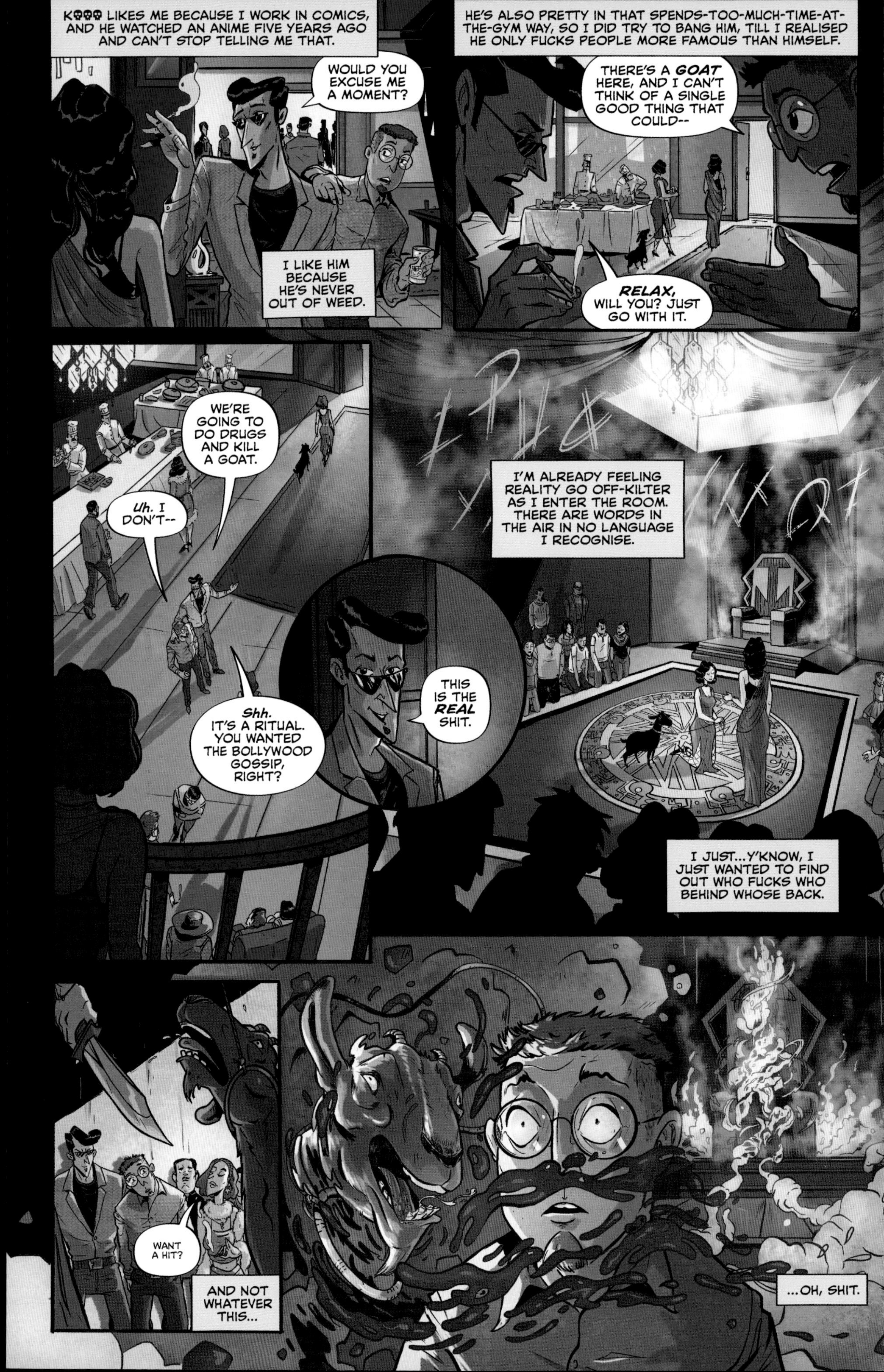
K☠☠☠ LIKES ME BECAUSE I WORK IN COMICS, AND HE WATCHED AN ANIME FIVE YEARS AGO AND CAN'T STOP TELLING ME THAT.
WOULD YOU EXCUSE ME A MOMENT?
I LIKE HIM BECAUSE HE'S NEVER OUT OF WEED.
HE'S ALSO PRETTY IN THAT SPENDS-TOO-MUCH-TIME-AT-THE-GYM WAY, SO I DID TRY TO BANG HIM, TILL I REALISED HE ONLY FUCKS PEOPLE MORE FAMOUS THAN HIMSELF.
THERE'S A ***GOAT*** HERE, AND I CAN'T THINK OF A SINGLE GOOD THING THAT COULD--
RELAX, WILL YOU? JUST GO WITH IT.
WE'RE GOING TO DO DRUGS AND KILL A GOAT.
Uh. I DON'T--
Shh. IT'S A RITUAL. YOU WANTED THE BOLLYWOOD GOSSIP, RIGHT?
THIS IS THE ***REAL*** SHIT.
I'M ALREADY FEELING REALITY GO OFF-KILTER AS I ENTER THE ROOM. THERE ARE WORDS IN THE AIR IN NO LANGUAGE I RECOGNISE.
I JUST...Y'KNOW, I JUST WANTED TO FIND OUT WHO FUCKS WHO BEHIND WHOSE BACK.
WANT A HIT?
AND NOT WHATEVER THIS...
...OH, SHIT.

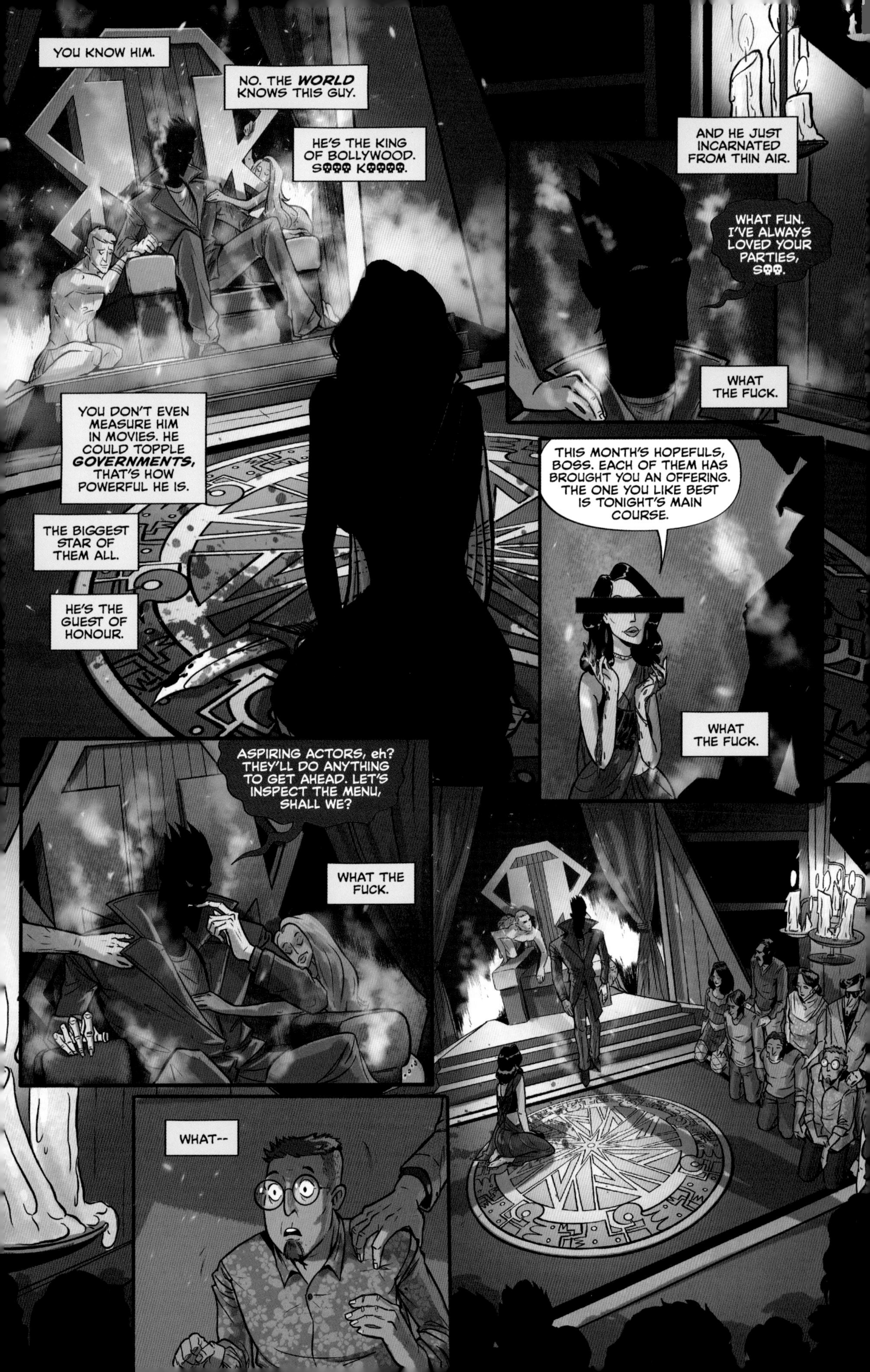
YOU KNOW HIM.
NO. THE ***WORLD*** KNOWS THIS GUY.
HE'S THE KING OF BOLLYWOOD. S☠☠☠ K☠☠☠☠.
AND HE JUST INCARNATED FROM THIN AIR.
WHAT FUN. I'VE ALWAYS LOVED YOUR PARTIES, S☠☠.
WHAT THE FUCK.
YOU DON'T EVEN MEASURE HIM IN MOVIES. HE COULD TOPPLE ***GOVERNMENTS,*** THAT'S HOW POWERFUL HE IS.
THE BIGGEST STAR OF THEM ALL.
HE'S THE GUEST OF HONOUR.
THIS MONTH'S HOPEFULS, BOSS. EACH OF THEM HAS BROUGHT YOU AN OFFERING. THE ONE YOU LIKE BEST IS TONIGHT'S MAIN COURSE.
WHAT THE FUCK.
ASPIRING ACTORS, eh? THEY'LL DO ANYTHING TO GET AHEAD. LET'S INSPECT THE MENU, SHALL WE?
WHAT THE FUCK.
WHAT--

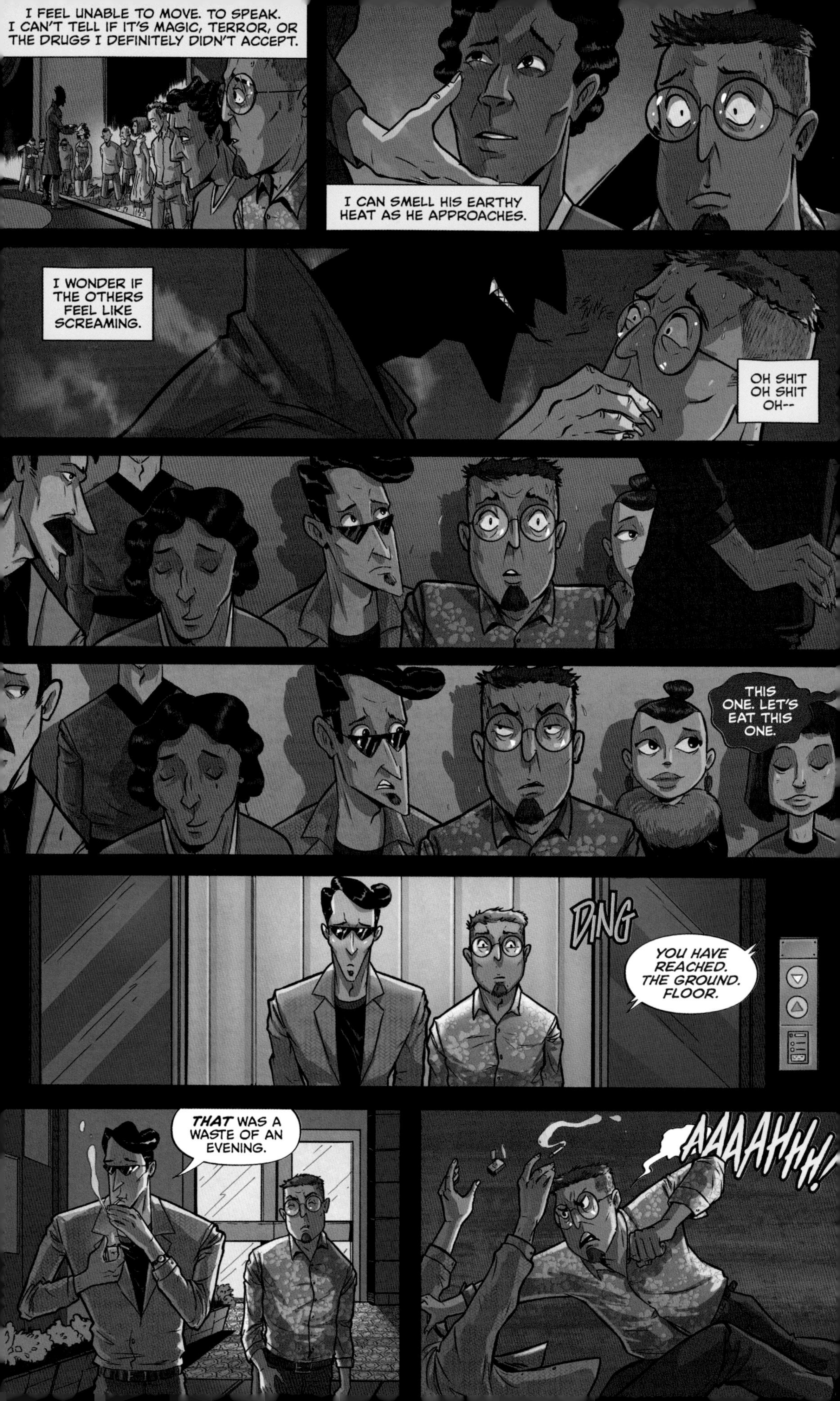
I FEEL UNABLE TO MOVE. TO SPEAK. I CAN'T TELL IF IT'S MAGIC, TERROR, OR THE DRUGS I DEFINITELY DIDN'T ACCEPT.
I CAN SMELL HIS EARTHY HEAT AS HE APPROACHES.
I WONDER IF THE OTHERS FEEL LIKE SCREAMING.
OH SHIT OH SHIT OH--
THIS ONE. LET'S EAT THIS ONE.
DING
YOU HAVE REACHED. THE GROUND. FLOOR.
THAT WAS A WASTE OF AN EVENING.
AAAAHHH!

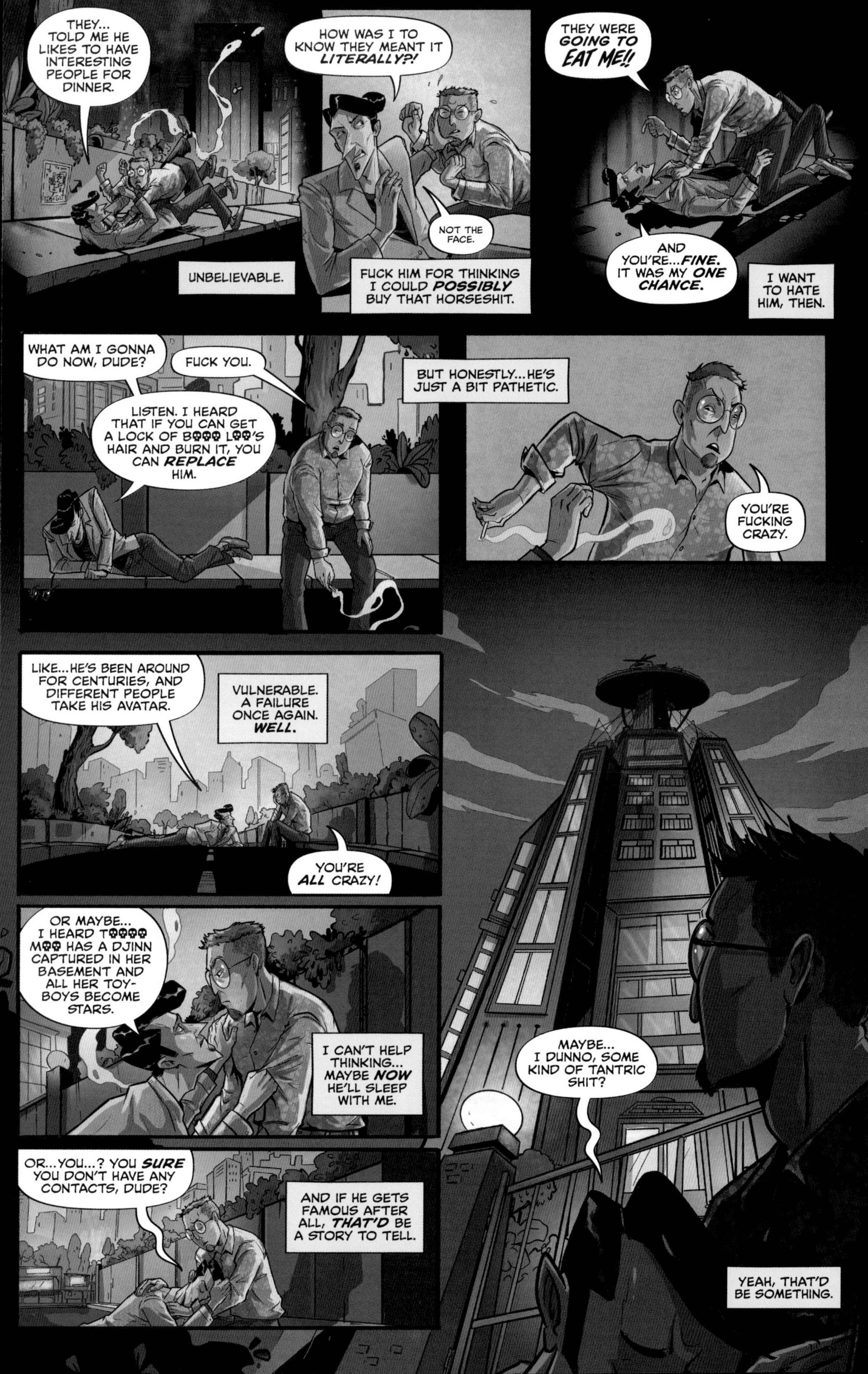
THEY... TOLD ME HE LIKES TO HAVE INTERESTING PEOPLE FOR DINNER.
UNBELIEVABLE.
HOW WAS I TO KNOW THEY MEANT IT *LITERALLY?!*
NOT THE FACE.
FUCK HIM FOR THINKING I COULD *POSSIBLY* BUY THAT HORSESHIT.
THEY WERE *GOING TO EAT ME!!*
AND YOU'RE...*FINE.* IT WAS MY *ONE CHANCE.*
I WANT TO HATE HIM, THEN.
WHAT AM I GONNA DO NOW, DUDE?
FUCK YOU.
LISTEN. I HEARD THAT IF YOU CAN GET A LOCK OF B☠☠☠ L☠☠'S HAIR AND BURN IT, YOU CAN *REPLACE* HIM.
BUT HONESTLY...HE'S JUST A BIT PATHETIC.
YOU'RE FUCKING CRAZY.
LIKE...HE'S BEEN AROUND FOR CENTURIES, AND DIFFERENT PEOPLE TAKE HIS AVATAR.
VULNERABLE. A FAILURE ONCE AGAIN. *WELL.*
YOU'RE *ALL* CRAZY!
OR MAYBE... I HEARD T☠☠☠☠ M☠☠ HAS A DJINN CAPTURED IN HER BASEMENT AND ALL HER TOY-BOYS BECOME STARS.
I CAN'T HELP THINKING... MAYBE *NOW* HE'LL SLEEP WITH ME.
OR...YOU...? YOU *SURE* YOU DON'T HAVE ANY CONTACTS, DUDE?
AND IF HE GETS FAMOUS AFTER ALL, *THAT'D* BE A STORY TO TELL.
MAYBE... I DUNNO, SOME KIND OF TANTRIC SHIT?
YEAH, THAT'D BE SOMETHING.

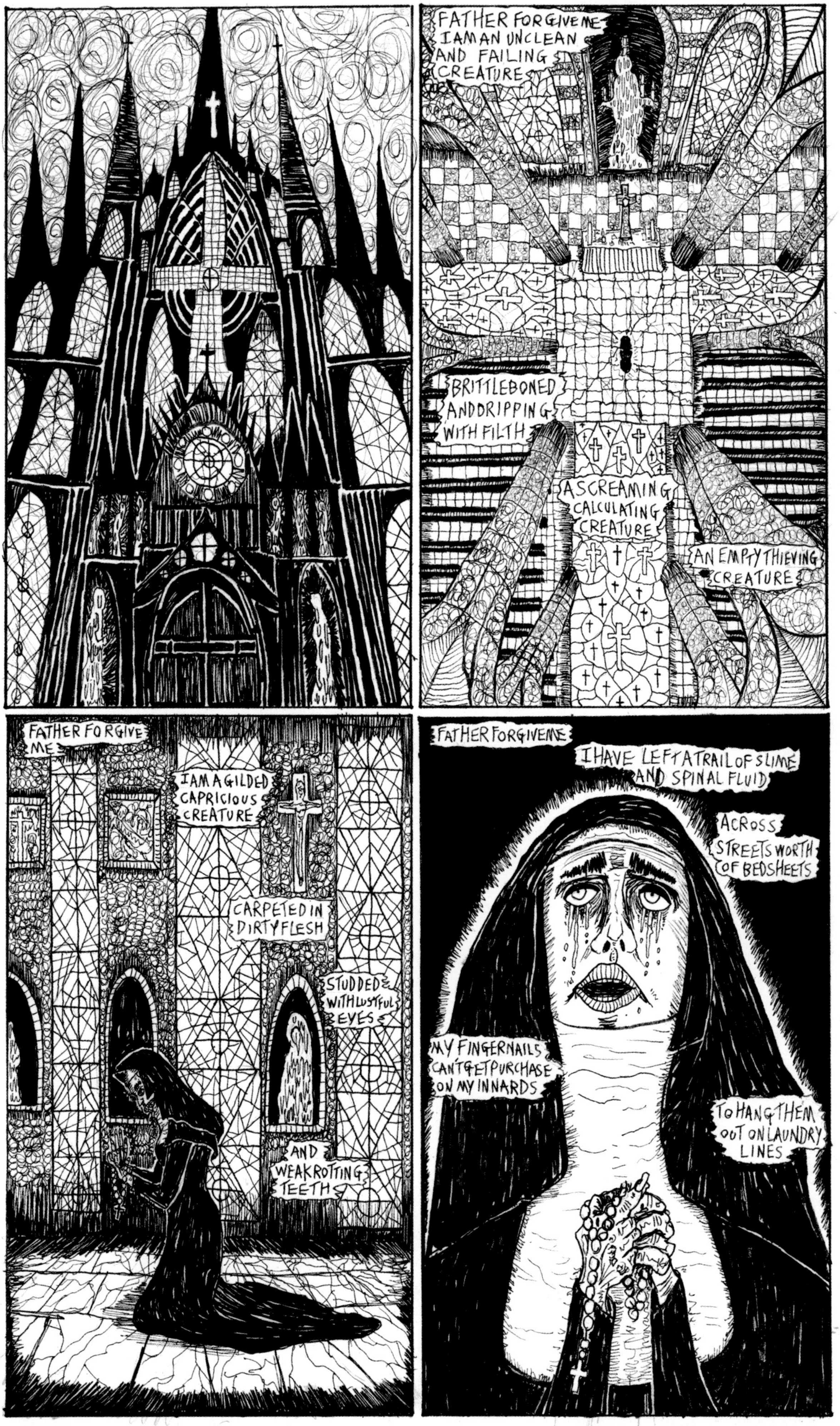
FATHER FORGIVE ME
I AM AN UNCLEAN AND FAILING CREATURE
BRITTLEBONED AND DRIPPING WITH FILTH
A SCREAMING CALCULATING CREATURE
AN EMPTY THIEVING CREATURE
FATHER FORGIVE ME
I AM A GILDED CAPRICIOUS CREATURE
CARPETED IN DIRTY FLESH
STUDDED WITH LUSTFUL EYES
AND WEAK ROTTING TEETH
FATHER FORGIVE ME
I HAVE LEFT A TRAIL OF SLIME AND SPINAL FLUID
ACROSS STREETS WORTH OF BEDSHEETS
MY FINGERNAILS CAN'T GET PURCHASE ON MY INNARDS
TO HANG THEM OUT ON LAUNDRY LINES

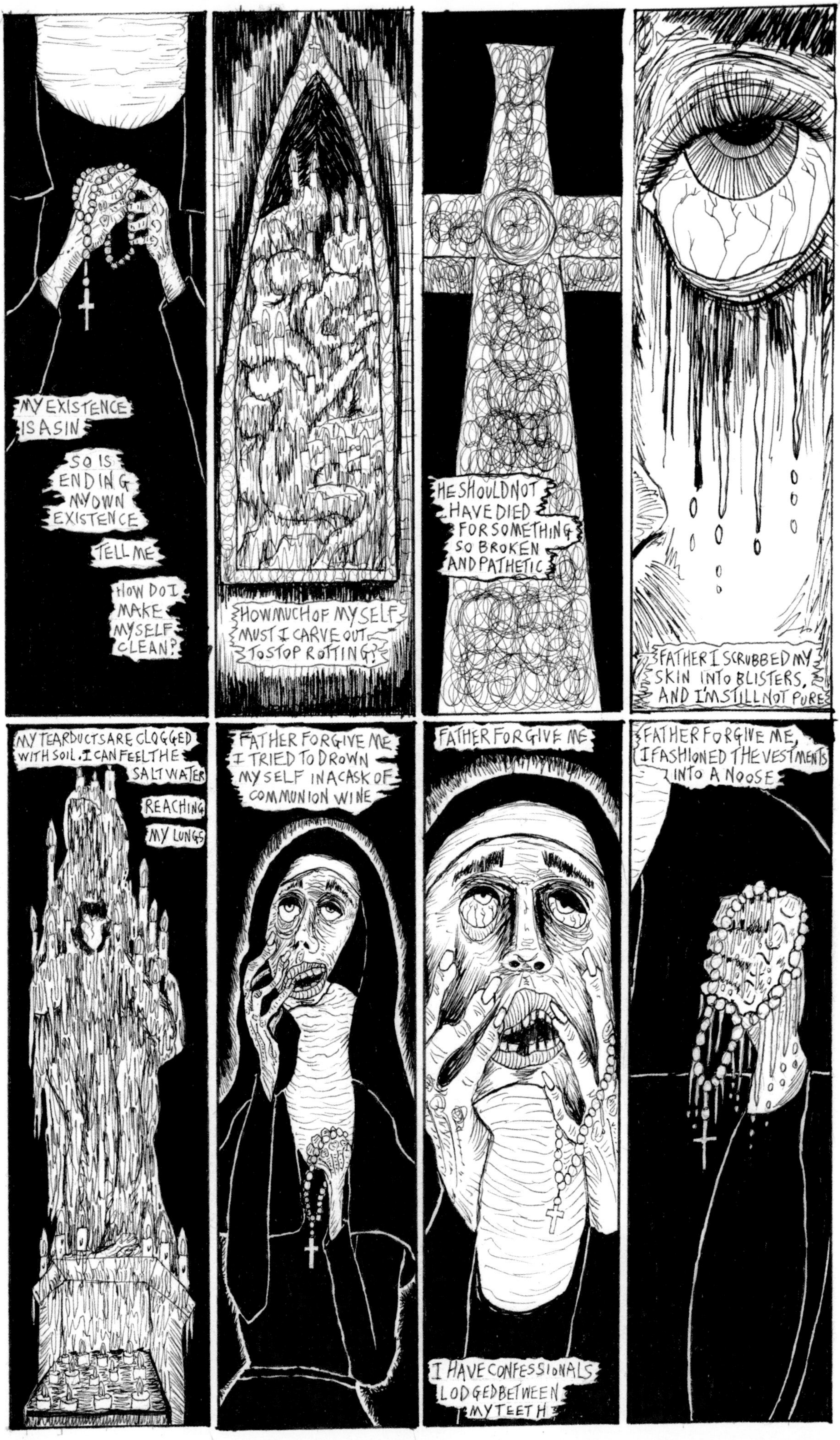
MY EXISTENCE IS A SIN
SO IS ENDING MY OWN EXISTENCE
TELL ME
HOW DO I MAKE MYSELF CLEAN?
HOW MUCH OF MYSELF MUST I CARVE OUT TO STOP ROTTING?
HE SHOULD NOT HAVE DIED FOR SOMETHING SO BROKEN AND PATHETIC
FATHER I SCRUBBED MY SKIN INTO BLISTERS, AND I'M STILL NOT PURE
MY TEARDUCTS ARE CLOGGED WITH SOIL. I CAN FEEL THE SALT WATER
REACHING
MY LUNGS
FATHER FORGIVE ME I TRIED TO DROWN MYSELF IN A CASK OF COMMUNION WINE
FATHER FORGIVE ME
I HAVE CONFESSIONALS LODGED BETWEEN MY TEETH
FATHER FORGIVE ME, I FASHIONED THE VESTMENTS INTO A NOOSE

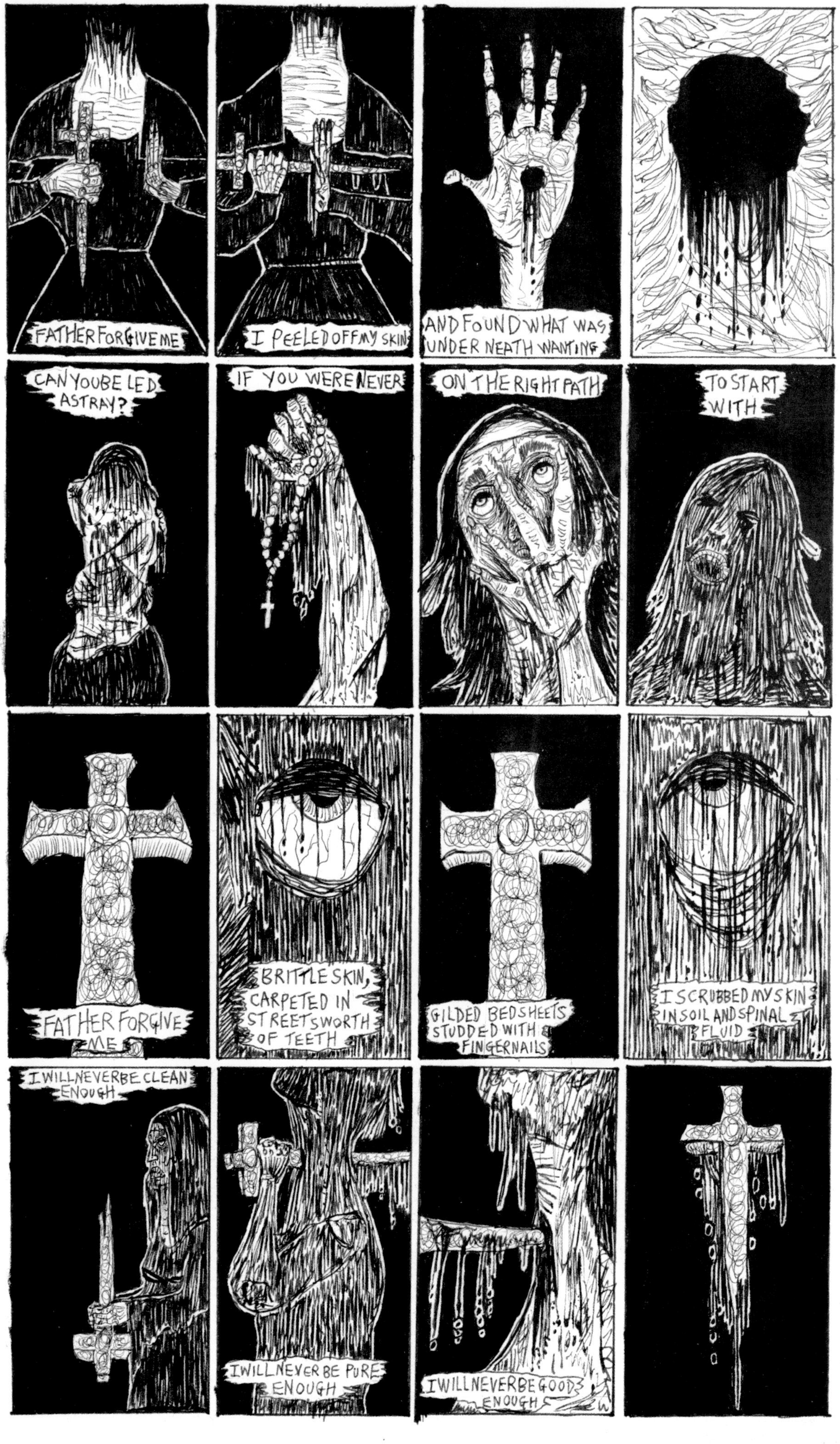
FATHER FORGIVE ME
I PEELED OFF MY SKIN
AND FOUND WHAT WAS UNDER NEATH WANTING
CAN YOU BE LED ASTRAY?
IF YOU WERE NEVER
ON THE RIGHT PATH
TO START WITH
FATHER FORGIVE ME
BRITTLE SKIN, CARPETED IN STREETS WORTH OF TEETH
GILDED BEDSHEETS STUDDED WITH FINGERNAILS
I SCRUBBED MY SKIN IN SOIL AND SPINAL FLUID
I WILL NEVER BE CLEAN ENOUGH
I WILL NEVER BE PURE ENOUGH
I WILL NEVER BE GOOD ENOUGH

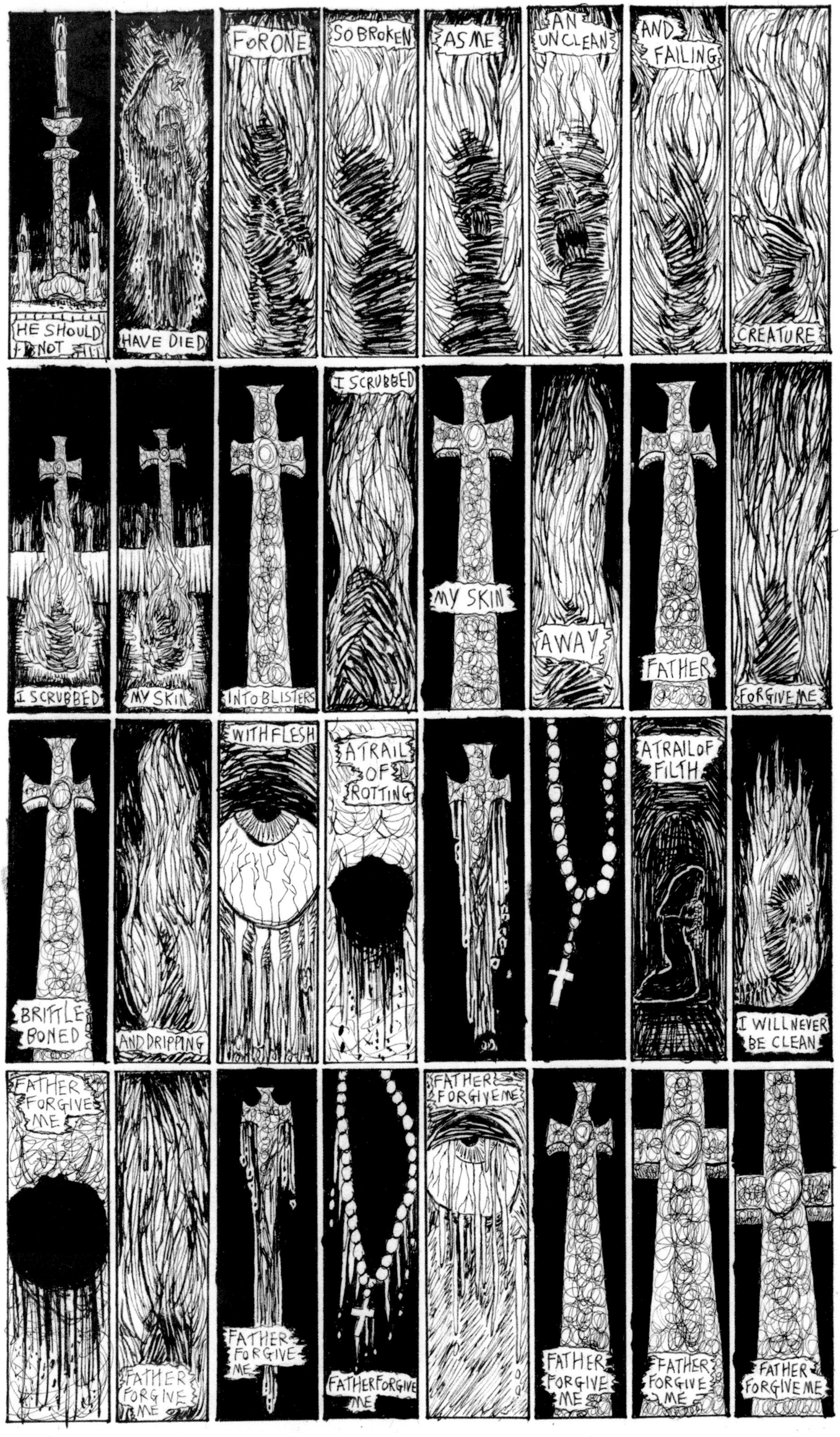
HE SHOULD NOT
HAVE DIED
FOR ONE
SO BROKEN
AS ME
AN UNCLEAN
AND FAILING
CREATURE
I SCRUBBED
MY SKIN
INTO BLISTERS
I SCRUBBED
MY SKIN
AWAY
FATHER
FORGIVE ME
BRITTLE BONED
AND DRIPPING
WITH FLESH
A TRAIL OF ROTTING
A TRAIL OF FILTH
I WILL NEVER BE CLEAN
FATHER FORGIVE ME
FATHER FORGIVE ME
FATHER FORGIVE ME
FATHER FORGIVE ME
FATHER FORGIVE ME
FATHER FORGIVE ME
FATHER FORGIVE ME
FATHER FORGIVE ME

LISTEN UP!! EVERYONE GO TO YOUR ASSIGNED CABIN AND GET UN*PACKED!* YOU KNOW WHERE YOU'RE SUPPOSED TO BE, IT'S ALL ON THE SCHEDULE!

LUNCH IS AT *TWELVE EXACTLY!* ANYONE LATE GOES *HUNGRY!*

THEN *FREE TIME* UNTIL *SIX,* AND MEET BACK AT THE MESS HALL FOR *DINNER!*

AND AFTER *THAT...*

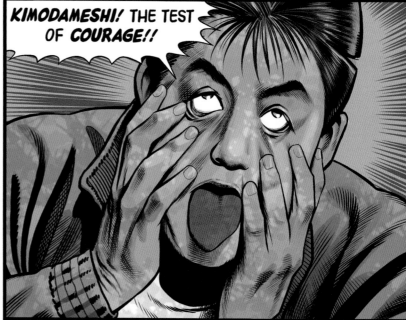

KIMODAMESHI! THE TEST OF *COURAGE!!*

PFFT.

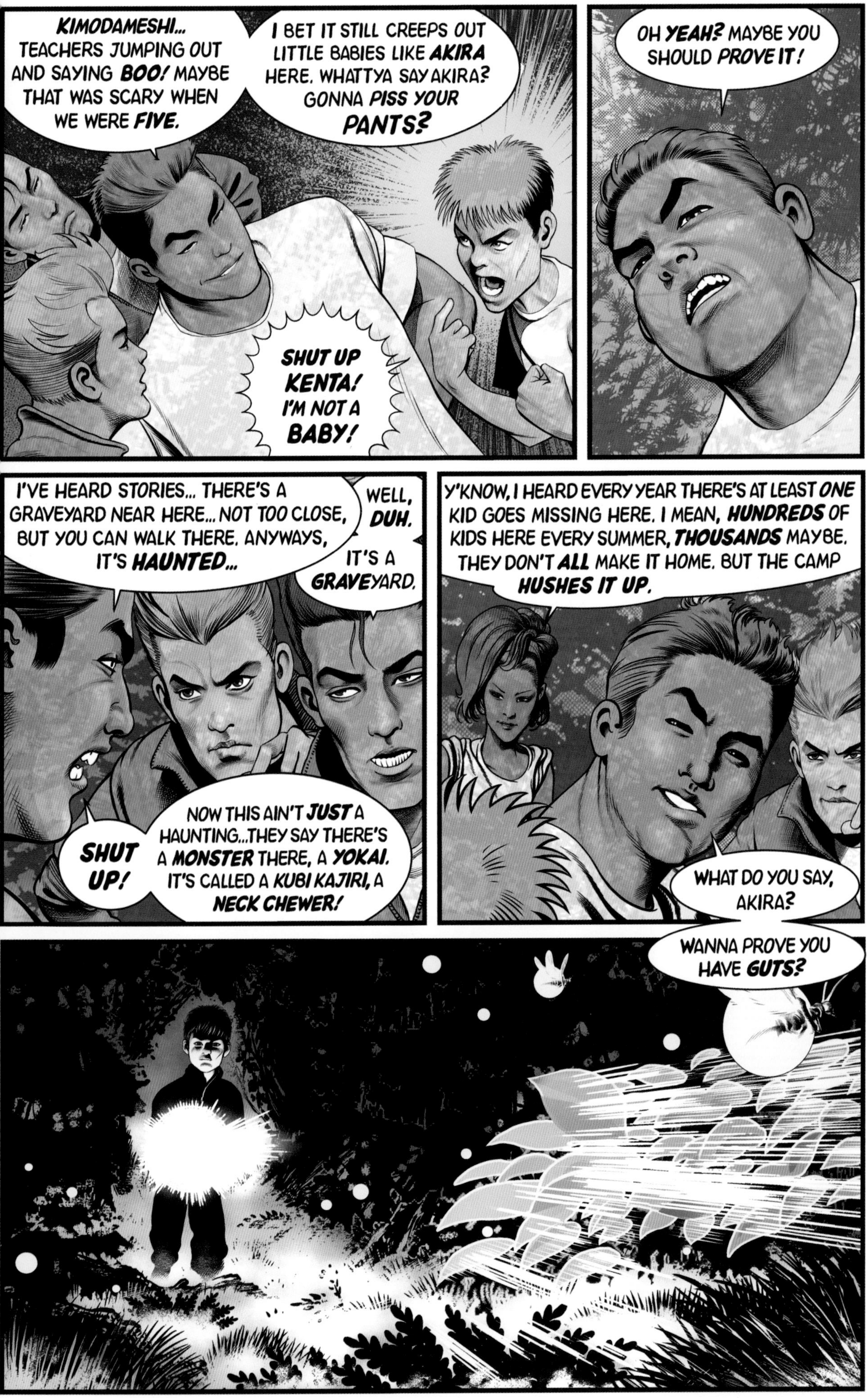
KIMODAMESHI... TEACHERS JUMPING OUT AND SAYING BOO! MAYBE THAT WAS SCARY WHEN WE WERE FIVE.
I BET IT STILL CREEPS OUT LITTLE BABIES LIKE AKIRA HERE. WHATTYA SAY AKIRA? GONNA PISS YOUR PANTS?
SHUT UP KENTA! I'M NOT A BABY!
OH YEAH? MAYBE YOU SHOULD PROVE IT!
I'VE HEARD STORIES... THERE'S A GRAVEYARD NEAR HERE... NOT TOO CLOSE, BUT YOU CAN WALK THERE. ANYWAYS, IT'S HAUNTED...
WELL, DUH.
IT'S A GRAVEYARD.
SHUT UP!
NOW THIS AIN'T JUST A HAUNTING...THEY SAY THERE'S A MONSTER THERE, A YOKAI. IT'S CALLED A KUBI KAJIRI, A NECK CHEWER!
Y'KNOW, I HEARD EVERY YEAR THERE'S AT LEAST ONE KID GOES MISSING HERE. I MEAN, HUNDREDS OF KIDS HERE EVERY SUMMER, THOUSANDS MAYBE. THEY DON'T ALL MAKE IT HOME. BUT THE CAMP HUSHES IT UP.
WHAT DO YOU SAY, AKIRA?
WANNA PROVE YOU HAVE GUTS?

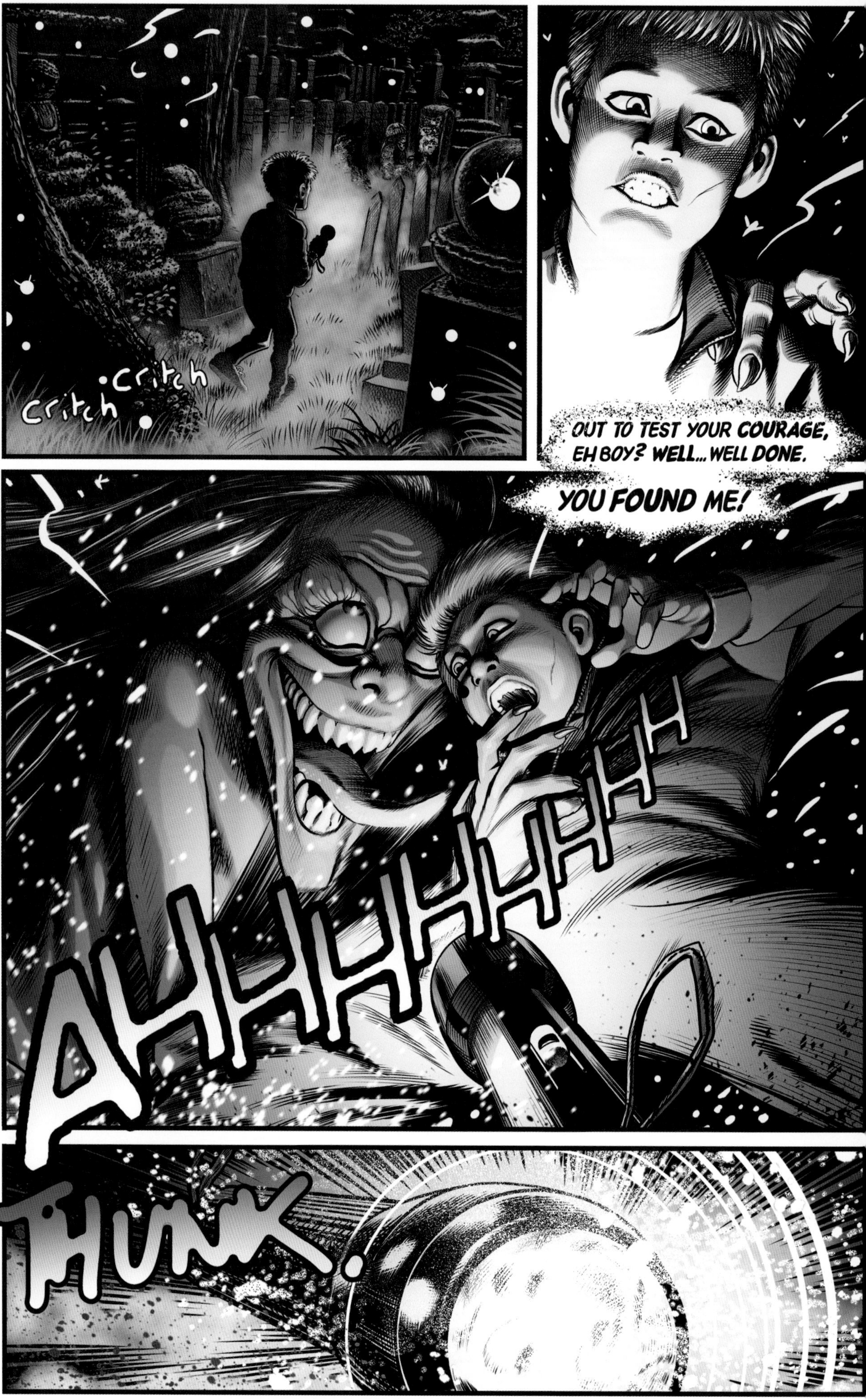
critch critch
OUT TO TEST YOUR COURAGE, EH BOY? WELL... WELL DONE.
YOU FOUND ME!
AHHHHHHHHH
THUNK.

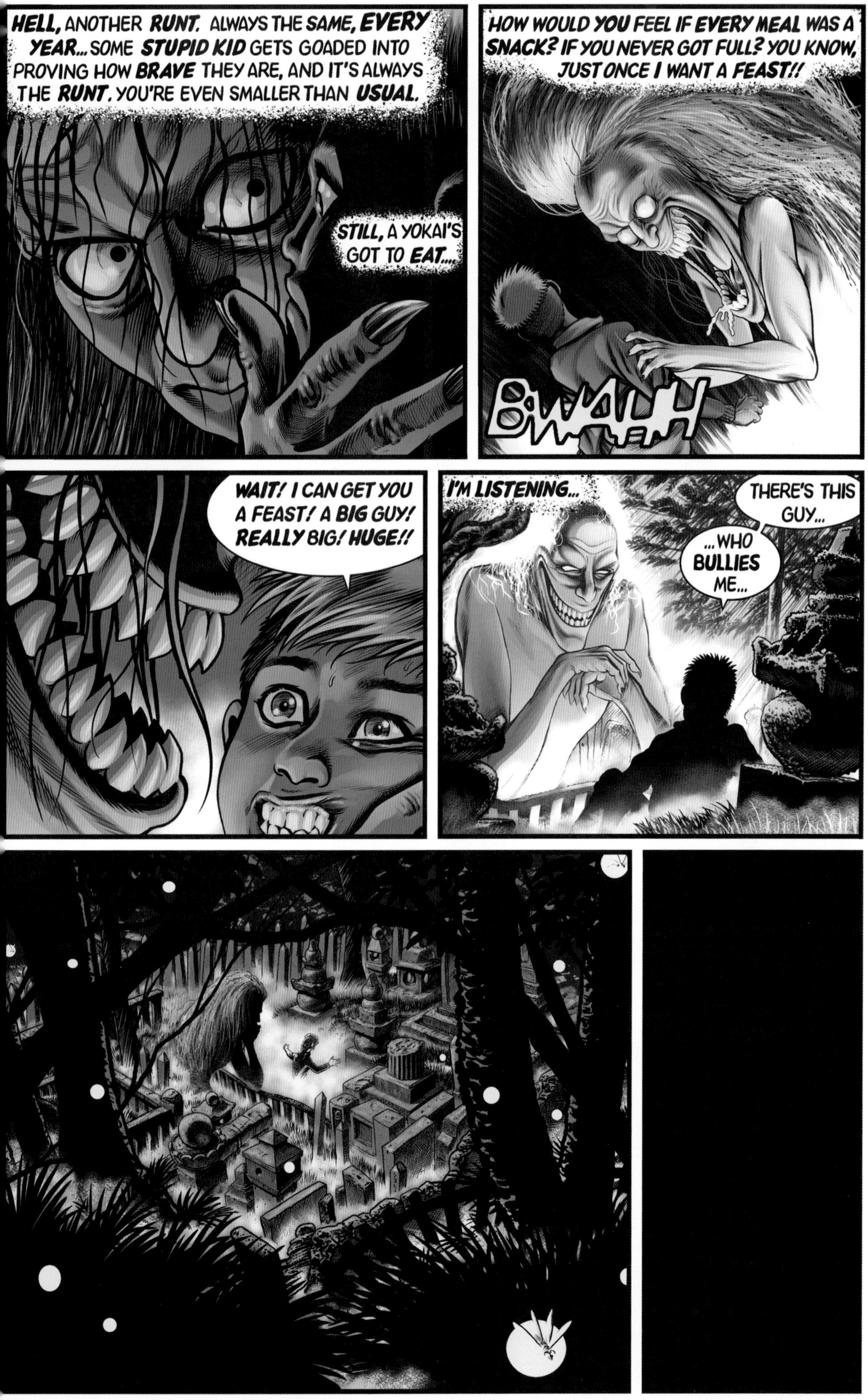
HELL, ANOTHER RUNT. ALWAYS THE SAME, EVERY YEAR... SOME STUPID KID GETS GOADED INTO PROVING HOW BRAVE THEY ARE, AND IT'S ALWAYS THE RUNT. YOU'RE EVEN SMALLER THAN USUAL.
STILL, A YOKAI'S GOT TO EAT...
HOW WOULD YOU FEEL IF EVERY MEAL WAS A SNACK? IF YOU NEVER GOT FULL? YOU KNOW, JUST ONCE I WANT A FEAST!!
BWAAH
WAIT! I CAN GET YOU A FEAST! A BIG GUY! REALLY BIG! HUGE!!
I'M LISTENING...
THERE'S THIS GUY...
...WHO BULLIES ME...

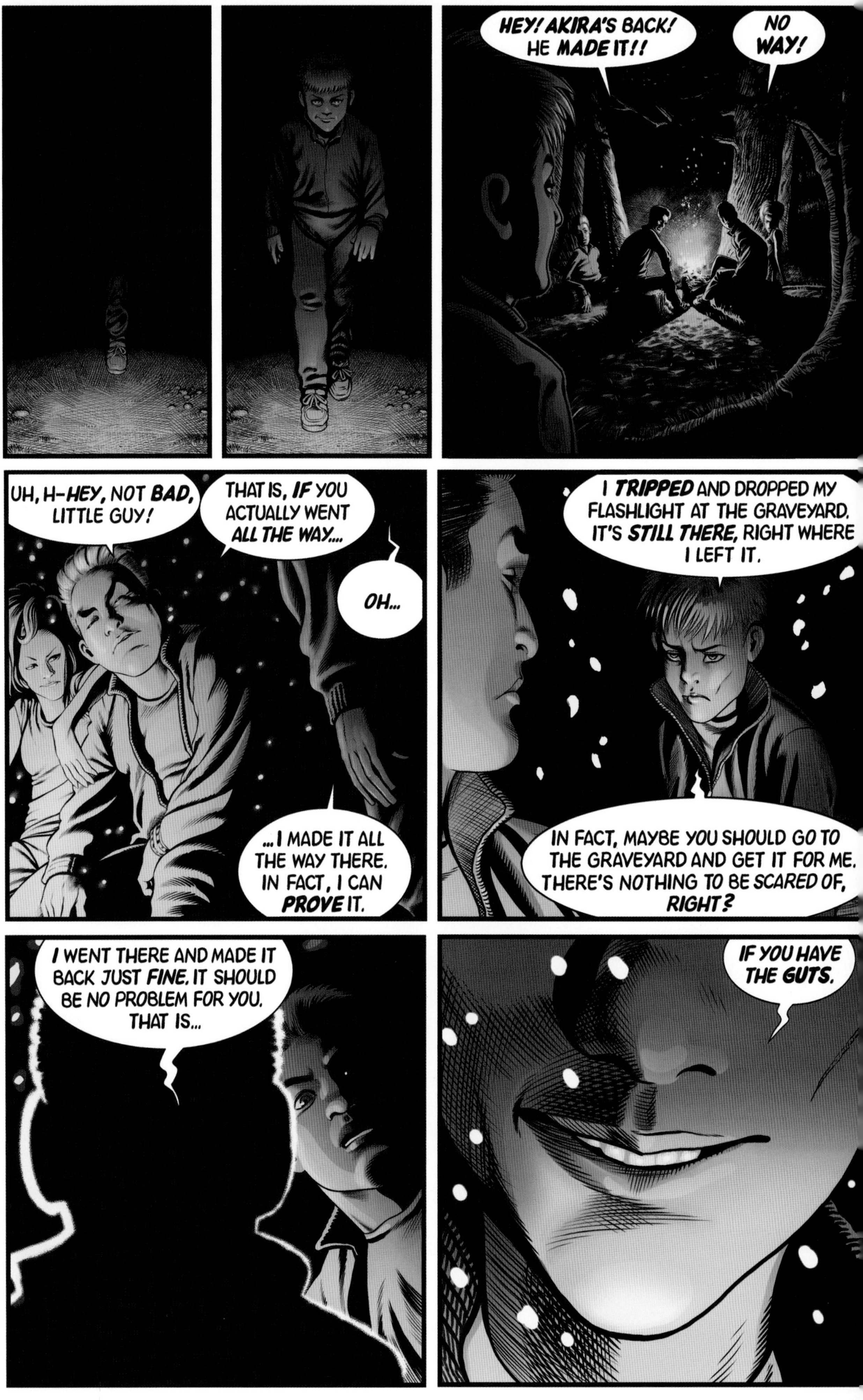
HEY! AKIRA'S BACK! HE MADE IT!!
NO WAY!
UH, H-HEY, NOT BAD, LITTLE GUY!
THAT IS, IF YOU ACTUALLY WENT ALL THE WAY....
OH...
...I MADE IT ALL THE WAY THERE. IN FACT, I CAN PROVE IT.
I TRIPPED AND DROPPED MY FLASHLIGHT AT THE GRAVEYARD. IT'S STILL THERE, RIGHT WHERE I LEFT IT.
IN FACT, MAYBE YOU SHOULD GO TO THE GRAVEYARD AND GET IT FOR ME. THERE'S NOTHING TO BE SCARED OF, RIGHT?
I WENT THERE AND MADE IT BACK JUST FINE. IT SHOULD BE NO PROBLEM FOR YOU. THAT IS...
IF YOU HAVE THE GUTS.

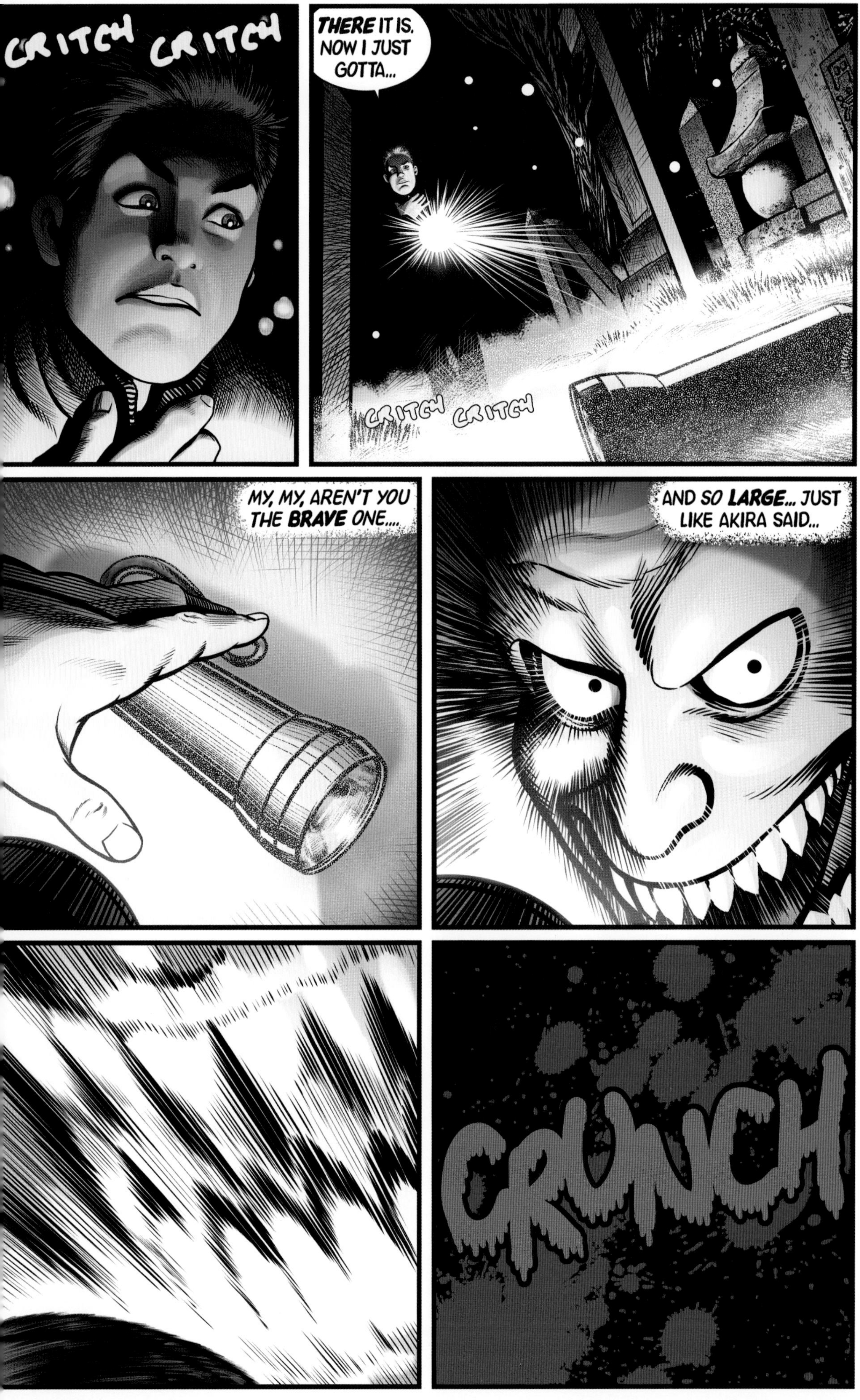
CRITCH CRITCH
THERE IT IS. NOW I JUST GOTTA...
CRITCH CRITCH
MY, MY, AREN'T YOU THE BRAVE ONE....
AND SO LARGE... JUST LIKE AKIRA SAID...
CRUNCH

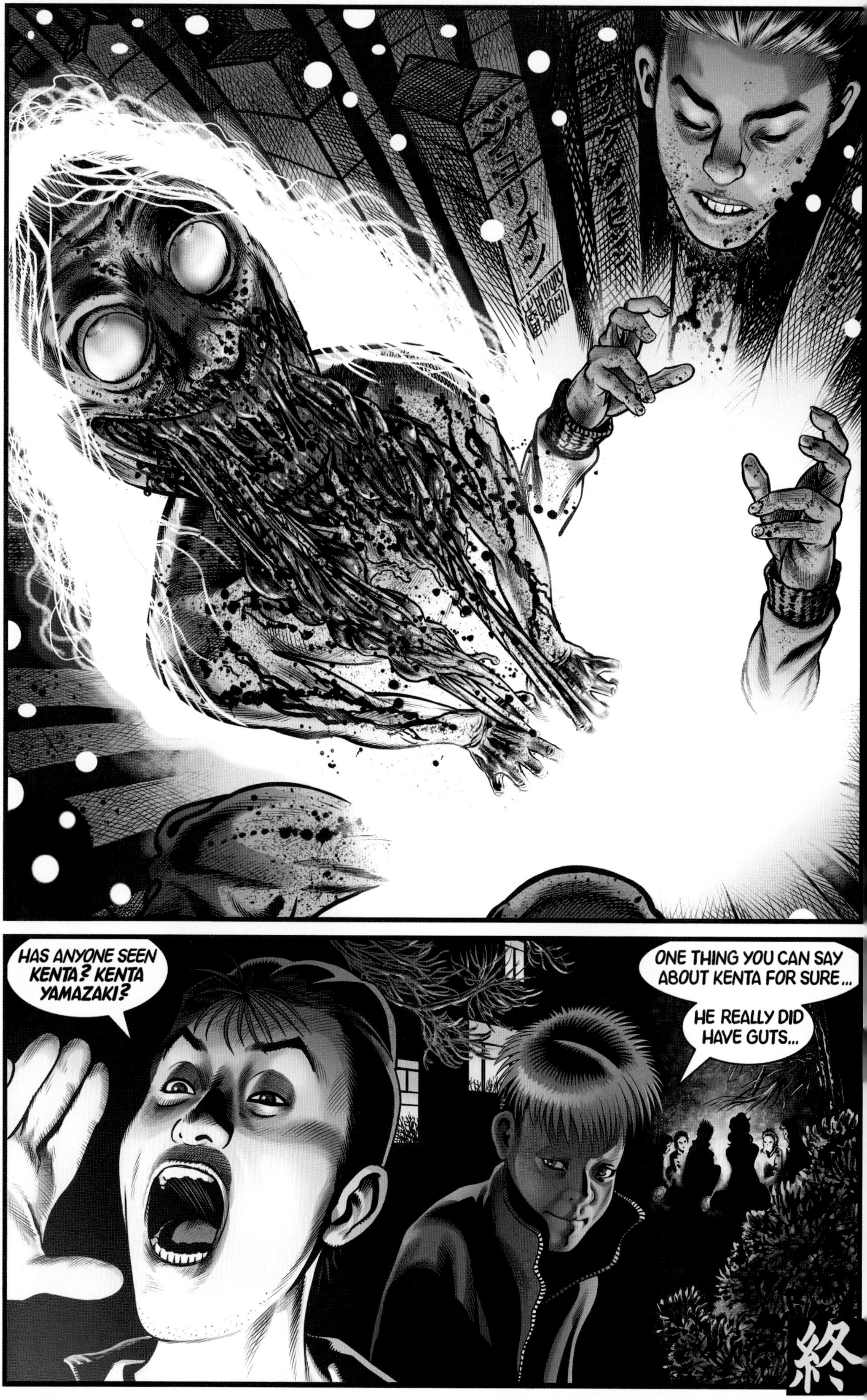
HAS ANYONE SEEN KENTA? KENTA YAMAZAKI?
ONE THING YOU CAN SAY ABOUT KENTA FOR SURE...
HE REALLY DID HAVE GUTS...
終

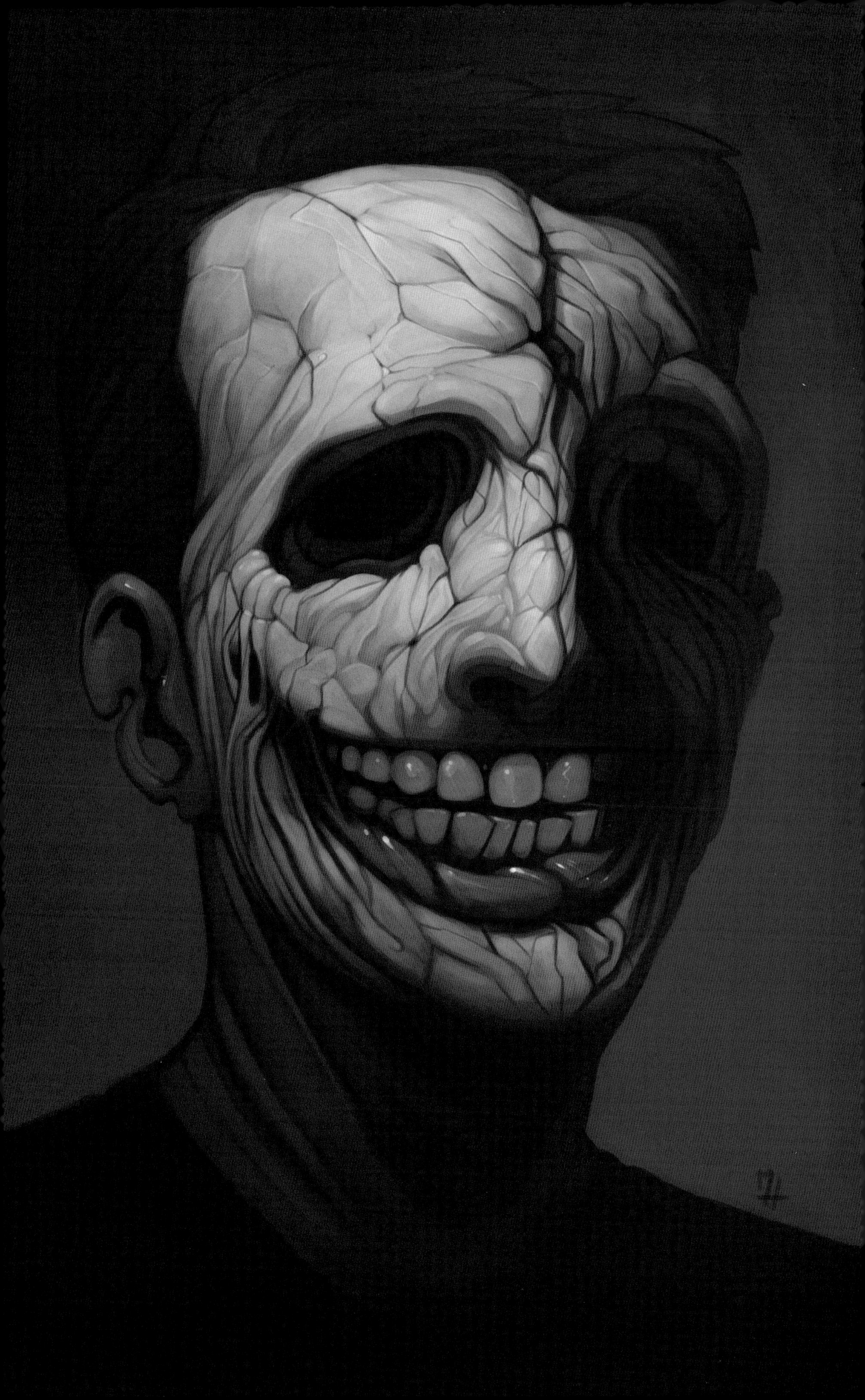

THE DOGS IN MY NEIGHBORHOOD

WRITTEN BY ADAM CESARE
ILLUSTRATION BY AARON CAMPBELL

It's called "phantom cries."

Parents will often wake up to their newborn needing to be fed or dried or swaddled, only to stumble over to the bassinet and find that the baby is still asleep.

We don't have a newborn.

Yet.

But we do have an old dog.

And Scooter's having just as much trouble adjusting to the suburbs as I am. More, actually.

Most nights he wakes at 2 or 3. Alone and needing to go to the bathroom, confused by the new layout of things, with that confusion compounded by his cataract blindness, he whines and barks. All of that makes him sound more pathetic than he actually is. He is pathetic, but he's still a happy guy, for the most part. He just has old-dog problems.

Some nights I make it downstairs in time. Some nights I'm scrubbing the carpet. Carpet we laid down so his back legs could get traction, since he has a difficult time keeping upright on tile or hardwood.

Tonight, I wake to a single, pained bark and hurry downstairs. And then downstairs again, since our bedroom is on the second floor.

But it's phantom cries.

He hasn't been barking. He's curled up, dozing soundly.

I look at my phone. It's 1:30. The house has been asleep for—what?—about three hours. If we're going by the schedule that Scooter's set forth, he's going to need to be walked in the next hour or so anyway.

I put my hand on the dimmer, bring the lights up a little. We repainted before moving in, but Scooter's nose has already smudged a brownish line two feet off the ground onto the basement's white walls.

He can feel his way around, remembering the layout well enough to find his food, water, and the plush dog bed I need to wash more than I'd like. He's in that bed now, feet gently twitching with a dream, ribs rising and falling.

Careful not to jostle him awake, I ease myself to the ground and begin petting his side. Then I coo nice things that I'm not sure he can hear, since he's pretty deaf. Eventually, his feet stop their dance and his age-grey eyes crack open.

I scratch up his neck, then put a knuckle in one ear and grind it around a little, a massage technique that keeps me from getting earwax on my fingertip.

Scooter groans, a sound more like an old man than an old dog. He's pissed to have been woken from his nice dream.

Fair is fair, pal.

I give him a kiss on his snout, dry and warm, then lift him up with both arms. He's a mutt. A 35-pound terrier mix who, when we got him, would turn absolutely psycho if you tried to pick him up. The shelter said it was likely residual trauma from an abusive upbringing.

Now, five years later, I can lift him no problem. The most I'll get is a slight growl of protest. But Scooter would never bite me.

I carry him upstairs, set him down, and get him clipped into his harness and leash.

There are four light switches by our front door, and I can still never remember which is the outdoor porch light. Tonight I find it on the second try, blinding myself with the overhead hall light in the process. I tell myself that once I've internalized these switches and what they light, that'll be when the house feels like a home. Or whatever.

I stomp down into my shoes, then use the handle on the back of Scooter's harness to get him pointed in the right direction. Once he's facing the door, I tug to guide him forward and out, carefully down the front steps, and we're on our way. Into the night.

I don't lock the front door. Why risk locking myself out if my key's not in my jacket?

It's quiet out here. Completely deserted.

In the city, when we went out for late-night walks like this, it was quiet too, but a different kind of quiet. Those city walks, even when we didn't see a single moving car, still had the ever-present susurrus of Ubers and ambulances, busy in the neighborhoods surrounding us.

Here in the burbs, even when there are sounds—the click of Scooter's nails on asphalt, a neighbor's air conditioner switching on—they're dampened by all the grass and trees.

We walk briskly down our driveway, as briskly as Scooter *can* walk. What I'm doing is attempting to reach the street before he lets loose with his bladder. Not that I necessarily care what the neighbors think, but if he pees on the concrete driveway, it leaves a stain. And I'll have to wash it away with the garden hose if it's not going to rain tomorrow.

Two steps from the gutter, almost there, he starts peeing.

First it's one leg up, marking his territory, but as the stream continues, the leg trembles, then wilts. He settles into an easier-on-the-joints squat before finishing.

You tried, bud.

We *could* call it quits here, walk back up into the house, hope he sleeps through the rest of the night. But that would be a risk.

I strain my memory, still mostly operating on autopilot, not full-awake, and try to remember his last bowel movement.

When it was. Its size and texture.

Was it yesterday morning? God. Sleeping so little is really beginning to get to me.

I remember reading somewhere that sleep deprivation as a form of torture or interrogation isn't about keeping a subject completely awake at all times. It's about waking them up thirty minutes or an hour into sleeping, giving them hope that they got *some* sleep, but keeping them from entering REM.

That kind of torture, it mixes up a person's thoughts, their sense of self.

Or maybe that isn't something I read. Maybe I made it up. Maybe it just sounds true because I'm sleep deprived.

Scooter sniffs at our garbage cans, rolled out for collection in a few hours. Before I can pull the leash taut, he bumps his muzzle on the corner of a cardboard box set out for recycling.

"Sorry pal," I say, bending to pat away his surprise.

Fucking recycling. In our apartment, nobody recycled. We all just tossed everything in the building's dumpster. I'm not even sure it was an option, that we were on a recycling route. Everyone here recycles. And they leave passive-aggressive messages in the neighborhood Facebook group if you mix up your plastic and paper days.

Stay focused. When was his last BM?

That I can't remember when Scooter last shit means that we need to walk a few blocks, in case he needs to shit.

I look both ways down our street.

There're no sidewalks here. It's that kind of suburb. So insulated that if the residents want to take a walk: why not just do it in the street? It's not like there's traffic.

To the left is a straightaway. Houses and houses. Probably safer at this time of night, because you'd see a car coming. The rare car driving these streets so late on a weeknight. Looking that way, I clock that one of the houses has deflated balloons tied to the mailbox and a plywood stork on the lawn.

I turn to our right.

That direction is a curved road and three-way stop. Very little shoulder to stick to, if someone was coming around the corner too fast. At the first stop, there's a little patch of grass and trees making a fork, and a block beyond that fork a baseball diamond and playground.

Fuck it, let's walk the more interesting direction. Even if it means getting run over by one of our wine-mom neighbors or their big-game-chicken-wing husbands.

On nights we go as far as the park, Scooter likes making circles on the grass. We tend to get better results, standing on the spongy grass, if he needs to go.

One thing age hasn't dulled is Scooter's ability to walk. He loves it. He may not be fast, but he never tires. As long as I'm there to guide him around obstacles, keep the leash tight if we're on uneven footing, the dog will walk indefinitely.

That's what the guy at the shelter had said when we'd got him, that—

I see something.

Not so much out of the corner of my eye, but in the area beyond where I'm looking.

There it is again.

Three houses down, further than the curve and the fork. There's something moving on that neighbor's lawn. A shadow that's darker than the rest of the shadows.

During the day, there's always something moving around on that lawn. They've got like four or five kids at that house. One set of twins even.

But this isn't a kid.

Our first night in our new house, I took Scooter out like this and we saw a fox. At first, I thought it was a big racoon, but then it'd moved, bounded off into someone's backyard, and the movement showed exactly what it was, even though I'd never seen a fox in real life.

Kind of sad that that brief encounter, or the occasional rabbit, or even squirrels with darker coloration than the grey-and-white type we saw in the city parks, qualifies as "nature," but to me it does. I'm not used to it. There are deer in the area too, but I haven't seen one yet, just cloven tracks on our lawn, a couple months ago, in a winter snow.

But the thing I glimpse on the neighbor's lawn feels like none of the above. And it's watching me. Watching Scooter. Standing still. Standing its ground.

We take a few more steps and it still doesn't move; we don't scare it off.

It's someone's dog. Alone in the night and standing on someone's front lawn.

It's not a particularly large dog. Hard to see much more than that from here, a few houses away.

At first I'm concerned for the dog. I think of that same, annoying Facebook group, how there's probably a post in there about a family dog who slipped under the fence. Has anyone seen it?

But then, considering how it seems to be watching Scooter, I'm concerned for me and my dog. My mind goes to those horror stories—violent dogs getting off-leash and mauling the first dog they see. Their person trying to intercede, getting chewed up.

I make the decision to turn around, but before I can pull Scooter's harness one-eighty, he's grunting and squatting. Scooter's begun the often very slow process of pooping.

"Always, bud. Always your timing," I whisper while digging into my jacket pocket for the roll of bags I keep there. I do this both one-handed and without looking, trying to keep my eye on the dog on the lawn, who's suddenly not there anymore.

Not there because it's closer. It has begun walking towards us, has crossed the road and is now standing on the stretch of grass at the fork. I can't see much. Its head is low to the ground, in shadows. My mind takes what I can see and fills in details. I couldn't guess at a breed, but it's one of those dogs with jowls and an underbite.

Uh oh.

I try for an extra second to get the bag I've torn off the roll open, then say screw it and leave the turd where it steams in the middle of the street.

Using the handle on his harness, I turn my wrist and get Scooter to about-face.

That's when I notice that Scooter's hackles are up. The fur between his shoulder blades puffs against the top of his harness and

his cropped tail is straight out. Hard to remember the last time he's done this. When we had the apartment, he'd go nuts whenever the maintenance guy needed come in to swap the air filter, but that was back when he could see and hear. Now when I take him for walks, he doesn't notice the neighbors or their dogs unless they come right up and touch him.

Scooter growls, like a ragged purr.

We begin walking back towards the house. Quickly. If I turn to look and the dog is running towards us, I tell myself, I'll pick Scooter up and run.

I turn to check and...

The strange dog's not running. It's walking. Still a comfortable distance away from us, two lawns, at least.

But now there are three dogs.

A smaller dog. White, almost reflective in the night. A lap dog.

And beside that one, standing three times its height, easy, is a greyhound. It's the only one of the three I can confidently tell the breed. This greyhound has such visible muscle definition that, in the streetlight, it's like it has no skin at all.

The three dogs walk in formation.

Their nails must be clipped short, because their approach doesn't make a sound.

I feel my lips mouth, *what the fuck?* and I bend, using Scooter's handle, not his leash, to hurry him back to the house and up the driveway.

Scooter's not growling anymore...he's whining.

I'm practically carrying him, since his harness loops under his armpits and I could puppy-lift him that way, if I needed to.

We make it to the front steps and I *will* myself not to check. Not to turn around and see if the trio—

now more?—has gotten any closer. Has followed us to our lawn. To our house.

Not that I'm that afraid of being mauled anymore; something about that specific spread of dogs: it's positively Disney-esque. How animators would choose a cast of dogs for *Oliver & Company* or something, making sure to vary their shapes and sizes so that each character had a unique silhouette. Hard to be afraid of a crew like that.

But still.

As I reach out for the doorknob, I wince. It's only a second or two after my mind's tried to turn the dogs into a joke and I am *actually* afraid. I'm positive that jaws are about to lock onto my ankle or calf. The Westie being the first to attack, bring me low so that his friends can close in.

Sure that then I'd have to watch them attack Scooter next. Pull my boy apart.

But that doesn't happen. Scooter and I make it inside and when I peek out the windows, there's nothing out there. Nothing in the night.

Four days later, I come downstairs, and it isn't phantom cries that bring me, just insomnia. Couldn't have been any kind of real cries because Scooter is dead.

He lays still. Half in and half out of his bed. Must've happened in the little over an hour I've been trying to sleep.

It wasn't a dramatic death. And I am so thankful for that.

For months—years if I'm being honest, since we adopted him, the shelter workers waiving the adoption fee, telling us how great we were for "taking a chance" on a "senior dog"—I'd been having nightmares about the day I was *sure* was coming: a sick dog, a doctor, and me holding him still for a needle.

I pet Scooter's body for a moment. Not crying.

Then I sit down on the basement couch and cry a little and fall asleep.

What wakes me is Scooter's final phantom bark.

I sit up on the couch, disoriented. Check my phone. 4 a.m. Nowhere near enough sleep.

Scooter's still half in, half out of his bed. A pose that would be cute, that I'd take a picture of, if he were alive, but doing so now seems undignified.

I move him back into the center of the dog bed. He feels heavier now. Then I find a towel to throw over him. A funerary shroud that we got at some New Jersey beach town.

I don't want her coming downstairs and finding him, having to see him.

Who do you even call at this point? The vet? I haven't had a dog since I was a teenager. And then I'd never dealt with this aspect of it. I don't know the procedure.

And as I'm thinking these questions, what to do in this scenario, I'm already up the stairs and facing the front door before I realize I've moved. Muscle memory. From taking Scooter out at this time of night. From not sleeping. From grief and confusion.

And once I'm this far, why not?

Why shouldn't I go for a walk?

I've got no socks on, but it doesn't matter. I step into my sneakers anyway.

As I reach for the knob, I hesitate. Remembering the dogs we saw the other night. Wild dogs? Feral dogs? Or just three missing dogs? Or a dream I had when I hadn't even taken my own dog out that night, the rare night he'd slept straight through to morning?

Whatever.

I want the air. I want the quiet.

There's nothing on our lawn. Nothing on our street. So I walk.

I'm so far from the house I can almost see the cage of the baseball diamond when I feel it.

The cold nose lightly touching the back of my hand as I walk towards the park.

I look down and it's the greyhound, standing there.

Something I couldn't tell four of five nights ago, whenever it was, when I saw the dogs from afar, was that they were all like my Scooter.

All old.

The greyhound, his ears down, a wide, slender smile I can see as he looks up at me, has cataracts too. So bad they reflect. Glistening in the last streetlight before the park like hologram stickers. Like a possum's eyes.

I look to the other side of me and there's the lap dog. This close, I can see it's a Westie.

I don't know why I was afraid of these dogs. Even for a moment.

His eyes are clearer. But he—she, actually. She's slender, I can see her hips and count her backbones—is old too. I can tell by her fur, the way it thins in spots, clumps in others. Not a matter of grooming, just a matter of: this is what an aging dog's final double coat will look like, towards the end.

At the entrance to the park, their leader waits. He's a boxer. We get closer, me and my escorts, and I can count the teeth he's missing. Not because he's baring his teeth in anger or intimidation, but because of his underbite.

Each of these dogs is old. But not gone. Not done yet. And they live here, in this neighborhood, and they patrol its streets when the kids birthday parties have been packed in, when the firepits have burned down, when the regulation-height street basketball hoops sit still.

And behind the boxer, where I didn't see them before, step more dogs. Dogs with masses, some benign and some cancerous. Dogs with arthritis and ones who can't seem to make the jump into the backseat anymore. Ones that tremble all the time and ones that are uncomfortably stiff. Ones that love fierce and outwardly and ones that sit quiet and warm.

And as we approach the boxer, I know that I—a person, not their kind, but the kind that *could* be their person—am being asked a question.

Yes.

I don't have to think about it for more than a few seconds.

Yes.

Yes.

I don't want to go back to that house.

Even if I did go back to the house, I can't even remember if I left the door unlocked. And I didn't take my keys.

I want to stay. Want to stay here with all of them.

And even though I left him under a towel, down in the basement, maybe Scooter's somehow already here among their number.

"Show me." I say out loud, though words probably aren't necessary.

And the dogs and I walk together into the park.

And I never do need a home.

End

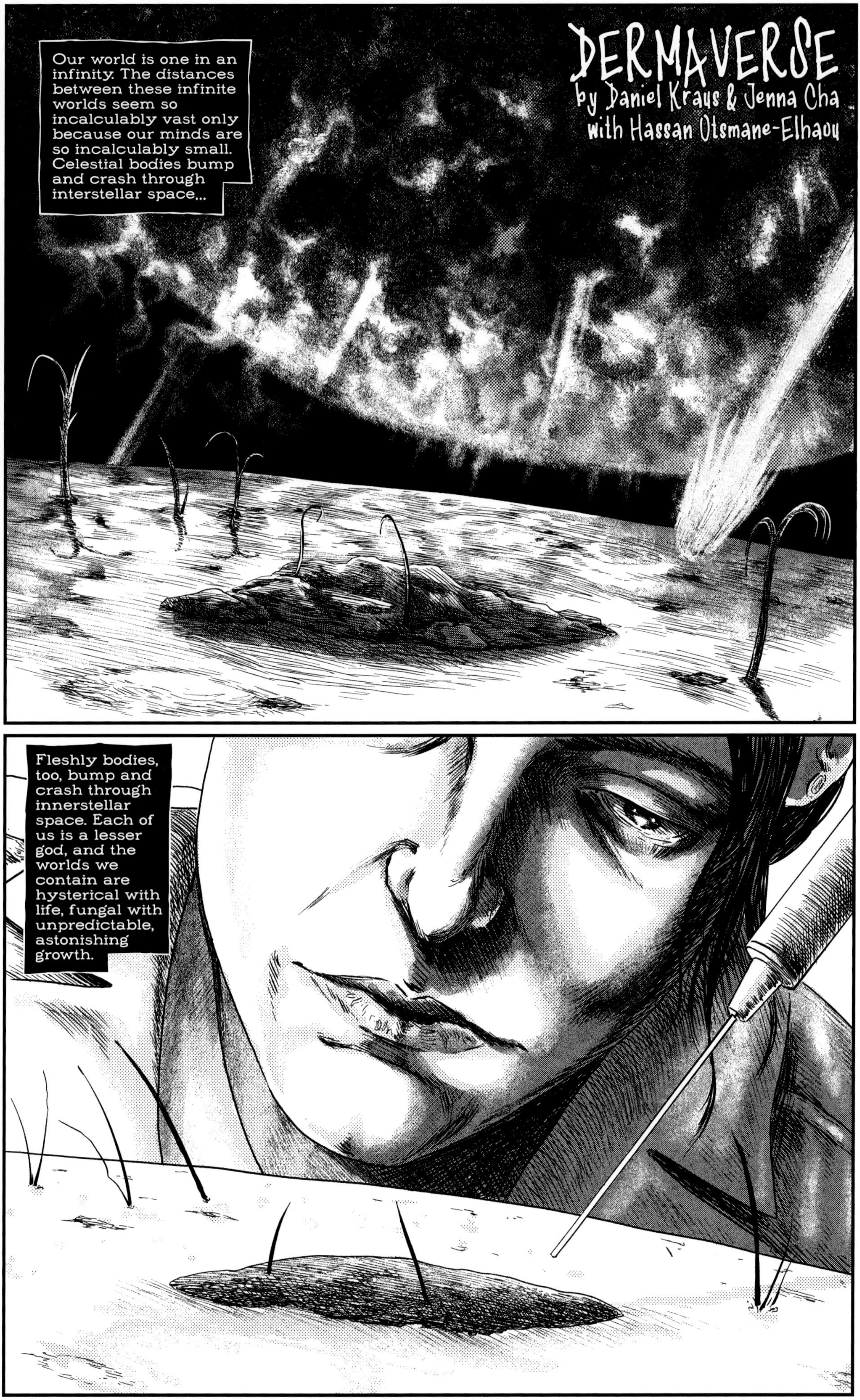

Our world is one in an infinity. The distances between these infinite worlds seem so incalculably vast only because our minds are so incalculably small. Celestial bodies bump and crash through interstellar space...
DERMAVERSE
by Daniel Kraus & Jenna Cha
with Hassan Otsmane-Elhaou
Fleshly bodies, too, bump and crash through innerstellar space. Each of us is a lesser god, and the worlds we contain are hysterical with life, fungal with unpredictable, astonishing growth.

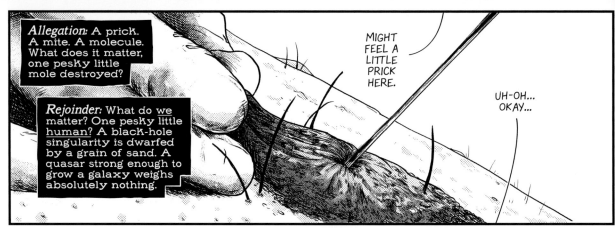

Allegation: A prick. A mite. A molecule. What does it matter, one pesky little mole destroyed?
Rejoinder: What do we matter? One pesky little human? A black-hole singularity is dwarfed by a grain of sand. A quasar strong enough to grow a galaxy weighs absolutely nothing.
MIGHT FEEL A LITTLE PRICK HERE.
UH-OH... OKAY...
THAT SHOULD NUMB YOU.
GREAT... HEH-HEH... I'M NOT A SUPER BIG FAN OF GETTING PIECES OF ME LOPPED OFF... HEH-HEH...
Yet you made this appointment, didn't you? No matter the pungent pregnancies your body birthed and nourished. Led by your lardy brain, you chose to extinguish a miracle.
SHINK
IS IT COOL IF WE...TALK? JUST CHIT-CHAT SO I DON'T FOCUS ON THE...
...HEY, WHAT DO YOU DO WITH THE MOLES ONCE YOU TAKE THEM OFF?
SAME THING AS AMPUTATED LIMBS OR ABORTED FETUSES. THEY GO INTO THE BIOHAZARD CREMATORIUM AT 2000°F.
I'M GOING TO SHAVE OFF THE MOLE NOW. YOU MIGHT FEEL DISTANT DISCOMFORT.
OH, GEEZ.
Distant. Discomfort.
I was "distant," they said. I made them "uncomfortable," they said.

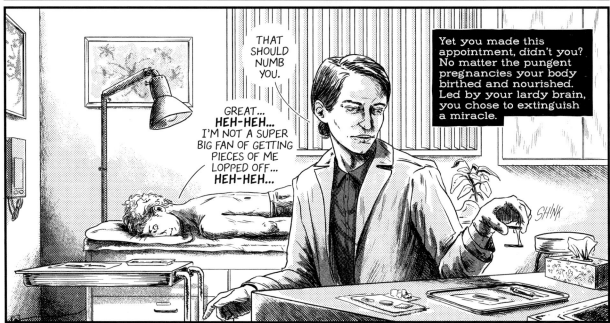

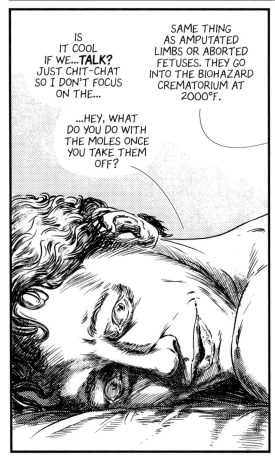

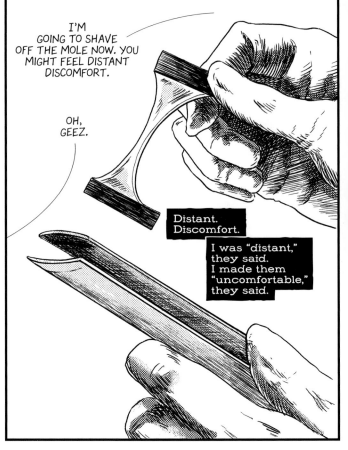

Early humans worshipped constellations in the sky. I've always done the same. My constellations are closer, but placed with the same divine inspiration.

JAYDEN, SHE'S OBSESSED WITH YOUR BACK! GROSS!

HAHAHA!

Nebulae – clouds of stardust dense enough to be seen by the eye, dots we can connect to divine the patterns of the universe.

A NEBULA IN THE TRIANGULUM GALAXY

HAHAHA!

Moles, melanocytic nevi – melanin dense enough to be seen by the eye, dots we can connect to divine the patterns of the innerverse.

SAY NO TO VAPING

Romances And Go

An STD is Forever

HAHAHA!

LAYERS OF HUMAN SKIN

MELANOCYTE

There are gods in the heavens. There must be gods inside us too.

THE FUCK? I THOUGHT YOU WERE GOING TO BLOW ME, NOT PLAY CONNECT THE DOTS!

HAHAHA!

PERFECT. MY SKIN IS PERFECT. WHY? WHY?

HAHAHA!

There is a hell. It's knowing what you must do to conjure these gods and yet lacking the natural ability to do it.

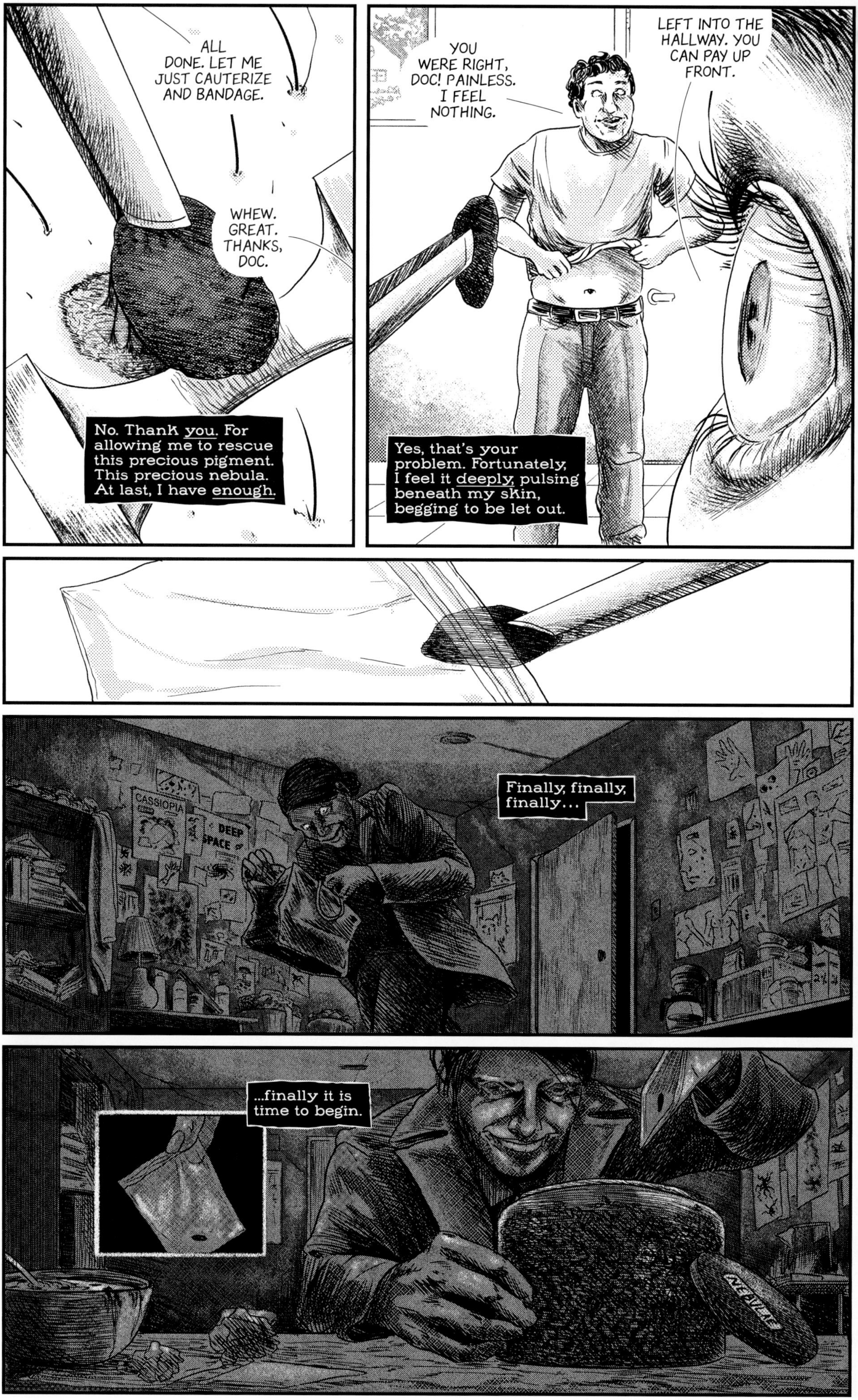
ALL DONE. LET ME JUST CAUTERIZE AND BANDAGE.
WHEW. GREAT. THANKS, DOC.
No. Thank you. For allowing me to rescue this precious pigment. This precious nebula. At last, I have enough.
YOU WERE RIGHT, DOC! PAINLESS. I FEEL NOTHING.
LEFT INTO THE HALLWAY. YOU CAN PAY UP FRONT.
Yes, that's your problem. Fortunately, I feel it deeply, pulsing beneath my skin, begging to be let out.
CASSIOPIA
DEEP SPACE
Finally, finally, finally...
...finally it is time to begin.

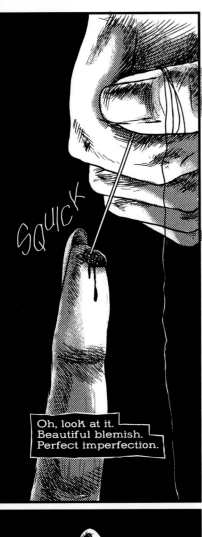

SQUICK

Oh, look at it. Beautiful blemish. Perfect imperfection.

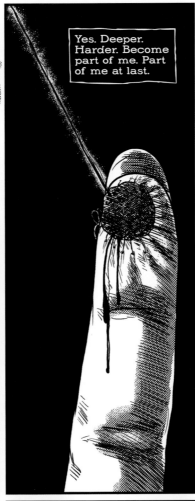

Yes. Deeper. Harder. Become part of me. Part of me at last.

Childhood... adolescence... college... med school... residency...

HI, DR. DERMITT. THIS IS TRACY AT CITY DERMATOLOGY'S FRONT DESK. YOU DIDN'T SHOW UP FOR WORK TODAY SO WE WERE JUST CHECKING IN...

DR. DERMITT, THIS IS TRACY AGAIN. IT'S BEEN THREE DAYS NOW, AND WE'RE HONESTLY GETTING A LITTLE CONCERNED...

No one ever understood. I was alone, always alone, always so very, very alone.

DR. DERMITT, THIS IS DIANE FROM HR. I REGRET TO INFORM YOU THAT YOU'VE BEEN LET GO FROM CITY DERMATOLOGY. YOUR FINAL CHECK WILL BE DELIVERED TO YOUR CURRENT ADDRESS...

Not anymore. Now my dots will connect. At last I'll connect to everyone... everything...

THUNK THUNK THUNK

I GOT COMPLAINTS OF A STENCH--AND I SMELL IT! YOU GOT THREE MONTHS' RENT DUE TOO! I DON'T HEAR FROM YOU TODAY AND I'M PUTTING IN THE EVICTION NOTICE.

YOU GO AHEAD. YOU'RE TOO LATE ANYWAY.

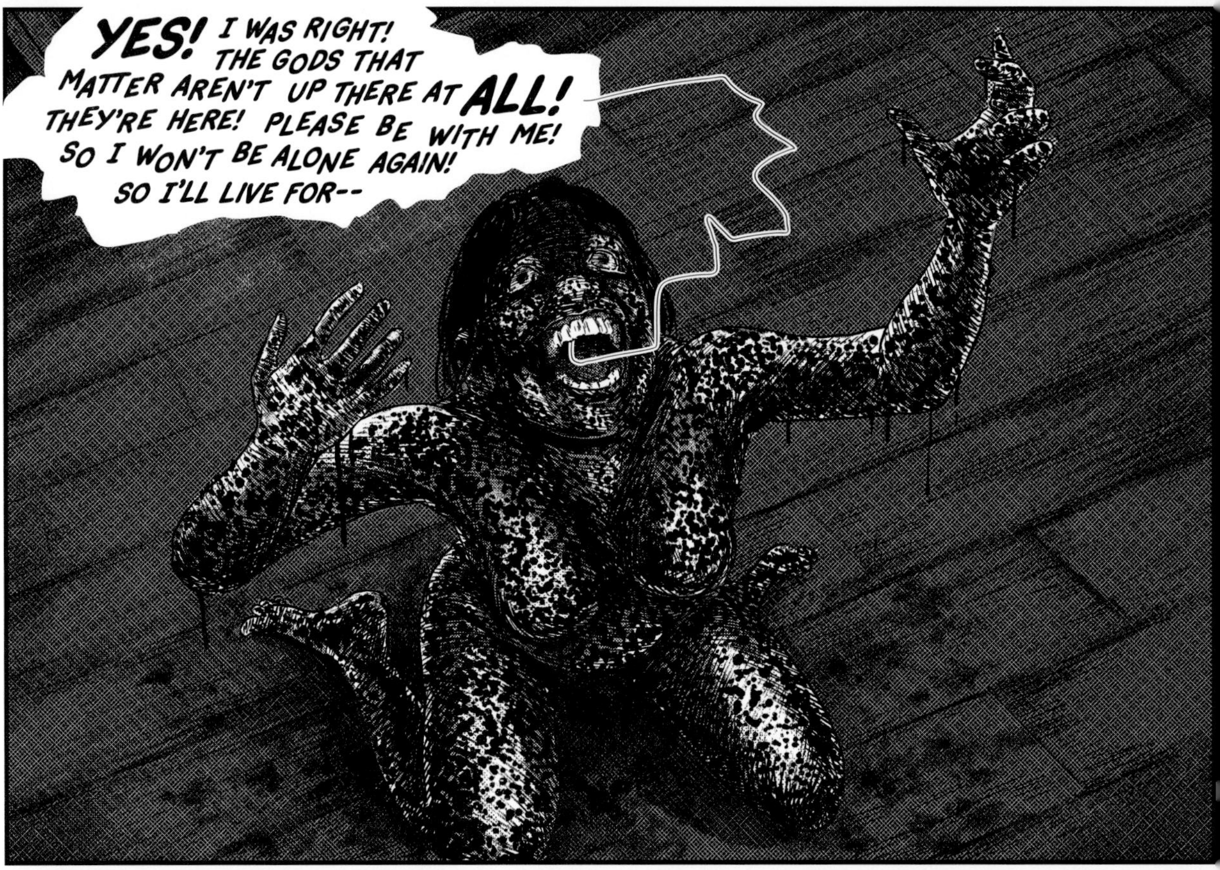
YES! I WAS RIGHT! THE GODS THAT MATTER AREN'T UP THERE AT ALL! THEY'RE HERE! PLEASE BE WITH ME! SO I WON'T BE ALONE AGAIN! SO I'LL LIVE FOR--

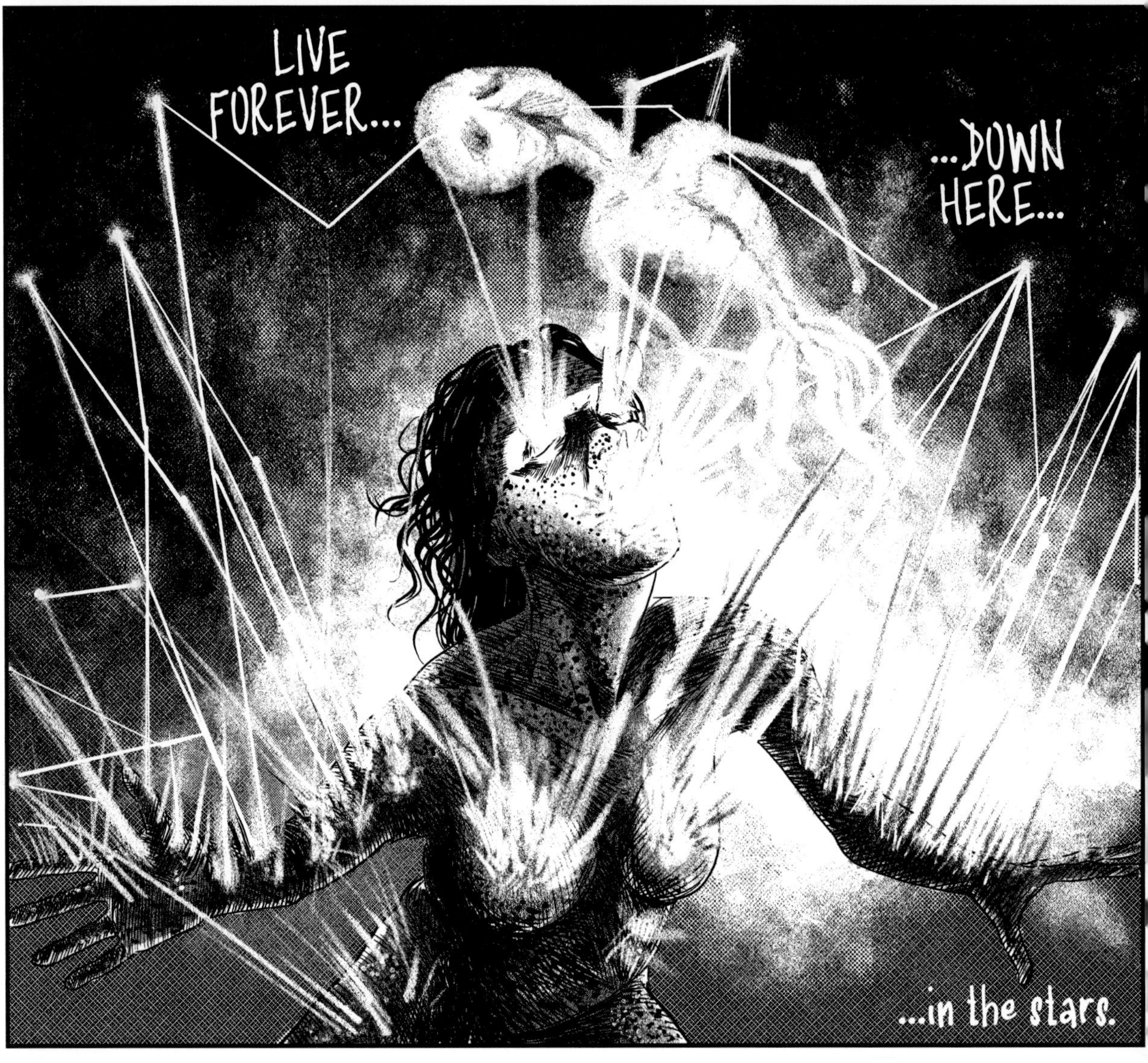
LIVE FOREVER...
...DOWN HERE...
...in the stars.

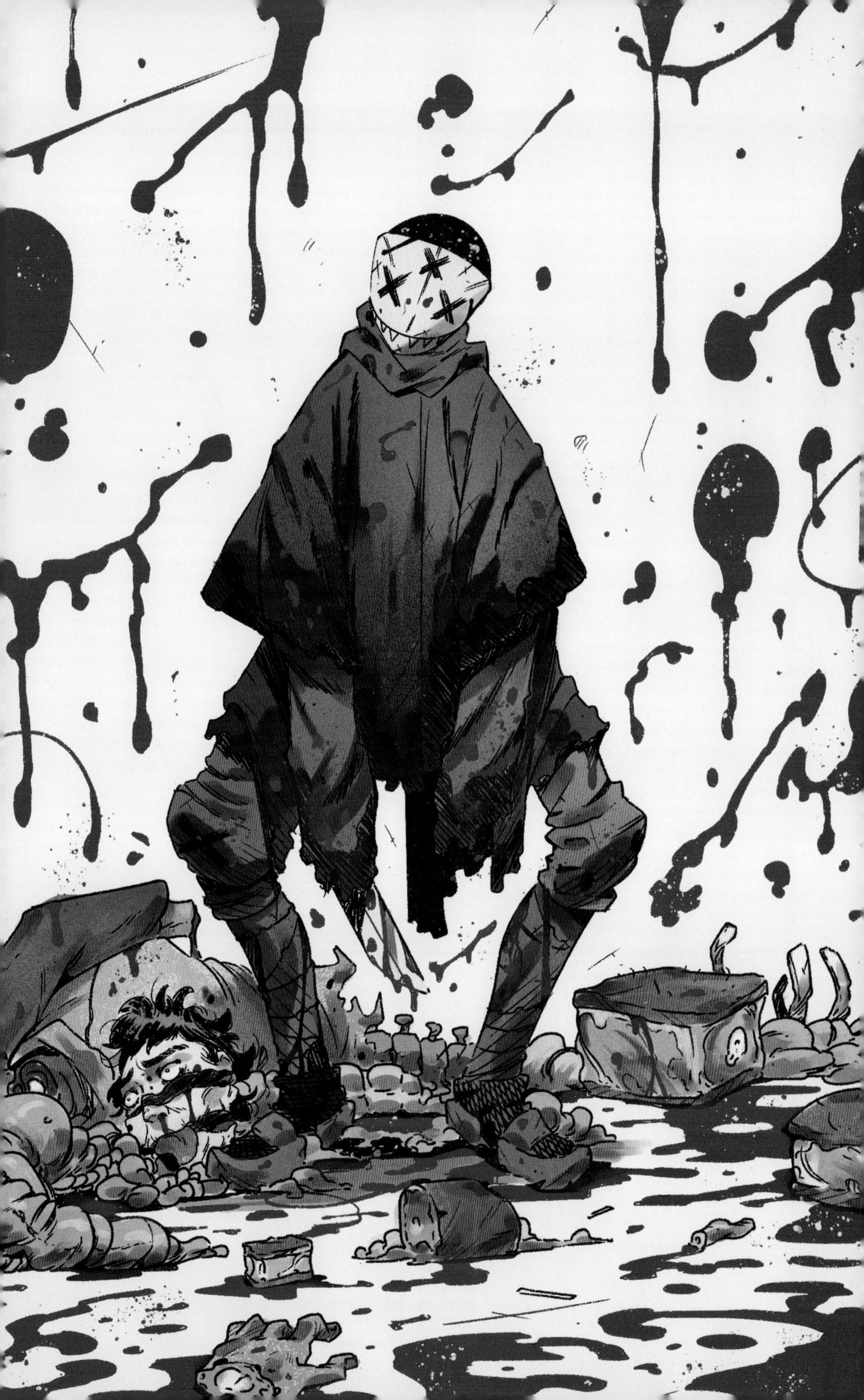

Becky Cloonan, or the Keats poem, "Isabella, or the Pot of Basil"

A discusion on the Razorblades issue #4 cover, a.k.a. Moan hither, all ye syllables of woe!

By Becky Cloonan, in case that wasn't obvious.

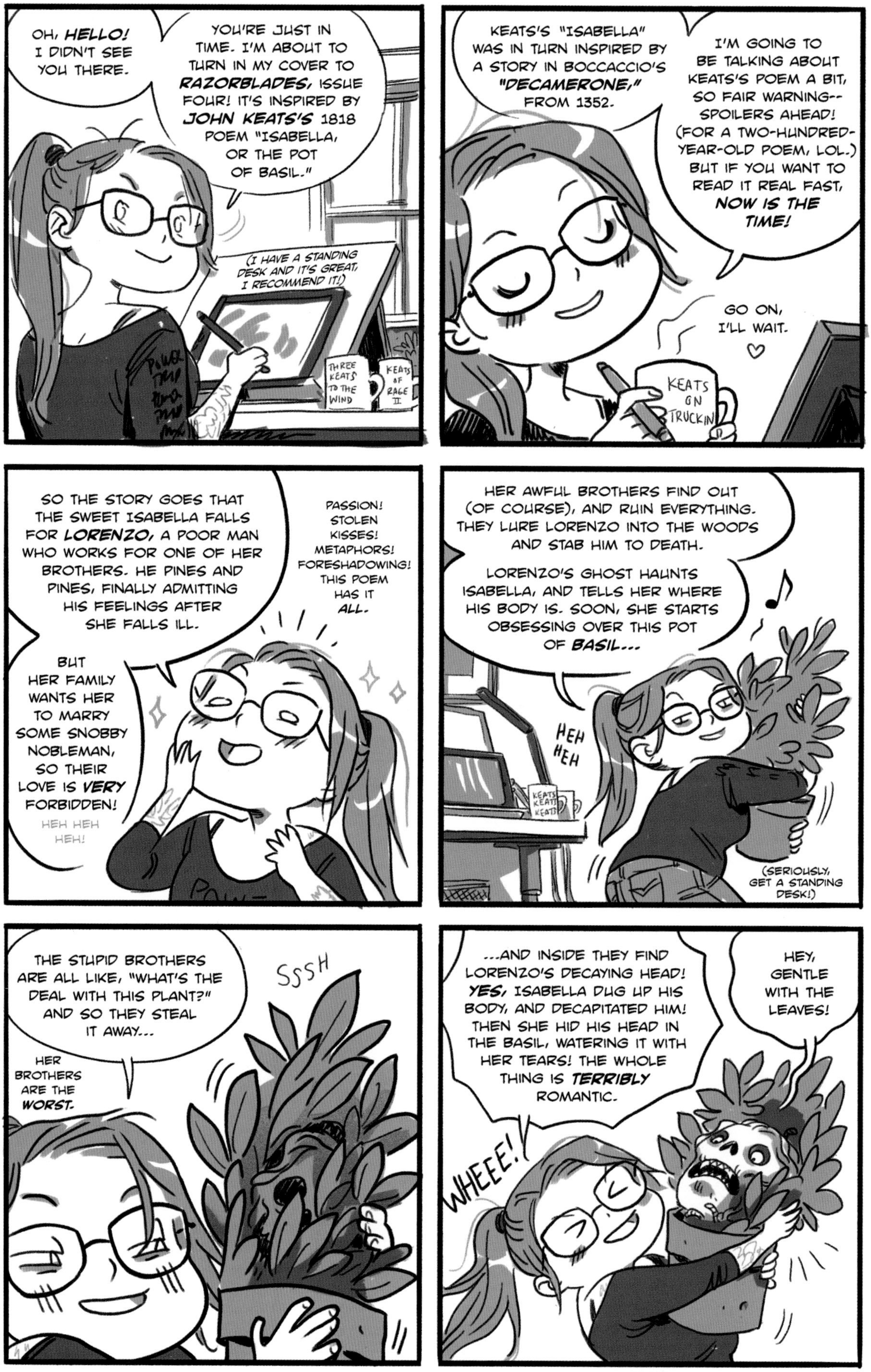

OH, HELLO! I DIDN'T SEE YOU THERE.
YOU'RE JUST IN TIME. I'M ABOUT TO TURN IN MY COVER TO RAZORBLADES, ISSUE FOUR! IT'S INSPIRED BY JOHN KEATS'S 1818 POEM "ISABELLA, OR THE POT OF BASIL."
(I HAVE A STANDING DESK AND IT'S GREAT, I RECOMMEND IT!)
THREE KEATS TO THE WIND
KEATS OF RAGE II
KEATS'S "ISABELLA" WAS IN TURN INSPIRED BY A STORY IN BOCCACCIO'S "DECAMERONE," FROM 1352.
I'M GOING TO BE TALKING ABOUT KEATS'S POEM A BIT, SO FAIR WARNING-- SPOILERS AHEAD! (FOR A TWO-HUNDRED-YEAR-OLD POEM, LOL.) BUT IF YOU WANT TO READ IT REAL FAST, NOW IS THE TIME!
GO ON, I'LL WAIT. ♡
KEATS ON TRUCKIN
SO THE STORY GOES THAT THE SWEET ISABELLA FALLS FOR LORENZO, A POOR MAN WHO WORKS FOR ONE OF HER BROTHERS. HE PINES AND PINES, FINALLY ADMITTING HIS FEELINGS AFTER SHE FALLS ILL.
BUT HER FAMILY WANTS HER TO MARRY SOME SNOBBY NOBLEMAN, SO THEIR LOVE IS VERY FORBIDDEN!
HEH HEH HEH!
PASSION! STOLEN KISSES! METAPHORS! FORESHADOWING! THIS POEM HAS IT ALL.
HER AWFUL BROTHERS FIND OUT (OF COURSE), AND RUIN EVERYTHING. THEY LURE LORENZO INTO THE WOODS AND STAB HIM TO DEATH.
LORENZO'S GHOST HAUNTS ISABELLA, AND TELLS HER WHERE HIS BODY IS. SOON, SHE STARTS OBSESSING OVER THIS POT OF BASIL...
HEH HEH
KEATS KEATS KEATS
(SERIOUSLY, GET A STANDING DESK!)
THE STUPID BROTHERS ARE ALL LIKE, "WHAT'S THE DEAL WITH THIS PLANT?" AND SO THEY STEAL IT AWAY...
SSSH
HER BROTHERS ARE THE WORST.
...AND INSIDE THEY FIND LORENZO'S DECAYING HEAD! YES, ISABELLA DUG UP HIS BODY, AND DECAPITATED HIM! THEN SHE HID HIS HEAD IN THE BASIL, WATERING IT WITH HER TEARS! THE WHOLE THING IS TERRIBLY ROMANTIC.
HEY, GENTLE WITH THE LEAVES!
WHEEE!

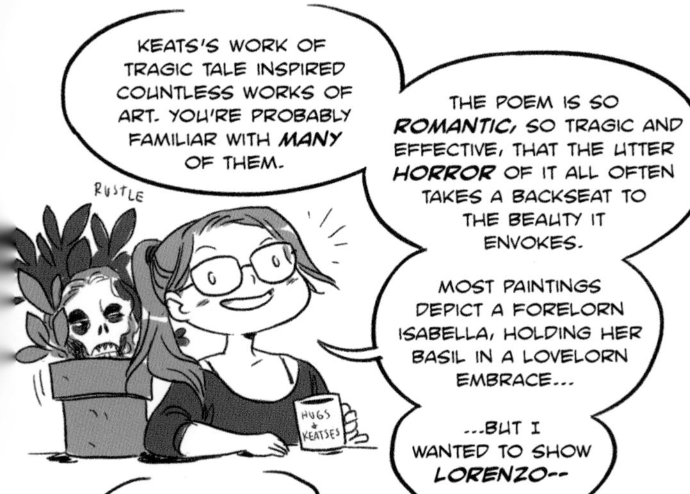
KEATS'S WORK OF TRAGIC TALE INSPIRED COUNTLESS WORKS OF ART. YOU'RE PROBABLY FAMILIAR WITH *MANY* OF THEM.
THE POEM IS SO ***ROMANTIC,*** SO TRAGIC AND EFFECTIVE, THAT THE UTTER ***HORROR*** OF IT ALL OFTEN TAKES A BACKSEAT TO THE BEAUTY IT ENVOKES.
MOST PAINTINGS DEPICT A FORELORN ISABELLA, HOLDING HER BASIL IN A LOVELORN EMBRACE...
...BUT I WANTED TO SHOW ***LORENZO--***
RUSTLE
HUGS + KEATSES

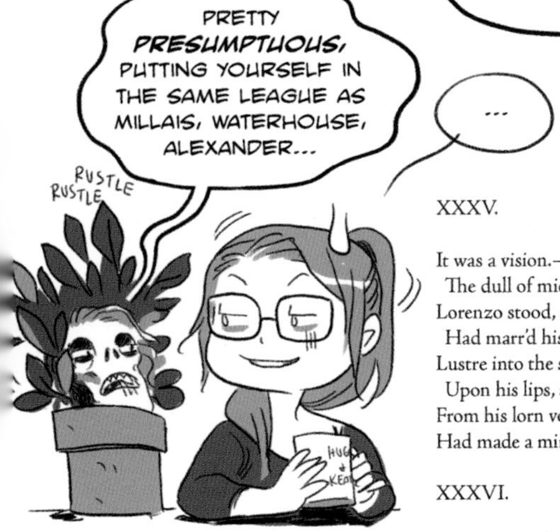
PRETTY ***PRESUMPTUOUS,*** PUTTING YOURSELF IN THE SAME LEAGUE AS MILLAIS, WATERHOUSE, ALEXANDER...
...
RUSTLE RUSTLE

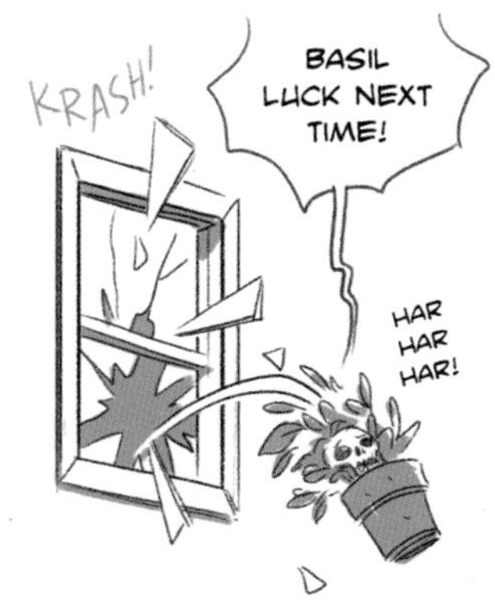
KRASH!
BASIL LUCK NEXT TIME!
HAR HAR HAR!

THESE ARE SOME OF MY FAVORITE STANZAS, FROM THE PART WHERE LORENZO'S GHOST APPEARS TO ISABELLA.

XXXV.

It was a vision.—In the drowsy gloom,
  The dull of midnight, at her couch's foot
Lorenzo stood, and wept: the forest tomb
  Had marr'd his glossy hair which once could shoot
Lustre into the sun, and put cold doom
  Upon his lips, and taken the soft lute
From his lorn voice, and past his loamed ears
Had made a miry channel for his tears.

XXXVI.

Strange sound it was, when the pale shadow spake;
  For there was striving, in its piteous tongue,
To speak as when on earth it was awake,
  And Isabella on its music hung:
Languor there was in it, and tremulous shake,
  As in a palsied Druid's harp unstrung;
And through it moan'd a ghostly under-song,
Like hoarse night-gusts sepulchral briars among.

XXXVII.

Its eyes, though wild, were still all dewy bright
  With love, and kept all phantom fear aloof
From the poor girl by magic of their light,
  The while it did unthread the horrid woof
Of the late darken'd time,—the murderous spite
  Of pride and avarice,—the dark pine roof
In the forest,—and the sodden turfed dell,
Where, without any word, from stabs he fell.

Detail of Isabella (1848-1849) by John Everett Millais.

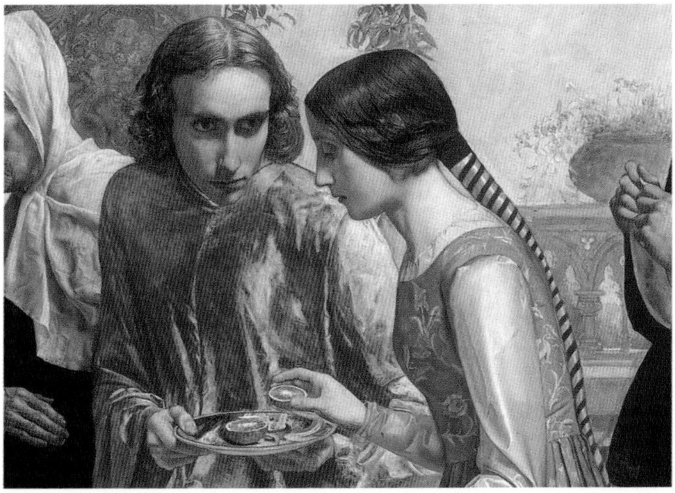

HERE ARE A COUPLE OF THE MANY, MANY PAINTINGS INSPIRED BY JOHN KEATS'S POEM! NEEDLESS TO SAY, I LOVE THEM ALL.

Isabella and the Pot of Basil (1907)
by John William Waterhouse

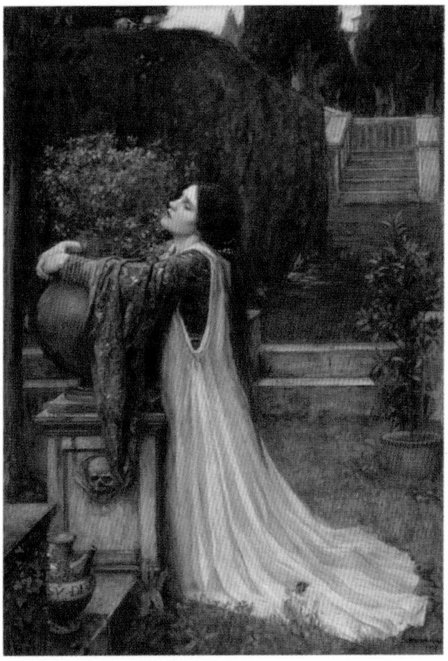

Isabella and the Pot of Basil (1904)
by Arthur Trevethin Nowell

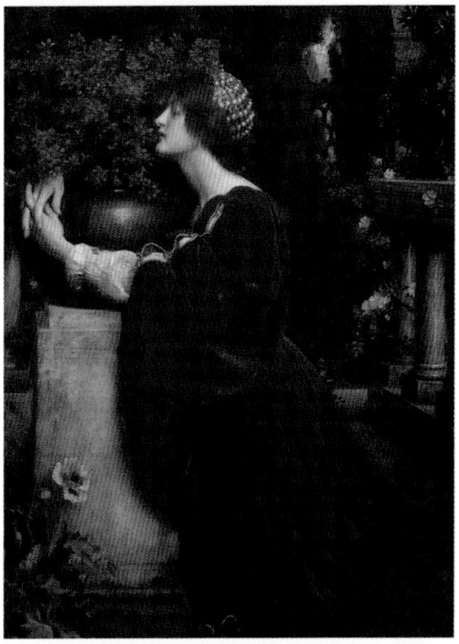

Isabella and the Pot of Basil (1868)
by William Holman Hunt.

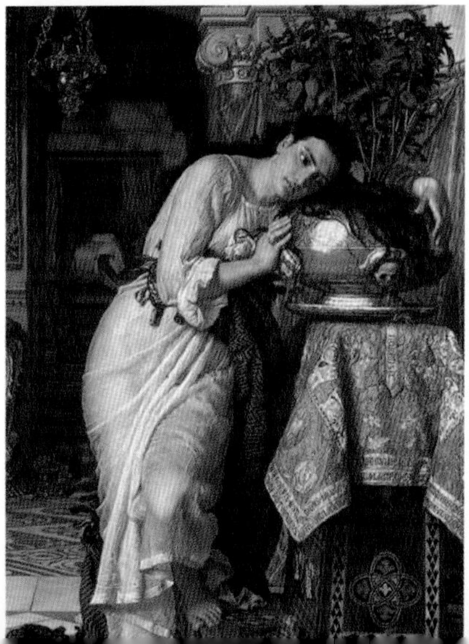

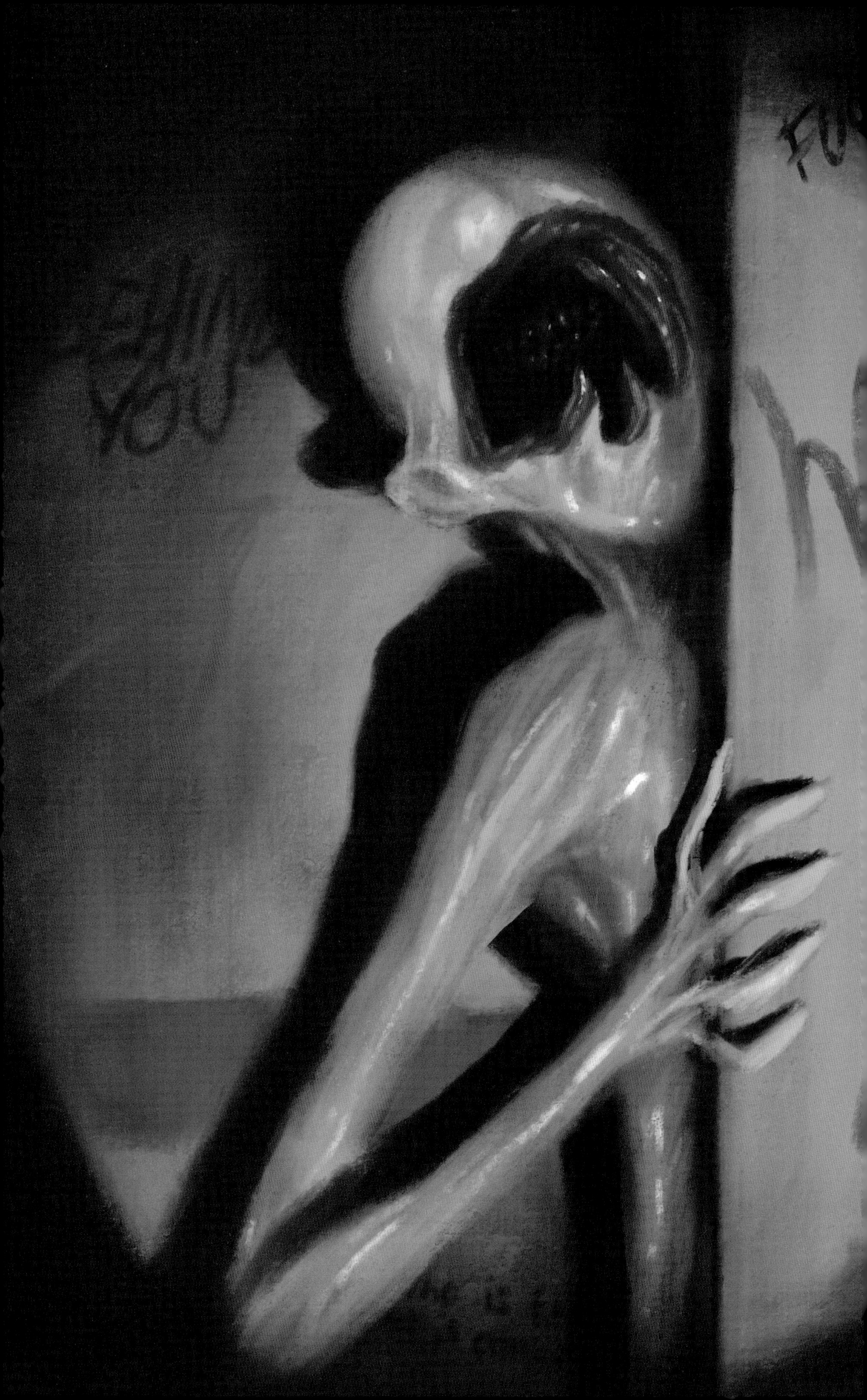
YOU

IF ANYONE FINDS THIS,
PLEASE GET HELP!
WE'VE BEEN STUCK DOWN HERE
FOR DAYS, IT GOES ON FOREVE
RE'S NO WAY OUT, WE'RE
RUNNING OUT of FOOD
AND THERE'S SOMETHING
DOWN HERE
WITH US

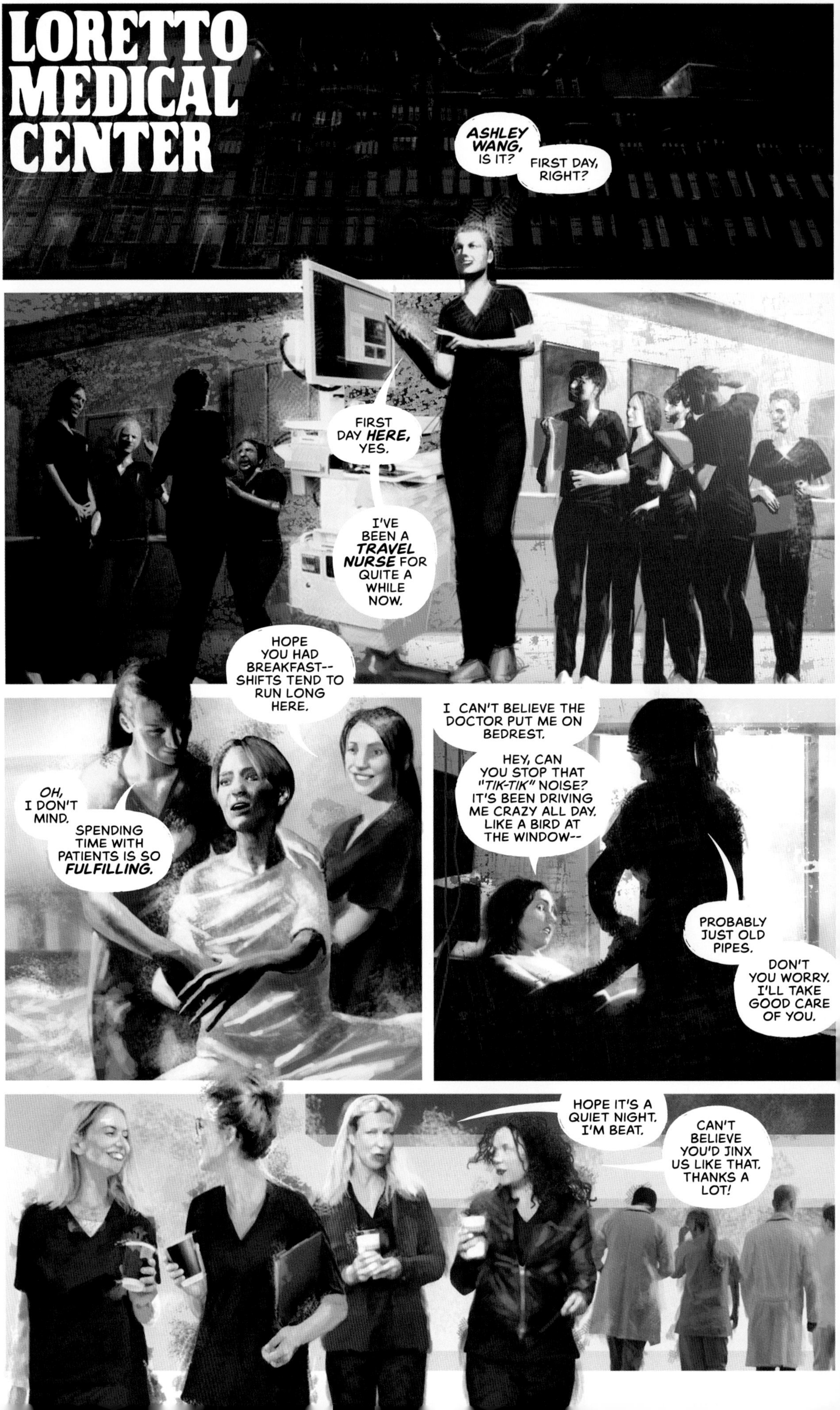
LORETTO MEDICAL CENTER
ASHLEY WANG, IS IT?
FIRST DAY, RIGHT?
FIRST DAY HERE, YES.
I'VE BEEN A TRAVEL NURSE FOR QUITE A WHILE NOW.
HOPE YOU HAD BREAKFAST-- SHIFTS TEND TO RUN LONG HERE.
OH, I DON'T MIND.
SPENDING TIME WITH PATIENTS IS SO FULFILLING.
I CAN'T BELIEVE THE DOCTOR PUT ME ON BEDREST.
HEY, CAN YOU STOP THAT "TIK-TIK" NOISE? IT'S BEEN DRIVING ME CRAZY ALL DAY. LIKE A BIRD AT THE WINDOW--
PROBABLY JUST OLD PIPES.
DON'T YOU WORRY. I'LL TAKE GOOD CARE OF YOU.
HOPE IT'S A QUIET NIGHT. I'M BEAT.
CAN'T BELIEVE YOU'D JINX US LIKE THAT. THANKS A LOT!

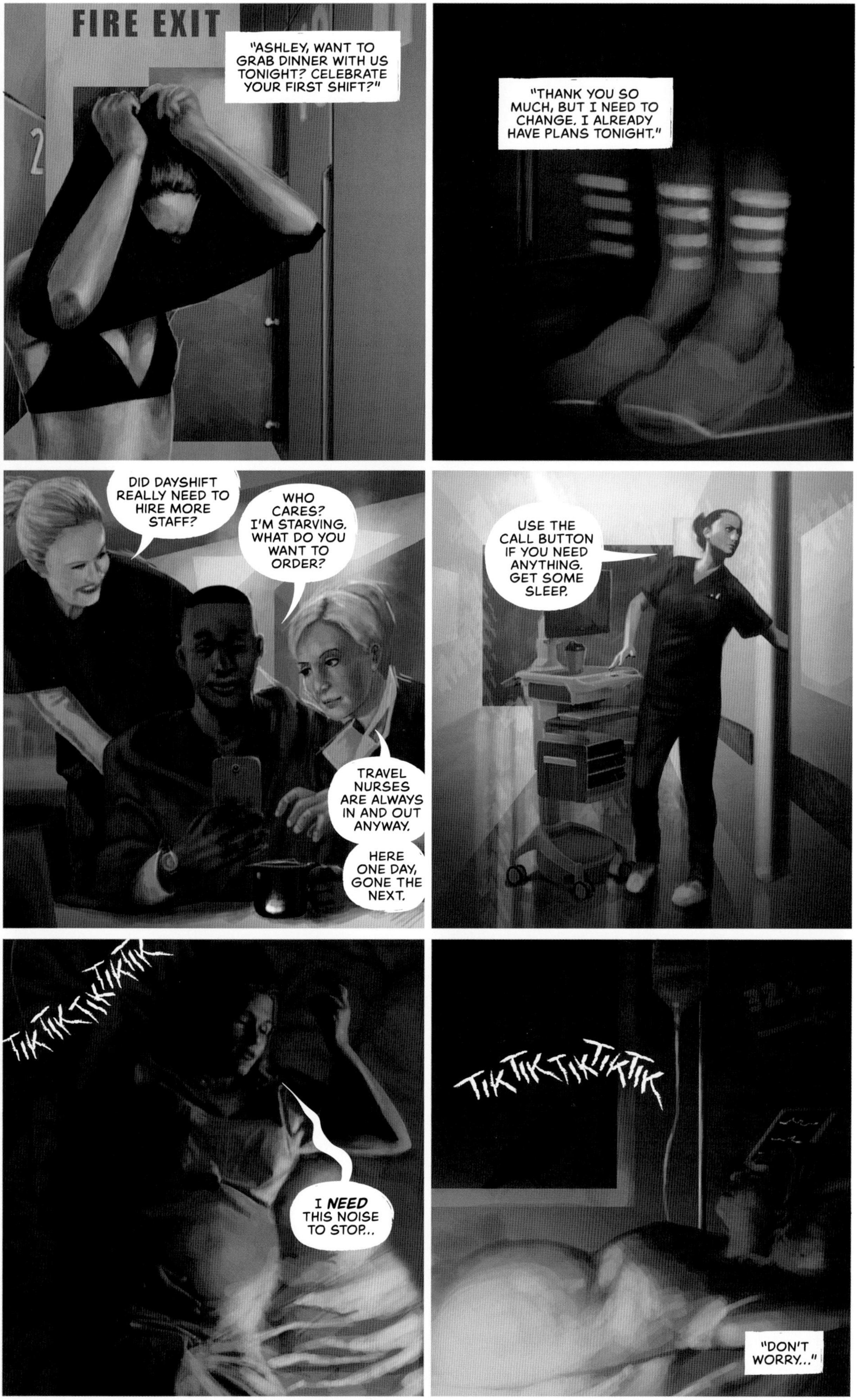
"ASHLEY, WANT TO GRAB DINNER WITH US TONIGHT? CELEBRATE YOUR FIRST SHIFT?"
FIRE EXIT
"THANK YOU SO MUCH, BUT I NEED TO CHANGE. I ALREADY HAVE PLANS TONIGHT."
DID DAYSHIFT REALLY NEED TO HIRE MORE STAFF?
WHO CARES? I'M STARVING. WHAT DO YOU WANT TO ORDER?
TRAVEL NURSES ARE ALWAYS IN AND OUT ANYWAY.
HERE ONE DAY, GONE THE NEXT.
USE THE CALL BUTTON IF YOU NEED ANYTHING. GET SOME SLEEP.
TIKTIKTIKTIKTIK
I ***NEED*** THIS NOISE TO STOP...
TIKTIKTIKTIKTIK
"DON'T WORRY..."

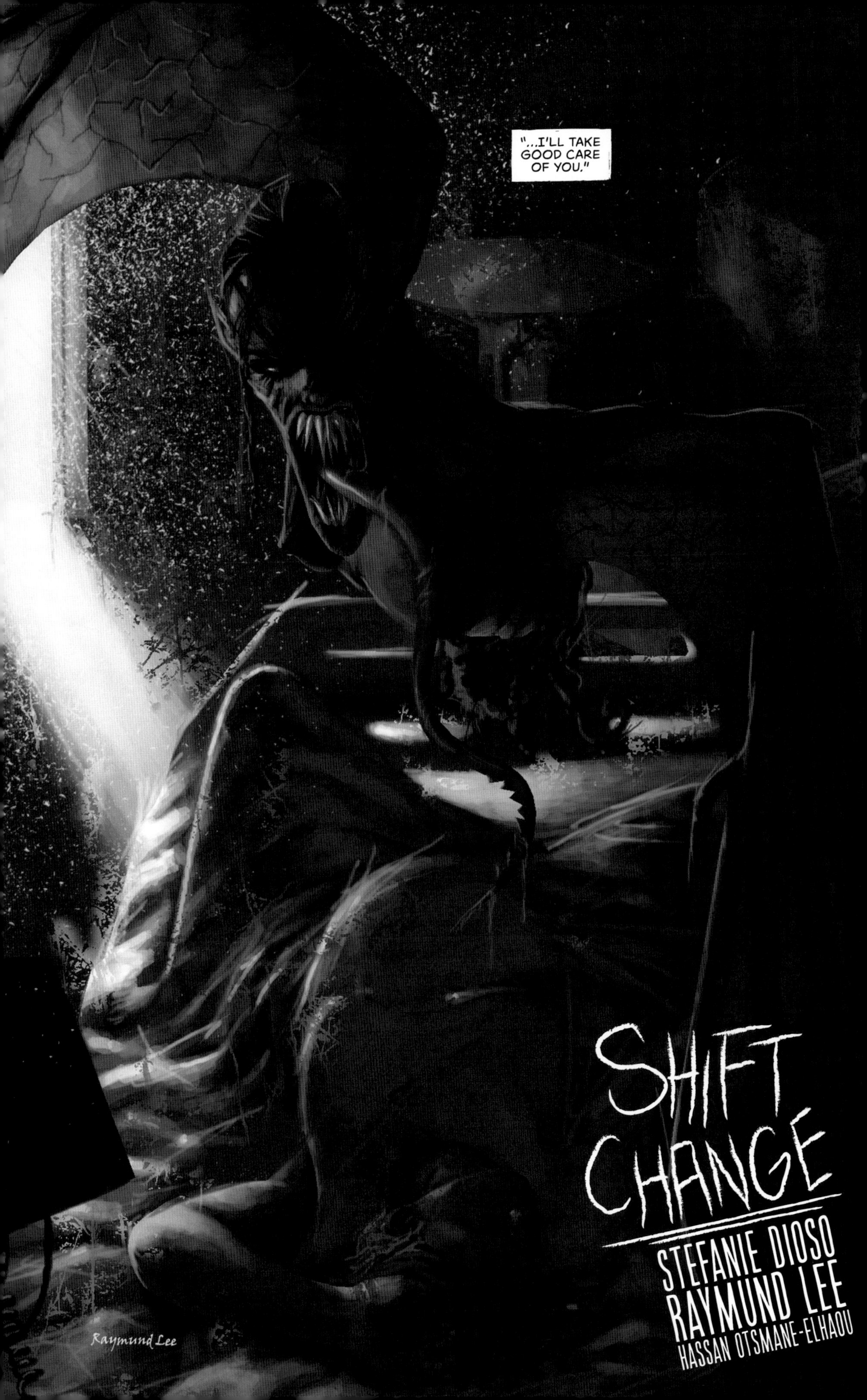
"...I'LL TAKE GOOD CARE OF YOU."
SHIFT CHANGE
STEFANIE DIOSO
RAYMUND LEE
HASSAN OTSMANE-ELHAOU
Raymund Lee

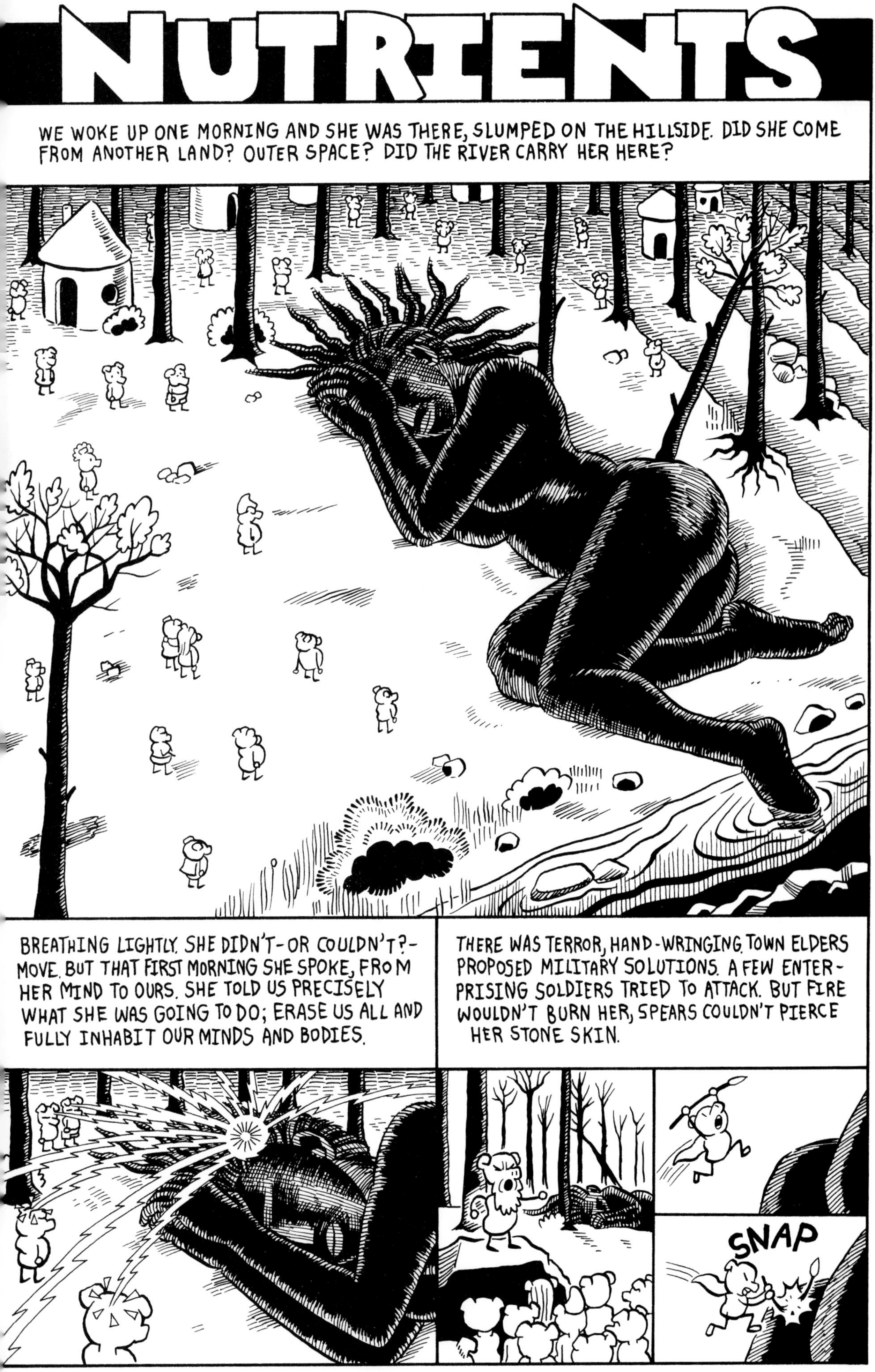
NUTRIENTS
WE WOKE UP ONE MORNING AND SHE WAS THERE, SLUMPED ON THE HILLSIDE. DID SHE COME FROM ANOTHER LAND? OUTER SPACE? DID THE RIVER CARRY HER HERE?
BREATHING LIGHTLY, SHE DIDN'T - OR COULDN'T? - MOVE, BUT THAT FIRST MORNING SHE SPOKE, FROM HER MIND TO OURS. SHE TOLD US PRECISELY WHAT SHE WAS GOING TO DO; ERASE US ALL AND FULLY INHABIT OUR MINDS AND BODIES.
THERE WAS TERROR, HAND-WRINGING, TOWN ELDERS PROPOSED MILITARY SOLUTIONS. A FEW ENTERPRISING SOLDIERS TRIED TO ATTACK. BUT FIRE WOULDN'T BURN HER, SPEARS COULDN'T PIERCE HER STONE SKIN.
SNAP

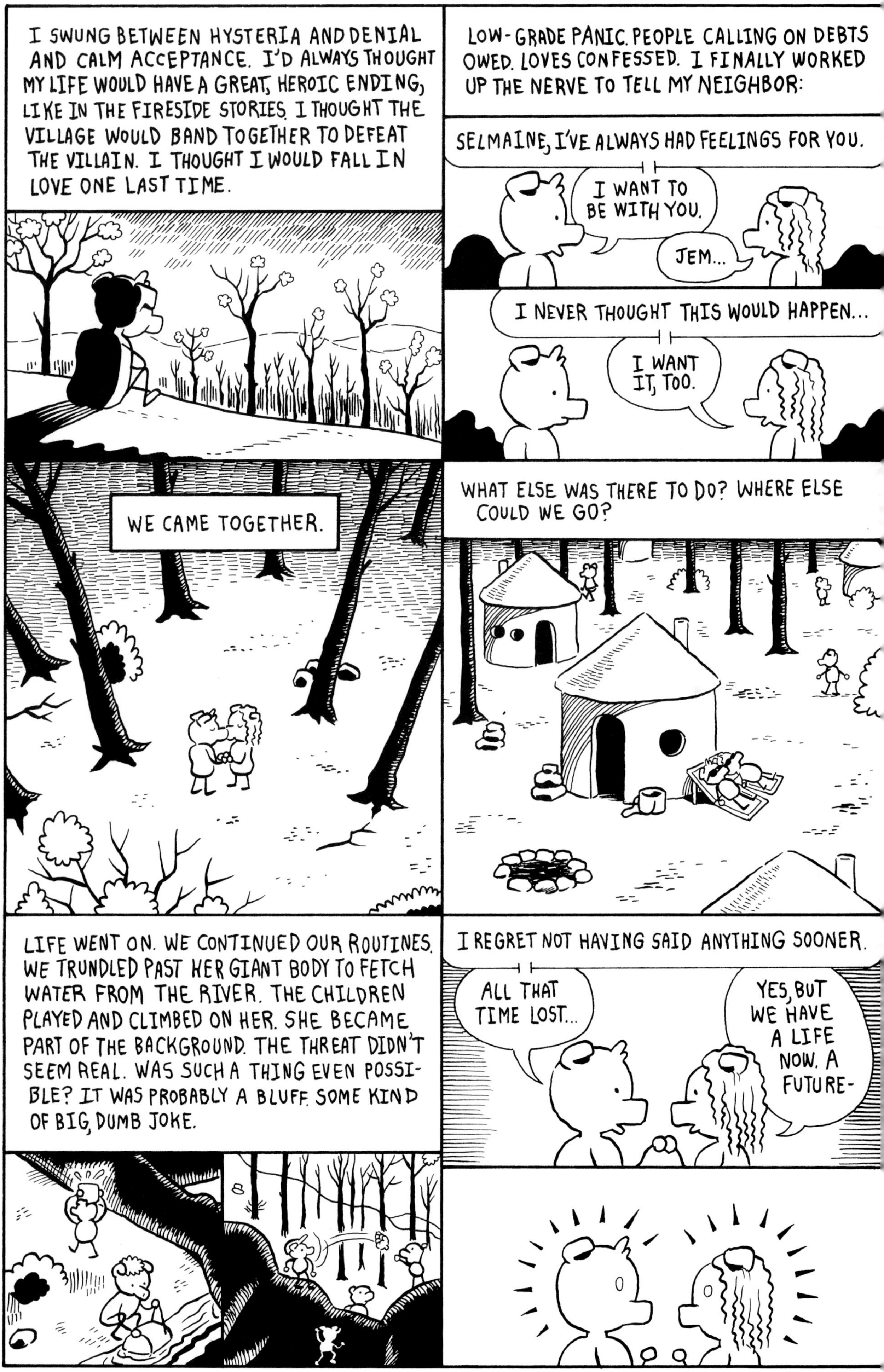
I SWUNG BETWEEN HYSTERIA AND DENIAL AND CALM ACCEPTANCE. I'D ALWAYS THOUGHT MY LIFE WOULD HAVE A GREAT, HEROIC ENDING, LIKE IN THE FIRESIDE STORIES. I THOUGHT THE VILLAGE WOULD BAND TOGETHER TO DEFEAT THE VILLAIN. I THOUGHT I WOULD FALL IN LOVE ONE LAST TIME.
LOW-GRADE PANIC. PEOPLE CALLING ON DEBTS OWED. LOVES CONFESSED. I FINALLY WORKED UP THE NERVE TO TELL MY NEIGHBOR:
SELMAINE, I'VE ALWAYS HAD FEELINGS FOR YOU.
I WANT TO BE WITH YOU.
JEM...
I NEVER THOUGHT THIS WOULD HAPPEN...
I WANT IT, TOO.
WE CAME TOGETHER.
WHAT ELSE WAS THERE TO DO? WHERE ELSE COULD WE GO?
LIFE WENT ON. WE CONTINUED OUR ROUTINES. WE TRUNDLED PAST HER GIANT BODY TO FETCH WATER FROM THE RIVER. THE CHILDREN PLAYED AND CLIMBED ON HER. SHE BECAME PART OF THE BACKGROUND. THE THREAT DIDN'T SEEM REAL. WAS SUCH A THING EVEN POSSIBLE? IT WAS PROBABLY A BLUFF. SOME KIND OF BIG, DUMB JOKE.
I REGRET NOT HAVING SAID ANYTHING SOONER.
ALL THAT TIME LOST...
YES, BUT WE HAVE A LIFE NOW. A FUTURE-

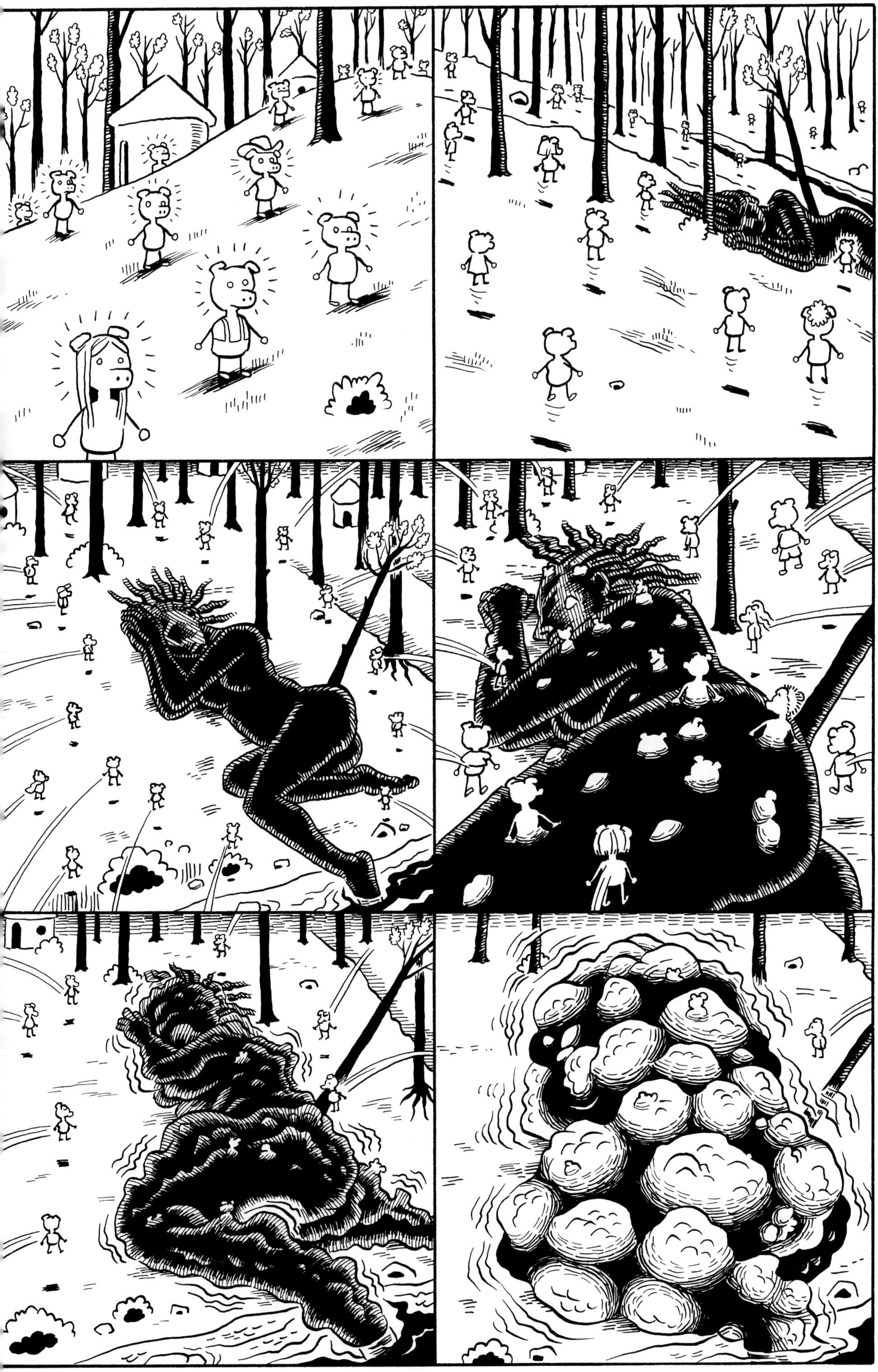

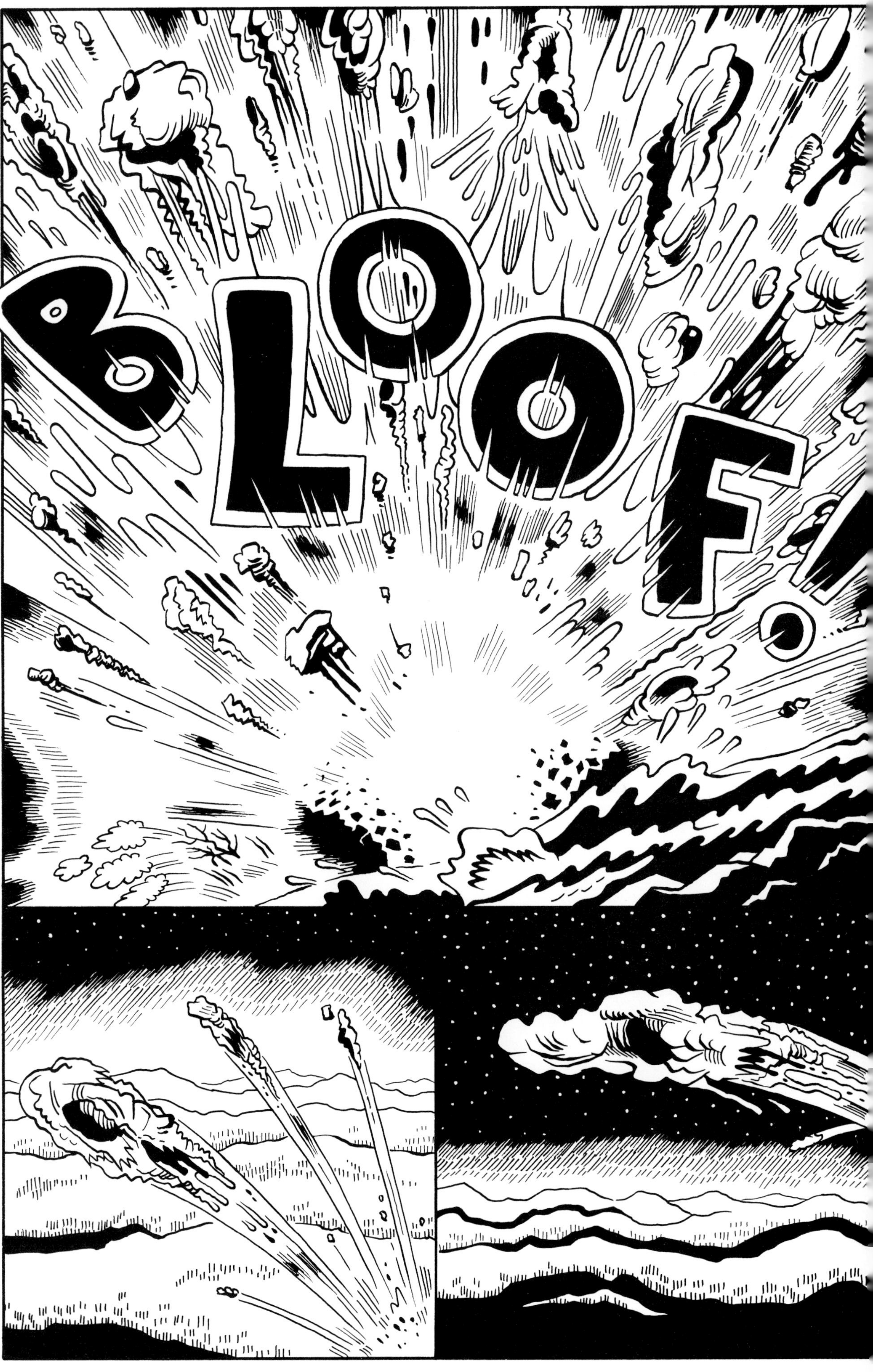
BLOOF!

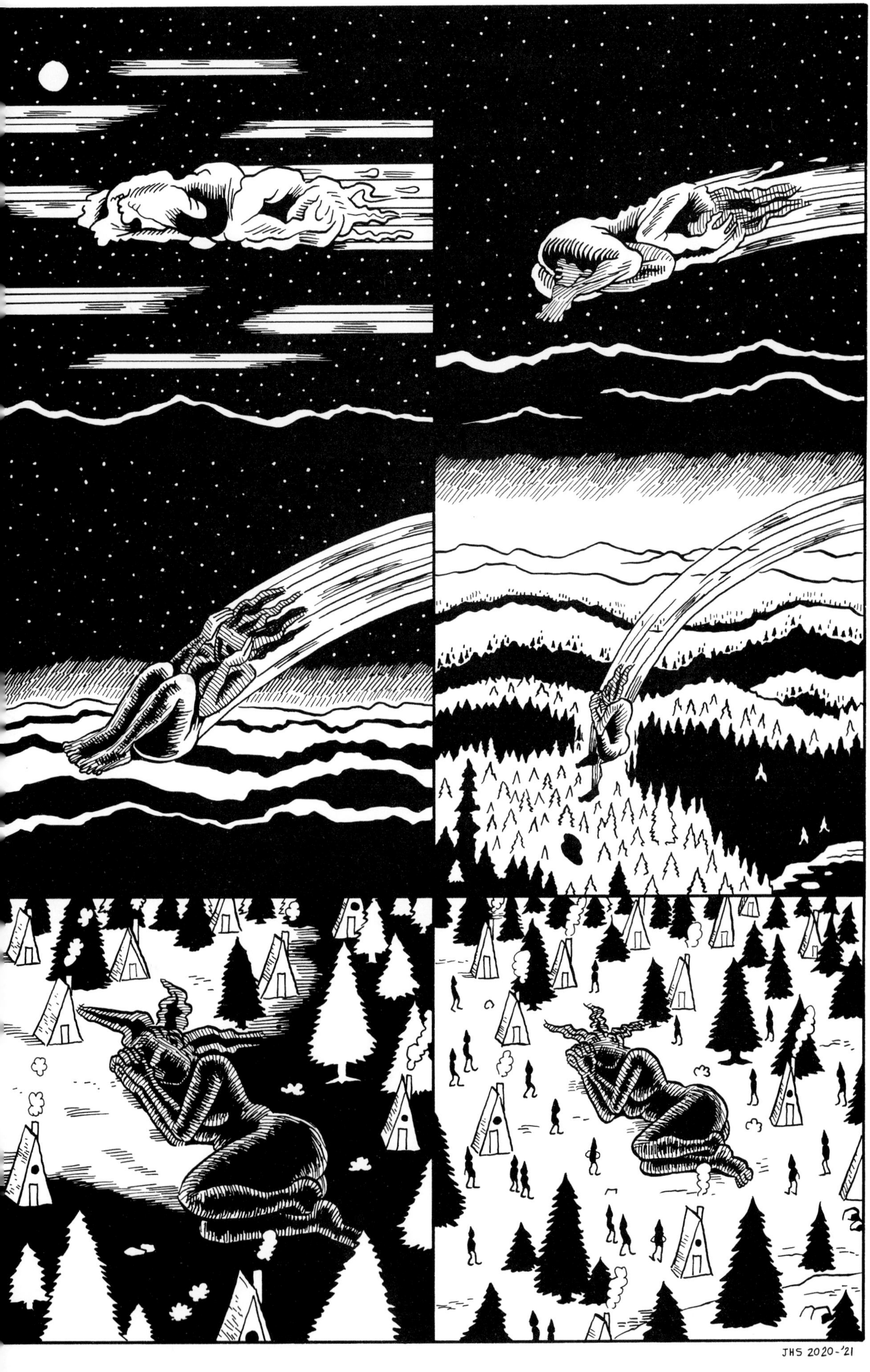

JHS 2020-'21

Origin of Man

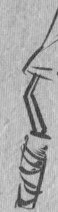

FIELD JOURNAL OF DR. MARA ALEXEYEV

After fifteen days together, I have finally convinced Michail to bring me to the village. Richard was right—the man is slow to trust but can see reason, and once I convinced him my intentions were honorable, he warmed to me.

The people here, even the young, are as weathered as the landscape, their faces cragged and cracked from the wind and cold, and they are not used to visitors. My credentials mean nothing to such an isolated, self-sufficient community (as my colleagues back at the institute warned me they wouldn't), but my gifts of packaged food and sleek tools to replace their older, cruder fare has ingratiated me to them somewhat.

After making a friend of the youngest villager—a boy of nine named Dominik, who appreciated the chocolate bars I smuggled—I was introduced to the elders of the place. They are:

-Yana, who looks the very definition of a crone, and the junior of the three at 98 years old

-Arseny, a smiling, toothless man of 101, whose mind is almost gone but whose advice is still keen

-A man they call Grigory, though he tells me that is not his true name. He claims to be over a thousand years old, but looks the fittest of the three

Two of the three bore the mark of the wolf on their face or hands. Only Grigory did not.

It was to them I pleaded my case.

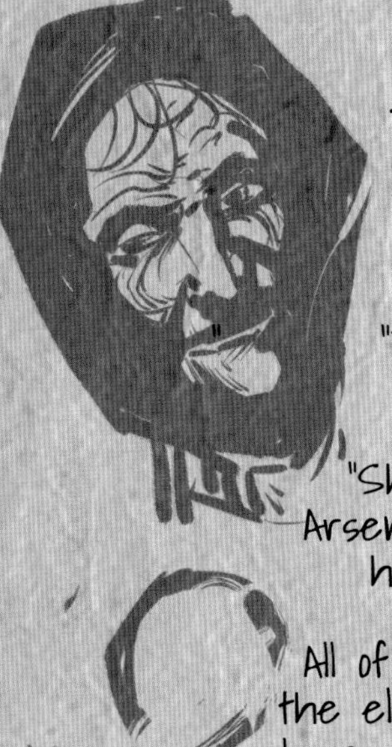

"I am here to trace the origins of legends," I told them. "I am here to see if we can find the truth of things, to understand the myths of your people." They asked me what story I sought, and I told them about my research.

"This is no myth," Yana spat, making motions with her hands. "This is truth. You already know."

"She knows, but she does not believe," Arseny said, nodding and grinning, and making hand motions of his own. "But...she will."

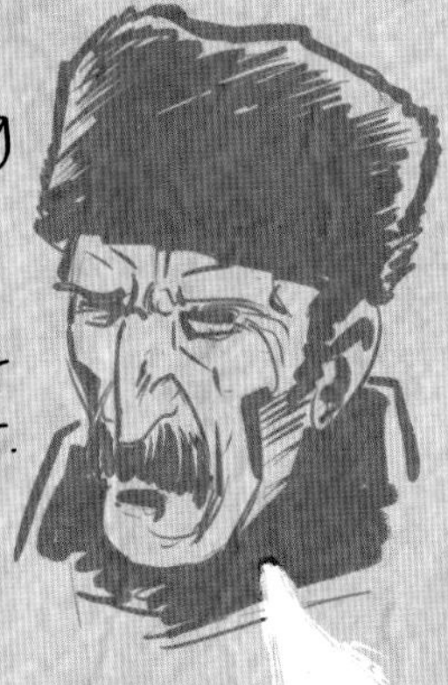

All of this was translated through Michail, as the elders and Dominik all spoke a dialect that I was quite unfamiliar with. Something rougher. Something older.

Grigory motioned our small group into his ancient-looking home, and we followed. He sparked a fire and sat us on the floor, so he could tower above us as he spoke.

He asked me what I knew, and I recounted the stories I had heard. Then he, like Yana, spat, chuckling darkly.

"No," he said. "I will speak now, and you will listen."

He was silent for a time, seeming to wrestle with where to start, before he nodded and straightened. "This is not myth, this is Truth," he began, inclining his head to Yana. "This is the Truth of my people, and I am the last who remembers. I am the last of the sons of the First Man."

Before he went on, he made me promise not to tell of where their village lay exactly, and to change the names of his kinsman, and leave out their distinguishing marks and customs if I must tell their story. I swore it, and will do so in my official papers.

Satisfied, he cleared his throat, and truly began.

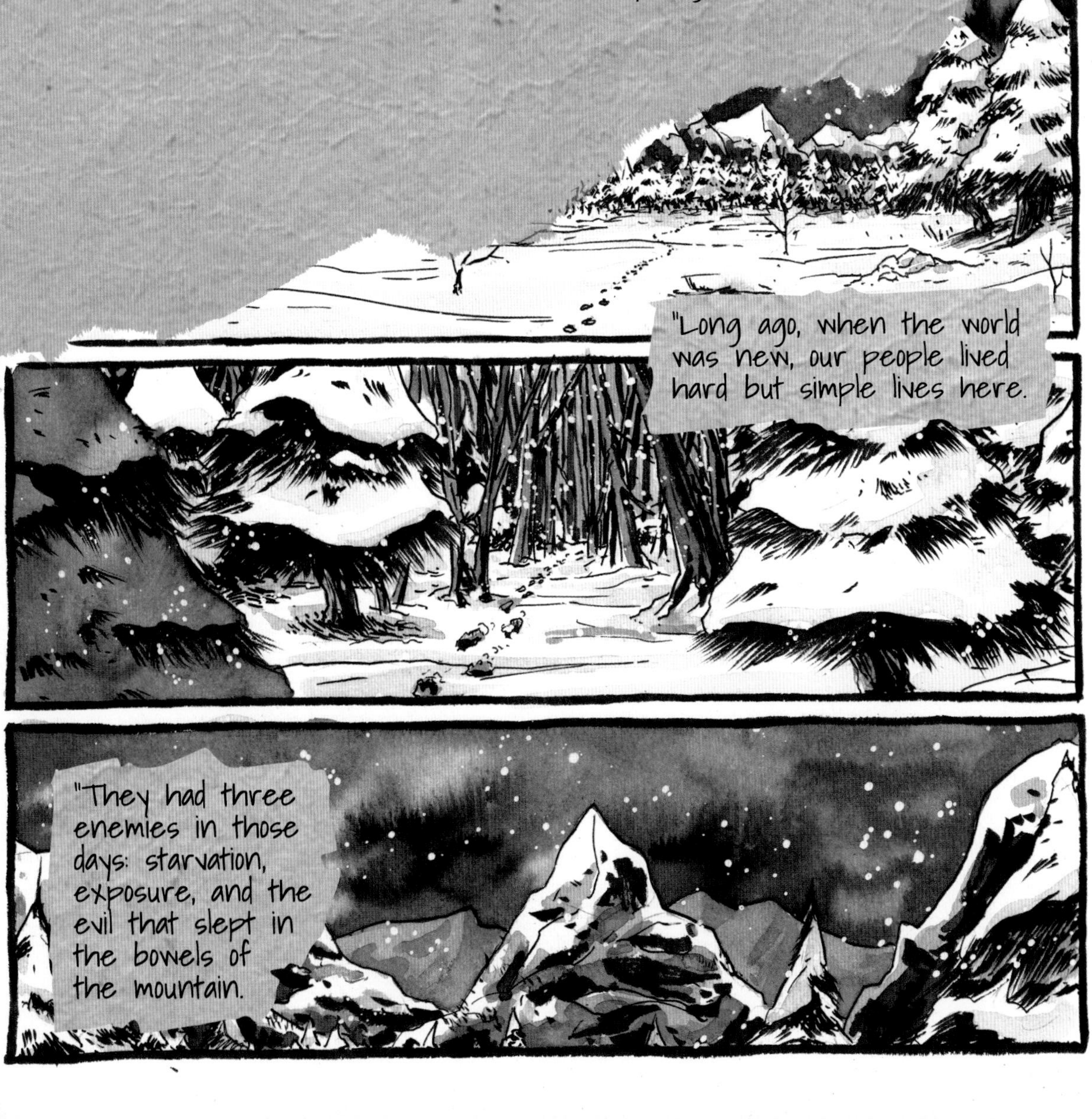
"Long ago, when the world was new, our people lived hard but simple lives here.
"They had three enemies in those days: starvation, exposure, and the evil that slept in the bowels of the mountain.

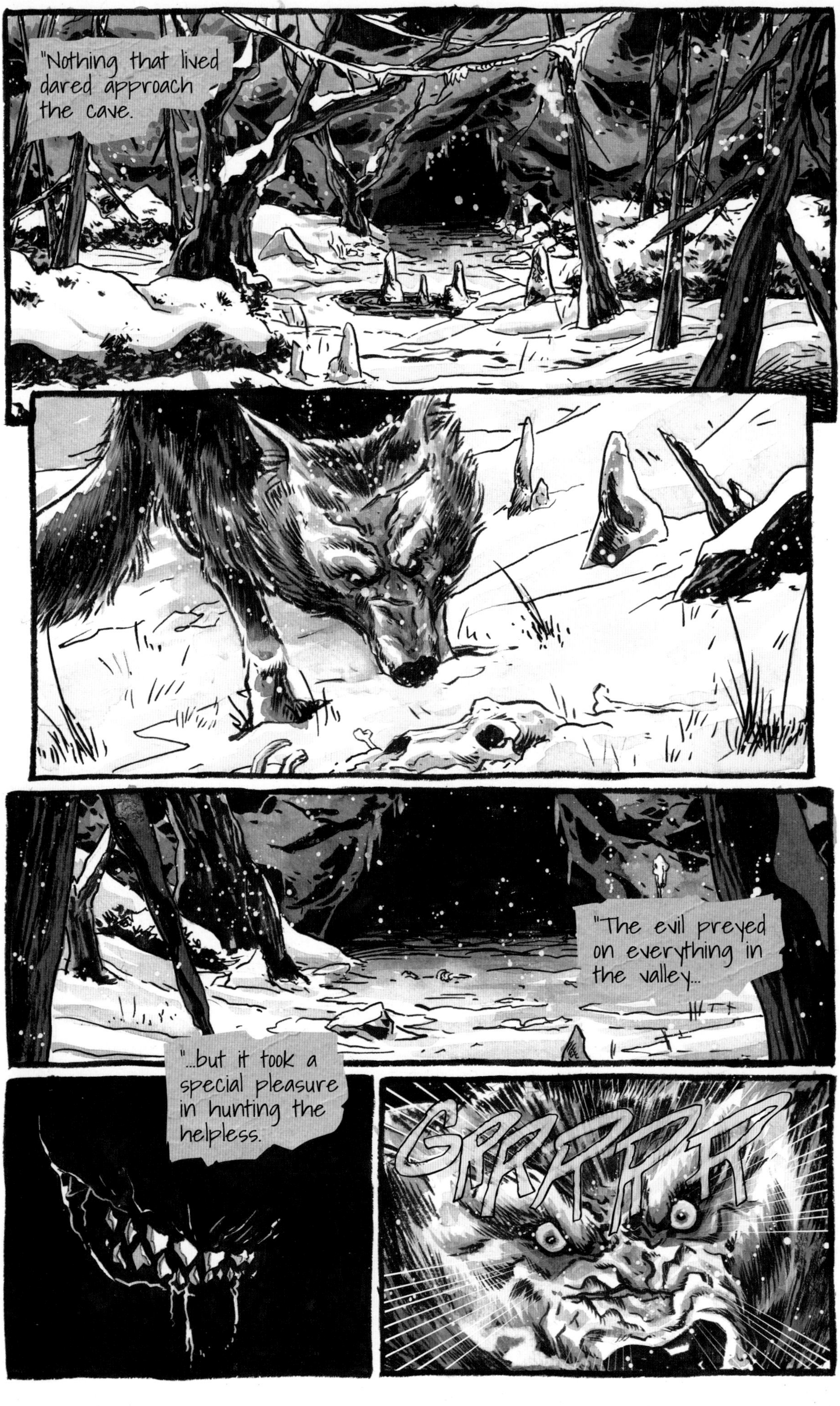
"Nothing that lived dared approach the cave.
"The evil preyed on everything in the valley...
"...but it took a special pleasure in hunting the helpless.
GRRRRRR

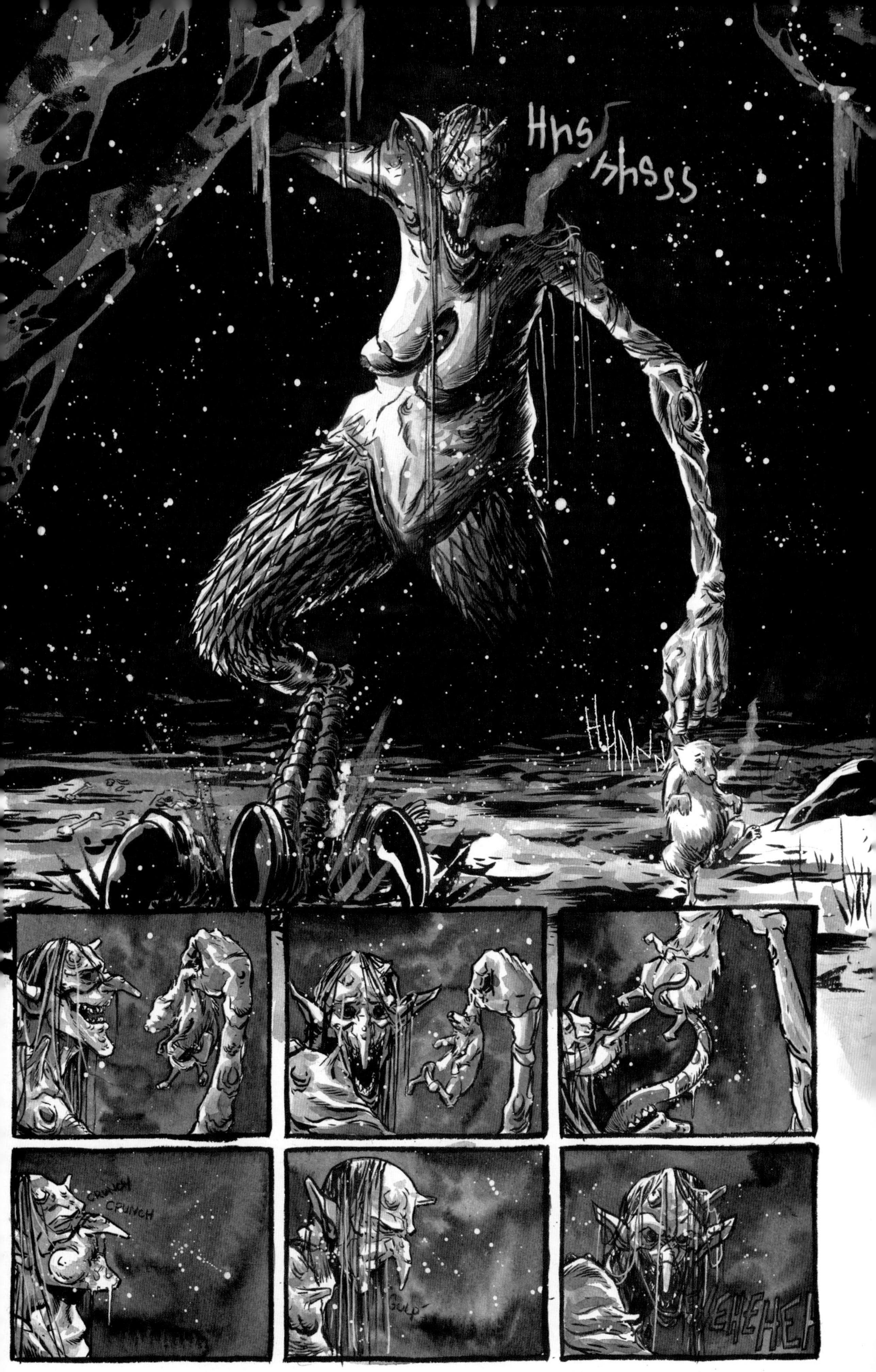
Hhs shsss
HUNNN
CRUNCH
CRUNCH
GULP
EHEHEH

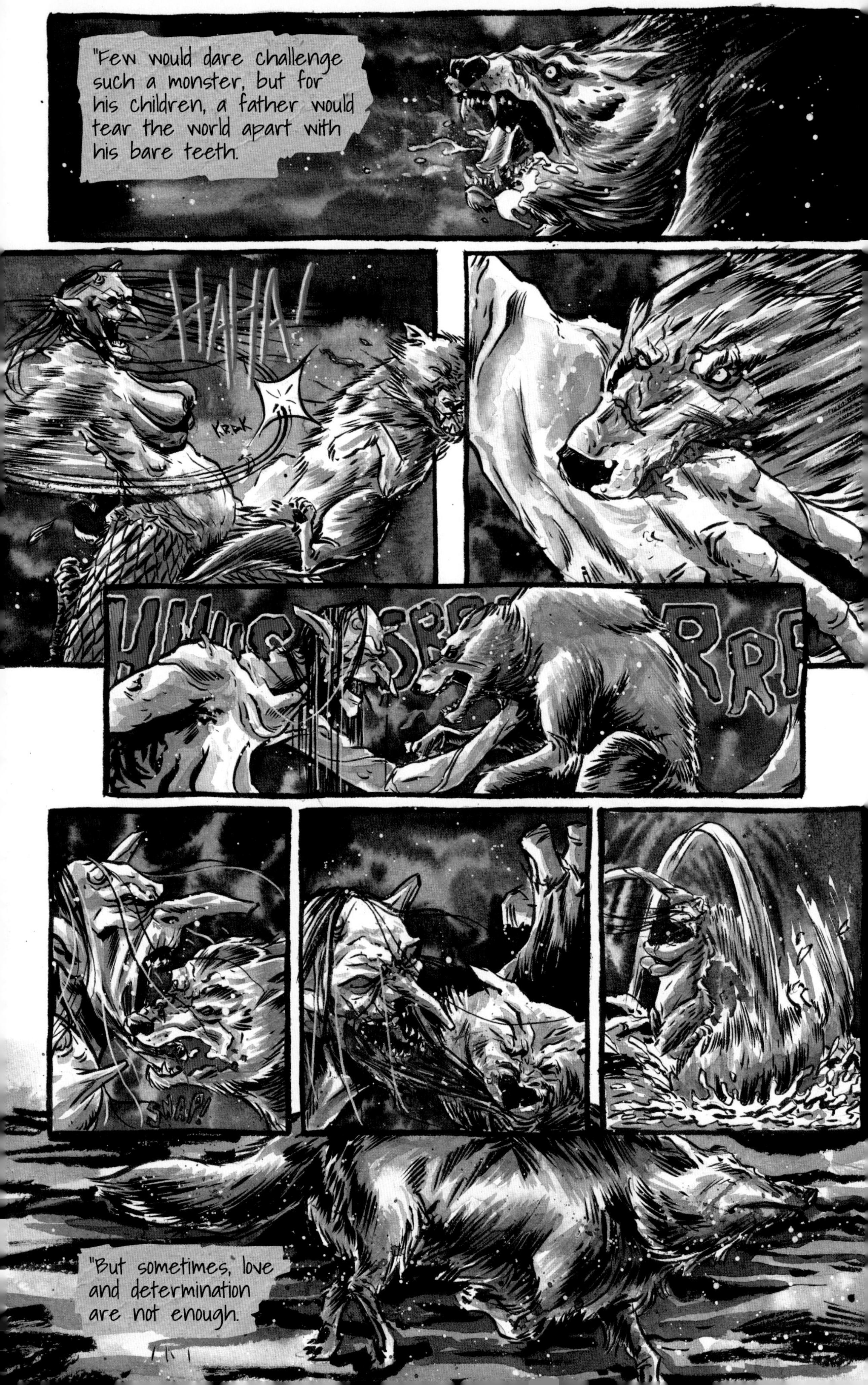
"Few would dare challenge such a monster, but for his children, a father would tear the world apart with his bare teeth.
HAHA!
KRAK
SNAP!
"But sometimes, love and determination are not enough.

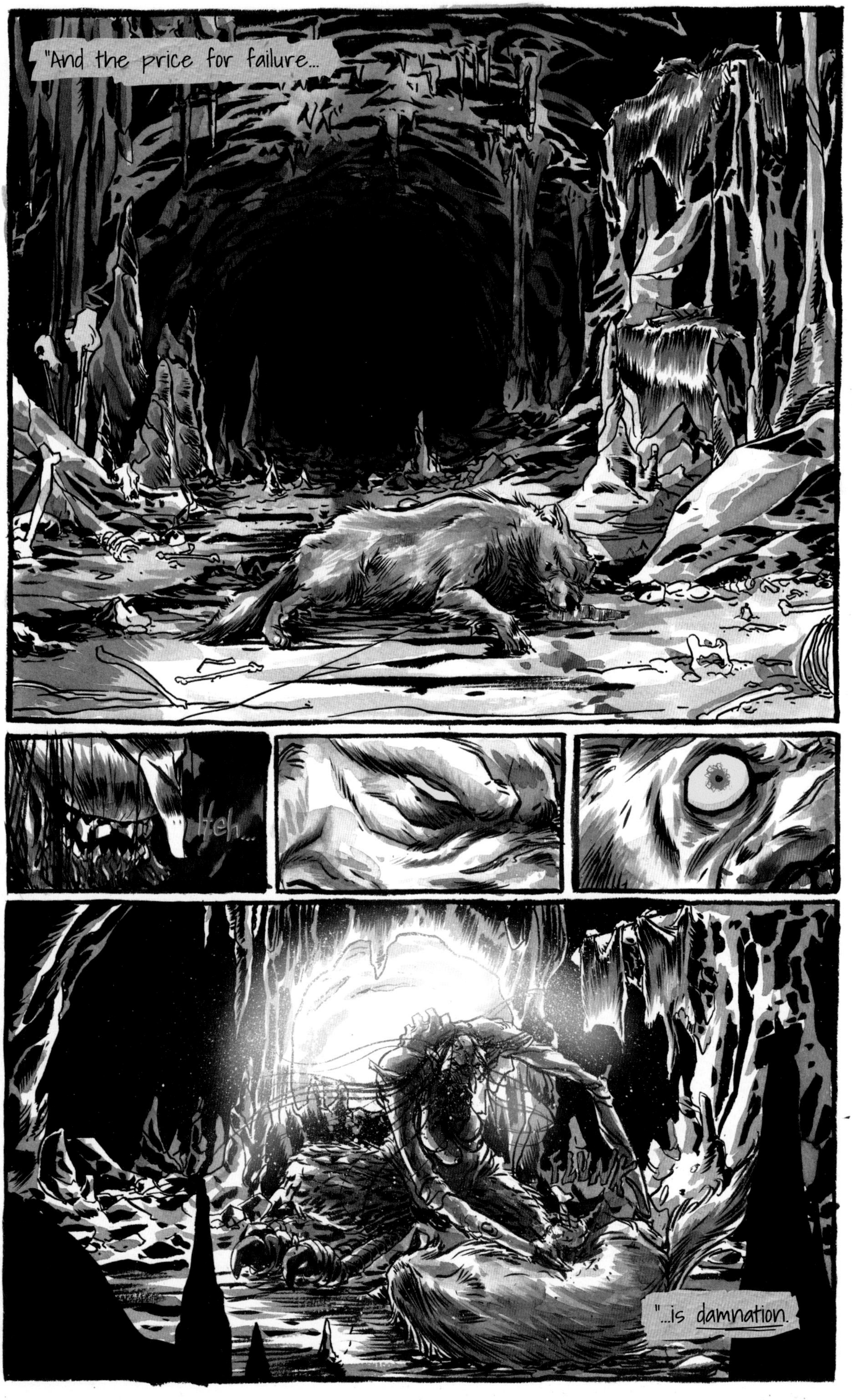
"And the price for failure...
Heh...
FLUNK
"...is damnation.

"When the Man returned to his pack, he found they had all changed, like him.

"They were cursed. This First Man, he was my father's father," the man known as Grigory said, opening his coat and pulling his layers of shirt up to reveal HIS mark of the Wolf—a large, angry-looking birthmark on his chest.

"All my children are mixed blood, and their children, and their children's children. I am the last of His line."

I thanked Grigory for his story, and gave him and the two others a gift of Scotch. Michail and I declined to drink it with them, as it was getting late and we had much traveling to do in the morning.

I am writing this all now while the story is fresh in my memories. Grigory knew some, but not as much as he thought. He left out important details, though perhaps the story is not passed down as faithfully in his family as it was in mine.

He did not seem to know that the witch had not always been a witch. That once she had been like the man, a leader of her people, though hers had feathers, not fur. She was known as a great healer, and an oracle.

He never mentioned that the Wolves had feared and hated her power, and had conspired to kill her, and it was by will alone that she had found the cave.

He did not seem to know that, in that cave, she had heard the promise the shadows whispered and had accepted their offer of revenge. She paid the price and she and her line were changed, cursed by her rage, much like the man.

The description of her body, while effectively frightening, was also exaggerated. Her form became more human, again, like the man, though she did tower over his people.

But unlike for him, there was an escape for her and her kin. That they would only be FREE when she destroyed the last blood of those who had driven her to the cave...life for life, a people for a people, a pact sealed in blood.

Some inquiring through Diminik has revealed that Grigory spoke true—that he is the last of the old blood, and further that his only living relative is Diminik himself, whom the old man cares for since the boy's parents took ill and died last year.

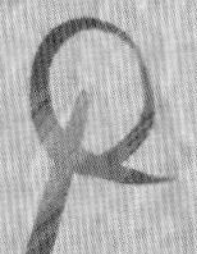

The True story, like the tools of deliverance, have been passed down to me by my mother, through her mother, and hers before her.

Soon, we will finally be free.

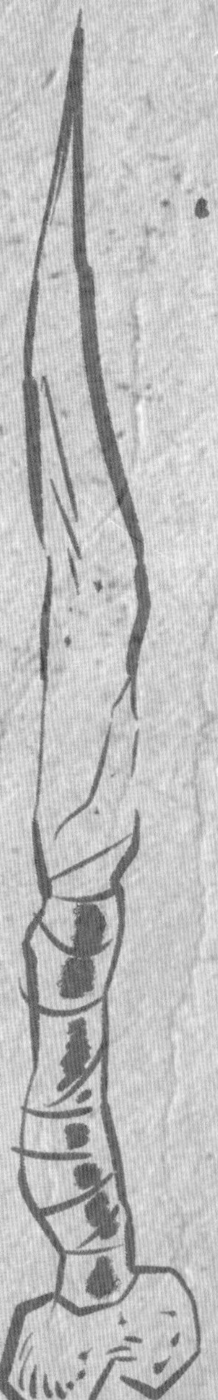

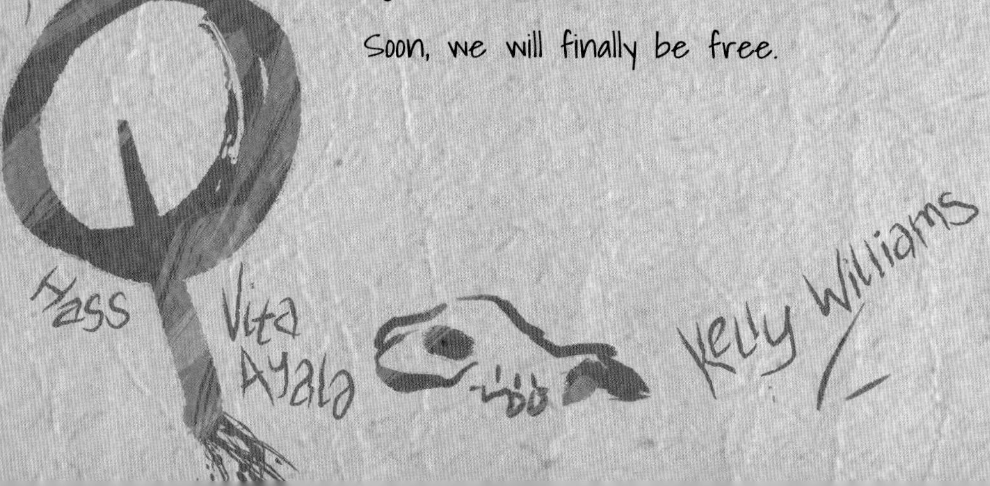
Hass
Vita Ayala
Kelly Williams

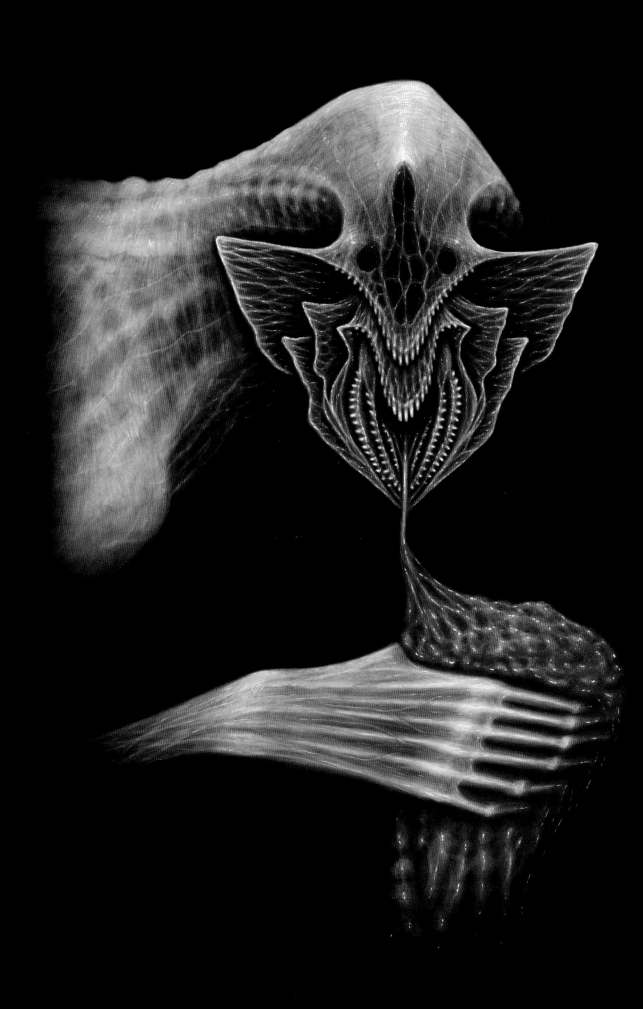

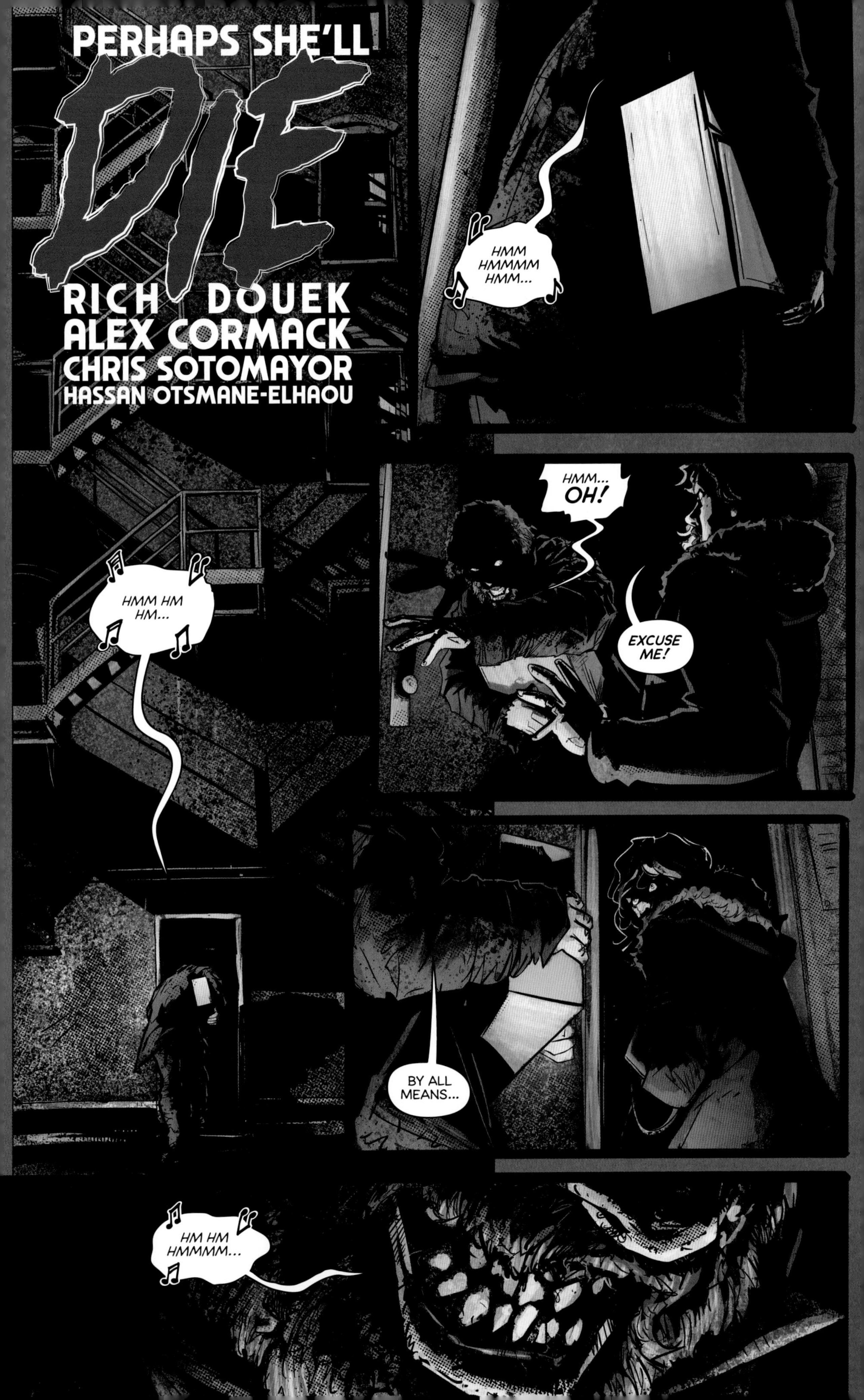
PERHAPS SHE'LL
DIE
RICH DOUEK
ALEX CORMACK
CHRIS SOTOMAYOR
HASSAN OTSMANE-ELHAOU
HMM HM HM...
HMM HMMMM HMM...
HMM... OH!
EXCUSE ME!
BY ALL MEANS...
HM HM HMMMM...

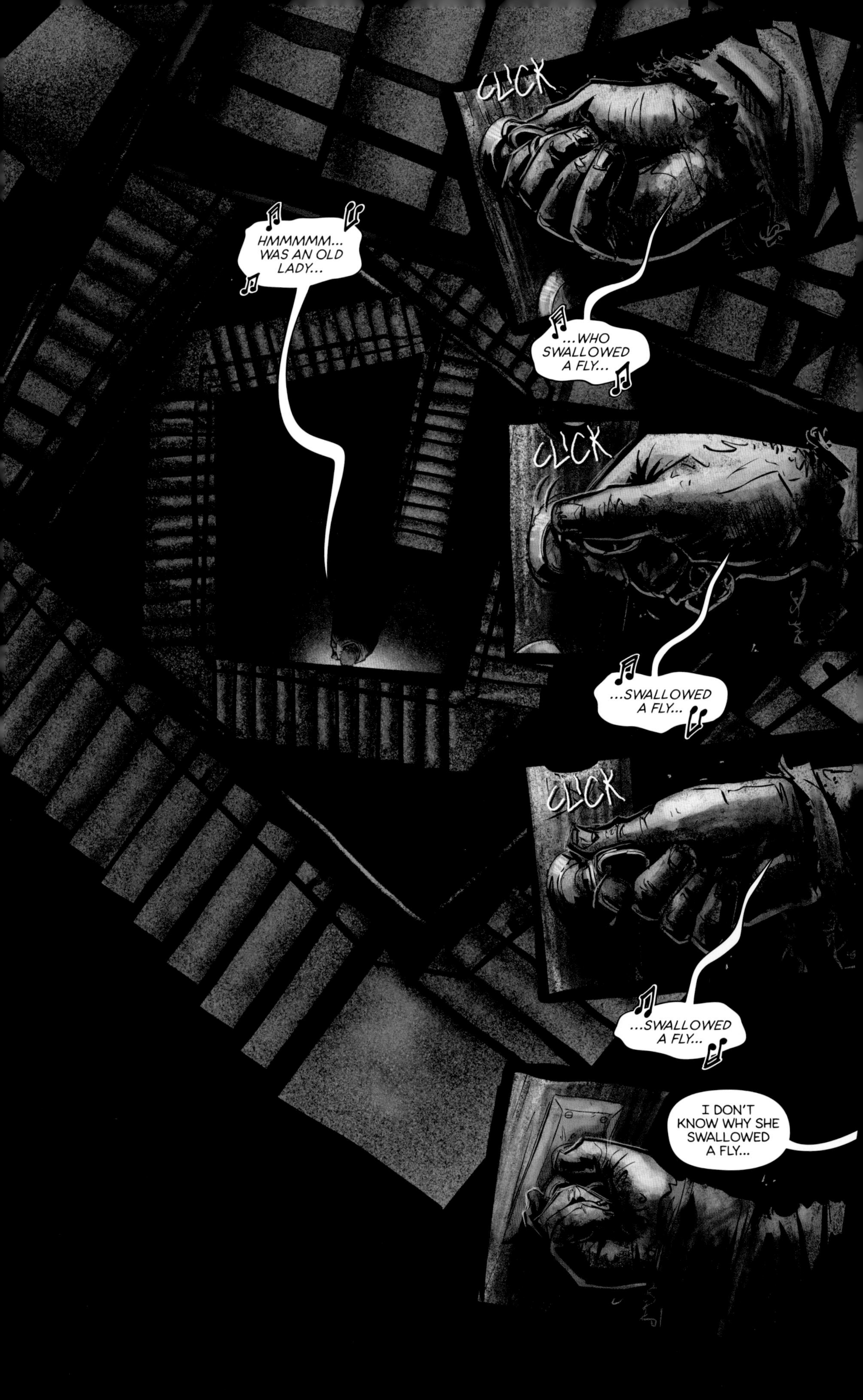
HMMMMM... WAS AN OLD LADY...
CLICK
...WHO SWALLOWED A FLY...
CLICK
...SWALLOWED A FLY...
CLICK
...SWALLOWED A FLY...
I DON'T KNOW WHY SHE SWALLOWED A FLY...

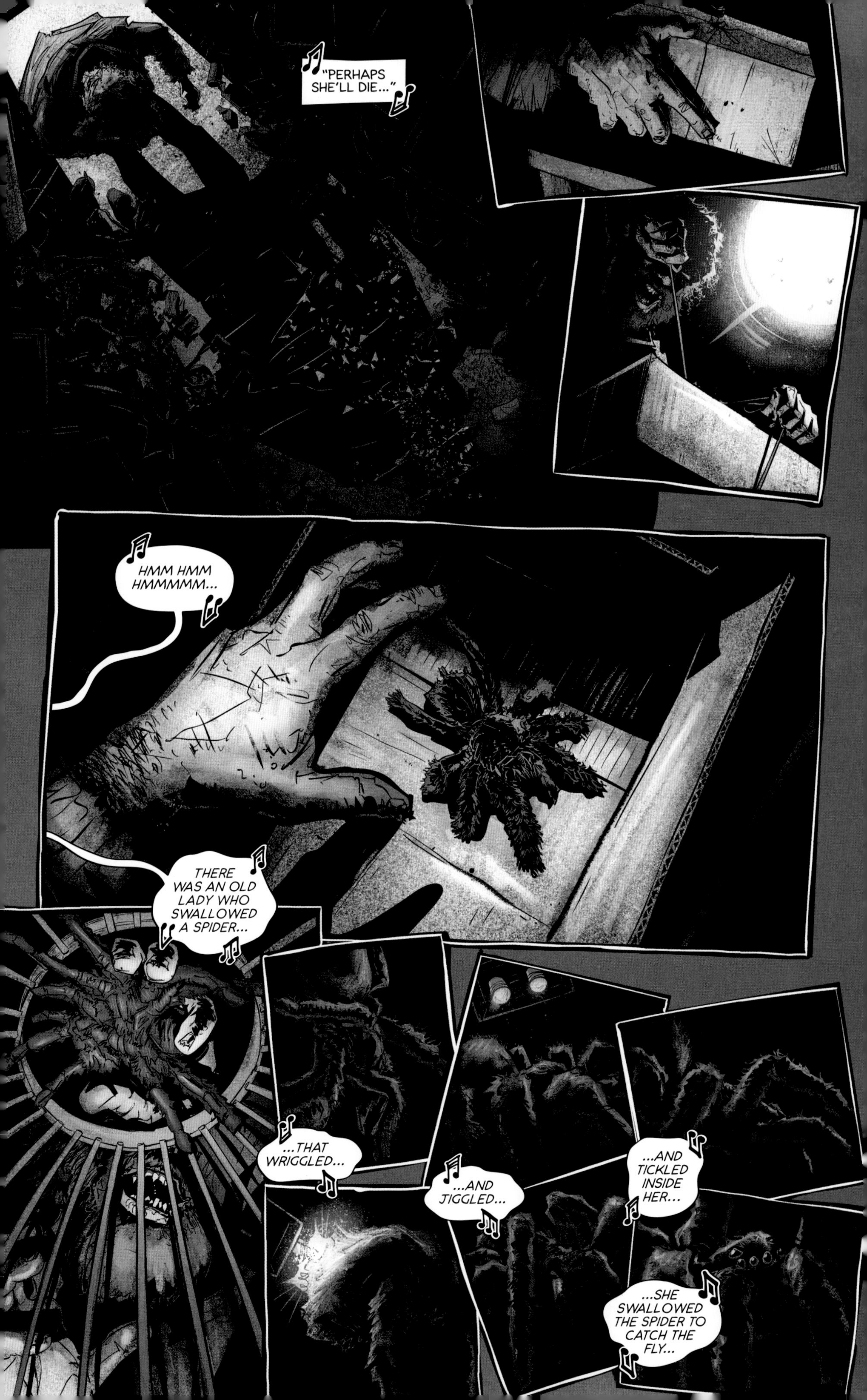
"PERHAPS SHE'LL DIE..."
HMM HMM HMMMMM...
THERE WAS AN OLD LADY WHO SWALLOWED A SPIDER...
...THAT WRIGGLED...
...AND JIGGLED...
...AND TICKLED INSIDE HER...
...SHE SWALLOWED THE SPIDER TO CATCH THE FLY...

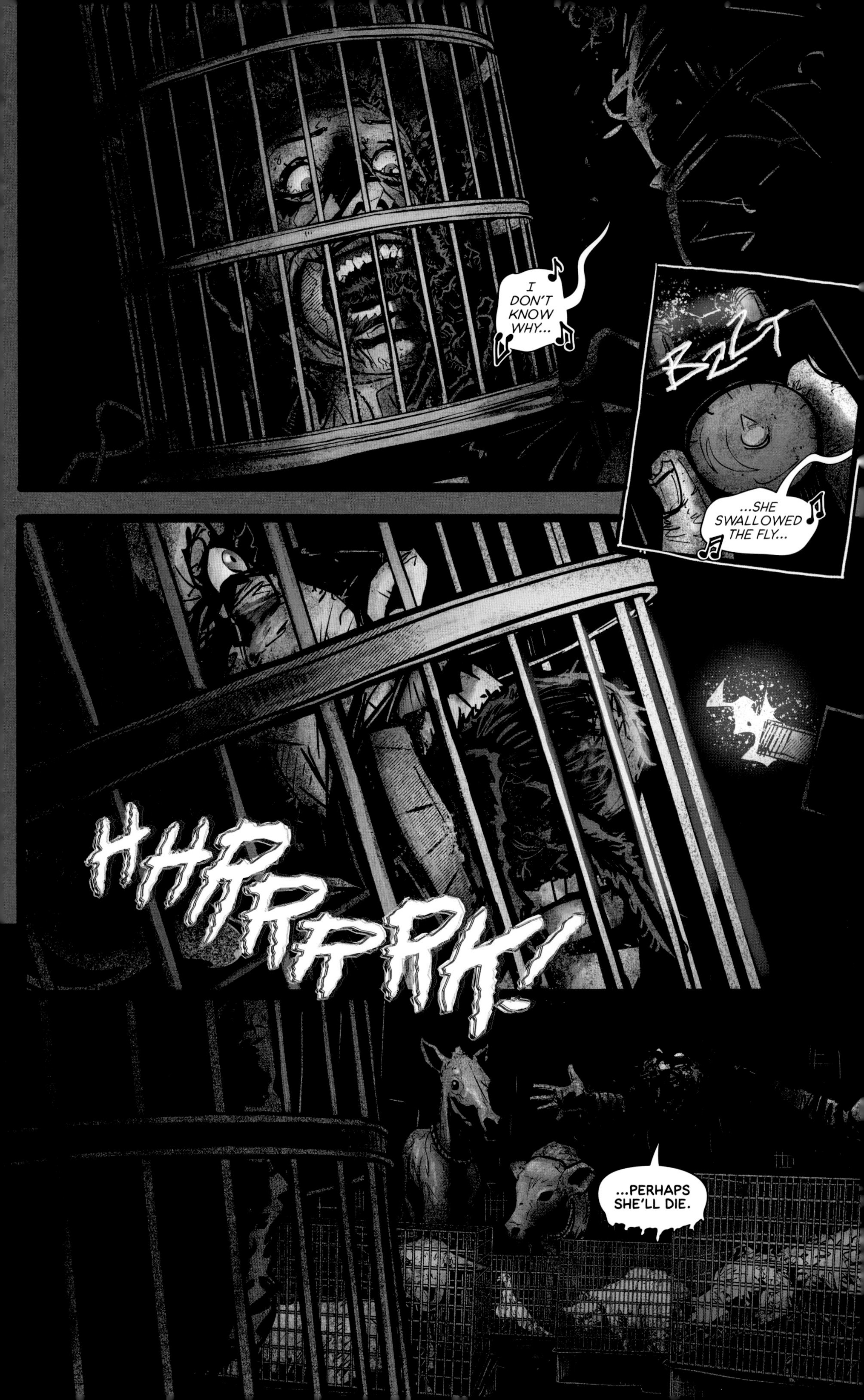
I DON'T KNOW WHY...
BZZT
...SHE SWALLOWED THE FLY...
HHRRRRK!
...PERHAPS SHE'LL DIE.

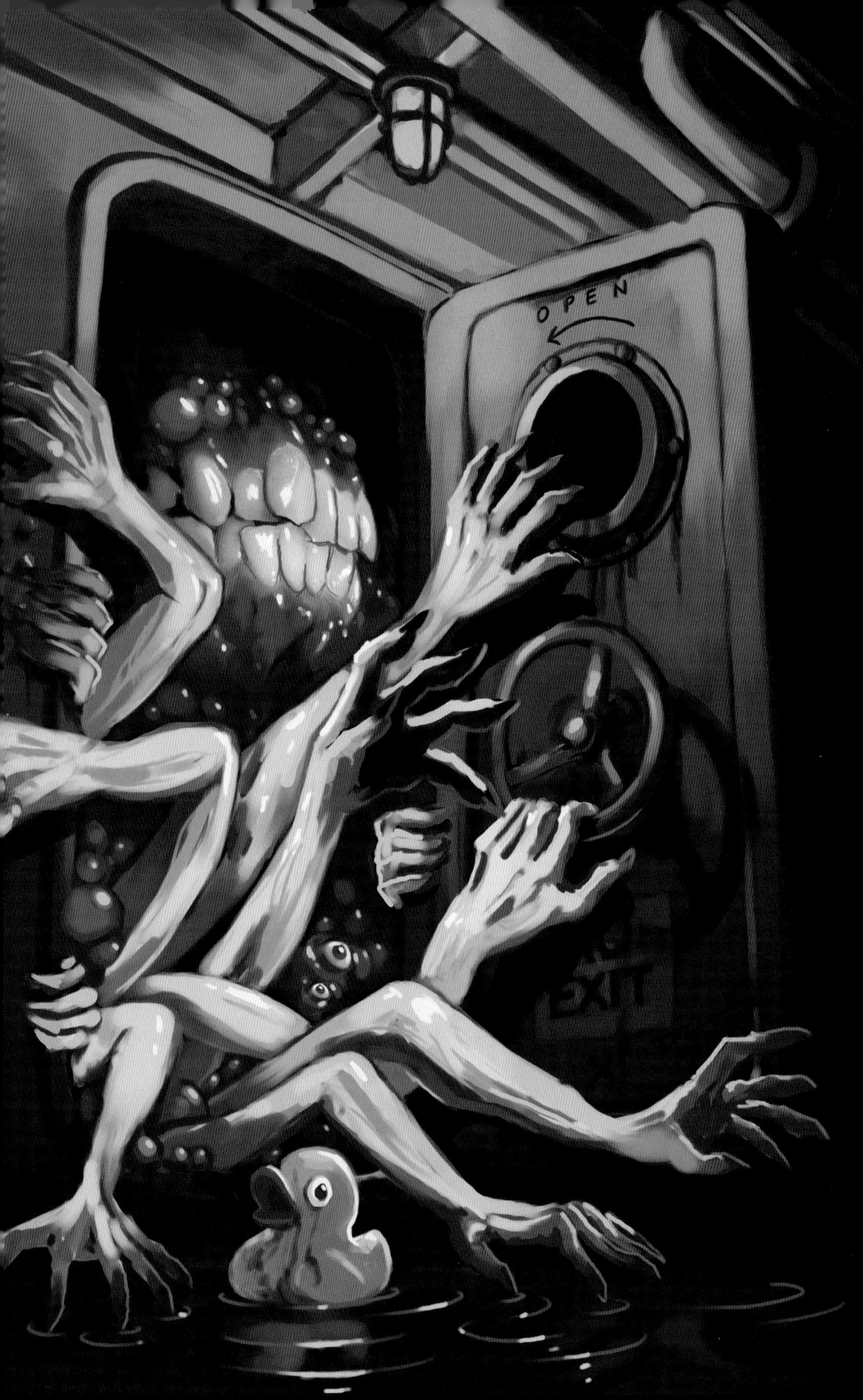
OPEN
EXIT

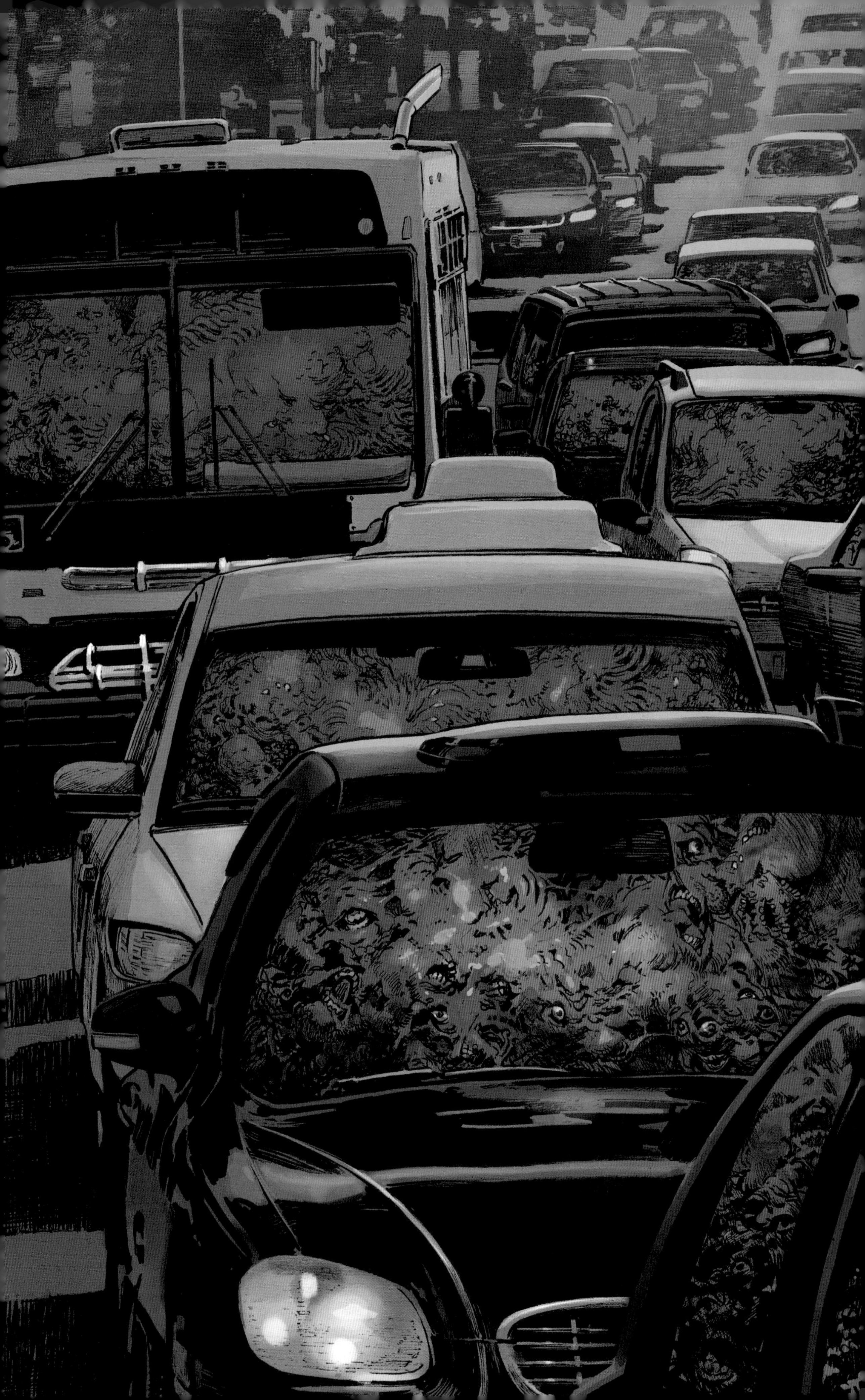

ISSUE #5

Cover Art By ALVARO MARTINEZ BUENO

"CLUB NIGHT"
By JAMES TYNION IV & LIANA KANGAS | *Lettered By* HASSAN OTSMANE-ELHAOU

"UNTITLED"
By SHINTARO KAGO

"ONE TUESDAY EVENING"
By PAUL HARRISON-DAVIES

"JUST RIDE IT OUT"
By EZRA CLAYTAN DANIELS

"MIDNIGHT SWIM"
By CHE GRAYSON & NAOMI FRANQUIZ | *Lettered By* HASSAN OTSMANE-ELHAOU

EXCERPT FROM "SLEEP STORIES"
By MICHAEL WALSH

"SELF-CARE"
Short Story By ALYSSA WONG | *Illustration By* AARON CAMPBELL

"THE TREE BY THE HILL"
By LESLÉ KIEU

"THE RIDE"
By JOHN J. PEARSON | *Lettered By* HASSAN OTSMANE-ELHAOU

"WATCHING YOU"
By VINCENZO RICCARDI

EXCERPT FROM "SLEEP STORIES"
By MICHAEL WALSH

"WE ARE ALL HERE"
By ZUZANNA KWIECIEN

"THE FINGER COLLECTOR"
By STEVE ORLANDO & ARTYOM TOPILIN | *Lettered By* HASSAN OTSMANE-ELHAOU

"PARASITOID"
By KHALIL VIVO

"THE DROWNED BOY"
By TREVOR HENDERSON

TREVOR HENDERSON MAKES MONSTERS:
TREVOR HENDERSON *Discusses His Creature Design Inspiration*

"THE PASSENGER"
By LONNIE NADLER, ZAC THOMPSON & IAN MCEWAN

EXCERPT FROM "SLEEP STORIES" *By* MICHAEL WALSH

"DIAMOND EYES"
By STEVE FOXE & PIOTR KOWALSKI | *Colored By* BRAD SIMPSON
Lettered By HASSAN OTSMANE-ELHAOU

"UNTITLED"
By CAM ADJODHA

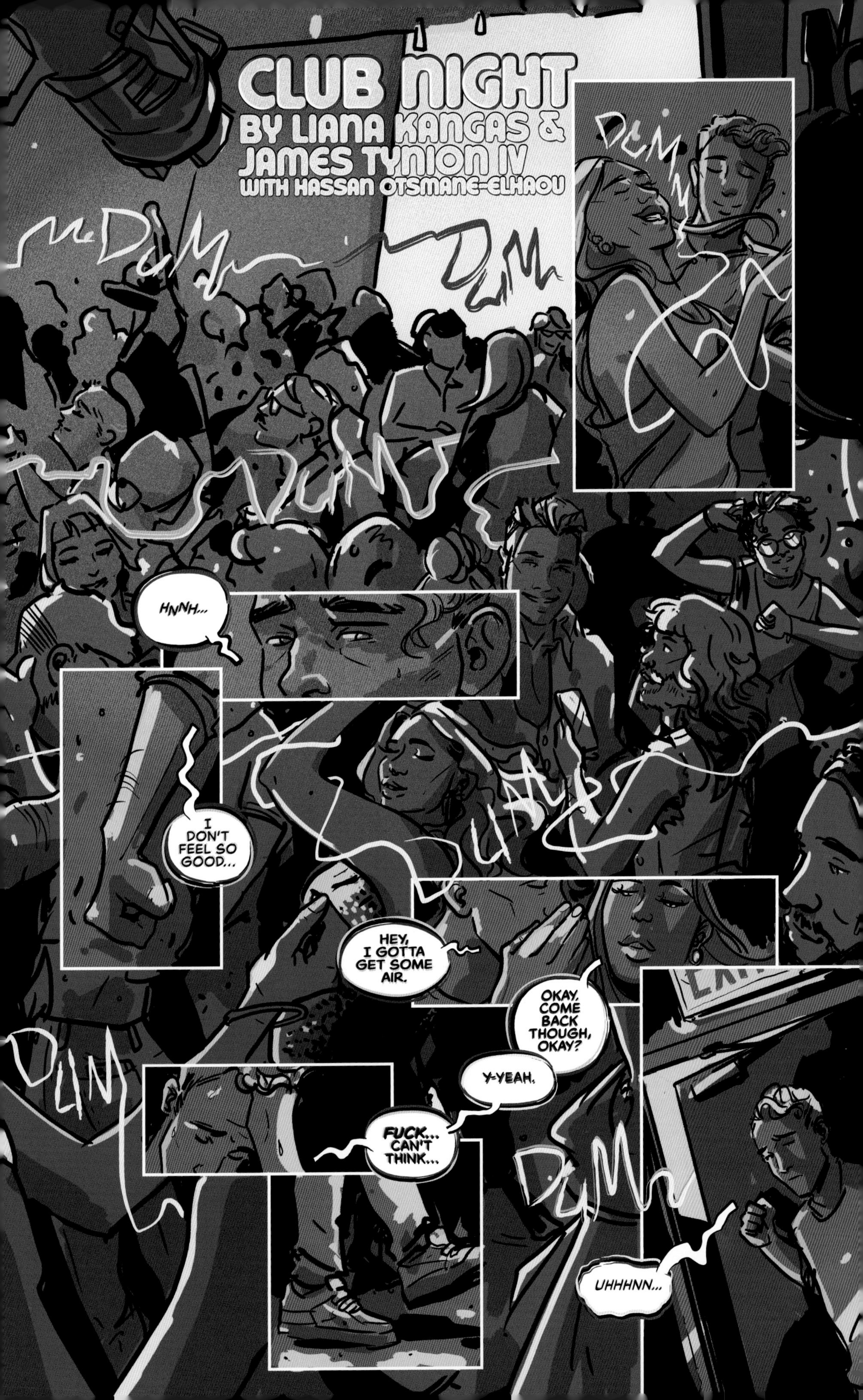
CLUB NIGHT
BY LIANA KANGAS & JAMES TYNION IV
WITH HASSAN OTSMANE-ELHAOU
DUM
DUM
DUM
DUM
HNNH...
I DON'T FEEL SO GOOD...
DUM
HEY, I GOTTA GET SOME AIR.
OKAY. COME BACK THOUGH, OKAY?
Y-YEAH.
DUM
FUCK... CAN'T THINK...
DUM
UHHHNN...

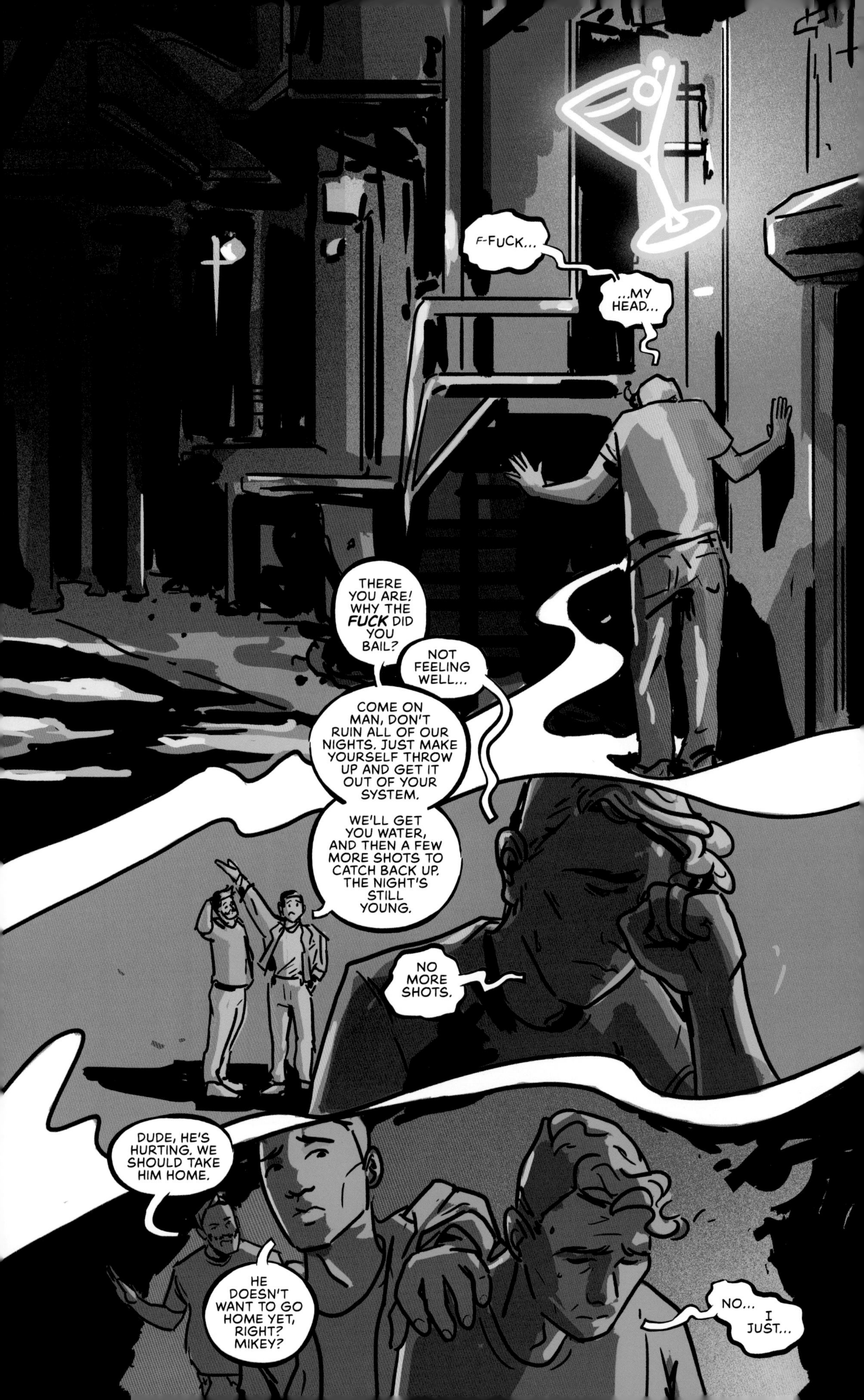
F-FUCK...
...MY HEAD...
THERE YOU ARE! WHY THE FUCK DID YOU BAIL?
NOT FEELING WELL...
COME ON MAN, DON'T RUIN ALL OF OUR NIGHTS. JUST MAKE YOURSELF THROW UP AND GET IT OUT OF YOUR SYSTEM.
WE'LL GET YOU WATER, AND THEN A FEW MORE SHOTS TO CATCH BACK UP. THE NIGHT'S STILL YOUNG.
NO MORE SHOTS.
DUDE, HE'S HURTING. WE SHOULD TAKE HIM HOME.
HE DOESN'T WANT TO GO HOME YET, RIGHT? MIKEY?
NO... I JUST...

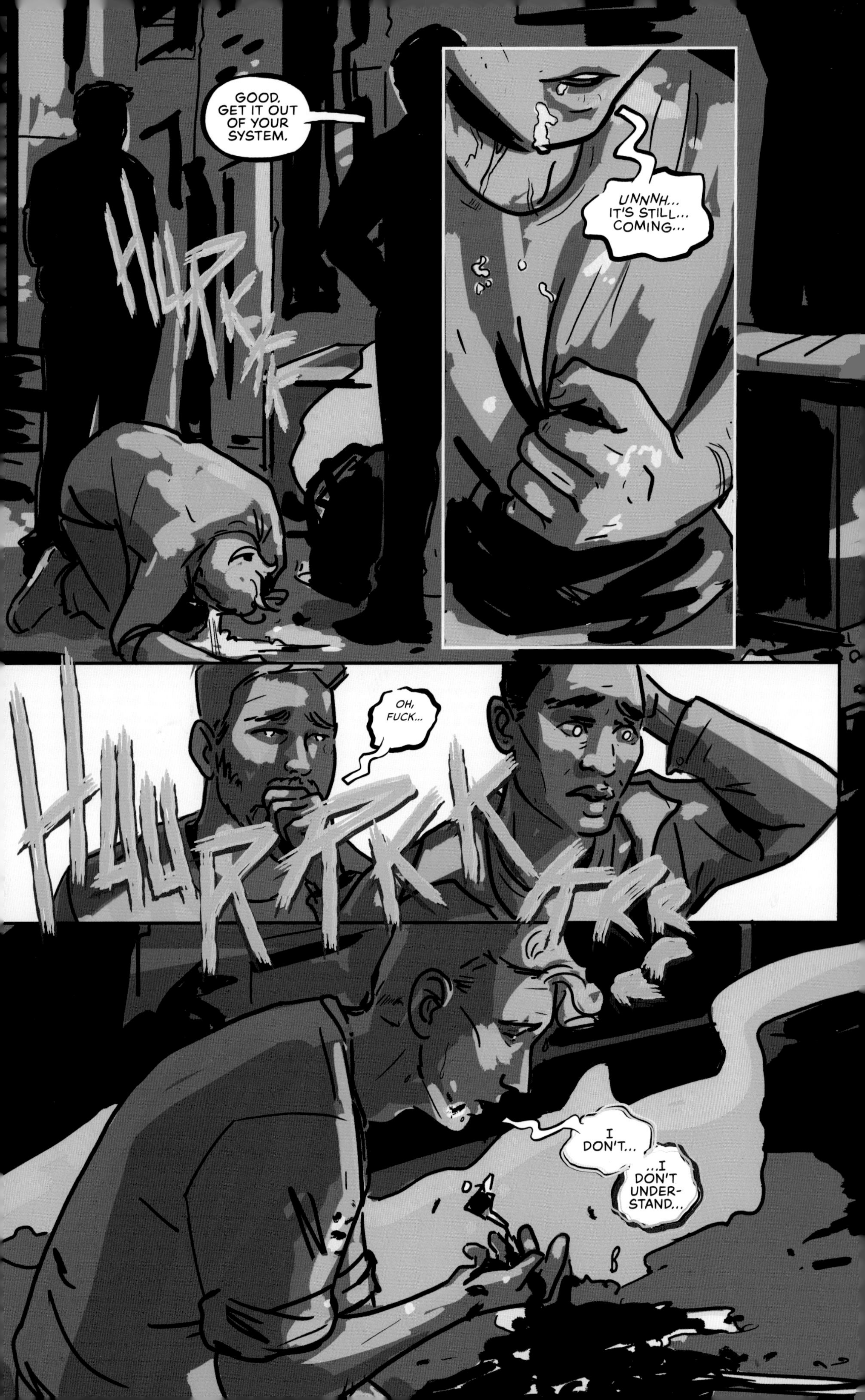
GOOD, GET IT OUT OF YOUR SYSTEM.
HURKKK
UNNNH... IT'S STILL... COMING...
HUURRKKKRR
OH, FUCK...
I DON'T...
...I DON'T UNDER-STAND...

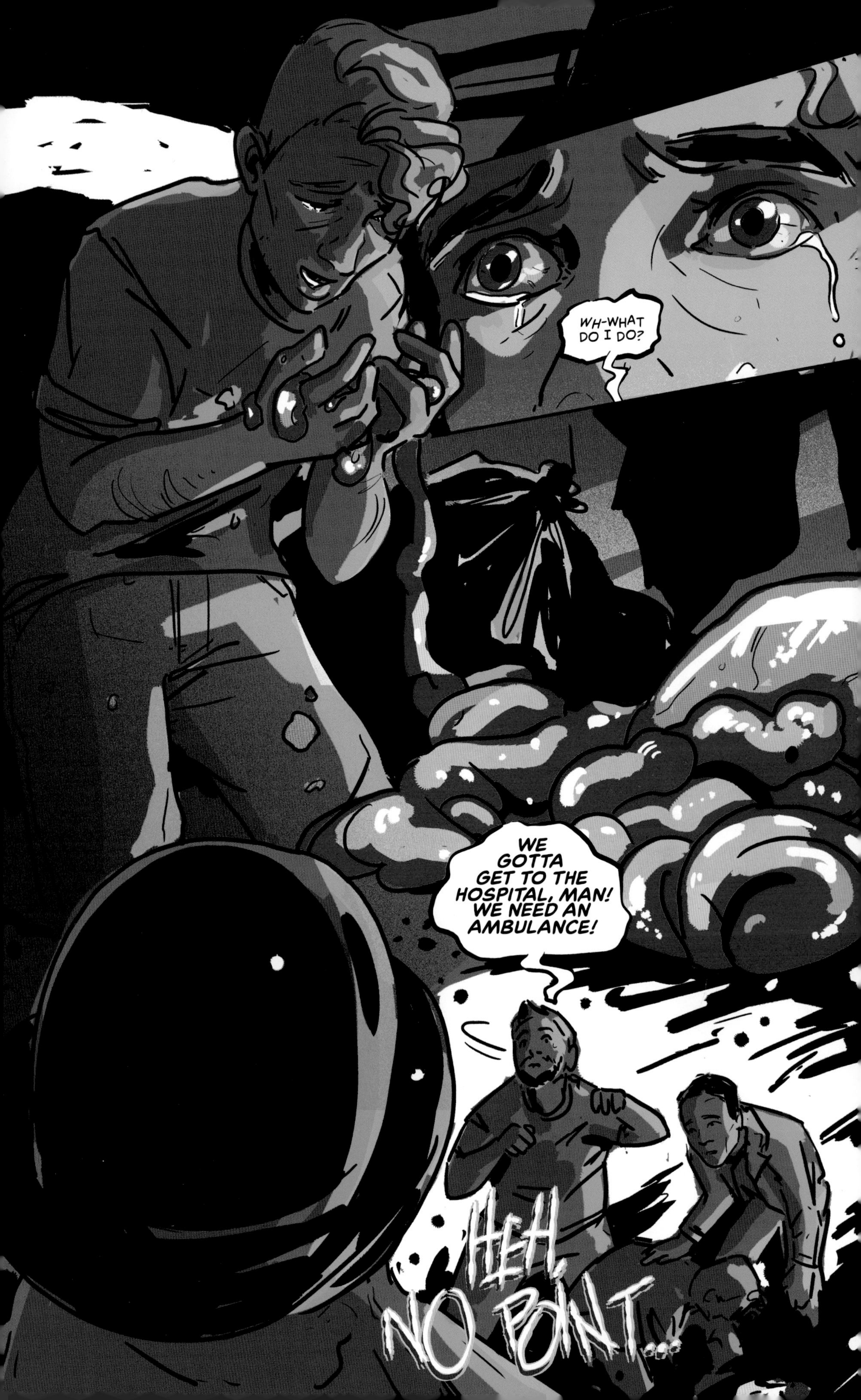
WH-WHAT DO I DO?
WE GOTTA GET TO THE HOSPITAL, MAN! WE NEED AN AMBULANCE!
HEH. NO POINT...

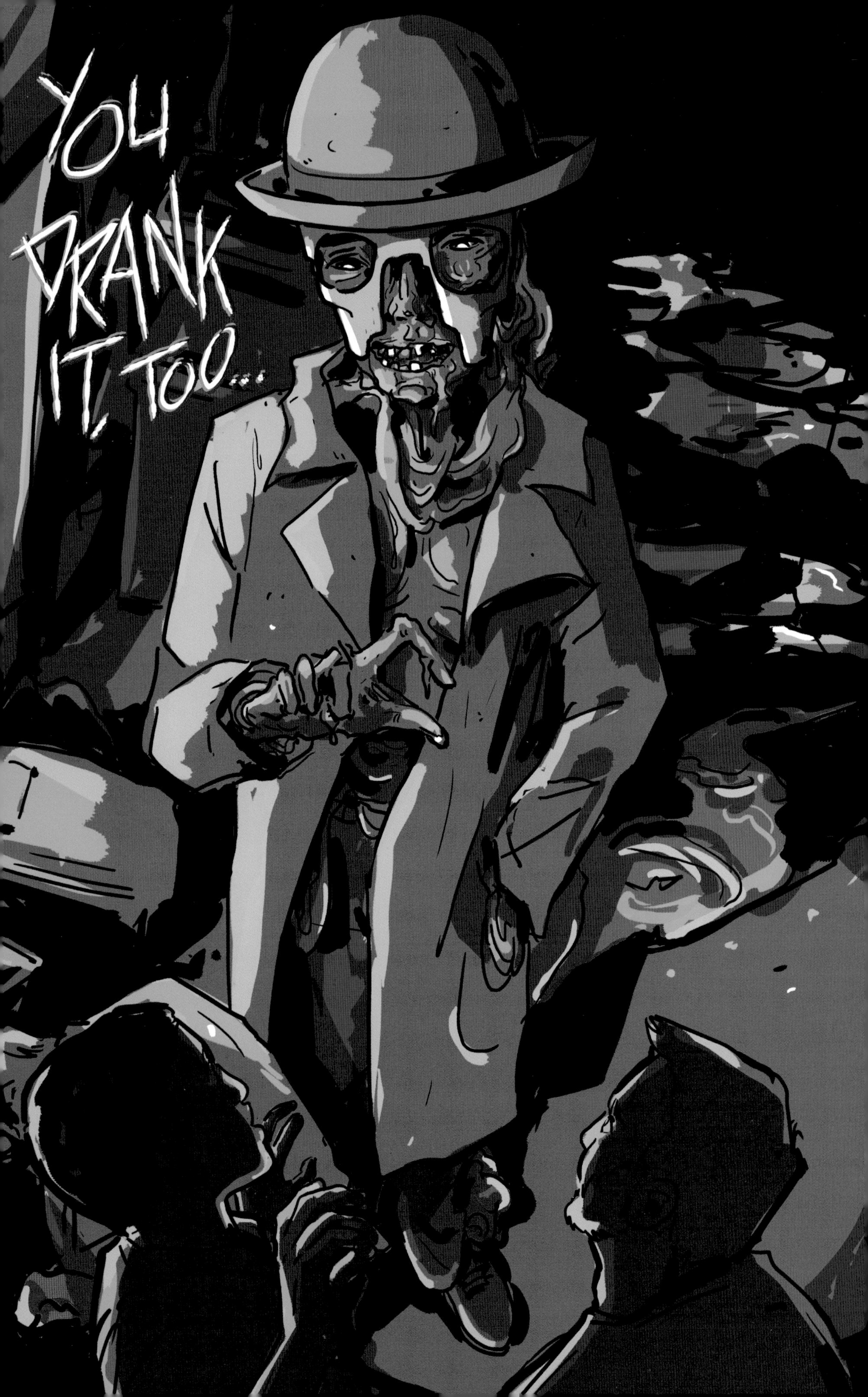
YOU DRANK IT, TOO...

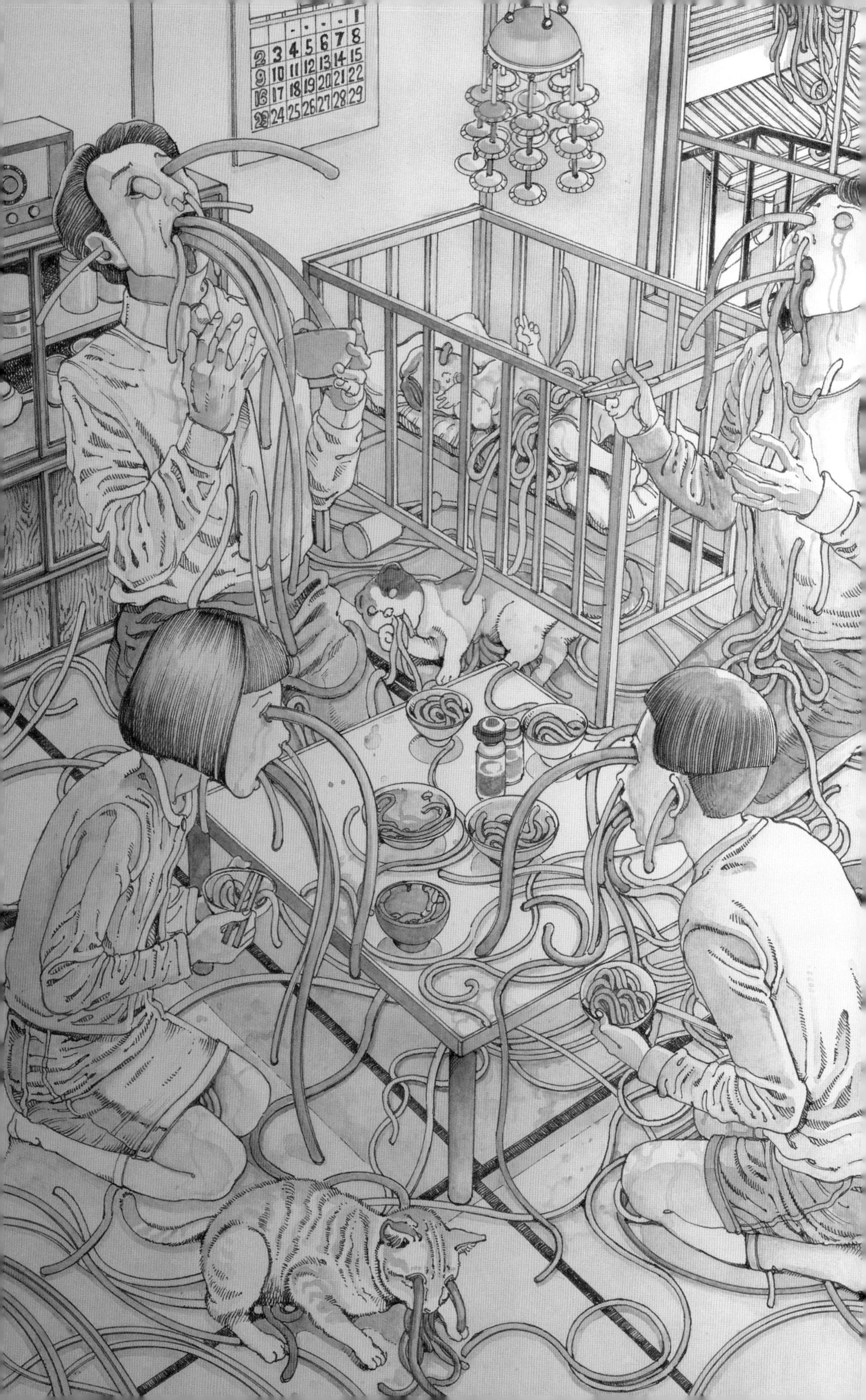

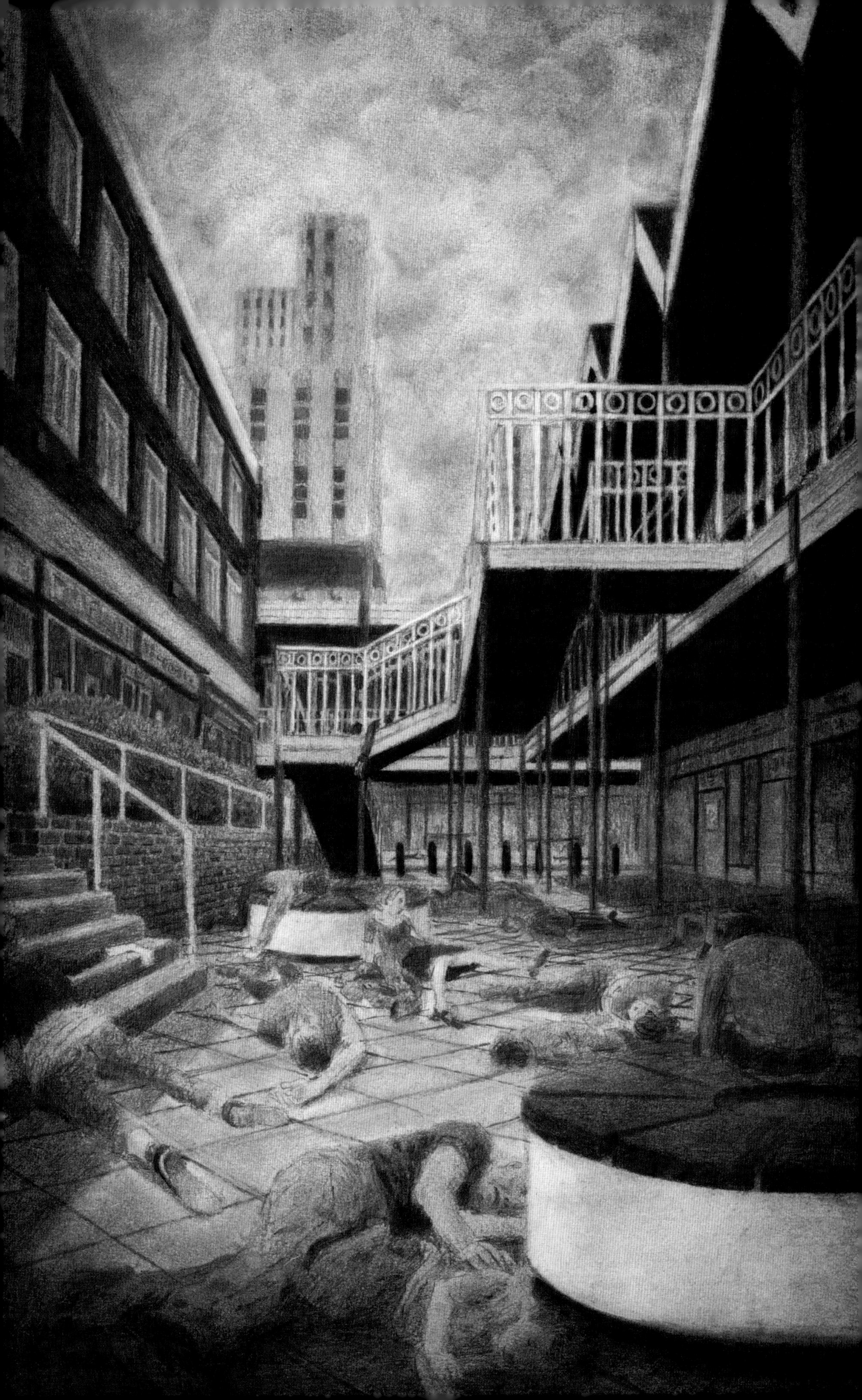

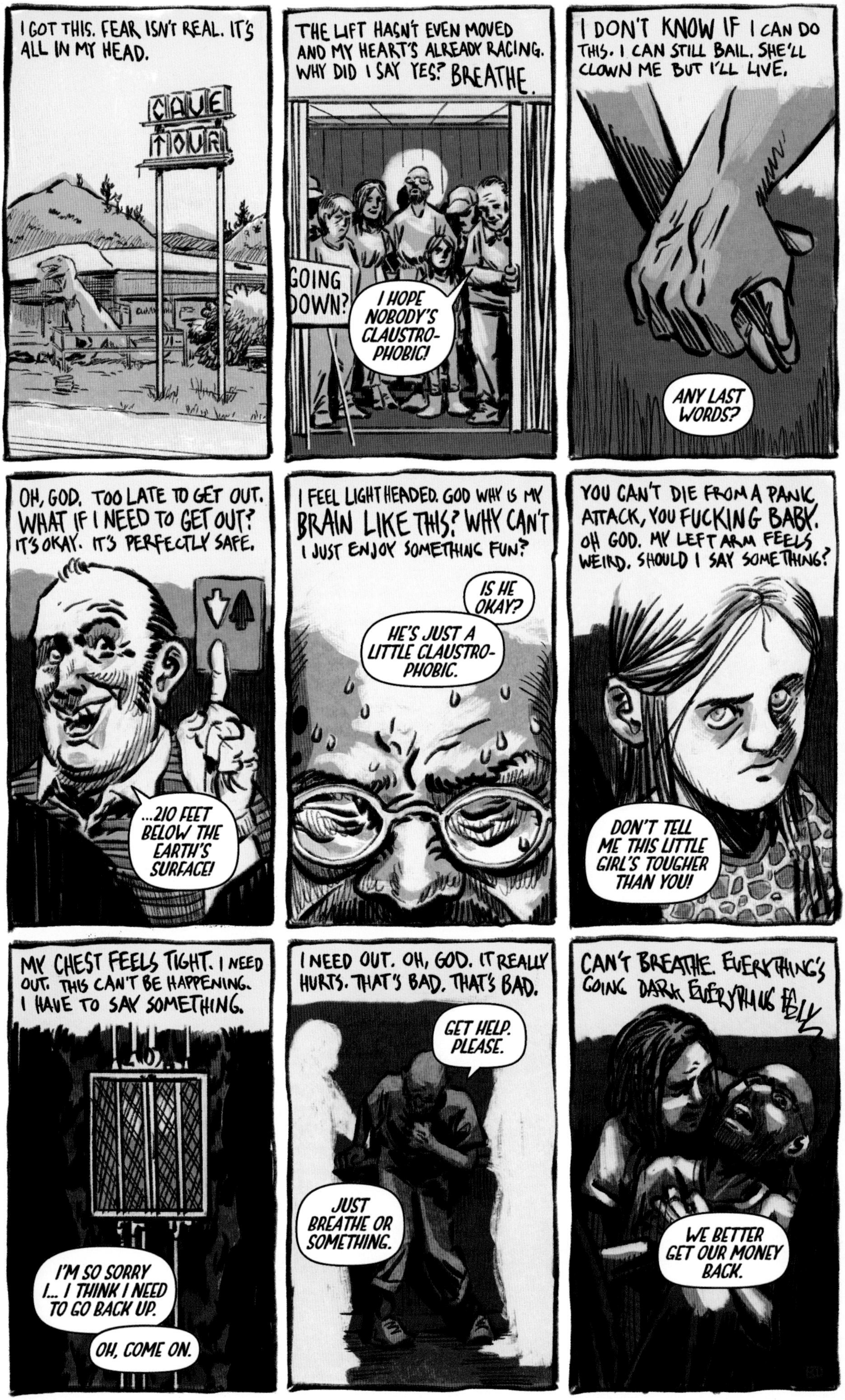
I GOT THIS. FEAR ISN'T REAL. IT'S ALL IN MY HEAD.
CAVE TOUR
THE LIFT HASN'T EVEN MOVED AND MY HEART'S ALREADY RACING. WHY DID I SAY YES? BREATHE.
GOING DOWN?
I HOPE NOBODY'S CLAUSTROPHOBIC!
I DON'T KNOW IF I CAN DO THIS. I CAN STILL BAIL. SHE'LL CLOWN ME BUT I'LL LIVE.
ANY LAST WORDS?
OH, GOD. TOO LATE TO GET OUT. WHAT IF I NEED TO GET OUT? IT'S OKAY. IT'S PERFECTLY SAFE.
...210 FEET BELOW THE EARTH'S SURFACE!
I FEEL LIGHTHEADED. GOD WHY IS MY BRAIN LIKE THIS? WHY CAN'T I JUST ENJOY SOMETHING FUN?
IS HE OKAY?
HE'S JUST A LITTLE CLAUSTROPHOBIC.
YOU CAN'T DIE FROM A PANIC ATTACK, YOU FUCKING BABY. OH GOD. MY LEFT ARM FEELS WEIRD. SHOULD I SAY SOMETHING?
DON'T TELL ME THIS LITTLE GIRL'S TOUGHER THAN YOU!
MY CHEST FEELS TIGHT. I NEED OUT. THIS CAN'T BE HAPPENING. I HAVE TO SAY SOMETHING.
I'M SO SORRY I... I THINK I NEED TO GO BACK UP.
OH, COME ON.
I NEED OUT. OH, GOD. IT REALLY HURTS. THAT'S BAD. THAT'S BAD.
GET HELP. PLEASE.
JUST BREATHE OR SOMETHING.
CAN'T BREATHE. EVERYTHING'S GOING DARK EVERYTHING
WE BETTER GET OUR MONEY BACK.

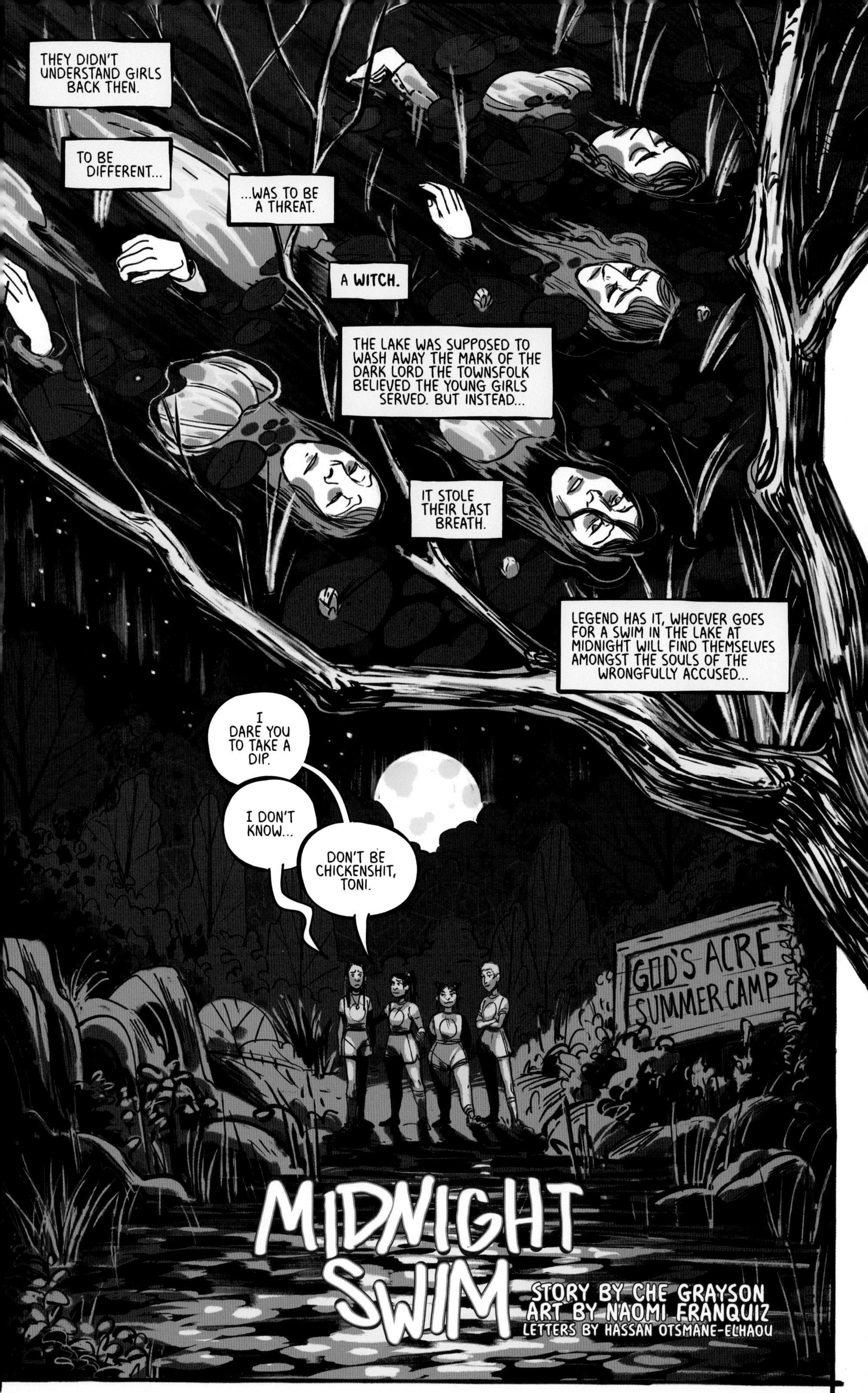
THEY DIDN'T UNDERSTAND GIRLS BACK THEN.
TO BE DIFFERENT...
...WAS TO BE A THREAT.
A WITCH.
THE LAKE WAS SUPPOSED TO WASH AWAY THE MARK OF THE DARK LORD THE TOWNSFOLK BELIEVED THE YOUNG GIRLS SERVED. BUT INSTEAD...
IT STOLE THEIR LAST BREATH.
LEGEND HAS IT, WHOEVER GOES FOR A SWIM IN THE LAKE AT MIDNIGHT WILL FIND THEMSELVES AMONGST THE SOULS OF THE WRONGFULLY ACCUSED...
I DARE YOU TO TAKE A DIP.
I DON'T KNOW...
DON'T BE CHICKENSHIT, TONI.
GOD'S ACRE SUMMER CAMP
MIDNIGHT SWIM
STORY BY CHE GRAYSON
ART BY NAOMI FRANQUIZ
LETTERS BY HASSAN OTSMANE-ELHAOU

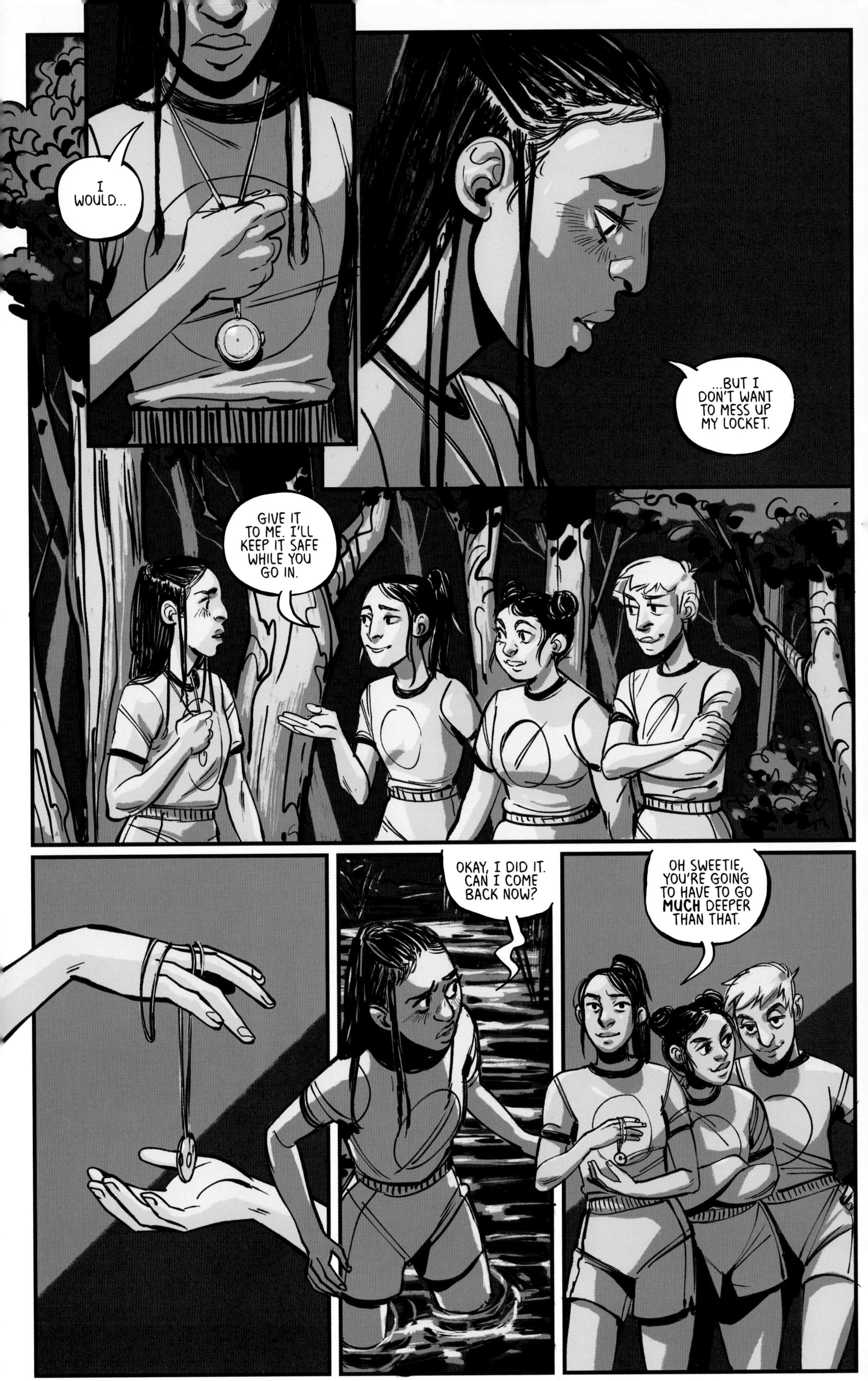
I WOULD...
...BUT I DON'T WANT TO MESS UP MY LOCKET.
GIVE IT TO ME. I'LL KEEP IT SAFE WHILE YOU GO IN.
OKAY, I DID IT. CAN I COME BACK NOW?
OH SWEETIE, YOU'RE GOING TO HAVE TO GO **MUCH** DEEPER THAN THAT.

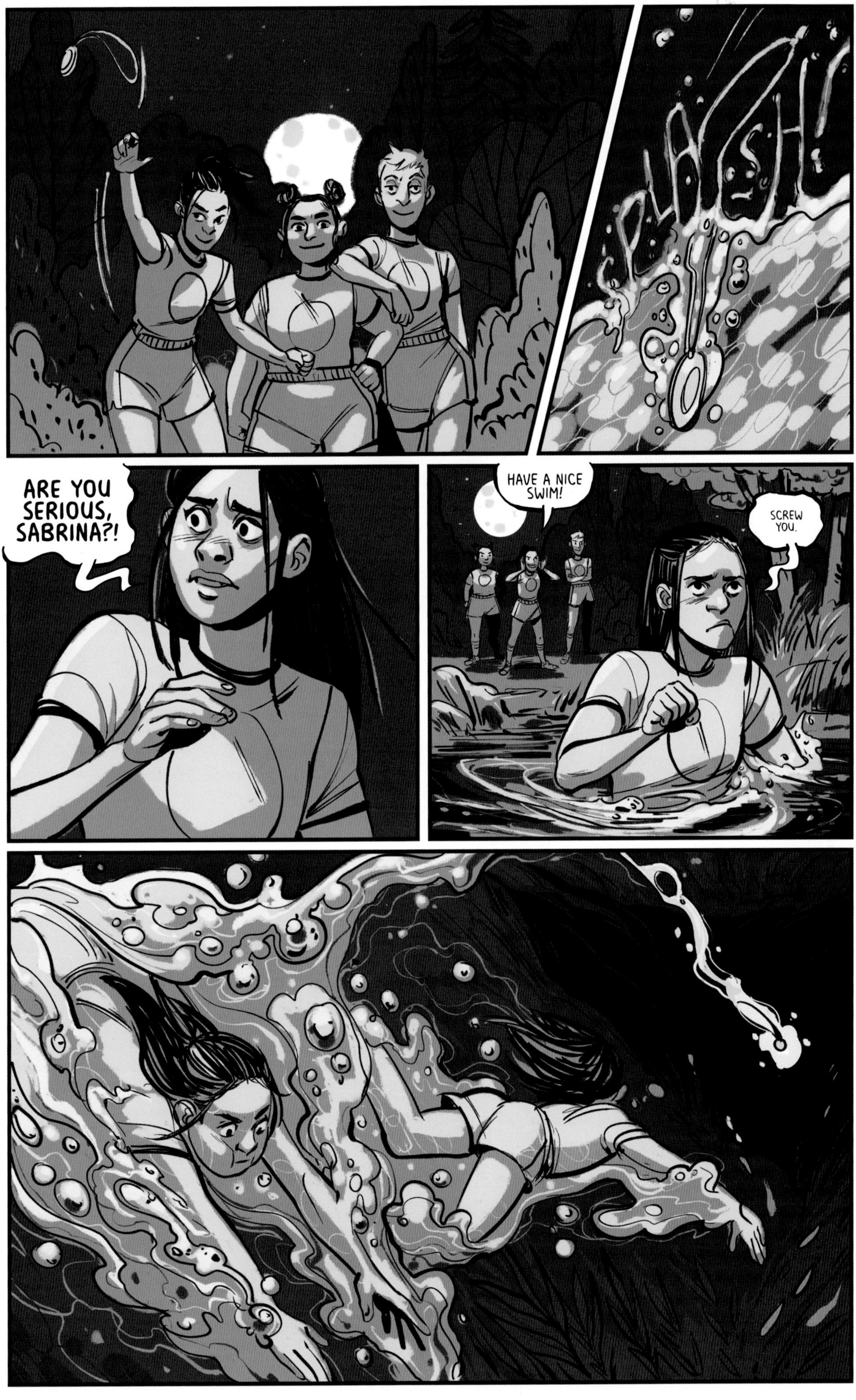
SPLASH!
ARE YOU SERIOUS, SABRINA?!
HAVE A NICE SWIM!
SCREW YOU.

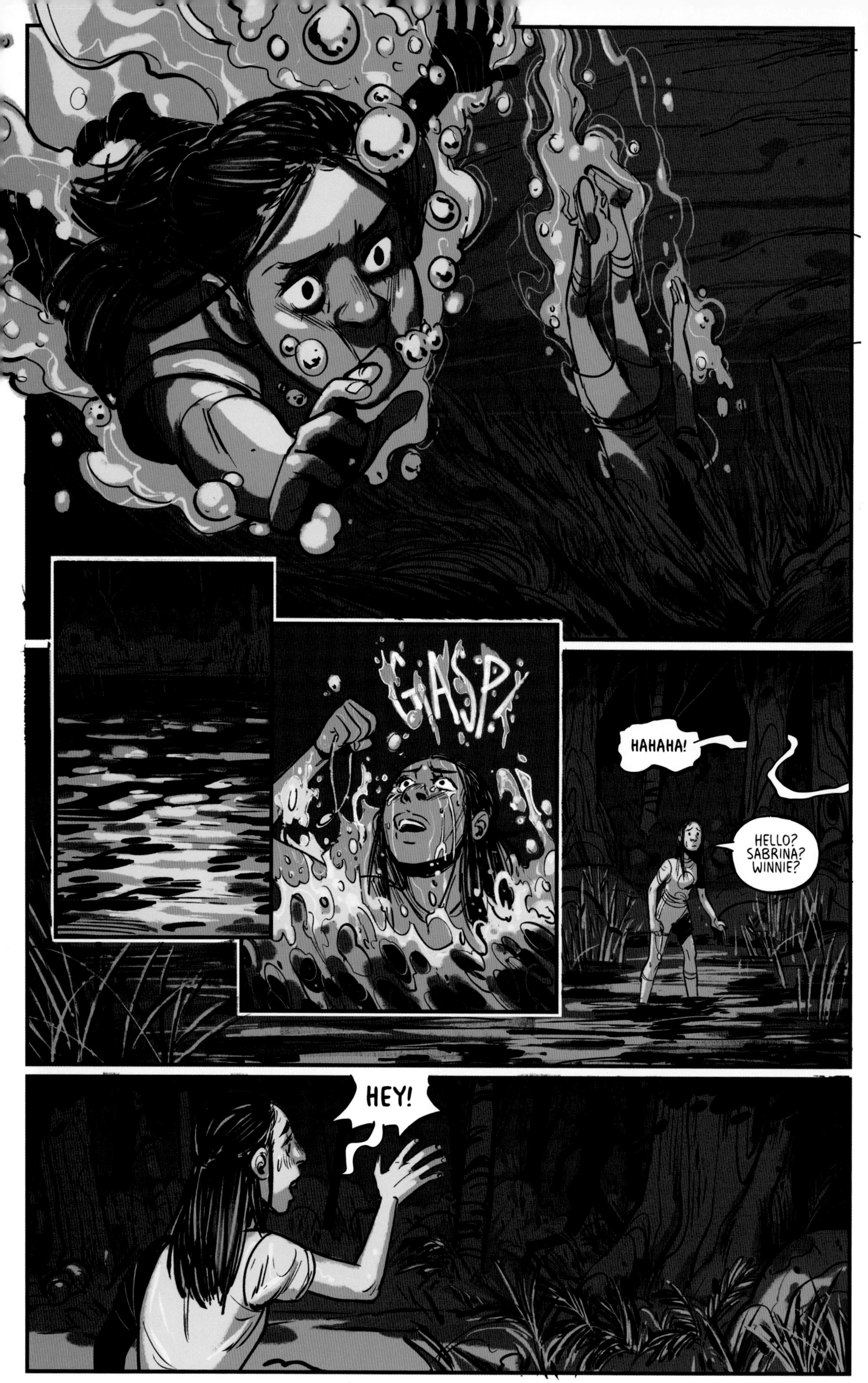
GASP!
HAHAHA!
HELLO? SABRINA? WINNIE?
HEY!

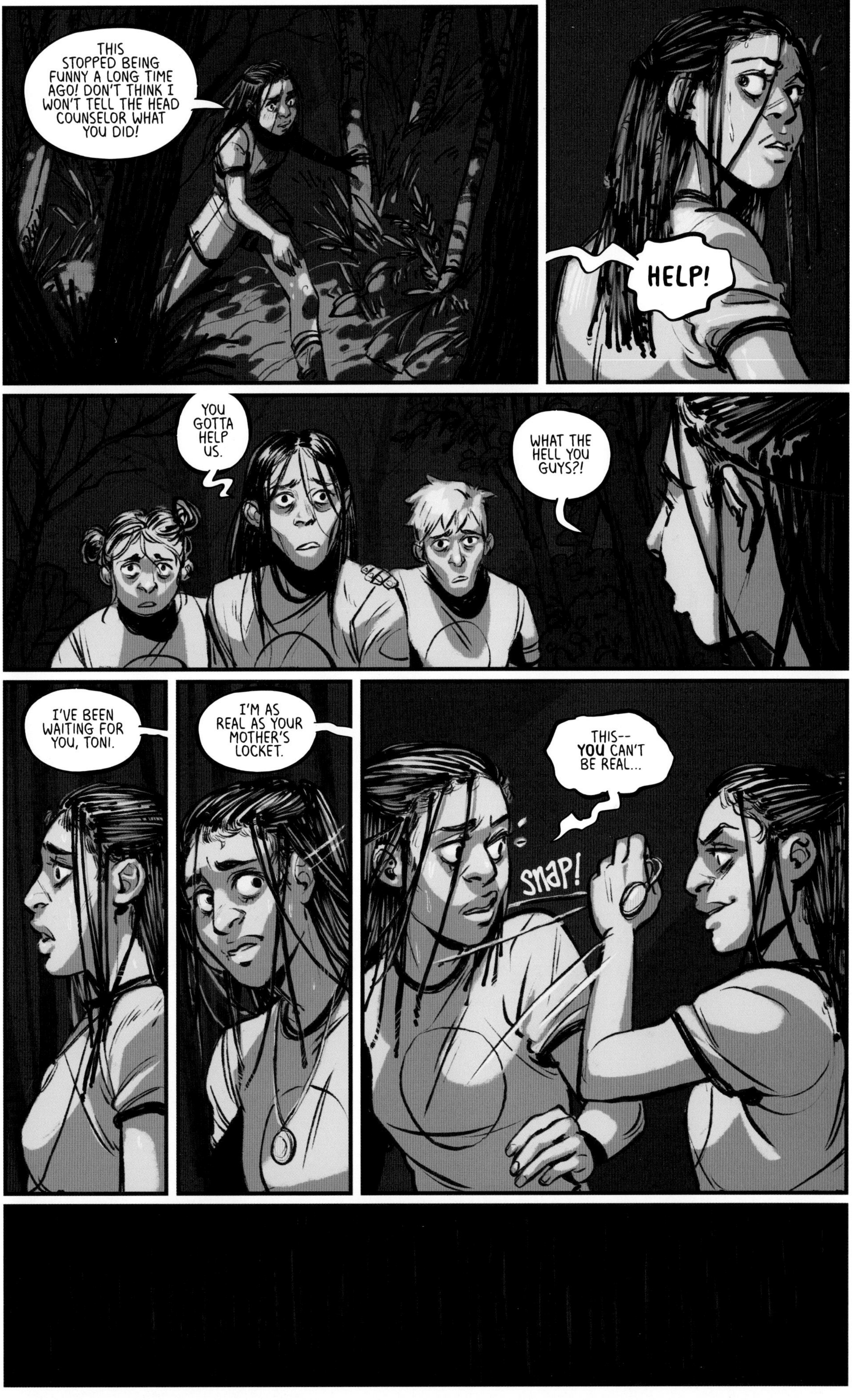
THIS STOPPED BEING FUNNY A LONG TIME AGO! DON'T THINK I WON'T TELL THE HEAD COUNSELOR WHAT YOU DID!
HELP!
YOU GOTTA HELP US.
WHAT THE HELL YOU GUYS?!
I'VE BEEN WAITING FOR YOU, TONI.
I'M AS REAL AS YOUR MOTHER'S LOCKET.
THIS-- **YOU** CAN'T BE REAL...
SNAP!

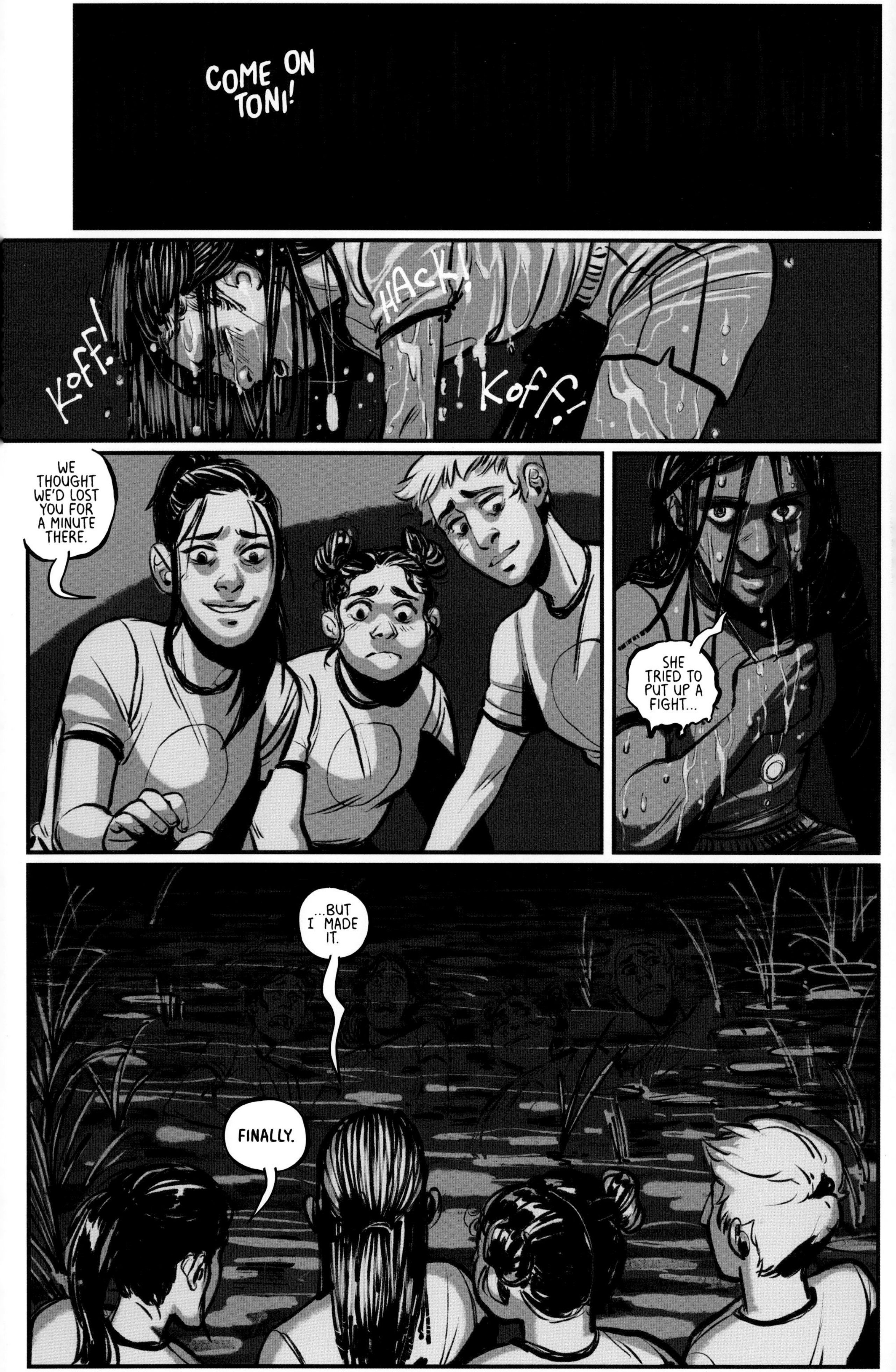
COME ON TONI!
KOFF!
HACK!
KOFF!
WE THOUGHT WE'D LOST YOU FOR A MINUTE THERE.
SHE TRIED TO PUT UP A FIGHT...
...BUT I MADE IT.
FINALLY.

THE **CORNER MAN** WAITS.

IN THE MIDDLE OF THE NIGHT, ON MY WAY TO THE BATHROOM,
WHEN THE FUZZY SHAPES MOVE AND MOLD IN SLIVERS OF LIGHT.

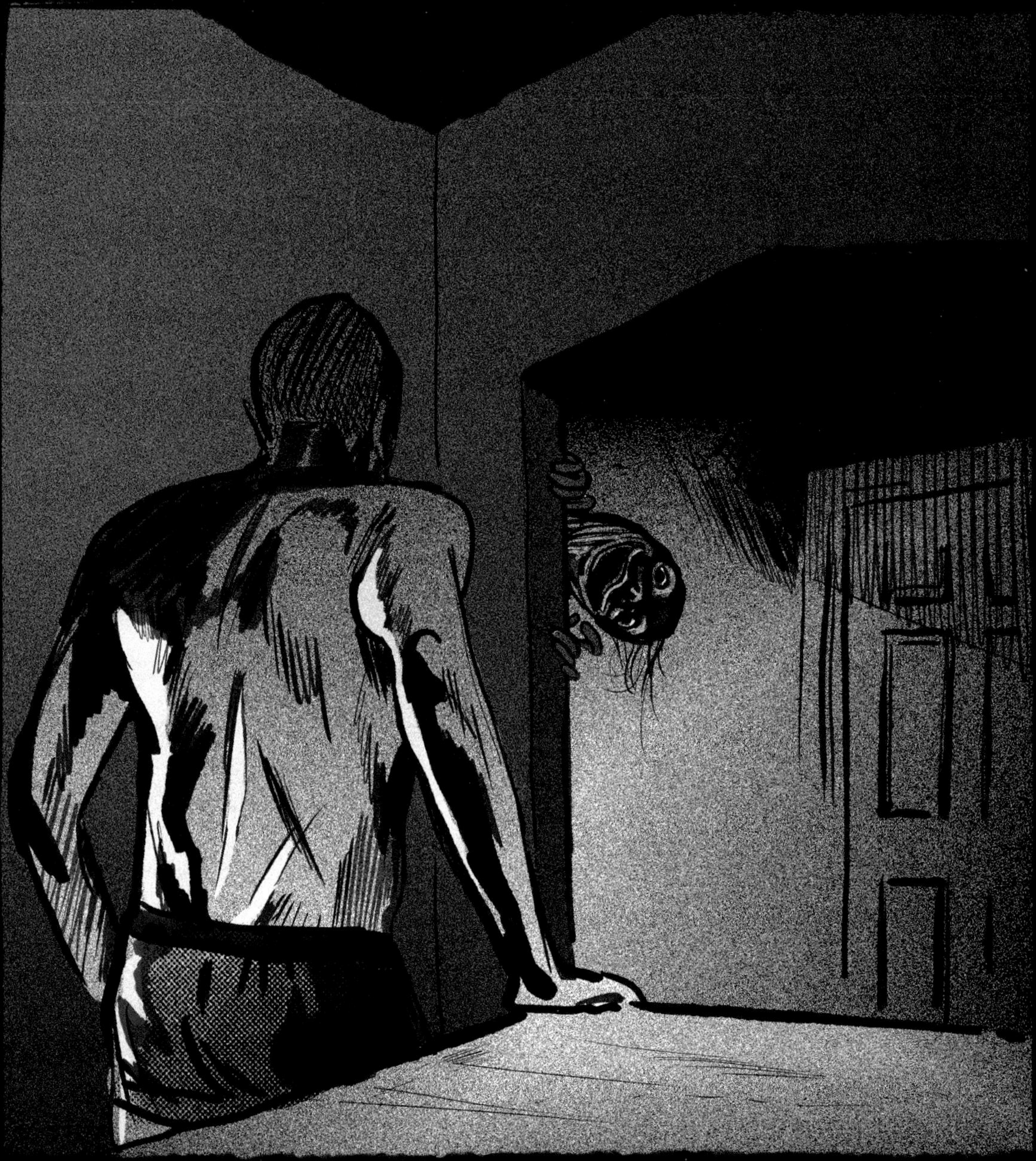

HIS GIGGLE SOUNDS LIKE **GLASS**.

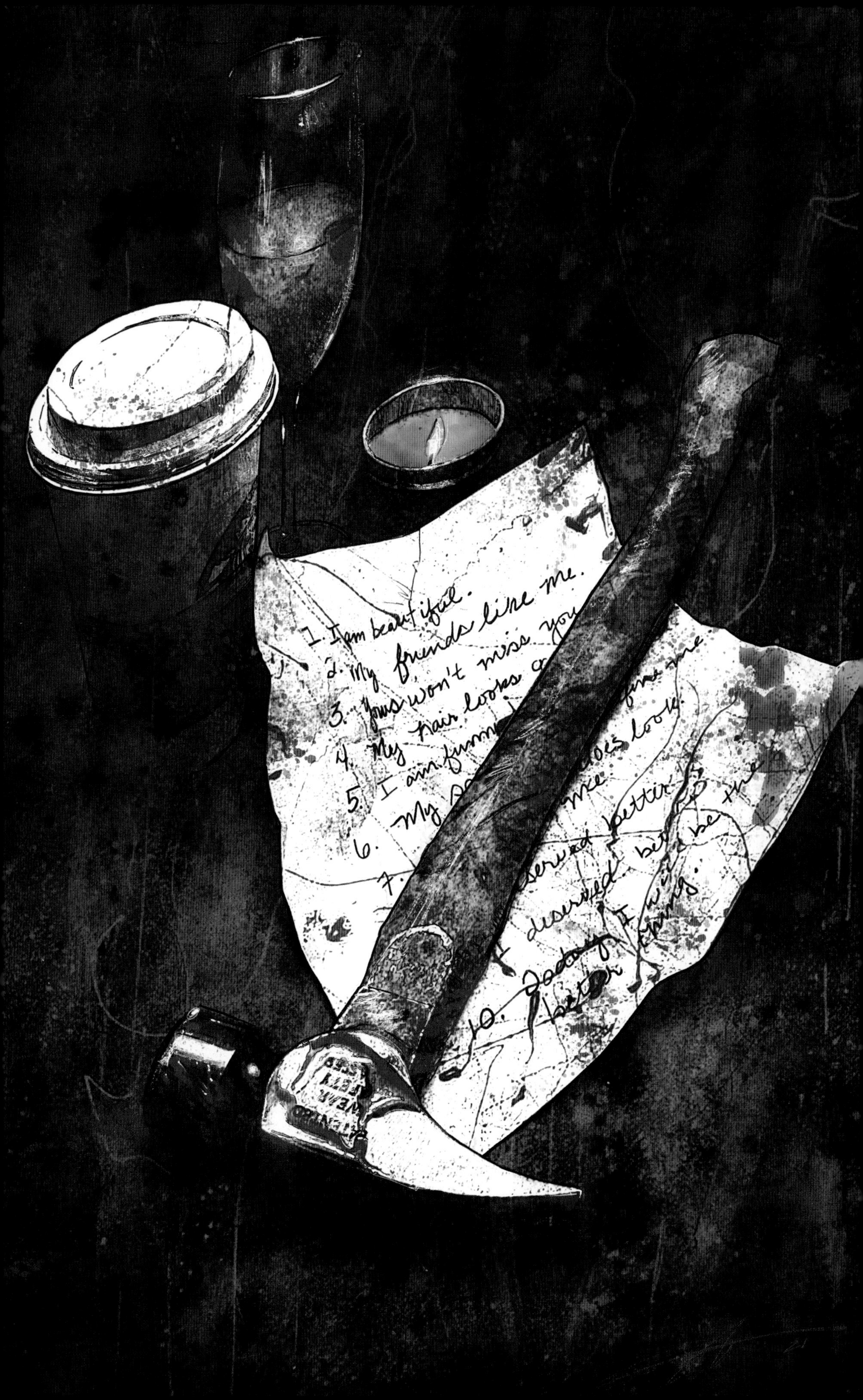
1. I am beautiful.
2. My friends like me.
3. Yous won't miss you
4. My hair looks
5. I am
6.
7.
deserved better
10. Today I will be the

SELF-CARE

WRITTEN BY ALYSSA WONG
ILLUSTRATION BY AARON CAMPBELL

Start with the knees. Aim to incapacitate, but remember that you're here to have fun! Work out that tension in your shoulders and arms. This should leave you feeling refreshed and ready to tackle the day.

Lean into the swinging motion, and breathe mindfully. In through your nose, out through your mouth. A relaxing, meditative breathing pattern helps cleanse your mind of anxiety. You should be able to feel your energy traveling through your body: gathering in your chest as you inhale, then traveling down to your fingertips on your exhale. Your hammer should feel comfortable in your palm. Like an organic extension of your body.

Feel free to personalize your hammer beforehand, to really cement your connection! JoAnn's offers a wide selection of acrylic paints and sealants.

From the knees, work downward. Shins are inviting targets, and invoke warm feelings of childhood nostalgia. Who hasn't kicked their crush in the shins? Embrace your inner child and recreate cherished memories.

Ankles and feet are full of tiny bones, and tiny things are cute! It can be tempting to leave them intact. But think about the way you were treated. Were you left intact?

It's like Marie Kondo said: Does this spark joy? If not, it doesn't belong in your life.

***

The first time he broke your arm, he said it was an accident. He cried and cried, and when that didn't work, he asked you why you'd hurt yourself like that. Why did you push him until he hurt you? It wasn't his fault. He cried until you started to believe him.

People are very good at making you believe things. That is why it's important to be assertive. Self-care is about being kind to you, even when it's hard. You have to be your own advocate.

Self-care is Korean face masks and Netflix in bed. It's getting a venti instead of a grande at Starbucks. It's making time to exercise and eat right, because even if it doesn't feel good now, soon you'll be strong enough to lift an unconscious man in and out of your Honda Civic. Plus, the squats make your butt look great.

The first step toward a better, healthier, happier you is acknowledging that you're worth it. Get the pretty gold zip-ties instead of the boring black ones. Buy the more expensive hammer with the grip that fits your hand perfectly. Say yes to the Costco-sized packet of teriyaki jerky and rolls of plastic sheeting.

Investing in yourself is investing in your future.

***

Take your time with the fingers, one by one. Indulgence is the name of the game! A giant case of Ferrero Rochers is meant to be savored, one perfect, foil-wrapped piece at a time. So, too, are fingers.

One way to make the process meaningful is to assign an affirmation to each finger:

1. I am beautiful.

2. My friends like me.

3. Yours won't miss you.

4. My hair looks great.

5. I am funny, smart, and loved.

6. My scars do not define me.

7. Red lipstick does look good on me.

8. I deserved better.

9. I deserved better.

10. Today, I will be the better thing.

***

As you work your way up the ribs, don't forget to take breaks! Stretch your hands every twenty minutes to avoid repetitive stress injuries. Without treatment, some conditions can become chronic. Prevention is your best friend.

Tendon glides are a close second.

Old injuries take longer to heal. Nine months after the EMTs carried you out of the bathtub, the smell of his sandalwood shampoo still sends you into a panic. Five months of occupational therapy, and your hands still ache on bad days.

Don't undo all that progress by going overboard. Tendon glide. Tendon glide. Roll your neck, rotate your shoulders. Hydrate.

He's not going anywhere.

You still have the voicemail he left you that night in May. You played it on speakerphone in the hospital, staring up at the white, speckled ceiling.

If you stay with him, he will kill you, the nurse told you as she reset your wrist again.

You're nothing without me, he told you.

Remember when you used to believe him?

***

Expert Tip: Self-care looks different for everybody! But everyone needs an alibi. So be good to Future You and plan yours early.

If you're an INTJ, using a bullet journal to organize your thoughts can be helpful. Just make sure to burn the pages afterward. You can even create your own ritual around it, a way to take control of letting things go.

***

The human body has 32 teeth. The world is your dental oyster.

Get creative! This is a great time to express yourself.

As you explore and play, it's important to manage your expectations. This may be therapeutic, but it isn't therapy. It won't make you whole. It won't make you feel less alone.

But it might make you feel better for a while! Like taking a long, luxurious bath with your favorite Lush bath bomb. And isn't it kind of sexy to have a naughty secret? Something you can think about late at night and enjoy, like a piece of chocolate melting on your tongue.

As with therapy, you get out what you put in. Allow yourself to experience emotional vulnerability, and embrace the depth of your feelings. Let yourself cry. Let yourself laugh. Tell him a secret, not as part of a dialogue—he can't answer anyway—but as an act of self-confirmation:

When I was five, I was scared of dogs.

Every time you hurt me, I forgave you.

I know about you and Jacinda.

I really thought you were the One.

For everything you give him, take something from him. You can keep them in a tasteful Hobby Lobby shadow box and craft something positive from the negative. Something new from the old.

Puffy paint won't fix you. A hammer won't fix him. And that's okay. Embrace radical acceptance, and close this chapter of your life as a better person, with better abs. The kind of person who drinks kale smoothies with yogurt, and owns Corkcicle water bottles and industrial-strength car detailing products. The kind of person who finishes their weekly bullet journal spreads early.

That could be you! Maybe it is already.

***

Don't forget about aftercare. That's important, too! Once you're done cleaning up, light your favorite candles, put on music that makes you happy, and sink into that hot bubble bath you've been craving all week. Be decadent and spoil yourself. You worked hard; you deserve it!

The high will wear off eventually. Even after it does, remember that red lipstick does look good on you, OxiClean is your friend, and you're stronger than people think you are.

And if your hands get itchy again? Well. You've got a whole bujo spread of names and dates. Your best friend, Jacinda, is written at the top in your favorite gel pen. Maybe you two should get brunch next week, with mimosas.

Your best self *loves* mimosas.

End

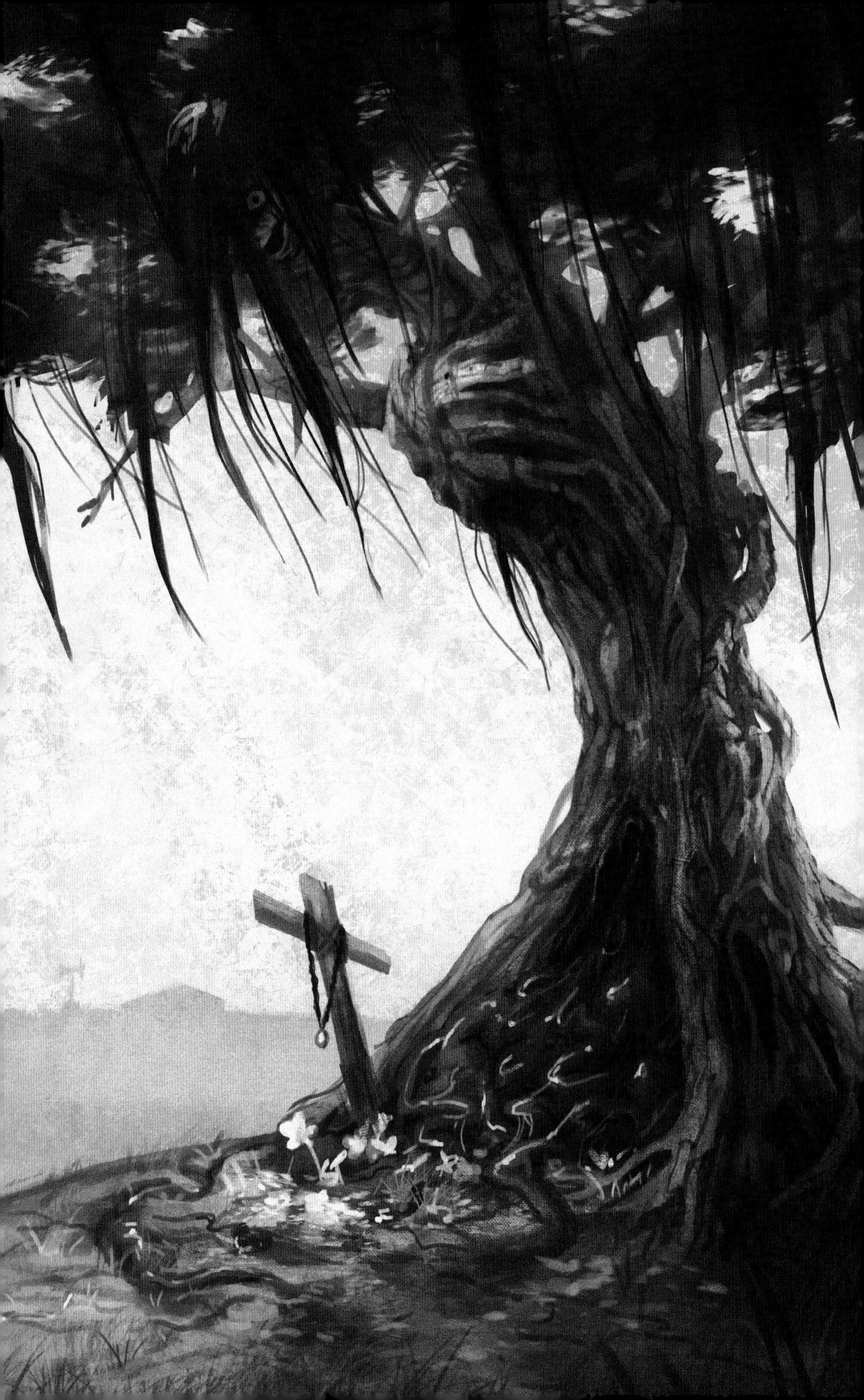

When the sickness would hit, my mum used to tell me to press my wrists against the glass.
As I grew older, I got into the habit of resting my head against the windows instead. It helped some.
But then I'd see the fingerprints, and that'd make the sickness double.
The thought of endless shit-smeared hands pressing against the glass I was resting on made the acid rise in my throat.
Sometimes the glass was so filthy you could barely see through it...
...no matter how hard you looked.
The warehouse, though.
It was impossible to miss that. Even if you wanted to, you couldn't escape it.
THE RIDE
Words + Art - John J. Pearson
Letters - Hassan Otsmane-Elhaou

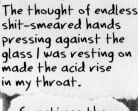

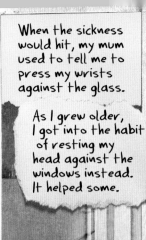

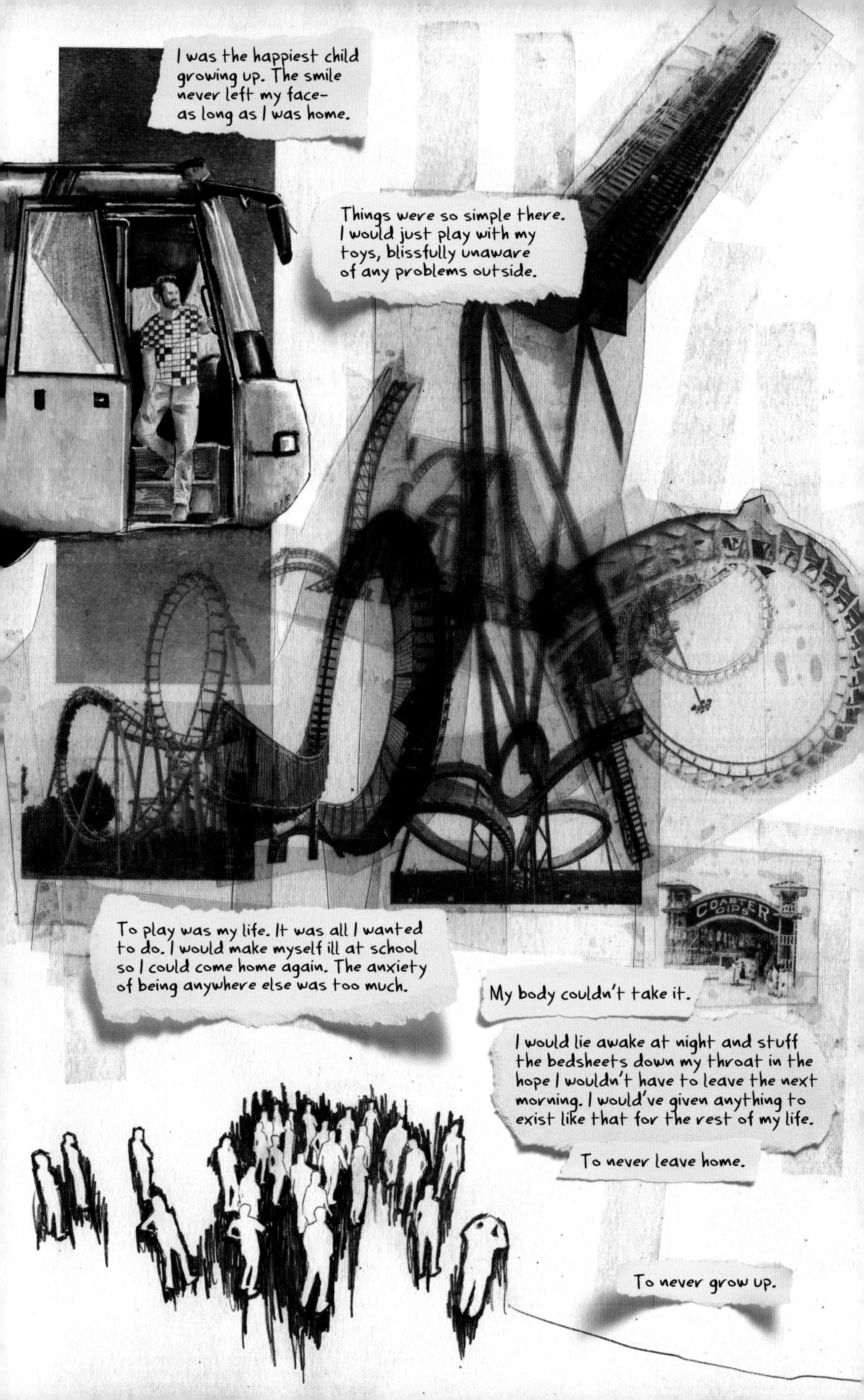
I was the happiest child growing up. The smile never left my face- as long as I was home.
Things were so simple there. I would just play with my toys, blissfully unaware of any problems outside.
COASTER DIPS
To play was my life. It was all I wanted to do. I would make myself ill at school so I could come home again. The anxiety of being anywhere else was too much.
My body couldn't take it.
I would lie awake at night and stuff the bedsheets down my throat in the hope I wouldn't have to leave the next morning. I would've given anything to exist like that for the rest of my life.
To never leave home.
To never grow up.

The thing is, we all have to leave home eventually.

I think with me, when I finally did leave, I never wanted to look back. I never wanted to stop.

I came to feel I'd spent my childhood hiding from the world, and now it was <u>my</u> time.

It broke my parents' hearts.

"Son, please don't."

I didn't listen.

"What the <u>fuck</u> are you doing!"

She tried as well. My love.

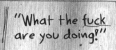

"Don't you fucking <u>dare</u>! You can't <u>do</u> this to me, you can't be so fucking selfish!"

I never listened.

I was going. There was nothing that would change that.

I can remember being scared of the stairs, not knowing what was in the darkness above.

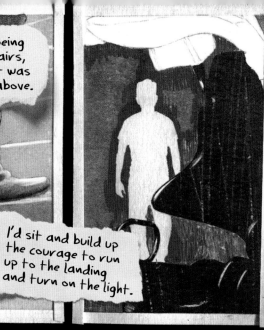

I'd sit and build up the courage to run up to the landing and turn on the light.

I'd feel the rush of adrenaline. Euphoric that I'd overcome my fear.

KER-CHINK

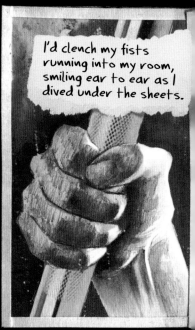

I'd clench my fists running into my room, smiling ear to ear as I dived under the sheets.

There was nothing I couldn't do. I'd made it to the sanctuary of my bed.

But then it would return. The anxiety.

I slowly stuffed the bedsheets down my throat once again.

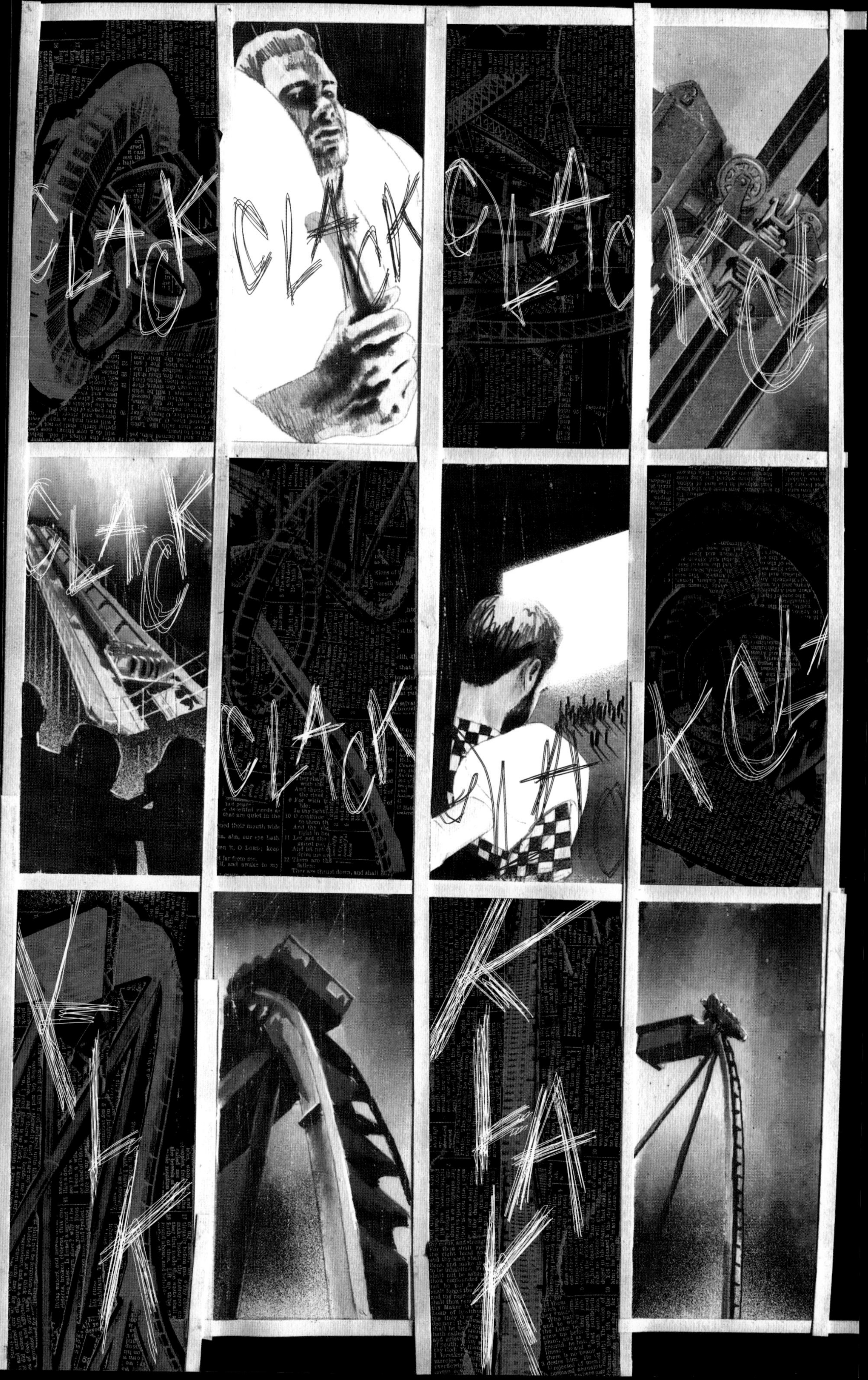
CLACK
CLACK
CLACK
CLACK
CLACK
K
L
A
K
K
L
A
K

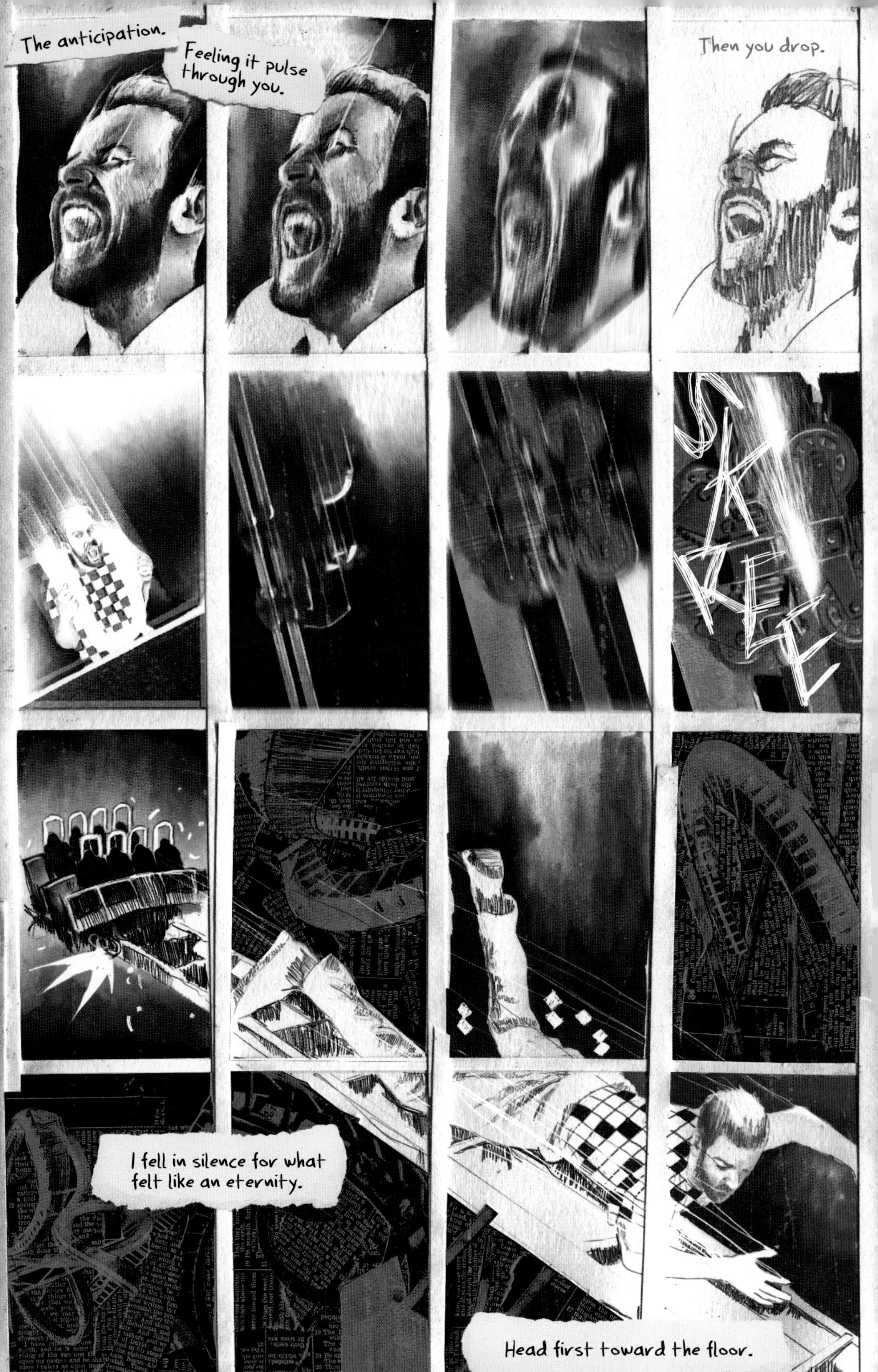

The anticipation.
Feeling it pulse through you.
Then you drop.
SKREE
I fell in silence for what felt like an eternity.
Head first toward the floor.

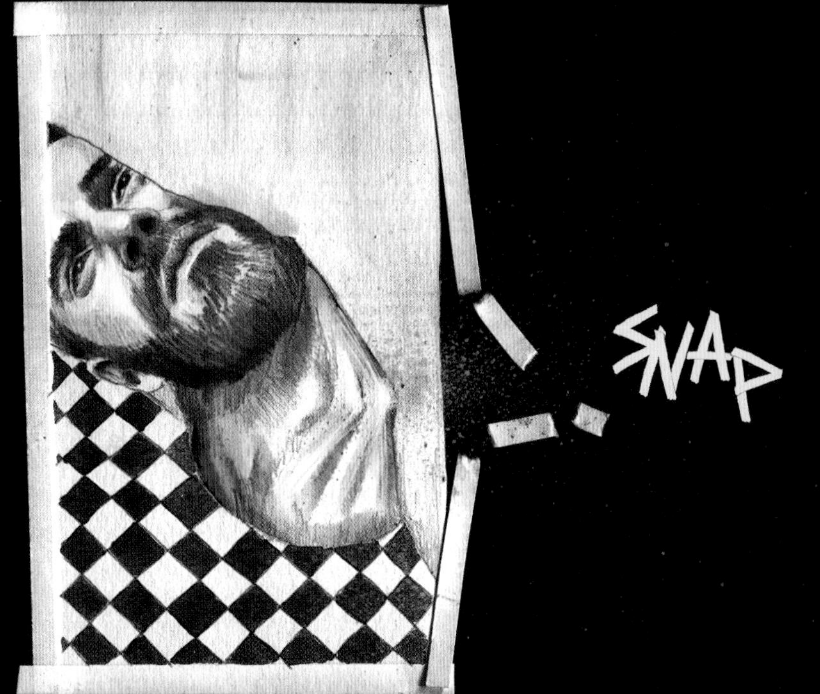
SNAP

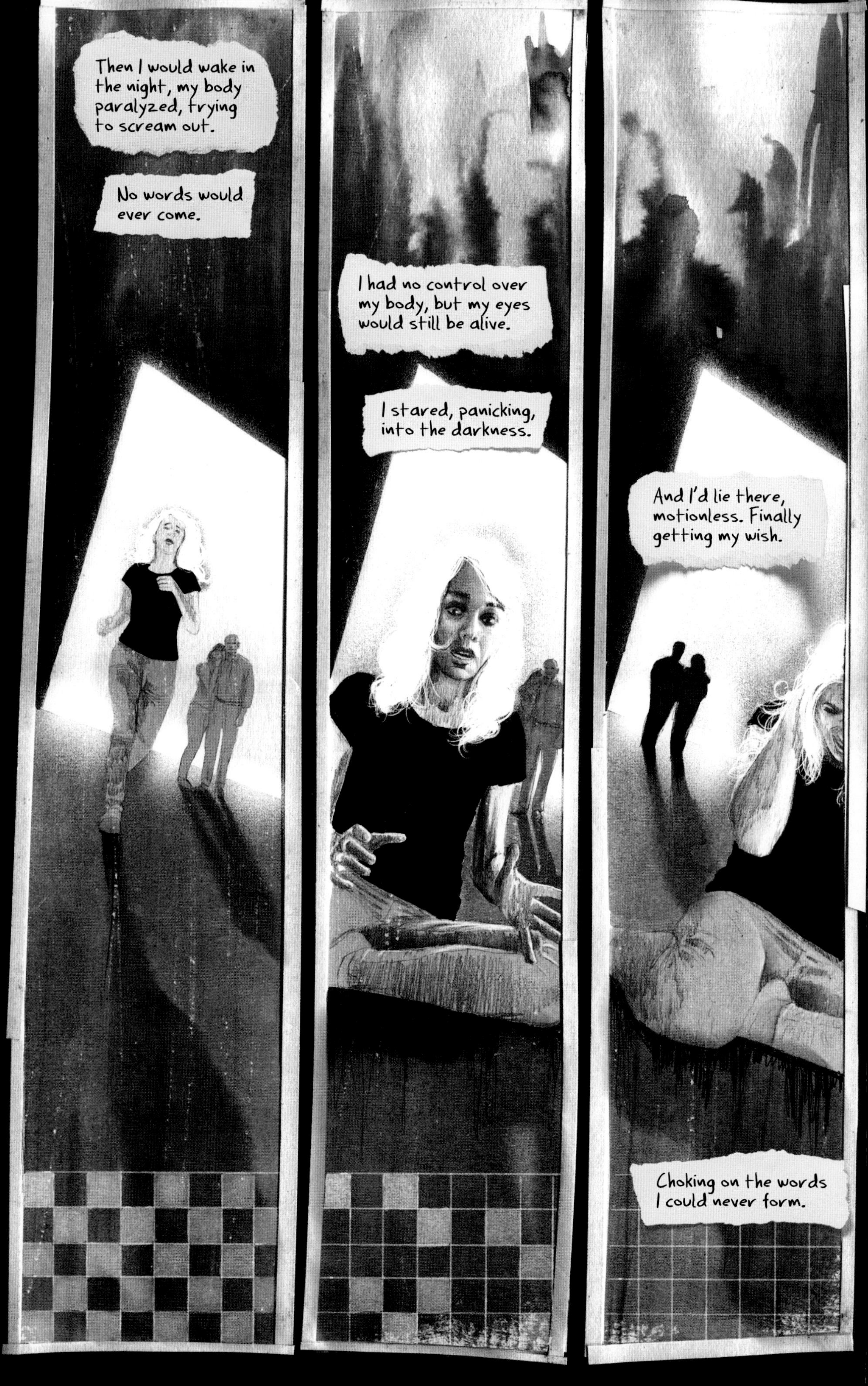
Then I would wake in the night, my body paralyzed, trying to scream out.
No words would ever come.
I had no control over my body, but my eyes would still be alive.
I stared, panicking, into the darkness.
And I'd lie there, motionless. Finally getting my wish.
Choking on the words I could never form.

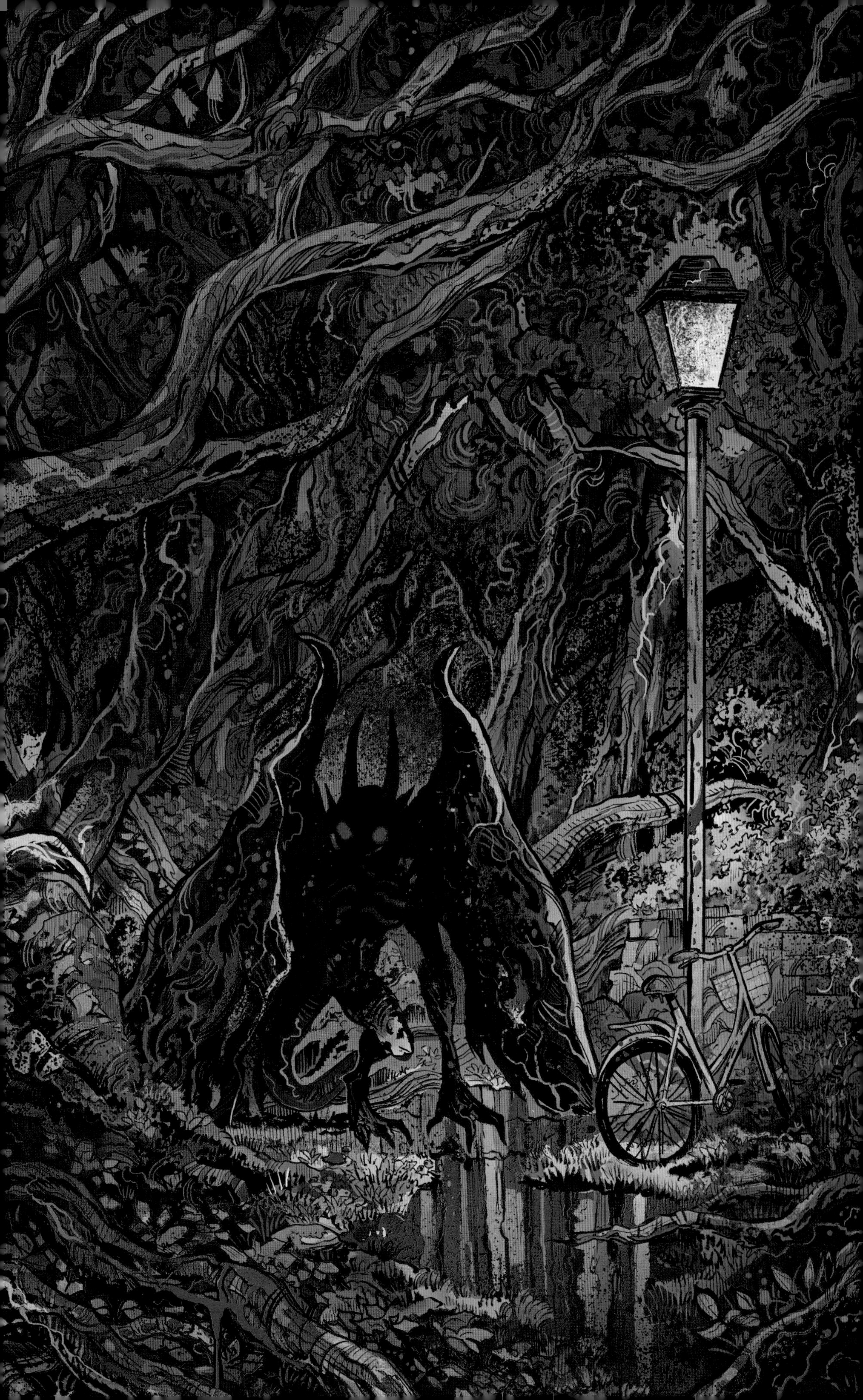

AS I WAS CLOSING THE DOOR, I HEARD HER SCREAM...

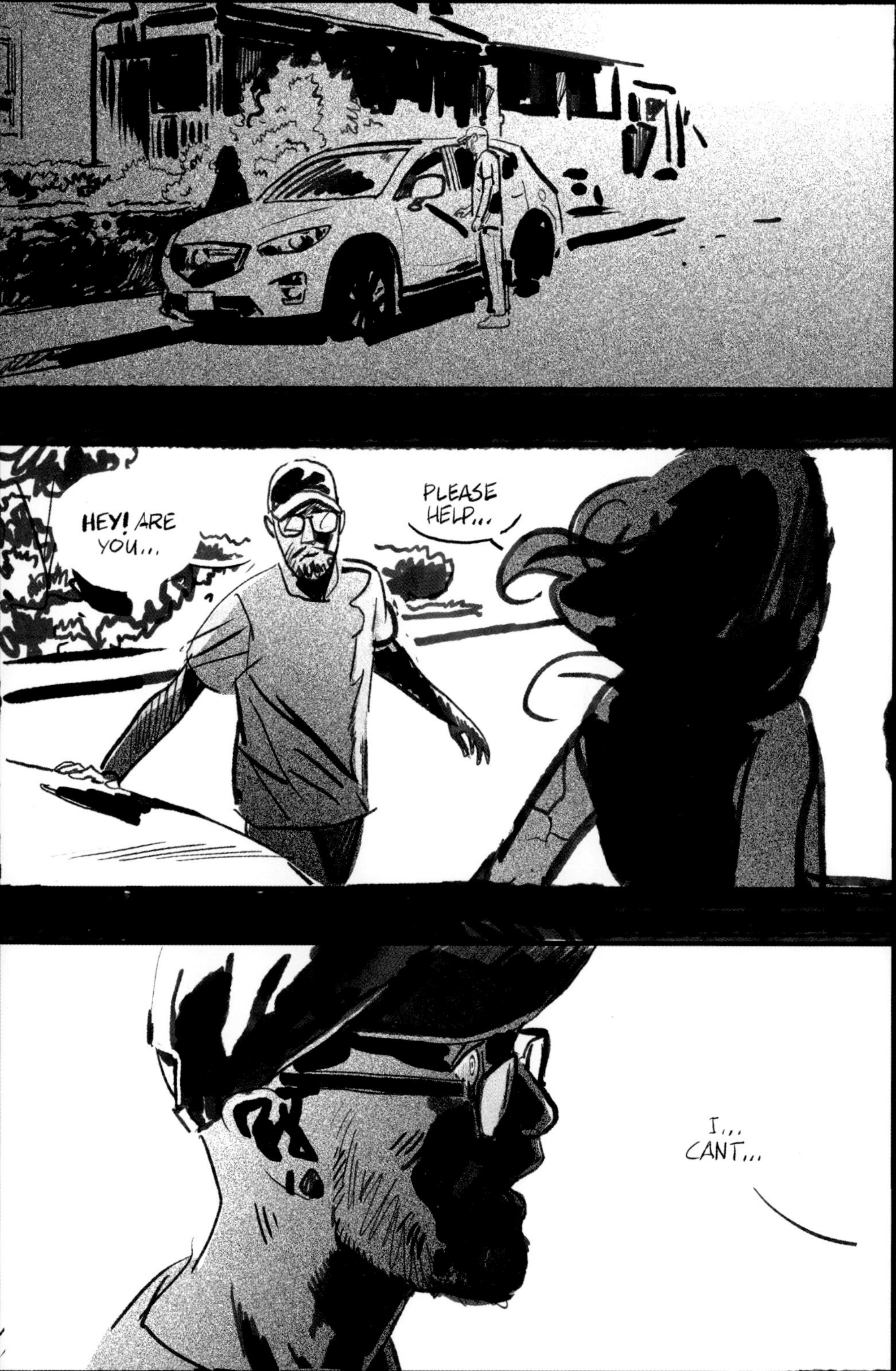
HEY! ARE YOU...
PLEASE HELP...
I... CANT...

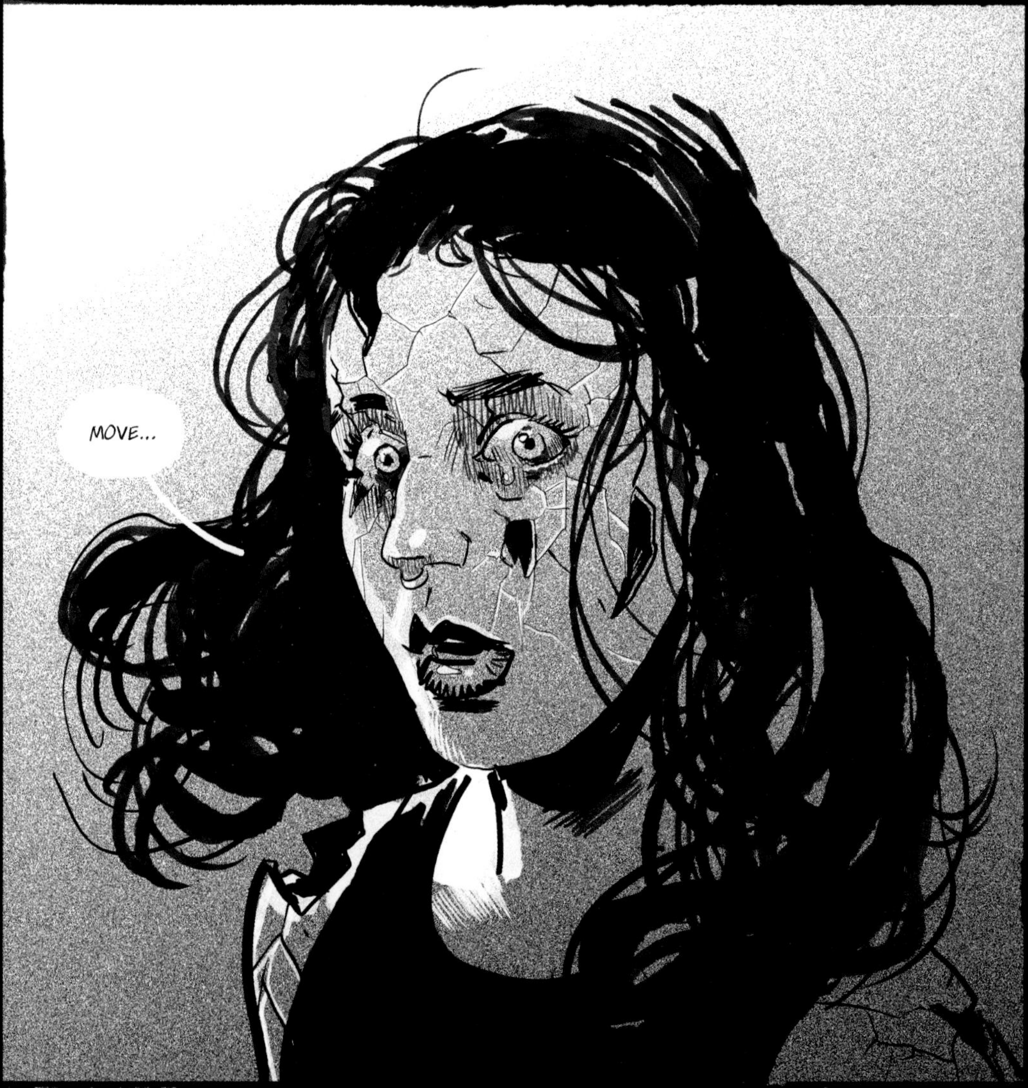
MOVE...

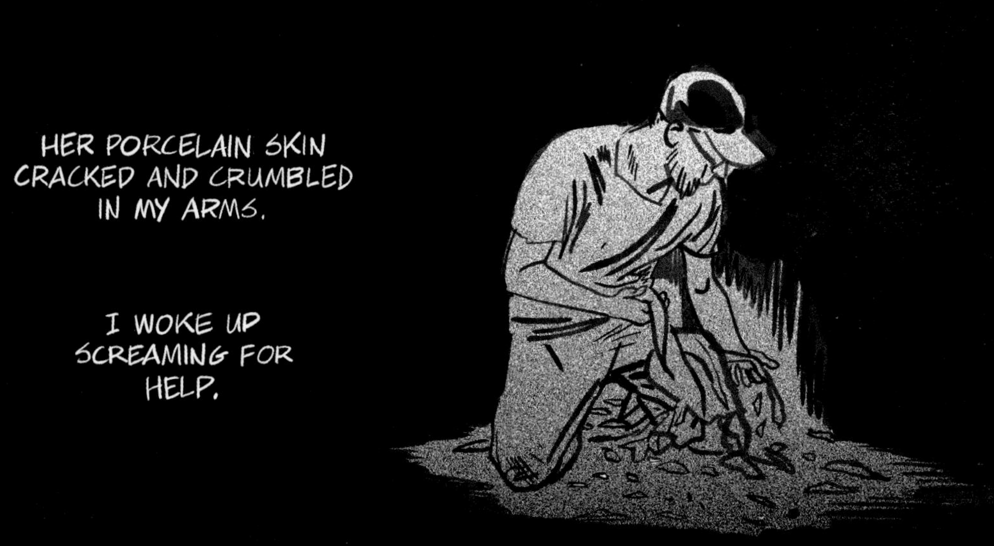
HER PORCELAIN SKIN
CRACKED AND CRUMBLED
IN MY ARMS.

I WOKE UP
SCREAMING FOR
HELP.

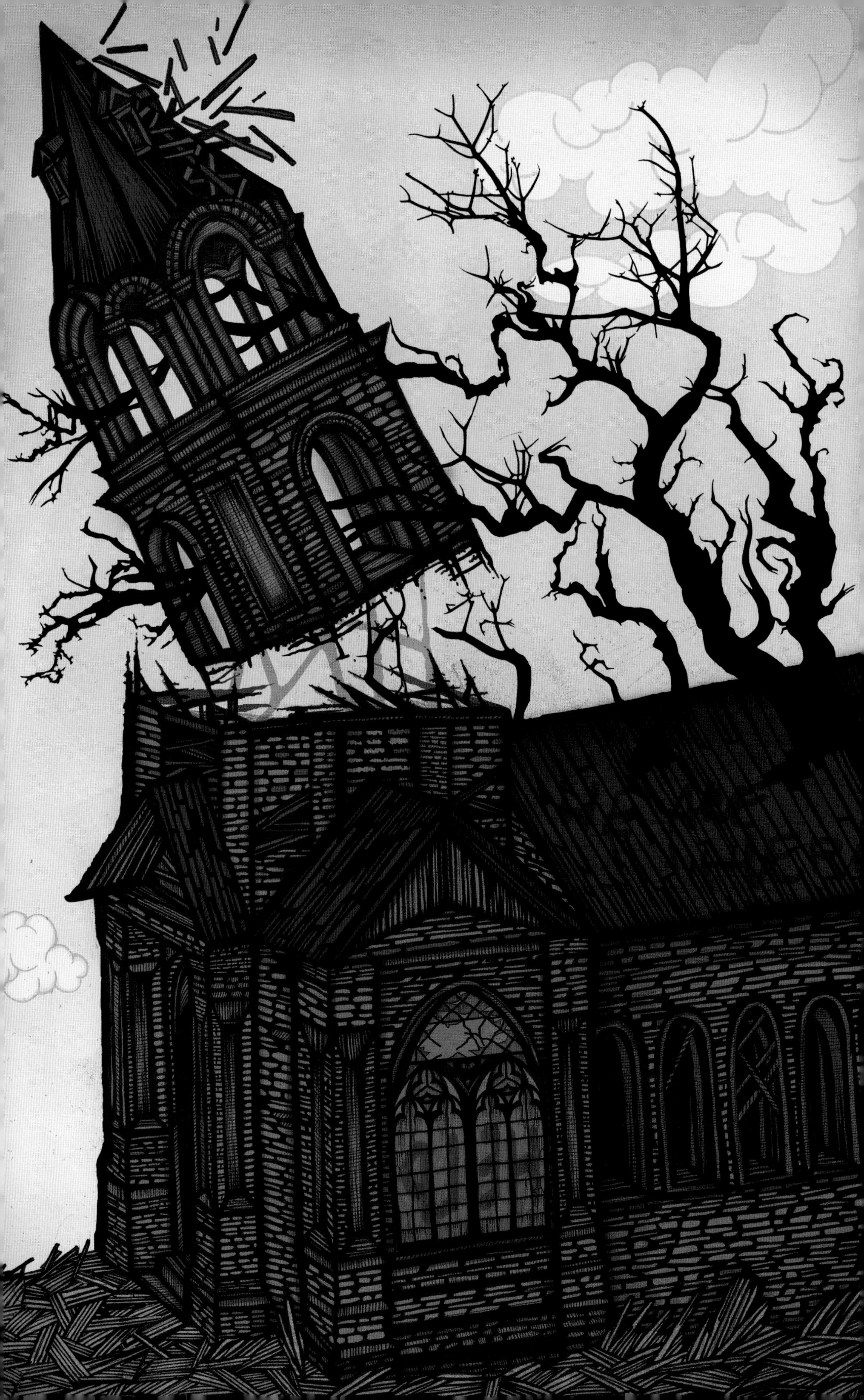

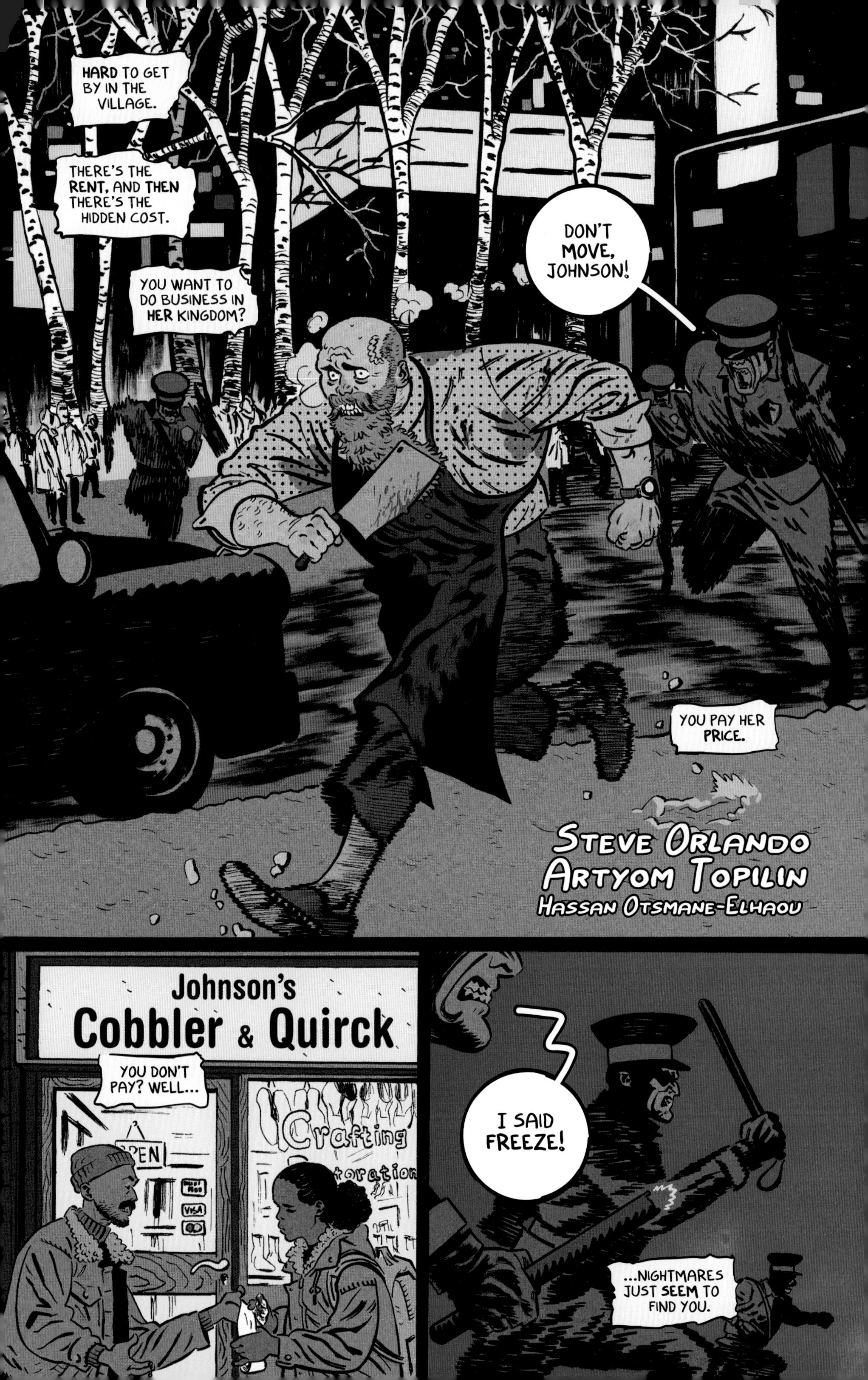

HARD TO GET BY IN THE VILLAGE.
THERE'S THE RENT, AND THEN THERE'S THE HIDDEN COST.
YOU WANT TO DO BUSINESS IN HER KINGDOM?
DON'T MOVE, JOHNSON!
YOU PAY HER PRICE.
STEVE ORLANDO
ARTYOM TOPILIN
HASSAN OTSMANE-ELHAOU
Johnson's
Cobbler & Quirck
YOU DON'T PAY? WELL...
Crafting
VISA
I SAID FREEZE!
...NIGHTMARES JUST SEEM TO FIND YOU.

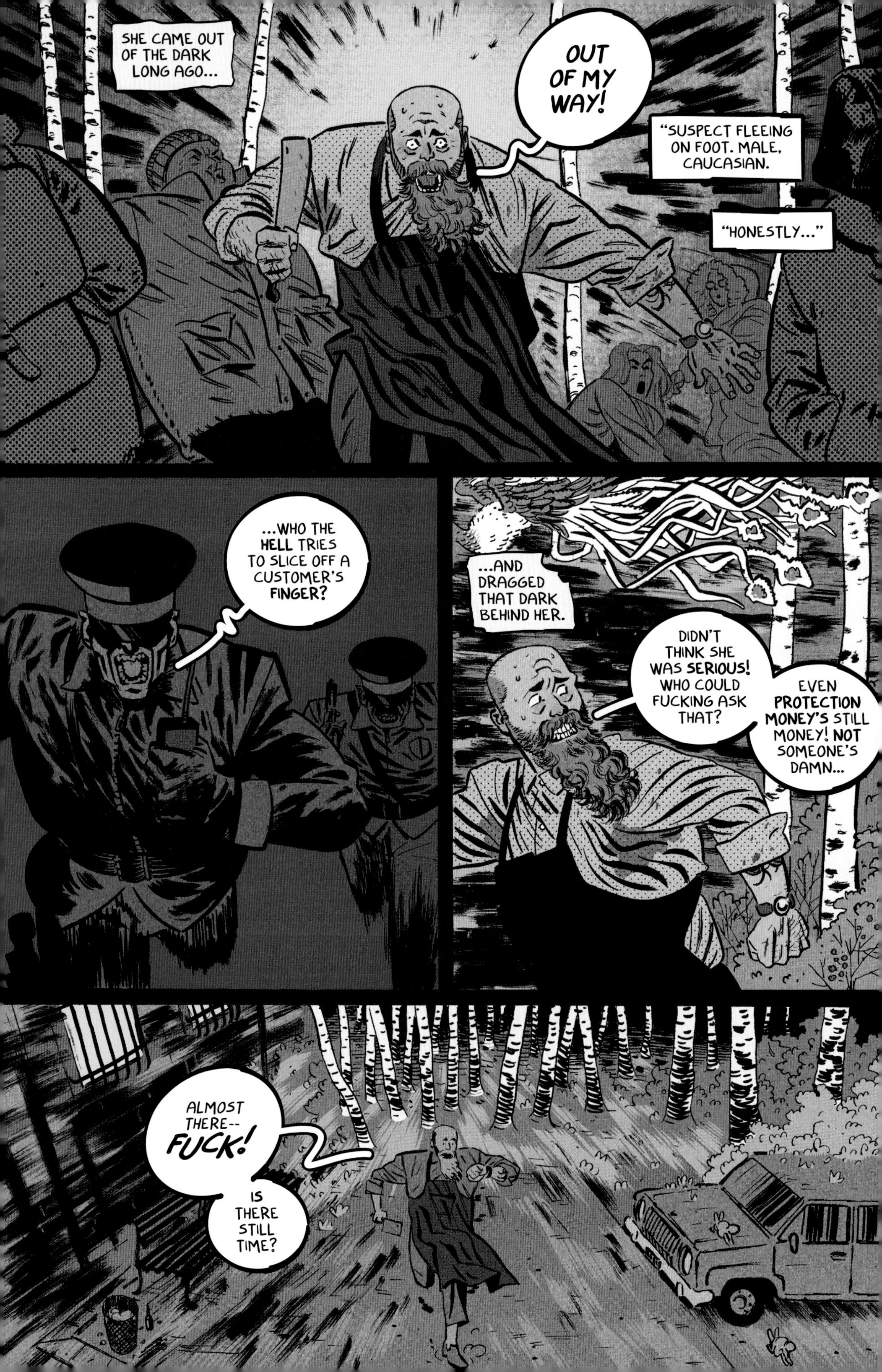
SHE CAME OUT OF THE DARK LONG AGO...
OUT OF MY WAY!
"SUSPECT FLEEING ON FOOT. MALE, CAUCASIAN.
"HONESTLY..."
...WHO THE HELL TRIES TO SLICE OFF A CUSTOMER'S FINGER?
...AND DRAGGED THAT DARK BEHIND HER.
DIDN'T THINK SHE WAS SERIOUS! WHO COULD FUCKING ASK THAT?
EVEN PROTECTION MONEY'S STILL MONEY! NOT SOMEONE'S DAMN...
ALMOST THERE-- FUCK!
IS THERE STILL TIME?

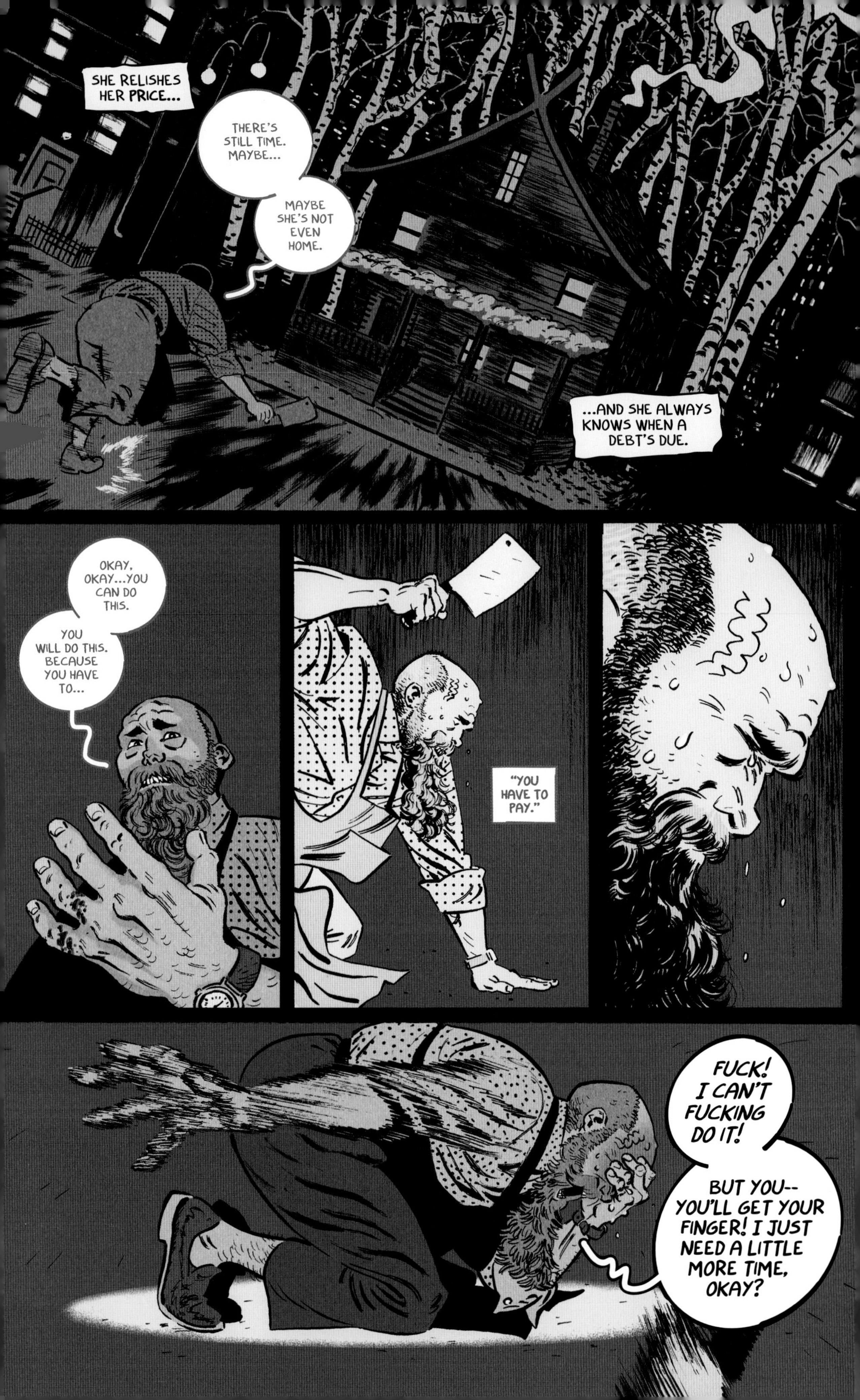
SHE RELISHES HER PRICE...
THERE'S STILL TIME. MAYBE...
MAYBE SHE'S NOT EVEN HOME.
...AND SHE ALWAYS KNOWS WHEN A DEBT'S DUE.
OKAY, OKAY...YOU CAN DO THIS.
YOU WILL DO THIS. BECAUSE YOU HAVE TO...
"YOU HAVE TO PAY."
FUCK! I CAN'T FUCKING DO IT!
BUT YOU-- YOU'LL GET YOUR FINGER! I JUST NEED A LITTLE MORE TIME, OKAY?

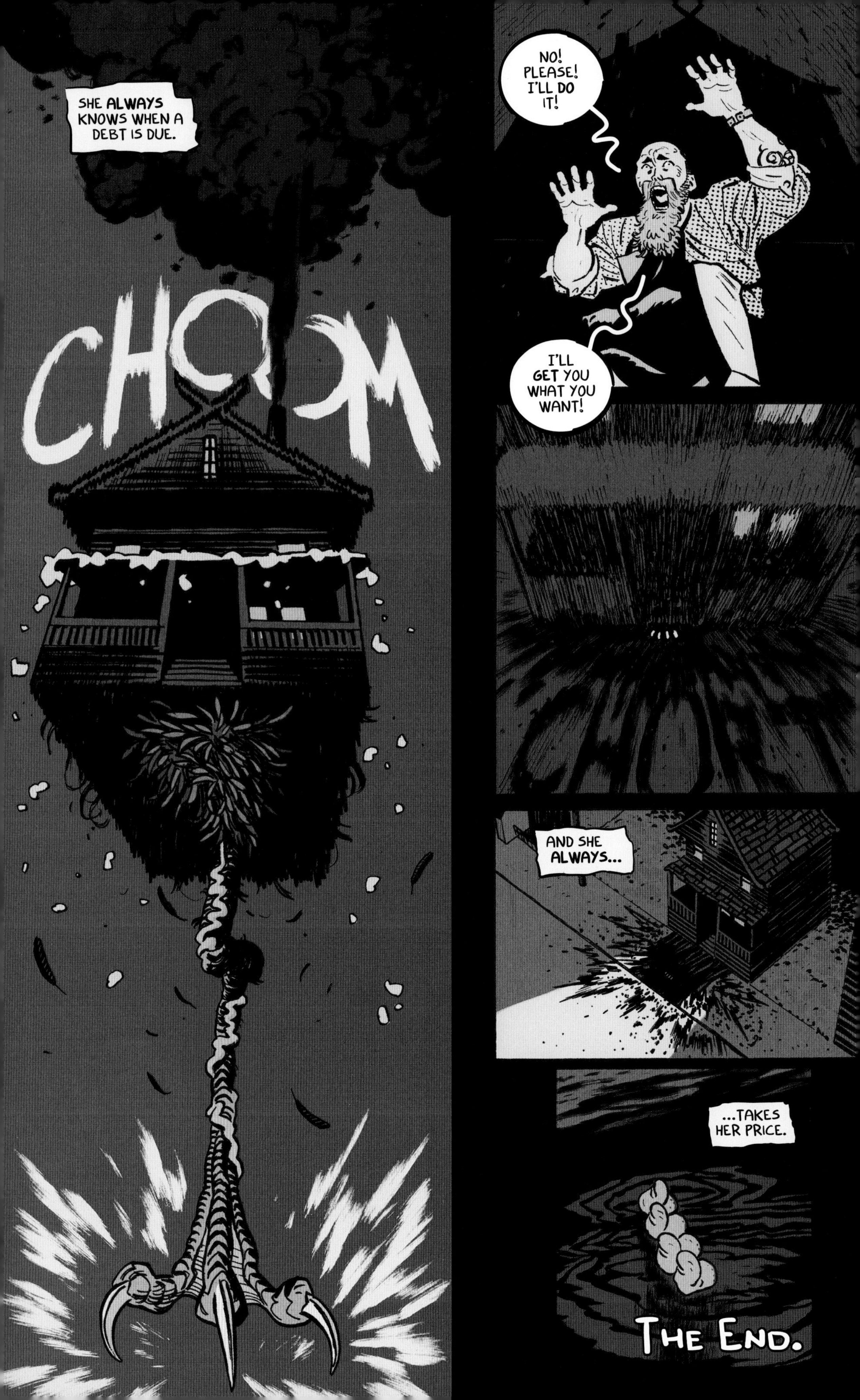
SHE ALWAYS KNOWS WHEN A DEBT IS DUE.
CHOOM
NO! PLEASE! I'LL DO IT!
I'LL GET YOU WHAT YOU WANT!
AND SHE ALWAYS...
...TAKES HER PRICE.
THE END.

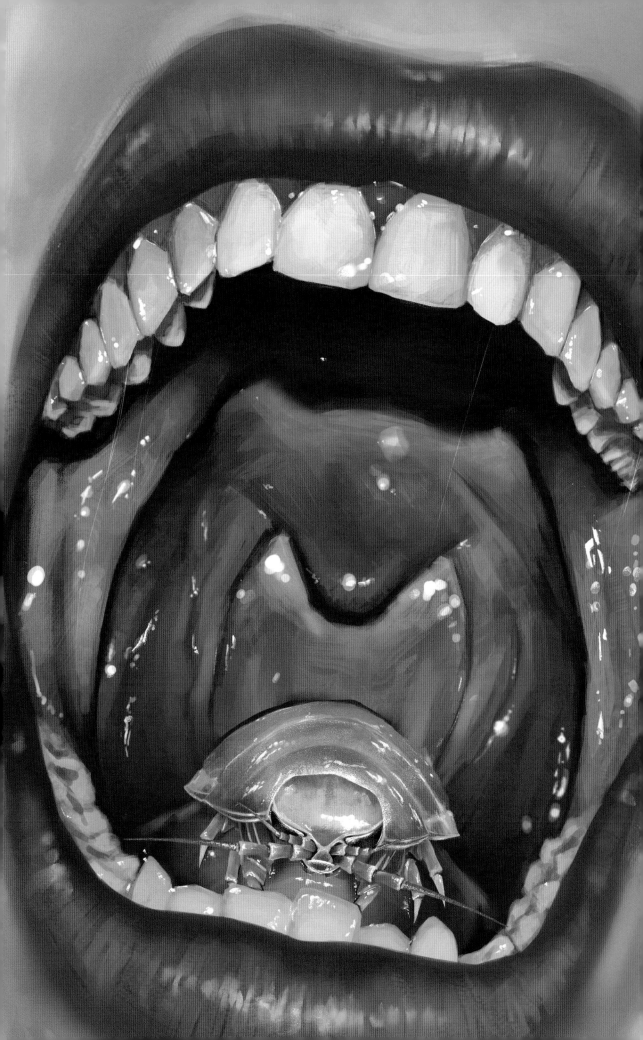

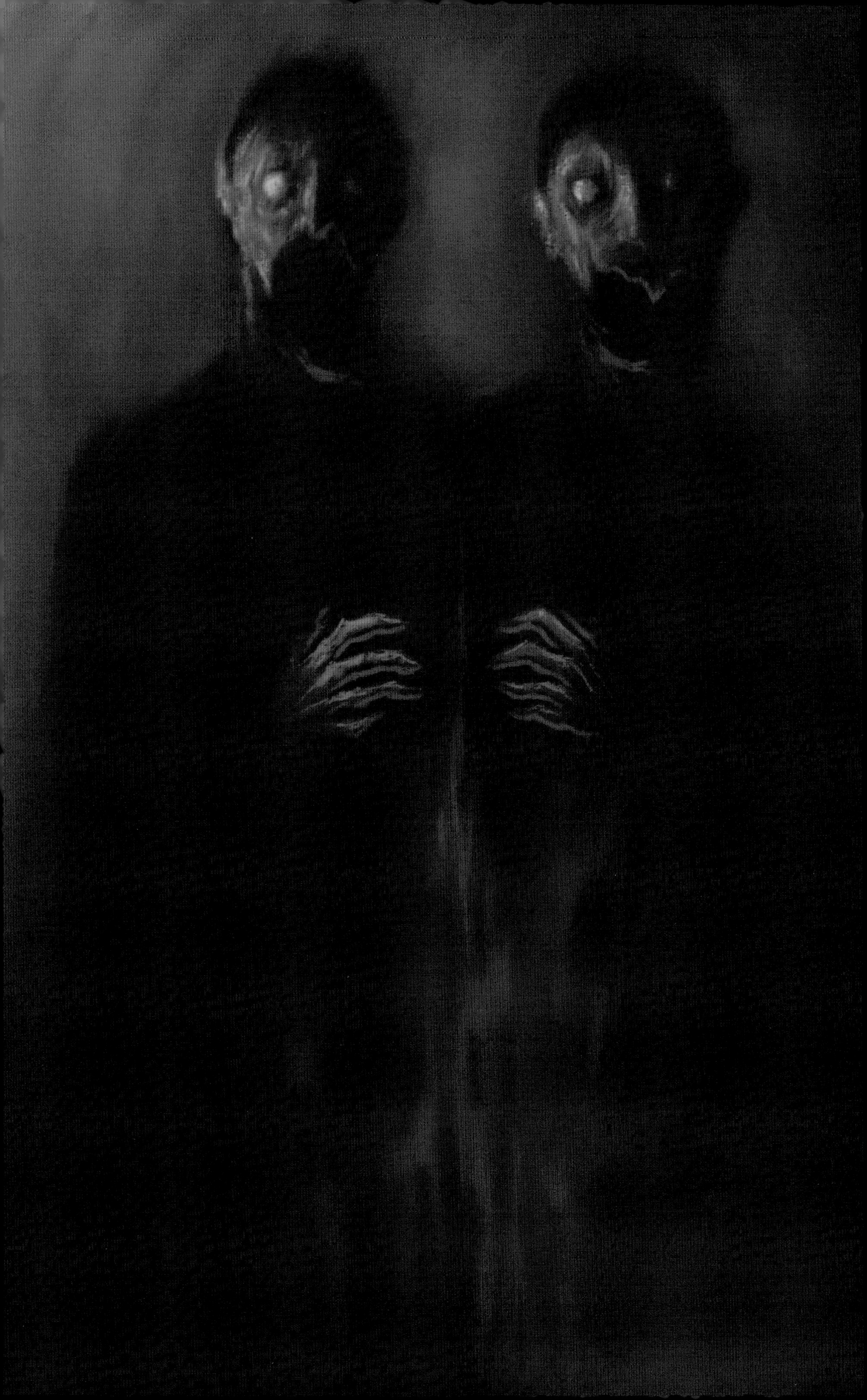

...rest Esther,

...regards to your latest curio, that blasted oil painting you've
...isted on welcoming into your home, I thought there were a few
...ngs you should be informed of.

...has quite the history, did you know? Before making its way to your
...ourite auction house, that painting (The Blind Paupers, as it has
...e to be known) had quite the long list of previous owners. And most
...them have met a miserable, violent end.

...e most famous story involved the hideous thing (and it is hideous!)
...rning up in a shop in Belgium in 1938, where it was purchased by one
...lia Trelawney. Julia, after having the filthy thing in her home for
...week or so, was quick to claim that one or both of the figures in
...e painting were prone to "shift around" in the peripheral of one's
...e when you weren't looking. Before long she was certain that the
...gures actually left the painting and walked around her house while
...e slept.

...lia was dead within the month. A fire ripped through her expansive
...nor house, and by the time anyone had arrived to help, it was almos
...er. They kept it quiet, but the cause was thought to be arson, that
...lia had struck the match that killed her herself. The expansive
...state and everything in it, reduced to ashes and scorched beams.
...verything except the painting, The Blind Paupers, which was
...ntouched. We know that it disappeared from police custody, and was
...issing for a time, before being discovered at the site of a double
...urder in the fall of 1945.

...lmost everyone who has been in contact with the painting has a
...imilar story. But no matter what, it always seems to come away
...nscathed. Maybe that has something to do with the beautifully low
...rice you obtained that horror at.

...s a friend and a colleague, I must strongly ask for you to reconsider
...your purchase. Even if it's just a string of coincidence, why tempt
...fate? Return it before it's too late.

...Best regards,

...Your friend, Patrick

TREVOR HENDERSON MAKES MONSTERS

My name is Trevor Henderson, and I'm a horror artist and creature designer based in Toronto. I was lucky enough to be asked to contribute to multiple issues of *Razorblades: The Horror Magazine,* including the cover for the first issue. It was a huge honor to have my art in the same pages as some of the most incredible horror writers and artists working today.

Sirenhead is probably my most popular design to date. I drew it for the first time in early 2018 and, while it was well received, I didn't really dwell on it. Despite revisiting the creature here and there, it wasn't until 2020 that he really exploded and went viral due to a fan game being reviewed by a lot of popular YouTubers. When I first drew Sirenhead, I was trying to reconcile my love of number stations (mysterious radio transmissions that broadcast seemingly random chains of numbers and words, often with creepy children's music) with lanky humanoid cryptids. I thought that pairing an elongated skeletal figure with the distinctive silhouette of the pole and sirens would make for an iconic image.

The very first drawing of Sirenhead was the one below, where I drew him onto a photo donated from a follower on Twitter. I started drawing monsters into photography primarily as an exercise in trying to match lighting, shadow, color, and tone with a pre-existing image, as well as working on distinctive silhouettes and shapes in my monsters. It became an easy way to practice without having to render a full piece after working retail all day.

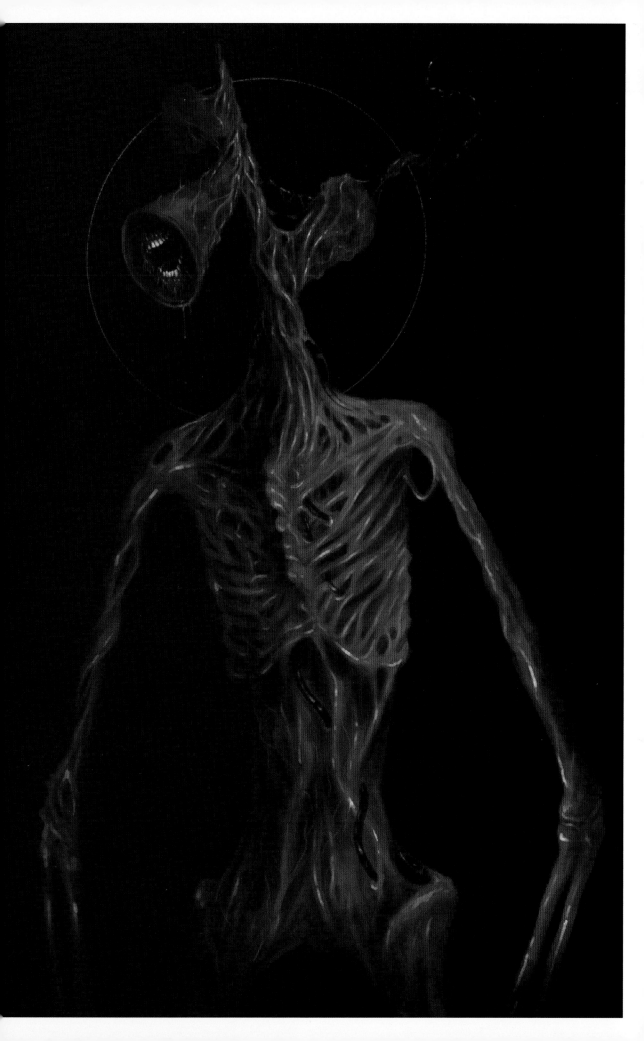

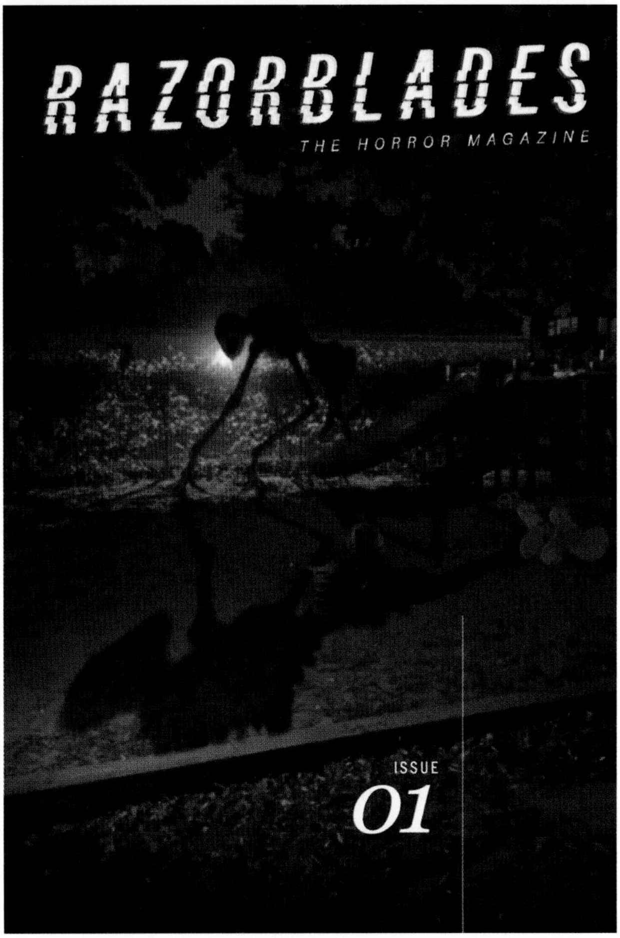
RAZORBLADES
THE HORROR MAGAZINE
ISSUE
01

When Steve Foxe and James Tynion IV asked me to do the cover for their (at-the-time) upcoming horror anthology magazine, I was over the moon. I went out after dark with a group of friends to scout for an appropriate photograph, and ended up taking a photo of a local playground that I felt was spooky enough. Then, after some back and forth with Steve where we discussed exactly what kind of weirdo he felt would work best in that space, I ended up drawing the bony, lanky creep above. I'm so happy the cover went over as well as it did.

When I was asked to include some art and writing in subsequent issues, I usually latched onto an idea after brainstorming a little bit, and let the image go where it went.

The writing always comes after the image for me, adding more context or story seeds in a way that hopefully works with the imagery to make a more alluring or interesting package.

I use Procreate on my iPad to draw, and usually favor the Damp Brush. I find that it's great for working with large swaths of color to give them a great amount of texture, as well as being able to focus in and add definition and detail when necessary. As always, color balance is how I secretly make the drawing not suck at the very end.

Making sure that an interesting texture comes across in my creature design is very important—and very fun for me! This guy's head below is supposed to feel like the rough and papery texture of papier-mâché, but also maybe dry and peeling skin. I really wanted to emphasize that this could be a mask, or his real head. We just don't know!

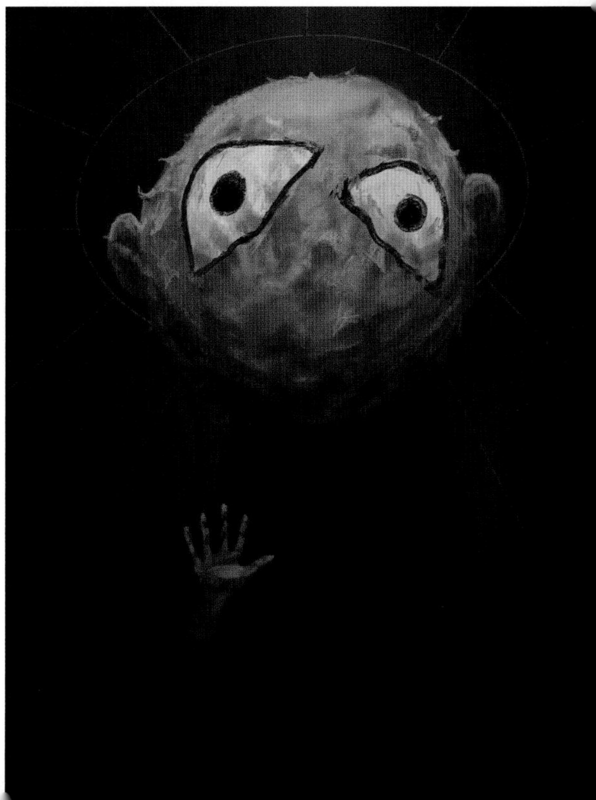

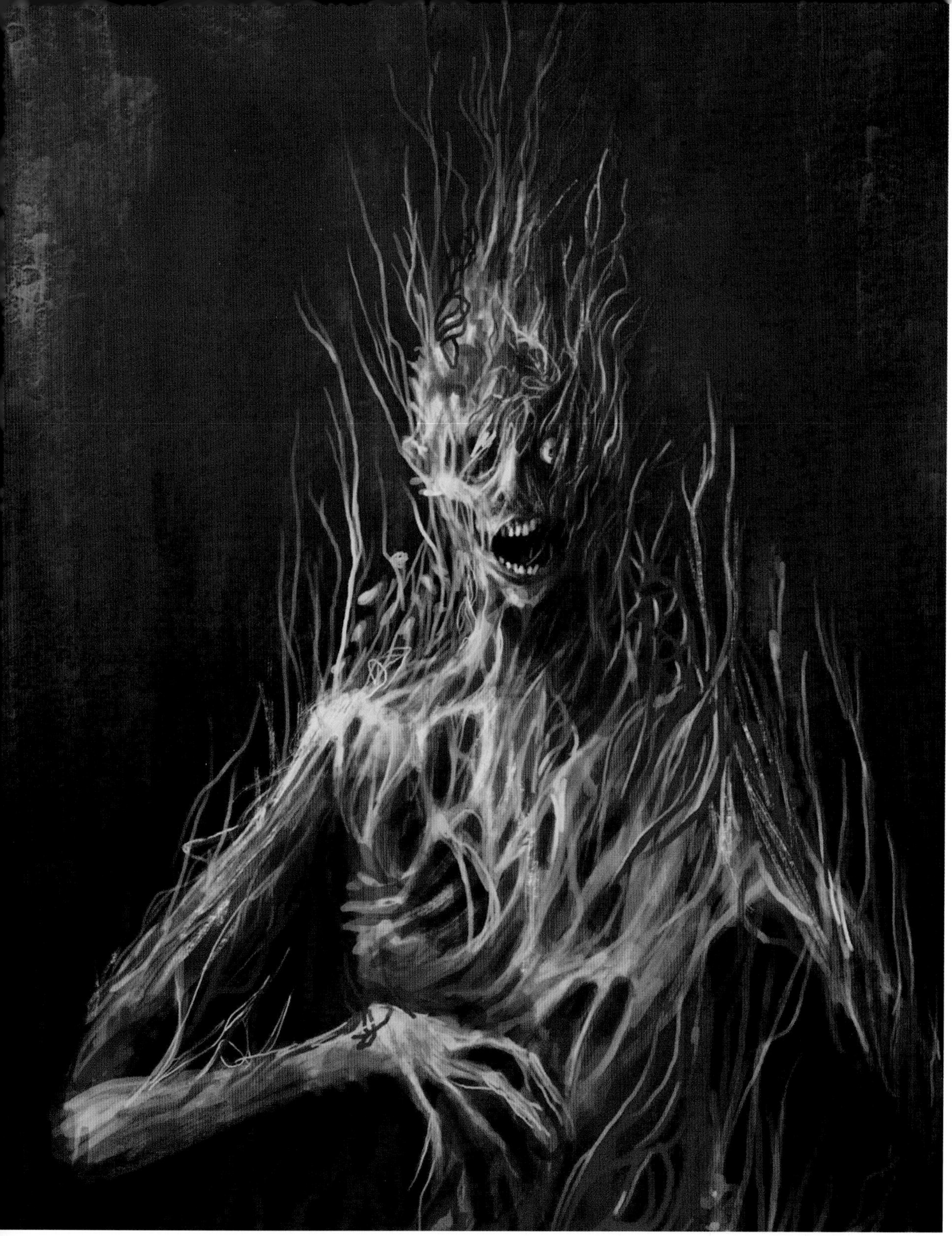

Image permitted for use by AfterShock Comics.

One of my favorite pieces I've ever done is this fungal corpse man, done for the AfterShock Comics series *I Breathed A Body* by Zac Thompson and Andy MacDonald. It was so exciting to be able to really lean into the details of the fruiting bodies growing from the cracks and crevices of this guy's body, and the vivid colors.

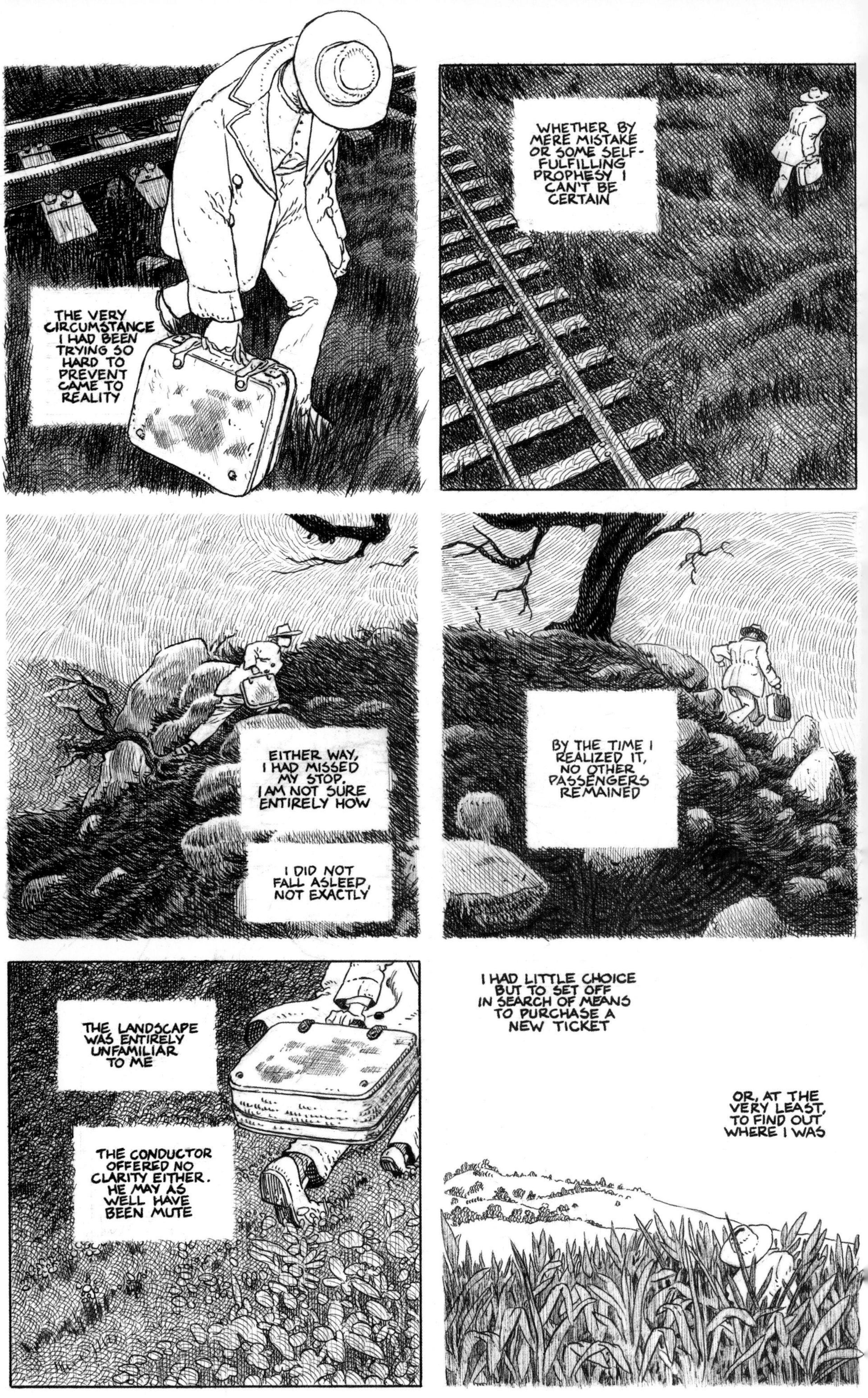
THE VERY CIRCUMSTANCE I HAD BEEN TRYING SO HARD TO PREVENT CAME TO REALITY
WHETHER BY MERE MISTAKE OR SOME SELF-FULFILLING PROPHESY I CAN'T BE CERTAIN
EITHER WAY, I HAD MISSED MY STOP. I AM NOT SURE ENTIRELY HOW
I DID NOT FALL ASLEEP, NOT EXACTLY
BY THE TIME I REALIZED IT, NO OTHER PASSENGERS REMAINED
THE LANDSCAPE WAS ENTIRELY UNFAMILIAR TO ME
THE CONDUCTOR OFFERED NO CLARITY EITHER. HE MAY AS WELL HAVE BEEN MUTE
I HAD LITTLE CHOICE BUT TO SET OFF IN SEARCH OF MEANS TO PURCHASE A NEW TICKET
OR, AT THE VERY LEAST, TO FIND OUT WHERE I WAS

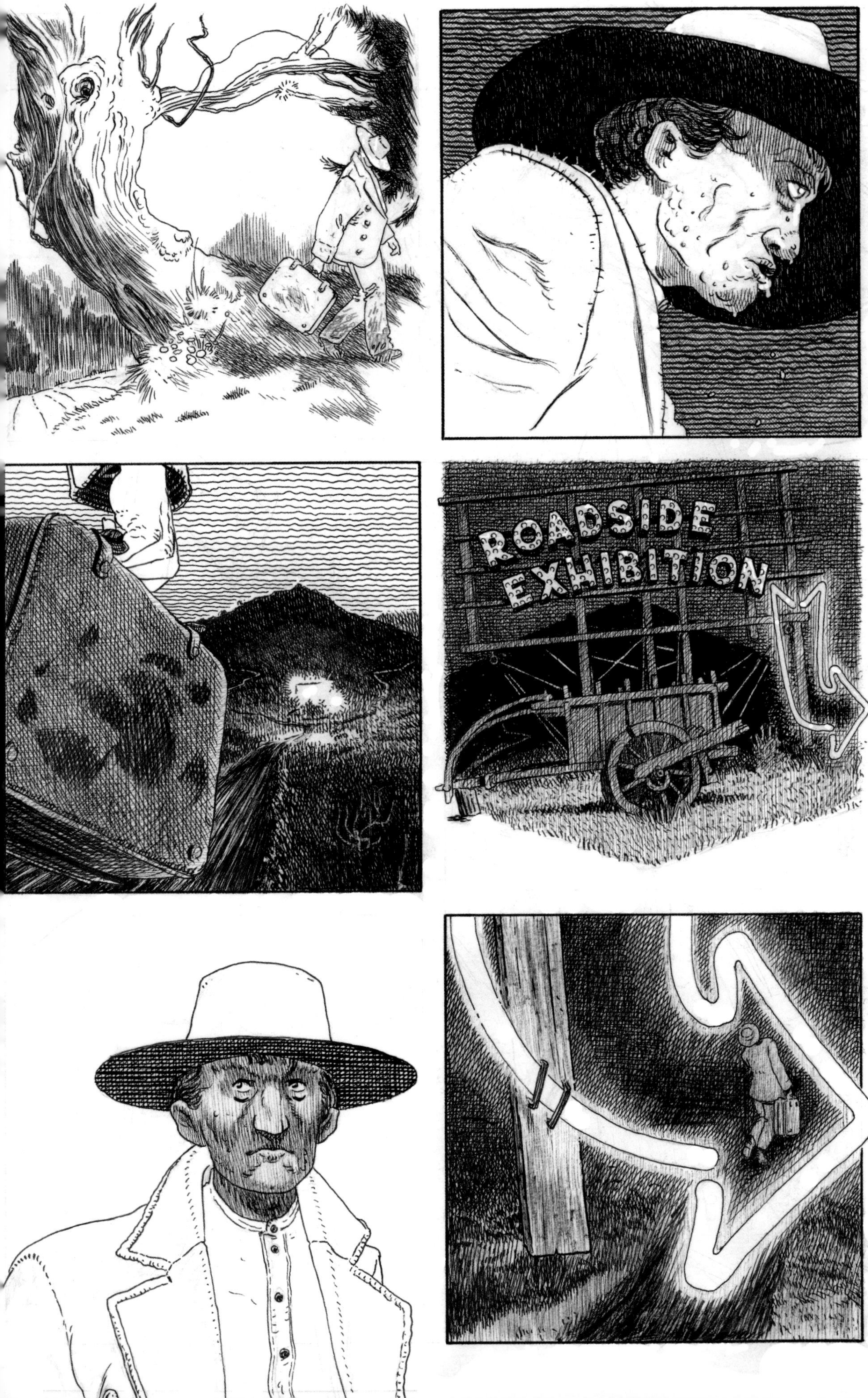
ROADSIDE
EXHIBITION

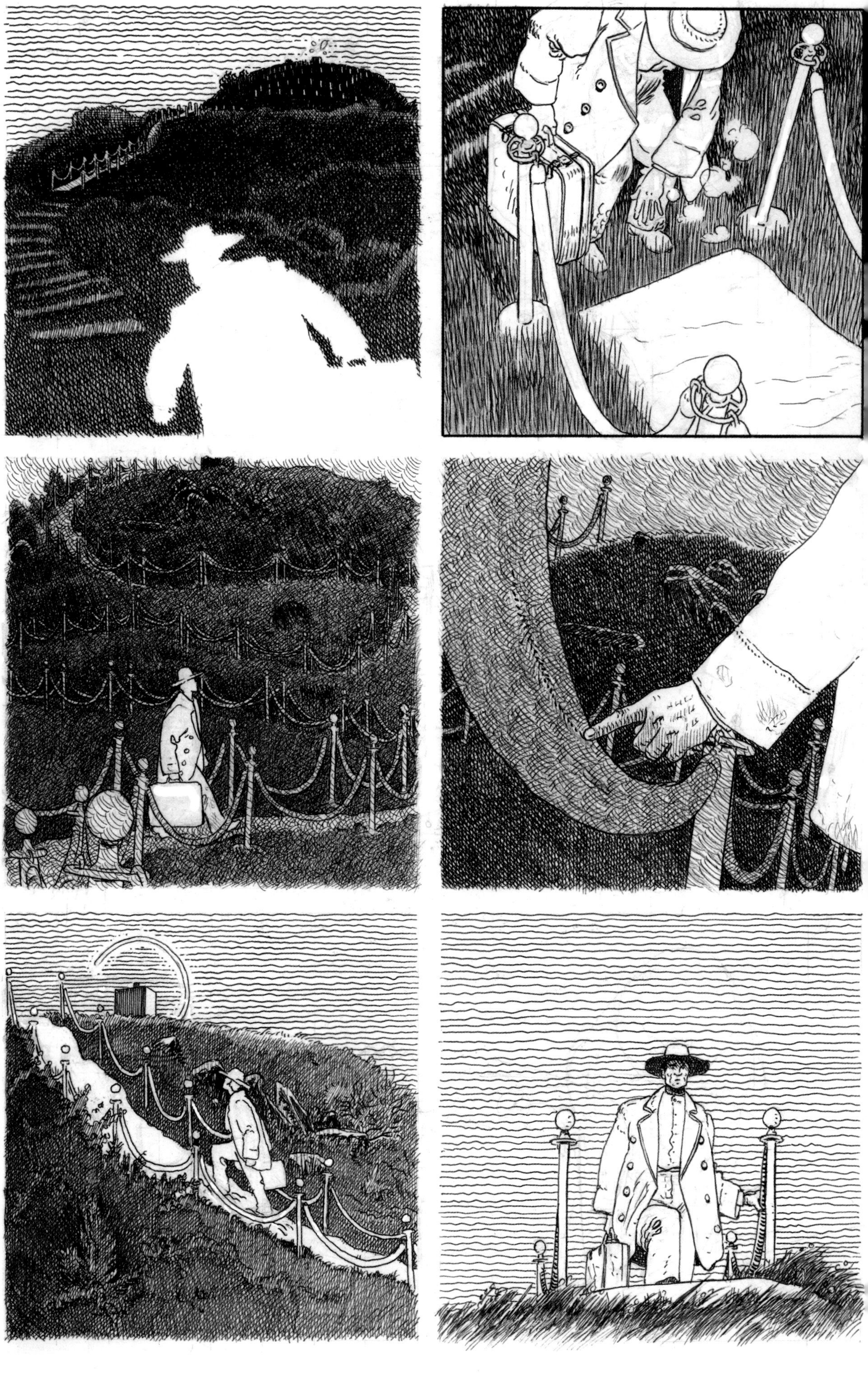

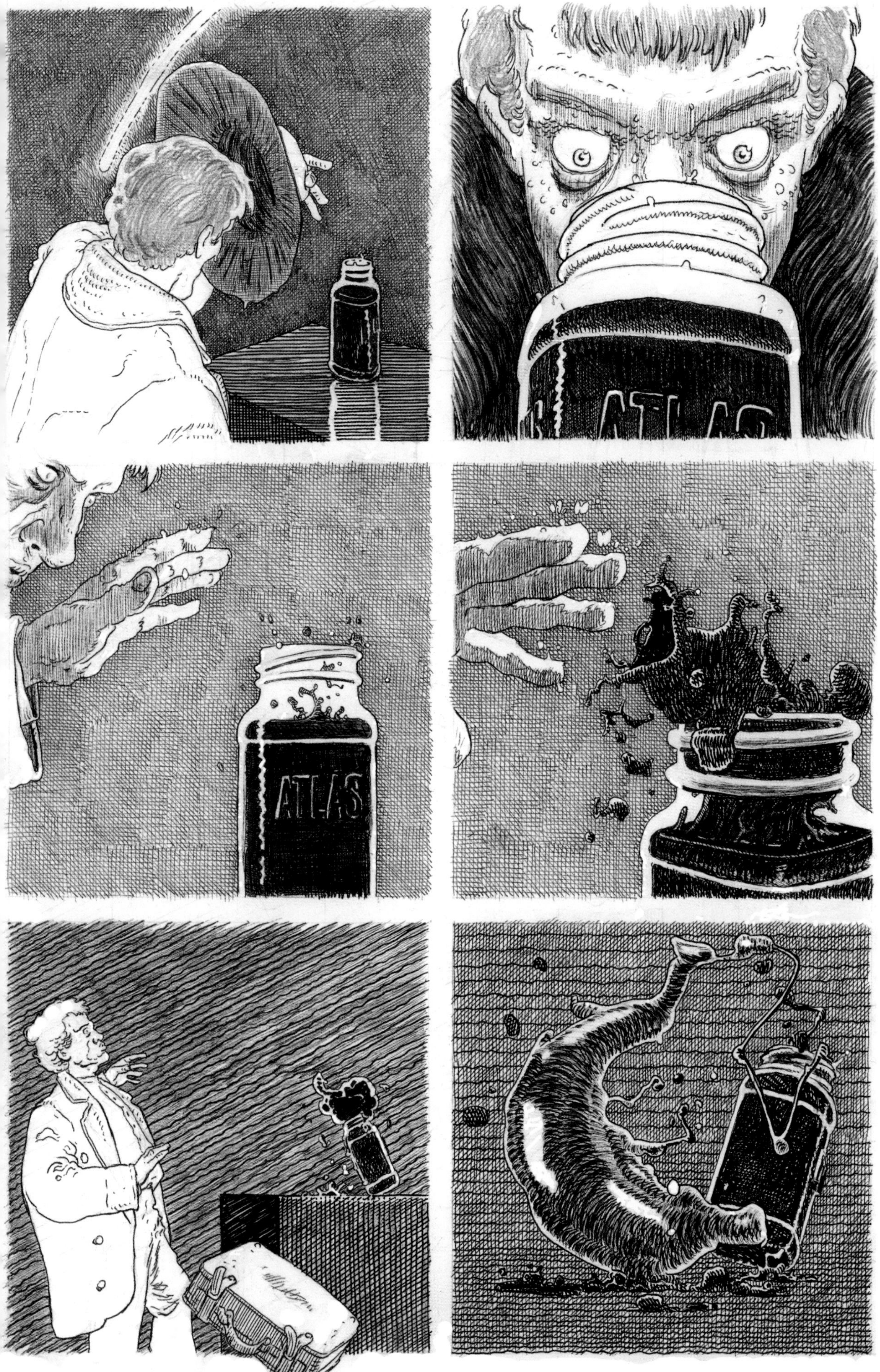
ATLAS
ATLAS

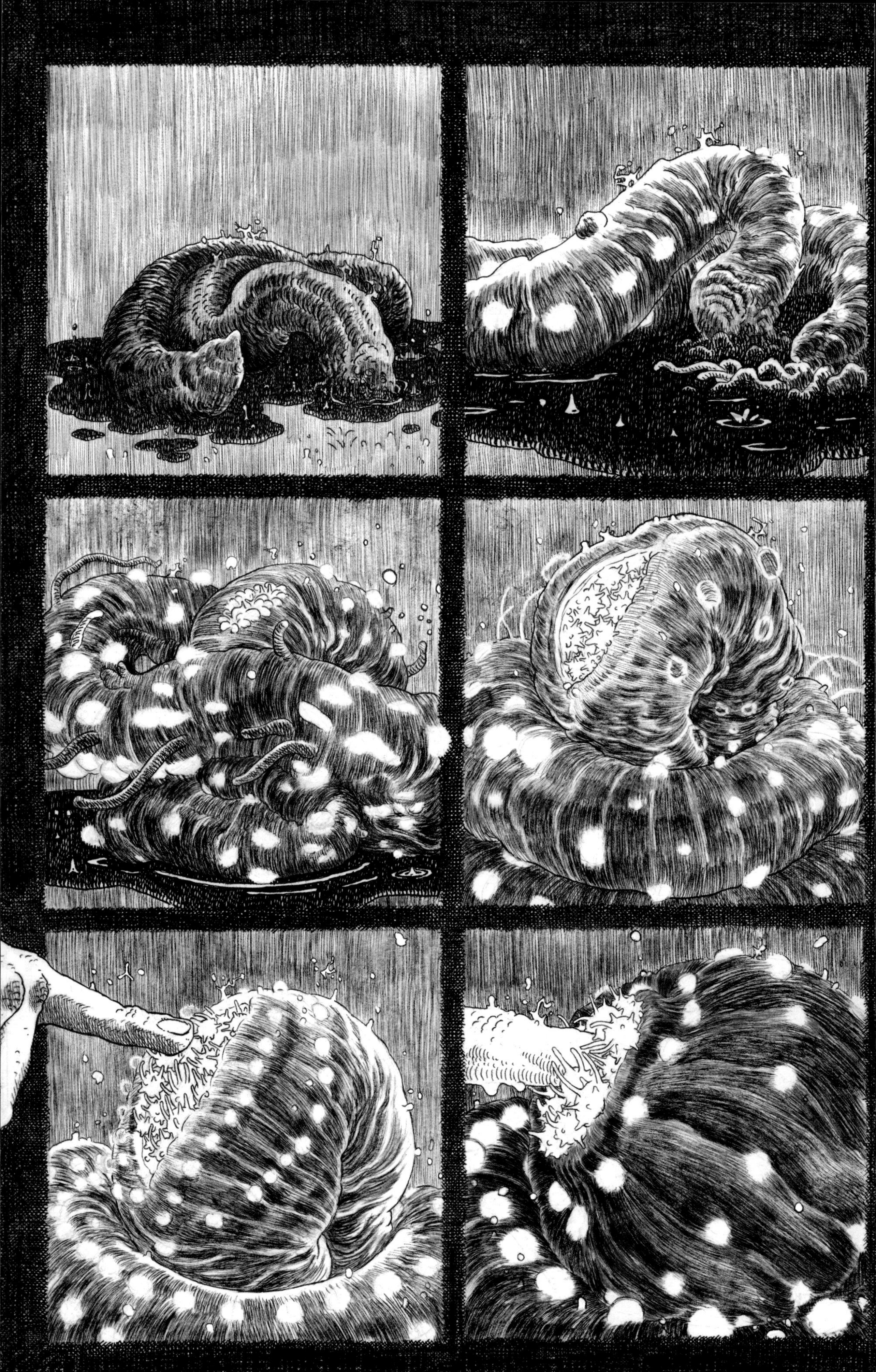

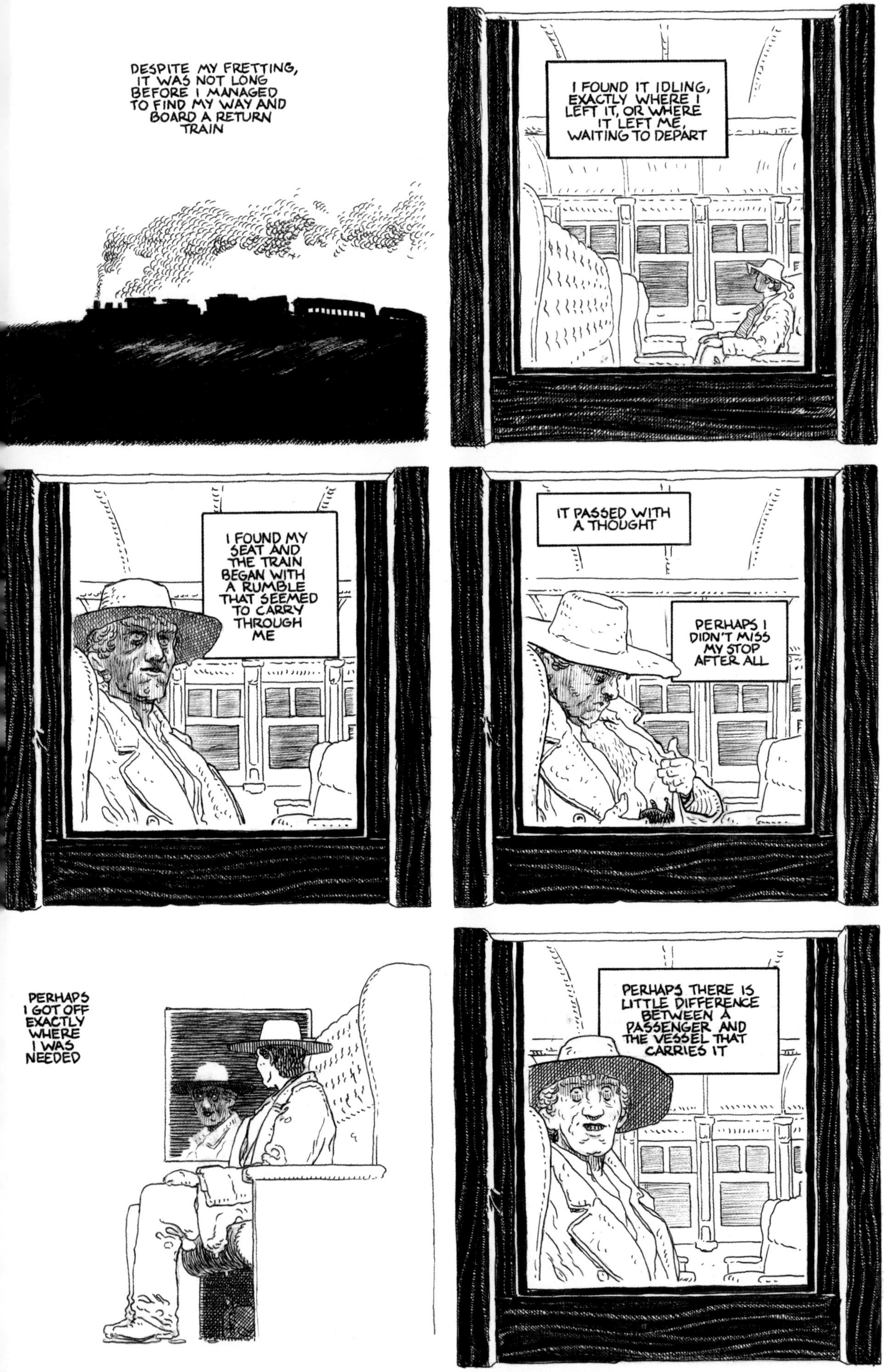
DESPITE MY FRETTING, IT WAS NOT LONG BEFORE I MANAGED TO FIND MY WAY AND BOARD A RETURN TRAIN
I FOUND IT IDLING, EXACTLY WHERE I LEFT IT, OR WHERE IT LEFT ME, WAITING TO DEPART
I FOUND MY SEAT AND THE TRAIN BEGAN WITH A RUMBLE THAT SEEMED TO CARRY THROUGH ME
IT PASSED WITH A THOUGHT
PERHAPS I DIDN'T MISS MY STOP AFTER ALL
PERHAPS I GOT OFF EXACTLY WHERE I WAS NEEDED
PERHAPS THERE IS LITTLE DIFFERENCE BETWEEN A PASSENGER AND THE VESSEL THAT CARRIES IT

THE WITCH HAD BEEN FLOATING THERE FOR WEEKS, SILENTLY STARING OUT AT THE HOUSES WITH HER GLASSY EYES.

OUR FOOD STORES DEPLETING, WE CAREFULLY WATCHED FROM THE WINDOW, PLANNING OUR ESCAPE.

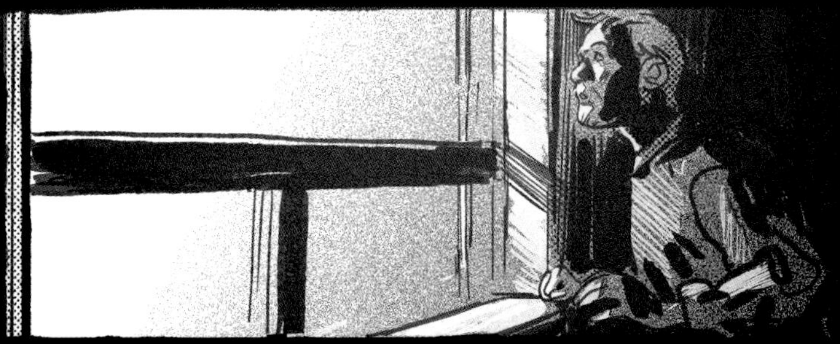

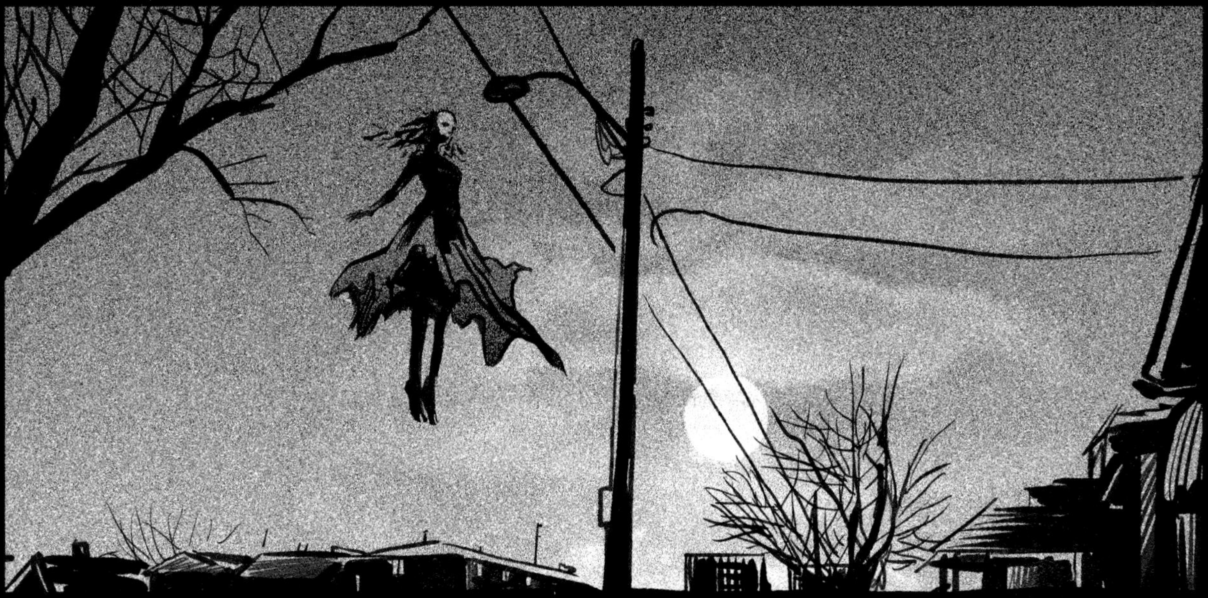

HER NECK CRACKED AND CREAKED AS SHE TURNED TOWARD ME.

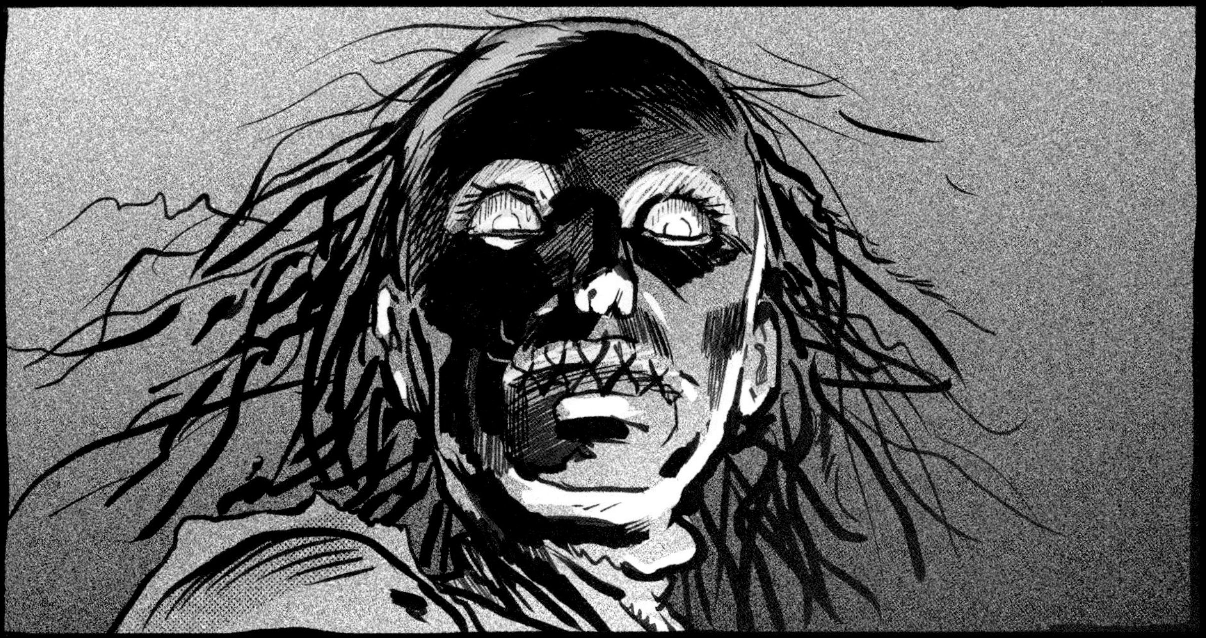

I FELT SOMETHING IN MY CHEST GO COLD.

New York City, 1997.

Foxe·Kowalski·
Simpson·Otsmane·Elhaou

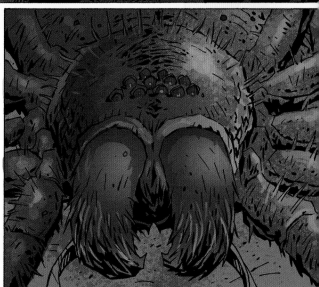

TRIP WIRES... TRICKY BASTARDS.

EXCUSE ME, SIR, BUT WE DON'T ALLOW--

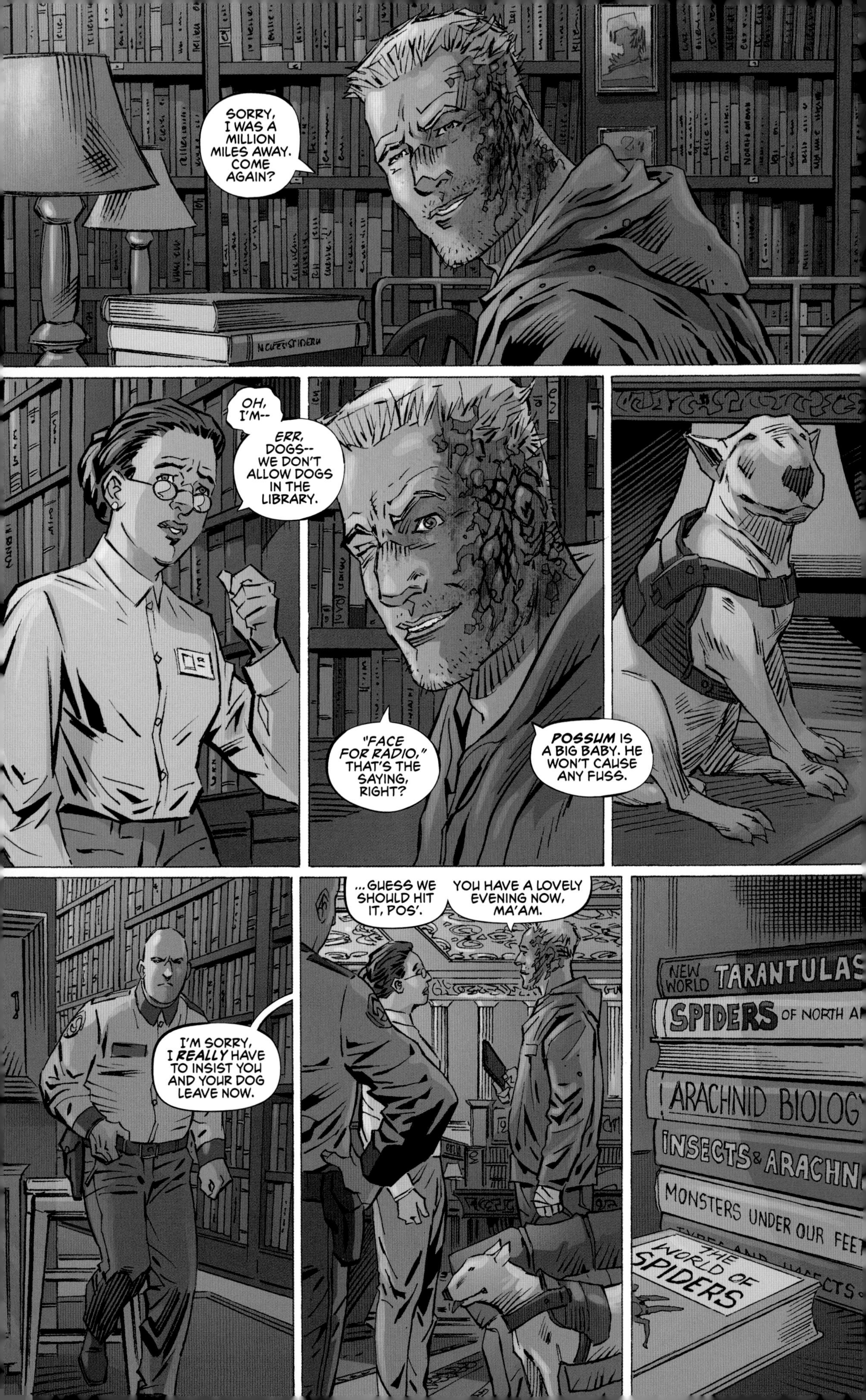
SORRY, I WAS A MILLION MILES AWAY. COME AGAIN?
OH, I'M--
ERR, DOGS-- WE DON'T ALLOW DOGS IN THE LIBRARY.
"FACE FOR RADIO," THAT'S THE SAYING, RIGHT?
POSSUM IS A BIG BABY. HE WON'T CAUSE ANY FUSS.
I'M SORRY, I REALLY HAVE TO INSIST YOU AND YOUR DOG LEAVE NOW.
...GUESS WE SHOULD HIT IT, POS'.
YOU HAVE A LOVELY EVENING NOW, MA'AM.
NEW WORLD TARANTULAS
SPIDERS OF NORTH A
ARACHNID BIOLOG
INSECTS & ARACHN
MONSTERS UNDER OUR FEE
THE WORLD OF SPIDERS

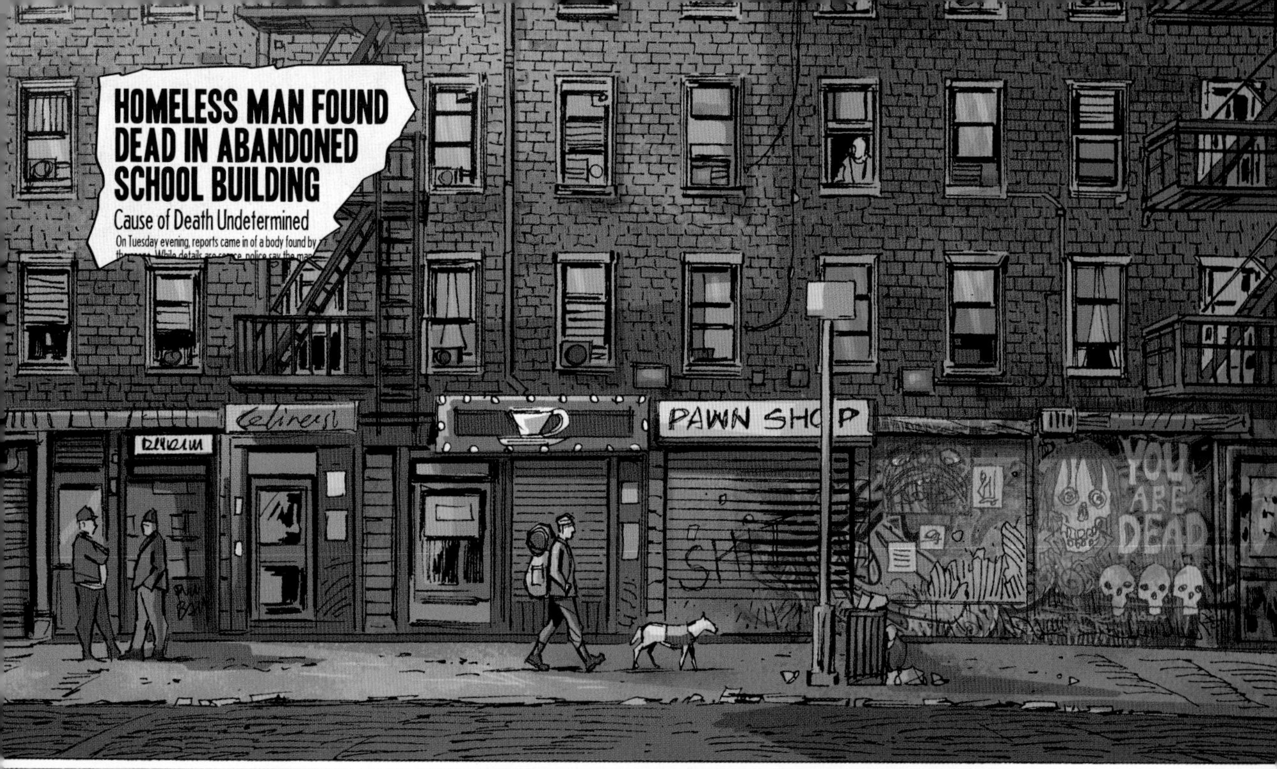
HOMELESS MAN FOUND DEAD IN ABANDONED SCHOOL BUILDING
Cause of Death Undetermined
On Tuesday evening, reports came in of a body found by
PAWN SHOP
YOU ARE DEAD
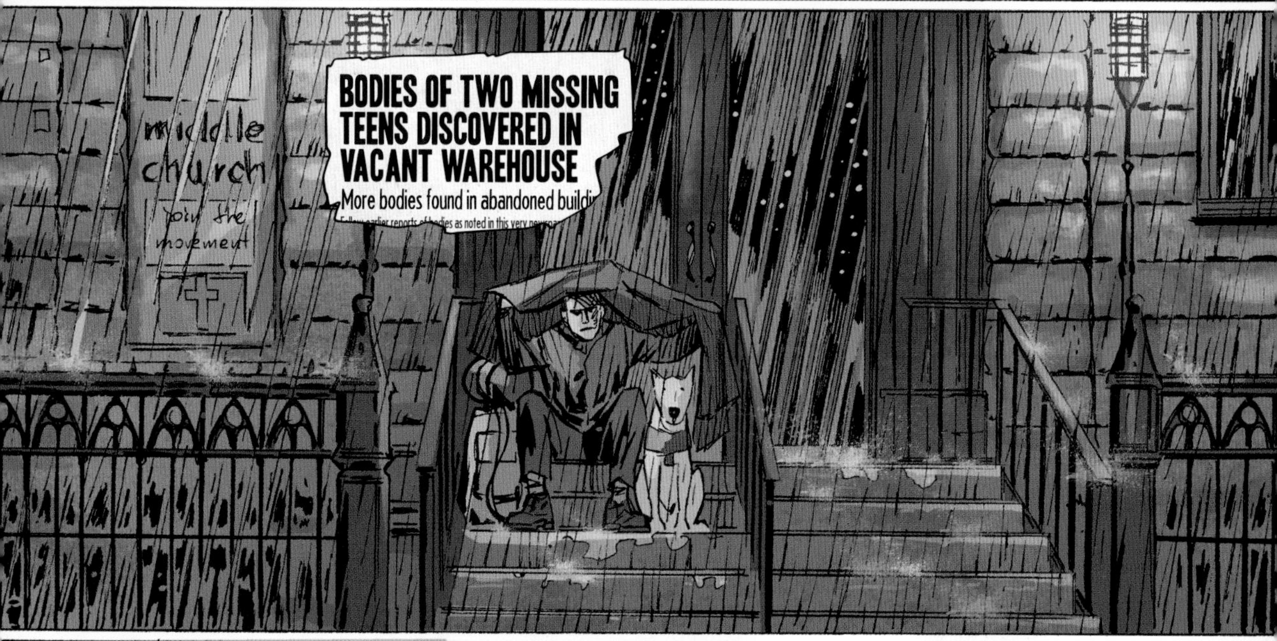
middle church
join the movement
BODIES OF TWO MISSING TEENS DISCOVERED IN VACANT WAREHOUSE
More bodies found in abandoned buildi
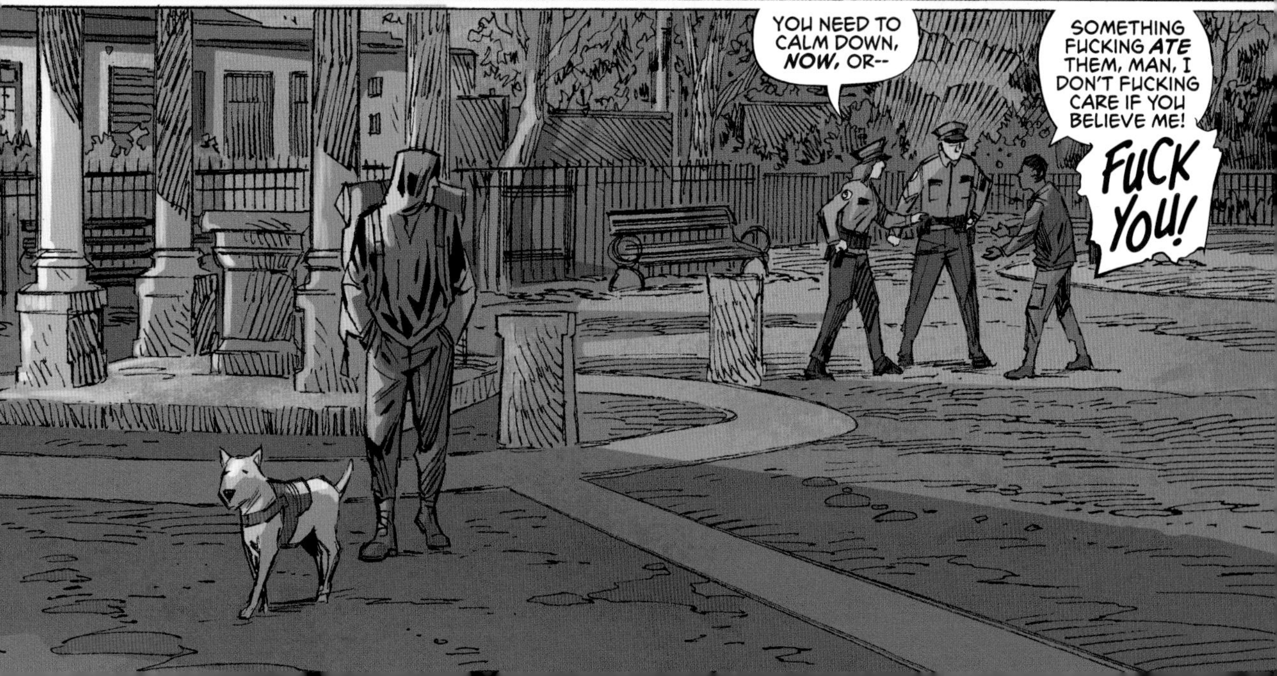
YOU NEED TO CALM DOWN, *NOW,* OR--
SOMETHING FUCKING *ATE* THEM, MAN, I DON'T FUCKING CARE IF YOU BELIEVE ME!
FUCK YOU!

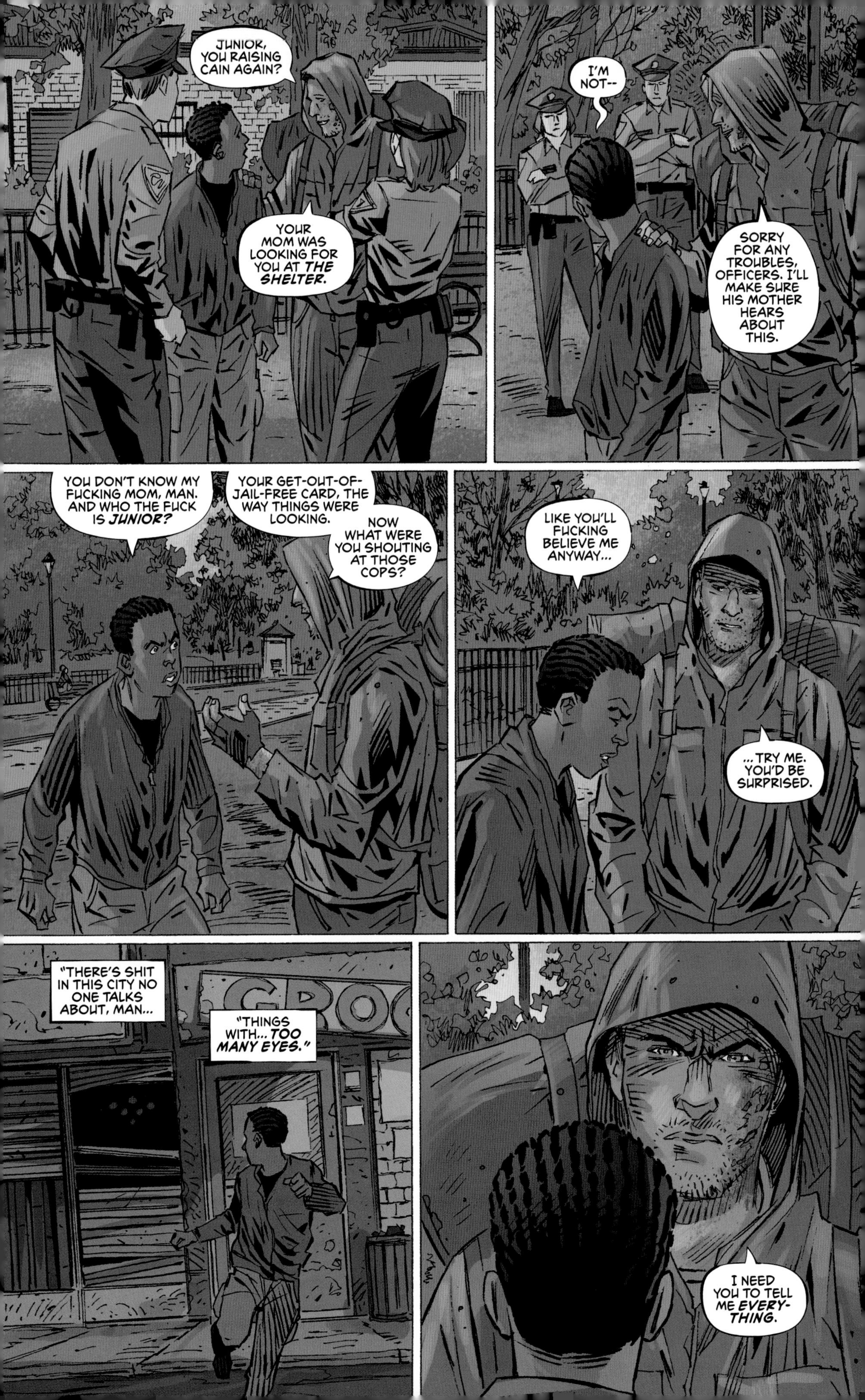
JUNIOR, YOU RAISING CAIN AGAIN?
YOUR MOM WAS LOOKING FOR YOU AT *THE SHELTER*.
I'M NOT--
SORRY FOR ANY TROUBLES, OFFICERS. I'LL MAKE SURE HIS MOTHER HEARS ABOUT THIS.
YOU DON'T KNOW MY FUCKING MOM, MAN. AND WHO THE FUCK IS *JUNIOR?*
YOUR GET-OUT-OF-JAIL-FREE CARD, THE WAY THINGS WERE LOOKING.
NOW WHAT WERE YOU SHOUTING AT THOSE COPS?
LIKE YOU'LL FUCKING BELIEVE ME ANYWAY...
...TRY ME. YOU'D BE SURPRISED.
"THERE'S SHIT IN THIS CITY NO ONE TALKS ABOUT, MAN...
"THINGS WITH... *TOO MANY EYES.*"
I NEED YOU TO TELL ME *EVERY-THING*.

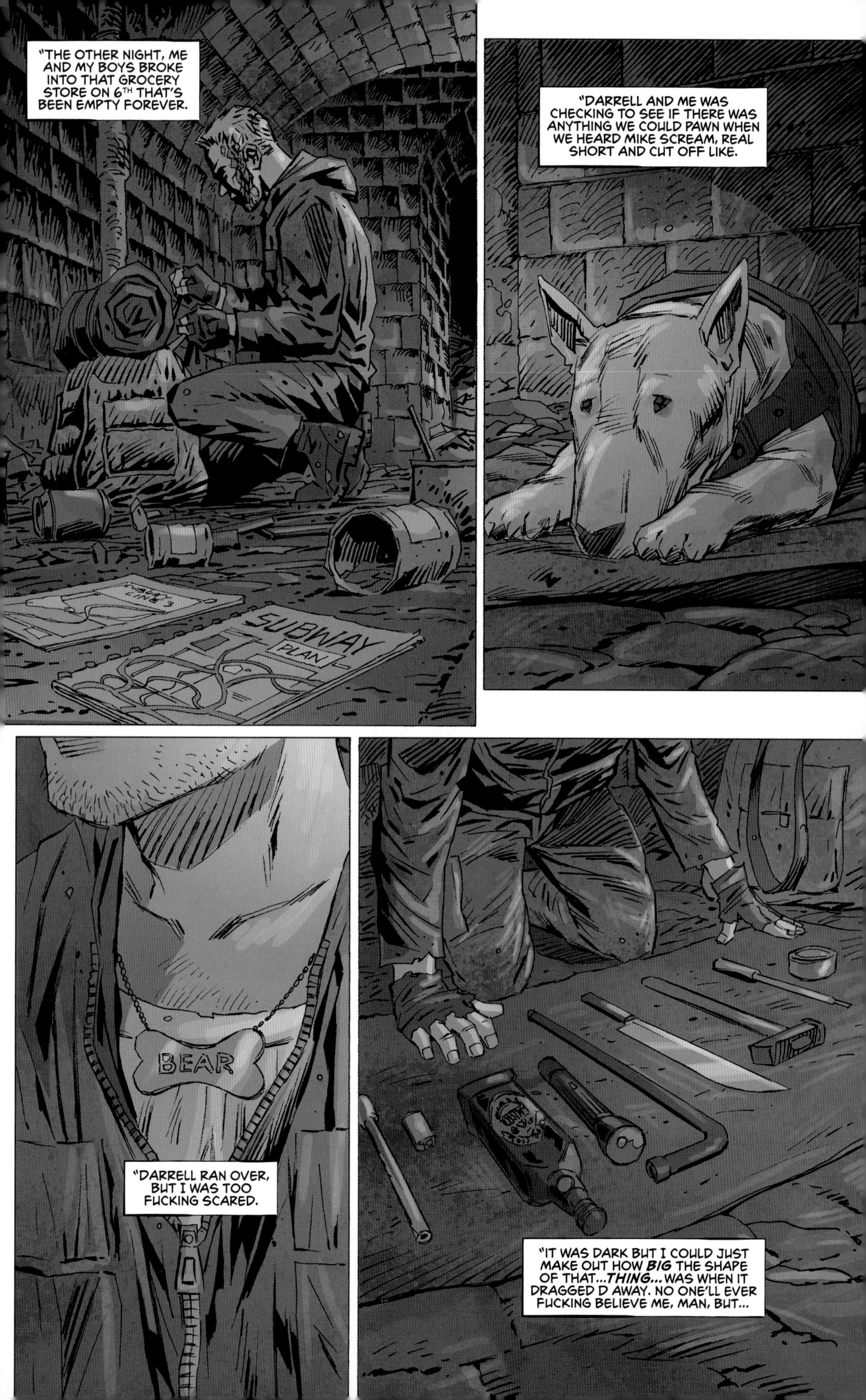
"THE OTHER NIGHT, ME AND MY BOYS BROKE INTO THAT GROCERY STORE ON 6TH THAT'S BEEN EMPTY FOREVER.
SUBWAY
PLAN
"DARRELL AND ME WAS CHECKING TO SEE IF THERE WAS ANYTHING WE COULD PAWN WHEN WE HEARD MIKE SCREAM, REAL SHORT AND CUT OFF LIKE.
BEAR
"DARRELL RAN OVER, BUT I WAS TOO FUCKING SCARED.
"IT WAS DARK BUT I COULD JUST MAKE OUT HOW *BIG* THE SHAPE OF THAT... *THING...* WAS WHEN IT DRAGGED D AWAY. NO ONE'LL EVER FUCKING BELIEVE ME, MAN, BUT...

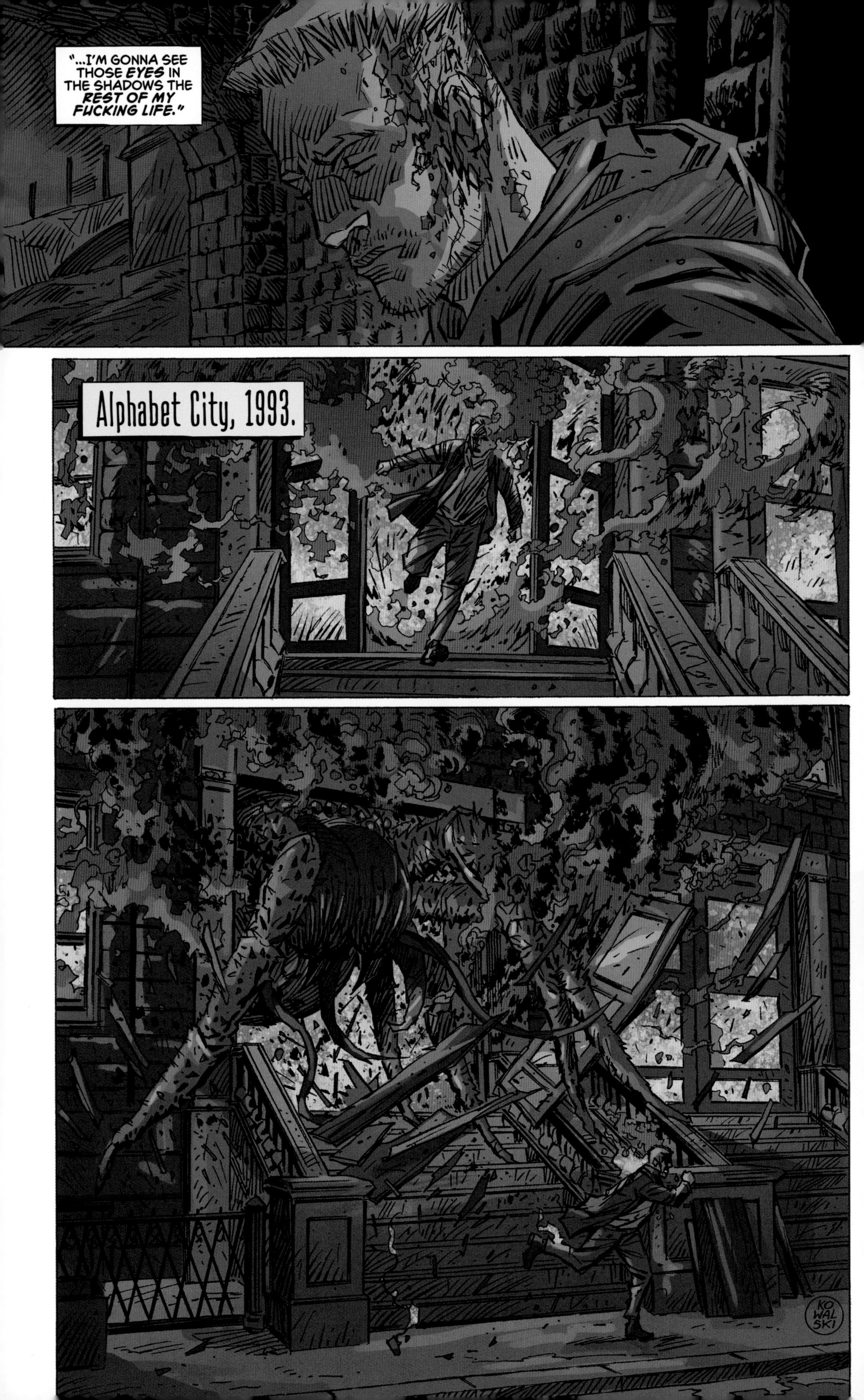
"...I'M GONNA SEE THOSE EYES IN THE SHADOWS THE REST OF MY FUCKING LIFE."
Alphabet City, 1993.
KOWALSKI

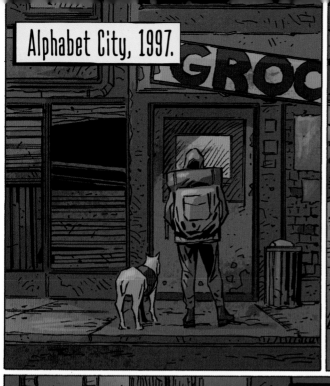

Alphabet City, 1997.

HAVEN'T REPLACED THE LOCKS YET. SAVES ME A STEP.

HRRRMMM

NOT RISKING IT, POS'. STAY.

WEBS...? BUT THEY DON'T--

CLK
CLK
CLK
CLK
CLK

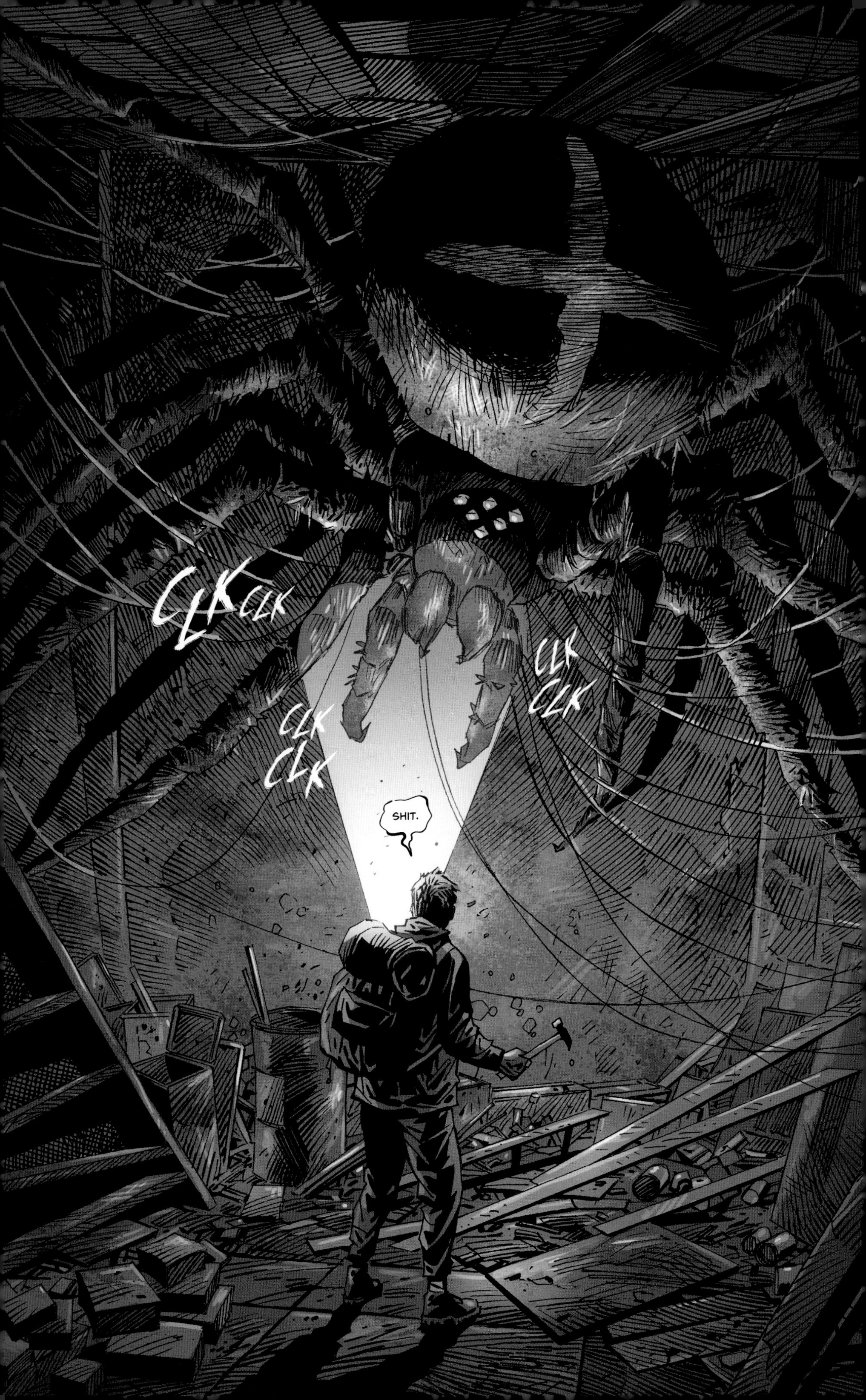
CLK CLK
CLK CLK
CLK CLK
SHIT.

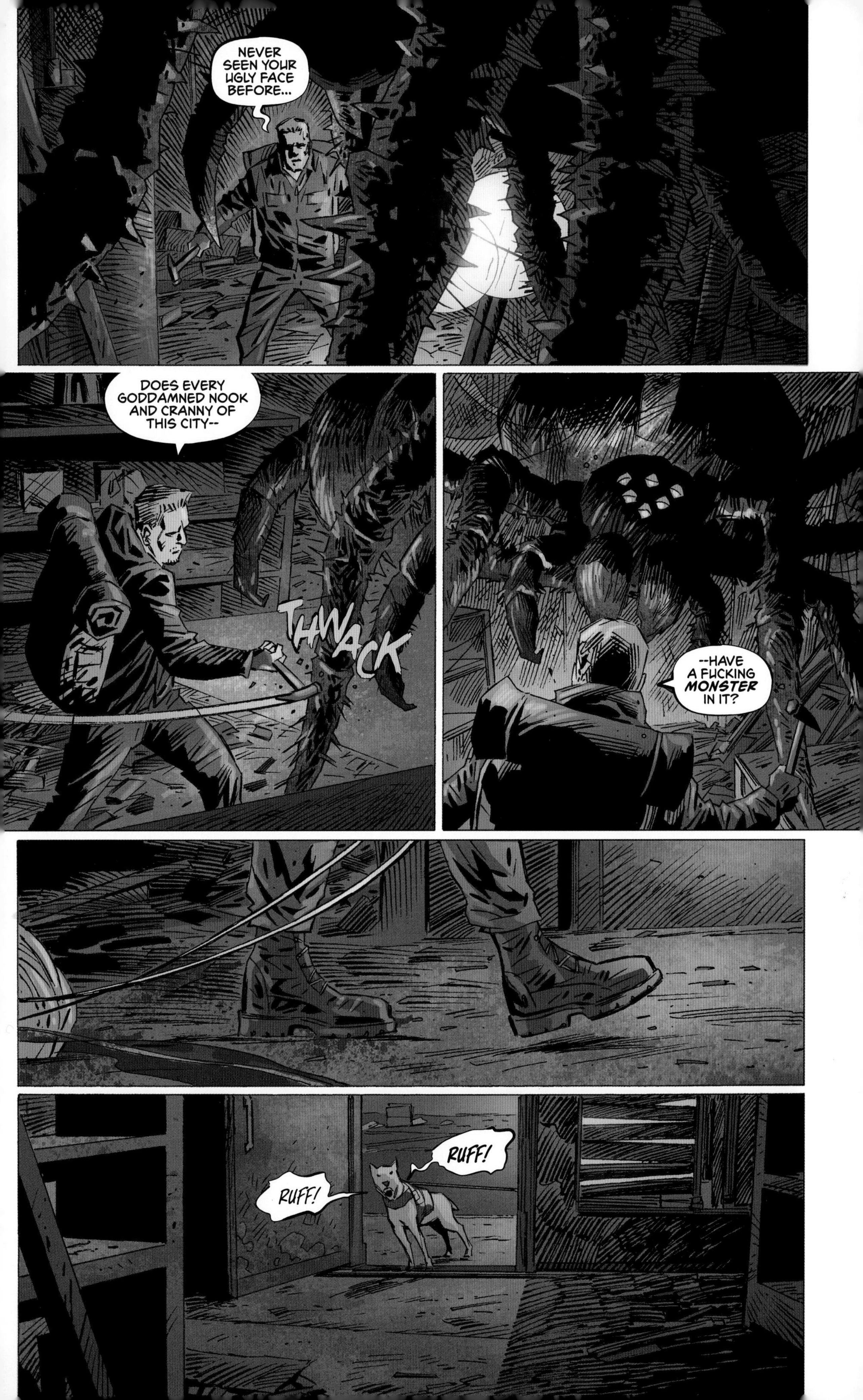
NEVER SEEN YOUR UGLY FACE BEFORE...
DOES EVERY GODDAMNED NOOK AND CRANNY OF THIS CITY--
THWACK
--HAVE A FUCKING MONSTER IN IT?
RUFF!
RUFF!

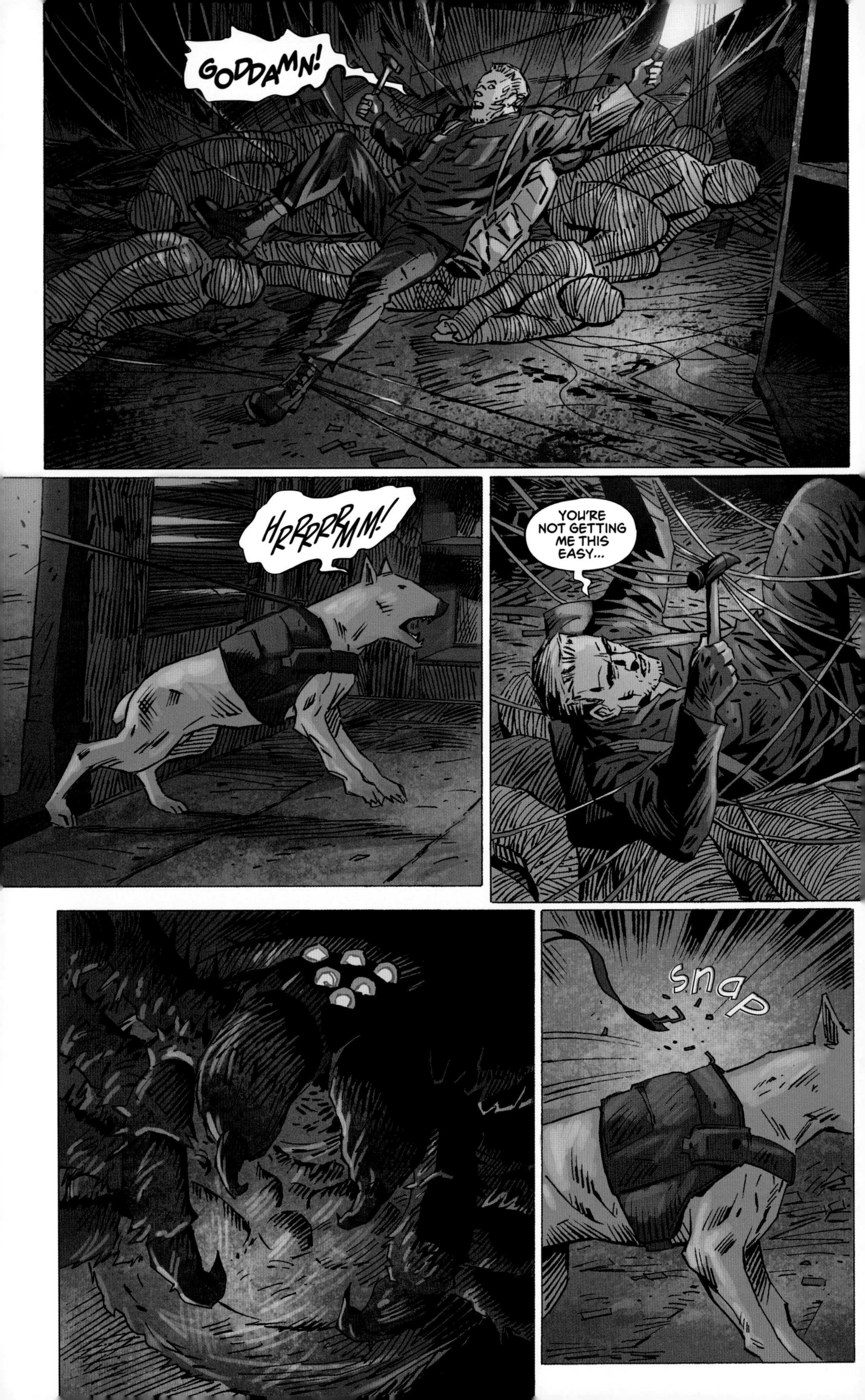
GODDAMN!
HRRRRRMM!
YOU'RE NOT GETTING ME THIS EASY...
SNAP

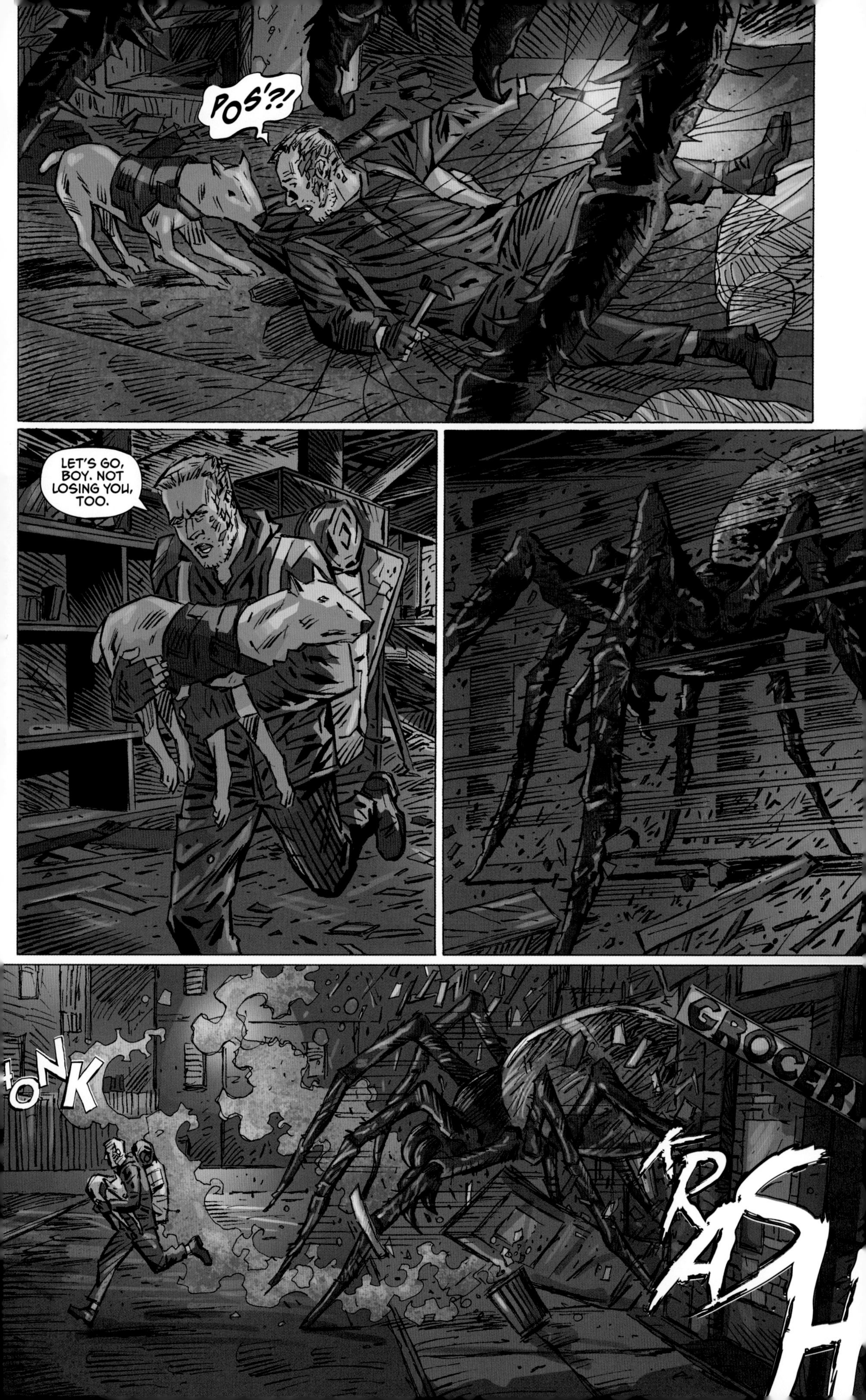
POS'?!
LET'S GO, BOY. NOT LOSING YOU, TOO.
HONK
GROCERY
KRASH

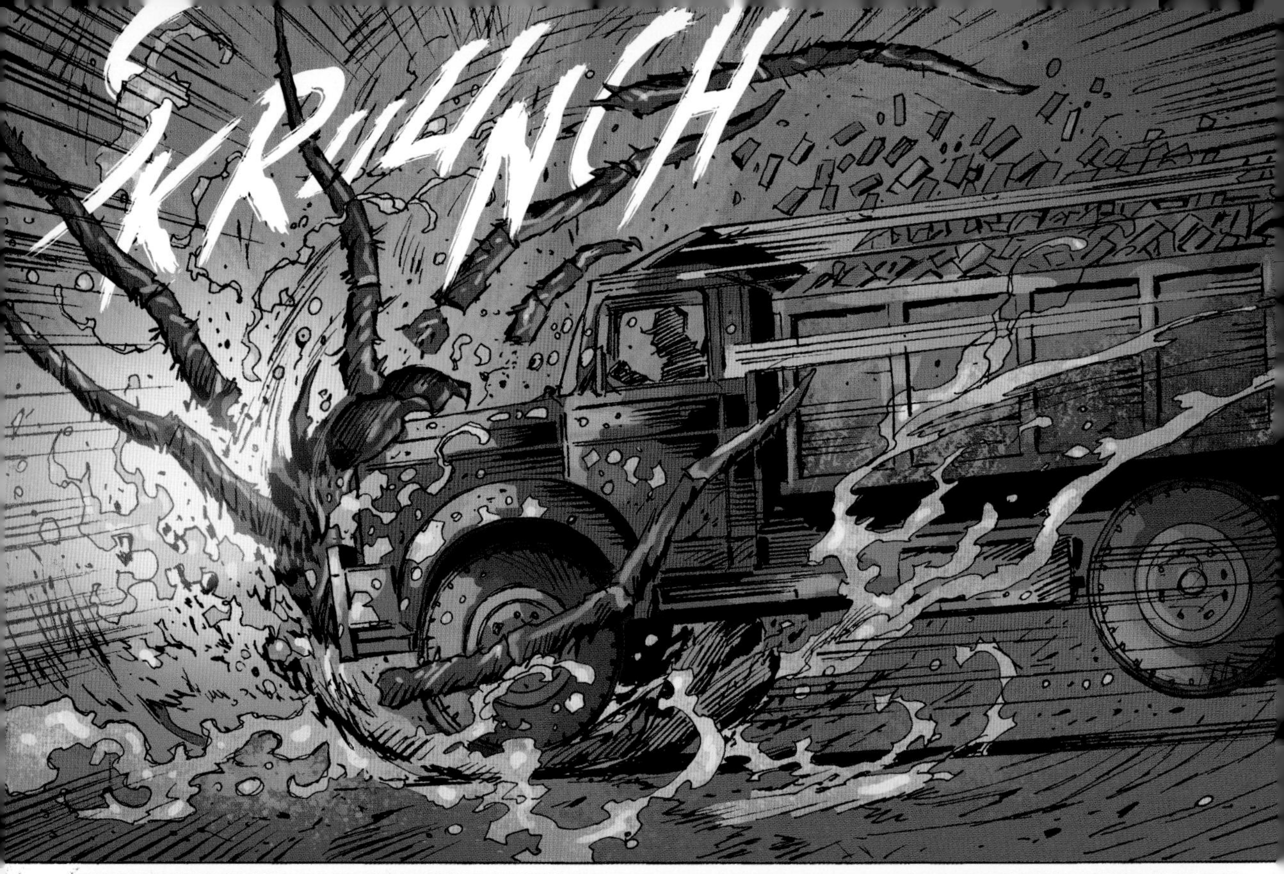
SKRUUNCH

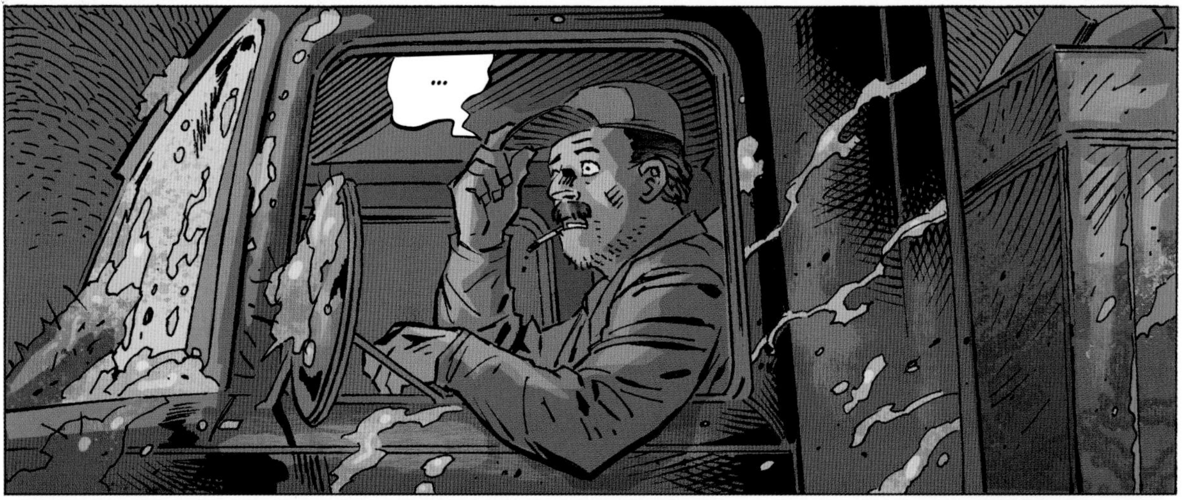
...

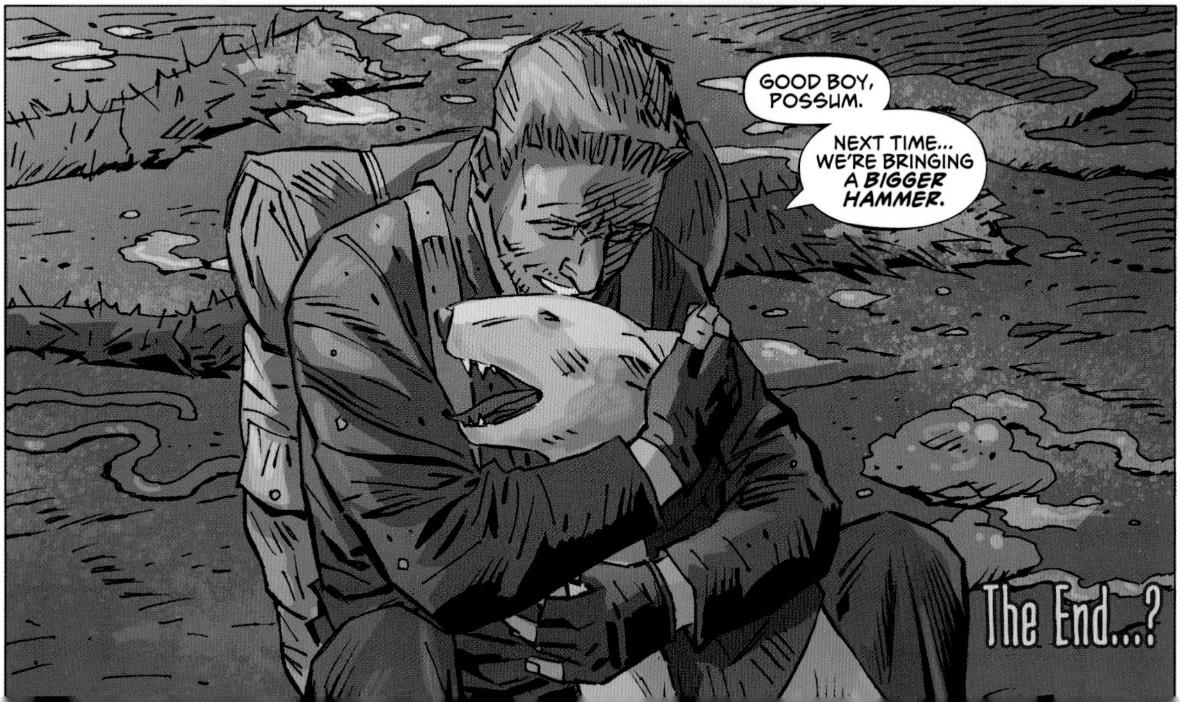
GOOD BOY, POSSUM.
NEXT TIME... WE'RE BRINGING A *BIGGER HAMMER.*
The End...?

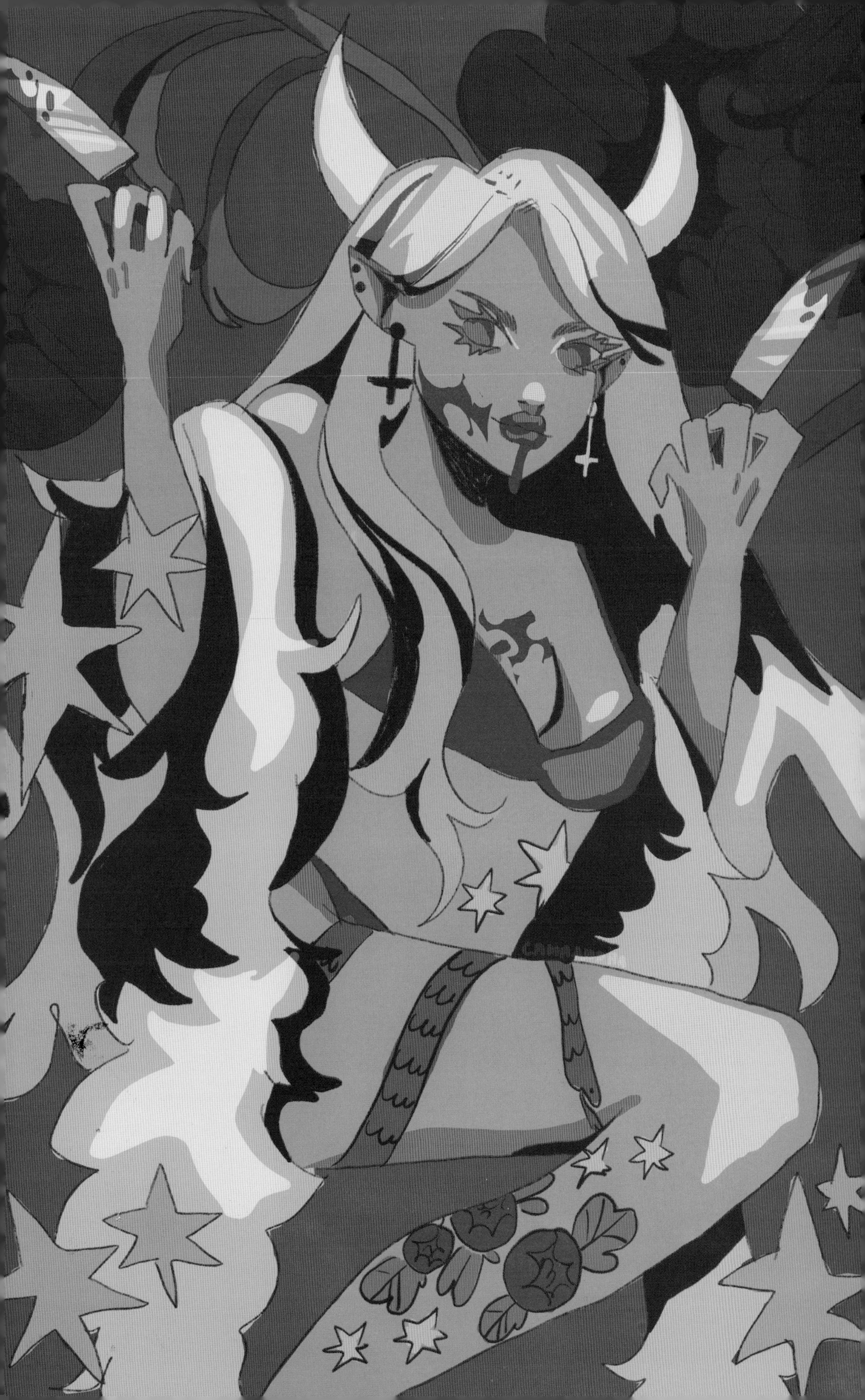

"CINDERSIDE"
By ALEX PAKNADEL & JASON LOO
Lettered By HASSAN OTSMANE-ELHAOU

CINDERSIDE originally ran as a serial in issues #2–#5.
It is presented here in its entirety.

"I DONT THINK"
By Brian Level
These pieces originally ran in issues #1–#3.
They are collected here with newly designed chapter
and end pages by Brian Level.

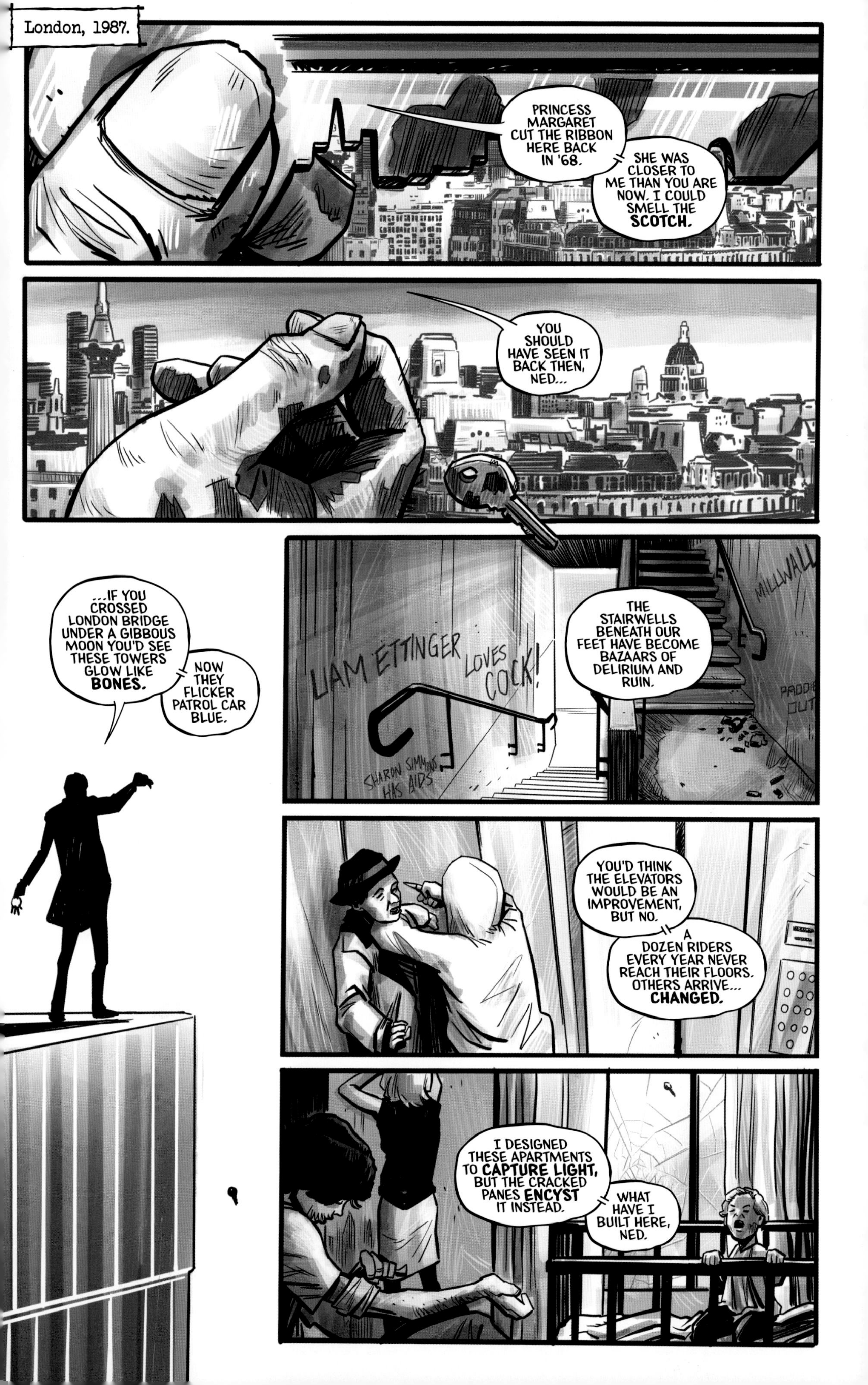
London, 1987.
PRINCESS MARGARET CUT THE RIBBON HERE BACK IN '68.
SHE WAS CLOSER TO ME THAN YOU ARE NOW. I COULD SMELL THE **SCOTCH.**
YOU SHOULD HAVE SEEN IT BACK THEN, NED...
...IF YOU CROSSED LONDON BRIDGE UNDER A GIBBOUS MOON YOU'D SEE THESE TOWERS GLOW LIKE **BONES.**
NOW THEY FLICKER PATROL CAR BLUE.
LIAM ETTINGER LOVES COCK!
MILLWALL
SHARON SIMMONS HAS AIDS
THE STAIRWELLS BENEATH OUR FEET HAVE BECOME BAZAARS OF DELIRIUM AND RUIN.
YOU'D THINK THE ELEVATORS WOULD BE AN IMPROVEMENT, BUT NO.
A DOZEN RIDERS EVERY YEAR NEVER REACH THEIR FLOORS. OTHERS ARRIVE... **CHANGED.**
I DESIGNED THESE APARTMENTS TO **CAPTURE LIGHT,** BUT THE CRACKED PANES **ENCYST** IT INSTEAD.
WHAT HAVE I BUILT HERE, NED.

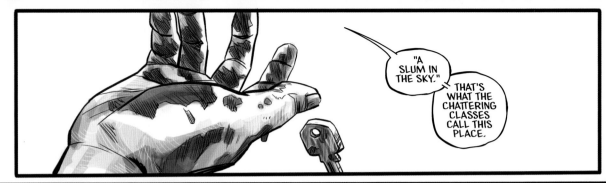

"A SLUM IN THE SKY." THAT'S WHAT THE CHATTERING CLASSES CALL THIS PLACE.

BUT I DIDN'T BUILD IT FOR **THEM.** I BUILT IT FOR THOSE **ORNAMENTLESS** SOULS BORN **DOWNWIND** OF THE CITY'S STEEPLES AND SMOKE-STACKS.

IT WAS TO BE A **MACHINE OF TRANSFORMATION.**

HERE, AMONG THE WILDING CLOUDS, THE DESERVING POOR WOULD FINALLY HAVE THE CHANCE TO **RISE.**

EXCEPT... THEY DIDN'T.

THE HIGHER I BUILT, THE LOWER THEY SANK. AND YOU **LET** THEM, NED.

YOU WERE THE **CARETAKER**-- THE **KEEPER** OF THE KEYS.

THERE'S NOTHING WRONG WITH THE BUILDING. THE HARDWARE **WORKS.**

IT'S THE SOFTWARE, NED...

"...IT'S THE PEOPLE."

MAYBE.... MAYBE IT'LL BE DIFFERENT TONIGHT.

HE PROMISED.

SHHH.

MAX, WHATEVER HAPPENS, DON'T SAY NOTHING. PRETEND YOU'RE ASLEEP.

STAY WITH ME, HELEN.

I'M RIGHT HERE. I WON'T LET HIM THIS TIME.

I PROMISE.

RIIISE AND SHIIINE, MY DOVES.

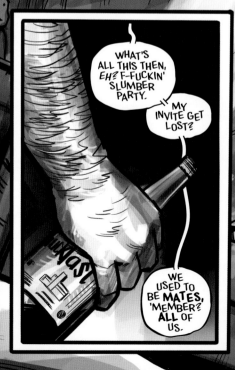

WHAT'S ALL THIS THEN, EH? F-FUCKIN' SLUMBER PARTY.

MY INVITE GET LOST?

WE USED TO BE MATES, 'MEMBER? ALL OF US.

COME ON, MAXY-BOY. HAVE A QUICK DRINK WITH ME.

JUSS... JUSS A LITTLE SNIFTER WITH YOUR OLD MAN, EH? PUT HAIRS ON YOUR TEETH.

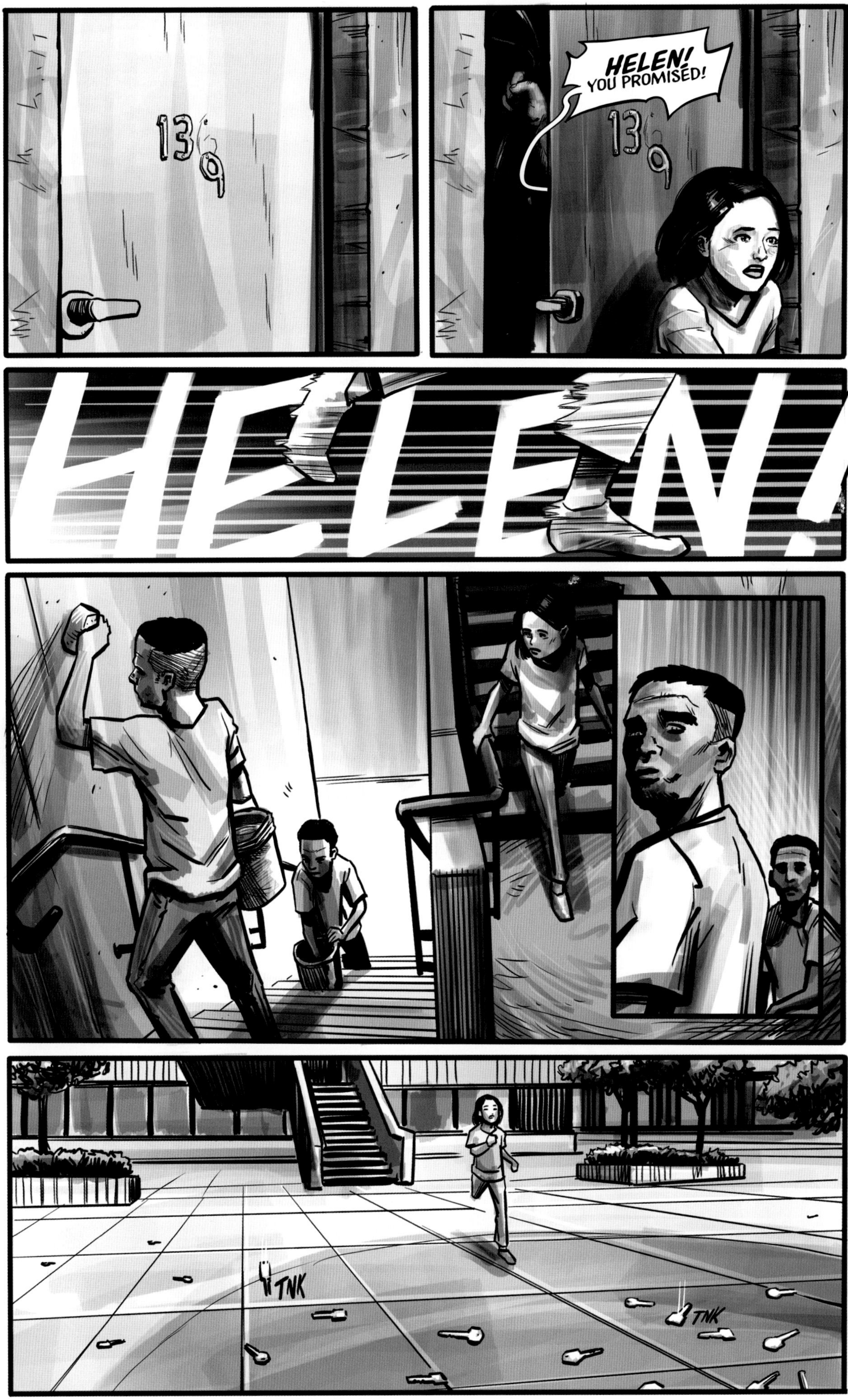
13
9
HELEN! YOU PROMISED!
HELEN!
TNK
TNK

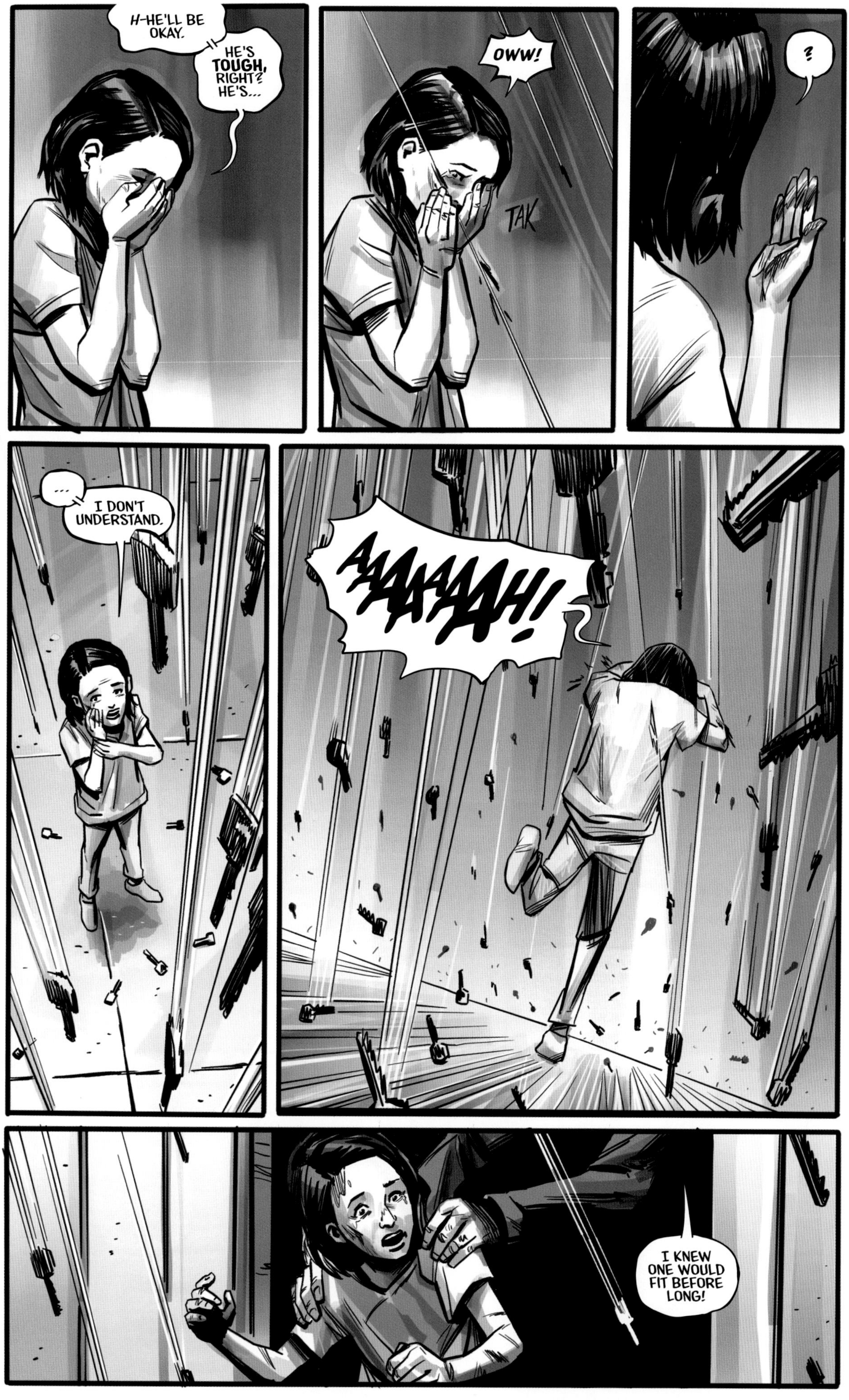
H-HE'LL BE OKAY.
HE'S TOUGH, RIGHT? HE'S...
OWW!
TAK
?
...
I DON'T UNDERSTAND.
AAAAAAAH!
I KNEW ONE WOULD FIT BEFORE LONG!

Morning.

Ingredients: Sodium Hypochlorite 0.52g per 100g

Chlorine based bleaching agents

<redacted>

Perfume

Methylisothiazolinone

<redacted>

Methylchloroisothialolinone

pfft

SNIFTER SLUMBER!

DOYE HAIR!

NOK NOK

HELEN? MAXY?

I'M SO SORRY.

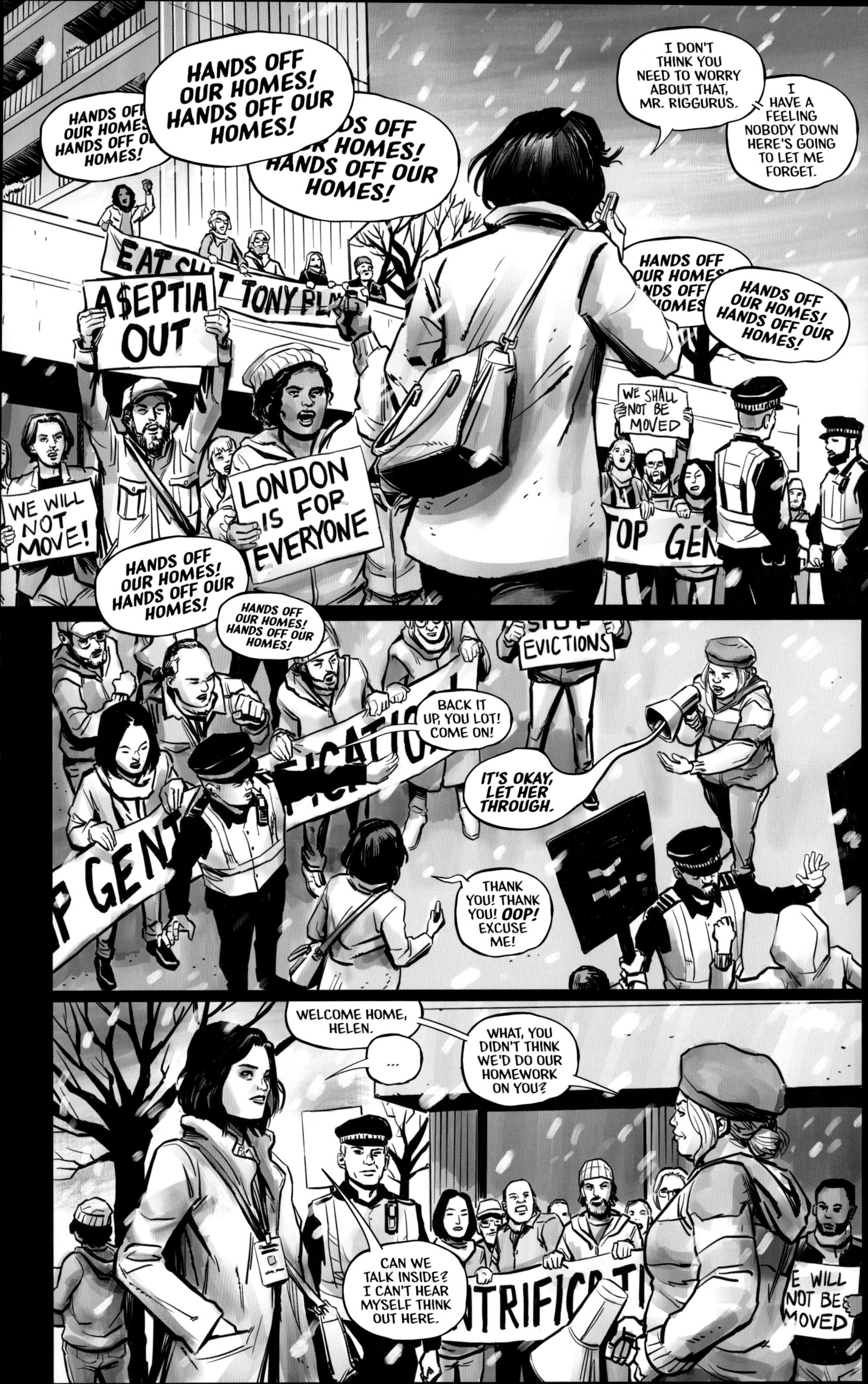
HANDS OFF OUR HOMES! HANDS OFF OUR HOMES!
HANDS OFF OUR HOMES! HANDS OFF OUR HOMES!
…DS OFF …R HOMES! HANDS OFF OUR HOMES!
EAT S… T TONY BL…
A$EPTIA OUT
I DON'T THINK YOU NEED TO WORRY ABOUT THAT, MR. RIGGURUS.
I HAVE A FEELING NOBODY DOWN HERE'S GOING TO LET ME FORGET.
HANDS OFF OUR HOMES! …NDS OFF …HOMES
HANDS OFF OUR HOMES! HANDS OFF OUR HOMES!
WE SHALL NOT BE MOVED
WE WILL NOT MOVE!
LONDON IS FOR EVERYONE
…TOP GEN…
HANDS OFF OUR HOMES! HANDS OFF OUR HOMES!
HANDS OFF OUR HOMES! HANDS OFF OUR HOMES!
EVICTIONS
BACK IT UP, YOU LOT! COME ON!
IT'S OKAY, LET HER THROUGH.
…P GENT…
THANK YOU! THANK YOU! OOP! EXCUSE ME!
WELCOME HOME, HELEN.
…
WHAT, YOU DIDN'T THINK WE'D DO OUR HOMEWORK ON YOU?
CAN WE TALK INSIDE? I CAN'T HEAR MYSELF THINK OUT HERE.
…NTRIFIC…TI…
…E WILL NOT BE MOVED

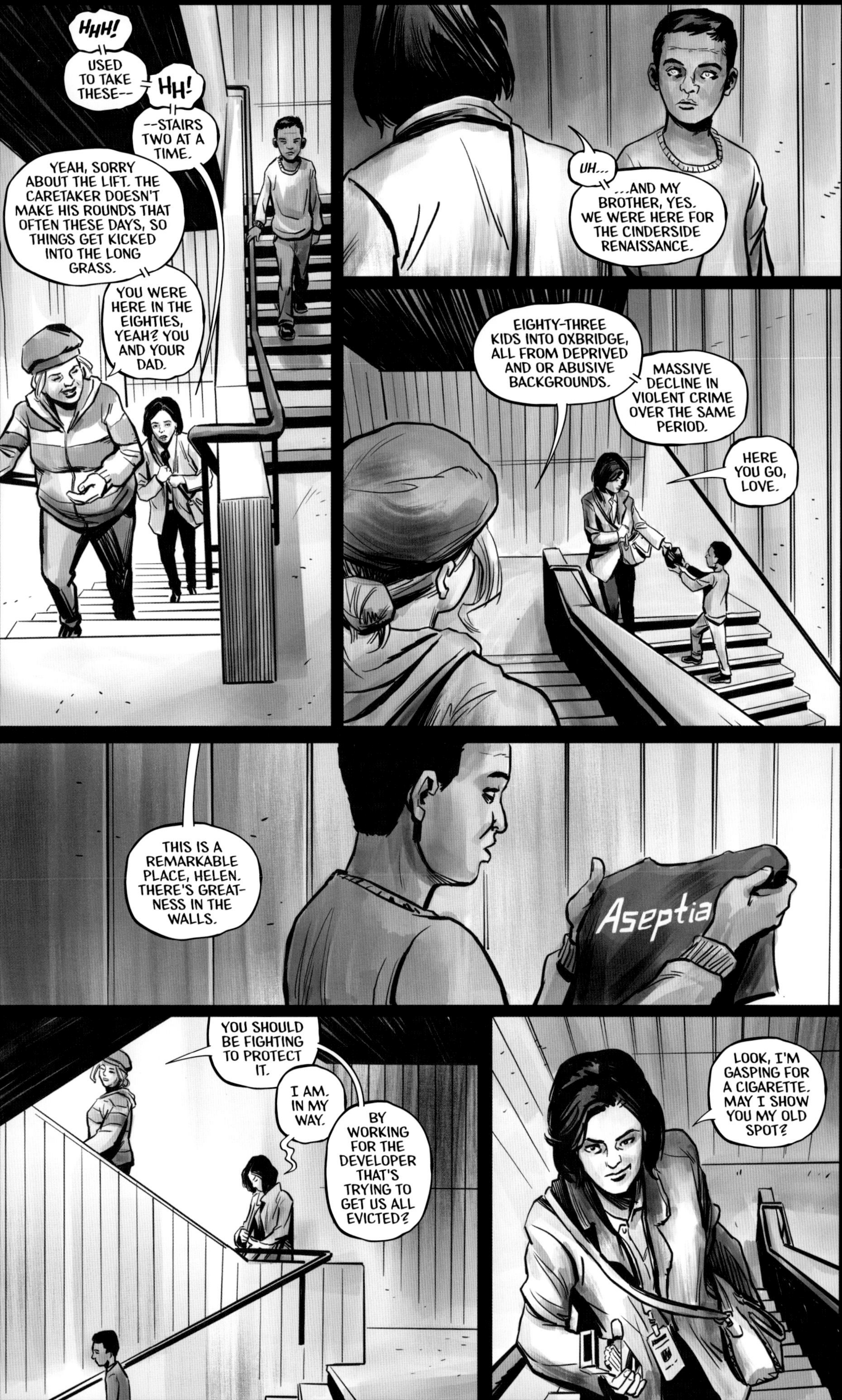
HHH!
USED TO TAKE THESE--
HH!
--STAIRS TWO AT A TIME.
YEAH, SORRY ABOUT THE LIFT. THE CARETAKER DOESN'T MAKE HIS ROUNDS THAT OFTEN THESE DAYS, SO THINGS GET KICKED INTO THE LONG GRASS.
YOU WERE HERE IN THE EIGHTIES, YEAH? YOU AND YOUR DAD.
UH...
...AND MY BROTHER, YES. WE WERE HERE FOR THE CINDERSIDE RENAISSANCE.
EIGHTY-THREE KIDS INTO OXBRIDGE, ALL FROM DEPRIVED AND OR ABUSIVE BACKGROUNDS.
MASSIVE DECLINE IN VIOLENT CRIME OVER THE SAME PERIOD.
HERE YOU GO, LOVE.
THIS IS A REMARKABLE PLACE, HELEN. THERE'S GREATNESS IN THE WALLS.
Aseptia
YOU SHOULD BE FIGHTING TO PROTECT IT.
I AM. IN MY WAY.
BY WORKING FOR THE DEVELOPER THAT'S TRYING TO GET US ALL EVICTED?
LOOK, I'M GASPING FOR A CIGARETTE. MAY I SHOW YOU MY OLD SPOT?

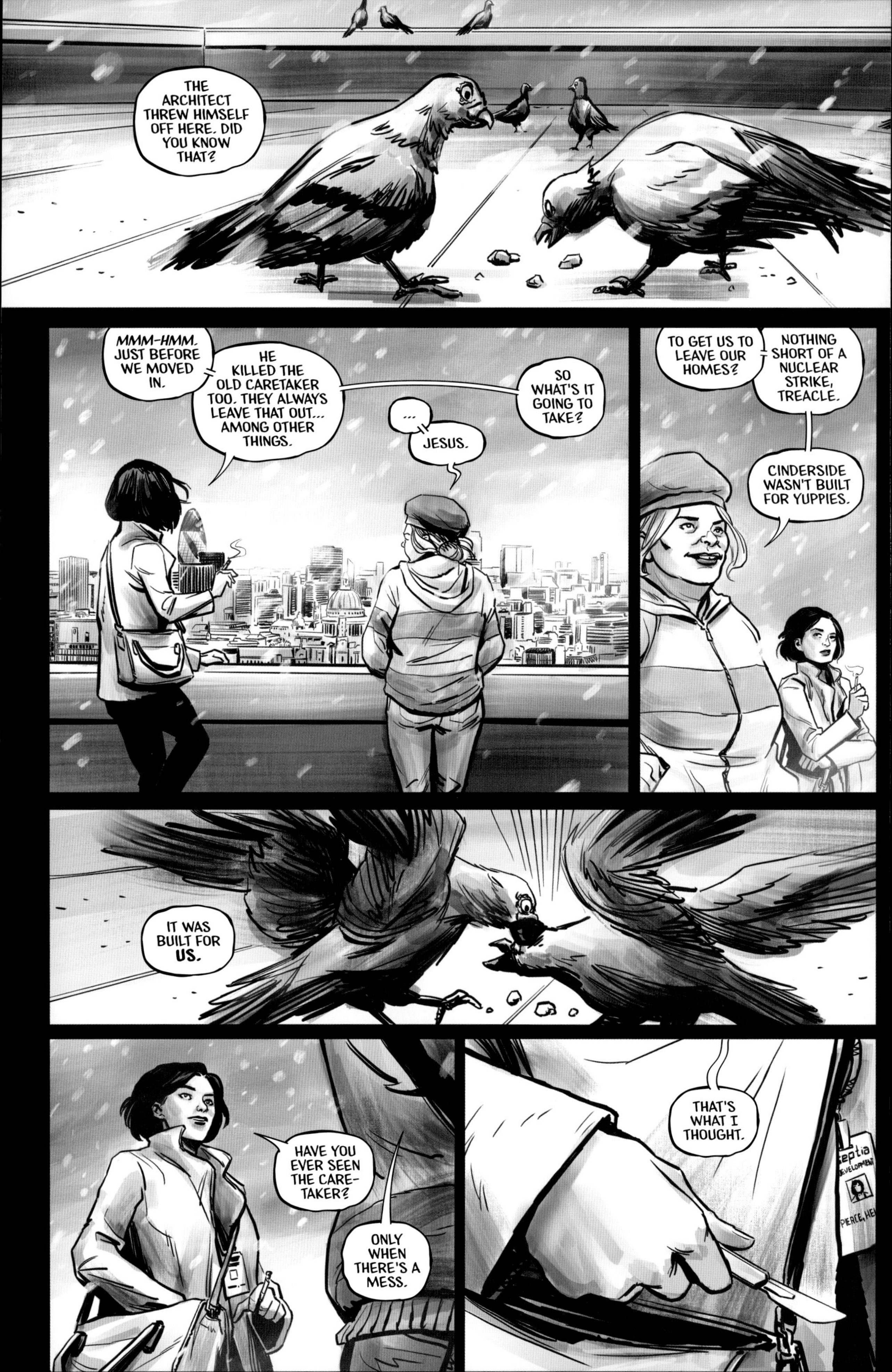
THE ARCHITECT THREW HIMSELF OFF HERE. DID YOU KNOW THAT?
MMM-HMM. JUST BEFORE WE MOVED IN.
HE KILLED THE OLD CARETAKER TOO. THEY ALWAYS LEAVE THAT OUT... AMONG OTHER THINGS.
...
JESUS.
SO WHAT'S IT GOING TO TAKE?
TO GET US TO LEAVE OUR HOMES?
NOTHING SHORT OF A NUCLEAR STRIKE, TREACLE.
CINDERSIDE WASN'T BUILT FOR YUPPIES.
IT WAS BUILT FOR US.
HAVE YOU EVER SEEN THE CARE-TAKER?
ONLY WHEN THERE'S A MESS.
THAT'S WHAT I THOUGHT.

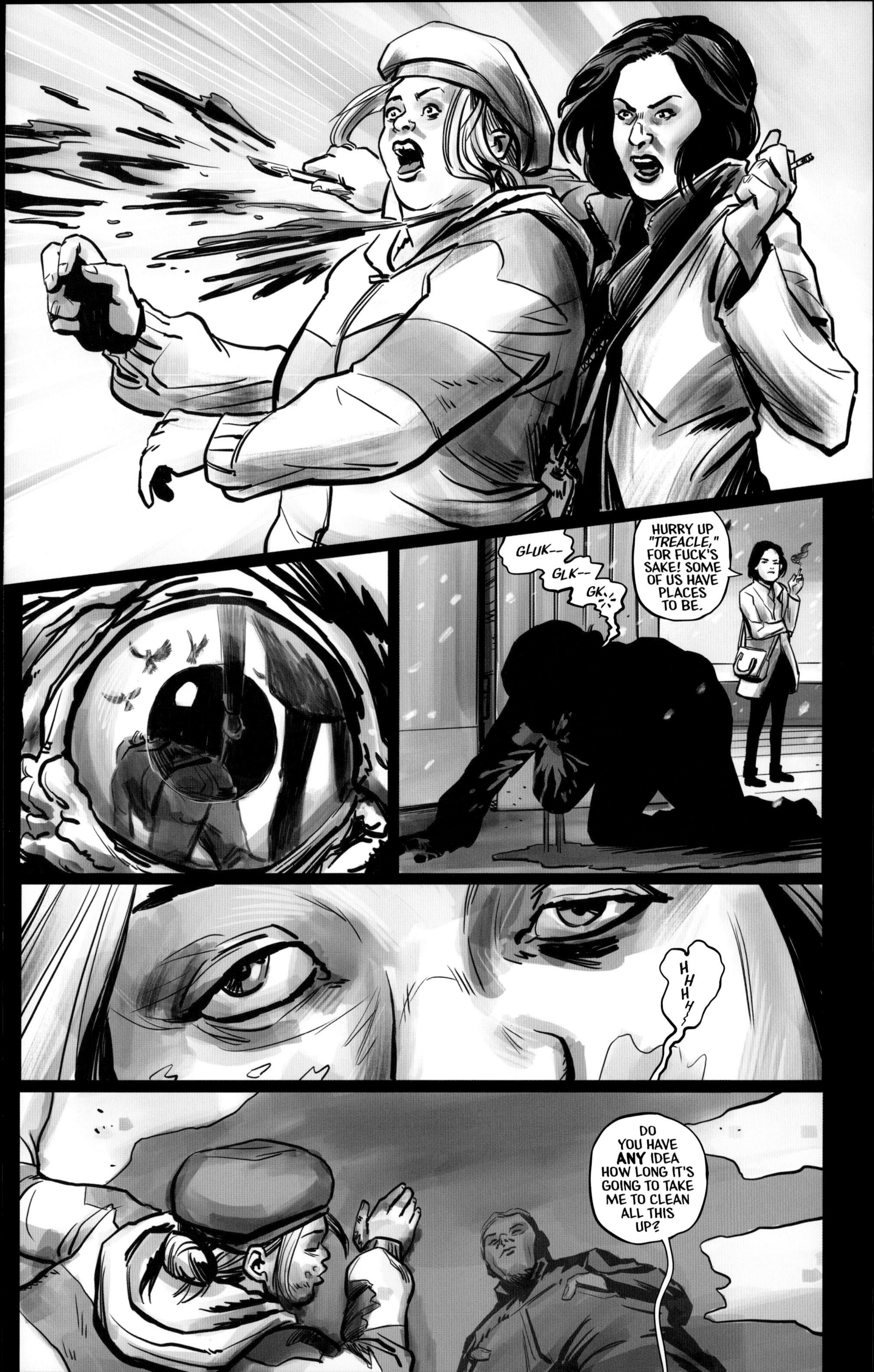
GLUK--
GLK--
GK
HURRY UP "TREACLE," FOR FUCK'S SAKE! SOME OF US HAVE PLACES TO BE.
HHHH--
DO YOU HAVE ANY IDEA HOW LONG IT'S GOING TO TAKE ME TO CLEAN ALL THIS UP?

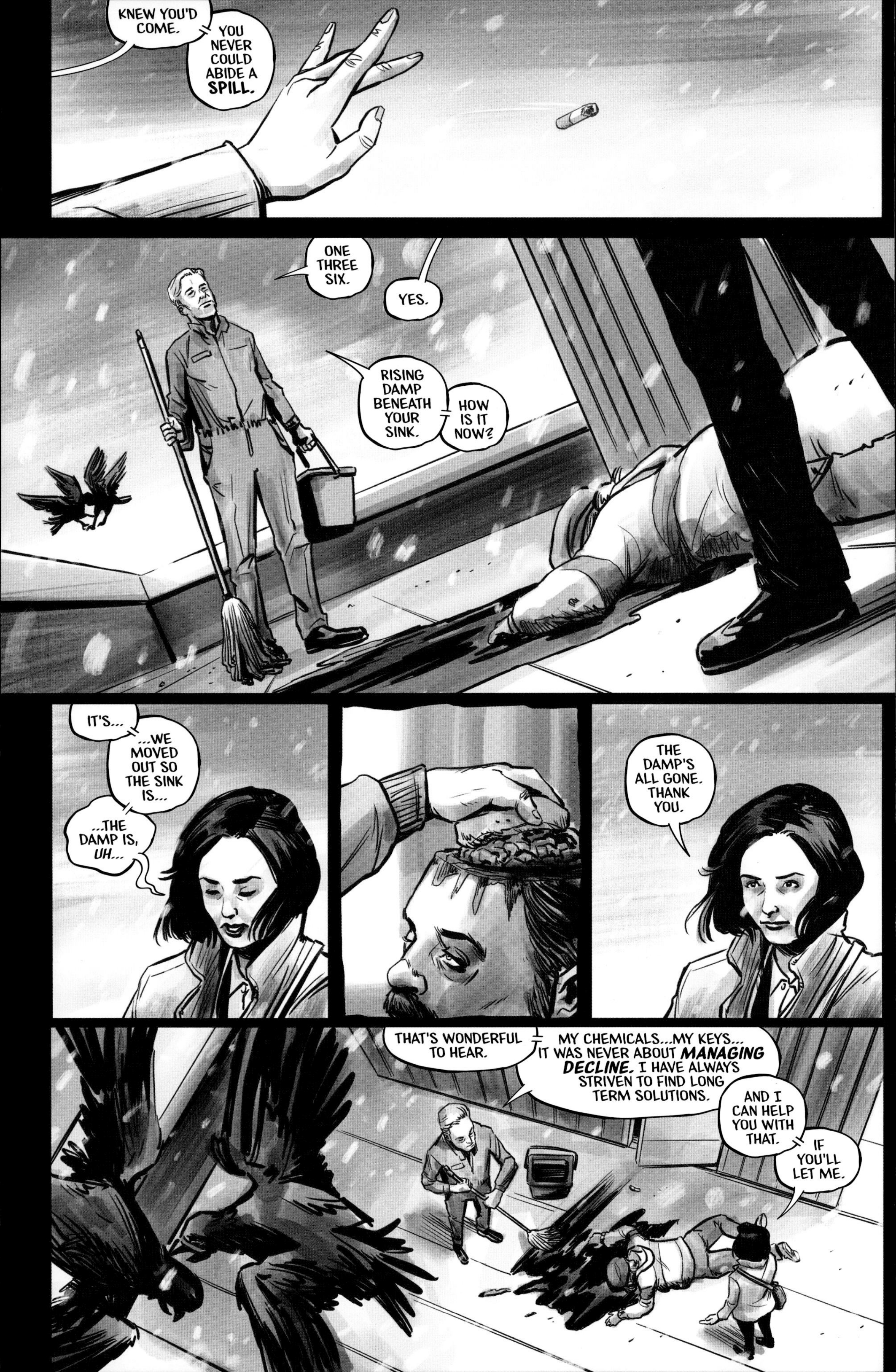
KNEW YOU'D COME.
YOU NEVER COULD ABIDE A **SPILL.**
ONE THREE SIX.
YES.
RISING DAMP BENEATH YOUR SINK.
HOW IS IT NOW?
IT'S...
...WE MOVED OUT SO THE SINK IS...
...THE DAMP IS, *UH...*
THE DAMP'S ALL GONE. THANK YOU.
THAT'S WONDERFUL TO HEAR.
MY CHEMICALS...MY KEYS... IT WAS NEVER ABOUT ***MANAGING DECLINE.*** I HAVE ALWAYS STRIVEN TO FIND LONG TERM SOLUTIONS.
AND I CAN HELP YOU WITH THAT.
IF YOU'LL LET ME.

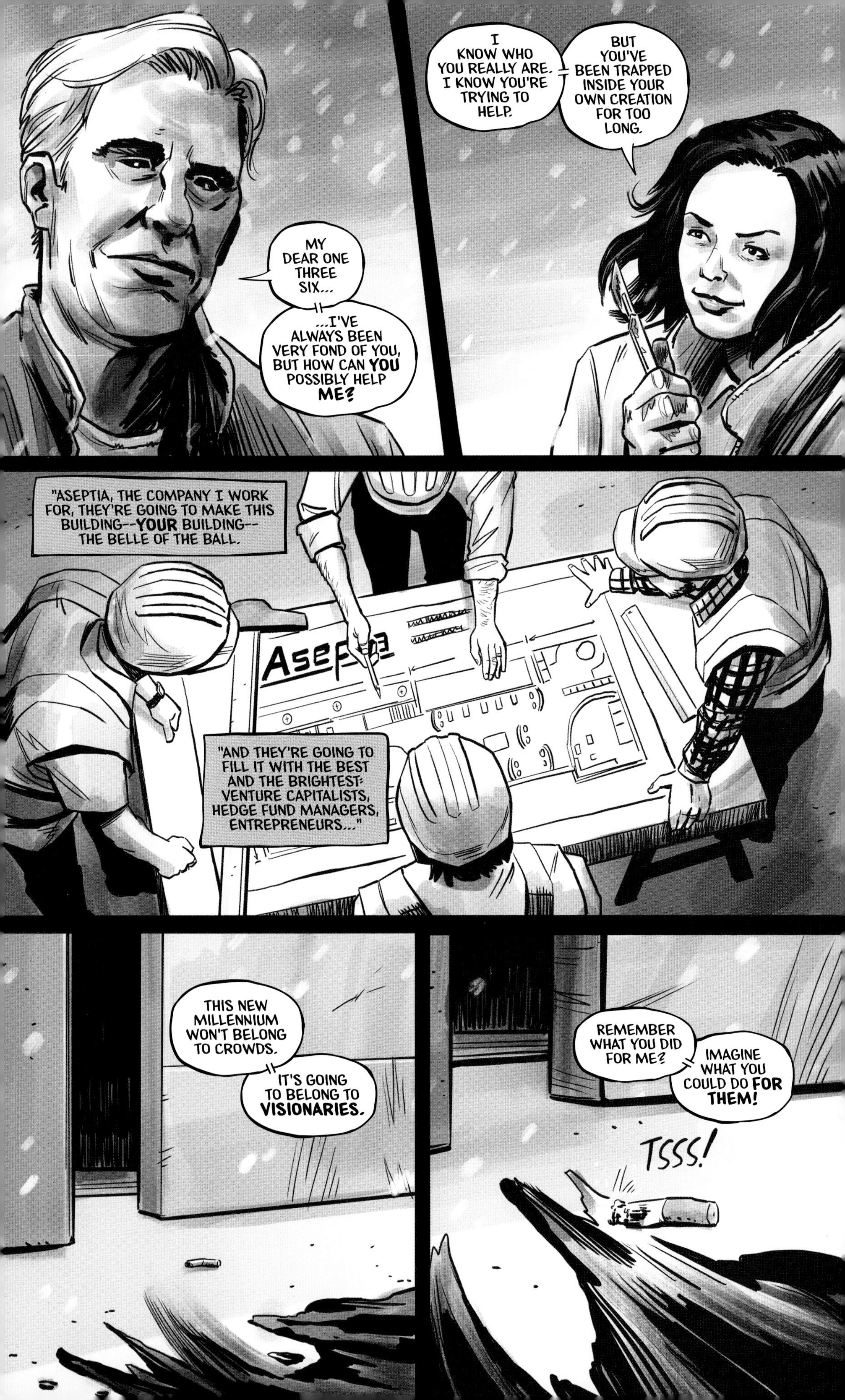
MY DEAR ONE THREE SIX...
...I'VE ALWAYS BEEN VERY FOND OF YOU, BUT HOW CAN **YOU** POSSIBLY HELP **ME?**
I KNOW WHO YOU REALLY ARE. I KNOW YOU'RE TRYING TO HELP.
BUT YOU'VE BEEN TRAPPED INSIDE YOUR OWN CREATION FOR TOO LONG.
"ASEPTIA, THE COMPANY I WORK FOR, THEY'RE GOING TO MAKE THIS BUILDING--**YOUR** BUILDING--THE BELLE OF THE BALL.
Asep
"AND THEY'RE GOING TO FILL IT WITH THE BEST AND THE BRIGHTEST: VENTURE CAPITALISTS, HEDGE FUND MANAGERS, ENTREPRENEURS..."
THIS NEW MILLENNIUM WON'T BELONG TO CROWDS.
IT'S GOING TO BELONG TO **VISIONARIES.**
REMEMBER WHAT YOU DID FOR ME?
IMAGINE WHAT YOU COULD DO **FOR THEM!**
TSSS!

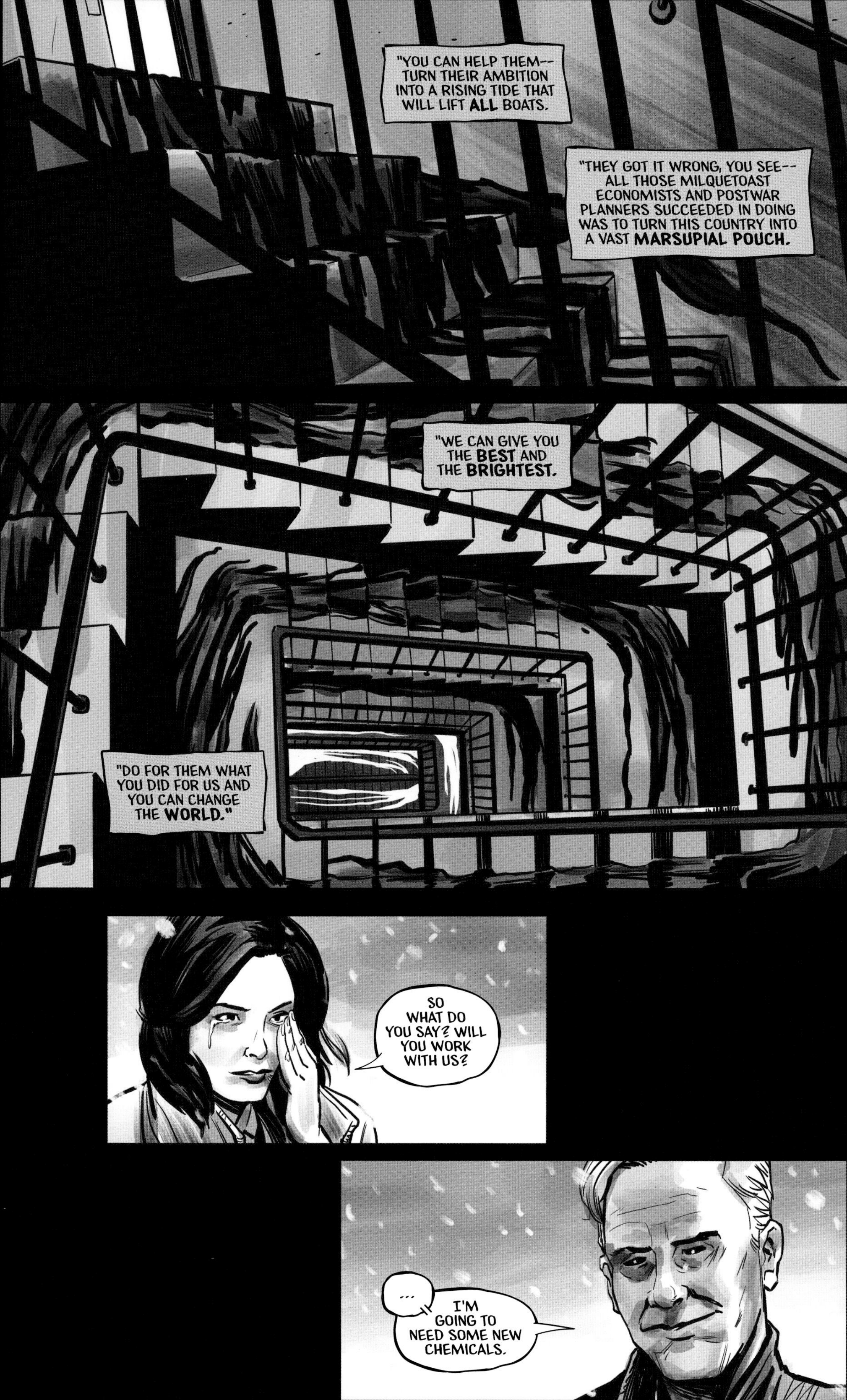
"YOU CAN HELP THEM--TURN THEIR AMBITION INTO A RISING TIDE THAT WILL LIFT **ALL** BOATS.
"THEY GOT IT WRONG, YOU SEE--ALL THOSE MILQUETOAST ECONOMISTS AND POSTWAR PLANNERS SUCCEEDED IN DOING WAS TO TURN THIS COUNTRY INTO A VAST **MARSUPIAL POUCH.**
"WE CAN GIVE YOU THE **BEST** AND THE **BRIGHTEST.**
"DO FOR THEM WHAT YOU DID FOR US AND YOU CAN CHANGE THE **WORLD.**"
SO WHAT DO YOU SAY? WILL YOU WORK WITH US?
...
I'M GOING TO NEED SOME NEW CHEMICALS.

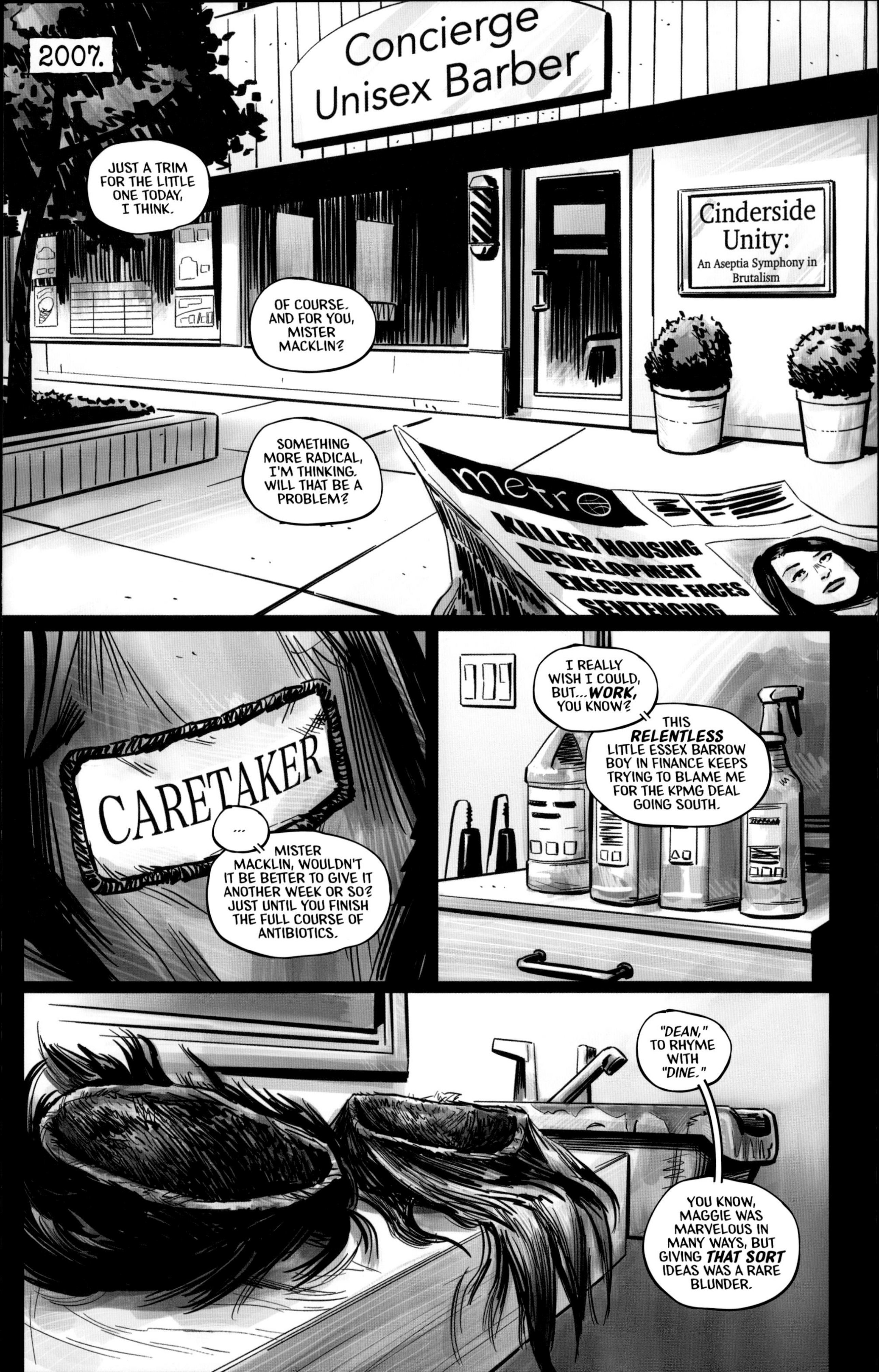
2007.
Concierge Unisex Barber
JUST A TRIM FOR THE LITTLE ONE TODAY, I THINK.
Cinderside Unity: An Aseptia Symphony in Brutalism
OF COURSE. AND FOR YOU, MISTER MACKLIN?
SOMETHING MORE RADICAL, I'M THINKING. WILL THAT BE A PROBLEM?
metro
KILLER HOUSING DEVELOPMENT EXECUTIVE FACES SENTENCING
CARETAKER
...
MISTER MACKLIN, WOULDN'T IT BE BETTER TO GIVE IT ANOTHER WEEK OR SO? JUST UNTIL YOU FINISH THE FULL COURSE OF ANTIBIOTICS.
I REALLY WISH I COULD, BUT... *WORK,* YOU KNOW?
THIS *RELENTLESS* LITTLE ESSEX BARROW BOY IN FINANCE KEEPS TRYING TO BLAME ME FOR THE KPMG DEAL GOING SOUTH.
"DEAN," TO RHYME WITH "DINE."
YOU KNOW, MAGGIE WAS MARVELOUS IN MANY WAYS, BUT GIVING *THAT SORT* IDEAS WAS A RARE BLUNDER.

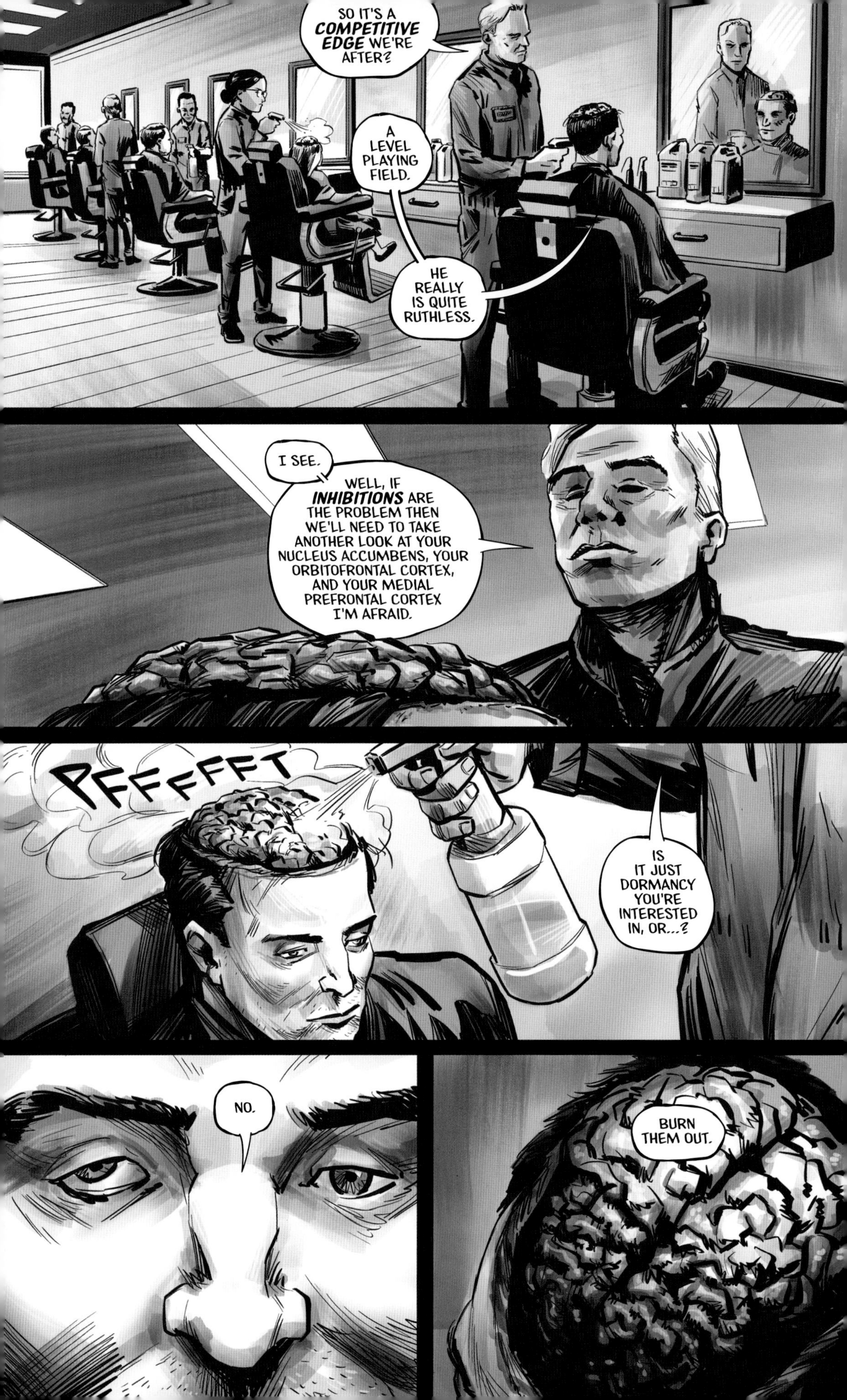
SO IT'S A **COMPETITIVE EDGE** WE'RE AFTER?
A LEVEL PLAYING FIELD.
HE REALLY IS QUITE RUTHLESS.
I SEE.
WELL, IF ***INHIBITIONS*** ARE THE PROBLEM THEN WE'LL NEED TO TAKE ANOTHER LOOK AT YOUR NUCLEUS ACCUMBENS, YOUR ORBITOFRONTAL CORTEX, AND YOUR MEDIAL PREFRONTAL CORTEX I'M AFRAID.
PFFFFFT
IS IT JUST DORMANCY YOU'RE INTERESTED IN, OR...?
NO.
BURN THEM OUT.

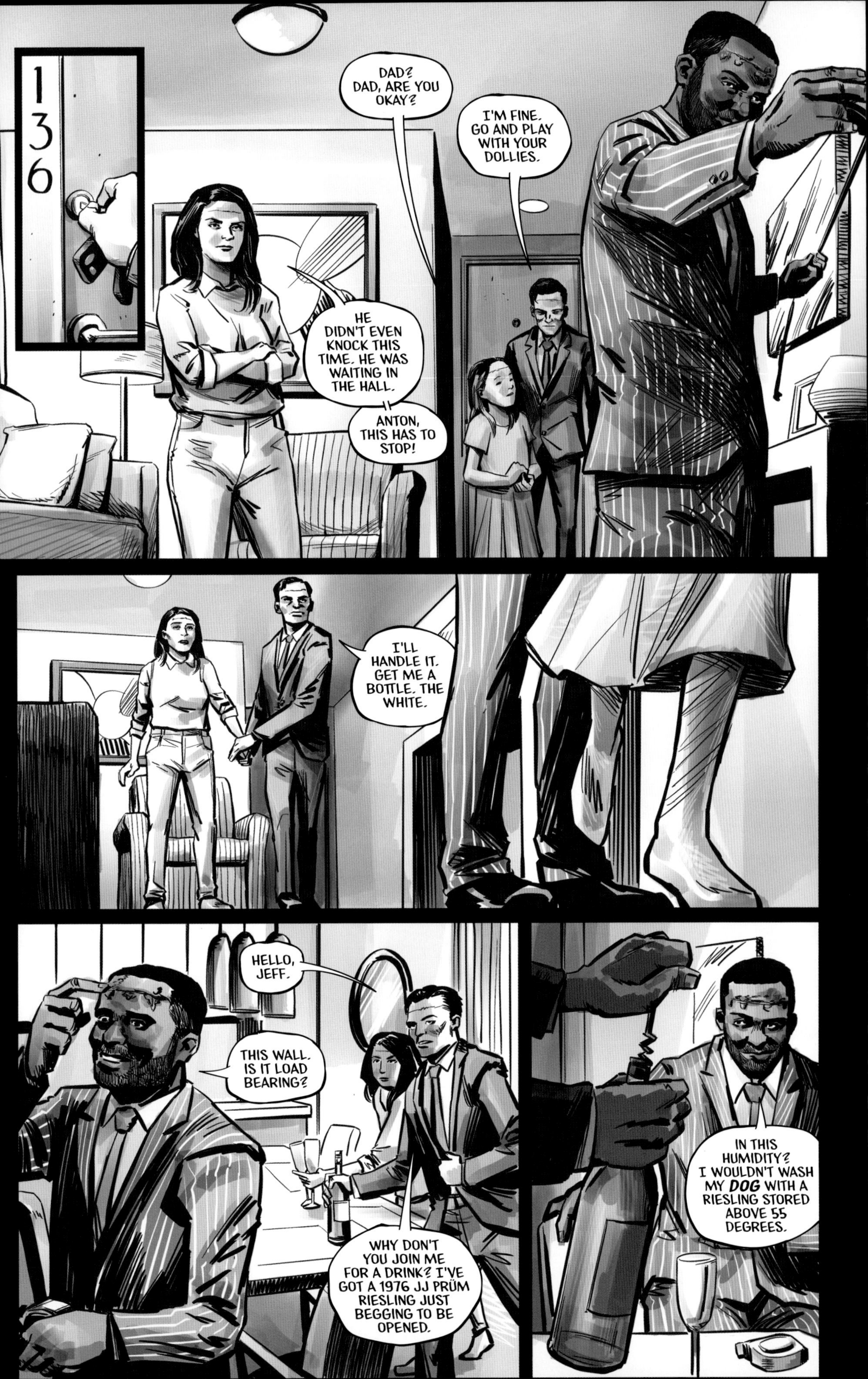
136
DAD? DAD, ARE YOU OKAY?
I'M FINE. GO AND PLAY WITH YOUR DOLLIES.
HE DIDN'T EVEN KNOCK THIS TIME. HE WAS WAITING IN THE HALL.
ANTON, THIS HAS TO STOP!
I'LL HANDLE IT. GET ME A BOTTLE. THE WHITE.
HELLO, JEFF.
THIS WALL. IS IT LOAD BEARING?
WHY DON'T YOU JOIN ME FOR A DRINK? I'VE GOT A 1976 JJ PRÜM RIESLING JUST BEGGING TO BE OPENED.
IN THIS HUMIDITY? I WOULDN'T WASH MY ***DOG*** WITH A RIESLING STORED ABOVE 55 DEGREES.

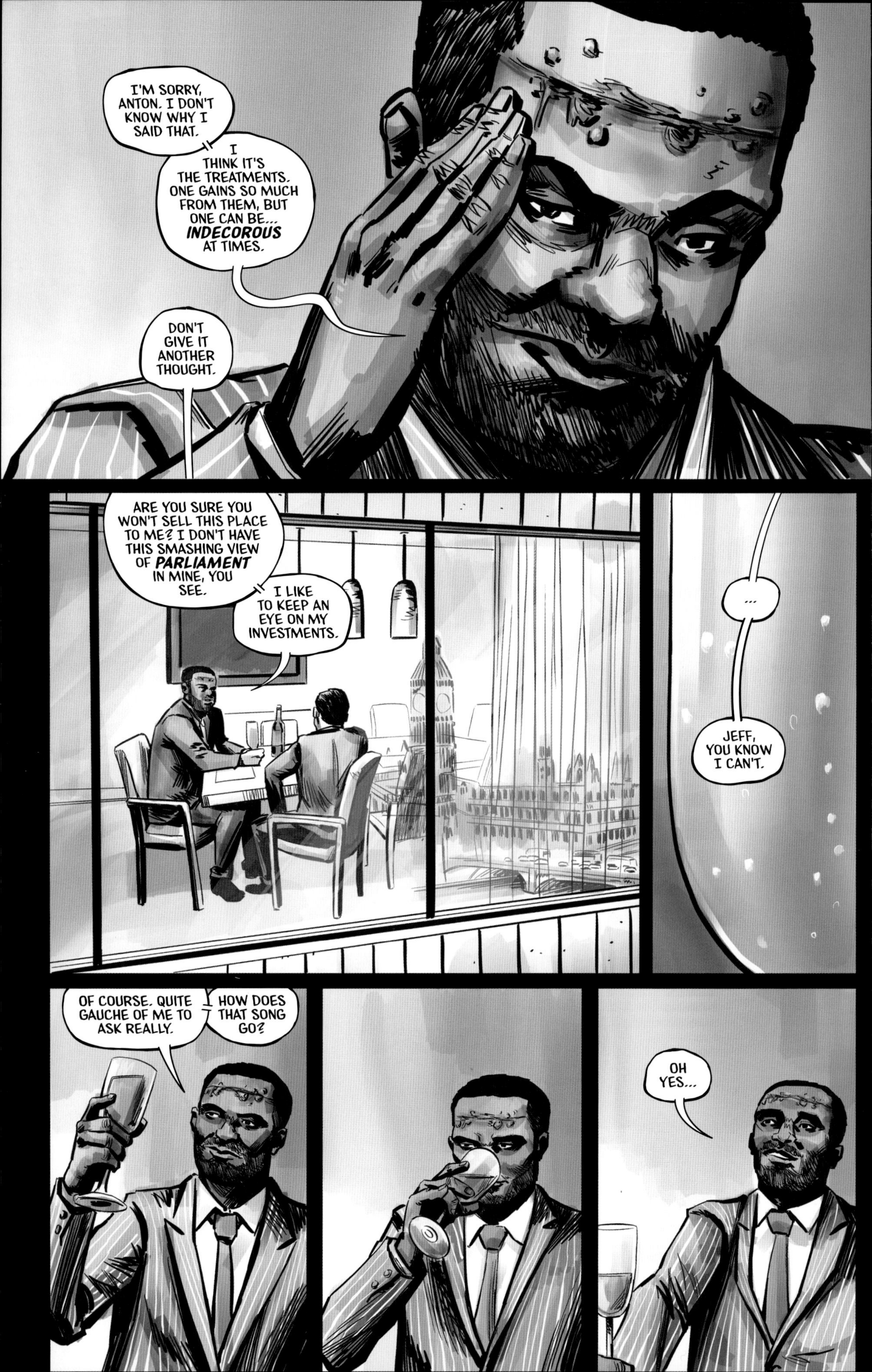
I'M SORRY, ANTON. I DON'T KNOW WHY I SAID THAT.
I THINK IT'S THE TREATMENTS. ONE GAINS SO MUCH FROM THEM, BUT ONE CAN BE... INDECOROUS AT TIMES.
DON'T GIVE IT ANOTHER THOUGHT.
ARE YOU SURE YOU WON'T SELL THIS PLACE TO ME? I DON'T HAVE THIS SMASHING VIEW OF PARLIAMENT IN MINE, YOU SEE.
I LIKE TO KEEP AN EYE ON MY INVESTMENTS.
...
JEFF, YOU KNOW I CAN'T.
OF COURSE. QUITE GAUCHE OF ME TO ASK REALLY.
HOW DOES THAT SONG GO?
OH YES...

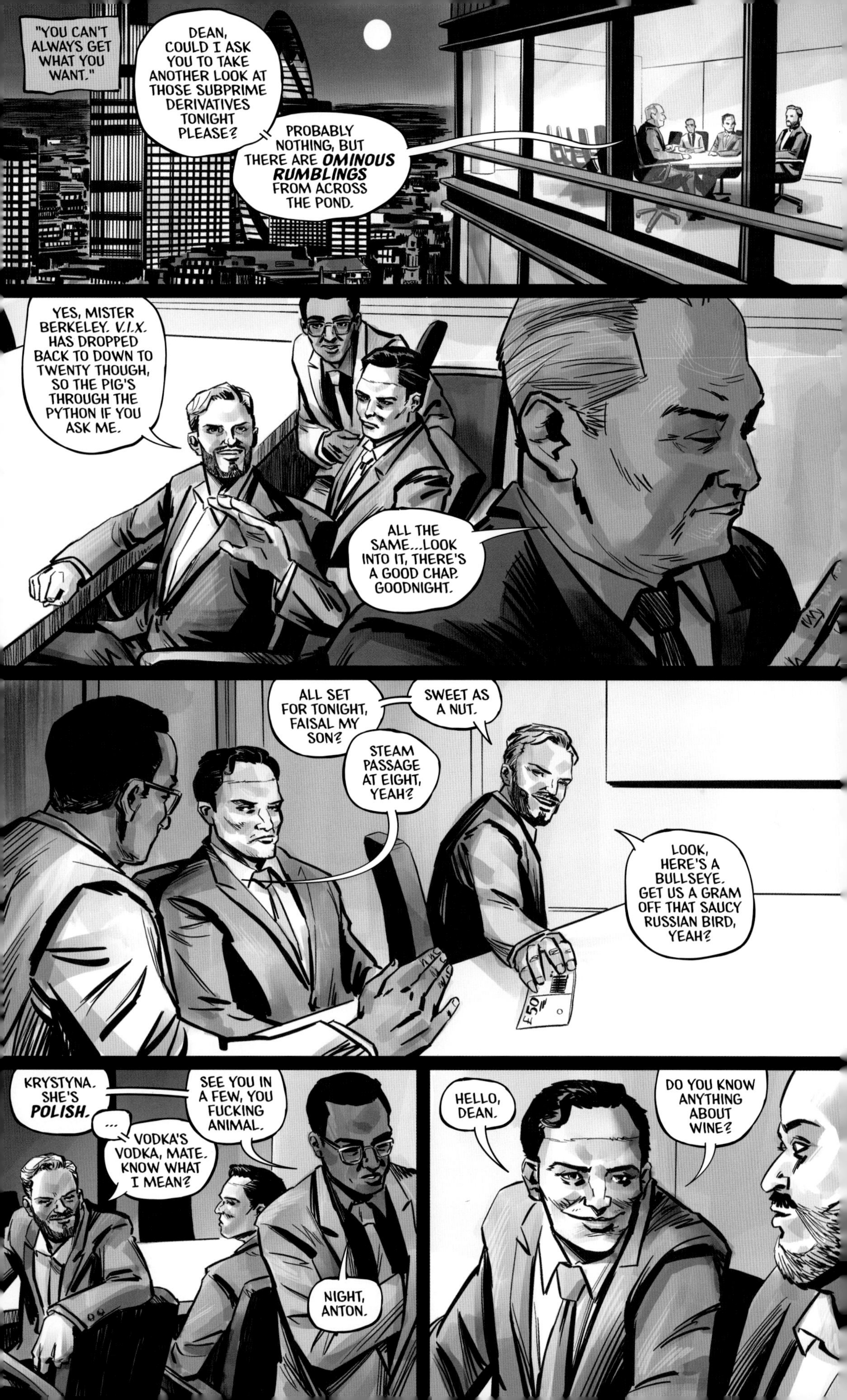
"YOU CAN'T ALWAYS GET WHAT YOU WANT."
DEAN, COULD I ASK YOU TO TAKE ANOTHER LOOK AT THOSE SUBPRIME DERIVATIVES TONIGHT PLEASE?
PROBABLY NOTHING, BUT THERE ARE ***OMINOUS RUMBLINGS*** FROM ACROSS THE POND.
YES, MISTER BERKELEY. *V.I.X.* HAS DROPPED BACK TO DOWN TO TWENTY THOUGH, SO THE PIG'S THROUGH THE PYTHON IF YOU ASK ME.
ALL THE SAME... LOOK INTO IT, THERE'S A GOOD CHAP. GOODNIGHT.
ALL SET FOR TONIGHT, FAISAL MY SON?
SWEET AS A NUT.
STEAM PASSAGE AT EIGHT, YEAH?
LOOK, HERE'S A BULLSEYE. GET US A GRAM OFF THAT SAUCY RUSSIAN BIRD, YEAH?
£50
KRYSTYNA. SHE'S ***POLISH.***
...
VODKA'S VODKA, MATE. KNOW WHAT I MEAN?
SEE YOU IN A FEW, YOU FUCKING ANIMAL.
NIGHT, ANTON.
HELLO, DEAN.
DO YOU KNOW ANYTHING ABOUT WINE?

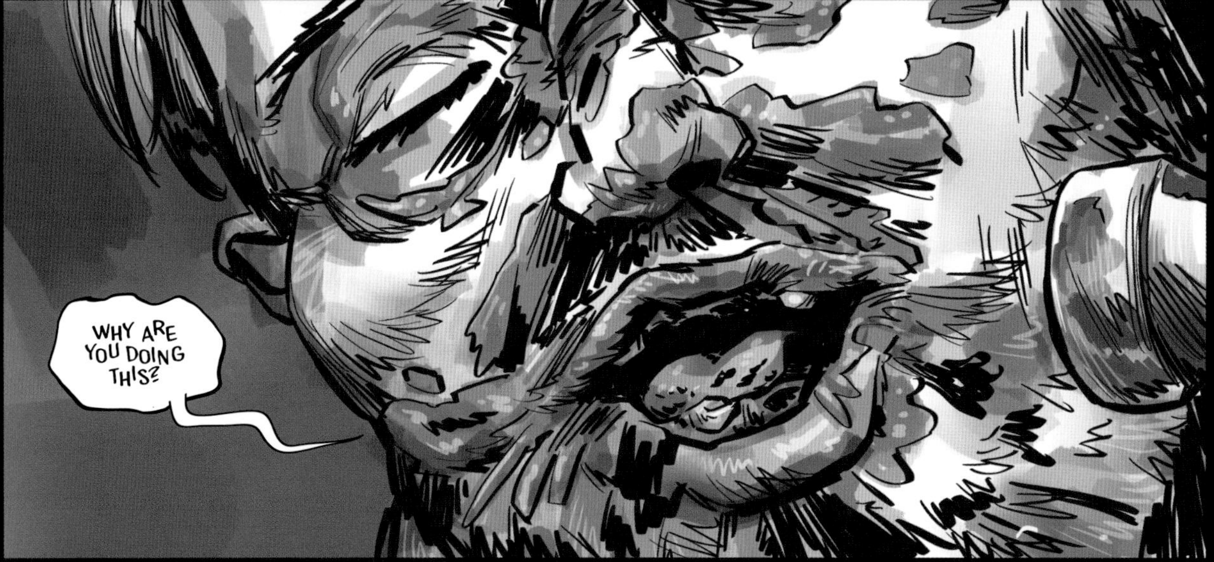
WHY ARE YOU DOING THIS?

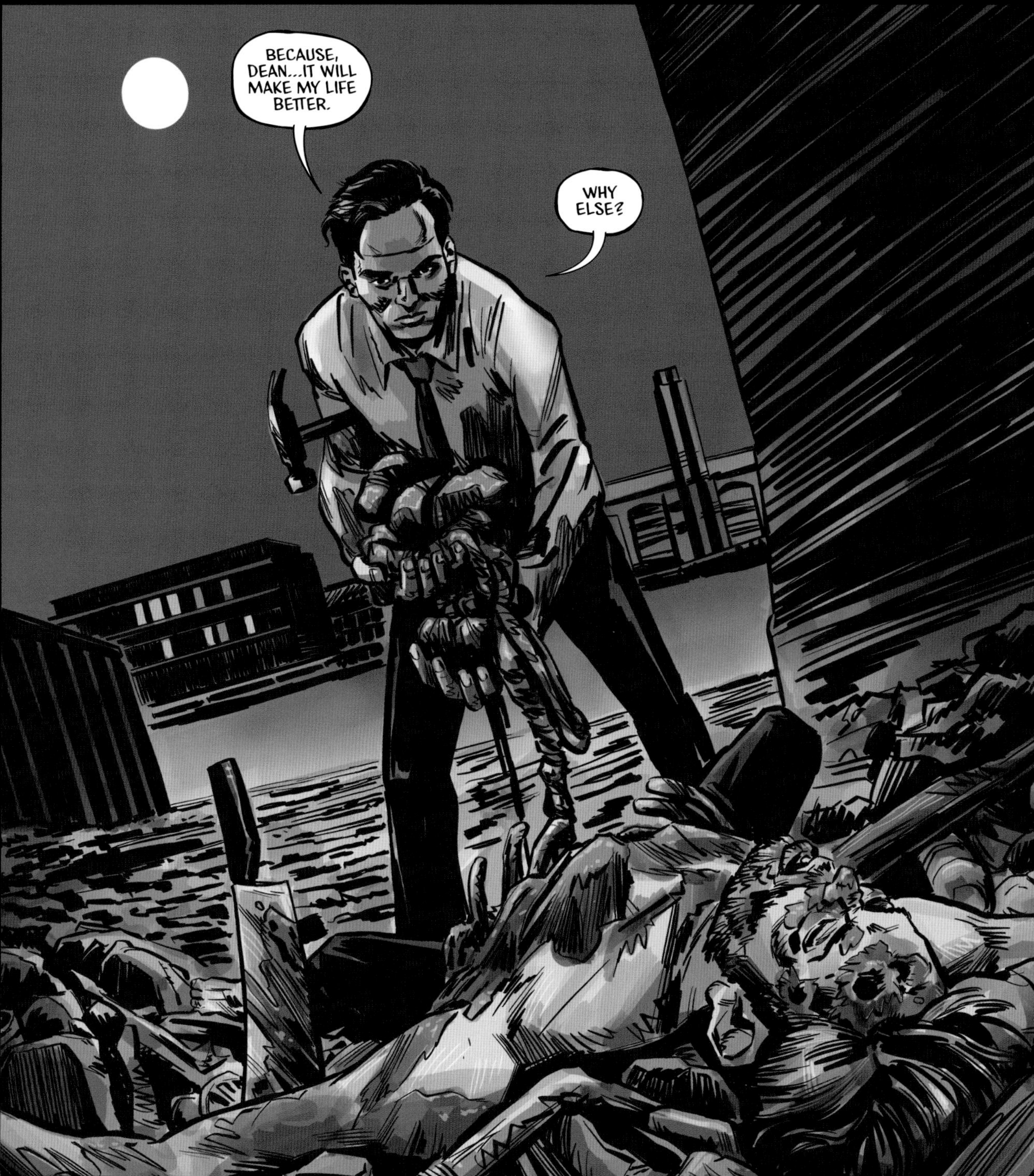
BECAUSE, DEAN...IT WILL MAKE MY LIFE BETTER.
WHY ELSE?

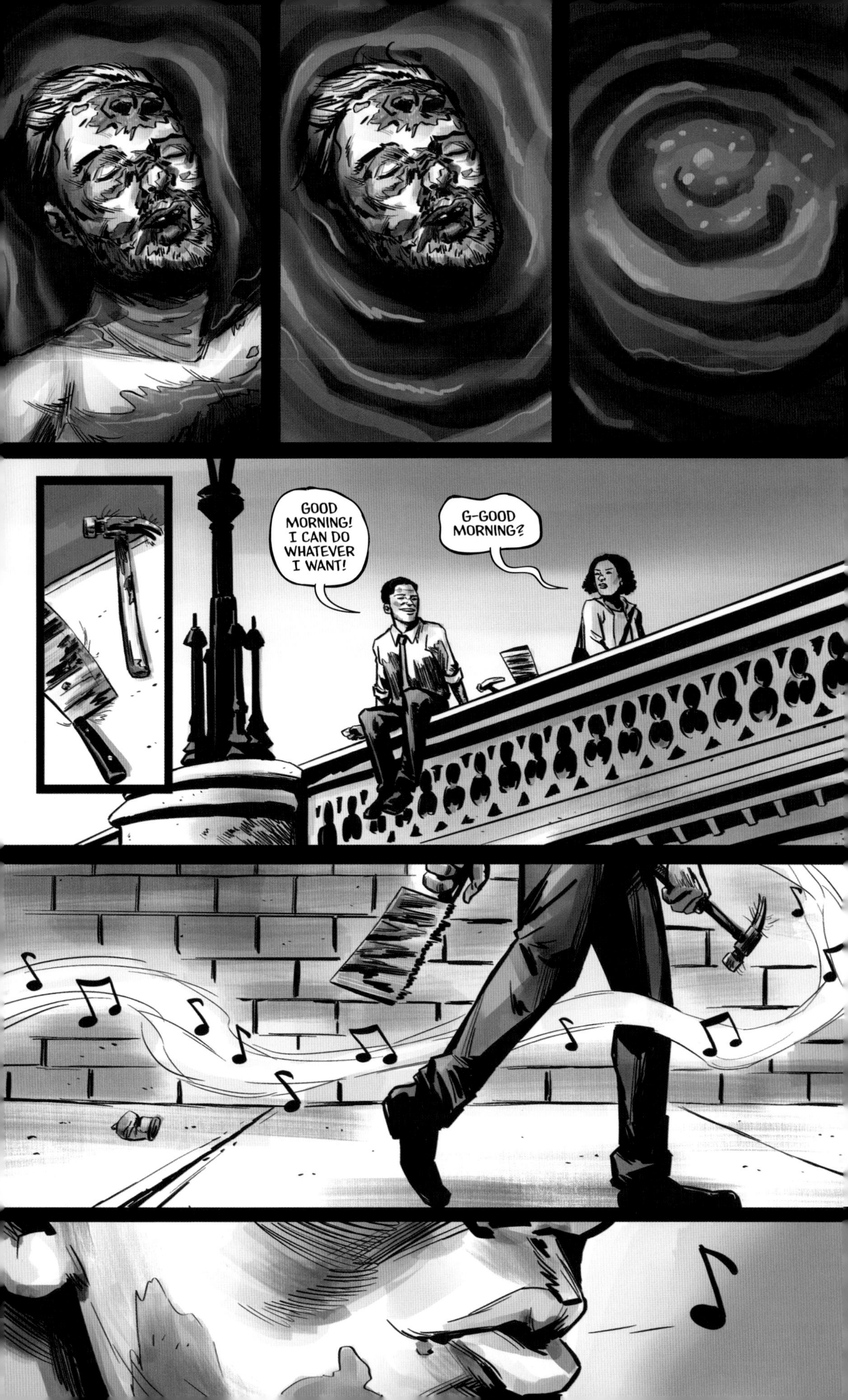
GOOD MORNING! I CAN DO WHATEVER I WANT!
G-GOOD MORNING?

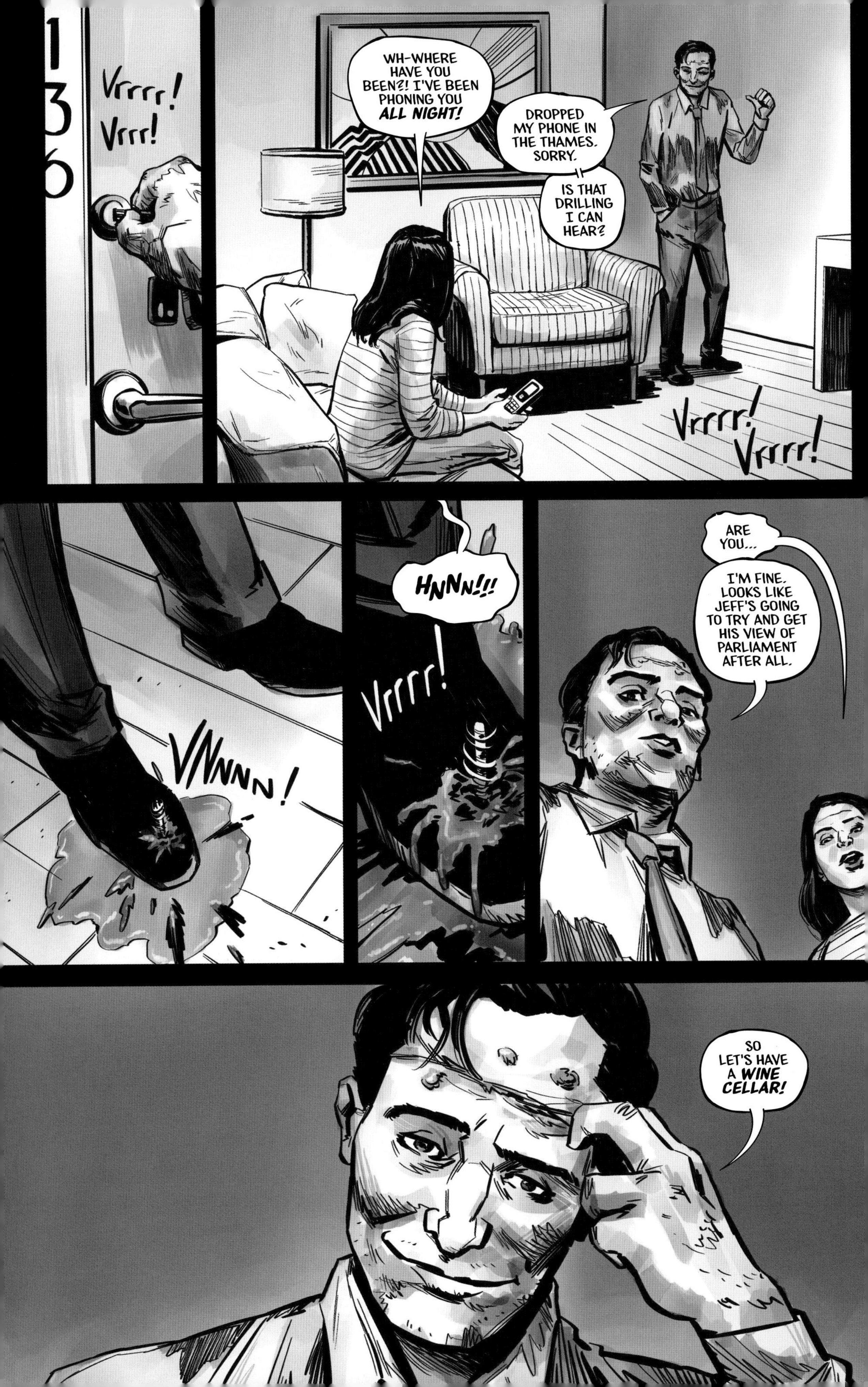
136
Vrrrr!
Vrrr!
WH-WHERE HAVE YOU BEEN?! I'VE BEEN PHONING YOU ALL NIGHT!
DROPPED MY PHONE IN THE THAMES. SORRY.
IS THAT DRILLING I CAN HEAR?
Vrrrr!
Vrrrr!
VNnnn!
HNNN!!!
Vrrrr!
ARE YOU...
I'M FINE. LOOKS LIKE JEFF'S GOING TO TRY AND GET HIS VIEW OF PARLIAMENT AFTER ALL.
SO LET'S HAVE A WINE CELLAR!

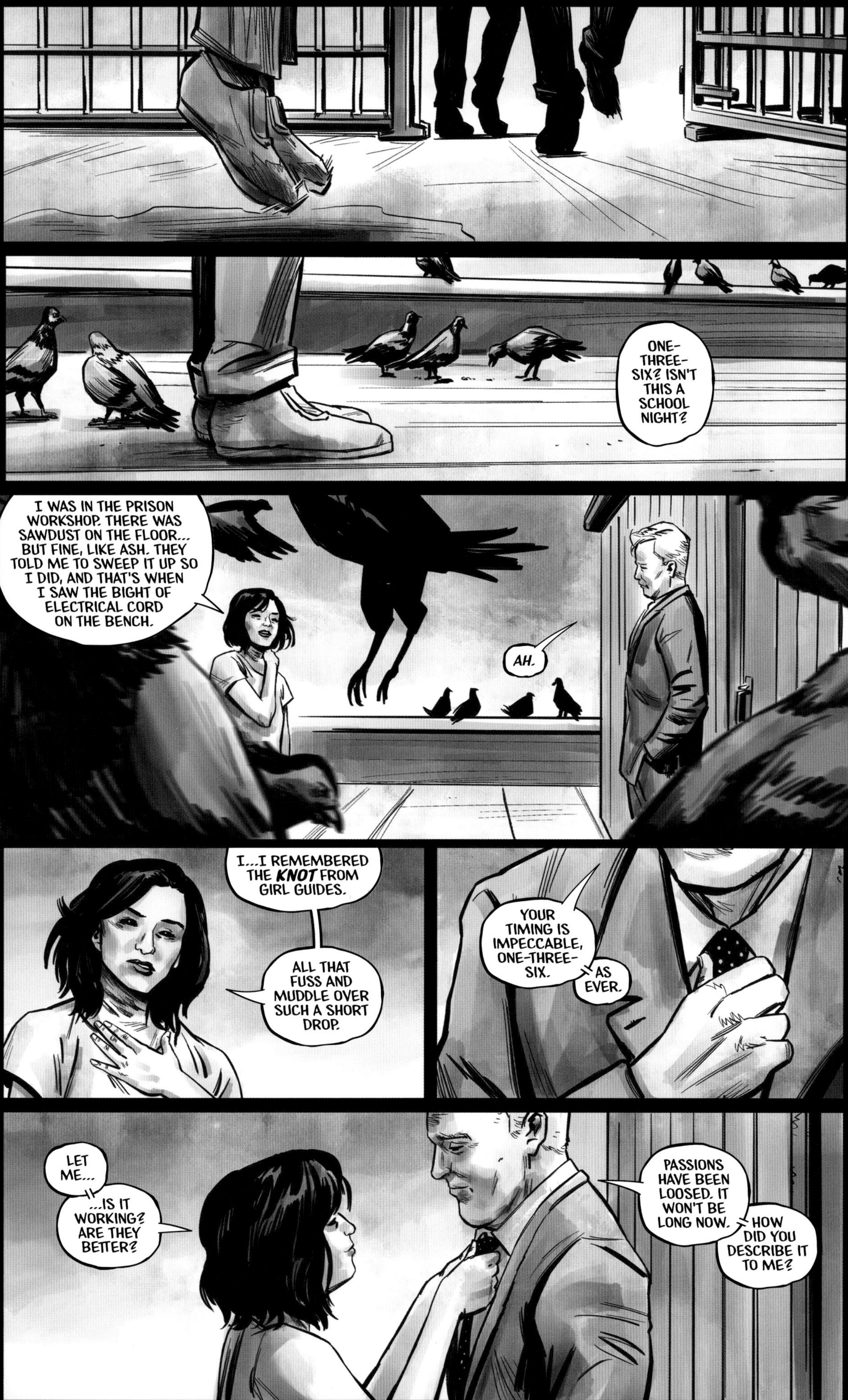
ONE-THREE-SIX? ISN'T THIS A SCHOOL NIGHT?
I WAS IN THE PRISON WORKSHOP. THERE WAS SAWDUST ON THE FLOOR... BUT FINE, LIKE ASH. THEY TOLD ME TO SWEEP IT UP SO I DID, AND THAT'S WHEN I SAW THE BIGHT OF ELECTRICAL CORD ON THE BENCH.
AH.
I...I REMEMBERED THE ***KNOT*** FROM GIRL GUIDES.
ALL THAT FUSS AND MUDDLE OVER SUCH A SHORT DROP.
YOUR TIMING IS IMPECCABLE, ONE-THREE-SIX.
AS EVER.
LET ME...
...IS IT WORKING? ARE THEY BETTER?
PASSIONS HAVE BEEN LOOSED. IT WON'T BE LONG NOW.
HOW DID YOU DESCRIBE IT TO ME?

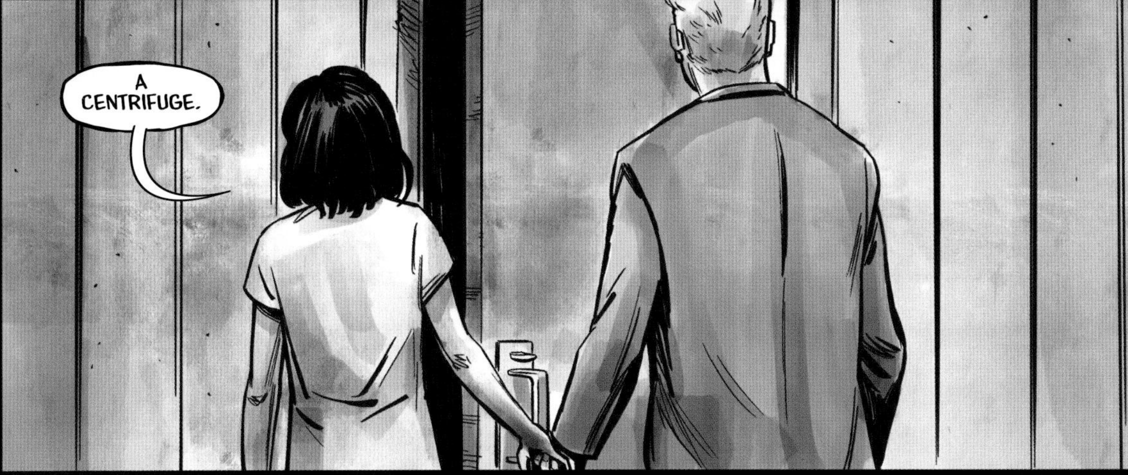
A CENTRIFUGE.

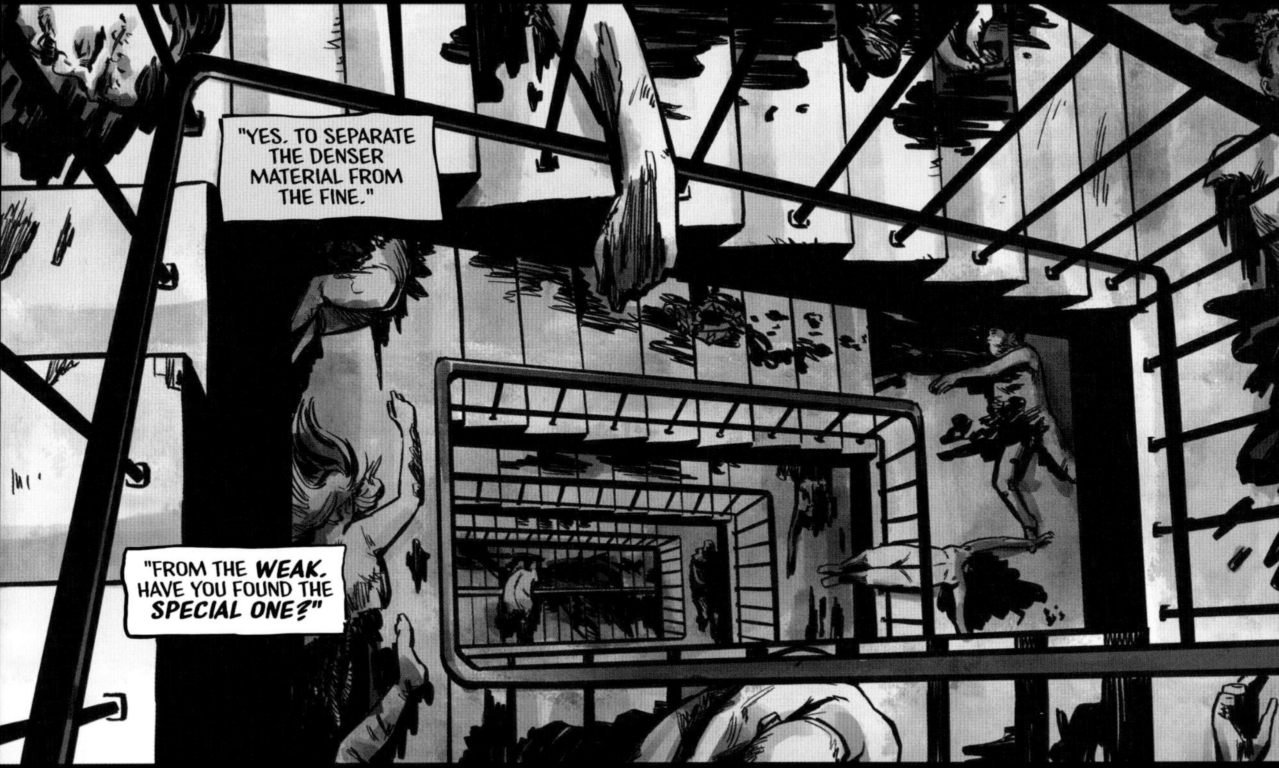
"YES. TO SEPARATE THE DENSER MATERIAL FROM THE FINE."
"FROM THE **WEAK.** HAVE YOU FOUND THE ***SPECIAL ONE?***"

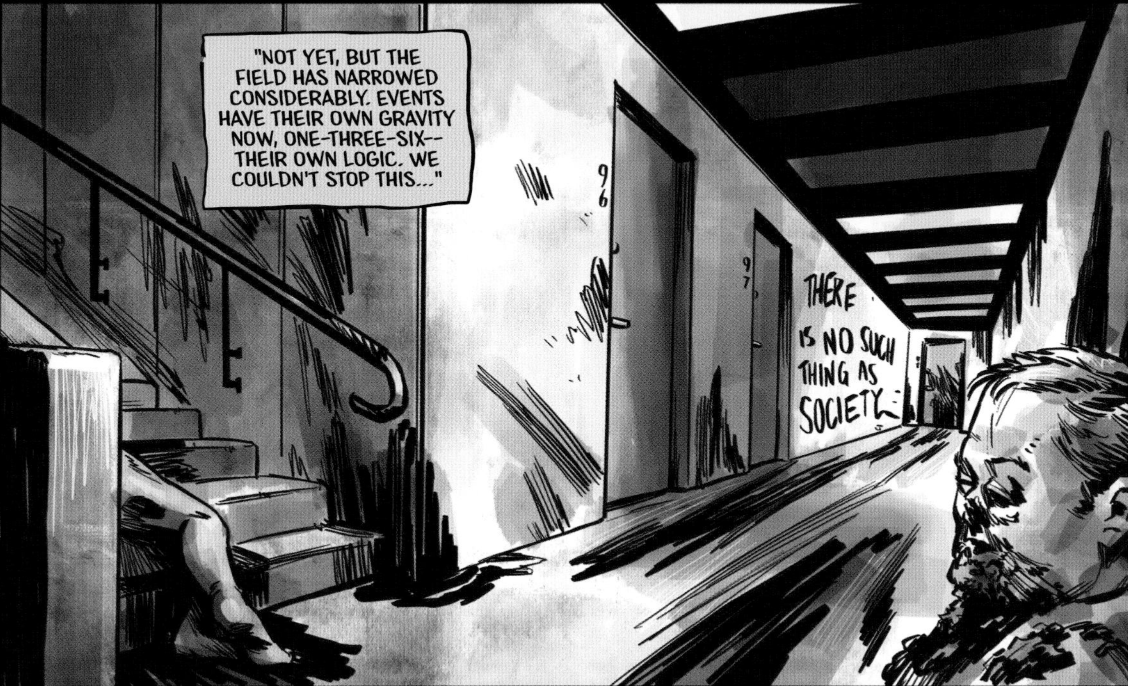
"NOT YET, BUT THE FIELD HAS NARROWED CONSIDERABLY. EVENTS HAVE THEIR OWN GRAVITY NOW, ONE-THREE-SIX-- THEIR OWN LOGIC. WE COULDN'T STOP THIS..."
96
97
THERE IS NO SUCH THING AS SOCIETY

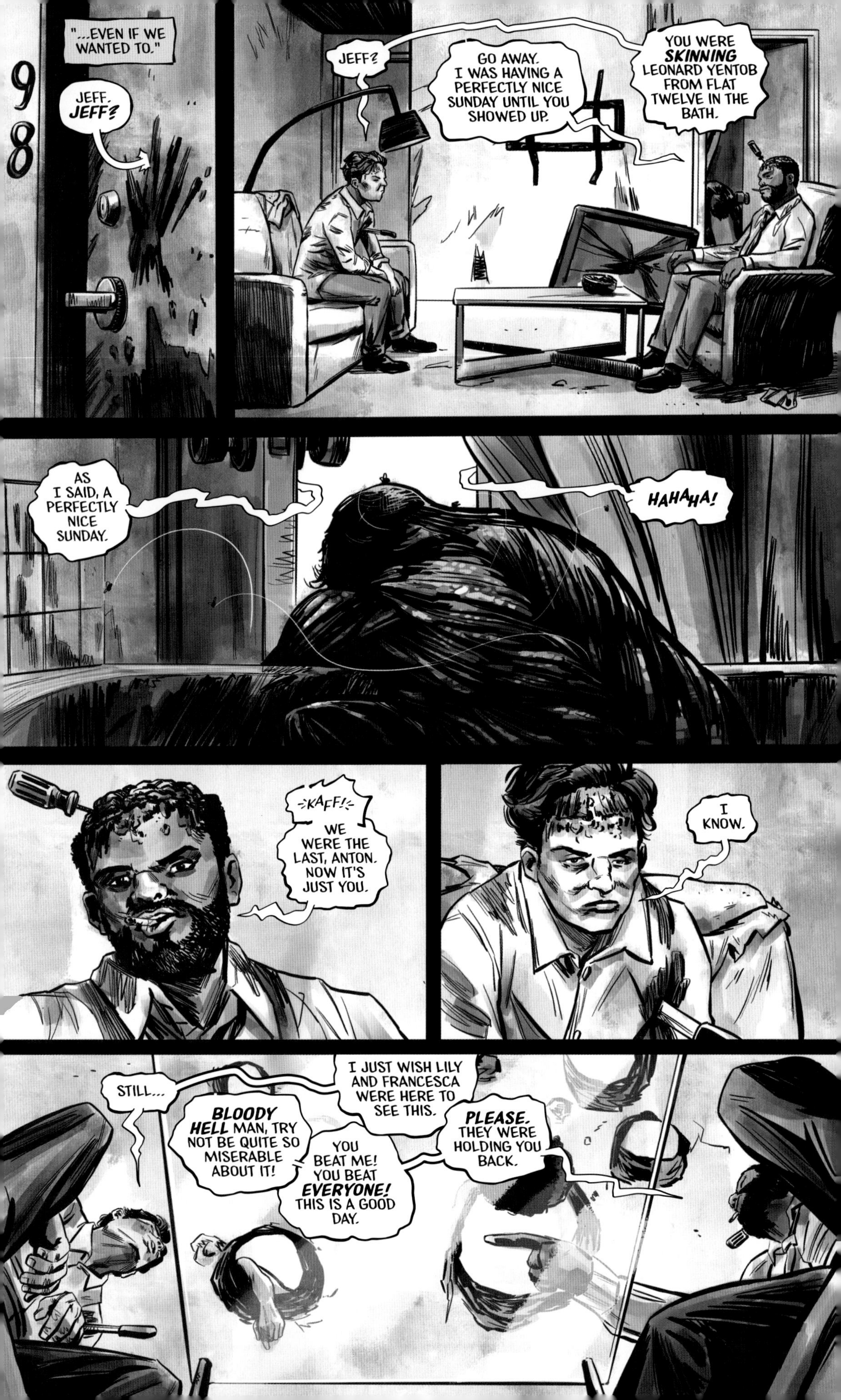
"...EVEN IF WE WANTED TO."
98
JEFF. JEFF?
JEFF?
GO AWAY. I WAS HAVING A PERFECTLY NICE SUNDAY UNTIL YOU SHOWED UP.
YOU WERE SKINNING LEONARD YENTOB FROM FLAT TWELVE IN THE BATH.
AS I SAID, A PERFECTLY NICE SUNDAY.
HAHAHA!
KAFF! WE WERE THE LAST, ANTON. NOW IT'S JUST YOU.
I KNOW.
STILL...
I JUST WISH LILY AND FRANCESCA WERE HERE TO SEE THIS.
BLOODY HELL MAN, TRY NOT BE QUITE SO MISERABLE ABOUT IT!
YOU BEAT ME! YOU BEAT EVERYONE! THIS IS A GOOD DAY.
PLEASE. THEY WERE HOLDING YOU BACK.

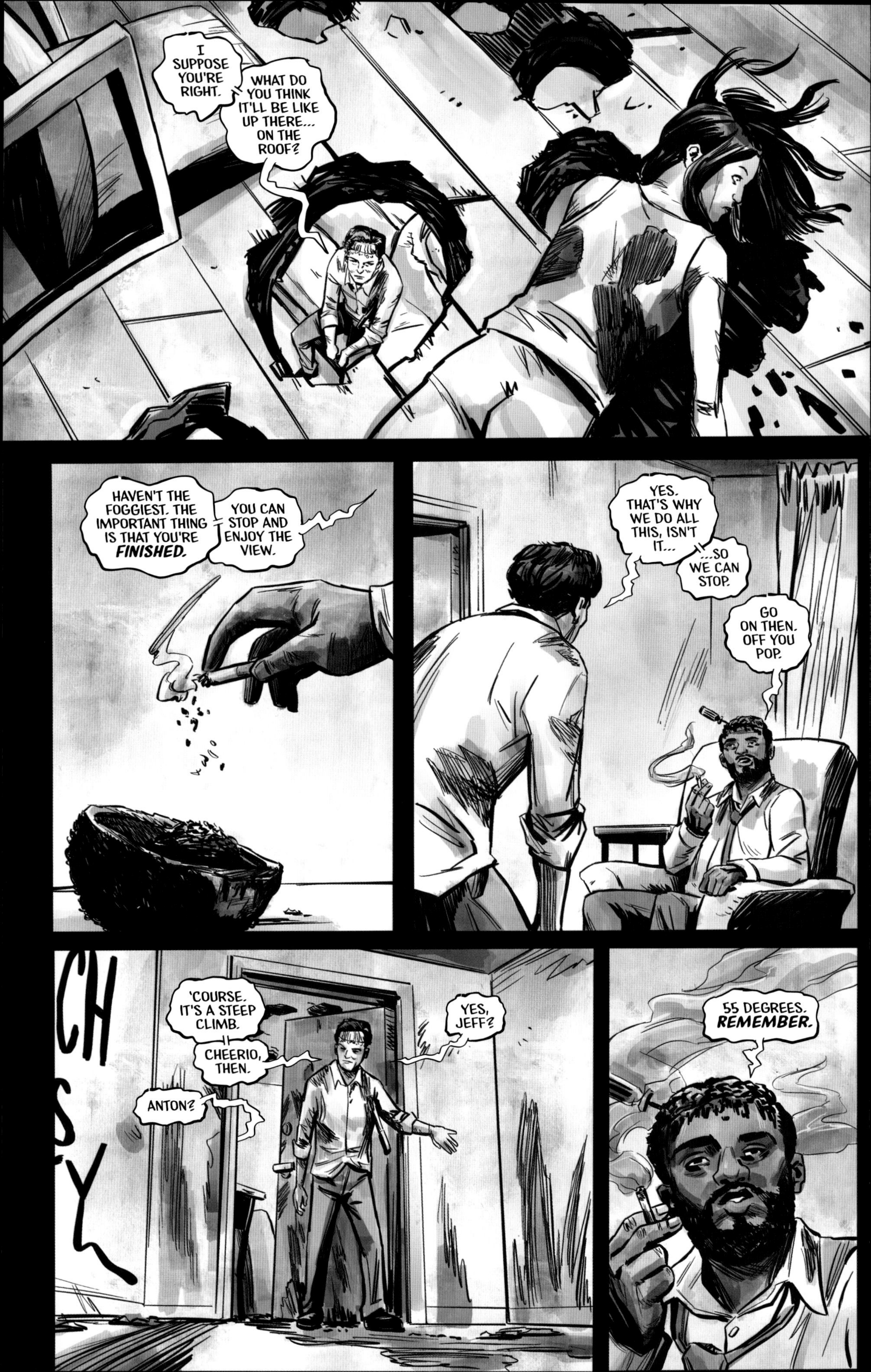
I SUPPOSE YOU'RE RIGHT.
WHAT DO YOU THINK IT'LL BE LIKE UP THERE... ON THE ROOF?
HAVEN'T THE FOGGIEST. THE IMPORTANT THING IS THAT YOU'RE ***FINISHED.***
YOU CAN STOP AND ENJOY THE VIEW.
YES. THAT'S WHY WE DO ALL THIS, ISN'T IT...
...SO WE CAN STOP.
GO ON THEN. OFF YOU POP.
'COURSE. IT'S A STEEP CLIMB.
CHEERIO, THEN.
ANTON?
YES, JEFF?
55 DEGREES. ***REMEMBER.***

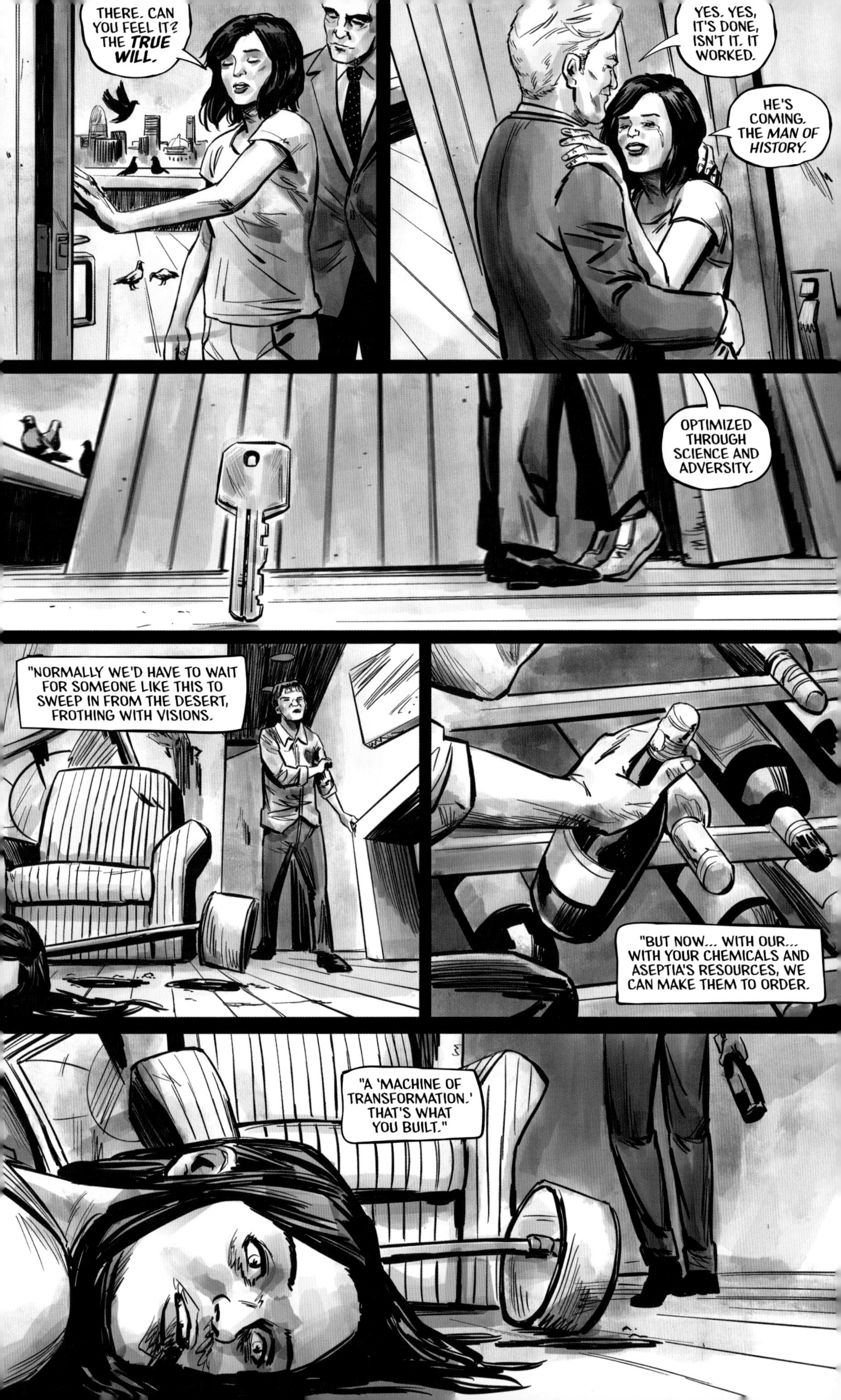
THERE. CAN YOU FEEL IT? THE **TRUE WILL.**
YES. YES, IT'S DONE, ISN'T IT. IT WORKED.
HE'S COMING. THE *MAN OF HISTORY.*
OPTIMIZED THROUGH SCIENCE AND ADVERSITY.
"NORMALLY WE'D HAVE TO WAIT FOR SOMEONE LIKE THIS TO SWEEP IN FROM THE DESERT, FROTHING WITH VISIONS.
"BUT NOW... WITH OUR... WITH YOUR CHEMICALS AND ASEPTIA'S RESOURCES, WE CAN MAKE THEM TO ORDER.
"A 'MACHINE OF TRANSFORMATION.' THAT'S WHAT YOU BUILT."

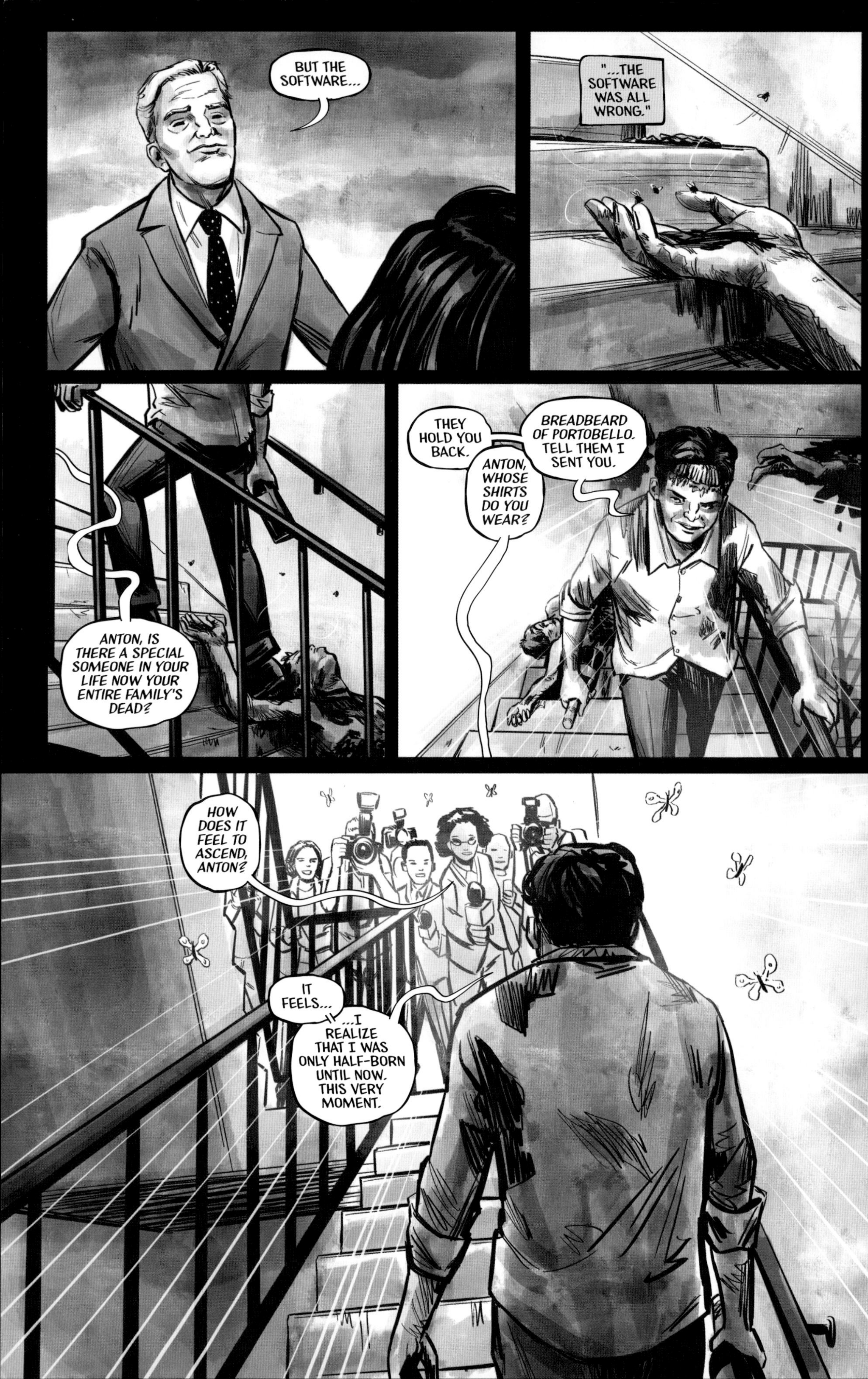
BUT THE SOFTWARE...
"...THE SOFTWARE WAS ALL WRONG."
ANTON, IS THERE A SPECIAL SOMEONE IN YOUR LIFE NOW YOUR ENTIRE FAMILY'S DEAD?
THEY HOLD YOU BACK.
BREADBEARD OF PORTOBELLO. TELL THEM I SENT YOU.
ANTON, WHOSE SHIRTS DO YOU WEAR?
HOW DOES IT FEEL TO ASCEND, ANTON?
IT FEELS...
...I REALIZE THAT I WAS ONLY HALF-BORN UNTIL NOW. THIS VERY MOMENT.

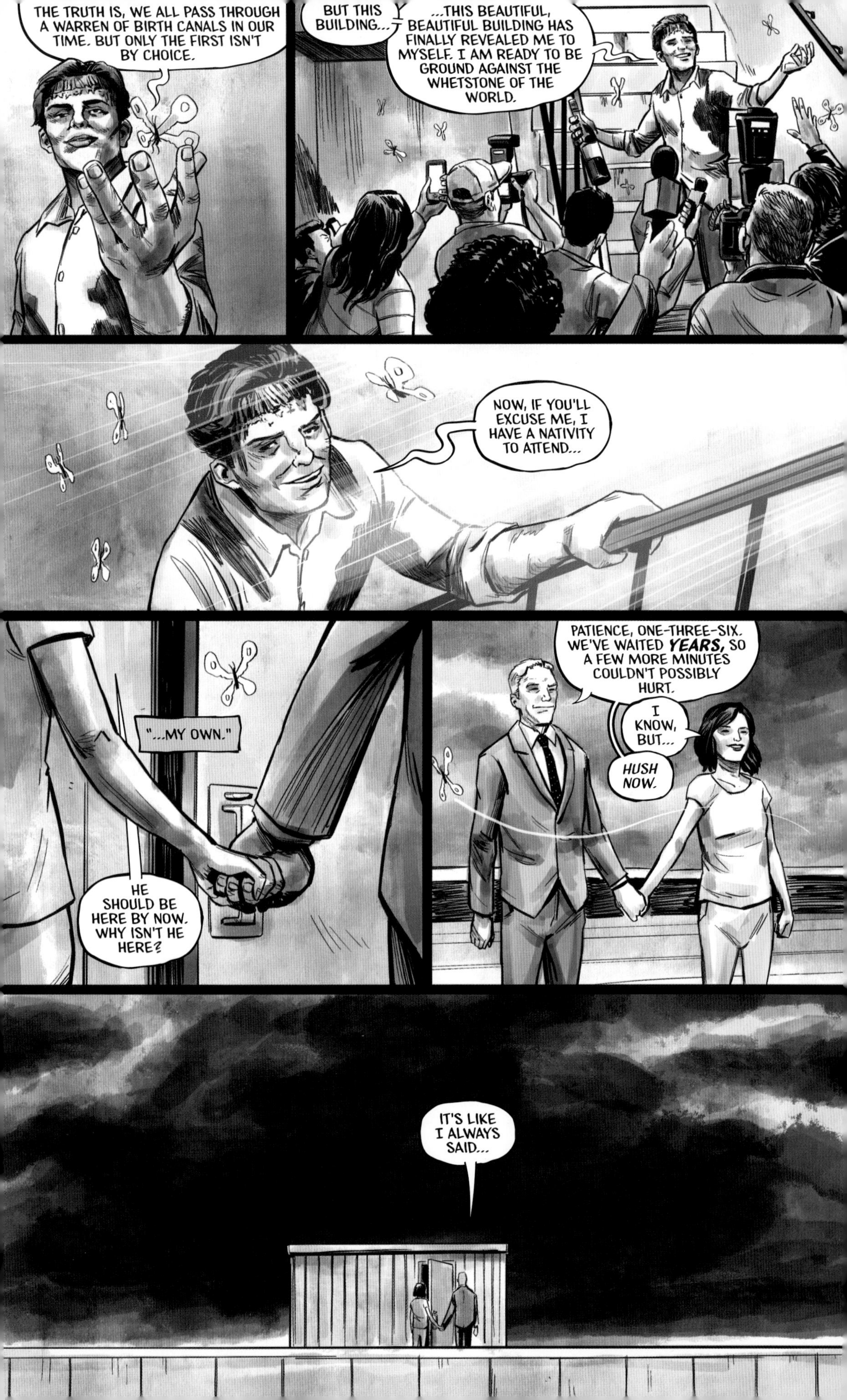
THE TRUTH IS, WE ALL PASS THROUGH A WARREN OF BIRTH CANALS IN OUR TIME. BUT ONLY THE FIRST ISN'T BY CHOICE.
BUT THIS BUILDING...
...THIS BEAUTIFUL, BEAUTIFUL BUILDING HAS FINALLY REVEALED ME TO MYSELF. I AM READY TO BE GROUND AGAINST THE WHETSTONE OF THE WORLD.
NOW, IF YOU'LL EXCUSE ME, I HAVE A NATIVITY TO ATTEND...
"...MY OWN."
HE SHOULD BE HERE BY NOW. WHY ISN'T HE HERE?
PATIENCE, ONE-THREE-SIX. WE'VE WAITED YEARS, SO A FEW MORE MINUTES COULDN'T POSSIBLY HURT.
I KNOW, BUT...
HUSH NOW.
IT'S LIKE I ALWAYS SAID...

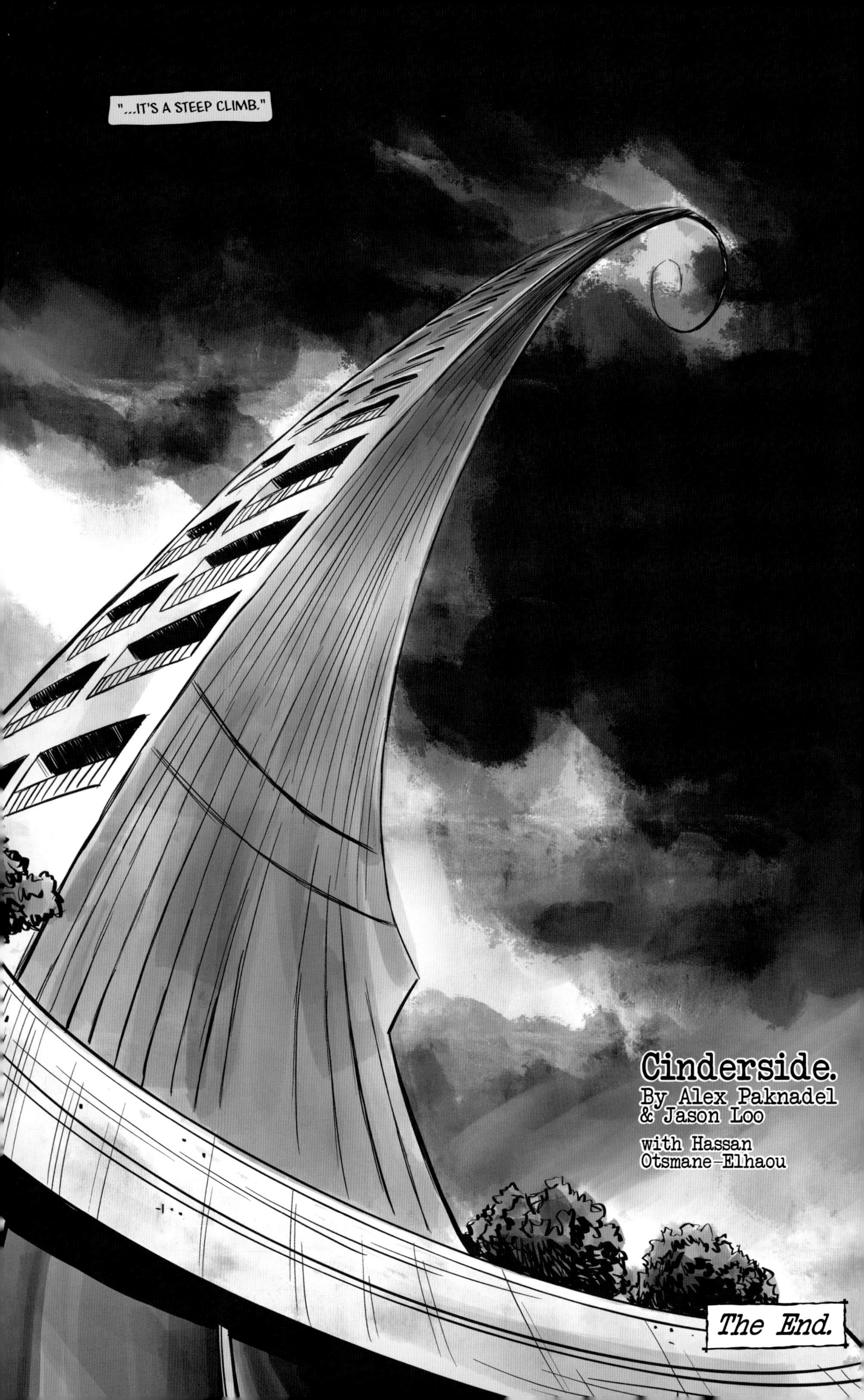
"...IT'S A STEEP CLIMB."
Cinderside.
By Alex Paknadel
& Jason Loo
with Hassan
Otsmane-Elhaou
The End.

"Nothing to Get Hung About"

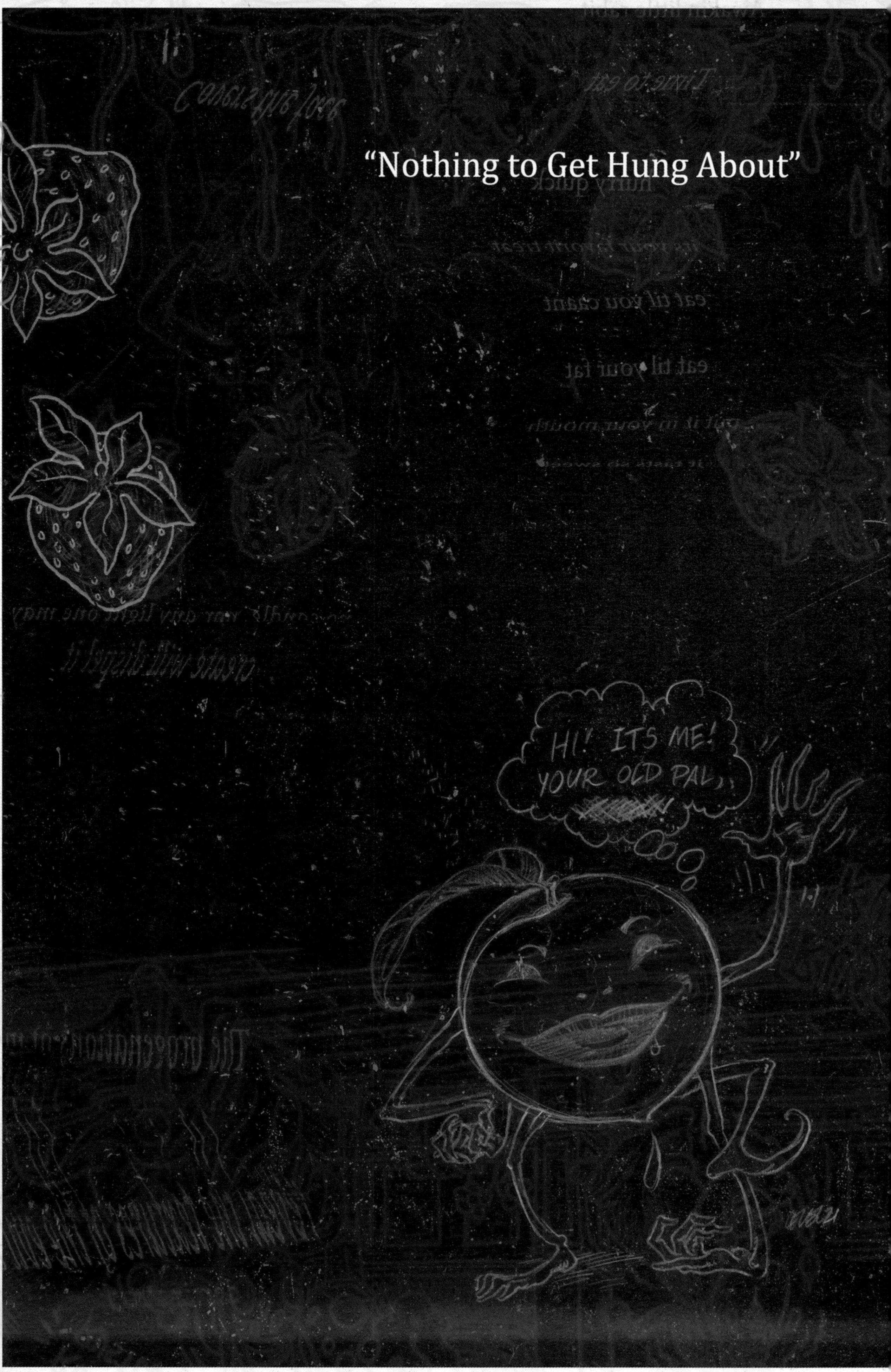
HI! ITS ME!
YOUR OLD PAL,

Chapter One

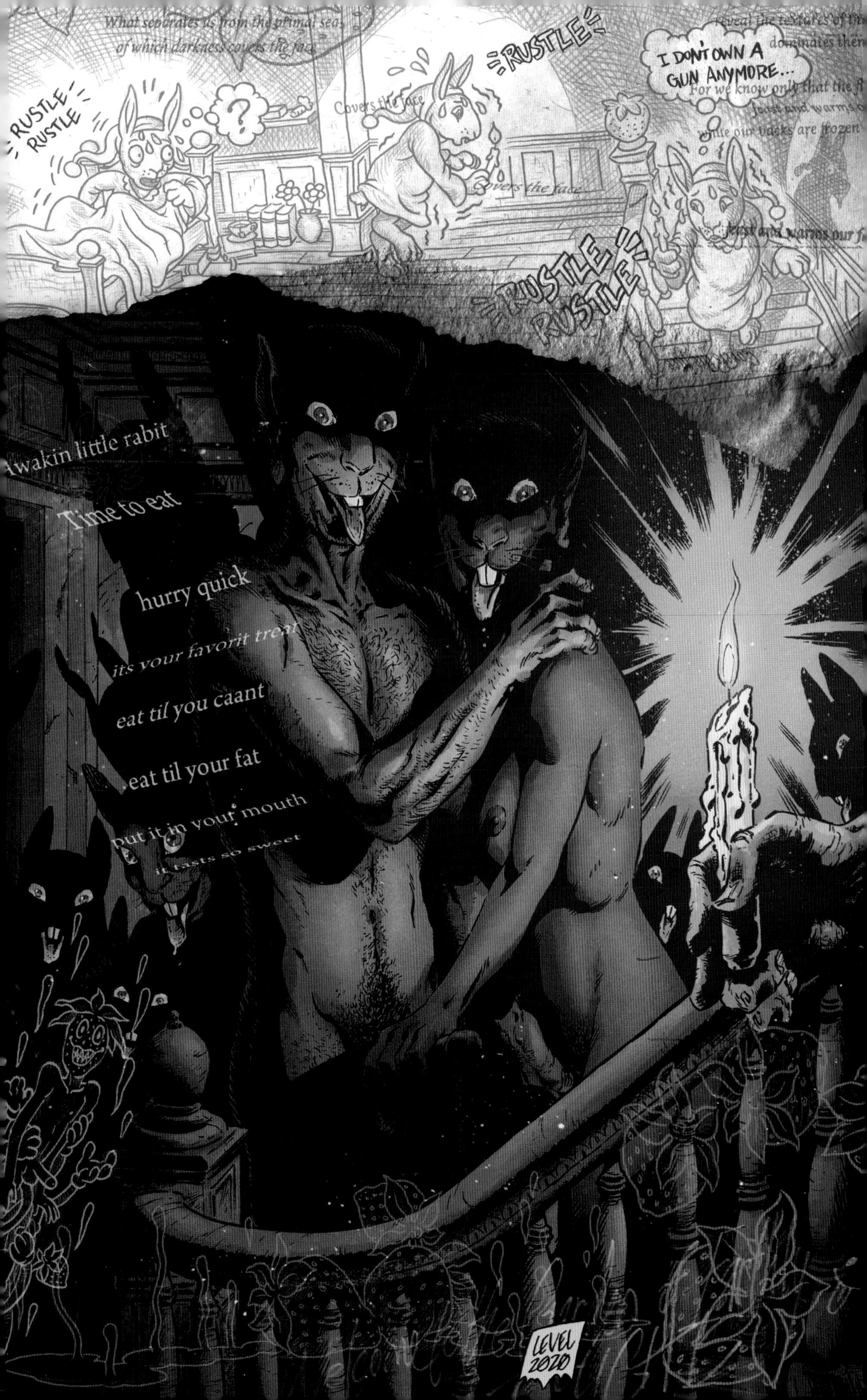
What separates us from the primal sea
of which darkness covers the face
RUSTLE RUSTLE
?
Covers the face
RUSTLE
Covers the face
reveal the textures of
dominates the
I DON'T OWN A GUN ANYMORE...
For we know only that the
feast and warms
while our backs are frozen
RUSTLE RUSTLE
awakin little rabit
Time to eat
hurry quick
its your favorit treat
eat til you caant
eat til your fat
put it in your mouth
it tasts so sweet
LEVEL 2020

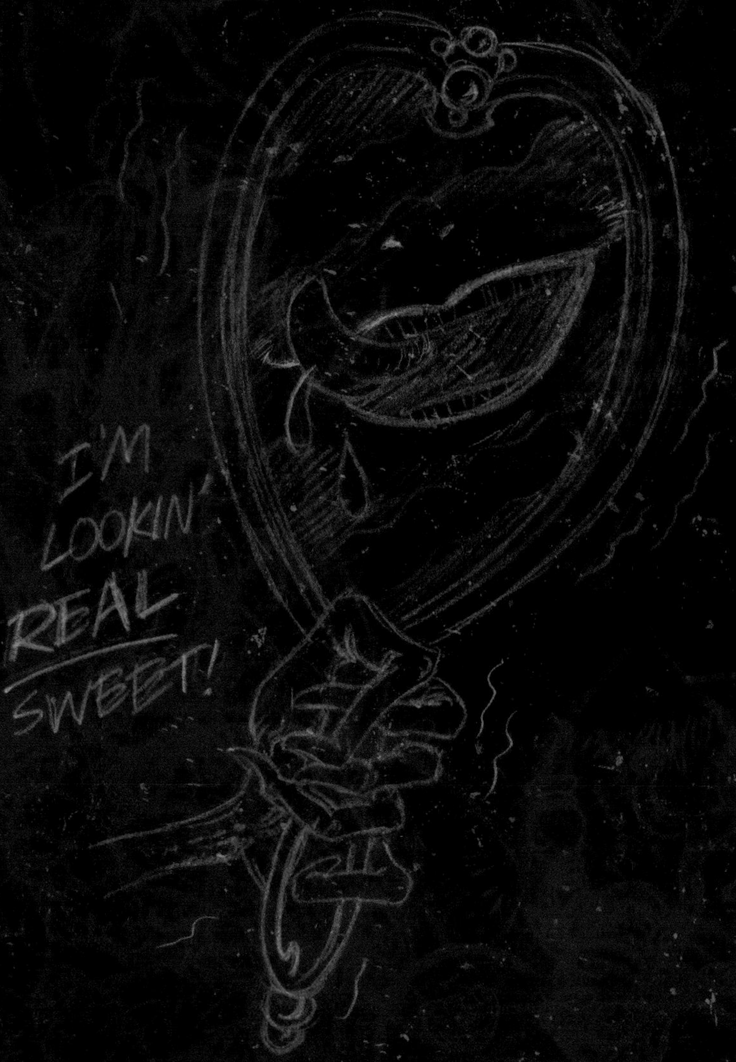
I'M LOOKIN' REAL SWEET!

"She's Giving Me the Excitations"

Chapter Two

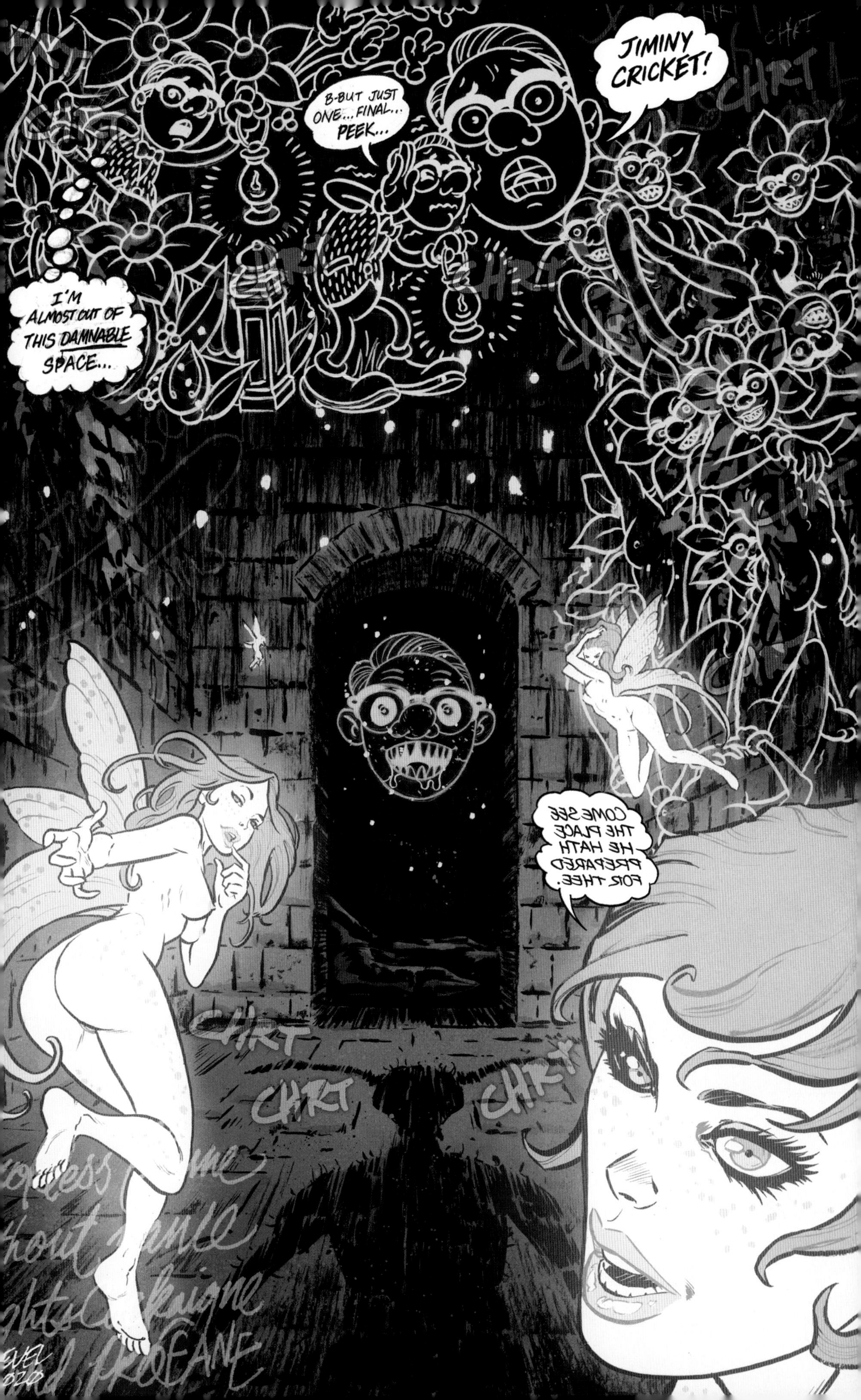
B-BUT JUST ONE... FINAL... PEEK...
JIMINY CRICKET!
I'M ALMOST OUT OF THIS DAMNABLE SPACE...
COME SEE THE PLACE HE HATH PREPARED FOR THEE.
CHRT
CHRT
CHRT

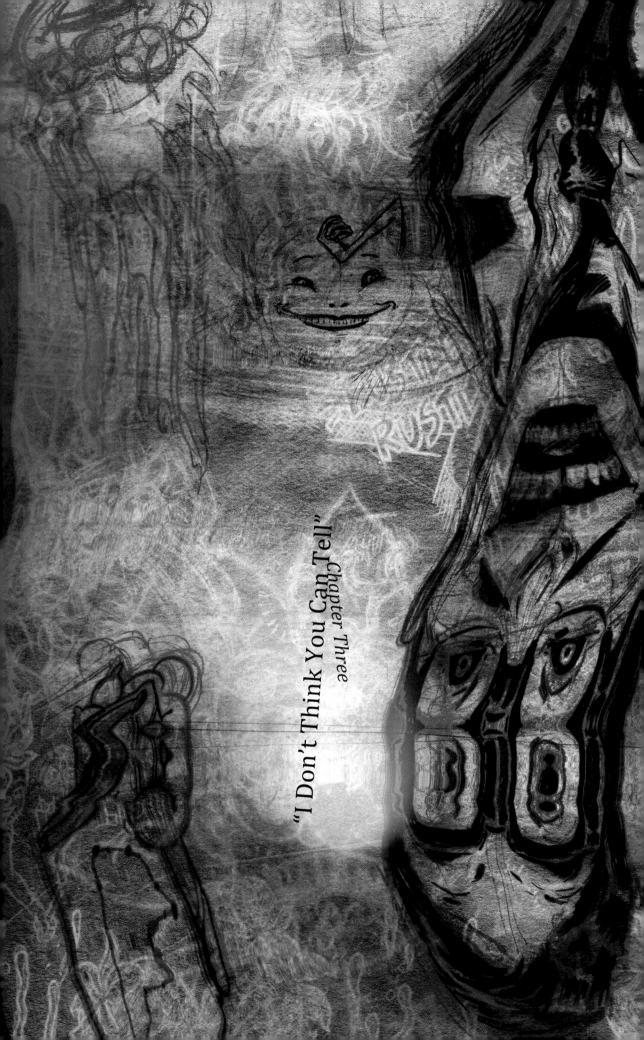

Chapter Three
"I Don't Think You Can Tell"

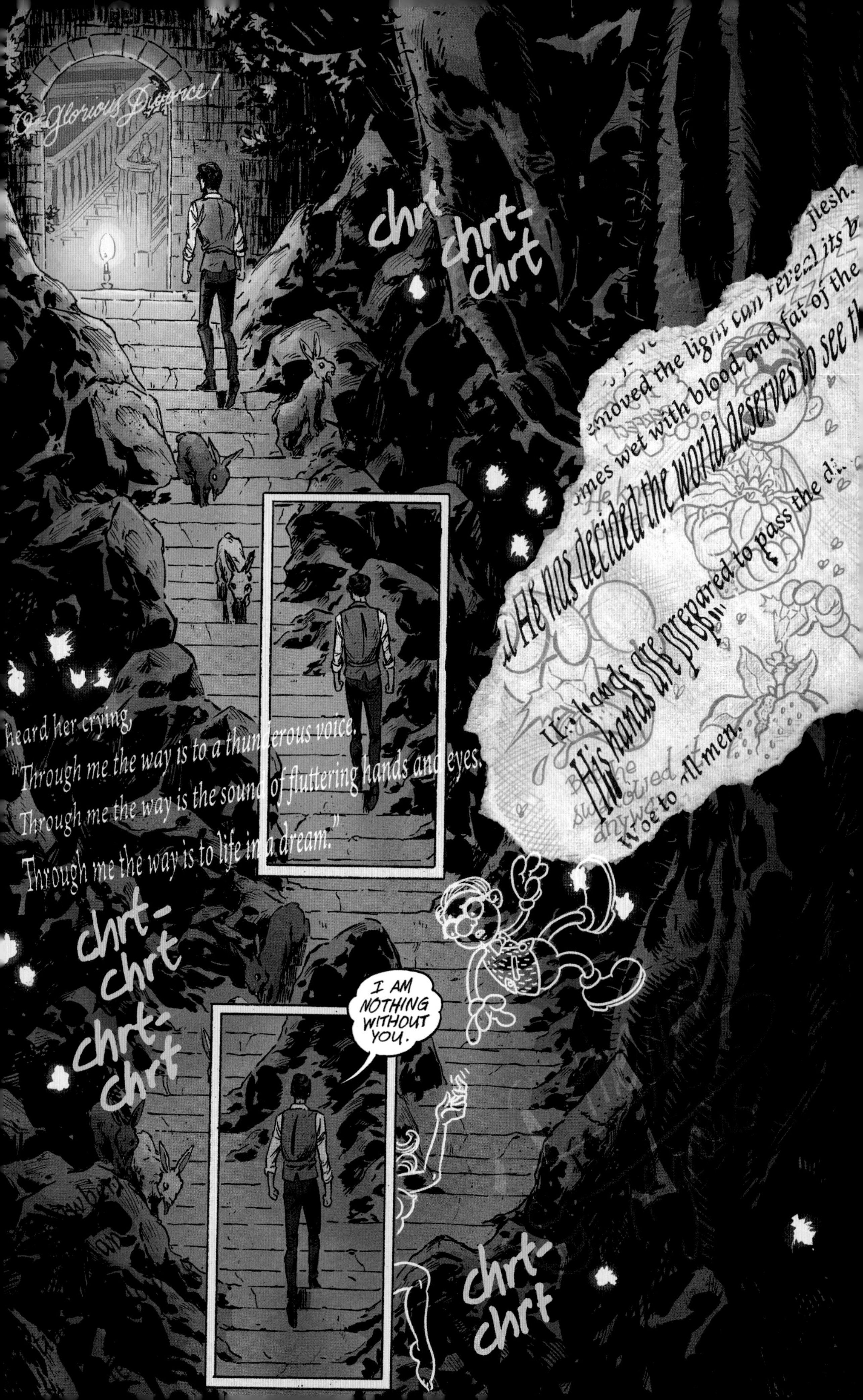
O Glorious Divorce!
chrt
chrt-chrt
flesh.
emoved the light can reveal its b
imes wet with blood and fat of the
He has decided the world deserves to see th
hands are prepared to pass the d
His hands are prep
Woe to all men.
heard her crying,
"Through me the way is to a thunderous voice.
Through me the way is the sound of fluttering hands and eyes.
Through me the way is to life in a dream."
chrt-chrt
chrt-chrt
I AM NOTHING WITHOUT YOU.
chrt-chrt

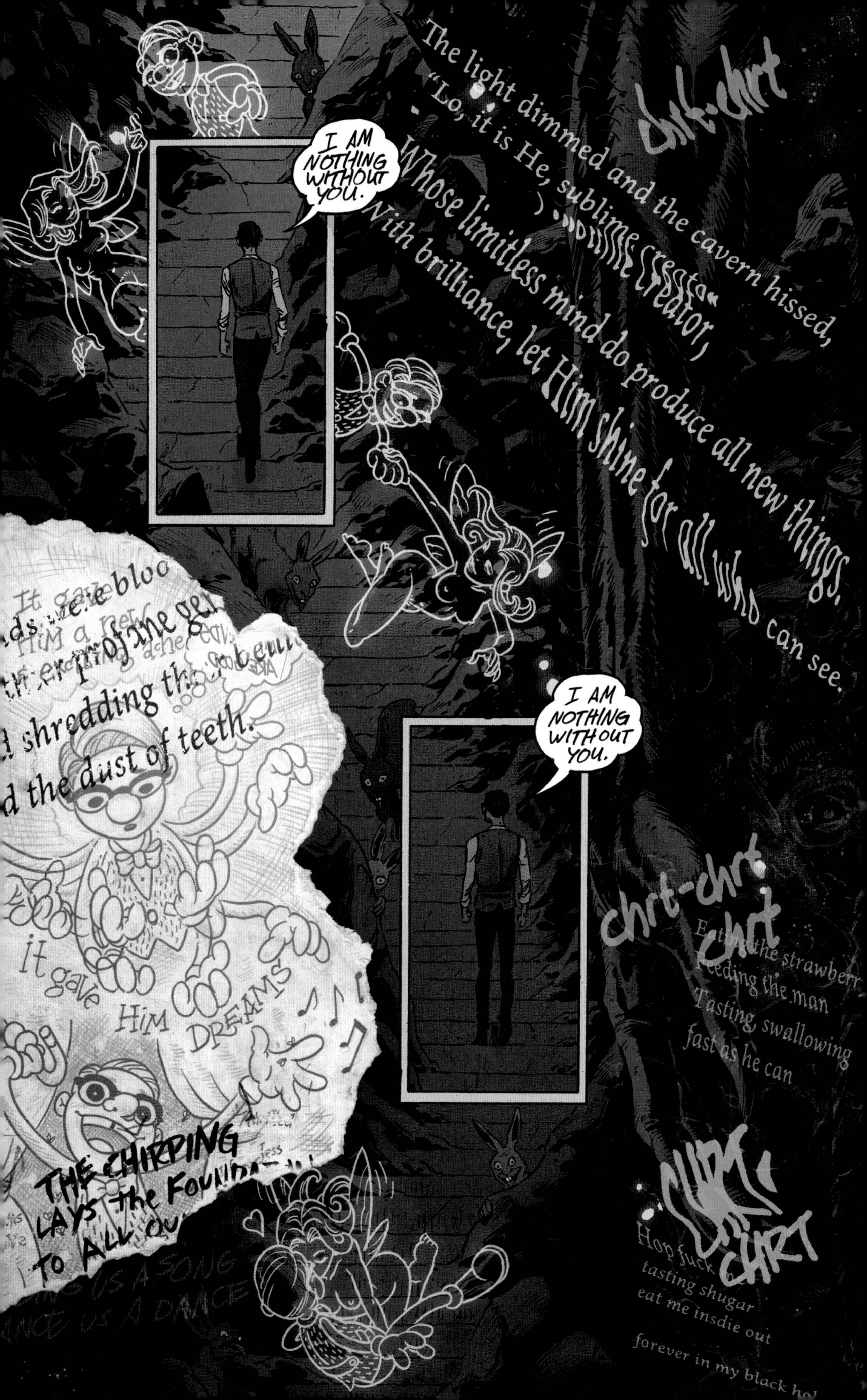
I AM NOTHING WITHOUT YOU.
The light dimmed and the cavern hissed,
"Lo, it is He, sublime creator,
Whose limitless mind do produce all new things,
With brilliance, let Him shine for all who can see.
chrt-chrt
d shredding th
d the dust of teeth.
it gave HIM DREAMS
THE CHIRPING LAYS the FOUNDA
TO ALL OU
I AM NOTHING WITHOUT YOU.
chrt-chrt chrt
Eating the strawberr
Feeding the man
Tasting, swallowing
fast as he can
chrt
tasting shugar
eat me insdie out
forever in my black ho

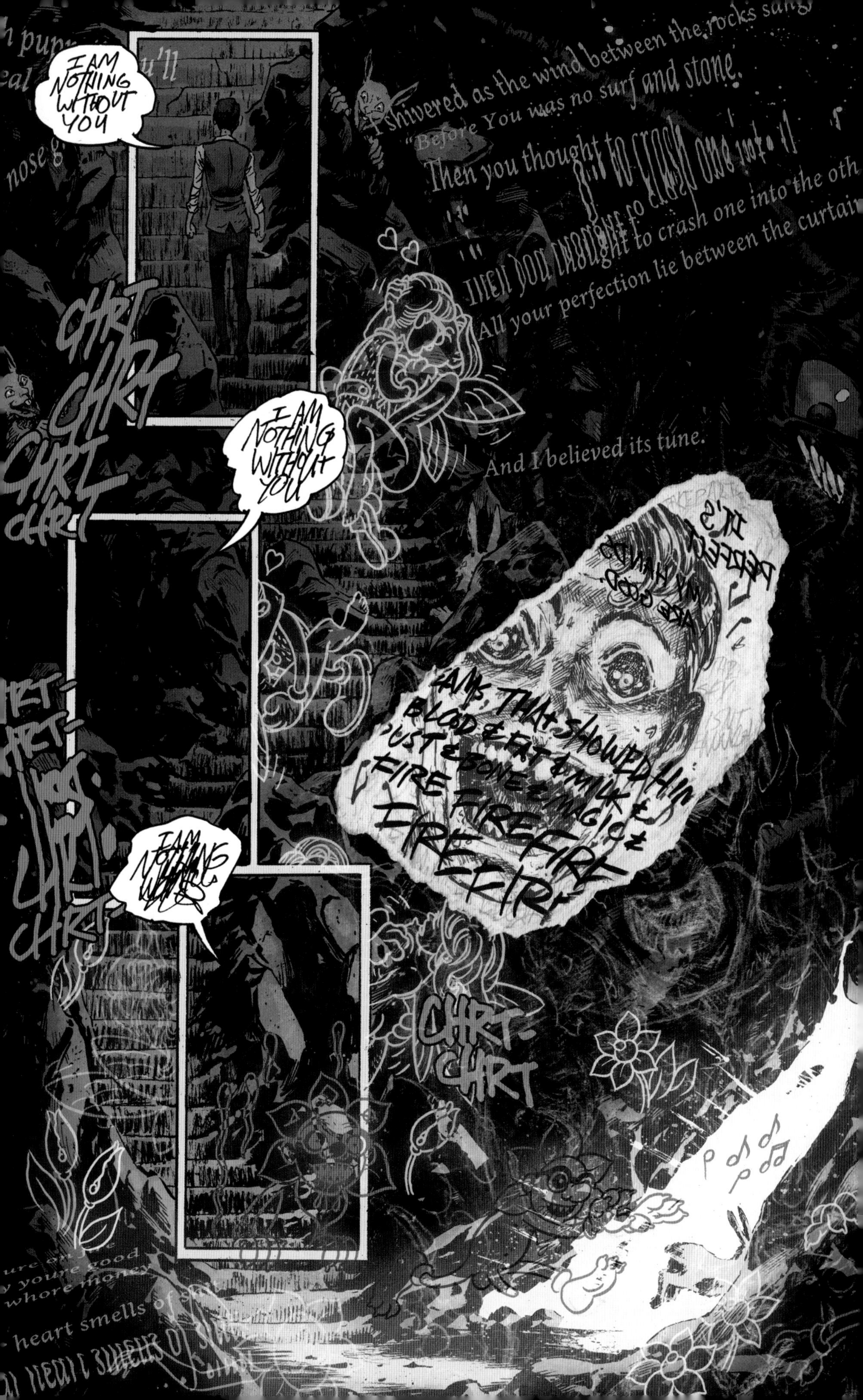
I shivered as the wind between the rocks sang
"Before You was no surf and stone.
Then you thought to crash one into the oth
All your perfection lie between the curtain
I AM NOTHING WITHOUT YOU
CHRT CHRT CHRT CHRT
I AM NOTHING WITHOUT YOU
And I believed its tune.
IT'S PERFECT
MY HANDS ARE GOOD.
HANDS THAT SHOWED HIM BLOOD & FAT & MILK & DUST & BONE & MAGIC & FIRE FIRE FIRE FIRE FIRE!
CHRT-CHRT

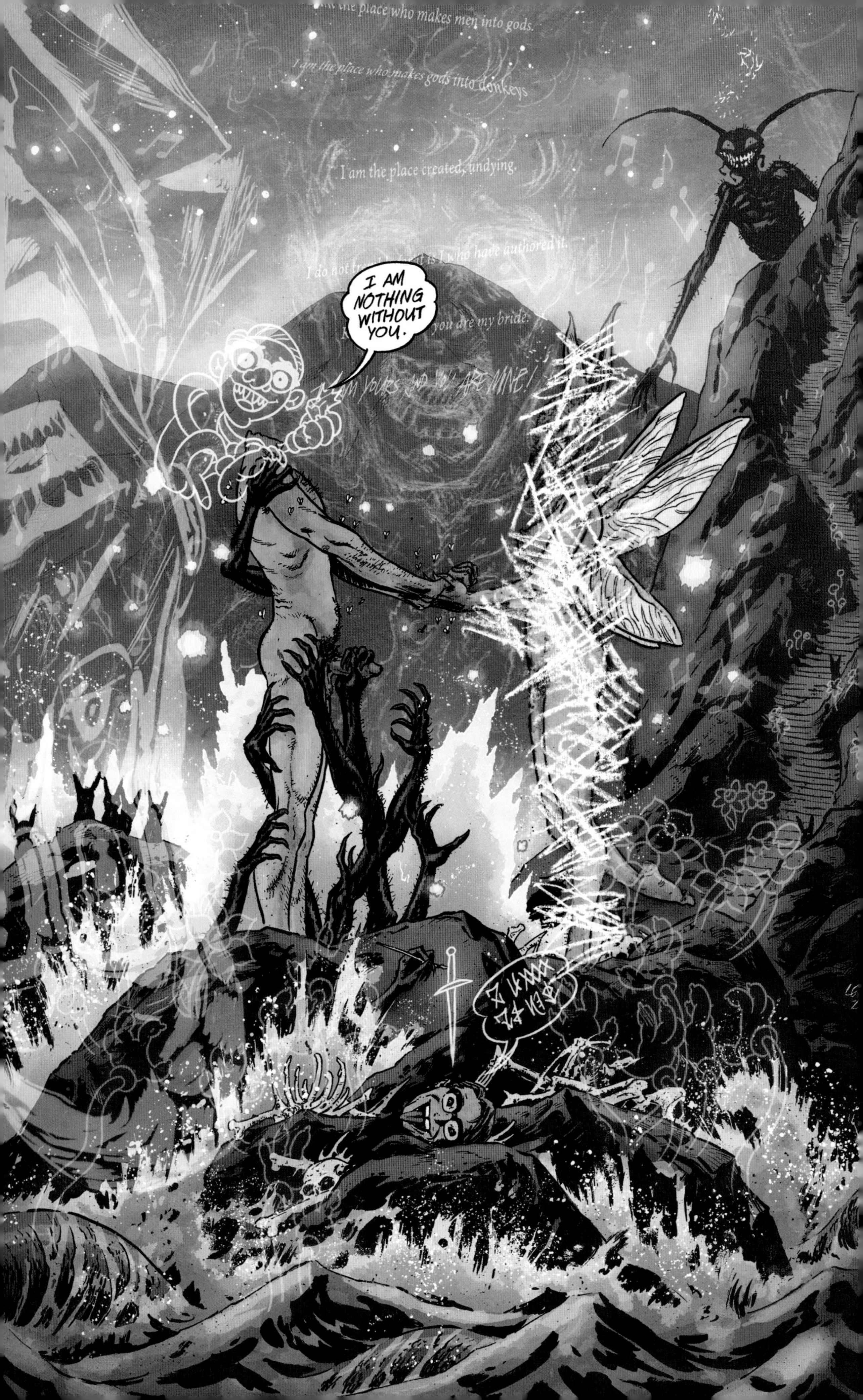

the place who makes men into gods.
I am the place who makes gods into donkeys
I am the place created, undying.
I do not
it is I who have authored it.
I AM NOTHING WITHOUT YOU.
you are my bride.
YOURS AND
ARE MINE!

this is always *The End*

VARIANT COVER GALLERY

RAZORBLADES: THE HORROR MAGAZINE #1
JJ'S COMICS & ART VARIANT
By *DOUG MAHNKE & DAVID BARON*

RAZORBLADES: THE HORROR MAGAZINE #2
SUBSCRIBER VARIANT
By *IAN BERTRAM & MIQUEL MUERTO*

RAZORBLADES: THE HORROR MAGAZINE #2
FORBIDDEN PLANET UK/JETPACK COMICS & GAMES VARIANT
By *NICK ROBLES*

RAZORBLADES: THE HORROR MAGAZINE #3
SUBSCRIBER VARIANT
By *DAVID ROMERO*

RAZORBLADES: THE HORROR MAGAZINE #4
SUBSCRIBER VARIANT
By *BECKY CLOONAN*

RAZORBLADES: THE HORROR MAGAZINE #4
SANCTUM SANCTORUM COMICS VARIANT
By *RAYMUND LEE*

RAZORBLADES: THE HORROR MAGAZINE #5
SUBSCRIBER VARIANT
By *ALVARO MARTINEZ BUENO*

RAZORBLADES: THE HORROR MAGAZINE—SMALL CUTS SPECIAL
By *DAVID ROMERO*

RAZORBLADES: THE HORROR MAGAZINE—SMALL CUTS SPECIAL
TINY ONION VARIANT
By *TYLER BOSS & ROMAN TITOV*

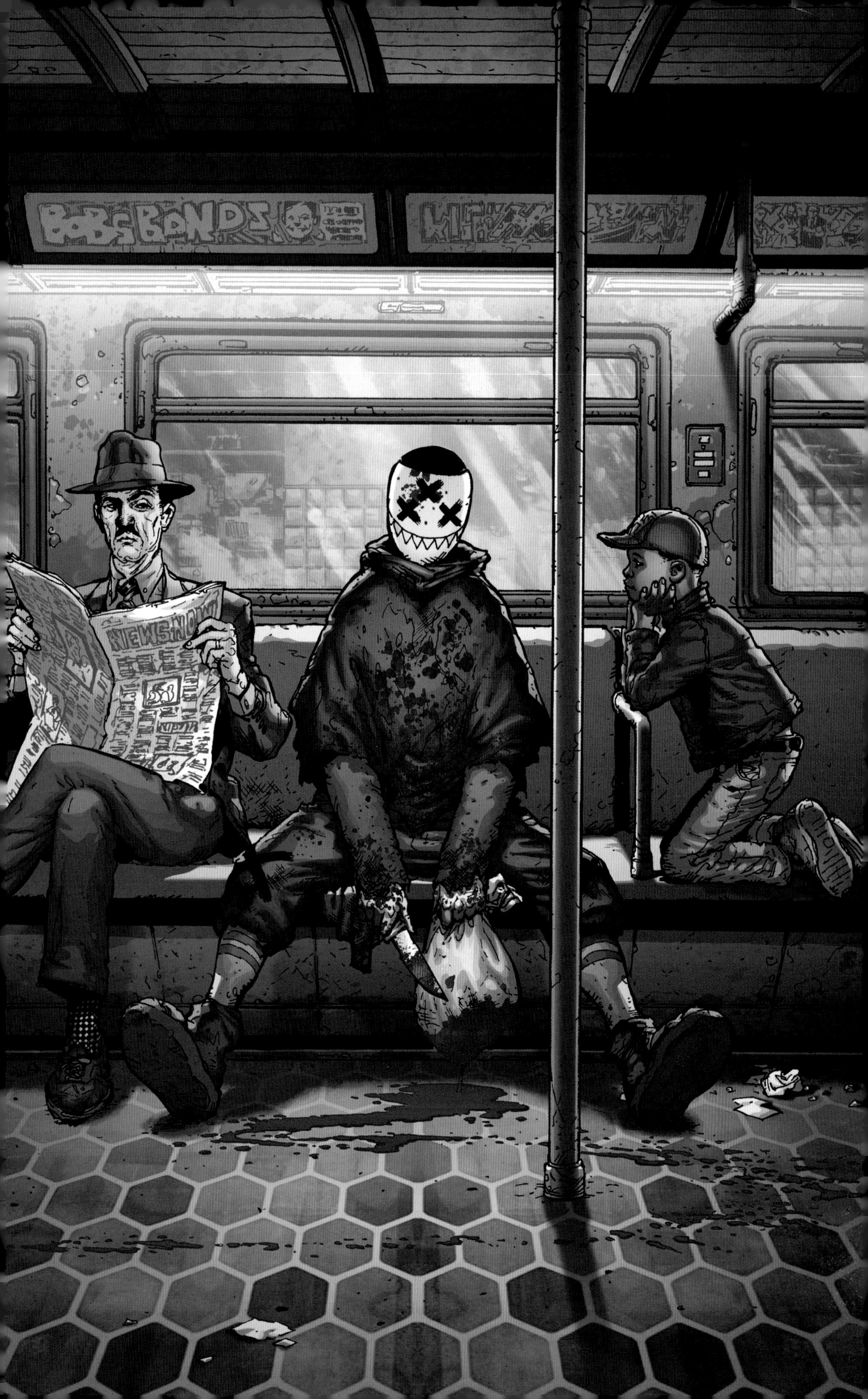
BOB'S BONDS
NEWS NOW

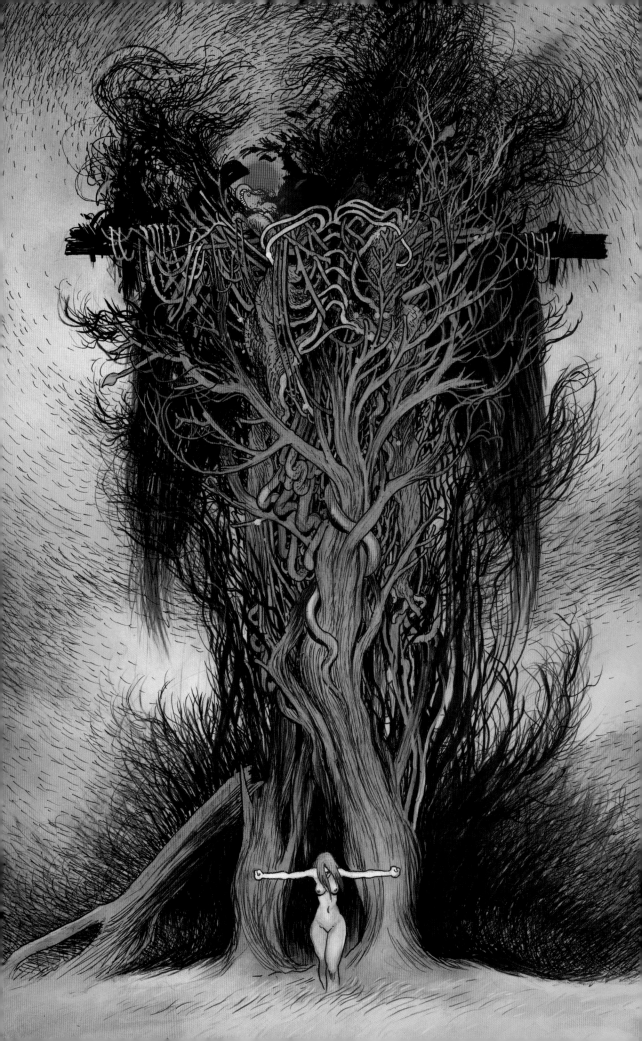

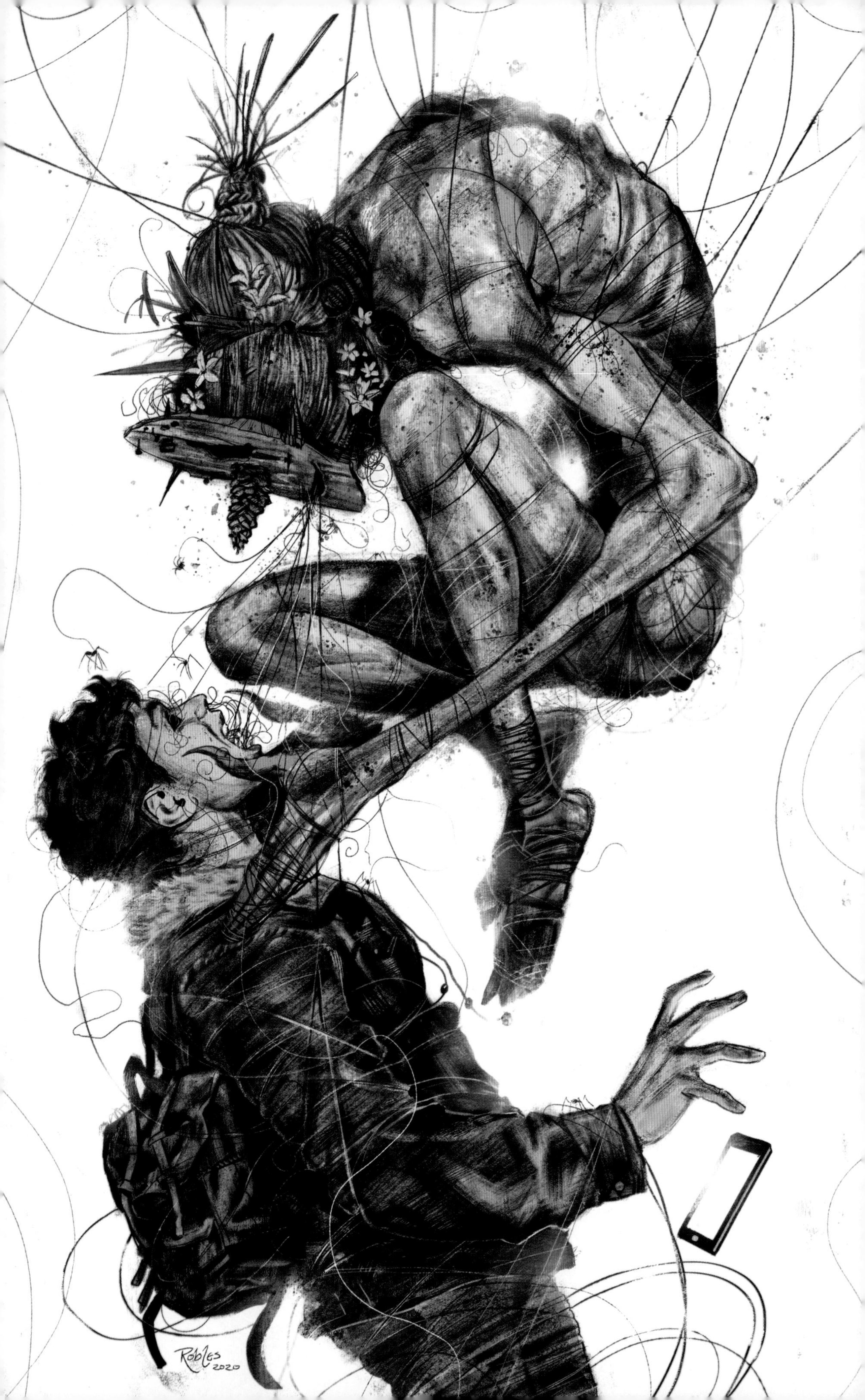
Robles
2020

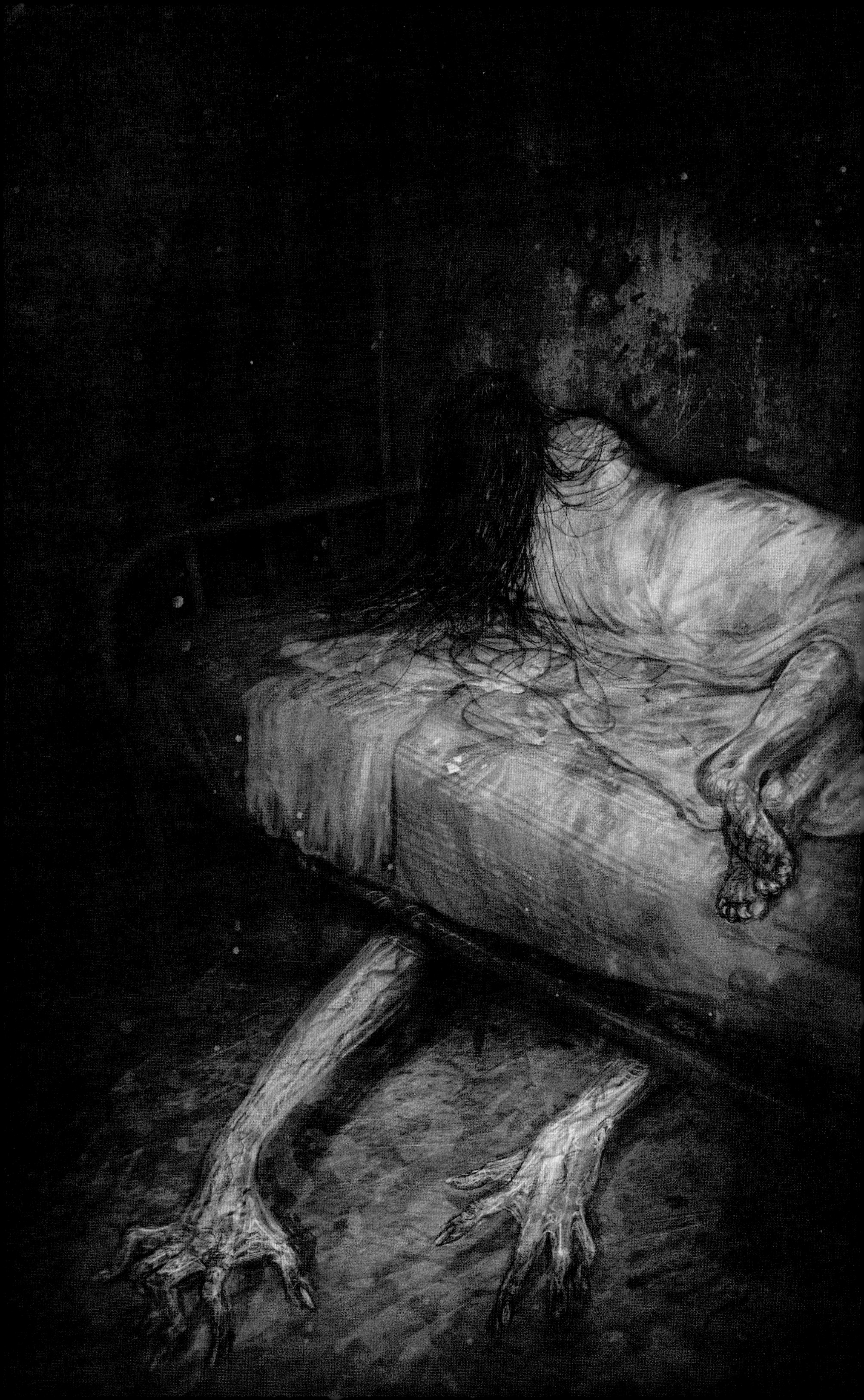

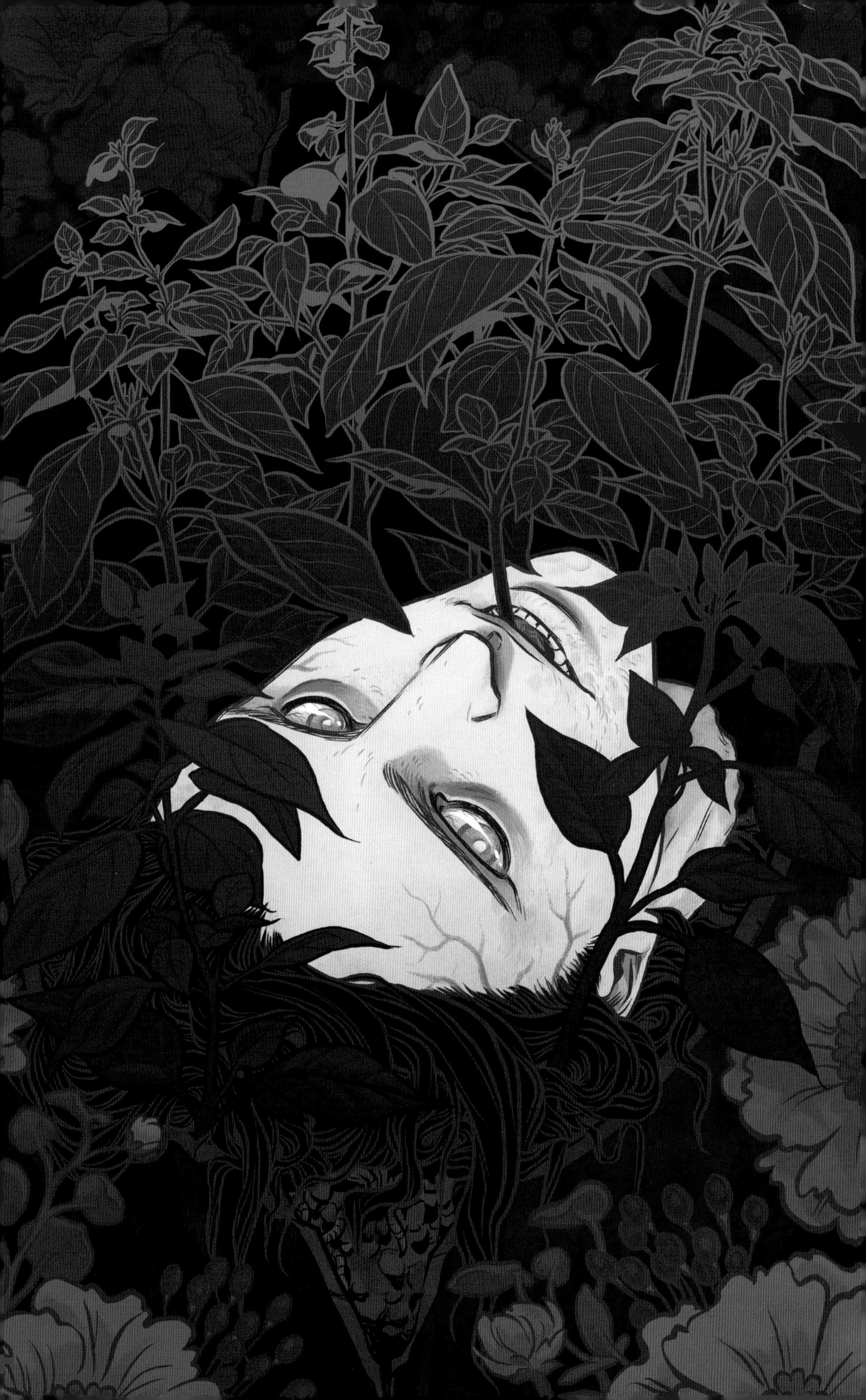

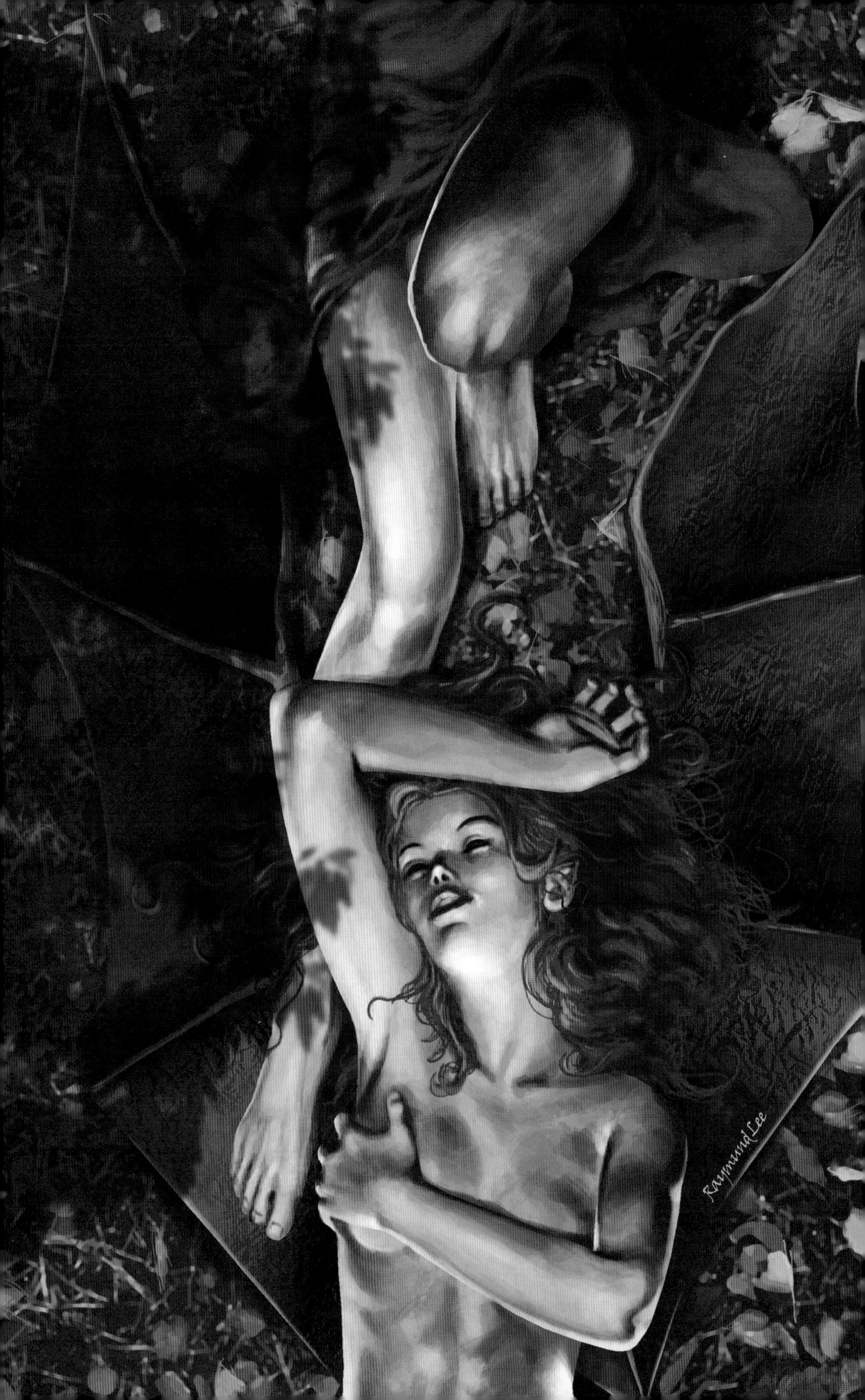
RaymundLee

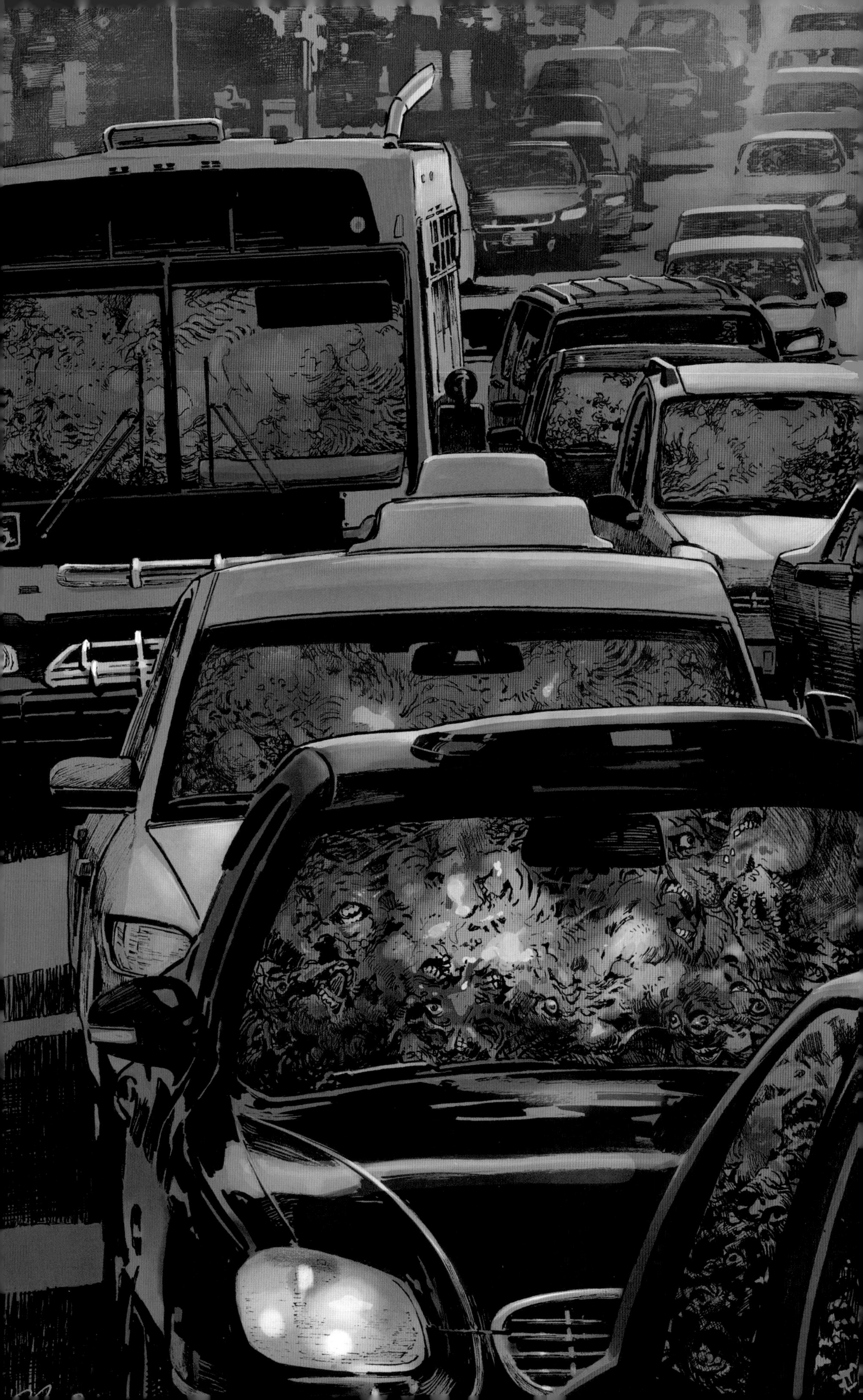

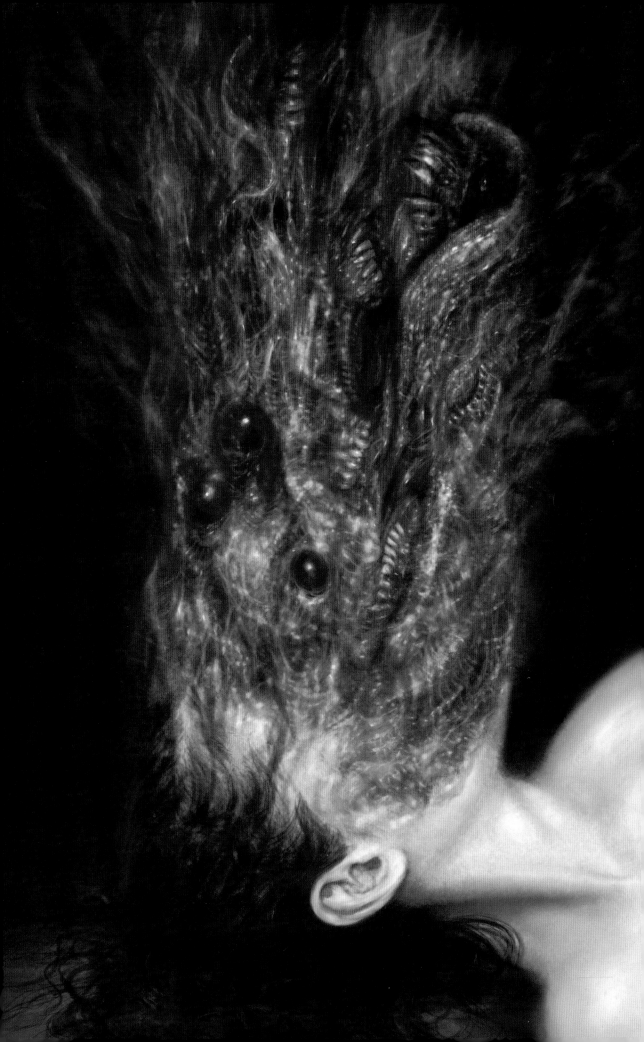

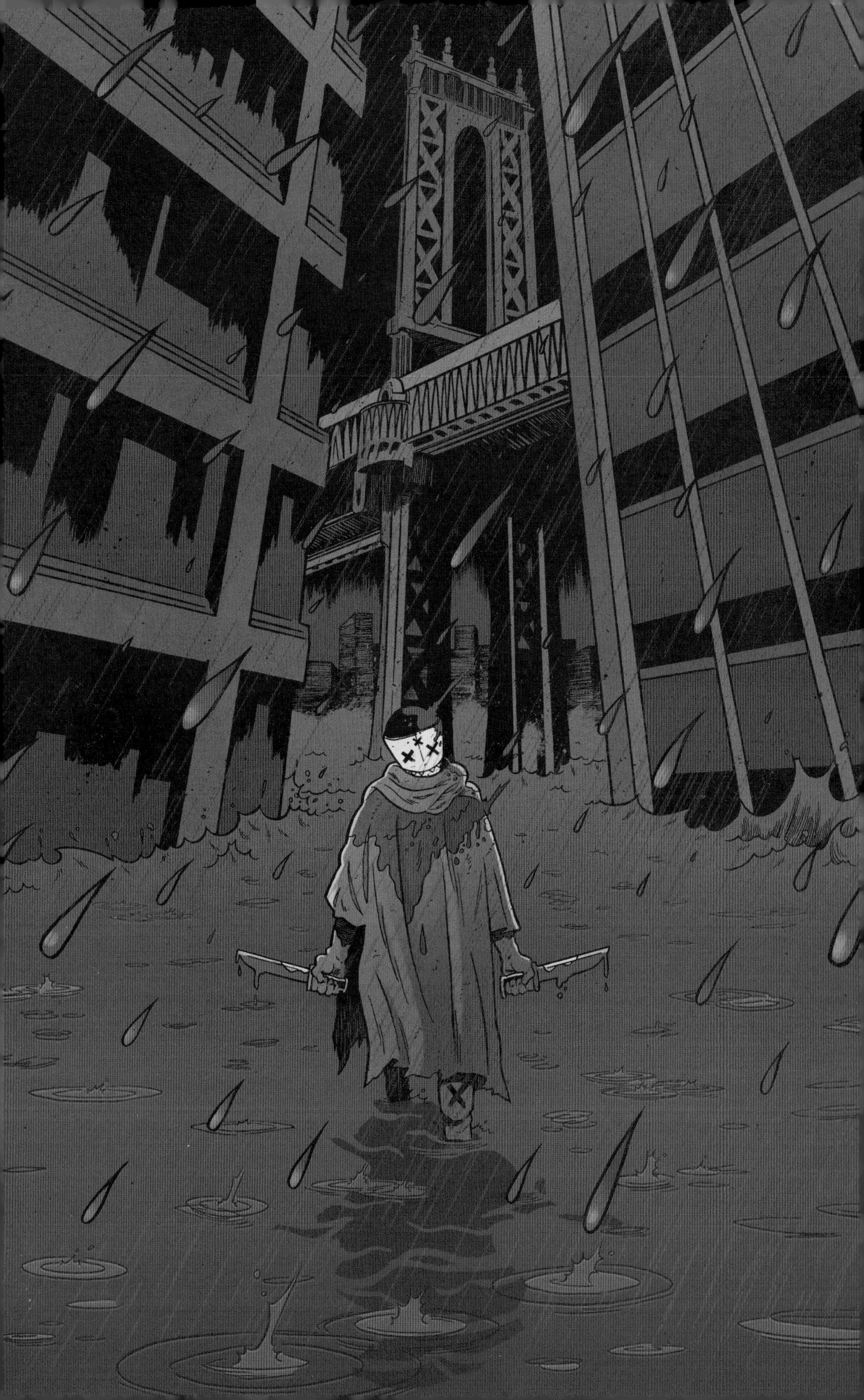

VARIANT COVERS **T-SHIRTS** **ENAMEL PINS**

EXCLUSIVE MERCHANDISE & MORE